THE LOEB CLASSICAL LIBRARY

FOUNDED BY JAMES LOEB, LL.D.

EDITED BY

G. P. GOOLD, PH.D.

FORMER EDITORS

† T. E. PAGE, C.H., LITT.D.   † E. CAPPS, PH.D., LL.D.

† W. H. D. ROUSE, LITT. D.   † L. A. POST, L.H.D.

E. H. WARMINGTON, M.A., F.R.HIST.SOC.

ACHILLES TATIUS

ACHILLES TATIUS

WITH AN ENGLISH TRANSLATION BY
S. GASELEE, M.A.

FELLOW AND LIBRARIAN OF MAGDALENE COLLEGE, CAMBRIDGE

CAMBRIDGE, MASSACHUSETTS
HARVARD UNIVERSITY PRESS

LONDON
WILLIAM HEINEMANN LTD

MCMLXXXIV

American ISBN 0–674–99050–1
British ISBN 0 434 99045 0

First printed 1917
Reprinted 1947, 1961
Revised and reprinted 1969, 1984

Printed in Great Britain

CONTENTS

PREFACE

THE work of S. Gaselee in the present reprint remains his, but the translation has been corrected and improved in a number of places; and the limited critical notes on the Greek text, and the Greek text itself, have been revised in the light of E. Vilborg's text, critical notes, and commentary (to which reference must be made for fuller information), with special regard to emendations by L. Castiglioni in *Byzantinisch-neugriech. Jahrbücher* (Bd. 4, 1923, 18–50), T. W. Lumb in *Classical Review*, XXXIV, 1920, 93–94 and *Classical Quarterly*, XIV, 1920, 147–149; and J. Jackson in *Classical Quarterly*, XXIX, 1935, 52–57, 96–112. Gaselee's original introduction has been partly retained, partly rewritten; and everything has been translated into English.

The critical notes as revised read as if they were a collaboration between Gaselee himself and the Editor; and in a sense they are indeed joint work, pieced or fused together. However, " I " is always Gaselee, not:—

E. H. WARMINGTON, 1968.

INTRODUCTION

I

WE know very little of the author of the *Clitophon and Leucippe*. "Suidas"[1] speaks of him thus: "Achilles Statius[2] of Alexandria: the writer of the story of Leucippe and Clitophon, as well as other episodes of love,[3] in eight books. He finally became a Christian and a bishop. He also wrote a treatise on the sphere, and works on etymology, and a mixed narration telling of many great and marvellous men. His novel is in all respects like that of the other writers of love-romances." It is possible that our author became a Christian later in his life (though there is certainly no sign of any such tendency in his work), but the statement that he ended in the episcopate should be looked upon with caution: it is probably a reflection of the similar story told of Heliodorus, the [later] novelist. His date is not easy to place with accuracy. [If the earlier of two papyri discovered after Gaselee wrote is to be dated late in

---

[1] The lexicographer who wrote in the tenth century, but made much (and usually accurate) use of earlier materials.

[2] *Sic.* We find the correct form of the name in the MSS. of our author and in other places where he is casually mentioned by late grammarians and scholiasts.

[3] This may either be interpreted that he wrote other novels with a love-interest, or as referring to the various loves, happy and unhappy, which are represented in the present work, subordinate to the main passion of the hero and heroine.

the second century, Achilles himself must be regarded as having composed his novel earlier in that century. See page xiii.—Ed.] There is no particular reason to doubt the statement of " Suidas " and of some of the MSS. of the novel that the author was a native of Alexandria, and the somewhat exaggerated description of the beauties of the city at the beginning of Book V. would seem to be evidence of the writer's patriotism. The scholiast Thomas Magister calls him an orator ($\dot{\rho}\acute{\eta}\tau\omega\rho$), and he may well have been an advocate: his general style is redolent of the rhetorician, and the lawsuit towards the end of the romance betrays a practised hand in the speeches on both sides. It will by now be apparent to the reader how much of our knowledge of Achilles Tatius is little more than conjecture on somewhat narrow grounds: one can only say that he seems to come [...from...] the school of the Greek novelists[1] which flourished from the first to the third century A.D., and he certainly became one of the most popular, for he was widely read throughout later Greek and Byzantine days.

Beyond the passage of " Suidas " mentioned above, the references to our author in antiquity are very few. Photius[2] in his great *Bibliotheca* has more than one reference to him, praising his literary art and powers as a *raconteur*, but censuring some of the episodes and digressions as inconsistent with the standard of purity that a Patriarch could desire:

[1] See a short general article on the Greek novelists printed as an appendix to the Loeb Series edition of Longus and Parthenius.

[2] Patriarch of Constantinople, 858–886: a man of real erudition, but not quite equal judgment.

" in this respect alone is Achilles Tatius inferior to
Heliodorus." We have a formal comparison of the
two authors from the pen of Michael Psellus; it
is too long to give here, but may be found on
pp. cvi–cxiv of Jacobs' edition [cp. 165–167 of
Vilborg's], and is an interesting example of eleventh
century criticism, for, besides ethical comparisons,
the styles of narration are set against one another
with plentiful illustration and considerable acumen.

[Another] reference to our author in ancient
literature is an epigram in the *Palatine Anthology*
(ix. 203), which is ascribed in the *lemma* as " by
Photius, patriarch of Constantinople: but others say
that it is by Leon the philosopher."

Φωτίου Πατριάρχου Κωνσταντινουπόλεως, ἄλλοι
δέ φασιν Λέοντος τοῦ φιλοσόφου

εἰς τὴν βίβλον Λευκίππης

Ἔρωτα πικρόν, ἀλλὰ σώφρονα βίον
ὁ Κλειτοφῶντος μὲν παρεμφαίνει λόγος·
ὁ Λευκίππης δὲ σωφρονέστατος βίος
ἅπαντας ἐξίστησι, πῶς τετυμμένη
κεκαρμένη τε καὶ κατηχρειωμένη,
τὸ δὴ μέγιστον, τρὶς θανοῦσ᾽ ἐκαρτέρει.
εἴπερ δὲ καὶ σὺ σωφρονεῖν θέλῃς, φίλος,
μὴ τὴν πάρεργον τῆς γραφῆς σκόπει θέαν,
τὴν τοῦ λόγου δὲ πρῶτα συνδρομὴν μάθε·
νυμφοστολεῖ γὰρ τοὺς ποθοῦντας ἐμφρόνως.

There are difficulties in both ascriptions: the style
of prosody is too late and accentual for Leon (and
his other epigrams are hardly of the same style),
and the sentiment of the little poem is rather more

favourable to the moral standard of the novel than we should expect if we judge from the other mentions by Photius. This attribution is, however, the more probable of the two—and the real point of the epigram is that the reader is not to allow himself to be distracted by any of the incidents of the novel, but to profit by the lesson of the main plot, which is undoubtedly, considered as a whole, a panegyric of chastity.

II

THE TEXT OF ACHILLES TATIUS

Papyri.

By far the earliest sources for the text of Achilles Tatius are provided by three papyri of which only one was known when Gaselee's volume in the Loeb Classical Library was published in 1917, and all afford fragments only : [1]

Π¹ Pap. Oxyrh. 1250, of the early (?) part of the fourth century after Christ, and now in the Bodleian Library, Oxford. B. Grenfell and A. Hunt, *The Oxyrhynchus Papyri*, Pt. X, pp. 135 ff.[2] C. F. Russo in Accad. d. Lincei, *Rendiconti della cl. di sc. mor., stor. e filolog.* Serie viii. v. x. fasc. 5–6, 1955, 397–403.

Π² Pap. Schubart 30, of the third century after Christ or earlier, and now it seems lost. W. Schubart, Griechische literarische Papyri. Berlin, 1950, pp. 59–60.

[1] Throughout we use the sigla for papyri and medieval manuscripts adopted by Vilborg in his edition of 1955, after collating all the manuscripts.

[2] Hence this papyrus is called GH by Gaselee.

Π³ Pap. Mediolanensis, of the late (?) second century after Christ, now at Milan. A. Vogliano, in Stud. ital. fil. class. N. S. XV, Florence, 1938, pp. 121–130.

Medieval Manuscripts.

Derived from a lost archetype which was on a line of tradition different from any of the papyri, are twenty-three extant medieval manuscripts, all but one belonging to one or other of two families (a) and (β). Of these MSS. the following, denoted by Vilborg's sigla, have independent authority.

Family (a).

M = Codex Marcianus graecus 409 (early? 13th century); there are MSS. copied from it. Contains Books I.1–VIII.16.

W = Vaticanus graecus 1349 (12th century); there are MSS. derived from it. Contains Books I.1–VIII.19.

D = Vaticanus graecus 914 (14th century); contains Book I and excerpts from Books II, III and IV.

Family (β) (which on the whole give a better tradition).

V = Vaticanus graecus 114 (13th century); there are MSS. copied from it. Contains Books I.1–VIII.19.

G = Marcianus graecus 607 (15th century); there is one MS. copied from it. Contains Books I.1–VIII.19.

T = Tubingensis M b 16 (16th century); there are
    MSS. derived from it. Contains Book I.1–10.
X = Parisinus graecus 2895 (early 16th century).
    Contains Book I.1–10.
E = Ambrosianus graecus 394 (15th or 16th cen-
    tury). Contains Books I.1–VII.9.
R = Vaticanus graecus 1348 (16th century); con-
    tains Books I.1–VIII.19.

A possible third family [γ] is suggested by

F = Laurentianus conv. soppr. 627 (13th century);
    contains Books I.1–IV.4.

For details see Vilborg's edition, pp. XV ff. There
is a stemma codicum on p. LXXII.

Gaselee's comments on what is now called Π¹.

The fragment is some thousand years older than
any extant MS. of our author, and naturally presents
a better text; those of its readings which are clearly
the true original have been incorporated into the
text of this edition, and attention has been called in a
footnote to other places where it is probably correct.
It is, however, satisfactory to find that our MSS., late
as they are, have not habitually lost the truth, and
that several places which have been doubted and
freely altered by modern editors are corroborated in
their traditional form by the new fragment.

There is, however, one important divergence in
the papyrus: it is a matter of order, chapters ii.
and iii. §§ 1–2 of Book II. being placed between
chapters viii. and ix. I will here quote the words
of Grenfell and Hunt, who express clearly and con-
cisely the exact state of affairs: " Some slight

INTRODUCTION

changes in the transitional phrases are made, so
that the passage as it stands runs quite smoothly.
But the last section of chapter iii. would not join
on to the end of chapter i., and there must have
been a larger modification at this point. The
abruptness of that section had already been observed by Jacobs, who suggested that something had
fallen out. These remarkable divergences of the
papyrus from the current version seem capable of
two explanations. Either there were two redac-
tions of the romance, a view which was suggested
long ago by Salmasius but was vigorously contested
by Jacobs, or possibly a leaf in the archetype from
which the medieval MSS. were derived was copied
in the wrong position and the dislocation has been
concealed by subsequent patching. The omission
in some MSS. of the words καὶ ἄρτι . . . . καιρὸς ἦν,
in others of καὶ πάλιν . . . καιρὸς ἦν at the
beginning of chapter ii. might be taken to point
in that direction." The second explanation, or
something like it, seems the more probable; but
after considerable hesitation no change from the
traditional order has been made in the present
edition. It would have been necessary to make
some kind of bridge between the end of chapter i.
and the latter part of chapter iii., which would
have presented considerable difficulties, and the
story, which now reads continuously, would run less
smoothly if such a course were adopted. It was
therefore thought sufficient to chronicle the fact of
the variant order in the papyrus, and to allow readers
to try for themselves the difference that this changed
order would have made.[1]

[1] See Vilborg, edition, pp. xv–xvii, xxxv–xliv.

INTRODUCTION

III

Editions

Before the first printing of a Greek text, Annibale della Croce (Cruceius) of Milan had produced a Latin translation of Books V–VIII at Lyon in 1544 and of all eight books at Basle in 1554. The editions of the Greek text are as follows.

H. Commelinus began and I. and N. Bonnvitius completed the *Editio Princeps* which was published at Heidelberg in 1601. It was followed by the edition of Salmasius (C. Saumaise) at Leyden in 1640. The next century saw the publication, in 1776 at Leipzig, of the edition by B. G. L. Boden, and in 1792, at Zweibrücken, that of C. G. Mitscherlich. In the nineteenth century came the edition by F. Jacobs (Leipzig, 1821), that of G. A. Hirschig (Paris, 1856), and that of R. Hercher (Leipzig, 1858–1859). The English translation, with Greek text, by S. Gaselee appeared in 1917.

We now have the important work of E. Vilborg (who writes in English), in two volumes: Achilles Tatius, *Leucippe and Clitophon*, Almquist and Wiksell, Stockholm and Göteborg, 1955, including bibliography, description of the papyri and the medieval manuscripts, Greek text, full critical notes, and *testimonia*; and Achilles Tatius, *Leucippe and Clitophon*. A commentary. Acta Universitatis Gothoburgensis, Stockholm and Göteborg, 1962.

ACHILLES TATIUS

ΑΧΙΛΛΕΩΣ ΤΑΤΙΟΥ

ΑΛΕΞΑΝΔΡΕΩΣ

ΤΩΝ ΚΑΤΑ

ΛΕΥΚΙΠΠΗΝ ΚΑΙ ΚΛΕΙΤΟΦΩΝΤΑ

Α′

1. Σιδὼν ἐπὶ θαλάσσῃ πόλις· Ἀσσυρίων [1] ἡ θάλασσα· μήτηρ Φοινίκων ἡ πόλις· Θηβαίων ὁ δῆμος πατήρ. δίδυμος λιμὴν ἐν κόλπῳ πλατύς, ἠρέμα κλείων τὸ πέλαγος. ᾗ γὰρ ὁ κόλπος κατὰ πλευρὰν ἐπὶ δεξιὰ κοιλαίνεται, στόμα δεύτερον ὀρώρυκται, καὶ τὸ ὕδωρ αὖθις εἰσρεῖ, καὶ γίνεται τοῦ λιμένος ἄλλος λιμήν, ὡς χειμάζειν μὲν ταύτῃ τὰς ὁλκάδας ἐν γαλήνῃ, θερίζειν δὲ τοῦ λιμένος εἰς τὸ προκόλπιον.

2 Ἐνταῦθα ἥκων ἐκ πολλοῦ χειμῶνος, σῶστρα ἔθυον ἐμαυτοῦ τῇ τῶν Φοινίκων θεᾷ· Ἀστάρτην αὐτὴν οἱ Σιδώνιοι καλοῦσιν. περιιὼν οὖν καὶ τὴν ἄλλην πόλιν καὶ περισκοπῶν τὰ ἀναθήματα, ὁρῶ γραφὴν ἀνακειμένην γῆς ἅμα καὶ θαλάσσης.

---

[1] Vilborg reads Συρίων.

ACHILLES TATIUS
OF ALEXANDRIA

THE ADVENTURES OF LEUCIPPE AND CLITOPHON

BOOK I

1. SIDON is on the sea-board of the Assyrian Ocean : it is the Phoenicians' mother city, and its people may be termed the father of the Theban race. There is a double harbour in the bay, wide within but with a narrow entrance so as to land-lock the sea by a gentle curve : where the bay makes an inward turn towards the right, a second inlet has been channelled out, for the water to run in, and thus there is formed a further harbour behind the first, so that in winter the ships can lie safely in the inner basin, while in summer they need not proceed further than the outer port.

On arriving there after a severe storm, I went to make my votive offerings for my safe arrival to the Phoenicians' goddess ; Astarte the people of Sidon call her : as I was thus walking about the city, paying especial attention to the temple-offerings, I saw a picture hanging up which was a landscape and a sea-

Εὐρώπης ἡ γραφή· Φοινίκων ἡ θάλασσα· Σιδῶνος
3 ἡ γῆ. ἐν τῇ γῇ λειμὼν καὶ χορὸς παρθένων· ἐν τῇ
θαλάσσῃ ταῦρος ἐνήχετο, καὶ τοῖς νώτοις καλὴ
παρθένος ἐπεκάθητο, ἐπὶ Κρήτην τῷ ταύρῳ
πλέουσα. ἐκόμα πολλοῖς ἄνθεσιν ὁ λειμών· δένδρων αὐτοῖς ἀνεμέμικτο φάλαγξ καὶ φυτῶν·
συνεχῆ τὰ δένδρα, συνηρεφῆ τὰ πέταλα· συνῆπτον
οἱ πτόρθοι τὰ φύλλα, καὶ ἐγίνετο τοῖς ἄνθεσιν
4 ὄροφος ἡ τῶν φύλλων συμπλοκή. ἔγραψεν ὁ
τεχνίτης ὑπὸ τὰ πέταλα καὶ τὴν σκιάν· καὶ ὁ
ἥλιος ἠρέμα τοῦ λειμῶνος κάτω σποράδην διέρρει,
ὅσον τὸ συνηρεφὲς τῆς τῶν φύλλων κόμης ἀνέῳ-
5 ξεν ὁ γραφεύς. ὅλον ἐτείχιζε τὸν λειμῶνα περι-
βολή· εἴσω δὲ τοῦ τῶν ὀρόφων στεφανώματος ὁ
λειμὼν ἐκάθητο. αἱ δὲ πρασιαὶ τῶν ἀνθέων ὑπὸ
τὰ πέταλα τῶν φυτῶν στοιχηδὸν ἐπεφύκεσαν,
νάρκισσος καὶ ῥόδα καὶ μύρριναι. ὕδωρ δὲ κατὰ
μέσον ἔρρει τοῦ λειμῶνος τῆς γραφῆς, τὸ μὲν
ἀναβλύζον κάτωθεν ἀπὸ τῆς γῆς, τὸ δὲ τοῖς
6 ἄνθεσι καὶ τοῖς φυτοῖς περιχεόμενον. ὀχετηγός
τις ἐγέγραπτο δίκελλαν κατέχων καὶ περὶ
μίαν ἀμάραν κεκυφὼς καὶ ἀνοίγων τὴν ὁδὸν τῷ
ῥεύματι.

Ἐν δὲ τῷ τοῦ λειμῶνος τέλει πρὸς ταῖς ἐπὶ θάλασσαν τῆς γῆς ἐκβολαῖς τὰς παρθένους ἔταξεν ὁ
7 τεχνίτης. τὸ σχῆμα ταῖς παρθένοις καὶ χαρᾶς καὶ
φόβου. στέφανοι περὶ τοῖς μετώποις δεδεμένοι·
κόμαι κατὰ τῶν ὤμων λελυμέναι· τὸ σκέλος πᾶν
γεγυμνωμέναι· τὸ μὲν ἄνω, τοῦ χιτῶνος, τὸ δὲ
κάτω, τοῦ πεδίλου, τὸ γὰρ ζῶσμα μέχρι γόνατος
ἀνεῖλκε τὸν χιτῶνα· τὸ πρόσωπον ὠχραί· σεση-
ρυῖαι τὰς παρειάς· τοὺς ὀφθαλμοὺς ἀνοίξασαι πρὸς

4

scape in one. The painting was of Europa: the sea
depicted was the Phoenician Ocean; the land,
Sidon. On the land part was a meadow and a troop
of girls: in the sea a bull was swimming, and on
his back sat a beautiful maiden, borne by the
bull towards Crete. The meadow was thick with all
kinds of flowers, and among them was planted a
thicket of trees and shrubs, the trees growing so
close that their foliage touched: and the branches,
intertwining their leaves, thus made a kind of
continuous roof over the flowers beneath. The
artist had also represented the shadows thrown by
the leaves, and the sun was gently breaking through,
here and there, on to the meadow, where the
painter had represented openings in the thick roof
of foliage. The meadow was surrounded on all sides
by an enclosure, and lay wholly within the embowering
roof; beneath the shrubs grass-beds of flowers grew
orderly—narcissus, roses, and bays; in the middle of
the meadow in the picture flowed a rivulet of water,
bubbling up on one side from the ground, and on
the other watering the flowers and shrubs; and a
gardener had been painted holding a pick, stooping
over a single channel and leading a path for the
water.

The painter had put the girls at one end of the
meadow where the land jutted out into the sea.
Their look was compounded of joy and fear: gar-
lands were bound about their brows; their hair had
been allowed to flow loose on their shoulders; their
legs were bare, covered neither by their tunics above
nor their sandals below, a girdle holding up their
skirts as far as the knee; their faces were pale and
their features distorted; their eyes were fixed wide

5

τὴν θάλασσαν· μικρὸν ὑποκεχηνυῖαι τὸ στόμα,
ὥσπερ ἀφήσειν ὑπὸ φόβου μέλλουσαι καὶ βοήν·
8 τὰς χεῖρας ὡς ἐπὶ τὸν βοῦν ὥρεγον. ἐπέβαινον
ἄκρας τῆς θαλάσσης, ὅσον ὑπεράνω μικρὸν τῶν
ταρσῶν ὑπερέχειν τὸ κῦμα· ἐῴκεσαν δὲ βούλεσθαι
μὲν ὡς ἐπὶ τὸν ταῦρον δραμεῖν, φοβεῖσθαι δὲ τῇ
θαλάσσῃ προσελθεῖν.

Τῆς δὲ θαλάσσης ἡ χροιὰ διπλῆ· τὸ μὲν γὰρ
πρὸς τὴν γῆν ὑπέρυθρον, κυάνεον δὲ τὸ πρὸς τὸ
9 πέλαγος. ἀφρὸς ἐπεποίητο καὶ πέτραι καὶ
κύματα· αἱ πέτραι τῆς γῆς ὑπερβεβλημέναι, ὁ
ἀφρὸς περιλευκαίνων τὰς πέτρας, τὸ κῦμα κορυφούμενον καὶ περὶ τὰς πέτρας λυόμενον εἰς τοὺς
ἀφρούς. ταῦρος ἐν μέσῃ τῇ θαλάσσῃ ἐγέγραπτο
τοῖς κύμασιν ἐποχούμενος, ὡς ὄρους ἀναβαίνοντος
τοῦ κύματος, ἔνθα καμπτόμενον τοῦ βοὸς κυρ-
10 τοῦται τὸ σκέλος. ἡ παρθένος μέσοις ἐπεκάθητο
τοῖς νώτοις τοῦ βοός, οὐ περιβάδην, ἀλλὰ κατὰ
πλευράν, ἐπὶ δεξιὰ συμβᾶσα τὼ πόδε, τῇ λαιᾷ
τοῦ κέρως ἐχομένη, ὥσπερ ἡνίοχος χαλινοῦ· καὶ
γὰρ ὁ βοῦς ἐπέστραπτο ταύτῃ μᾶλλον πρὸς τὸ
τῆς χειρὸς ἕλκον ἡνιοχούμενος. χιτὼν ἀμφὶ τὰ
στέρνα τῆς παρθένου μέχρις αἰδοῦς· τοὐντεῦθεν
ἐπεκάλυπτε χλαῖνα τὰ κάτω τοῦ σώματος.
λευκὸς ὁ χιτών· ἡ χλαῖνα πορφυρᾶ· τὸ δὲ σῶμα
11 διὰ τῆς ἐσθῆτος ὑπεφαίνετο. βαθὺς ὀμφαλός·
γαστὴρ τεταμένη· λαπάρα στενή· τὸ στενὸν εἰς
ἰξὺν καταβαῖνον ηὐρύνετο· μαζοὶ τῶν στέρνων
ἠρέμα προκύπτοντες· ἡ συνάγουσα ζώνη τὸν
χιτῶνα καὶ τοὺς μαζοὺς ἔκλειε, καὶ ἐγίνετο τοῦ
12 σώματος κάτοπτρον ὁ χιτών. αἱ χεῖρες ἄμφω
διετέταντο, ἡ μὲν ἐπὶ κέρας, ἡ δὲ ἐπ᾽ οὐράν·

open upon the sea, and their lips were slightly
parted, as if they were about to utter a cry of fear;
their hands were stretched out in the direction of
the bull. They were standing on the water's edge,
so that the surge just wetted their feet: and they
seemed to be anxious to run after the bull, but to be
afraid of entering the water.

The sea had two different tinges of colour;
towards the land it was almost red, but out towards
the deep water it was dark blue : and foam, and
rocks, and wave crests had been painted in it.
The rocks ran out from the shore and were whitened
with foam, while the waves rose into crests and
were then dashed into foam by breaking upon the
rocks. Far out in the ocean was painted a bull
breasting the waves, while a billow rose like a
mountain where his leg was bent in swimming : the
maiden sat on the middle of his back, not astride
but sideways, with her feet held together on the
right : with her left hand she clung to his horn,
like a charioteer holding the reins, and the bull
inclined a little in that direction, guided by the
pressure of her hand. On the upper part of her
body she wore a tunic down to her groin, and
then a robe covered the lower part of her body :
the tunic was white, the robe purple : and her
figure could be traced under the clothes—the
deep-set navel, the long slight curve of the belly,
the narrow waist, broadening down to the loins,
the breasts gently swelling from her bosom and
confined, as well as her tunic, by a girdle : and
the tunic was a kind of mirror of the shape of
her body. Her hands were held widely apart, the
one to the bull's horn, the other to his tail ; and

ἤρτητο δὲ ἀμφοῖν ἑκατέρωθεν ὑπὲρ τὴν κεφαλὴν
καλύπτρα κύκλῳ τῶν νώτων ἐμπεπετασμένη· ὁ
δὲ κόλπος τοῦ πέπλου πάντοθεν ἐτέτατο κυρτού-
μενος· καὶ ἦν οὗτος ἄνεμος τοῦ ζωγράφου. ἡ
δὲ δίκην ἐπεκάθητο τῷ ταύρῳ πλεούσης νεώς,
13 ὥσπερ ἱστίῳ τῷ πέπλῳ χρωμένη. περὶ δὲ τὸν
βοῦν ὠρχοῦντο δελφῖνες, ἔπαιζον Ἔρωτες· εἶπες
ἂν αὐτῶν γεγράφθαι καὶ τὰ κινήματα. Ἔρως
εἷλκε τὸν βοῦν· Ἔρως, μικρὸν παιδίον, ἡπλώκει
τὸ πτερόν, ἤρτητο τὴν¹ φαρέτραν, ἐκράτει τὸ
πῦρ· ἐπέστραπτο δὲ ὡς ἐπὶ τὸν Δία καὶ ὑπε-
μειδία, ὥσπερ αὐτοῦ καταγελῶν, ὅτι δι᾽ αὐτὸν
γέγονε βοῦς.

2. Ἐγὼ δὲ καὶ τἆλλα μὲν ἐπῄνουν τῆς
γραφῆς, ἅτε δὲ ὢν ἐρωτικὸς περιεργότερον ἔβλεπον τὸν ἄγοντα τὸν βοῦν Ἔρωτα, καὶ "Οἷον,"
εἶπον, "ἄρχει βρέφος οὐρανοῦ καὶ γῆς καὶ
θαλάσσης." ταῦτά μου λέγοντος, νεανίσκος καὶ
αὐτὸς παρεστώς, "Ἐγὼ ταῦτ᾽ ἂν ἐδείκνυν," ἔφη,
2 "τοσαύτας ὕβρεις ἐξ ἔρωτος παθών." "Καὶ τί

---

¹ It seems necessary to supply, with Hercher, the definite article, in order to make the expression balance with
the others of the same sentence.

---

¹ This picture may be compared with the short description
in Ovid, *Metamorphoses*, vi. 101 *seq*.:—

A Lydian maiden in her web did portray to the full
How Europe was by royal Jove beguiled in shape of Bull.
A swimming bull, a swelling sea, so lively had she wrought
The lady seemed looking back to landward and to cry
Upon her women, and to fear the water sprinkling high,
And shrinking up her fearful feet.

with both she held above her head the ends of
her veil which floated down about her shoulders,
bellying out through its whole length and so giving
the impression of a painted breeze. Thus she was
seated on the bull like a vessel under way, using the
veil as a sail; about the bull dolphins gambolled,
Cupids sported: they actually seemed to move in
the picture. Love himself led the bull—Love, in
the guise of a tiny boy, his wings stretched out,
wearing his quiver, his lighted torch in his hands:
he was turning towards Zeus with a smile on his
face, as if he were laughing at him for becoming a
bull for his sake.[1]

2. I was admiring the whole of the picture, but—
a lover myself—paid particular attention to that
part of it where love was leading the bull; and
" Look," I said, " how that imp dominates over sky
and land and sea ! " As I was speaking, a young man
standing by me broke in: " I may term myself a
living example of it," he said; " I am one who has
suffered many buffets from the hand of Love." " How
is that ? " said I. " What have your sufferings been,

The subject was closely connected with Sidon, and is represented, almost exactly as in Achilles Tatius' description (so

far as the bull and his burden are concerned) on the Sidonian
coins.

πέπονθας," εἶπον, "ὦγαθέ; καὶ γὰρ ὁρῶ σου τὴν
ὄψιν οὐ μακρὰν τῆς τοῦ θεοῦ τελετῆς." "Σμῆνος
ἀνεγείρεις," εἶπε, "λόγων· τὰ γὰρ ἐμὰ μύθοις
ἔοικε." "Μὴ κατοκνήσῃς, ὦ βέλτιστε," ἔφην,
"πρὸς τοῦ Διὸς καὶ τοῦ Ἔρωτος αὐτοῦ, ταύτῃ
3 μᾶλλον ἥσειν, εἰ καὶ μύθοις ἔοικε." καὶ ταῦτα
δὴ λέγων, δεξιοῦμαί τε αὐτὸν καὶ ἐπί τινος
ἄλσους ἄγω γείτονος, ἔνθα πλάτανοι μὲν ἐπεφύκεσαν πολλαὶ καὶ πυκναί, παρέρρει δὲ ὕδωρ
ψυχρόν τε καὶ διαυγές, οἷον ἀπὸ χιόνος ἄρτι
λυθείσης ἔρχεται. καθίσας οὖν αὐτὸν ἐπί τινος
θώκου χαμαιζήλου καὶ αὐτὸς παρακαθισάμενος,
"Ὥρα σοι," ἔφην, "τῆς τῶν λόγων ἀκροάσεως·
πάντως δὲ ὁ τόπος [1] ἡδὺς καὶ μύθων ἄξιος ἐρω-
τικῶν."

3. Ὁ δὲ ἄρχεται τοῦ λέγειν ὧδε· Ἐμοὶ Φοινίκη
γένος, Τύρος πατρίς, ὄνομα Κλειτοφῶν, πατὴρ
Ἱππίας, ἀδελφὸς πατρὸς Σώστρατος, οὐ πάντα
δὲ ἀδελφός, ἀλλ᾽ ὅσον ἀμφοῖν εἷς πατήρ· αἱ γὰρ
μητέρες, τῷ μὲν ἦν Βυζαντία, τῷ δὲ ἐμῷ πατρὶ
Τυρία. ὁ μὲν οὖν τὸν πάντα χρόνον εἶχεν ἐν
Βυζαντίῳ· πολὺς γὰρ ὁ τῆς μητρὸς κλῆρος ἦν
2 αὐτῷ· ὁ δὲ ἐμὸς πατὴρ ἐν Τύρῳ κατῴκει. τὴν
δὲ μητέρα οὐκ οἶδα τὴν ἐμήν· ἐπὶ νηπίῳ γάρ
μοι τέθνηκεν. ἐδέησεν οὖν τῷ πατρὶ γυναικὸς
ἑτέρας, ἐξ ἧς ἀδελφή μοι Καλλιγόνη γίνεται.
καὶ ἐδόκει μὲν τῷ πατρὶ συνάψαι μᾶλλον ἡμᾶς
γάμῳ· αἱ δὲ Μοῖραι τῶν ἀνθρώπων κρείττονες
ἄλλην ἐτήρουν μοι γυναῖκα.

---

[1] MSS. ὁ τοιοῦτος τόπος. Hirschig and Hercher, following
Scaliger, seem right to omit τοιοῦτος.

my friend? I can see by your looks that you are not far from being one of the god's initiates." "You are stirring a whole swarm of stories," said he; "my adventures are really like fiction." "I hope, Sir," said I, "in the name of Zeus and that very god Love, that you will not hesitate to give me all the same the pleasure of hearing them, even if they are like fiction": and while I was speaking I took him by the hand and led him to a grove at no great distance, where many thick plane-trees were growing, and a stream of water flowing through, cool and translucent, as if it came from freshly melted snow. There I bade him sit down on a low bench, and I sat by him, and said: "Now is the time to hear your tale; and the surroundings are pleasant and altogether suitable for listening to a love-story."

3. This is how he began: I am a Phoenician by nation, my country is Tyre; my name is Clitophon, my father is called Hippias, my uncle Sostratus; but he was only my father's half-brother, on the father's side, for my grandfather was twice married: my uncle's mother was a Byzantine woman, my father's a Tyrian. My uncle has lived all his life at Byzantium, having inherited there a very considerable property from his mother; my father stayed in Tyre. My mother I never knew, as she died when I was a baby; and then my father took a second wife, who was the mother of my sister Calligone. To this sister my father determined to unite me in marriage[1]; but Fate, stronger than the will of man, was reserving another to be my wife.

---

[1] Marriage was allowed in ancient Greece between half-brothers and half-sisters descended from the same father, but not between *uterine* half-brothers and half-sisters.

Φιλεῖ δὲ τὸ δαιμόνιον τὸ μέλλον ἀνθρώποις νύκτωρ πολλάκις λαλεῖν· οὐχ ἵνα φυλάξωνται μὴ παθεῖν (οὐ γὰρ εἱμαρμένης δύνανται κρατεῖν)
3 ἀλλ' ἵνα κουφότερον πάσχοντες φέρωσι. τὸ μὲν γὰρ ἐξαίφνης ἀθρόον καὶ ἀπροσδόκητον ἐκπλήσσει τὴν ψυχὴν ἄφνω προσπεσὸν καὶ κατεβάπτισε· τὸ δὲ πρὸ τοῦ παθεῖν προσδοκώμενον προκατηνάλωσε κατὰ μικρὸν μελετώμενον τοῦ πάθους τὴν ἀκμήν. ἐπεὶ γὰρ εἶχον ἔννατον ἔτος ἐπὶ τοῖς δέκα, καὶ παρεσκεύαζεν ὁ πατὴρ εἰς νέωτα ποιήσων τοὺς γάμους, ἤρχετο τοῦ
4 δράματος ἡ τύχη. ὄναρ ἐδόκουν συμφῦναι τῇ παρθένῳ τὰ κάτω μέρη μέχρις ὀμφαλοῦ, δύο δὲ ἐντεῦθεν τὰ ἄνω σώματα· ἐφίσταται δέ μοι γυνὴ φοβερὰ καὶ μεγάλη, τὸ πρόσωπον ἀγρία. ὀφθαλμὸς ἐν αἵματι, βλοσυραὶ παρειαί, ὄφεις αἱ κόμαι· ἅρπην ἐκράτει τῇ δεξιᾷ, δᾷδα τῇ λαιᾷ. ἐπιπεσοῦσα οὖν μοι θυμῷ καὶ ἀνατείνασα τὴν ἅρπην, καταφέρει τῆς ἰξύος, ἔνθα τῶν δύο σωμάτων ἦσαν αἱ συμβολαί, καὶ ἀποκόπτει
5 μου τὴν παρθένον. περιδεὴς οὖν ἀναθορὼν ἐκ τοῦ δείματος,[1] φράζω μὲν πρὸς οὐδένα, κατ' ἐμαυτὸν δὲ πονηρὰ ἐσκεπτόμην.

Ἐν δὲ τούτῳ συμβαίνει τοιάδε. ἦν ἀδελφός, ὡς ἔφην, τοῦ πατρὸς Σώστρατος· παρὰ τούτου τις ἔρχεται κομίζων ἐπιστολὰς ἀπὸ Βυζαντίου· καὶ ἦν τὰ γεγραμμένα τοιάδε·

6   Ἱππίᾳ τῷ ἀδελφῷ χαίρειν Σώστρατος.

Ἥκουσι πρὸς σὲ θυγάτηρ ἐμὴ Λευκίππη καὶ Πάνθεια γυνή· πόλεμος γὰρ περιλαμβάνει

---

[1] Knox proposes δεμνίου or στρώματος.

Providence sometimes foreshews the future to men in dreams, not so that they may be able to avoid the sufferings fated for them, for they can never get the better of destiny, but in order that they may bear them with the more patience when those sufferings come : for when disasters come all together and unexpectedly, they strike the spirit with so severe and sudden a blow that they overwhelm it ; while if they are anticipated, the mind, by dwelling on them beforehand, is able little by little to turn the edge of sorrow. Well, I was nineteen years of age, and my father was making preparations to celebrate my marriage in the following year, when Fate began the drama of my fortunes. I had a dream, in which I seemed to have grown into one with Calligone from the belly downwards, while above we had two separate bodies : then there stood over me a tall woman of fearful appearance ; she had a savage countenance, blood-shot eyes, grim, rough cheeks, and snakes for hair ; in her right hand she held a sickle, and in her left a torch. She advanced angrily upon me, brandishing the sickle : and then struck with it at my waist, where the two bodies joined, and so cut the maiden away from me. In mortal fear I jumped up, terrified : I told nobody the dream, but revolved inwardly the most gloomy forebodings.

Meanwhile, the following events were happening. My father's brother, as I told you, was Sostratus ; and a messenger came from him bringing letters from Byzantium. This was the purport of them :—

Sostratus, to his brother Hippias, greeting.

My daughter Leucippe and my wife Panthea are on their way to you : war has been declared by the Thracians

Βυζαντίους Θρακικός. σῶζε δή μοι τὰ φίλτατα
τοῦ γένους μέχρι τῆς τοῦ πολέμου τύχης.

4. Ταῦτα ὁ πατὴρ ἀναγνοὺς ἀναπηδᾷ καὶ ἐπὶ
τὴν θάλασσαν ἐκτρέχει καὶ μικρὸν ὕστερον
αὖθις ἐπανῆκεν. εἵποντο δὲ αὐτῷ κατόπιν πολὺ
πλῆθος οἰκετῶν καὶ θεραπαινίδων, ἃς συνεκ-
πέμψας ὁ Σώστρατος ἐτύγχανε ταῖς γυναιξίν· ἐν
μέσοις δὲ ἦν γυνὴ μεγάλη καὶ πλουσία τῇ
2 στολῇ. ὡς δὲ ἐπέτεινα τοὺς ὀφθαλμοὺς ἐπ'
αὐτήν, ἐν ἀριστερᾷ παρθένος ἐκφαίνεταί μοι,
καὶ καταστράπτει μου τοὺς ὀφθαλμοὺς τῷ
3 προσώπῳ. τοιαύτην εἶδον ἐγώ ποτε ἐπὶ ταύρῳ
γεγραμμένην Εὐρώπην·[1] ὄμμα γοργὸν ἐν ἡδονῇ·
κόμη ξανθή, τὸ ξανθὸν οὖλον· ὀφρὺς μέλαινα,
τὸ μέλαν ἄκρατον· λευκὴ παρειά, τὸ λευκὸν
εἰς μέσον ἐφοινίσσετο καὶ ἐμιμεῖτο πορφύραν
οἵαν εἰς[2] τὸν ἐλέφαντα Λυδία βάπτει γυνή· τὸ
στόμα ῥόδων ἄνθος ἦν, ὅταν ἄρχηται τὸ ῥόδον
4 ἀνοίγειν τῶν φύλλων τὰ χείλη. ὡς δὲ εἶδον,
εὐθὺς ἀπωλώλειν· κάλλος γὰρ ὀξύτερον τιτρώσκει βέλους καὶ διὰ τῶν ὀφθαλμῶν εἰς τὴν
ψυχὴν καταρρεῖ· ὀφθαλμὸς γὰρ ὁδὸς ἐρωτικῷ
5 τραύματι. πάντα δέ με εἶχεν ὁμοῦ, ἔπαινος,
ἔκπληξις, τρόμος, αἰδώς, ἀναίδεια· ἐπήνουν τὸ
μέγεθος, ἐξεπεπλήγμην τὸ κάλλος, ἔτρεμον τὴν
καρδίαν, ἔβλεπον ἀναιδῶς, ἠδούμην ἁλῶναι. τοὺς
δὲ ὀφθαλμοὺς ἀφέλκειν μὲν ἀπὸ τῆς κόρης
ἐβιαζόμην· οἱ δὲ οὐκ ἤθελον, ἀλλ' ἀνθεῖλκον

---

[1] The MSS. all have Σελήνην: but it seems necessary to
adopt the reading of the β MSS. Εὐρώπην, to give some point
to the introduction of the story. But cf. Vilborg's commentary, pp. 21–22.

*against the Byzantines.   Keep safe these, the dearest of
my family, until the war is decided one way or the other.*

4. Directly my father had read these words, he
jumped up and hurried down to the sea-shore.   He
was not long in returning, and then there followed
him a great number of men-servants and maid-
servants, sent by Sostratus to accompany his ladies :
in the middle of them walked a tall woman richly
dressed ; and as I gazed at her, I suddenly saw a
maiden on her left, who blinded my eyes, as with a
stroke of lightning, by the beauty of her face.
She was like that picture of Europa on the bull
which I saw but just now : an eye at once piercing
and voluptuous ; golden hair in golden curls ; black
eyebrows—jet black ; pale cheeks, the pallor shading
in the centre into a ruddy hue, like that stain
wherewith the Lydian women tint ivory ; and a
mouth that was a rose—a rose-bud just beginning to
uncurl its petals.   Directly I saw her, I was lost :
for beauty wounds deeper than any arrow and
strikes down through the eyes into the soul ; the
eye is the passage for love's wound.` All manner
of feelings took possession of me at once—admira-
tion, stupefaction, fear, shame, shamelessness. I admired her tall form, I was stupefied by her beauty,
I shewed my fear by the beating of my heart; I
stared shamelessly at her, but I was ashamed to be
caught doing so.   Try as I would to drag my eyes away
from gazing upon her, they would not obey me, but

---

² εἰς οἵαν Vilborg: οἵαν εἰς the MSS. Wifstrand deletes εἰς.

ἑαυτοὺς ἐκεῖ τῷ τοῦ κάλλους ἑλκόμενοι πείσματι,
καὶ τέλος ἐνίκησαν.

5. Αἱ μὲν δὴ κατήγοντο πρὸς ἡμᾶς, καὶ αὐταῖς
ὁ πατὴρ μέρος τι τῆς οἰκίας ἀποτεμόμενος,
εὐτρεπίζει δεῖπνον. καὶ ἐπεὶ καιρὸς ἦν, συνεπίνομεν κατὰ δύο τὰς κλίνας διαλαχόντες (οὕτω
γὰρ ἔταξεν ὁ πατήρ), αὐτὸς κἀγὼ τὴν μέσην,
αἱ μητέρες αἱ δύο τὴν ἐν ἀριστερᾷ, τὴν δεξιὰν
2 εἶχον αἱ παρθένοι. ἐγὼ δὲ ὡς ταύτην ἤκουσα
τὴν εὐταξίαν, μικροῦ προσελθὼν κατεφίλησα
τὸν πατέρα, ὅτι μοι κατ᾽ ὀφθαλμοὺς ἀνέκλινε
3 τὴν παρθένον. τί μὲν οὖν ἔφαγον, μὰ τοὺς
θεούς, ἔγωγε οὐκ ᾔδειν· ἐῴκειν γὰρ τοῖς ἐν
ὀνείροις ἐσθίουσιν. ἐρείσας δὲ κατὰ τῆς στρωμνῆς τὸν ἀγκῶνα καὶ ἐγκλίνας ἐμαυτόν, ὅλοις
ἔβλεπον τὴν κόρην τοῖς προσώποις, κλέπτων ἅμα
τὴν θέαν· τοῦτο γάρ μοι ἦν τὸ δεῖπνον. ὡς δὲ
4 ἦμεν ἀπὸ τοῦ δείπνου, παῖς εἰσέρχεται κιθάραν
ἁρμοσάμενος, τοῦ πατρὸς οἰκέτης, καὶ ψιλαῖς

---

[1] The dinner couches were thus arranged :

	HIPPIAS	CLITOPHON	
PANTHEA		Table	LEUCIPPE
CLITOPHON'S STEPMOTHER			CALLIGONE

As the guests at a Greek dinner-party reclined on their
left elbows, leaving the right arm free for eating and

16

remained fixed upon her by the force of her beauty, and at length they won the day against my will.

5. Such was the manner of their arrival. My father then set aside for their use a part of the house, and ordered dinner to be made ready. When the hour for it came, we sat down two on each couch. my father arranged that he and I should occupy the middle one, the two mothers that on the left, and the two maidens the right-hand one. I was overjoyed when I heard of this arrangement,[1] and I could hardly restrain myself from publicly embracing my father for thus putting the girl under my very eyes. I swear that I have not the slightest idea what I ate—I was like a man eating in a dream. I rested myself firmly on my elbow on the couch, and, leaning forward, devoured the maiden with my eyes, sometimes intercepting a glance on her part; for that was my dinner. After it was over, a young slave (one of my father's servants) came in with a lute ready tuned; first of all he played it with his

---

drinking, the expressions *left* and *right* in the text, describing the benches on which the ladies of the party reclined, must be from the point of view of a spectator looking up towards the middle bench occupied by the two men.

τὸ πρῶτον διατινάξας ταῖς χερσί, τὰς χορδὰς
ἔκρουε, καί τι κρουμάτιον ὑπολιγήνας ὑποψιθυρί-
ζουσι τοῖς δακτύλοις, μετὰ τοῦτο ἤδη τῷ πλήκ-
τρῳ τὰς χορδὰς ἔκρουε, καὶ ὀλίγον ὅσον κιθαρί-
5 σας συνῇδε τοῖς κρούμασι. τὸ δὲ ᾆσμα ἦν,
Ἀπόλλων μεμφόμενος τὴν Δάφνην φεύγουσαν
καὶ διώκων ἅμα καὶ μέλλων καταλαμβάνειν,
καὶ γινομένη φυτὸν ἡ κόρη, καὶ Ἀπόλλων τὸ
φυτὸν στεφανούμενος. τοῦτό μοι μᾶλλον ἀσθὲν
6 εἰς τέλος τὴν ψυχὴν ἐξέκαυσεν· ὑπέκκαυμα γὰρ
ἐπιθυμίας λόγος ἐρωτικός· κἂν εἰς σωφροσύνην
τις ἑαυτὸν νουθετῇ, τῷ παραδείγματι πρὸς τὴν
μίμησιν ἐρεθίζεται, μάλιστα ὅταν ἐκ τοῦ κρείττονος ᾖ τὸ παράδειγμα· ἡ γὰρ ὧν ἁμαρτάνει
τις αἰδὼς τῷ τοῦ βελτίονος ἀξιώματι παρρησία
7 γίνεται. καὶ ταῦτα πρὸς ἐμαυτὸν ἔλεγον· "Ἰδοὺ
καὶ Ἀπόλλων ἐρᾷ, κἀκεῖνος παρθένου, καὶ ἐρῶν
οὐκ αἰσχύνεται, ἀλλὰ διώκει τὴν παρθένον· σὺ δὲ
ὀκνεῖς, καὶ αἰδῇ, καὶ ἀκαίρως σωφρονεῖς; μὴ
κρείττων εἶ τοῦ θεοῦ;"

6. Ὡς δὲ ἦν ἑσπέρα, πρότεραι μὲν πρὸς
ὕπνον ἐτράπησαν αἱ γυναῖκες· μικρὸν δὲ ὕστερον
καὶ ἡμεῖς· οἱ μὲν δὴ ἄλλοι τῇ γαστρὶ μετρή-
σαντες τὴν ἡδονήν, ἐγὼ δὲ τὴν εὐωχίαν ἐν τοῖς
ὀφθαλμοῖς φέρων, τῶν τε τῆς κόρης προσώπων
γεμισθεὶς καὶ ἀκράτῳ θεάματι καὶ μέχρι κόρου
2 προελθών, ἀπῆλθον μεθύων ἔρωτι. ὡς δὲ εἰς τὸ
δωμάτιον παρῆλθον, ἔνθα μοι καθεύδειν ἔθος ἦν,
οὐδὲ ὕπνου τυχεῖν ἠδυνάμην. ἔστι μὲν γὰρ

hands alone, sweeping over the strings and producing a subdued tone by twanging them with his
fingers ; then he struck the strings with the plectrum,
and having played a short prelude he sang in concert
with the music. The subject of his song was the
chiding of Apollo as Daphne fled from him ; his
pursuit, and how he all but caught her; and then
how the maid became a tree, and how Apollo made
himself a crown out of its leaves. This story, as
he sang it, at last set my heart more fiercely ablaze :
for love stories are the very fuel of desire ; and however much a man may school himself to continence,
by the force of example he is stimulated to imitate
it, especially when that example proceeds from one
in a higher position than himself: for that shame,
which prevents a man going astray, is converted
into boldness by the approval of one of higher
rank. So I said to myself : " Look, here is Apollo
in love, and like you in love with a maiden ; and
when he is in love, he feels no shame about it,
but pursues his maiden, while you hesitate and
profess to be ashamed, and encourage a most untimely continence : do you put yourself above a
god ?"

6. When the evening came, the women went
first to bed, and we followed their example after
a short interval. The others had taken their
pleasure by the satisfying of their appetite, but
all *my* feast was through my eyes : so that I retired
to rest gorged with the vision of the maiden's face
and sated with undiluted gazing upon her. Indeed,
I was drunk with love ; but when I reached the
chamber where I always lay I was unable to get
to sleep. For Nature will have it that diseases and

φύσει καὶ τἆλλα νοσήματα καὶ τὰ τοῦ σώματος
τραύματα ἐν [1] νυκτὶ χαλεπώτερα, καὶ ἐπανίσταται
μᾶλλον ἡμῖν ἡσυχάζουσι καὶ ἐρεθίζει τὰς
3 ἀλγηδόνας· ὅταν γὰρ ἀναπαύηται τὸ σῶμα,
τότε σχολάζει τὸ ἕλκος νοσεῖν· τὰ δὲ τῆς
ψυχῆς τραύματα, μὴ κινουμένου τοῦ σώματος,
πολὺ μᾶλλον ὀδυνᾷ. ἐν ἡμέρᾳ μὲν γὰρ ὀφθαλμοὶ
καὶ ὦτα πολλῆς γεμιζόμενα περιεργίας ἐπικου-
φίζει τῆς νόσου τὴν ἀκμήν, ἀντιπεριάγοντα
τὴν ψυχὴν τῆς εἰς τὸ πονεῖν σχολῆς· ἐὰν δὲ
ἡσυχίᾳ τὸ σῶμα πεδηθῇ, καθ' ἑαυτὴν ἡ ψυχὴ
4 γενομένη τῷ κακῷ κυμαίνεται. πάντα γὰρ
ἐξεγείρεται τότε τὰ τέως κοιμώμενα· τοῖς πεν-
θοῦσιν αἱ λῦπαι· τοῖς μεριμνῶσιν αἱ φροντίδες·
τοῖς κινδυνεύουσιν οἱ φόβοι· τοῖς ἐρῶσι τὸ πῦρ.
περὶ δὲ τὴν ἔω μόλις ἐλεήσας μέ τις ὕπνος
5 ἀνέπαυσεν ὀλίγον. ἀλλ' οὐδὲ τότε μου τῆς
ψυχῆς ἀπελθεῖν ἤθελεν ἡ κόρη· πάντα γὰρ ἦν
μοι Λευκίππη τὰ ἐνύπνια· διελεγόμην αὐτῇ,
συνέπαιζον, συνεδείπνουν, ἡπτόμην, πλείονα
εἶχον ἀγαθὰ τῆς ἡμέρας. καὶ γὰρ κατεφίλησα,
καὶ ἦν τὸ φίλημα ἀληθινόν· ὥστε ἐπειδή με
ἤγειρεν ὁ οἰκέτης, ἐλοιδορούμην αὐτῷ τῆς
ἀκαιρίας, ὡς ἀπολέσας ὄνειρον οὕτω γλυκύν.
6 ἀναστὰς οὖν ἐβάδιζον ἐξεπίτηδες εἴσω τῆς οἰκίας
κατὰ πρόσωπον τῆς κόρης, βιβλίον ἅμα κρατῶν,
καὶ ἐγκεκυφὼς ἀνεγίνωσκον· τὸν δὲ ὀφθαλμόν,
εἰ κατὰ τὰς θύρας γενοίμην, ὑπείλιττον κάτωθεν,

---

[1] ἐν was inserted by Cobet. I do not feel quite certain
that νυκτί alone would not bear the sense. Hercher suggested
νυκτός, which is not impossible, though he did not admit it
into his text.

bodily wounds are worse at night: while we are at rest they obtain more power to attack us and aggravate the pain that they cause; for when the body is still, the wound has the more leisure to hurt. In like manner the wounds of the soul are far more painful when the body is at rest: for during the daytime the eyes and ears have plenty of occupation and so turn the edge of the disease, distracting the soul so that it has less leisure for its grief; but when the body is bound fast by bodily rest, the soul has the greater freedom to be tossed about by its woe: all the sensations which were lately at rest are then aroused; mourners feel their grief anew, the anxious their cares, those in danger their fears, and lovers their consuming flame. Hardly about daybreak did sleep of a kind take pity upon me and give me a little respite: but not even then could I banish the maiden from my mind; Leucippe was all my dreams—I spoke with her, I sported with her, I ate with her, I touched her; yes, I obtained a greater degree of happiness than in the daytime; for I kissed her, and it was a real kiss: the natural result was that when my servant came to wake me, I upbraided him bitterly for his untimely coming, so that I thus lost so sweet a dream. I arose therefore, and determined to walk up and down somewhere in the house, into my sweetheart's presence. I took a book, and bent over it, and pretended to read; but every time that I was at the door, my eyes, off the book, ogled her slyly. So making several journeys, and

καί τινας ἐμπεριπατήσας διαύλους, καὶ ἐποχε-
τευσάμενος ἐκ τῆς θέας ἔρωτα, σαφῶς ἀπῄειν
ἔχων τὴν ψυχὴν κακῶς. καὶ ταῦτά μοι τριῶν
ἡμερῶν ἐπυρσεύετο.

7. Ἦν δέ μοι Κλεινίας ἀνεψιός, ὀρφανὸς καὶ
νέος, δύο ἀναβεβηκὼς ἔτη τῆς ἡλικίας τῆς ἐμῆς,
ἔρωτι τετελεσμένος· μειρακίου δὲ ὁ ἔρως ἦν.
οὕτω δὲ εἶχε φιλοτιμίας πρὸς αὐτό, ὥστε καὶ
ἵππον πριάμενος, ἐπεὶ θεασάμενον τὸ μειράκιον
ἐπῄνεσεν, εὐθὺς ἐχαρίσατο φέρων αὐτῷ τὸν ἵπ-
2 πον. ἔσκωπτον οὖν αὐτὸν ἀεὶ τῆς ἀμεριμνίας, ὅτι
σχολάζει φιλεῖν καὶ δοῦλός ἐστιν ἐρωτικῆς ἡδονῆς·
ὁ δέ μοι μειδιῶν καὶ τὴν κεφαλὴν ἐπισείων
ἔλεγεν· "Ἔσῃ ποτὲ καὶ σύ μοι δοῦλος ταχύ."
3 πρὸς τοῦτον ἀπιὼν καὶ ἀσπασάμενος καὶ παρακαθισάμενος, "Ἔδωκα," ἔφην, "Κλεινία, σοι δίκην
τῶν σκωμμάτων. δοῦλος γέγονα κἀγώ." ἀνα-
κροτήσας οὖν τὰς χεῖρας ἐξεγέλασε, καὶ ἀναστὰς
κατεφίλησέ μου τὸ πρόσωπον, ἐμφαῖνον ἐρωτικὴν ἀγρυπνίαν· καί, "Ἐρᾷς," εἶπεν, "ἐρᾷς
ἀληθῶς· οἱ ὀφθαλμοί σου λέγουσιν."

Ἄρτι δὲ λέγοντος αὐτοῦ, Χαρικλῆς εἰστρέχει
(τοῦτο γὰρ ἦν ὄνομα τῷ μειρακίῳ) τεθορυβημένος,
4 "Οἴχομαί σοι," λέγων, "Κλεινία." καὶ συνε-
στέναξεν ὁ Κλεινίας, ὥσπερ ἐκ τῆς ἐκείνου
ψυχῆς κρεμάμενος· καὶ τῇ φωνῇ τρέμων,
"Ἀποκτενεῖς," εἶπε, "σιωπῶν· τί σε λυπεῖ;
τίνι δεῖ μάχεσθαι;" καὶ ὁ Χαρικλῆς, "Γάμον,"
εἶπεν, "ὁ πατήρ μοι προξενεῖ, καὶ γάμον
ἀμόρφου κόρης, ἵνα διπλῷ συνοικῶ κακῷ. πονηρὸν μὲν γὰρ γυνή, κἂν εὔμορφος ᾖ· ἐὰν δὲ καὶ

drawing in fresh draughts of love every time I saw her, I returned with my heart in ill case indeed. And those flames went on burning up in me for the next three days.

7. Now I had a cousin called Clinias. Both his parents were dead, and he was young, two years older than myself; one of Love's adepts. But the object of his affections was a youth; and so strong were his feelings towards him that once when he had bought a horse, and the boy saw it and admired it, he at once sent it to him as a present. So I used constantly to be laughing at him for neglecting all his proper pursuits and having leisure for nought but his affections, a slave to love and pleasure; but he always used to smile, wagging his head and saying: "Mark my words, some day you will be a slave too." To him then I went, and greeted him, and said: "At last, Clinias, I have been paid out for all my scoffing: I too have become a slave." He clapped his hands and burst out laughing; then he rose and kissed me—my face bore every sign of a lover's sleeplessness—and, "Yes," he said, "you are really in love: your tell-tale eyes shew it."

He was still speaking, when Charicles (that was the name of his dear youth) burst in, greatly disordered, crying: "It is all over with me, Clinias." Clinias gave a deep groan, as though his life hung on his friend's, and murmured with a trembling voice: "You will kill me if you do not tell me at once; what is your trouble? What have we to fight against?" "Marriage!" Charicles answered, "which my father is arranging for me, and a marriage with an ugly girl, to give me double agony. Any woman is bad enough, however fair; but if she

ACHILLES TATIUS

5 ἀμορφίαν δυστυχῆ, διπλοῦν τὸ κακόν. ἀλλὰ
πρὸς τὸν πλοῦτον ὁ πατὴρ ἀποβλέπων σπουδάζει
τὸ κῆδος. ἐκδίδομαι ὁ δυστυχὴς τοῖς ἐκείνης
χρήμασιν, ἵνα γήμω πωλούμενος."
8. Ὡς οὖν ταῦτα ἤκουσεν ὁ Κλεινίας.
ὠχρίασεν. ἐπιπαρώξυνεν οὖν τὸ μειράκιον
ἀπωθεῖσθαι τὸν γάμον, τὸ τῶν γυναικῶν γένος
λοιδορῶν. "Γάμον," εἶπεν, "ἤδη σοι δίδωσιν ὁ
2 πατήρ; τί γὰρ ἠδίκηκας, ἵνα καὶ πεδηθῇς; οὐκ
ἀκούεις τοῦ Διὸς λέγοντος

Τοῖς δ' ἐγὼ ἀντὶ πυρὸς δώσω κακόν, ᾧ κεν
ἅπαντες
τέρπωνται κατὰ θυμόν, ἑὸν κακὸν ἀμφαγα-
πῶντες;

αὕτη γυναικῶν[1] ἡδονή· καὶ ἔοικε τῇ τῶν Σειρήνων
φύσει· κἀκεῖναι γὰρ ἡδονῇ φονεύουσιν ᾠδῆς.
3 ἔστι δέ σοι συνιέναι τὸ μέγεθος τοῦ κακοῦ καὶ
ἀπ' αὐτῆς τῆς τοῦ γάμου παρασκευῆς. βόμβος
αὐλῶν, δικλίδων κτύπος, πυρσῶν δᾳδουχία.
ἐρεῖ τις ἰδὼν τοσοῦτον κυδοιμόν· 'Ἀτυχὴς ὁ
μέλλων γαμεῖν· ἐπὶ πόλεμον, δοκῶ μοι, πέμ-
4 πεται.' ἀλλ' εἰ μὲν ἰδιώτης ἦσθα μουσικῆς,
ἠγνόεις ἂν τὰ τῶν γυναικῶν δράματα· νῦν
δὲ κἂν ἄλλοις λέγοις, ὅσων ἐνέπλησαν μύθων
γυναῖκες τὴν σκηνήν. ὁ[2] ὅρμος Ἐριφύλης,

[1] Göttling's correction for the MSS. κακῶν.
[2] Inserted by Cobet. The article seems clearly necessary.

24

has the bad luck to be ugly, the business is twice as bad. But she has a fortune; that is what my father looks at in arranging the match: so that I am unhappy enough to be bartered for her money: I am to be sold into marriage."

8. When Clinias heard this, he grew suddenly pale; and then he urged the youth to refuse the marriage absolutely, abusing the whole female sex. "Marriage!" he said, "is that what your father is arranging for you already? What have you done, to be so fettered? Do you not remember the words of Zeus:

' The stolen fire must be avenged, and so
   Men must seem joyful and hug close their woe'?[1]

Such is the pleasure of woman; she is like the Sirens, who kill men by the charm of their song. Why, the magnitude of the evil can be conjectured from the very preparations for a marriage, the whistling of the flutes, the banging of doors, the carrying of torches; anyone who sees all this disturbance would naturally say: ' How wretched is a bridegroom—he looks to me like one being sent off to the wars.' If you were one that were uninstructed in the examples of poetry, you might perhaps be unaware of women's doings; but, as it is, you know enough even to teach others the kind of stories with which women have filled the stage—

---

[1] Hesiod, *Works and Days*, 57. The punishment sent to men for the fire stolen for them by Prometheus was the gift of woman.

Φιλομήλας ἡ τράπεζα, Σθενοβοίας ἡ διαβολή,
5 Ἀερόπης ἡ κλοπή, Πρόκνης ἡ σφαγή. ἂν τὸ
Χρυσηΐδος κάλλος Ἀγαμέμνων ποθῇ, λοιμὸν τοῖς
Ἕλλησι ποιεῖ· ἂν τὸ Βρισηΐδος κάλλος
Ἀχιλλεύς,[1] πένθος αὐτῷ προξενεῖ· ἐὰν ἔχῃ
γυναῖκα Κανδαύλης καλήν, φονεύει Κανδαύλην ἡ
6 γυνή. τὸ μὲν γὰρ Ἑλένης τῶν γάμων πῦρ
ἀνῆψε κατὰ τῆς Τροίας ἄλλο πῦρ· ὁ δὲ
Πηνελόπης γάμος τῆς σώφρονος πόσους νυμφίους
ἀπώλεσεν; ἀπέκτεινεν Ἱππόλυτον φιλοῦσα
Φαίδρα, Κλυταιμνήστρα δὲ Ἀγαμέμνονα μὴ
7 φιλοῦσα. ὦ πάντα τολμῶσαι γυναῖκες· κἂν
φιλῶσι, φονεύουσι· κἂν μὴ φιλῶσι, φονεύουσιν.
Ἀγαμέμνονα ἔδει φονευθῆναι τὸν καλόν, οὗ
κάλλος ἐπουράνιον ἦν,

Ὄμματα καὶ κεφαλὴν ἴκελος Διΐ τερπικε-
ραύνῳ·

καὶ ταύτην ἀπέκοψεν, ὦ Ζεῦ, τὴν κεφαλὴν
8 γυνή. καὶ ταῦτα μὲν περὶ τῶν εὐμόρφων τις ἂν
εἴποι γυναικῶν, ἔνθα καὶ μέτριον τὸ ἀτύχημα.
τὸ γὰρ κάλλος ἔχει τινὰ[2] παρηγορίαν τῶν κακῶν,
καὶ τοῦτ' ἔστιν ἐν ἀτυχήμασιν εὐτύχημα· εἰ δὲ

---

[1] After Ἀχιλλεύς the MSS. again read ποθῇ (G has ἐρᾷ), the
deletion of which is due to Cobet.
[2] Headlam's correction from MSS. τήν.

---

[1] Amphiaraus, who was a prophet, knew that he was
destined to perish if he joined in the famous attack of the
Seven against Thebes. Polynices, the leader of the invaders,
bribed his wife Eriphyle with a golden necklace to indicate
Amphiaraus' hiding-place and to persuade him to go to his
doom.
[2] Tereus, the husband of Procne, violated her sister Philo-

Eriphyle's necklace,[1] Philomela's feast,[2] Stheno-
boea's false accusation,[3] Aerope's wicked stratagem,[4]
Procne's murder.[5] When Agamemnon desires the
beauty of Chryseis, he brings destruction upon the
Greek army ; when Achilles desires Briseis' beauty,
he makes sorrow for himself. If Candaules[6] has a
fair wife, his wife murders Candaules. The fire of
Helen's marriage-torches lit another fire for Troy.
But Penelope's marriage, chaste creature, how many
suitors did that destroy? Phaedra destroyed Hip-
polytus by loving him, Clytemnestra Agamemnon
because she loved him not. O women, women, that
stay at nothing ! If they love, they kill : and if they
do not love, they kill all the same. Agamemnon
was fated to be murdered—Agamemnon whose
beauty was described to be as of heaven.

> ' In eyes and head like thunder-hurling Zeus,' [7]

and, O Zeus, a woman lopped off that very head.
And all these are the accusations which can be
brought against fair women, where the ill-fortune of
having to do with them is moderated, for beauty is
some consolation in distress, and a certain amount of
good luck amid the bad ; but if the woman is not

mela. To avenge themselves, the women served to him a
cannibal feast of his own son Itys. The story is given at
length in V. v.
  [3] The Potiphar's wife of Greek mythology : Proteus was
Potiphar, Bellerophon Joseph.
  [4] The wicked wife of Atreus, who sinned with her husband's
brother Thyestes.   [5] See footnote 2 above.
  [6] Herodotus, i. 12. Candaules, king of Lydia, was so
infatuated with the beauty of his wife, that he must needs
shew her naked to his friend Gyges : in revenge for the
insult, she plotted with Gyges to kill him and seize his
throne.   [7] Homer, *Iliad*, ii. 478.

μηδὲ εὔμορφος, ὡς φῄς, ἡ συμφορὰ διπλῆ. καὶ
πῶς ἄν τις ἀνάσχοιτο, καὶ ταῦτα μειράκιον οὕτω
9 καλόν; μή, πρὸς θεῶν, Χαρίκλεις, μήπω μοι
δοῦλος γένῃ, μηδὲ τὸ ἄνθος πρὸ καιροῦ τῆς ἥβης
ἀπολέσῃς· πρὸς γὰρ τοῖς ἄλλοις καὶ τοῦτ' ἔστι
τοῦ γάμου τὸ ἀτύχημα· μαραίνει τὴν ἀκμήν. μή,
δέομαι, Χαρίκλεις, μήπω μοι μαρανθῇς· μὴ παρα-
δῶς εὔμορφον τρυγῆσαι ῥόδον ἀμόρφῳ γεωργῷ."
10 καὶ ὁ Χαρικλῆς, "Ταῦτα μέν," ἔφη, "καὶ θεοῖς
κἀμοὶ μελήσει· καὶ γὰρ εἰς τὴν προθεσμίαν τῶν
γάμων χρόνος ἐστὶν ἡμερῶν, πολλὰ δὲ ἂν γένοιτο
καὶ ἐν νυκτὶ μιᾷ· καὶ κατὰ σχολὴν ζητήσομεν.
11 τὸ δὲ νῦν ἔχον, ἐφ' ἱππασίαν ἄπειμι. ἐξ ὅτου
γάρ μοι τὸν ἵππον ἐχαρίσω τὸν καλόν, οὔπω σου
τῶν δώρων ἀπέλαυσα. ἐπικουφιεῖ δέ μοι τὸ
γυμνάσιον τῆς ψυχῆς τὸ λυπούμενον." ὁ μὲν
οὖν ἀπῄει τὴν τελευταίαν ὁδὸν ὕστατα καὶ
πρῶτα μελλήσων ἱππάζεσθαι.

9. Ἐγὼ δὲ πρὸς τὸν Κλεινίαν καταλέγω μου
τὸ δρᾶμα πῶς ἐγένετο, πῶς πάθοιμι, πῶς ἴδοιμι,
τὴν καταγωγήν, τὸ δεῖπνον, τὸ κάλλος τῆς κόρης.
τελευτῶν δὲ τῷ λόγῳ συνίην ἀσχημονῶν, "Οὐ
φέρω," λέγων, "Κλεινία, τὴν ἀνίαν· ὅλος γάρ
μοι προσέπεσεν ὁ ἔρως, καὶ αὐτόν μου διώκει
τὸν ὕπνον τῶν ὀμμάτων· πάντοτε Λευκίππην
2 φαντάζομαι. οὐ γέγονεν ἄλλῳ τινὶ τοιοῦτον
ἀτύχημα· τὸ γὰρ κακόν μοι καὶ συνοικεῖ." καὶ ὁ
Κλεινίας, "Ληρεῖς," εἶπεν, "οὕτως εἰς ἔρωτα εὐτυχῶν. οὐ γὰρ ἐπ' ἀλλοτρίας θύρας ἐλθεῖν σε δεῖ,
οὐδὲ διάκονον παρακαλεῖν· αὐτήν σοι δέδωκε τὴν
3 ἐρωμένην ἡ τύχη καὶ φέρουσα ἔνδον ἵδρυσεν. ἄλλῳ

even **fair**, as you tell me, the misfortune is double. No one could tolerate such a thing—least of all a youth as fair as you. I pray you, Charicles, by all that you hold holy, do not allow yourself to become a slave, do not throw away untimely the flower of your youth; in addition to all its other disadvantages marriage has this, that it does away with the bloom of vigour and beauty. Do not wither yet, Charicles, I implore you; do not hand over a lovely rose to be plucked by an ill-favoured rustic clown." "This whole affair," said Charicles, "must be left to providence and to me; I have, after all, a certain number of days before the day ordained. A great deal can happen even in a single night; and we must think over all this at our leisure. Now, at any rate, I am going riding. I have never made use of your present since you gave me that splendid horse; the exercise will lighten the grief on my mind." So with this he went away, on what was to be his first and last ride.

9. I related to Clinias my whole story—how it came about, my feelings, how I first saw her, the arrival, the dinner, the great beauty of the maiden. At last I felt that I was talking in a very unseemly way, and burst out: "I cannot bear the pain, Clinias; Love with all his forces has attacked me and drives sleep away from my eyes; I see Leucippe always. No one has ever been in such misery as I am; my grief lives always with me." "What nonsense you talk," cried Clinias, "you, who are a fortunate lover. You do not have constantly to be going to the doors of another's house; you have no need of a messenger; fortune has given her to you, has brought her and established her at your

μὲν γὰρ ἐραστῇ καὶ βλέμμα μόνον ἤρκεσε τηρου-
μένης παρθένου, καὶ μέγιστον τοῦτο ἀγαθὸν
νενόμικεν ἐραστής, ἐὰν καὶ μέχρι τῶν ὀμμάτων
εὐτυχῇ, οἱ δὲ εὐδαιμονέστεροι τῶν ἐραστῶν, ἂν
τύχωσι κἂν ῥήματος μόνον. σὺ δὲ βλέπεις ἀεὶ
καὶ ἀκούεις ἀεὶ καὶ συνδειπνεῖς καὶ συμπίνεις·
4 καὶ τούτοις εὐτυχῶν ἐγκαλεῖς· ἀχάριστος εἶ
πρὸς ἔρωτος δωρεάν· οὐκ οἶδας οἷόν ἐστιν
ἐρωμένη βλεπομένη· μείζονα τῶν ἔργων ἔχει
τὴν ἡδονήν. ὀφθαλμοὶ γὰρ ἀλλήλοις ἀντανακλώ-
μενοι ἀπομάττουσιν ὡς ἐν κατόπτρῳ τῶν σωμάτων τὰ εἴδωλα· ἡ δὲ τοῦ κάλλους ἀπορροή,
δι' αὐτῶν εἰς τὴν ψυχὴν καταρρέουσα, ἔχει
5 τινὰ μίξιν ἐν ἀποστάσει. καὶ ὀλίγον [1] ἐστὶ τῆς
τῶν σωμάτων μίξεως· καινὴ γάρ ἐστι σωμάτων
συμπλοκή. ἐγὼ δέ σοι καὶ τὸ ἔργον ἔσεσθαι
ταχὺ μαντεύομαι· μέγιστον γάρ ἐστιν ἐφόδιον
εἰς πειθὼ συνεχὴς πρὸς ἐρωμένην ὁμιλία. ὀφθαλμὸς γὰρ φιλίας πρόξενος καὶ τὸ σύνηθες
6 τῆς κοινωνίας εἰς χάριν ἀνυσιμώτερον. εἰ γὰρ
τὰ ἄγρια τῶν θηρίων συνηθείᾳ τιθασεύεται,
πολλῷ μᾶλλον ταύτῃ μαλαχθείη καὶ γυνή. ἔχει
δέ τι πρὸς παρθένον ἐπαγωγὸν ἡλικιώτης ἐρῶν· τὸ
δὲ ἐν ὥρᾳ τῆς ἀκμῆς ἐπεῖγον εἰς τὴν φύσιν καὶ
τὸ συνειδὸς τοῦ φιλεῖσθαι τίκτει πολλάκις ἀντέρ-
ωτα. θέλει γὰρ ἑκάστη τῶν παρθένων εἶναι
καλή, καὶ φιλουμένη χαίρει, καὶ ἐπαινεῖ τῆς
μαρτυρίας τὸν φιλοῦντα· κἂν μὴ φιλήσῃ τις

---

[1] Göttling suggested γλυκίων for ὀλίγον (G has ὀλίγων), and
the sense would indeed be more consistent with μείζονα τῶν
ἔργων just above. Vilborg rightly rejects Knox's suggestion
of inserting παρ' before ὀλίγον. Schmidt suggests ἢ (omitting
καὶ) καλλίων.

very side. Some lovers have to be content with a
mere look at their sweetheart, so well guarded is she,
and to think themselves very lucky if they can obtain
this pleasure of the eye; others are more fortunate,
if they can but get a word with her : but you—you
are constantly seeing her and hearing her; you eat
with her and drink with her : and yet, with all this
good fortune, you grumble; let me tell you that you
are ungrateful for this gift that Love has made you.
You do not know what it is to be able to see the
one you love ; it is a greater pleasure than further
favours. When the eyes meet one another they
receive the impression of the body as in a mirror,
and this emanation of beauty, which penetrates
down into the soul through the eyes, effects a kind of
union however the bodies are sundered; 'tis something
of a bodily union—a new kind of bodily embrace.
But I prophesy to you that you will soon get all
you want. There is no more ready road to over-
coming the resistance of the beloved than constantly
to be in her presence ; the eye is the go-between
of affection, and the habit of being regularly in one
another's society is a quick and successful way to
full favour. Wild beasts can be tamed by habit,
as they become used to their masters ; how much
more easily can a woman's heart be softened by the
same means ! And then the fact that her lover is
of the same age as herself is a powerful impulse to a
maiden. Those feelings which are natural in the
heyday of youth, and her knowledge that she is
adored, will often inspire her to return your passion ;
for every maiden wishes to be fair, is pleased to
be loved, and is grateful to the lover for the witness
that he bears to her charms—if no one were in

7 αὐτήν, οὔπω πεπίστευκεν εἶναι καλή. ἐν οὖν
σοι παραινῶ μόνον, ἐρᾶσθαι πιστευσάτω, καὶ
ταχέως σε μιμήσεται." "Πῶς ἂν οὖν," εἶπον,
"γένοιτο τοῦτο τὸ μάντευμα; δός μοι τὰς
ἀφορμάς· σὺ γὰρ ἀρχαιότερος μύστης ἐμοῦ καὶ
συνηθέστερος ἤδη τῇ τελετῇ τοῦ θεοῦ. τί λέγω;
τί ποιῶ; πῶς ἂν τύχοιμι τῆς ἐρωμένης; οὐκ
οἶδα γὰρ τὰς ὁδούς."

10. "Μηδέν," εἶπεν ὁ Κλεινίας, "πρὸς ταῦτα
ζήτει παρ' ἄλλου μαθεῖν· αὐτοδίδακτος γάρ ἐστιν
ὁ θεὸς σοφιστής. ὥσπερ γὰρ τὰ ἀρτίτοκα τῶν
βρεφῶν οὐδεὶς διδάσκει τὴν τροφήν, αὐτόματα
γὰρ ἐκμανθάνει καὶ οἶδεν ἐν τοῖς μαζοῖς οὖσαν
αὐτοῖς τὴν τράπεζαν, οὕτω καὶ νεανίσκος ἔρωτος
πρωτοκύμων οὐ δεῖται διδασκαλίας πρὸς τὸν
2 τοκετόν. ἐὰν γὰρ ἡ ὠδὶς παραγένηται καὶ
ἐνστῇ τῆς ἀνάγκης ἡ προθεσμία, μηδὲν πλανηθείς, κἂν πρωτοκύμων ᾖς, εὑρήσεις τεκεῖν ὑπ'
αὐτοῦ μαιωθεὶς τοῦ θεοῦ. ὅσα δέ ἐστι κοινὰ
καὶ μὴ τῆς εὐκαίρου τύχης δεόμενα, ταῦτα ἀκούσας
μάθε. μηδὲν μὲν εἴπῃς πρὸς τὴν παρθένον
ἀφροδίσιον· τὸ δὲ ἔργον ζήτει πῶς γένηται σιωπῇ.
3 παῖς γὰρ καὶ παρθένος ὅμοιοι μέν εἰσιν εἰς
αἰδῶ· πρὸς δὲ τὴν τῆς Ἀφροδίτης χάριν κἂν
γνώμης τι[1] ἔχωσιν, ἃ πάσχουσιν ἀκούειν οὐ θέ-

---

[1] The MSS. have γνώμης ἔχωσιν: it is necessary either to
write γνώμην, as Jacobs (τὴν γνώμην Hercher), or to insert τι
as I have done in the text. Schmidt proposes ὁρμήν.

love with her, she could have so far no grounds of confidence that she was beautiful. One only piece of advice then I have to give you: let her be sure that she is loved, and she will soon return your affection." "But how," said I, "is this prophecy of yours to be accomplished? Indicate to me at any rate how to begin; you were initiated before me into the mysteries of the god and are better acquainted with the course required to become an adept. What am I to say? What am I to do? How am I to win the object of my passion? I have no idea of the way to proceed."

10. "On this subject," said Clinias, "you have no need to enquire of another: Love is a self-instructed expert. He is like the new-born babe which needs no teaching from anybody where to look for its nourishment; for that is an accomplishment which it learns of itself, knowing that its table is spread in its mother's breasts; in the same way a young man for the first time big with love needs no instruction as to how to bring it to birth. For when you begin to feel the pangs and it is clear that the destined day is at hand, you cannot go wrong, even though it be your first labour, but you will find the way to bring forth and the god himself will deliver you. However, you may as well listen to the ordinary maxims which are applicable at any time and need no fortunate occasion. In the first place, say nothing to the maiden of the actual fruition of love, but rather look for a means for your passion silently to be translated into action: boys and girls are alike shamefaced creatures; however much they may be inclined towards the pleasures that Aphrodite can afford, they do not care to hear their experi-

λουσι· τὴν γὰρ αἰσχύνην κεῖσθαι νομίζουσιν ἐν
4 τοῖς ῥήμασι. γυναῖκας μὲν γὰρ εὐφραίνει καὶ
τὰ ῥήματα· παρθένος δὲ τοὺς μὲν ἔξωθεν ἀκρο-
βολισμοὺς τῶν ἐραστῶν εἰς πεῖραν φέρει καὶ
ἄφνω συντίθεται τοῖς νεύμασιν· ἐὰν δὲ αἰτή-
σῃς τὸ ἔργον προσελθών, ἐκπλήξεις αὐτῆς τὰ
ὦτα τῇ φωνῇ, καὶ ἐρυθριᾷ καὶ μισεῖ τὸ ῥῆμα
καὶ λοιδορεῖσθαι δοκεῖ· κἂν ὑποσχέσθαι θέλῃ
τὴν χάριν, αἰσχύνεται. τότε γὰρ πάσχειν νομίζει
τὸ ἔργον, ὅτε μᾶλλον τὴν πεῖραν ἐκ τῆς τῶν
5 λόγων ἡδονῆς ἀκούει. ἐὰν δέ, τὴν πεῖραν προσ-
άγων τὴν ἄλλην, καὶ εὐάγωγον αὐτὴν παρασκευάσας, ἡδέως ἤδη προσέρχῃ, σιώπα μὲν οὖν τὰ
πολλὰ ὡς ἐν μυστηρίῳ, φίλησον δὲ προσελθὼν
ἠρέμα. τὸ γὰρ ἐραστοῦ φίλημα πρὸς ἐρωμένην
θέλουσαν μὲν παρέχειν, αἴτησίς ἐστι,[1] πρὸς ἀπει-
6 θοῦσαν δέ, ἱκετηρία. κἂν μὲν προσῇ τις συνθήκη
τῆς πράξεως,[2] πολλάκις δὲ καὶ ἑκοῦσαι πρὸς τὸ
ἔργον ἐρχόμεναι θέλουσι βιάζεσθαι δοκεῖν, ἵνα
τῇ δόξῃ τῆς ἀνάγκης ἀποτρέπωνται τῆς αἰσχύνης
τὸ ἑκούσιον. μὴ τοίνυν ὀκνήσῃς, ἐὰν ἀνθιστα-
μένην αὐτὴν ἴδῃς, ἀλλ' ἐπιτήρει πῶς ἀνθίσταται·
7 σοφίας γὰρ κἀνταῦθα δεῖ. κἂν μὲν προσκαρ-
τερῇ, ἐπίσχες τὴν βίαν· οὔπω γὰρ πείθεται·

---

[1] The MSS. after ἐστί read σιωπῇ, which is omitted on the
suggestion of Jacobs. σιωπηλὴ Castiglioni.
[2] Jacobs thought there must be a lacuna after πράξεως, and
in any case there is something of an anacoluthon—a dis-
jointure of the grammatical construction.

ences mentioned aloud: they think that modesty is a matter of words, while grown women, on the other hand, take a pleasure in the words too. A girl bears calmly the long-range skirmishes that a lover uses to feel his way, and will suddenly express her complacency by a gesture; but if you go bluntly to her with a verbal call to action, you will only shock her ears by the words you employ. She will blush, affect to regard your proposal with horror, and think that an insult is being offered to her; even if she is desirous to afford you her favours, she is ashamed, for it seems to her that she is already yielding, when the pleasure she derives from your words seems to transform your tentative into reality. If, however, you act upon the other tack, gradually moulding her to your wishes and gaining easy access to her, be as silent as in church, but approach her gently and kiss her: if the beloved is compliant, the lover's kiss is an invitation to her to accord him all her favours; if reluctant, it is a kind of supplication and prayer. Then, even when they have promised and are certain to yield, many of them, however willingly they come into action, prefer the appearance of coercion, so that by a shew of force they can avoid the charge of compliance which would be a reproach to their modesty. Even if you find her persistently obdurate, do not relax your efforts, but rather watch closely for the means of converting her: here too tact is wanted. Do not in any case, if she remains obstinate, employ force; she is not yet sufficiently softened: but if you desire her to melt,

35

ἐὰν δὲ μαλθακώτερον ἤδη θέλῃς, χορήγησον τὴν
ὑπόκρισιν, μὴ ἀπολέσῃς σου τὸ δρᾶμα."

11. Κἀγὼ δέ, "Μεγάλα μέν," ἔφην, "ἐφόδια
μοι δέδωκας καὶ εὔχομαι τυχεῖν, Κλεινία· φοβοῦμαι δὲ ὅμως μὴ κακῶν γένηταί μοι τὸ εὐτύχημα
μειζόνων ἀρχὴ καὶ ἐπιτρίψῃ με πρὸς ἔρωτα
πλείονα. ἂν γοῦν αὐξηθῇ τὸ δεινόν, τί δράσω;
2 γαμεῖν μὲν οὐκ ἂν δυναίμην· ἄλλῃ γὰρ δέδομαι
παρθένῳ. ἐπίκειται δέ μοι πρὸς τοῦτον τὸν γάμον
ὁ πατήρ, δίκαια αἰτῶν, οὐ ξένην οὐδὲ αἰσχρὰν
γῆμαι κόρην, οὐδὲ ὡς Χαρικλέα πλούτῳ με
πωλεῖ, ἀλλ' αὑτοῦ μοι δίδωσι θυγατέρα, καλὴν
μέν, ὦ θεοί, πρὶν Λευκίππην ἰδεῖν· νῦν δὲ καὶ
πρὸς τὸ κάλλος αὐτῆς τυφλώττω καὶ πρὸς
3 Λευκίππην μόνην τοὺς ὀφθαλμοὺς ἔχω. ἐν
μεθορίῳ κεῖμαι δύο ἐναντίων· ἔρως ἀνταγωνίζεται
καὶ πατήρ. ὁ μὲν ἕστηκεν αἰδοῖ κρατῶν, ὁ δὲ
κάθηται πυρπολῶν. πῶς κρίνω τὴν δίκην;
ἀνάγκη μάχεται καὶ φύσις. καὶ θέλω μὲν σοὶ
δικάσαι, πάτερ, ἀλλ' ἀντίδικον ἔχω χαλεπώτερον.
βασανίζει τὸν δικαστήν, ἕστηκε μετὰ βελῶν,
κρίνεται μετὰ πυρός. ἂν ἀπειθήσω, πάτερ, αὐτοῦ
καίομαι τῷ πυρί."[1]

12. Ἡμεῖς μὲν οὖν ταῦτα ἐφιλοσοφοῦμεν περὶ
τοῦ θεοῦ· ἐξαίφνης δέ τις εἰστρέχει τῶν τοῦ

---

[1] The last words of this paragraph contain rather an
elaborate metaphor from the Attic system of the production
of plays, which is difficult to render into appropriate

you must be prepared to act a part, or else you will lose all the trouble of your plot." [1]

11. " By your advice, Clinias," said I, "you have given me the most admirable provision for my journey, and I pray that I may arrive safely ; but at the same time I cannot help fearing that my very success may be the beginning of worse troubles and expose me to the more violent flames of love ; and at any rate if they do become more savage, what am I to do ? I cannot marry her—I am pledged to another maiden ; and my father is greatly set on this match. Nor is his object an unreasonable one : he does not ask me to marry a foreigner, or an ugly girl ; he does not sell me for gold, as Charicles is to be sold ; but he intends for me his own daughter, who was beautiful enough, God knows, before I saw Leucippe ; but now I am blind to her beauty and have eyes for Leucippe alone. I am on the horns of a dilemma—Love and my father wait on opposite sides of me : my father stands behind me, holding me back by the respect which I owe to him ; Love sits before me, brandishing his torch of fire. How am I to decide the contest, when affection is at war with the promptings of nature ? I desire to give my verdict for you, father, but I have a stronger adversary—he puts the judge to the torture, he stands in court armed with his arrows, he pleads his cause with flame ; if I do not decide against you, father, I must be utterly consumed by his fire."

12. We were engaged in this kind of philosophical discussion about Love, when one of Charicles'

English. "You must stage-manage (χορηγεῖν) your own acting, or else you will not get your play accepted, and so will have wasted all the trouble you took in composing it."

Χαρικλέους οἰκετῶν, ἔχων ἐπὶ τοῦ προσώπου τὴν
ἀγγελίαν τοῦ κακοῦ, ὡς καὶ τὸν Κλεινίαν εὐθὺς
ἀνακραγεῖν θεασάμενον, "Κακόν τι γέγονε
Χαρικλεῖ." ἅμα δὲ αὐτοῦ λέγοντος, συνεξεφώ-
2 νησεν ὁ οἰκέτης, "Τέθνηκε Χαρικλῆς." τὸν μὲν
οὖν Κλεινίαν πρὸς τὴν ἀγγελίαν ἀφῆκεν ἡ φωνὴ
καὶ ἔμεινεν ἀκίνητος, ὥσπερ τυφῶνι βεβλημένος
τῷ λόγῳ. ὁ δὲ οἰκέτης διηγεῖται· "Ἐπὶ τὸν ἵππον
τὸν σὸν ἐκάθισεν, ὦ Κλεινία, ὃς τὰ μὲν πρῶτα
ἤλαυνεν ἠρέμα, δύο δὲ ἢ τρεῖς δρόμους περιελθών,
τὴν ἱππασίαν ἐπέσχε καὶ τὸν ἵππον ἱδροῦντα
κατέψα καθήμενος, τοῦ ῥυτῆρος ἀμελήσας.
3 ἀπομάττοντος δὲ τῆς ἕδρας τοὺς ἱδρῶτας, ψόφος
κατόπιν γίνεται, καὶ ὁ ἵππος ἐκταραχθεὶς πηδᾷ
ὄρθιος¹ ἀρθεὶς καὶ ἀλογίστως ἐφέρετο. τὸν γὰρ
χαλινὸν ἐνδακὼν καὶ τὸν αὐχένα σιμώσας,
φρίξας τε τὴν κόμην, οἰστρηθεὶς τῷ φόβῳ
διαέριος² ἵπτατο. τῶν δὲ ποδῶν οἱ μὲν ἔμπροσθεν ἤλλοντο, οἱ δὲ ὄπισθεν τοὺς ἔμπροσθεν
ἐπειγόμενοι φθάσαι, τὸν δρόμον ἐπέσπευδον,
4 διώκοντες τὸν ἵππον. ὁ δὲ ἵππος τῇ τῶν ποδῶν
κυρτούμενος ἁμίλλῃ, ἄνω τε καὶ κάτω πηδῶν
πρὸς τὴν ἑκατέρων σπουδὴν δίκην νεὼς χειμαζο-
μένης τοῖς νώτοις ἐκυμαίνετο. ὁ δὲ κακοδαίμων
Χαρικλῆς ὑπὸ τοῦ τῆς ἱππείας ταλαντευόμενος
κύματος, ἐκ τῆς ἕδρας ἐσφαιρίζετο, ποτὲ μὲν ἐπ'
οὐρὰν κατολισθάνων, ποτὲ δὲ ἐπὶ τράχηλον
κυβιστῶν· ὁ δὲ τοῦ κλύδωνος ἐπίεζεν αὐτὸν
5 χειμών. τῶν δὲ ῥυτήρων οὐκέτι κρατεῖν δυνά-

---

¹ So Bergler: ὄρθιον.
² The adjective διαέριος of some MSS. seems slightly preferable to the δι' ἀέρος of the other MSS. and editions.

servants rushed in, with evil tidings so clearly
written upon his face that Clinias instantly cried
out : "Something has happened to Charicles." He
had not yet finished speaking, when the servant
exclaimed in the same breath : " Charicles is dead."
At this announcement Clinias was stricken utterly
dumb and stood motionless, as though he had been
struck by a whirlwind. The servant went on : " He
mounted your horse, Clinias, and at first rode quietly
enough upon him ; after two or three turns, he pulled
him up, and, dropping the reins on his back, began
to rub down the sweating animal as he sat. While
he was wiping by the saddle, there was a sudden
noise behind ; the horse was frightened, reared,
and bolted wildly. He took the bit between his
teeth, tossed up his head, shook his mane, and
seemed to fly through the air spurred on by
fear; his hinder feet seemed to be trying to catch
up his galloping fore-quarters, increasing the speed
of his flight and spurring on his pace; his body
arched by reason of the contest between his feet,
bounding up and down at each stride, the motion
of his back was like a ship tossed in a storm. Poor
Charicles, thrown up and down rather as if by a
wave than on a horse, bounded from the saddle like
a ball, at one time slipping back on to the horse's
quarters, at another hurled forward on to his neck,
while the tempest-like motion ever more and more
overcame his efforts. At last, no longer able to hold

μενος, δοὺς δὲ ἑαυτὸν ὅλως [1] τῷ τοῦ δρόμου
πνεύματι, τῆς τύχης ἦν. ὁ δὲ ἵππος ῥύμῃ θέων
ἐκτρέπεται τῆς λεωφόρου καὶ ἐς ὕλην ἐπήδησε
καὶ εὐθὺς τὸν ἄθλιον Χαρικλέα περιρρήγνυσι
δένδρῳ. ὁ δέ, ὡς ἀπὸ μηχανῆς προσαραχθείς,
ἐκκρούεται μὲν τῆς ἕδρας, ὑπὸ δὲ τῶν τοῦ
δένδρου κλάδων τὸ πρόσωπον αἰσχύνεται καὶ
τοσούτοις περιδρύπτεται τραύμασιν, ὅσαι τῶν
6 κλάδων ἦσαν αἱ αἰχμαί. οἱ δὲ ῥυτῆρες αὐτῷ
περιδεθέντες οὐκ ἤθελον ἀφεῖναι τὸ σῶμα, ἀλλ᾿
ἀνθεῖλκον αὐτό, περισύροντες θανάτου τρίβον.
ὁ δὲ ἵππος ἔτι μᾶλλον ἐκταραχθεὶς τῷ πτώματι
καὶ ἐμποδιζόμενος εἰς τὸν δρόμον τῷ σώματι
κατεπάτει τὸν ἄθλιον, ἐκλακτίζων τὸν δεσμὸν
τῆς φυγῆς· ὥστε οὐκ ἂν αὐτόν τις ἰδὼν οὐδὲ
γνωρίσειεν."

13. Ταῦτα μὲν οὖν ἀκούων ὁ Κλεινίας ἐσίγα
τινὰ χρόνον ὑπ᾿ ἐκπλήξεως· μεταξὺ δὲ νήψας ἐκ
τοῦ κακοῦ διωλύγιον ἐκώκυσε, καὶ ἐκδραμεῖν ἐπὶ
τὸ σῶμα μὲν ἠπείγετο, ἐπηκολούθουν δὲ κἀγώ,
2 παρηγορῶν ὡς ἠδυνάμην. καὶ ἐν τούτῳ φοράδην
Χαρικλῆς ἐκομίζετο, θέαμα οἴκτιστον καὶ ἐλεεινόν·
ὅλος γὰρ τραῦμα ἦν, ὥστε μηδένα τῶν παρόντων
κατασχεῖν τὰ δάκρυα. ἐξῆρχε δὲ τοῦ θρήνου ὁ
πατὴρ πολυτάρακτον βοῶν· "Οἷος ἀπ᾿ ἐμοῦ
προελθών, οἷος ἐπανέρχῃ μοι, τέκνον; ὦ πονηρῶν
ἱππασμάτων. οὐδὲ κοινῷ μοι θανάτῳ τέθνηκας·

---

[1] ὅλως Boissonade: ὅμως MSS. which Hercher deletes.
Salmasius added ὅλος before τῆς τύχης.

the reins, he completely let himself drive with the
storm and was at the mercy of fortune: then the
horse, still at top speed, turned aside from the high
road, bounded into a wood, and straightway dashed
the miserable Charicles against a tree. He left the
saddle, shot like a stone from a sling; his face
was cut to pieces by the tree's branches and he was
covered with as many wounds as there were sharp
points on the boughs. The reins twisted round his
body,[1] which he was unable to extricate, and then
dragged it along with them, making a very path of
death. The horse, still more alarmed by the fall and
finding his speed checked by the body dragging
behind him, trampled upon the unhappy boy,
kicking out at what he found to be a check upon
his flight; so that now no one who saw him could
possibly recognize him as the Charicles they once
knew."

13. At this news Clinias was struck with utter
silence for a considerable period ; then, as if suddenly
awaked from a swoon of grief, he cried out very
pitifully and hurried to run to meet the corpse,
while I followed him, affording him such poor
comfort as I was able. At that moment Charicles
was brought in on a bier, a sight most pitiful and
sad ; he appeared to be all one wound, so that
none of the standers-by were able to refrain from
tears. His father led the chorus of lamentation,
greatly disordered and crying out: "Look on this
picture and on that—how you left me and how
you come back to me ; a curse on all riding of
horses ! A worse than common death is yours, which

---

[1] The Greek rider had the reins carried round behind his
waist.

3 οὐδὲ εὐσχήμων φαίνῃ νεκρός. τοῖς μὲν γὰρ
ἄλλοις τῶν ἀποθανόντων τὸ ἴχνος τῶν γνωρι-
σμάτων διασώζεται, κἂν τὸ ἄνθος τις τῶν
προσώπων ἀπολέσῃ, τηρεῖ τὸ εἴδωλον καὶ παρη-
γορεῖ τὸ λυπούμενον καθεύδοντα μιμούμενος· τὴν
μὲν γὰρ ψυχὴν ἐξεῖλεν ὁ θάνατος, ἐν δὲ τῷ
4 σώματι τηρεῖ τὸν ἄνθρωπον. σοῦ δὲ ὁμοῦ καὶ
ταῦτα διέφθειρεν ἡ τύχη, καί μοι τέθνηκας
θάνατον διπλοῦν, ψυχῇ καὶ σώματι. ὄντως[1]
σου τέθνηκε καὶ τῆς εἰκόνος ἡ σκιά· ἡ μὲν γὰρ
ψυχή σου πέφευγεν· οὐχ εὑρίσκω δέ σε οὐδ' ἐν
5 τῷ σώματι. πότε μοι, τέκνον, γαμεῖς; πότε σου
θύσω τοὺς γάμους, ἱππεῦ καὶ νυμφίε; νυμφίε μὲν
ἀτελής, ἱππεῦ δὲ δυστυχής. τάφος μέν σοι,
τέκνον, ὁ θάλαμος· γάμος δὲ ὁ θάνατος· θρῆνος δὲ
ὁ ὑμέναιος· ὁ δὲ κωκυτὸς οὗτος τῶν γάμων ὠδαί.
6 ἄλλο σοι, τέκνον, προσεδόκων πῦρ ἀνάψειν·
ἀλλὰ τοῦτο μὲν ἔσβεσεν ἡ πονηρὰ τύχη μετὰ
σοῦ· ἀνάπτει δέ σοι δᾷδας κακῶν. ὦ πονηρᾶς
ταύτης δᾳδουχίας. ἡ νυμφική σοι δᾳδουχία
ταφὴ γίνεται."

14. Ταῦτα μὲν οὖν οὕτως ἐκώκυεν ὁ πατήρ·
ἑτέρωθεν δὲ καθ' αὑτὸν ὁ Κλεινίας· καὶ ἦν

---

[1] Hercher's ingenious conjecture for MSS. οὗτω or οὗτως.

---

[1] Cf. St. Gregory of Nyssa, *De deitate Filii et Spiritus
Sancti* (ed. Paris. 1615, ii. p. 906 A), where Abraham laments
over the approaching sacrifice of Isaac: καὶ ἄψω ἐπ' αὐτῷ
οὐχὶ λαμπάδα γαμήλιον, ἀλλὰ πῦρ ἐπιτάφιον; "Am I to kindle
for him no marriage lights, but the torches for his

leaves you an unsightly corpse; when others die, at
least the lineaments of their features are preserved,
and even if the living bloom of beauty be gone, at
least the face keeps a semblance of its former
appearance and affords some comfort to the mourner
by its mimicry of sleep; death may have snatched
away the soul, but at least it leaves in the body the
one we knew. But with you even this has been
destroyed by fate—so you are doubly dead to me,
soul and body too; even the very shadow of your
likeness is gone—your soul is fled and I cannot find
my Charicles in this corpse. When, my child, shall
the day of your wedlock be? When shall I perform
at your marriage the rites that religion demands,
horseman and bridegroom—bridegroom that shall
never wed, most unfortunate of horsemen? Your
bridal chamber is the grave; your wedlock is with
death; the dirge your bridal song; these wailings
your marriage lays. A very different fire from this,
my child, did I hope to kindle for you; but cruel
fate has extinguished both it and you, and lit up in
its place the torches of a funeral. A cruel illumina-
tion this! The tapers of your marriage rite have
become the flambeaux of a requiem." [1]

14. So wailed his father, and on the other side of
the body Clinias was reproaching himself: it was a

burial?" We might also compare *Anth. Pal.* vii. 185 and
712, and our Herrick's (ed. Moorman, p. 109)

> That morn which saw me made a bride,
> That evening witnessed that I died.
> Those holy lights, wherewith they guide
> Unto the bed the bashful bride,
> Served but as tapers, for to burn
> And light my reliques to their urn.
> This epitaph, which here you see,
> Supplied the Epithalamy.

θρήνων ἅμιλλα, ἐραστοῦ καὶ πατρός· "'Εγώ μου τὸν δεσπότην ἀπολώλεκα. τί γὰρ αὐτῷ τοιοῦτον δῶρον ἐχαριζόμην; φιάλη γὰρ οὐκ ἦν χρυσῆ, ἵν' ἐσπένδετο πίνων καὶ ἐχρῆτό μου τῷ δώρῳ

2 τρυφῶν; ἐγὼ δὲ ὁ κακοδαίμων ἐχαριζόμην θηρίον μειρακίῳ καλῷ, ἐκαλλώπιζον δὲ καὶ τὸ πονηρὸν θηρίον προστερνιδίοις, προμετωπιδίοις, φαλάροις ἀργυροῖς, χρυσαῖς ἡνίαις. οἴμοι Χαρίκλεις· ἐκόσμησά σου τὸν φονέα χρυσῷ. ἵππε πάντων θηρίων ἀγριώτατε, πονηρὲ καὶ ἀχάριστε καὶ ἀναί-

3 σθητε κάλλους, ὁ μὲν κατέψα σου τοὺς ἱδρῶτας καὶ τροφὰς ἐπηγγέλλετο πλείονας καὶ ἐπῄνει τὸν δρόμον, σὺ δὲ ἀπέκτεινας ἐπαινούμενος. οὐχ ἥδου προσαπτομένου σου τοιούτου σώματος, οὐκ ἦν σοι τοιοῦτος ἱππεὺς τρυφή, ἀλλ' ἔρριψας, ἄστοργε, τὸ κάλλος χαμαί. οἴμοι δυστυχής· ἐγώ σοι τὸν φονέα, τὸν ἀνδροφόνον ἐωνησάμην."

15. Μετὰ δὲ τὴν ταφὴν εὐθὺς ἔσπευδον ἐπὶ τὴν κόρην· ἡ δὲ ἦν ἐν τῷ παραδείσῳ τῆς οἰκίας. ὁ δὲ παράδεισος ἄλσος ἦν, μέγα τι χρῆμα πρὸς ὀφθαλμῶν ἡδονήν· καὶ περὶ τὸ ἄλσος τειχίον ἦν αὔταρκες εἰς ὕψος καὶ ἑκάστη πλευρὰ τειχίου (τέσσαρες δὲ ἦσαν πλευραί) κατάστεγος ὑπὸ χορῷ κιόνων· ὑπὸ δὲ τοῖς κίοσιν ἔνδον ἦν ἡ τῶν

2 δένδρων πανήγυρις. ἔθαλλον οἱ κλάδοι, συνέπιπτον ἀλλήλοις ἄλλος ἐπ' ἄλλον, αἱ γείτονες τῶν πετάλων περιπλοκαί, τῶν φύλλων περιβολαί, τῶν καρπῶν συμπλοκαί. τοιαύτη τις ἦν

3 ὁμιλία τῶν φυτῶν. ἐνίοις δὲ τῶν δένδρων τῶν ἁδροτέρων κιττὸς καὶ σμῖλαξ παρεπεφύκει· ἡ μὲν ἐξηρτημένη πλατάνου καὶ περιπυκάζουσα ῥαδινῇ

very rivalry of laments, the loving friend and the father. "It is I," said he, "that have destroyed him that was the master of my heart. Why did I give him such a gift as that? Why not rather a cup of gold for libations when he drank, to use and pride himself on my present? As it is, wretched fool that I was, I gave this fair lad a wild beast, and I decked out the cursed brute with martingales and frontlets, silver trappings and gold-embroidered reins; yes, alas, Charicles, I furbished up your murderer with gold. Vile horse, the most savage of all beasts, wicked, thankless brute, sense-less of beauty, he was wiping away your sweat and promising you a fuller manger and praising your paces; and you killed him as you were being flattered —you took no pleasure in the touch of that beautiful body, that fair horseman was no source of pride in you; you entertained no feelings of affection for him, but dashed his beauty to the ground. Woe is me: it was I that bought for you the cause of your death, your murderer!"

15. When the entombment was over, I hurried to my sweetheart, who was in the garden of our house. This garden was a meadow, a very object of beauty to the eyes; round it ran a wall of sufficient height, and each of the four sides of the wall formed a portico standing on pillars, within which was a close plantation of trees. Their branches, which were in full foliage, intertwined with one another; their neighbouring flowers mingled with each other, their leaves overlapped, their fruits joined. Such was the way in which the trees grew together; to some of the larger of them were ivy and smilax attached, the smilax hanging from planes and filling all the

45

τῇ κόμῃ· ὁ δὲ κιττὸς περὶ πεύκην εἰλιχθεὶς
ᾠκειοῦτο τὸ δένδρον ταῖς περιπλοκαῖς, καὶ
ἐγίνετο τῷ κιττῷ ὄχημα τὸ φυτόν, στέφανος δὲ ὁ
4 κιττὸς τοῦ φυτοῦ. ἄμπελοι δὲ ἑκατέρωθεν τοῦ
δένδρου, καλάμοις ἐποχούμεναι, τοῖς φύλλοις
ἔθαλλον, καὶ ὁ καρπὸς ὡραίαν εἶχε τὴν ἄνθην καὶ
διὰ τῆς ὀπῆς τῶν καλάμων ἐξεκρέματο καὶ ἦν
βόστρυχος τοῦ φυτοῦ· τῶν δὲ φύλλων ἄνωθεν
αἰωρουμένων, ὑφ᾽ ἡλίῳ πρὸς ἄνεμον συμμιγεῖ
5 ὠχρὰν ἐμάρμαιρεν ἡ γῆ τὴν σκιάν. τὰ δὲ ἄνθη
ποικίλην ἔχοντα τὴν χροιάν, ἐν μέρει συνεξέφαινε
τὸ κάλλος, καὶ ἦν τοῦτο τῆς γῆς πορφύρα καὶ
νάρκισσος καὶ ῥόδον· μία μὲν τῷ ῥόδῳ καὶ τῷ
ναρκίσσῳ ἡ κάλυξ, ὅσον εἰς περιγραφήν· καὶ ἦν
φιάλη τοῦ φυτοῦ. ἡ χροιὰ δὲ τῶν περὶ τὴν
κάλυκα φύλλων ἐσχισμένων, τῷ ῥόδῳ μὲν
αἵματος τὸ ἄνω [1] καὶ γάλακτος, τὸ κάτω τοῦ
φύλλου, καὶ ὁ νάρκισσος ἦν τὸ πᾶν ὅμοιον τῷ
6 κάτω τοῦ ῥόδου. τῷ ἴῳ κάλυξ μὲν οὐδαμοῦ,
χροιὰ δὲ οἵαν ἡ τῆς θαλάσσης ἀστράπτει γαλήνη.
ἐν μέσοις δὲ τοῖς ἄνθεσι πηγὴ ἀνέβλυζε καὶ
περιεγέγραπτο τετράγωνος χαράδρα χειροποίητος
τῷ ῥεύματι. τὸ δὲ ὕδωρ τῶν ἀνθέων ἦν κάτοπτρον, ὡς δοκεῖν τὸ ἄλσος εἶναι διπλοῦν, τὸ μὲν
7 τῆς ἀληθείας, τὸ δὲ τῆς σκιᾶς. ὄρνιθες δέ, οἱ
μὲν χειροήθεις περὶ τὸ ἄλσος ἐνέμοντο, οὓς
ἐκολάκευον αἱ τῶν ἀνθρώπων τροφαί, οἱ δὲ
ἐλεύθερον ἔχοντες τὸ πτερόν, περὶ τὰς τῶν
δένδρων κορυφὰς ἔπαιζον· οἱ μὲν ᾄδοντες τὰ
ὀρνίθων ᾄσματα, οἱ δὲ τῇ τῶν πτερῶν ἀγλαϊζό-

---

[1] τὸ ἄνω Vilborg: ἄνωθεν Lumb: ὁμοῦ the MSS. After ὁμοῦ
the MSS. give ἴων, which Jacobs removed.

interstices between the boughs with its soft foliage, the ivy twisting up the pines and embracing the trunks, so that the tree formed a support for the ivy, and the ivy a garland for the tree. On either side of each tree grew vines, creeping upon reed supports, with luxuriant foliage; these, now in full fruitage, hung from the joints of the reeds, and formed as it were the ringlets of the tree. The leaves higher up were in gentle motion, and the rays of the sun penetrating them as the wind moved them gave the effect of a pale, mottled shadow on the ground. Flowers too of many hues displayed each their own beauty, and this formed the earth's gay colour—the narcissus and the rose. Now the calyx of the rose and the narcissus was alike so far as shape goes—the cup in fact of the plants. As for the colour of the much-divided petals round the calyx, the rose was like blood above and milk below, whereas the narcissus was wholly of the colour of the lower part of the rose; there were violets too, whose cup-shaped blossoms you could not distinguish, but their colour was as that of a shining calm at sea. In the mist of all these flowers bubbled up a spring, the waters of which were confined in a square artificial basin; the water served as a mirror for the flowers, giving the impression of a double grove, one real and the other a reflexion. Birds there were too: some, tame, sought for food in the grove, pampered and domesticated by the rearing of men; others, wild and on the wing, sported around the summits of the trees; some chirping their birds' songs, others brilliant in their gorgeous plumage.

8 μενοι στολῇ. οἱ ᾠδοὶ δέ, τέττιγες καὶ χελιδόνες·
οἱ μὲν τὴν Ἠοῦς ᾄδοντες εὐνήν, αἱ δὲ τὴν Τηρέως
τράπεζαν. οἱ δὲ χειροήθεις, ταῶς καὶ κύκνος καὶ
ψιττακός· ὁ κύκνος περὶ τὰς τῶν ὑδάτων πίδακας
νεμόμενος, ὁ ψιττακὸς ἐν οἰκίσκῳ περὶ δένδρον
κρεμάμενος, ὁ ταῶς τοῖς ἄνθεσι περισύρων τὸ
πτερόν. ἀντέλαμπε δὲ ἡ τῶν ἀνθέων θέα τῇ τῶν
ὀρνίθων χροιᾷ καὶ ἦν ἄνθη πτερῶν.

16. Βουλόμενος οὖν εὐάγωγον τὴν κόρην εἰς
ἔρωτα παρασκευάσαι, λόγων πρὸς τὸν Σάτυρον
ἠρχόμην, ἀπὸ τοῦ ὄρνιθος λαβὼν τὴν εὐκαιρίαν·
διαβαδίζουσα γὰρ ἔτυχεν ἅμα τῇ Κλειοῖ καὶ
2 ἐπιστᾶσα τῷ ταῷ κατάντιον.[1] ἔτυχε γὰρ τύχῃ
τινὶ συμβὰν τότε τὸν ὄρνιν ἀναπτερῶσαι τὸ κάλλος
καὶ τὸ θέατρον ἐπιδεικνύναι τῶν πτερῶν. "Τοῦτο μέντοι οὐκ ἄνευ τέχνης ὁ ὄρνις," ἔφην, "ποιεῖ·
ἀλλ' ἔστι γὰρ ἐρωτικός· ὅταν γοῦν ἐπαγαγέσθαι
θέλῃ τὴν ἐρωμένην, τότε οὕτως καλλωπίζεται.
3 ὁρᾷς ἐκείνην τὴν τῆς πλατάνου πλησίον;"
(δείξας θήλειαν ταῶνα) "ταύτῃ νῦν οὗτος τὸ
κάλλος ἐπιδείκνυται λειμῶνα πτερῶν. ὁ δὲ τοῦ
ταῶ λειμὼν εὐανθέστερος, πεφύτευται γὰρ αὐτῷ
καὶ χρυσὸς ἐν τοῖς πτεροῖς, κύκλῳ δὲ τὸ ἁλουργὲς

---

[1] κατάντιον Jacobs. The MSS. have κατ' αὐτὸν (κατὰ
ταὐτὸν G). Hercher deletes.

---

[1] Tithonus, the human spouse of the goddess of the Dawn,
asked for and obtained the gift of immortality ; but neglecting also to demand perpetual youth, he shrivelled up in
extreme old age until it was the truest mercy to change him
into a grasshopper.
[2] See I. viii. and V. iii. After the cannibal feast, Philo-

The songsters were grasshoppers and swallows: the former sang of Aurora's marriage-bed,[1] the latter of the banquet of Tereus.[2] There were tame birds too, a peacock, a swan, and a parrot; the swan fed round about the sources of the spring, the parrot was hung in a cage from the branches of a tree, the peacock spread his tail among the flowers, and there was a kind of rivalry between the brilliance of the flowers and the hues of the peacock, whose plumage seemed itself to consist of very flowers.

16. Desiring to influence the thoughts of the maiden so as to make her amenable to love, I began to address myself to Satyrus,[3] taking the birds as my text. Now my sweetheart happened to be walking with Clio and had stopped opposite the peacock, who chanced at that moment to be making a display of all his finery and shewing off his tail to its best advantage. "This bird," said I, "does not behave thus without intent: he is really an amorous creature; at least he shews off this gorgeous livery when he wishes to attract the object of his passion. Do you not see her (and as I spoke I pointed to the hen) near that plane tree? It is for her that he is shewing his beauties, his train which is a garden in itself—a garden which contains more beautiful flowers than a natural garden, for there is gold in the plumage, with an outer circle of purple running

mela was changed into a nightingale, Procne into a swallow, Tereus into an owl, and Itys, miraculously revived, into a pheasant.

[3] Satyrus and Clio are rather inartistically introduced without further description. Satyrus was a male slave of the household, Clio Leucippe's chambermaid : they form another pair of lovers.

τὸν χρυσὸν περιθέει τὸν ἴσον κύκλον, καί ἐστιν
ὀφθαλμὸς ἐν τῷ πτερῷ."

17. Καὶ ὁ Σάτυρος συνεὶς τοῦ λόγου μου τὴν
ὑπόθεσιν, ἵνα μοι μᾶλλον εἴη περὶ τούτου λέγειν,
"Ἦ γὰρ ὁ ἔρως," ἔφη, "τοσαύτην ἔχει τὴν
ἰσχύν, ὡς καὶ μέχρις ὀρνίθων πέμπειν τὸ
πῦρ;" "Οὐ μέχρις ὀρνίθων," ἔφην, "τοῦτο γὰρ
οὐ θαυμαστόν, ἐπεὶ καὶ αὐτὸς ἔχει πτερόν, ἀλλὰ
καὶ ἑρπετῶν καὶ φυτῶν, ἐγὼ δὲ δοκῶ μοι,[1]
2 καὶ λίθων. ἐρᾷ γοῦν ἡ μαγνησία λίθος τοῦ
σιδήρου· κἂν μόνον ἴδῃ καὶ θίγῃ, πρὸς αὑτὴν
εἵλκυσεν, ὥσπερ ἐρωτικόν τι ἔνδον ἔχουσα. καὶ
μή τι τοῦτό ἐστιν ἐρώσης λίθου καὶ ἐρωμένου
3 σιδήρου φίλημα; περὶ δὲ τῶν φυτῶν λέγουσι
παῖδες σοφῶν· καὶ μῦθον ἔλεγον ἂν[2] τὸν λόγον
εἶναι, εἰ μὴ καὶ παῖδες ἔλεγον γεωργῶν. ὁ δὲ
λόγος· ἄλλο μὲν ἄλλου φυτὸν ἐρᾶν, τῷ δὲ
φοίνικι τὸν ἔρωτα μᾶλλον ἐνοχλεῖν· λέγουσι δὲ
4 τὸν μὲν ἄρρενα τῶν φοινίκων, τὸν δὲ θῆλυν. ὁ
ἄρρην οὖν τοῦ θήλεος ἐρᾷ· κἂν ὁ θῆλυς ἀπῳκισ-
μένος ᾖ τῇ τῆς φυτείας στάσει, ὁ ἐραστὴς[3] αὐαί-
νεται. συνίησιν οὖν ὁ γεωργὸς τὴν λύπην τοῦ
φυτοῦ, καὶ εἰς τὴν τοῦ χωρίου περιωπὴν ἀνελθών,
ἐφορᾷ ποῖ[4] νένευκε· κλίνεται γὰρ εἰς τὸ ἐρώμενον·
καὶ μαθών, θεραπεύει τοῦ φυτοῦ τὴν νόσον.
5 πτόρθον γὰρ τοῦ θήλεος φοίνικος λαβών, εἰς
τὴν τοῦ ἄρρενος καρδίαν ἐντίθησι, καὶ ἀνέψυξε

---

[1] The MSS. W and M omit μοι.
[2] Not in the MSS. Supplied by Cobet.
[3] After this word the MSS. have ὁ ἄρρην, which Cobet saw
to be a gloss.
[4] ποῖ Cobet: ποῦ MSS.

round the whole circle of gold, and on every feather an eye."

17. Satyrus, perceiving the trend and object of my discourse, was desirous of assisting me to enlarge further on the subject, and, " Has then Love," said he, " such mighty power that he is able to inflame even birds?" " Not birds only," I answered; " that would be no marvel, for you too know that he is winged himself, but creeping snakes and plants too, and I believe even stones as well: at least the loadstone[1] loves the iron, and if it may but see it and touch it, it attracts it towards itself as though possessed of the passion of love. May this not be the kiss of the loving stone and the beloved metal? As for plants, the children of wisdom have a tale to tell, one that I should deem a fable were it not that it was borne out by countrymen; and this it is. Plants, they say, fall in love with one another, and the palm is particularly susceptible to the passion: there are both male and female palms; the male falls in love with the female; and if the female be planted at any considerable distance, the loving male begins to wither away. The gardener realises what is the cause of the tree's grief, goes to some slight eminence in the ground, and observes in which direction it is drooping (for it always inclines towards the object of its passion); and when he has discovered this, he is soon able to heal its disease: for he takes a shoot of the female palm and grafts it into the very heart of the male. This refreshes the

[1] The French call it *l'aimant.*

μὲν τὴν ψυχὴν τοῦ φυτοῦ, τὸ δὲ σῶμα ἄποθνῆ-
σκον πάλιν ἀνεζωπύρησε καὶ ἐξανέστη, χαῖρον
ἐπὶ τῇ τῆς ἐρωμένης συμπλοκῇ. καὶ τοῦτό ἐστι
γάμος φυτῶν.

18. "Γίνεται δὲ καὶ γάμος ἄλλος ὑδάτων δια-
πόντιος. καί ἐστιν ὁ μὲν ἐραστὴς ποταμὸς Ἠλεῖος,
ἡ δὲ ἐρωμένη κρήνη Σικελική. διὰ γὰρ τῆς θαλάτ-
2 της ὁ ποταμὸς ὡς διὰ πεδίου τρέχει. ἡ δὲ οὐκ
ἀφανίζει γλυκὺν ἐραστὴν ἁλμυρῷ κύματι, σχί-
ζεται δὲ αὐτῷ ῥέοντι, καὶ τὸ σχίσμα τῆς θαλάτ-
της χαράδρα τῷ ποταμῷ γίνεται· καὶ ἐπὶ τὴν
Ἀρέθουσαν οὕτω τὸν Ἀλφειὸν νυμφοστολεῖ.
ὅταν οὖν ᾖ ἡ¹ τῶν Ὀλυμπίων ἑορτή, πολλοὶ
μὲν εἰς τὰς δίνας τοῦ ποταμοῦ καθιᾶσιν ἄλλος
ἄλλα δῶρα· ὁ δὲ εὐθὺς πρὸς τὴν ἐρωμένην κομίζει
καὶ ταῦτά ἐστιν ἔδνα ποταμοῦ.

3 Γίνεται δὲ καὶ ἐν τοῖς ἑρπετοῖς ἄλλο ἔρωτος
μυστήριον, οὐ τοῖς ὁμοιογενέσι μόνον πρὸς ἄλληλα,
ἀλλὰ καὶ τοῖς ἀλλοφύλοις. ὁ ἔχις ὁ τῆς γῆς ὄφις
εἰς τὴν σμύραιναν οἰστρεῖ· ἡ δὲ σμύραινά ἐστιν
ἄλλος ὄφις θαλάσσιος, εἰς μὲν τὴν μορφὴν ὄφις,
4 εἰς δὲ τὴν χρῆσιν ἰχθύς. ὅταν οὖν εἰς τὸν γάμον
ἐθέλωσιν ἀλλήλοις συνελθεῖν, ὁ μὲν εἰς τὸν
αἰγιαλὸν ἐλθὼν συρίζει πρὸς τὴν θάλασσαν τῇ
σμυραίνῃ σύμβολον, ἡ δὲ γνωρίζει τὸ σύνθημα
καὶ ἐκ τῶν κυμάτων ἀναδύεται. ἀλλ' οὐκ εὐθέως
πρὸς τὸν νυμφίον ἐξέρχεται (οἶδε γάρ, ὅτι θάνα-

----

¹ Not in the MSS. Supplied by Jacobs.

----

¹ Pliny, N.H. xxxi. 5. "Over and besides, is not this a
strange miracle, that the fountain Arethusa in Syracuse
should have a scent or smell of dung during the solemn
games and exercises at Olympia? But there is some pro-

tree's spirit, and the trunk, which seemed on the point of death, revives and gains new vigour in joy at the embrace of the beloved: it is a kind of vegetable marriage.

18. "There is even an example of wedlock between waters, which takes place across the sea. In this case [1] the lover is a river of Elis, the beloved a fountain in Sicily; the river traverses the sea as though it were a plain, and the sea, far from overwhelming the lover's fresh waters with its salt billows, makes an opening for the river's flow and thus becomes a sort of watercourse for it; so that it may fairly be said to be the match-maker between the spring Arethusa and the river Alpheus: thus when the Olympic games are in progress, it is the custom for many of those present at the Festival to throw various objects into the waters of the river, and these are borne directly by the river to the beloved, serving as wedding presents.

Among reptiles, there is an even more extraordinary mystery of love, because it is not merely the affection of two individuals of the same race towards one another, but that of a member of one species for a member of another. The viper, which is a land snake, has a burning passion for the murry, a snake of the sea, which has the outward appearance indeed of a snake, but is essentially a fish; so when these wish to join together in matrimony, the viper goes down to the shore and hisses seaward, as a signal to the murry, who recognizes it as the agreed sign, and comes out of the water. However, she does not go straight to the bridegroom, knowing

bable reason to be rendered hereof, because the river Alpheus passeth from Olympus under the very bottom of the sea into that Island of Sicily where Syracuse standeth, and so cometh to the foresaid fountain."

τον ἐν τοῖς ὀδοῦσι φέρει) ἀλλ' ἄνεισιν εἰς τὴν
πέτραν καὶ περιμένει τὸν νυμφίον καθῆραι τὸ
5 στόμα. ἑστᾶσιν οὖν ἀμφότεροι πρὸς ἀλλήλους
βλέποντες, ὁ μὲν ἠπειρώτης ἐραστής, ἡ δὲ ἐρωμένη
νησιῶτις. ὅταν οὖν ὁ ἐραστὴς ἐξεμέσῃ τῆς
νύμφης τὸν φόβον, ἡ δὲ ἐρριμμένον ἤδη τὸν
θάνατον χαμαί, τότε καταβαίνει τῆς πέτρας καὶ
εἰς τὴν ἤπειρον ἐξέρχεται καὶ τὸν ἐραστὴν περι-
πτύσσεται καὶ οὐκέτι φοβεῖται τὰ φιλήματα."

19. Ταῦτα λέγων ἔβλεπον ἅμα τὴν κόρην,[1] πῶς
ἔχει πρὸς τὴν ἀκρόασιν τὴν ἐρωτικήν· ἡ δὲ
ὑπεσήμαινεν οὐκ ἀηδῶς ἀκούειν. τὸ δὲ κάλλος
ἀστράπτον τοῦ ταῶ ἧττον ἐδόκει μοι τοῦ Λευκίπ-
της εἶναι προσώπου. τὸ γὰρ τοῦ σώματος
κάλλος αὐτῆς πρὸς τὰ τοῦ λειμῶνος ἤριζεν ἄνθη·
ναρκίσσου μὲν τὸ πρόσωπον ἔστιλβε χροιάν, ῥόδον
δὲ ἀνέτελλεν ἐκ τῆς παρειᾶς, ἴον δὲ ἡ τῶν ὀφθαλμῶν ἐμάρμαιρεν αὐγή, αἱ δὲ κόμαι βοστρυχού-
2 μεναι μᾶλλον εἱλίττοντο κιττοῦ· τοιοῦτος ἦν
Λευκίππης ἐπὶ τῶν προσώπων ὁ λειμών. ἡ μὲν
οὖν μετὰ μικρὸν ἀπιοῦσα ᾤχετο· τῆς γὰρ κιθάρας
αὐτὴν ὁ καιρὸς ἐκάλει· ἐμοὶ δὲ ἐδόκει παρεῖναι,
ἀπελθοῦσα γὰρ τὴν μορφὴν ἐπαφῆκέ μου τοῖς
3 ὀφθαλμοῖς. ἑαυτοὺς οὖν ἐπῃνοῦμεν ἐγώ τε καὶ
ὁ Σάτυρος· ἐγὼ μὲν ἐμαυτὸν τῆς μυθολογίας, ὁ
δὲ ὅτι μοι τὰς ἀφορμὰς παρέσχεν.[2]

[1] Jacobs suggested ἐνέβλεπον τῇ κόρῃ. MSS. W and M
have ἔβλεπον τῇ κόρῃ. Compare ταύτην βλέπε in II. v. § 2,
where, however, the meaning is " stare at," rather than " cast
a glance at."

[2] After παρέσχεν the MSS. have the words καὶ μετὰ μικρὸν
τοῦ δείπνου καιρὸς ἦν καὶ πάλιν ὁμοίως συνεπίνομεν, which Jacobs
saw to be an insertion derived from II. ix. § 1. They are
totally inconsistent with the opening words of Book II.

that he carries a deathly poison in his fangs, but climbs a rock and waits until he has been able to purify his mouth, and so they stay looking at one another, the lover of the land and the beloved of the sea. After the lover has been able to vomit forth that which has so greatly frightened his bride, and she has seen the death spat out on the ground, she comes down from the rock to the mainland and embraces her lover, and is no longer in terror of his kisses."

19. While recounting all these stories, I kept at the same time glancing at the maiden, to see how she felt while hearing all this talk of love; and there were some indications that she was not listening without pleasure. The gleaming beauty of the peacock seemed to me nothing in comparison with Leucippe's lovely face; indeed, her beauty was rival of the flowers of the meadow. Her skin was bright with the hue of the narcissus, roses sprang from her cheeks, the dark gleam of her eyes shone like the violet, the ringlets of her hair curled more tightly than the ivy—Leucippe's whole appearance was that of a flowery meadow. She soon turned and left the garden, as the time for her harp-playing claimed her : but she seemed to me to be still present, as even when she had gone she was able to fix the image of her form in my eyes. So Satyrus and I were then equally well satisfied with ourselves—I for the learned subjects I had been able to discuss, and he because he had given me my starting-cue.

B′

1. Ἅμα δὲ ἑαυτοὺς ἐπαινοῦντες ἐπὶ τὸ δωμάτιον ἐβαδίζομεν τῆς κόρης, ἀκροασόμενοι δῆθεν
τῶν κιθαρισμάτων· οὐ γὰρ ἠδυνάμην ἐμαυτοῦ
κἂν ἐπ᾽ ὀλίγον κρατεῖν τοῦ μὴ ὁρᾶν τὴν κόρην.
ἡ δὲ πρῶτον μὲν ᾖσεν Ὁμήρου τὴν πρὸς τὸν
λέοντα τοῦ συὸς μάχην· ἔπειτα δέ τι καὶ τῆς
ἁπαλῆς μούσης ἐλίγαινε· ῥόδον γὰρ ἐπῄνει τὸ
2 ᾆσμα. εἴ τις τὰς καμπὰς τῆς ᾠδῆς περιελὼν
ψιλὸν ἔλεγεν ἁρμονίας τὸν λόγον, οὕτως ἂν
εἶχεν ὁ λόγος· " Εἰ τοῖς ἄνθεσιν ἤθελεν ὁ Ζεὺς
ἐπιθεῖναι βασιλέα, τὸ ῥόδον ἂν τῶν ἀνθέων
ἐβασίλευε. γῆς ἐστι κόσμος, φυτῶν ἀγλάϊσμα,
ὀφθαλμὸς ἀνθέων, λειμῶνος ἐρύθημα, κάλλος
3 ἀστράπτον· ἔρωτος πνέει, Ἀφροδίτην προξενεῖ,
εὐώδεσι φύλλοις κομᾷ, εὐκινήτοις πετάλοις τρυφᾷ, τὸ πέταλον τῷ Ζεφύρῳ γελᾷ." ἡ μὲν ταῦτα
ᾖδεν· ἐγὼ δὲ ἐδόκουν τὸ ῥόδον ἐπὶ τῶν χειλέων
αὐτῆς ἰδεῖν, ὡς εἴ τις κάλυκος τὸ περιφερὲς εἰς
τὴν τοῦ στόματος ἔκλεισε μορφήν.

2. Καὶ ἄρτι ἐπέπαυτο τῶν κιθαρισμάτων καὶ
πάλιν τοῦ δείπνου καιρὸς ἦν. ἦν γὰρ [1] ἑορτὴ
προτρυγαίου Διονύσου τότε· τὸν γὰρ Διόνυσον
Τύριοι νομίζουσιν ἑαυτῶν, ἐπεὶ καὶ τὸν Κάδμου

---

[1] With these words begins col. 1, line 33 of the papyrus
GH = Π¹, but with this part of the story put after Book II. 8.

BOOK II

1. Thus congratulating one another we repaired to the maiden's chamber to hear her play on the harp, for I could not bear, even for a short time, to let her out of my sight. First of all she performed Homer's fight [1] between the boar and the lion, then she changed to a tenderer strain, her song celebrating the praises of the rose. Neglecting the modulations of the music, one might describe thus the bare theme of the composition: "If Zeus had wished to give the flowers a king, that king would have been the rose; for it is the ornament of the world, the glory of the plants, the eye of all flowers, the meadows' blush, beauty itself glowing; it has the breath of Love, it is the go-between of Aphrodite; its foliage is of sweet-smelling leaves, it glories in its rustling petals which seem to smile at the approach of the Zephyr." Thus she sang; but to me it seemed as if I saw that rose upon her lips, as it were a flower converted into the shape of her sweet mouth.

2. Hardly had she ended when the time of dinner was again at hand. It happened at that season to be the festival of Dionysus Lord of the Vintage; for the Tyrians claim him as their own proper deity, singing on the subject Cadmus' [2] myth, which

[1] *Iliad*, xvi. 823.

[2] Cadmus, the mythical founder of Thebes and introducer into Greece of the art of writing, was himself a Tyrian.

2 μῦθον ᾄδουσι· καὶ τῆς ἑορτῆς διηγοῦνται πατέρα
μῦθον, οἶνον οὐκ εἶναί πω παρ' ἀνθρώποις,[1] οὐ
τὸν μέλανα, τὸν ἀνθοσμίαν, οὐ τὸν τῆς Βιβλίας
ἀμπέλου, οὐ τὸν Μάρωνος τὸν Θράκιον, οὐ Χῖον
ἐκ Λακαίνης,[2] οὐ τὸν Ἰκάρου τὸν νησιώτην, ἀλλὰ
τούτους μὲν ἅπαντας ἀποίκους εἶναι Τυρίων
ἀμπέλων·[3] τὴν δὲ πρώτην παρ' αὐτοῖς φῦναι τῶν
3 οἴνων μητέρα. εἶναι γὰρ ἐκεῖ τινὰ φιλόξενον
ποιμένα. οἷον Ἀθηναῖοι τὸν Ἰκάριον[4] λέγουσι,
καὶ τοῦτον ἐνταῦθα τοῦ μύθου γενέσθαι πατέρα,
ὅσον Ἀττικὸν εἶναι δοκεῖν. ἐπὶ τοῦτον ἧκεν ὁ
Διόνυσος τὸν βουκόλον· ὁ δὲ αὐτῷ παρατίθησιν
ὅσα γῆ τρέφει καὶ μαζοὶ βοῶν· ποτὸν δὲ ἦν παρ'
αὐτοῖς οἷον καὶ ὁ βοῦς ἔπινεν· οὔπω γὰρ τὸ
4 ἀμπέλινον ἦν. ὁ Διόνυσος καὶ ἐπαινεῖ τῆς φιλο-
φροσύνης τὸν βουκόλον καὶ αὐτῷ προπίνει κύλικα
φιλοτησίαν· τὸ δὲ ποτὸν οἶνος ἦν. ὁ δὲ πιὼν ὑφ'
ἡδονῆς βακχεύεται καὶ λέγει πρὸς τὸν θεόν·
" Πόθεν, ὦ ξένε, σοὶ τὸ ὕδωρ τοῦτο τὸ πορφυροῦν;
πόθεν οὕτως εὖρες αἷμα γλυκύ; οὐ γάρ ἐστιν
5 ἐκεῖνο τὸ χαμαὶ ῥέον. τὸ μὲν γὰρ εἰς τὰ στέρνα
καταβαίνει καὶ λεπτὴν ἔχει τὴν ἡδονήν· τοῦτο δὲ

---

[1] After ἀνθρώποις MSS. have μήπω παρ' αὑτοῖς—removed by
Cobet as a gloss: but the papyrus GH = Π[1] also has
οπ[. . . . .]ου παρ αυτοις.

[2] χῖον ἐκ Λακαίνης Jackson: χῖον τὸν ἐκ Λ. MSS.: ἔκλευκον Π[1].

[3] Jacobs' conjecture for the pointless ἀνθρώπων of the MSS.
and of Π[1].

[4] It is possible that we should here read Ἴκαρον with
Boden. Both forms seem to be found. The whole passage
is difficult and probably corrupt.

---

[1] A doubtful name, found also in Hesiod, Works and Days,
587, and Theocritus, xiv. 15. It is variously derived from
a district in Thrace or as a generic term for wine in Crete.

they relate as the origin of the festival; and this
is it. In early days men had no wine; neither the
dark, fragrant kind, nor that from the Biblian [1] vine,
not Maron's [2] Thracian sort, not Chian "from a
Laconian cup," [3] not the island wine of Icarus, [4] but
all these, they said, were derived from Tyrian vines,
the original mother of all wines being a plant of their
country. There was a certain shepherd noted for his
hospitality, just as the Athenians describe Icarus,
from whom this Tyrian story derives its origin, so
that it almost seems an Attic tale. Dionysus once
paid a visit to this herdsman, who set before him the
produce of the earth and the result of the strength
of his oxen: but their drink was the same as that of
the oxen, since vines did not yet exist. Dionysus
thanked the herdsman for his kindly cheer, and
pledged him in a friendly cup; but his drink was wine.
The herdsman, drinking of it, danced for joy, and said
to the god: "Where did you get this purple water,
my friend? Wherever did you find blood so sweet?
For it is not that water which flows on the ground
—that, as it descends into the midriff, affords but a
faint pleasure, while this delights the sense of smell

[2] Ulysses' wine which proved so fatal to the Cyclops was
a present to him from Maron, priest of Apollo (*Od.* ix. 197).

[3] Chian wine was very good. For the saying "from a
Laconian cup" see Athenaeus XI. 484 from Aristophanes'
Daitaleis, and Hesychius Χῖον ... ἐκ Λακαίνης.

[4] Icarus, who was a friend of Bacchus, was given a cutting
of the vine by him. Cultivating this, and manufacturing
wine from the grapes, he wished to impart the new gift to
men: but unfortunately he began by administering it to
some ignorant shepherds, who at first drank greedily of it,
but when they began to feel its effects they thought that
they were poisoned, and killed their unlucky benefactor.

καὶ πρὸ τοῦ στόματος τὰς ῥῖνας εὐφραίνει καὶ
θιγόντι μὲν ψυχρόν ἐστιν, εἰς τὴν γαστέρα δὲ
καταθορὸν ἀνάπτει κάτωθεν ἡδονῆς πῦρ." καὶ ὁ
Διόνυσος ἔφη· "Τοῦτ' ἔστιν ὀπώρας ὕδωρ, τοῦτ'
6 ἔστιν αἷμα βότρυος." ἄγει πρὸς τὴν ἄμπελον ὁ
θεὸς τὸν βουκόλον, καὶ τῶν βοτρύων λαβὼν ἅμα
καὶ θλίβων καὶ δεικνὺς τὴν ἄμπελον, "Τοῦτο μέν
ἐστιν," ἔφη, "τὸ ὕδωρ· τοῦτο δὲ ἡ πηγή." ὁ μὲν
οὖν οἶνος οὕτως ἐς ἀνθρώπους παρῆλθεν, ὡς ὁ
Τυρίων λόγος, (3) ἑορτὴν δὲ ἄγουσιν ἐκείνην τὴν
ἡμέραν ἐκείνῳ τῷ θεῷ.

Φιλοτιμούμενος οὖν ὁ πατὴρ τά τε ἄλλα
παρασκευάσας εἰς τὸ δεῖπνον ἔτυχε πολυτελέσ-
τερα καὶ κρατῆρα παρεθήκατο ἱερὸν τοῦ θεοῦ
πολυτελή, μετὰ τὸν Γλαύκου τοῦ Χίου δεύτερον.
2 ὑάλου μὲν τὸ πᾶν ἔργον ὀρωρυγμένης· κύκλῳ δὲ
αὐτὸν ἄμπελοι περιέστεφον ἀπ' αὐτοῦ τοῦ
κρατῆρος πεφυτευμέναι· οἱ δὲ βότρυες πάντη
περικρεμάμενοι· ὄμφαξ μὲν αὐτῶν ἕκαστος ἐφ'
ὅσον ἦν κενὸς ὁ κρατήρ· ἐὰν δὲ ἐγχέῃς οἴνου, κατὰ
μικρὸν ὁ βότρυς ὑποπερκάζεται καὶ σταφυλὴν
τὴν ὄμφακα ποιεῖ. Διόνυσος δὲ ἐντετύπωται τῶν
βοτρύων πλησίον, ἵνα τὴν ἄμπελον οἴνῳ γεωργῇ.[1]
3 τοῦ δὲ πότου προϊόντος ἤδη καὶ ἀναισχύντως ἐς
αὐτὴν ἑώρων. Ἔρως δὲ καὶ Διόνυσος, δύο βίαιοι
θεοί, ψυχὴν κατασχόντες, ἐκμαίνουσιν εἰς ἀναισχυντίαν, ὁ μὲν καίων αὐτὴν τῷ συνήθει πυρί, ὁ δὲ

---

[1] After γεωρ[, GH = Π¹ passes to Book II. 9. I have
adopted a fair number of unimportant corrections from it.

---

[1] Or, perhaps, "the water of fruit."

before ever it reaches the mouth; when you touch
it, it is cold, but it leaps down into the belly and
there, far down, lights up the fires of delight."
"This," said Dionysus, "is harvest[1] water, the blood
of the grape": then the god led the herdsman to
the vine, and took hold of the clusters and squeezed
them; and then, pointing to the vine, "Here is your
water," said he, "this is its source." That is the
way in which wine came to men, as the Tyrian story
goes, (3) and they keep that day as Dionysus'
festival.

My father, wishing to celebrate it with splendour,
had set out all that was necessary for the dinner in a
rich and costly fashion; but especially a precious cup
to be used for libations to the god, one only second
to the famous goblet[2] of Glaucus of Chios. The
material of it was wrought rock-crystal; vines crowned
its rim, seeming to grow from the cup itself, their
clusters drooped down in every direction: when the
cup was empty, each grape seemed green and unripe,
but when wine was poured into it, then little by
little the clusters became red and dark, the green
crop turning into the ripe fruit; Dionysus too was
represented hard by the clusters, to be the husband-
man of the vine and the vintner.[3] As we drank
deeper, I began to look more boldly and with less shame at
my sweetheart: Cupid and Dionysus are two of the
most violent of the gods, they can grasp the soul
and drive it so far towards madness that it loses all
restraint; Cupid fires it with the flames which are
his attribute, while Dionysus supplies wine which is

[2] Presumably that mentioned in Herodotus, i. 25. Glaucus
was a contemporary of Gyges.
[3] It is hard to see how οἴνῳ should be rendered.

τὸν οἶνον ὑπέκκαυμα φέρων· οἶνος γὰρ ἔρωτος
τροφή. ἤδη δὲ καὶ αὐτὴ περιεργότερον εἰς ἐμὲ
βλέπειν ἐθρασύνετο. καὶ ταῦτα μὲν ἡμῖν ἡμερῶν
ἐπράττετο δέκα· καὶ πλέον τῶν ὀμμάτων ἐκερ-
δαίνομεν ἢ ἐτολμῶμεν οὐδέν.

4. Κοινοῦμαι δὴ τῷ Σατύρῳ τὸ πᾶν καὶ συμ-
πράττειν ἠξίουν· ὁ δὲ ἔλεγε καὶ αὐτὸς μὲν
ἐγνωκέναι πρὶν παρ᾽ ἐμοῦ μαθεῖν, ὀκνεῖν δὲ
ἐλέγχειν βουλόμενον λαθεῖν. ὁ γὰρ μετὰ κλοπῆς
ἐρῶν ἂν ἐλεγχθῇ πρός τινος, ὡς ὀνειδίζοντα τὸν
2 ἐλέγξαντα μισεῖ. "'Ἤδη δέ," ἔφη, " καὶ τὸ αὐτόματον ἡμῶν προυνόησεν.[1] ἡ γὰρ τὸν θάλαμον
αὐτῆς πεπιστευμένη Κλειὼ κεκοινώνηκέ μοι καὶ
ἔχει πρός με ὡς ἐραστήν. ταύτην παρασκευάσω
κατὰ μικρὸν πρὸς ἡμᾶς οὕτως ἔχειν, ὡς καὶ
3 συναίρεσθαι πρὸς τὸ ἔργον. δεῖ δέ σε καὶ τὴν
κόρην μὴ μέχρι τῶν ὀφθαλμῶν[2] πειρᾶν, ἀλλὰ
καὶ ῥῆμα δριμύτερον εἰπεῖν. τότε δὲ πρόσαγε
4 τὴν δευτέραν μηχανήν· θίγε χειρός, θλῖψον
δάκτυλον, θλίβων στέναξον. ἢν δὲ ταῦτά σου
ποιοῦντος καρτερῇ καὶ προσίηται, σὸν ἔργον ἤδη
δέσποινάν τε καλεῖν καὶ φιλῆσαι τράχηλον."
" Πιθανῶς μέν," ἔφην, " νὴ τὴν Ἀθηνᾶν, εἰς
τὸ ἔργον παιδοτριβεῖς· δέδοικα δὲ μὴ ἄτολμος[3]
5 καὶ δειλὸς ἔρωτος ἀθλητὴς γένωμαι." "'Ἔρως, ὦ

---

[1] After προυνόησεν some MSS. have ἡ τύχη. But it is probably a marginal gloss on τὸ αὐτόματον which has crept into the
text. Berger deleted it. Lumb reads ᾗ τύχῃ. cf. ch. vi. § 3.

[2] Here in M follows μόνον, in W μόνων: but Jacobs was
probably right in omitting it with MSS. β, F, as the insertion
of a reader trying to make the text easier: μέχρι τῶν ὀφθαλμῶν
really means in itself " by glances of the eyes only."

[3] ὦν, which here followed in the MSS., is omitted on the
authority of Cobet.

as fuel to the fire: for wine is the very sustenance of love. She too became more hardy, and scrutinized me more curiously. In this state of affairs ten days passed, but we made no other progress nor ventured further than this duel of eyes.

4. I imparted the whole story to Satyrus and asked for his assistance: he replied that he had perceived how things were before I had told him, but had hesitated to question me since I wanted to hide my feelings; for the secret lover, when questioned, often contracts a hatred of the questioner as if he were offering him some insult. "However," said he, "things have already of their own accord fallen out to our advantage; for Clio, the serving-maid entrusted with the care of your sweetheart's chamber, confides in me and regards me as her lover. I hope little by little to be able to wheedle her and make her so favourably disposed to us that she will lend her assistance to the final effort. But as for you, you must not be content with making advances to her with glances of your eyes alone; you must use a direct and outright form of speech. Then bring forward your second line, touch her hand, squeeze a finger, and sigh as you squeeze; if she allows you to do this and seems to approve, your next step is to call her your princess and to kiss her on the neck." "You are a plausible trainer, I vow," said I, "for the difficult accomplishment; but I fear that I shall prove a backward and cowardly performer." "Love," he answered, "tolerates no

γενναῖε," ἔφη, "δειλίας οὐκ ἀνέχεται. ὁρᾷς
αὐτοῦ τὸ σχῆμα ὡς ἐστι στρατιωτικόν· τόξα καὶ
φαρέτρα καὶ βέλη καὶ πῦρ, ἀνδρεῖα πάντα καὶ
τόλμης γέμοντα. τοιοῦτον οὖν ἐν σεαυτῷ θεὸν
ἔχων, δειλὸς εἶ καὶ φοβῇ; ὅρα μὴ καταψεύσῃ[1]
6 τοῦ θεοῦ. ἀρχὴν δέ σοι ἐγὼ παρέξω· τὴν Κλειὼ
γὰρ ἀπάξω μάλιστα ὅταν ἐπιτήδειον ἴδω καιρὸν
τοῦ σε τῇ παρθένῳ δύνασθαι καθ᾽ αὑτὸν συνεῖναι
μόνῃ."

5. Ταῦτα εἰπὼν ἐχώρησεν ἔξω τῶν θυρῶν· ἐγὼ
δὲ κατ᾽ ἐμαυτὸν γενόμενος καὶ ὑπὸ τοῦ Σατύρου
παροξυνθείς, ἤσκουν ἐμαυτὸν εἰς εὐτολμίαν πρὸς
τὴν παρθένον. "Μέχρι τίνος, ἄνανδρε, σιγᾷς; τί
δὲ δειλὸς εἶ στρατιώτης ἀνδρείου θεοῦ; τὴν κόρην
2 προσελθεῖν σοὶ περιμένεις;" εἶτα προσετίθην·
"Τί γάρ, ὦ κακόδαιμον, οὐ σωφρονεῖς; τί δὲ οὐκ
ἐρᾷς ὧν σε δεῖ; παρθένον ἔνδον ἔχεις ἄλλην
καλήν· ταύτης ἔρα, ταύτην βλέπε, ταύτην
ἔξεστί σοι γαμεῖν." ἐδόκουν πεπεῖσθαι· κάτωθεν
δὲ ὥσπερ ἐκ τῆς καρδίας ὁ ἔρως ἀντεφθέγγετο.
"Ναί, τολμηρέ, κατ᾽ ἐμοῦ στρατεύῃ καὶ ἀντι-
παρατάττῃ; ἵπταμαι καὶ τοξεύω καὶ φλέγω.
πῶς δυνήσῃ με φυγεῖν; ἂν φυλάξῃ μου τὸ τόξον,
οὐκ ἔχεις φυλάξασθαι τὸ πῦρ· ἂν δὲ κατασβέσῃς
σωφροσύνῃ τὴν φλόγα, αὐτῷ σε καταλήψομαι
τῷ πτερῷ."

6. Ταῦτα διαλεγόμενος ἔλαθον ἐπιστὰς ἀπρο-
οράτως τῇ κόρῃ καὶ ὠχρίασα ἰδὼν ἐξαίφνης·
εἶτ᾽ ἐφοινίχθην. μόνη δὲ ἦν καὶ οὐδὲ ἡ Κλειὼ
συμπαρῆν. ὅμως οὖν, ὡς ἂν τεθορυβημένος οὐκ

[1] So W and M, giving better grammar. The other MSS.
have καταψεύδῃ.

cowardice at all: look how warlike is his appearance—bow, quiver, arrows, and fire—all of them the
furniture of courage and enterprise. With such
a god as that within you, can you be backward and fearful? Be careful not to give him
the lie. However, I will give you an opening: I
will distract Clio directly I see the most favourable
time for you to be alone and by yourself to have a
private conversation with the maiden."

5. This said, he left the room: when I was by
myself, stimulated by Satyrus' words, I began to
screw up my courage for the coming attack. "How
long," said I, "do you mean to keep silent, you
coward? Why are you so fearful a soldier of so
brave a god? Do you expect the maiden to make
the first advances toward you?" Then I went on:
"But why cannot you control yourself, fool? Why
not love where duty bids you? You have another
in the house—a virgin, and fair: love her, look at
her, marriage with her is in your power." I thought
that I had persuaded myself, but deep down love
answered, as though speaking from my heart: "Ha,
insolent, do you dare to take arms and set yourself
up to do battle with me? I can fly, I can shoot, I
can burn, how can you avoid me? If you escape my
bow, you cannot escape my fire; and if you can
quench my fire by your self-control, I shall yet catch
you with my wings."

6. While I was thus arguing with myself, I unexpectedly found that I was standing in the maiden's
presence, and at the sudden sight of her I turned
pale and then blushed red: she was all alone, not
even Clio with her. However, I could say nothing in

2 ἔχων τί εἴπω, "Χαῖρε," ἔφην, "δέσποινα." ἡ δὲ
μειδιάσασα γλυκὺ καὶ ἐμφανίσασα διὰ τοῦ
γέλωτος, ὅτι συνῆκε πῶς εἶπον τὸ "Χαῖρε,
δέσποινα," εἶπεν· "᾿Εγὼ σή; μὴ τοῦτ᾿ εἴπῃς."
"Καὶ μὴν πέπρακε μέ τίς σοι θεῶν ὥσπερ καὶ τὸν
3 ῾Ηρακλέα τῇ ᾿Ομφάλῃ." "Τὸν ῾Ερμῆν λέγεις;
τούτῳ τὴν πρᾶσιν ἐκέλευσεν ὁ Ζεύς," καὶ ἅμα
ἐγέλασε. "Ποῖον ῾Ερμῆν; τί ληρεῖς," εἶπον,
"εἰδυῖα σαφῶς ὃ λέγω·" ὡς δὲ περιέπλεκον
λόγους ἐκ λόγων, τὸ αὐτόματόν μοι συνήργησεν.

7. ῎Ετυχε τῇ προτεραίᾳ ταύτης ἡμέρᾳ περὶ
μεσημβρίαν ἡ παῖς ψάλλουσα κιθάρᾳ, ἐπιπαρῆν
δὲ αὐτῇ καὶ ἡ Κλειὼ καὶ παρεκάθητο, διεβάδιζον
δὲ ἐγώ· καί τις ἐξαίφνης μέλιττά ποθεν ἐπιπτᾶσα
2 τῆς Κλειοῦς ἐπάταξε τὴν χεῖρα. καὶ ἡ μὲν
ἀνέκραγεν· ἡ δὲ παῖς ἀναθοροῦσα καὶ καταθεμένη
τὴν κιθάραν κατενόει τὴν πληγήν, καὶ ἅμα
παρῆνει, λέγουσα μηδὲν ἄχθεσθαι· παύσειν γὰρ
αὐτὴν τῆς ἀλγηδόνος δύο ἐπάσασαν ῥήματα·
διδαχθῆναι γὰρ αὐτὴν ὑπό τινος Αἰγυπτίας εἰς
3 πληγὰς σφηκῶν καὶ μελιττῶν. καὶ ἅμα ἐπῇδε·
καὶ ἔλεγεν ἡ Κλειὼ μετὰ μικρὸν ῥάων γεγονέναι.
τότε οὖν κατὰ τύχην μέλιττά τις ἢ σφὴξ
περιβομβήσασα, κύκλῳ μου τὸ πρόσωπον περι-
έπτη· κἀγὼ λαμβάνω τὸ ἐνθύμιον καὶ τὴν
χεῖρα ἐπιβαλὼν τοῖς προσώποις, προσεποιούμην
4 πεπλῆχθαι καὶ ἀλγεῖν. ἡ δὲ παῖς προσελθοῦσα,

my agitation, but did my best with " Greetings, my princess." She smiled very sweetly, showing through her smile that she understood why I greeted her as my princess, and said : " I your princess ? Do not call me by such a name." " Say not so," said I : " one of the gods has sold me into captivity to you, as he did Hercules[1] to Omphale." " Is it Hermes you mean," said she, " whom Zeus sent to effect the sale ? " and burst out laughing. " Hermes, indeed !" I answered. " How can you talk such nonsense, when you know well enough what I mean ? " One such repartee led to another, and my good luck helped me.

7. Now it had happened on the day before that while the maiden was playing on her harp, Clio was sitting by her and I myself was walking to and fro : and suddenly a bee flew in from somewhere and stung Clio on the hand, who gave a loud scream. Leucippe jumped up, laid down her harp, examined the wound, and did her best to comfort her, telling her not to complain ; for she could ease her of the pain by saying over it a couple of charms which she had learned of a gipsy against the stings of wasps and bees : and she pronounced them, and almost immediately Clio said that she was much better. Well, on this second occasion there happened to be some wasp or bee buzzing about and flying round my face, so I adopted the idea, and putting my hand to my face, pretended that I had been stung and was in pain. The maiden came over

---

[1] Hercules had committed some crime ; opinions differ as to whether he had killed somebody or stolen a tripod from Apollo's shrine. To expiate this he was ordered by Zeus, using Hermes as messenger, to be a slave for a time of Omphale, Queen of Lydia.

εἷλκε τὴν χεῖρα καὶ ἐπυνθάνετο ποῦ ἐπαταχθην·
κἀγώ, "Κατὰ τοῦ χείλους," ἔφην. "ἀλλὰ τι
οὐκ ἐπᾴδεις, φιλτάτη;" ἡ δὲ προσῆλθέ τε καὶ
ἀνέθηκεν, ὡς ἐπάσουσα, τὸ στόμα, καί τι ἐψι-
θύριζεν, ἐπιπολῆς ψαύουσά μου τῶν χειλέων.
5 κἀγὼ κατεφίλουν σιωπῇ, κλέπτων τῶν φιλημάτων τὸν ψόφον, ἡ δὲ ἀνοίγουσα καὶ κλείουσα
τῶν χειλέων τὴν συμβολὴν τῷ τῆς ἐπῳδῆς
ψιθυρίσματι, φιλήματα ἐποίει τὴν ἐπῳδήν· κἀγὼ
τότε δὴ περιβαλὼν φανερῶς κατεφίλουν· ἡ δὲ διασχοῦσα, "Τί ποιεῖς;" ἔφη, "καὶ σὺ κατεπᾴδεις;"
"Τὴν ἐπῳδόν," εἶπον,[1] "φιλῶ, ὅτι μου τὴν ὀδύνην
6 ἰάσω." ὡς δὲ συνῆκεν ὁ λέγω καὶ ἐμειδίασε,
θαρρήσας εἶπον· "Οἴμοι, φιλτάτη, πάλιν τέτρω-
μαι χαλεπώτερον· ἐπὶ γὰρ τὴν καρδίαν κατέρ-
ρευσε τὸ τραῦμα καὶ ζητεῖ σου τὴν ἐπῳδήν. ἦ
που καὶ σὺ μέλιτταν ἐπὶ τοῦ στόματος φέρεις·
καὶ γὰρ μέλιτος γέμεις, καὶ τιτρώσκει σου τὰ
7 φιλήματα. ἀλλὰ δέομαι,[2] κατέπασον αὖθις καὶ
μὴ ταχὺ τὴν ἐπῳδὴν παραδράμῃς καὶ πάλιν
ἀγριάνῃς τὸ τραῦμα." καὶ ἅμα λέγων τὴν χεῖρα
βιαιότερον περιέβαλλον καὶ ἐφίλουν ἐλευθερω-
τερον· ἡ δὲ ἠνείχετο, κωλύουσα δῆθεν. 8. ἐν τούτῳ
πόρρωθεν ἰδόντες προσιοῦσαν τὴν θεράπαιναν
διελύθημεν, ἐγὼ μὲν ἄκων καὶ λυπούμενος, ἡ δὲ
οὐκ οἶδ' ὅπως εἶχεν.

Ῥάων οὖν ἐγεγόνειν καὶ μεστὸς ἐλπίδων,
ᾐσθόμην δὲ ἐπικαθημένου μοι τοῦ φιλήματος
ὡς σώματος. καὶ ἐφύλαττον ἀκριβῶς ὡς θησαυρὸν τὸ φίλημα τηρῶν ἡδονῆς, ὁ πρῶτόν ἐστιν

---

[1] The MSS. read ὅτι φιλῶ ὅτι (not G).
[2] Here begins GH = Π¹, col. 1, l. 1.

to me, drew my hand away, and asked me where the sting was: "On the lip," said I: "will you not repeat the charm, my dearest?" She came close to me and put her mouth close to mine, so as to work the charm, and murmured something while she touched the tip of my lips; and I gently kissed her, avoiding all the noise of an ordinary salute, until, in the successive opening and shutting of her lips as she murmured it, she converted the charm into a series of kisses: then at last I actually threw my arms round her and kissed her fully without further pretence. At this she started back, crying: "What are you doing? Are you saying a charm too?" "No," said I, "I am kissing the charmer who has cured me of my pain." As she did not misunderstand my words, and smiled, I plucked up my courage and went on: "Ah, my dearest, I am stung again, and worse: this time the wound has reached my heart and needs your charm to heal it. I think you must have a bee on your lips, so full of honey are you, and your kisses sting. I implore you to repeat your charm once more, and do not hurry over it and make the wound worse again." So speaking, I put my arm more boldly round her and kissed her with more freedom than before: and she let me do it, while pretending to resist. **8.** At that moment we saw her serving-maid approaching from a distance and sprang apart: with me it went much against the grain and to my displeasure—what her feelings were I do not know.

This experience made me feel less unhappy, and I began to be full of hope: I felt as if the kiss, like some material object, were still on my lips and preserved it jealously, keeping it as a kind of treasury

2 ἐραστῇ γλυκύ. καὶ γὰρ ἀπὸ τοῦ καλλίστου τῶν
τοῦ σώματος ὀργάνων τίκτεται· στόμα γὰρ φωνῆς
ὄργανον· φωνὴ δὲ ψυχῆς σκιά. αἱ γὰρ τῶν στομά-
των συμβολαὶ κιρνάμεναι καὶ ἐκπέμπουσαι κάτω
τῶν στέρνων τὴν ἡδονὴν ἕλκουσι τὰς ψυχὰς πρὸς
3 τὰ φιλήματα. οὐκ οἶδα δὲ οὕτω πρότερον ἡσθεὶς
ἐκ τῆς καρδίας· καὶ τότε πρῶτον ἔμαθον ὅτι
μηδὲν ἐρίζει πρὸς ἡδονὴν φιλήματι ἐρωτικῷ.[1]

9. Ἐπειδὴ δὲ τοῦ δείπνου καιρὸς ἦν, πάλιν[1]
ὁμοίως συνεπίνομεν· ᾠνοχόει δὲ ὁ Σάτυρος ἡμῖν καί
τι ποιεῖ πρᾶγμα[2] ἐρωτικόν. διαλλάσσει τὰ ἐκπώματα καὶ τὸ μὲν ἐμὸν τῇ κόρῃ προστίθησι, τὸ δὲ
ἐκείνης ἐμοί, καὶ ἐγχέων ἀμφοτέροις καὶ κερασάμε-
2 νος ὤρεγεν. ἐγὼ δὲ ἐπιτηρήσας τὸ μέρος τοῦ
ἐκπώματος, ἔνθα τὸ χεῖλος ἡ κόρη πίνουσα
προσέθηκεν, ἐναρμοσάμενος[3] ἔπινον, ἀποστολι-
μαῖον τοῦτο φίλημα ποιῶν, καὶ ἅμα κατεφίλουν
3 τὸ ἔκπωμα. ἡ δὲ ὡς εἶδεν, συνῆκεν ὅτι[4] τοῦ
χείλους αὐτῆς καταφιλῶ καὶ τὴν σκιάν. ἀλλ' ὅ
γε Σάτυρος συμφωρήσας[5] πάλιν τὰ ἐκπώματα
ἐνήλλαξεν ἡμῖν. τότε δὴ καὶ τὴν κόρην εἶδον τὰ
ἐμὰ μιμουμένην καὶ ταὐτὰ πίνουσαν, καὶ ἔχαιρον
ἤδη πλέον, καὶ τρίτον ἐγένετο τοῦτο καὶ τέταρτον
καὶ τὸ λοιπὸν τῆς ἡμέρας οὕτως ἀλλήλοις προὐπί-
νομεν τὰ φιλήματα.

10. Μετὰ δὲ τὸ δεῖπνον ὁ Σάτυρός μοι προσελθὼν ἔφη· "Νῦν μὲν ἀνδρίζεσθαι καιρός. ἡ γὰρ

---

[1] ερωτικω [ε]σπερας γενομενης παλιν Π[1].
[2] πραγμα Π[1]. Omitted by MSS.
[3] Here Vilborg adds τὸ ἐμὸν.   [4] With συνηκεν ο [ends Π[1].
[5] συμφορήσας MSS. α: συμφυράσας MSS. β: συμφρονήσας
Jacobs: I have preferred to suggest συμφωρήσας. συμφύρας
Cobet.

of delight; the kiss is the lover's first favour. It is of the fairest part of the whole body—the mouth, which is the instrument of the voice, and the voice is the reflection of the soul. When lovers' lips meet and mingle together they send down a stream of pleasure beneath the breast and draw up the soul to the lips.[1] I know that never before this did I feel such pleasure in my inmost heart: then for the first time I learned that there is no pleasure on earth comparable with a lover's kiss.

9. When the time for dinner came, we drank with one another as before. Satyrus was serving the wine, and he devised a trick such as lovers enjoy. He exchanged our cups, giving mine to Leucippe and hers to me, after he had put in the wine and made the mixture: I had observed which part of the cup she had touched when drinking, and then set my own lips upon the same place when I drank myself, so that as my mouth touched the brim I seemed to be sending her a kiss by proxy: when she saw this, she comprehended at once that I was glad enough to kiss even the shadow of her lips. Presently Satyrus once more stole away the cups and again exchanged them: then I saw her copying my procedure and drinking from the same spot where I had drunk, and at this I was still more delighted. This happened a third and a fourth time, and indeed for the rest of that evening we were thus pledging kisses to one another.

10. When the dinner was over Satyrus came up to me and said: "Now is the time to play

---

[1] *Cf.* ch. xxxvii. The idea is a commonplace of Greek and Latin literature, from a famous epigram of Plato's onward; and Tennyson's *Fatima*: "With one long kiss he drew My whole soul through my lips."

μήτηρ τῆς κόρης, ὡς οἶδας, μαλακίζεται καὶ καθ'
αὐτὴν ἀναπαύεται· μόνη δὲ ἡ παῖς βαδιεῖται
κατὰ τὰ εἰθισμένα τῆς Κλειοῦς ἑπομένης, πρὶν
2 ἐπὶ τὸν ὕπνον τραπῆναι. ἐγὼ δέ σοι καὶ ταύτην
ἀπάξω διαλεγόμενος." ταῦτα εἰπών, τῇ Κλειοῖ
μὲν αὐτός, ἐγὼ δὲ τῇ παιδὶ διαλαχόντες ἐφη-
δρεύομεν. καὶ οὕτως ἐγένετο. ἀπεσπάσθη μὲν
ἡ Κλειώ, ἡ δὲ παρθένος ἐν τῷ περιπάτῳ κατε-
3 λέλειπτο. ἐπιτηρήσας οὖν ὅτε[1] τὸ πολὺ τῆς
αὐγῆς ἐμαραίνετο, πρόσειμι πρὸς αὐτὴν[2]
θρασύτερος γενόμενος ἐκ τῆς πρώτης προσβολῆς,
ὥσπερ στρατιώτης ἤδη νενικηκὼς καὶ τοῦ
πολέμου καταπεφρονηκώς· πολλὰ γὰρ ἦν τὰ τότε
ὁπλίζοντά με θαρρεῖν, οἶνος, ἔρως, ἐλπίς, ἐρημία·
καὶ οὐδὲν εἰπών, ἀλλ' ὡς ἐπὶ συγκείμενον ἔργον,
4 ὡς εἶχον, περιχυθεὶς τὴν κόρην κατεφίλουν. ὡς
δὲ καὶ ἐπεχείρουν τι προὔργου ποιεῖν, ψόφος τις
ἡμῶν κατόπιν γίνεται· καὶ ταραχθέντες ἀνε-
πηδήσαμεν. καὶ ἡ μὲν ἐπέκεινα τρέπεται ἐπὶ
τὸ δωμάτιον αὐτῆς, ἐγὼ δὲ ἐπὶ θάτερα, σφόδρα
ἀνιώμενος, ἔργον οὕτω καλὸν ἀπολέσας, καὶ τὸν
5 ψόφον λοιδορῶν. ἐν τούτῳ δὲ[3] ὁ Σάτυρος
ὑπαντιάζει μοι φαιδρῷ τῷ προσώπῳ· καθορᾶν
γάρ μοι ἐδόκει ὅσα ἐπράττομεν, ὑπό τινι τῶν
δένδρων λοχῶν μή τις ἡμῖν ἐπέλθῃ· καὶ αὐτὸς ἦν
ὁ ποιήσας τὸν ψόφον, προσιόντα θεασάμενός τινα.

---

[1] Here followed in the MSS. τοῦ φωτός, which was rightly
expunged by Spitzner as a gloss on τῆς αὐγῆς.

[2] πρὸς αὐτήν is found in the MSS. after γενόμενος. I prefer
this transposition to removing it altogether, with Hercher.

[3] Some MSS. have δὲ καί, but the second word is better
omitted with the Codex Vaticanus graecus 114 and also E
and R.

the man. Your sweetheart's mother, as you
know, is not in good health and is gone to
rest alone: while Leucippe will take a stroll, before
retiring to sleep, with no other escort than her
maid Clio, her regular attendant: I will fall into
conversation with Clio and lead her apart." Acting
on this suggestion, we lay in wait for them, I
devoting my energies to the maiden, and he to
Clio: and all turned out well; Clio disappeared,
and Leucippe was left walking in the court. I thus
bided my time until the greater part of the sun's
light was obscured, and then advanced to the attack,
a bolder man since the success of my first onslaught,
like a soldier that has already gained the victory and
made light of war: for the arms that gave me
such confidence were not a few—wine, love, hope,
solitude: so that I uttered never a word, but without
other preliminaries, as if all had been arranged
between us beforehand, I threw my arms round
her and kissed her. I was even beginning to make
further advances, when we suddenly heard a noise
behind us, and in our anxiety jumped apart: she
retired to her chamber and I to the other part
of the house, very angry at the spoiling of such
a good beginning, and cursing the noise. While
so engaged Satyrus met me with a smiling face:
it appeared that he had seen all our proceedings,
hiding behind some bushes in case anybody should
come; and it was he that had made the noise,
because he had seen someone approaching.

11. Ὀλίγων δὲ ἡμερῶν διελθουσῶν, ὁ πατήρ μοι τοὺς γάμους συνεκρότει θᾶττον ἢ διεγνώκει. ἐνύπνια γὰρ αὐτὸν διετάραττε πολλά· ἔδοξεν ἄγειν ἡμῶν τοὺς γάμους, ἤδη δὲ ἅψαντος αὐτοῦ τὰς δᾷδας, ἀποσβεσθῆναι τὸ πῦρ[1] . . . . ἢ καὶ
2 μᾶλλον ἠπείγετο συναγαγεῖν ἡμᾶς· τοῦτο δὲ εἰς τὴν ὑστεραίαν παρεσκευάζετο. ἐώνητο δὲ τῇ κόρῃ τὰ πρὸς τὸν γάμον· περιδέραιον μὲν λίθων ποικίλων· ἐσθῆτα δὲ τὸ πᾶν μὲν πορφυρᾶν, ἔνθα δὲ ταῖς ἄλλαις ἐσθῆσιν ἡ χώρα τῆς πορφύρας, ἐκεῖ χρυσὸς ἦν. ἤριζον δὲ πρὸς ἀλλήλους
3 οἱ λίθοι. ὑάκινθος μὲν ῥόδον ἦν ἐν λίθῳ· ἀμέθυστος δὲ ἐπορφύρετο τοῦ χρυσοῦ πλησίον. ἐν μέσῳ δὲ τρεῖς ἦσαν λίθοι, τὴν χροιὰν ἐπάλληλοι· συγκείμενοι δὲ ἦσαν οἱ τρεῖς· μέλαινα μὲν ἡ κρηπὶς τοῦ λίθου, τὸ δὲ μέσον σῶμα λευκὸν τῷ μέλανι συνεφαίνετο, ἑξῆς δὲ τῷ λευκῷ τὸ λοιπὸν ἐπυρρία κορυφούμενον· ὁ λίθος δὲ τῷ χρυσῷ στεφανούμενος, ὀφθαλμὸν ἐμιμεῖτο
4 χρυσοῦν. τῆς δὲ ἐσθῆτος οὐ πάρεργον εἶχεν ἡ πορφύρα τὴν βαφήν, ἀλλ' οἵαν μυθολογοῦσι Τύριοι τοῦ ποιμένος εὑρεῖν τὸν κύνα, ᾗ καὶ μέχρι τούτου βάπτουσιν Ἀφροδίτης τὸν πέπλον.

---

[1] Jacobs saw that something was missing in the Greek. The Latin translation of Annibale della Croce (published in 1554 before the appearance of the Greek text) contains words which may be rendered " and, a thing that gave him even keener anguish, the bride and I disappeared from his sight. ' Whether or not any MS. ever contained the original of these words, the sense is not unlike that which is required.

11. A few days later, my father began to push on
the preparations for my marriage with more haste
than he had originally intended, because he was
being troubled by frequent dreams. He thought
that he was conducting our marriage ceremonies, and
had already lit the torches, when the fire was
suddenly put out [and, what disturbed him even
more deeply, both Calligone and I vanished]. This
made him in the greater hurry to unite us, and
preparations were made for the wedding to be on
the following day. All the bridal ornaments had
been bought for the maiden : she had a necklace of
various precious stones and a dress of which the
whole ground was purple ; where, on ordinary dresses
there would be braidings of purple, on this they
were of gold. In the necklace the gems seemed at
rivalry with one another; there was a jacinth that
might be described as a rose crystallized in stone[1] and
an amethyst that shone so brightly that it seemed
akin to gold ; in between were three stones of
graded colours, all mounted together, forming a gem
black at the base, white streaked with black in the
middle, and the white shaded off into red at the
top : the whole jewel was encircled with gold and
presented the appearance of a golden eye. As for
the dress, the purple with which it was dyed was no
casual tint, but that kind which (according to the
story the Tyrians tell) was discovered by the shepherd's dog, with which they dye Aphrodite's robe

[1] This does not refer to the shape of the gem, but to its
colour.

ἦν γὰρ χρόνος ὅτε τῆς πορφύρας ὁ κόσμος
ἀνθρώποις ἀπόρρητος ἦν· μικρὸς δὲ αὐτὴν ἐκά-
5 λυπτε κόχλος ἐγκύκλῳ μυχῷ. ἁλιεὺς ἀγρεύει
τὴν ἄγραν ταύτην· καὶ ὁ μὲν ἰχθὺν προσεδό-
κησεν, ὡς δὲ εἶδε τοῦ κόχλου τὴν τραχύτητα,
ἐλοιδόρει τὴν ἄγραν καὶ ἔρριψεν ὡς θαλάσσης
σκύβαλον. εὑρίσκει δὲ κύων τὸ ἕρμαιον καὶ
καταθραύει τοῖς ὀδοῦσι, καὶ τῷ στόματι τοῦ
κυνὸς περιρρέει τοῦ ἄνθους τὸ αἷμα καὶ βάπτει
τὸ αἷμα τὴν γένυν καὶ ὑφαίνει τοῖς χείλεσι τὴν
6 πορφύραν. ὁ ποιμὴν ὁρᾷ τὰ χείλη τοῦ κυνὸς
ἡμαγμένα καὶ τραῦμα νομίσας τὴν βαφὴν πρόσεισι καὶ ἀπέπλυνε τῇ θαλάσσῃ, καὶ τὸ αἷμα
λαμπρότερον ἐπορφύρετο· ὡς δὲ καὶ ταῖς χερσὶν
7 ἔθιγε, τὴν πορφύραν εἶχε καὶ ἡ χείρ. συνῆκεν
οὖν τοῦ κόχλου τὴν φύσιν ὁ ποιμήν, ὅτι φάρμακον ἔχει κάλλους πεφυτευμένον· καὶ λαβὼν
μαλλὸν ἐρίου, καθῆκεν εἰς τὸν χηραμὸν αὐτοῦ
τὸ ἔριον, ζητῶν τοῦ κόχλου τὰ μυστήρια· τὸ δὲ
κατὰ τὴν γένυν τοῦ κυνὸς ἡμάσσετο· καὶ τότε
8 τὴν εἰκόνα[1] τῆς πορφύρας ἐδιδάσκετο. λαβὼν
δή τινας λίθους περιθραύει τὸ τεῖχος τοῦ φαρμάκου καὶ τὸ ἄδυτον ἀνοίγει τῆς πορφύρας, καὶ
θησαυρὸν εὑρίσκει βαφῆς.

---

[1] For τὴν εἰκόνα Hercher suggested τὸν οἶκον (Knox,
better, τὴν οἰκίαν), the "home" of the dye instead of its
"appearance." But the change does not seem absolutely
necessary. Jackson proposes τὴν μήκωνα.

---

[1] This interruption of the action by a description of the
origin of the purple dye seems strangely inartistic to us.
Compare the account in ch. ii. above of the discovery of
wine, and the account of the hippopotamus in Bk. IV. ii. *sqq.*:

to this day. There[1] was once a time, you must
know, when purple was still an ornament forbidden
to men ; it lay concealed in the round cavity of a
tiny shell. A fisherman captured some of these ; he
at first thought that he had obtained some fish, but
when he saw that the shell was rough and hard, he
was vexed with what he had caught, and threw it
away as the mere offal of the sea. A dog found
this windfall, and crunched it with its teeth ; the
blood of the dye streamed all over the dog's mouth,
staining its muzzle and indelibly imprinting the
purple on its lips. The shepherd,[2] seeing his dog's
lips thus blood-stained, thought that the colour
arose from a wound, and went and washed it in
sea-water ; but the blood only shone the brighter,
and when he touched it with his hands, some of the
purple appeared on the hand. He then realised
the character of the shell, how it contained within
it a medicament of great beauty ; he took a fleece
of wool and pressed it into the interior of the shell,
trying to find out its secret ; and the wool too
appeared as though blood-stained, like the dog's
muzzle ; thence he learned the appearance of the
dye. He therefore took some stones and broke
the outer shell which hid the substance, opened the
hiding-place of the purple, and thus discovered what
was a very treasury of dye.

there are many other instances. It may perhaps here be
mentioned that the famous purple was probably more like
our scarlet or crimson.

[2] It does not seem quite certain whether the "shepherd"
and the "fisherman" are identical : the scribe of one manu-
script clearly thought so, by here altering ποιμήν into ἁλιεύς.
But a fisherman would perhaps not have possessed a dog, and
the two seem better regarded as quite separate persons.

12. Ἔθυεν οὖν τότε ὁ πατὴρ προτέλεια τῶν γάμων. ὡς δὲ ἤκουσα, ἀπωλώλειν καὶ ἐζήτουν μηχανὴν δι᾽ ἧς[1] ἀναβαλέσθαι δυναίμην τὸν γάμον. σκοποῦντος δέ μου, θόρυβος ἐξαίφνης γίνεται κατὰ τὸν ἀνδρῶνα τῆς οἰκίας. ἐγεγόνει 2 δέ τι τοιοῦτον· ἐπειδὴ θυσάμενος ὁ πατὴρ ἔτυχε καὶ τὰ θύματα ἐπέκειτο τοῖς βωμοῖς, ἀετὸς ἄνωθεν καταπτὰς ἁρπάζει τὸ ἱερεῖον· σοβούντων δὲ πλέον οὐδὲν ἦν· ὁ γὰρ ὄρνις ᾤχετο φέρων τὴν ἄγραν. ἐδόκει τοίνυν οὐκ ἀγαθὸν εἶναι, καὶ δὴ ἐπέσχον ἐκείνην τὴν ἡμέραν τοὺς γάμους· καλεσάμενος δὲ μάντεις ὁ πατὴρ καὶ τερατο- 3 σκόπους τὸν οἰωνὸν διηγεῖται. οἱ δὲ ἔφασαν δεῖν καλλιερῆσαι Ξενίῳ Διὶ νυκτὸς μεσούσης ἐπὶ θάλασσαν ἥκοντας· ὁ γὰρ ὄρνις ἔτυχεν ἱπτά- μενος ἐκεῖ.[2] ἐγὼ δὲ ταῦτα ὡς ἐγένετο τὸν ἀετὸν ὑπερεπήνουν καὶ δικαίως ἔλεγον ἁπάντων ὀρνίθων εἶναι βασιλέα· οὐκ εἰς μακρὰν δὲ ἀπέβη τοῦ τέρατος τὸ ἔργον.

13. Νεανίσκος ἦν Βυζάντιος, ὄνομα Καλλι- σθένης, ὀρφανὸς καὶ πλούσιος, ἄσωτος δὲ καὶ πολυτελής. οὗτος ἀκούων τῷ Σωστράτῳ θυγα- τέρα εἶναι καλήν, ἰδὼν δὲ οὐδέποτε, ἤθελεν αὐτῷ ταύτην γενέσθαι γυναῖκα, καὶ ἦν ἐξ ἀκοῆς ἐραστής· τοσαύτη γὰρ τοῖς ἀκολάστοις ὕβρις,

---

[1] Cobet would here insert ἄν, believing that it had fallen out because it consisted of the same two letters as the opening of the next word. It would be necessary in classical Greek, but its absence may perhaps be excused in a writer of so late a date as this.

[2] After this the MSS. have the sentence τὸ δὲ ἔργον εὐθὺς ἀπέβη· τὸν γὰρ ἀετὸν ἀναπτάντα ἐπὶ τὴν θάλασσαν συνέβη φανῆναι οὐκέτι, which Jacobs rejects, Vilborg retains.

12. My father then began to perform the sacrifices which are the necessary preliminaries to a wedding; and when I heard of this, I gave myself up for lost and began to look for some excuse to defer it, While I was thus engaged, a sudden tumult arose throughout the men's part of the house: and this was what had occurred. My father was in the act of sacrificing, and had just placed the victims upon the altar, when an eagle swooped down from above and carried off the offering. It was of no avail that those present tried to scare him away; he flew off carrying away his prey. Now this seemed to bode no good, so that they postponed the wedding for that day: my father called in soothsayers and augurs and related the omen to them; and they answered that he must perform a sacrifice at midnight to Zeus as god of strangers upon the sea-shore, for that was the direction in which the bird had flown. [And that was the end of the matter: for it had indeed so chanced that the eagle had flown seaward and appeared no more.] At all this I was greatly delighted with the eagle, and I remarked that it was certainly true that the eagle was the king of all birds. Nor was it long before the event followed the prodigy which had foreshadowed it.

13. There was a certain youth of Byzantium, named Callisthenes. His father and mother were dead; he was rich, but profligate and extravagant. He, hearing that Sostratus had a beautiful daughter, wished, although he had never seen her, to make her his wife, and became her lover by hearsay; for such is the lack of self-control in the lewd, that

ὡς καὶ τοῖς ὠσὶν εἰς ἔρωτα τρυφᾶν καὶ ταὐτὰ
πάσχειν ὑπὸ ῥημάτων, ἃ τῇ ψυχῇ τρωθέντες
2 διακονοῦσιν ὀφθαλμοί. προσελθὼν οὖν τῷ Σωστράτῳ πρὶν τὸν πόλεμον τοῖς Βυζαντίοις ἐπιπε-
σεῖν, ᾐτεῖτο τὴν κόρην· ὁ δὲ βδελυττόμενος αὐτοῦ
τοῦ βίου τὴν ἀκολασίαν, ἠρνήσατο. θυμὸς ἴσχει
τὸν Καλλισθενην καὶ ἠτιμάσθαι νομίσαντα ὑπὸ
τοῦ Σωστράτου καὶ ἄλλως ἐρῶντα· ἀναπλάττων
γὰρ ἑαυτῷ τῆς παιδὸς τὸ κάλλος καὶ φανταζό-
μενος τὰ ἀόρατα, ἔλαθε σφόδρα κακῶς διακεί-
3 μενος. ἐπιβουλεύει δ᾽ οὖν καὶ τὸν Σώστρατον
ἀμύνασθαι τῆς ὕβρεως, καὶ αὑτῷ τὴν ἐπιθυμίαν
τελέσαι· νόμου γὰρ ὄντος Βυζαντίοις, εἴ τις
ἁρπάσας παρθένον φθάσας ποιήσει γυναῖκα,
γάμον ἔχειν τὴν ζημίαν, προσεῖχε τούτῳ τῷ νόμῳ.
καὶ ὁ μὲν ἐζήτει καιρὸν πρὸς τὸ ἔργον.

14. Ἐν τούτῳ δὲ τοῦ πολέμου περιστάντος
καὶ τῆς παιδὸς εἰς ἡμᾶς ὑπεκκειμένης, ἐμεμαθήκει
μὲν ἕκαστα τούτων· οὐδὲν δὲ ἧττον τῆς ἐπιβουλῆς εἴχετο· καὶ τοιοῦτό τι αὐτῷ συνήργησε.
χρησμὸν ἴσχουσιν οἱ Βυζάντιοι τοιόνδε·

Νῆσός τις πόλις ἐστὶ φυτώνυμον αἷμα λαχοῦσα,
ἰσθμὸν ὁμοῦ καὶ πορθμὸν ἐπ᾽ ἠπείροιο φέρουσα,

---

[1] The Greek word thus translated might also mean that
he escaped the notice of others (ἔλαθεν ἄλλους) rather than
ἔλαθεν ἑαυτόν, "he escaped his own notice," or did it

they are led into the passion of love by means of their ears, and report has the same effect upon them as the ministry of the love-smitten eyes, acting upon the mind, has upon others. Before, then, the war broke out in which the Byzantines were engaged, he approached Sostratus, and asked him for his daughter's hand, but Sostratus refused it because he loathed Callisthenes' loose life. This enraged him, not only because he considered himself slighted by Sostratus, but because he actually was in love : for he pictured in his imagination the beauty of the maiden, conceiving inwardly that which he had never seen, and in this manner he fell, before he knew where he was,[1] into a very bitter state of mind. The result was that he began to plot how he might at the same time be revenged upon Sostratus for the injury and accomplish his own desires ; and to this end he purposed to have recourse to a law of the Byzantines, to the effect that if a man carried off a virgin and instantly made her his wife, the penalty exacted was simply the fact of the marriage itself : so that he began to look about for an occasion to accomplish his ends.

14. Meanwhile the war broke out and the maiden came to live with us, but his knowledge of these facts did not restrain him from his plotting. He was assisted by the following circumstance ; an oracle was current among the Byzantines to this effect :—

" There is an island city : they who dwell
    Therein are named from trees. It makes as well

unwittingly. In the former case the rendering would be " he secretly worked himself into a very bitter state of mind."

ἔνθ᾽ Ἥφαιστος ἔχων χαίρει γλαυκῶπιν Ἀθήνην
κεῖθι θυηπολίην σε φέρειν κέλομαι Ἡρακλεῖ.[1]

2 ἀπορούντων δὲ αὐτῶν τί λέγει τὸ μάντευμα,
Σώστρατος (τοῦ πολέμου γάρ, ὡς ἔφην, στρατηγὸς
ἦν οὗτος), "῟Ωρα πέμπειν ἡμᾶς θυσίαν εἰς
Τύρον," εἶπεν, "Ἡρακλεῖ· τὰ γὰρ τοῦ χρησμοῦ
ἐστὶ πάντα ἐνταῦθα. φυτώνυμον γὰρ ὁ θεὸς
εἶπεν αὐτήν, ἐπεὶ Φοινίκων ἡ νῆσος· ὁ δὲ φοῖνιξ
φυτόν. ἐρίζει δὲ περὶ ταύτης γῆ καὶ θάλασσα·
ἕλκει <μὲν ἡ θάλασσα, ἕλκει>[2] δὲ ἡ γῆ, ἡ δὲ εἰς
3 ἀμφότερα αὐτὴν ἥρμοσε. καὶ γὰρ ἐν θαλάσσῃ
κάθηται καὶ οὐκ ἀφῆκε τὴν γῆν· συνδεῖ γὰρ
αὐτὴν πρὸς τὴν ἤπειρον στενὸς αὐχήν, καί ἐστιν
4 ὥσπερ τῆς νήσου τράχηλος. οὐκ ἐρρίζωται δὲ
κατὰ τῆς θαλάσσης, ἀλλὰ τὸ ὕδωρ ὑπορρεῖ
κάτωθεν. ὑπόκειται δὲ πορθμὸς κάτωθεν ἰσθμῷ·
καὶ γίνεται τὸ θέαμα καινόν, πόλις ἐν θαλάσσῃ
5 καὶ νῆσος ἐν γῇ. Ἀθηνᾶν δὲ Ἥφαιστος ἔχει·
εἰς τὴν ἐλαίαν ᾐνίξατο καὶ τὸ πῦρ, ἃ παρ᾽ ἡμῖν
ἀλλήλοις συνοικεῖ. τὸ δὲ χωρίον ἱερὸν ἐν περι-
βόλῳ· ἐλαίαν μὲν ἀναθάλλει φαιδροῖς τοῖς

---

[1] This oracle is also found in the *Anthologia Palatina*,
xiv. 34, where a line of doubtful meaning, ἔνθ᾽ ἀπ᾽ ἐμῆς ἴσθ᾽
αἷμα ὁμοῦ καὶ Κέκροπος αἷμα, is inserted between ll. 2 and 3. It
is supposed to indicate that there were many foreigners in
Tyre, such as Byzantines and Athenians, as well as the
Tyrians of native stock.

[2] The words within brackets are an ingenious suggestion
by Cobet : they might easily have dropped out from a copyist
looking on from the first ἕλκει to the second.

An isthmus on the sea, a bay on shore,
Where, to Hephaestus' joy, for evermore
Consorts with him Athene, grey-eyed maid.
There let your rites to Hercules be paid."

Now they had no idea what the oracle meant; but
Sostratus, who was, as I said,[1] one of the generals in
the war, spoke as follows: "It is time," said he,
"to send to Tyre and sacrifice to Hercules: the
particulars of the oracle all agree with that spot.
The god called it 'named from trees,' because it is
an island belonging to the Phoenicians, and the
phoenix-palm is a tree. It is a subject of contention
to both land and sea, the sea striving for it in one
direction, the land in the other; but it partakes of
both, for it is founded in the sea and is yet not dis-
connected with the shore: there is a narrow strip of
land which joins it to the mainland, forming a kind
of neck to the island.[2] Nor is it rooted to the
bottom of the sea, but the water flows beneath it,
and also beneath the isthmus, so that it presents the
curious spectacle of a city in the sea and an island
on land. As for the expression of 'Hephaestus
consorting with Athene,' the riddling allusion is to
the connection of the olive with fire, which are also
found in company in our own country. There is
there a sacred piece of ground walled in, where the
olive grows with its gleaming foliage, and there is

[1] A mistake of the writer: we only know (from I. iii.) that
Sostratus lived all his life at Byzantium, and sent his wife
and daughter to Tyre on the outbreak of hostilities.
[2] Pliny, *Natural History*, v. 19: "Then followeth the
noble city Tyrus, in old time an Island, lying almost 3
quarters of a mile within the deepe sea: but now, by the
great travaile and devises wrought by *Alexander* the Great
at the siege thereof, joyned to the firme ground."

κλάδοις, πεφύτευται δὲ σὺν αὐτῇ τὸ πῦρ καὶ ἀνάπτει περὶ τοὺς πτόρθους ¹ πολλὴν τὴν φλόγα· ἡ
6 δὲ τοῦ πυρὸς αἰθάλη τὸ φυτὸν γεωργεῖ. αὕτη
πυρὸς φιλία καὶ φυτοῦ· οὕτως οὐ φεύγει τὸν
"Ηφαιστον 'Αθήνη." καὶ ὁ Χαιρεφῶν συστρά-
τηγος ὢν τοῦ Σωστράτου μείζων, ἐπεὶ πατρόθεν
ἦν Τύριος,² ἐκθειάζων αὐτόν, "Πάντα μὲν τὸν
χρησμόν," εἶπεν, "ἐξηγήσω καλῶς· μὴ μέντοι
θαύμαζε τὴν τοῦ πυρὸς μόνον, ἀλλὰ καὶ τὴν τοῦ
7 ὕδατος φύσιν. ἐθεασάμην γὰρ ἐγὼ τοιαῦτα
μυστήρια. τὸ γοῦν τῆς Σικελικῆς πηγῆς ὕδωρ
κεκερασμένον ἔχει πῦρ· καὶ φλόγα μὲν ὄψει
κάτωθεν ἀπ' αὐτῆς ἀλλομένην ἄνωθεν· θιγόντι
δέ σοι τὸ ὕδωρ ψυχρόν ἐστιν οἷόνπερ ³ χιών, καὶ
οὔτε τὸ πῦρ ὑπὸ τοῦ ὕδατος κατασβέννυται, οὔτε
τὸ ὕδωρ ὑπὸ τοῦ πυρὸς φλέγεται, ἀλλ' ὕδατός
8 εἰσιν ἐν τῇ κρήνῃ καὶ πυρὸς σπονδαί. ἐπεὶ καὶ
ποταμὸς 'Ιβηρικός, εἰ μὲν ἴδοις αὐτὸν εὐθύς,
οὐδενὸς ἄλλου κρείττων ἐστὶ ποταμοῦ· ἢν δὲ
ἀκοῦσαι θέλῃς τοῦ ὕδατος λαλοῦντος, μικρὸν
ἀνάμεινον ἐκπετάσας τὰ ὦτα. ἐὰν γὰρ ὀλίγος
ἄνεμος εἰς τὰς δίνας ἐμπέσῃ, τὸ μὲν ὕδωρ ὡς
χορδὴ κρούεται, τὸ δὲ πνεῦμα τοῦ ὕδατος
πλῆκτρον γίνεται, τὸ ῥεῦμα δὲ ὡς κιθάρα λαλεῖ.
9 ἀλλὰ καὶ λίμνη Λιβυκὴ μιμεῖται γῆν 'Ινδικήν,

---

¹ Here began Π², verso.

² Jacobs would replace Τύριος by Βυζάντιος. If Τύριος be
retained, the words give the reason why Chaerephon agreed
with Sostratus in his interpretation: if we accept the alteration, Βυζάντιος, they are an explanation why Chaerephon, a
full-blooded Byzantine, was an officer of higher rank than
Sostratus, who was of a Byzantine mother but a Tyrian
father (I. iii.).

³ Here ended (with ὥσπερ for οἷόνπερ) Π², verso.

also fire in the ground which sends up a great blaze among the branches, the soot of which manures the trees.[1] This is the affection existing between the fire and the plant, and it may thus be said that Athene flees not from Hephaestus." Chaerephon, who was a fellow-general with Sostratus of superior rank, was a native of Tyre on his father's side, and congratulated him on his interpretation. " You have explained the whole oracle admirably," said he : " but it is not fire only, but water as well, which has properties not unworthy of wonder. I myself have seen some of these miraculous sights : there is, for example, a spring in Sicily which has fire mixed with its waters ; if you look down you can see the flame shooting up from beneath, and yet if you touch the water it is as cold as snow : the fire is not put out by the water, nor is the water heated by the fire, but a truce reigns in the spring between the two elements. Then there is a river in Spain which does not seem at first sight different from any other river ; but if you wish to hear the water talking, open your ears and wait a little : for if a gentle breeze strikes its eddies, the water thrills like a string : the wind acts as a plectrum upon the water, and the water sings like a lyre. Again, there is in Libya a lake [2] which may be compared to

---

[1] Volcanic ground suits the olive, as it does the vine.

[2] Was Bishop Heber thinking of some such story when he wrote of places " Where Afric's sunny fountains Roll down their golden sand " ? Perhaps he was referring to the colour of the soil alone. This account seems to be taken, with some modifications, from Herodotus iv. 195, who relates how the maidens of the island of Cyrannis, on the east coast of Africa, obtain gold from a lake by means of feathers smeared with pitch. He had also mentioned (iii. 102) that the sand, or soil, of parts of India is gold-bearing.

καὶ ἴσασιν αὐτῆς τὸ ἀπόρρητον αἱ Λιβύων παρθένοι, ὅτι ὕδωρ ἔχει πλούσιον. ὁ δὲ πλοῦτος ταύτῃ κάτωθεν τεταμίευται τῇ τῶν ὑδάτων ἰλύϊ δεδεμένος· καὶ ἔστιν ἐκεῖ χρυσοῦ πηγή. κοντὸν οὖν εἰς τὸ ὕδωρ βαπτίζουσι πίσσῃ πεφαρμαγμένον καὶ ἀνοίγουσι τοῦ ποταμοῦ τὰ κλεῖθρα. 10 ὁ δὲ κοντὸς πρὸς τὸν χρυσὸν οἷον πρὸς τὸν ἰχθὺν ἄγκιστρον γίνεται, ἀγρεύει γὰρ αὐτόν, ἡ δὲ πίσσα δέλεαρ γίνεται τῆς ἄγρας, ὅ τι γὰρ ἂν εἰς αὐτὴν ἐμπέσῃ τῆς τοῦ χρυσοῦ γονῆς, τὸ μὲν προσήψατο μόνον, ἡ πίσσα δὲ εἰς τὴν ἤπειρον ἥρπασε τὴν ἄγραν. οὕτως ἐκ ποταμοῦ Λιβυκοῦ χρυσὸς ἁλιεύεται."

15. Ταῦτα εἰπὼν τὴν θυσίαν ἐπὶ τὴν Τύρον ἔπεμπε, καὶ τῇ πόλει συνδοκοῦν. ὁ γοῦν Καλλισθένης διαπράττεται τῶν θεωρῶν εἰς γενέσθαι· καὶ ταχὺ καταπλεύσας εἰς τὴν Τύρον καὶ ἐκμαθὼν τὴν τοῦ πατρὸς οἰκίαν, ἐφήδρευε ταῖς γυναιξίν. αἱ δὲ ὀψόμεναι τὴν θυσίαν ἐξῄεσαν· καὶ γὰρ 2 ἦν πολυτελής. πολλὴ μὲν ἡ τῶν θυμιαμάτων πομπή, ποικίλη δὲ ἡ τῶν ἀνθέων συμπλοκή. τὰ θυμιάματα, κασσία καὶ λιβανωτὸς καὶ κρόκος· τὰ ἄνθη, νάρκισσος καὶ ῥόδα καὶ μυρρίναι· ἡ δὲ τῶν ἀνθέων ἀναπνοὴ πρὸς τὴν τῶν θυμιαμάτων ἤριζεν ὀδμήν· τὸ δὲ πνεῦμα ἀναπεμπόμενον εἰς τὸν ἀέρα τὴν ὀδμὴν ἐκεράννυ, καὶ ἦν ἄνεμος 3 ἡδονῆς. τὰ δὲ ἱερεῖα πολλὰ μὲν ἦν καὶ ποικίλα, διέπρεπον δὲ ἐν αὐτοῖς οἱ τοῦ Νείλου βόες. βοῦς

the soil of India : the Libyan maidens know its
secret, that its water contains a store of wealth ; this
is preserved below as in a treasury, being intermingled with the mud of the lake, which is a very
spring of gold. So they smear with pitch the end
of a pole and thrust it down beneath the water :
thus they open its concealed store-house, the pole
being with respect to the gold what the hook is to
a fish, for it does the fishing, while the pitch acts as
bait ; since all the gold which touches it (and nothing
else) sticks to it and thus the pitch draws its capture
to the land. That is the manner of the gold fisheries
in this Libyan stream."

15. After thus speaking, Chaerephon gave his
opinion in favour of sending the sacrifice to be
performed at Tyre, and the city also agreed.
Callisthenes was successful in getting himself appointed one of the envoys,[1] and at once, after arriving
at Tyre by sea and finding out where my father
lived, laid his snares for the women. They had
gone out to see the sacrifice, which was indeed a
very sumptuous affair : there was a great variety of
different kinds of burnt perfumes, and many different
nosegays of flowers ; of the former, cinnamon, frank-
incense, and saffron ; of the latter, jonquil, rose,
and myrtle ; the smell of the flowers competed with
the scent of the perfumes, and the breeze as it
travelled up into the air mingled the two together,
so that it formed a gale of delight. The victims
were many in number and various in kind : con-
spicuous among them were the cattle from the Nile.

---

[1] The θεωροί were strictly the quasi-sacred messengers sent
by Athens to the Delphic Oracle and the great Hellenic
games. But in later Greek the word came to be used for any
kind of ambassador.

γὰρ Αἰγύπτιος οὐ τὸ μέγεθος μόνον ἀλλὰ καὶ
τὴν χροιὰν εὐτυχεῖ· τὸ μὲν γὰρ μέγεθος πάνυ
μέγας, τὸν αὐχένα παχύς, τὸν νῶτον πλατύς, τὴν
γαστέρα πολύς, τὸ κέρας οὐχ ὡς ὁ Σικελικὸς
εὐτελὴς οὐδὲ ὡς ὁ Κύπριος δυσειδής, ἀλλ᾽ ἐκ
τῶν κροτάφων ὄρθιον ἀναβαῖνον, κατὰ μικρὸν
ἑκατέρωθεν κυρτούμενον τὰς κορυφὰς συνάγει
τοσοῦτον, ὅσον αἱ τῶν κεράτων διεστᾶσιν ἀρχαί·
καὶ τὸ θέαμα κυκλουμένης σελήνης ἐστὶν εἰκών·
ἡ χροιὰ δὲ οἵαν Ὅμηρος τοὺς[1] τοῦ Θρακὸς ἵππους
4 ἐπαινεῖ. βαδίζει δὲ ταῦρος ὑψαυχενῶν καὶ ὥσπερ
ἐπιδεικνύμενος ὅτι τῶν ἄλλων βοῶν ἐστι βασιλεύς. εἰ δὲ ὁ μῦθος Εὐρώπης ἀληθής, Αἰγύπτιον
βοῦν ὁ Ζεὺς ἐμιμήσατο.

16. Ἔτυχεν οὖν ἡ μὲν ἐμὴ μητηρ τοτε μαλα-
κῶς ἔχουσα· σκηψαμένη δὲ καὶ ἡ Λευκίππη
νοσεῖν, ἔνδον ὑπέμεινε (συνέκειτο γὰρ ἡμῖν εἰς
ταὐτὸν ἐλθεῖν, ὡς ἂν τῶν πολλῶν ἐξιόντων),
ὥστε συνέβη τὴν ἀδελφὴν τὴν ἐμὴν μετὰ τῆς
2 Λευκίππης μητρὸς προελθεῖν. ὁ δὲ Καλλισθένης
τὴν μὲν Λευκίππην οὐχ ἑωρακώς ποτε, τὴν δὲ
Καλλιγόνην ἰδὼν τὴν ἐμὴν ἀδελφήν, νομίσας
Λευκίππην εἶναι (ἐγνώρισε γὰρ τοῦ Σωστράτου
τὴν γυναῖκα), πυθόμενος οὐδέν, ἦν γὰρ ἑαλωκὼς

---

[1] The grammar is a little loose, but not impossible, so that
it does not seem necessary to alter with Hercher into ἐν τοῖς
... ἵπποις.

For the Egyptian ox is especially favoured, both in bulk and in colouring: he is of very great size, with a brawny neck, a broad back, a great belly, horns neither small like those of the Sicilian cattle, nor ugly like those from Cyprus; but they spring up straight from the forehead, bending outward a little on either side, and their tips are the same distance apart as their roots, giving the appearance of the moon coming to the full: their colour is like that for which Homer so greatly commends the horses of the Thracian.[1] The bull paces with neck well lifted up, as though he would shew that he was the king of all other cattle. If the story of Europa be true, Zeus put on the appearance of an Egyptian bull.

16. It so happened that at that time my mother[2] was in delicate health: and Leucippe also pretended that she was ill and remained indoors, for by such means it was arranged by us to contrive to meet, while the others were away: the result of this was my sister went out to the spectacle with Leucippe's mother alone. Callisthenes, who had never set eyes on Leucippe, when he saw my sister Calligone, thought that she was Leucippe, because he recognized Sostratus' wife; without asking any questions,

---

[1]   'Ρῆσος βασιλεύς, παῖς Ἠιονῆος.
   τοῦ δὴ καλλίστους ἵππους ἴδον ἠδὲ μεγίστους·
   λευκότεροι χιόνος, θείειν δ' ἀνέμοισιν ὁμοῖοι.
                                        (Iliad x. 435.)

                          King Rhesus, of Eïones the son,
Whose horses, very fair and great, did make a goodly show:
They faster ran than any wind, and whiter were than snow.

   These lines were also imitated by Virgil in the account of the horses which Orithyia gave to Pilumnus (Aen. xii. 84):
Qui candore nives anteirent, cursibus auras.

[2] i.e. his step-mother.

ἐκ τῆς θέας, δείκνυσιν ἑνὶ τῶν οἰκετῶν τὴν κόρην,
ὃς ἦν αὐτῷ πιστότατος, καὶ κελεύει λῃστὰς
ἐπ᾽ αὐτὴν συγκροτῆσαι, καταλέξας τὸν τρόπον
τῆς ἁρπαγῆς. πανήγυρις δὲ ἐπέκειτο, καθ᾽ ἣν
ἠκηκόει πάσας τὰς παρθένους ἀπαντᾶν ἐπὶ
θάλασσαν.

Ὁ μὲν οὖν ταῦτα εἰπὼν καὶ τὴν θεωρίαν ἀφω-
σιωμένος ἀπῆλθε· **17.** ναῦν δὲ εἶχεν ἰδίαν, τοῦτο
προκατασκευάσας οἴκοθεν εἰ τύχοι τῆς ἐπιχειρή-
σεως. οἱ μὲν δὴ ἄλλοι θεωροὶ ἀπέπλευσαν, αὐτὸς
δὲ μικρὸν ἀπεσάλευε τῆς γῆς, ἅμα μὲν ὡς[1] δοκοίη
τοῖς πολίταις ἕπεσθαι, ἅμα δὲ ἵνα μὴ πλησίον
τῆς Τύρου τοῦ σκάφους ὄντος, κατάφωρος γένοιτο
2 μετὰ τὴν ἁρπαγήν. ἐπεὶ δὲ ἐγένετο κατὰ Σά-
ραπτα κώμην Τυρίων ἐπὶ θαλάσσῃ κειμένην,
ἐνταῦθα προσπορίζεται λέμβον, δίδωσι δὲ τῷ
Ζήνωνι, τοῦτο γὰρ ἦν ὄνομα τῷ οἰκέτῃ ὃν ἐπὶ
3 τὴν ἁρπαγὴν παρεσκευάκει. ὁ δέ (ἦν γὰρ καὶ
ἄλλως εὔρωστος τὸ σῶμα καὶ φύσει πειρατικός)
ταχὺ μὲν ἐξεῦρε λῃστὰς ἁλιεῖς ἀπὸ τῆς κώμης
ἐκείνης καὶ δῆτα ἀπέπλευσεν ἐπὶ τὴν Τύρον. ἔστι
δὲ μικρὸν ἐπίνειον Τυρίων, νησίδιον ἀπέχον ὀλίγον
τῆς Τύρου (Ῥοδόπης αὐτὸ τάφον οἱ Τύριοι
λέγουσιν) ἔνθα ὁ λέμβος ἐφήδρευε.

18. Πρὸ δὲ τῆς πανηγύρεως, ἣν ὁ Καλλισθένης[2]
προσεδόκα, γίνεται δὴ τὰ τοῦ ἀετοῦ καὶ τῶν
μάντεων· καὶ εἰς τὴν ὑστεραίαν παρεσκευαζόμεθα

---

[1] Hercher here inserts ἄν. It is a question whether
Achilles Tatius is a sufficiently correct writer thus to make
him conform to the strict Attic standard.

[2] καὶ after Καλλισθένης was deleted anonymously.

for he was carried away by the sight of her, he pointed her out to his most trusty servant, bidding him get together a band of robbers to carry her off, and instructed him how the attempt was to be made: a holiday was near at hand, on which, he had heard, it was customary for all the maidens of the place to come together on the sea-shore.

After giving these instructions, and after performing the sacrifice for which he had formed part of the embassy, he retired. 17. He had a vessel of his own—he had made all these preparations at home, in case he should succeed in such an attempt: so when the rest of the envoys sailed off, he weighed anchor and rode a little off the land, waiting in order that he might seem to be accompanying his fellow-citizens on their homeward journey, and that after the carrying off of the girl his vessel might not be too close to Tyre and so himself be taken in the act. When he had arrived at Sarepta, a Tyrian village on the sea-board, he acquired a small boat and entrusted it to Zeno; that was the name of the servant in whose charge he had placed the abduction—a fellow of a robust body and the nature of a brigand. Zeno picked up with all speed some fishermen from that village who were really pirates as well, and with them sailed away for Tyre: the boat came to anchor, waiting in ambush, in a little creek in a small island not far from Tyre, which the Tyrians call Rhodope's Tomb.

18. However, the omen of the eagle and the soothsayers happened before the holiday for which Callisthenes was waiting, and for the next day we made the prescribed preparations at night for sacri-

νύκτωρ, ὡς θυσόμενοι τῷ θεῷ. Τούτων δὲ τὸν
Ζήνωνα ἐλάνθανεν οὐδέν· ἀλλ᾽ ἐπειδὴ καιρὸς ἦν
βαθείας ἑσπέρας, ἡμεῖς μὲν προήλθομεν, αὐτὸς
2 δὲ εἵπετο. ἄρτι δὲ γενομένων ἡμῶν ἐπὶ τῷ
χείλει τῆς θαλάσσης, ὁ μὲν τὸ συγκείμενον
ἀνέτεινε σημεῖον, ὁ δὲ λέμβος ἐξαίφνης προσέ-
πλει, καὶ ἐπεὶ πλησίον ἐγένετο, ἐφάνησαν ἐν
3 αὐτῷ νεανίσκοι δέκα. ὀκτὼ δὲ ἑτέρους ἐπὶ τῆς
γῆς εἶχον προλοχίσαντες, οἳ γυναικείας μὲν εἶχον
ἐσθῆτας καὶ τῶν γενείων ἐψίλωντο τὰς τρίχας,
ἔφερον δὲ ἕκαστος ὑπὸ κόλπῳ ξίφος, ἐκόμιζον
δὲ καὶ αὐτοὶ θυσίαν, ὡς ἂν ἥκιστα ὑποπτευθεῖεν·
4 ἡμεῖς δὲ ᾠόμεθα γυναῖκας εἶναι. ἐπεὶ δὲ συνετί-
θεμεν τὴν πυράν, ἐξαίφνης βοῶντες συντρέχουσι
καὶ τὰς μὲν δᾷδας ἡμῶν ἀποσβεννύουσι, φευγόν-
των δὲ ἀτάκτως ὑπὸ τῆς ἐκπλήξεως, τὰ ξίφη
γυμνώσαντες ἁρπάζουσι τὴν ἀδελφὴν τὴν ἐμὴν
καὶ ἐνθέμενοι τῷ σκάφει, ἐμβάντες εὐθύς, ὄρνιθος
5 δίκην ἀφίπτανται. ἡμῶν δὲ οἱ μὲν ἔφευγον, οὐδὲν
οὔτε εἰδότες οὔτε ἑωρακότες, οἱ δὲ ἅμα τε εἶδον
καὶ ἐβόων, "Λῃσταὶ Καλλιγόνην ἔχουσι." τὸ
δὲ πλοῖον ἤδη μέσην ἐπέραινε τὴν θάλασσαν·
ὡς δὲ τοῖς Σαράπτοις προσέσχον, πόρρωθεν ὁ
Καλλισθένης τὸ σημεῖον ἰδών, ὑπηντίασεν ἐπι-
πλεύσας καὶ δέχεται μὲν τὴν κόρην, πλεῖ δὲ
6 εὐθὺς πελάγιος. ἐγὼ δὲ ἀνέπνευσα μὲν οὕτω
διαλυθέντων μοι τῶν γάμων παραδόξως, ἠχθόμην
δὲ ὅμως ὑπὲρ ἀδελφῆς περιπεσούσης τοιαύτῃ
συμφορᾷ.

ficing to the god. Nothing of all this escaped Zeno's notice: when evening was now far advanced, we went forth, and he was following us. Hardly had we arrived at the water's edge, when he hoisted the preconcerted signal; the boat rapidly sailed toward the shore, and when it had come close, it was apparent that it contained ten youths. They had already secretly posted eight others on land, dressed like women and with their faces closely shaved of all hair; each was wearing under his gown a sword, and they too carried a sacrifice in order to avoid all suspicion: we thought that they were women. No sooner had we raised our pyre, when they suddenly gave a shout, ran all together upon us, and put out our torches; and as we fled, all in disorder from the sudden surprise, they drew their swords, seized my sister, put her aboard the boat, quickly embarked themselves, and were off like a bird. Some of our party were flying, knowing and seeing nothing; others did see, and cried out, "Calligone has been carried off by brigands." Their boat, however, was already far out at sea. When they began to approach Sarepta, Callisthenes observed their signal from a distance; he sailed to meet them, put the girl on board his ship, and quickly sailed for the open sea. I felt a great relief at my wedding being thus all unexpectedly made impossible, and yet at the same time I was of course much distressed at the way this great disaster had befallen my sister.

ACHILLES TATIUS

19. Ὀλίγας δὲ ἡμέρας διαλιπών, πρὸς τὴν Λευκίππην διελεγόμην· "Μέχρι τίνος ἐπὶ τῶν φιλημάτων ἱστάμεθα, φιλτάτη; καλὰ[1] τὰ προοίμια. προσθῶμεν ἤδη τι καὶ ἐρωτικόν.[2] φέρε, ἀνάγκην ἀλλήλοις ἐπιθῶμεν πίστεως. ἂν γὰρ ἡμᾶς Ἀφροδίτη μυσταγωγήσῃ, οὐ μή τις ἄλλος 2 κρείττων γένηται τῆς θεοῦ." ταῦτα πολλάκις κατεπᾴδων ἐπεπείκειν τὴν κόρην ὑποδέξασθαί με νυκτὸς τῷ θαλάμῳ, τῆς Κλειοῦς συνεργούσης, ἥτις ἦν αὐτῇ θαλαμηπόλος. εἶχε δὲ ὁ θάλαμος 3 αὐτῆς οὕτως· χωρίον ἦν μέγα τέτταρα οἰκήματα ἔχον, δύο μὲν ἐπὶ δεξιά, δύο δὲ ἐπὶ θάτερα· μέσος δὲ διεῖργε στενωπὸς[3] τὰ οἰκήματα· θύρα δὲ ἐν ἀρχῇ τοῦ στενωποῦ μία ἐκλείετο.[4] ταύτην 4 εἶχον τὴν καταγωγὴν αἱ γυναῖκες· καὶ τὰ μὲν ἐνδοτέρω τῶν οἰκημάτων ἥ τε παρθένος καὶ ἡ μήτηρ αὐτῆς διειλήχεσαν, ἑκάτερα τὰ ἀντικρύ, τὰ δὲ ἔξω δύο τὰ πρὸς τὴν εἴσοδον, τὸ μὲν ἡ Κλειὼ τὸ κατὰ τὴν παρθένον, τὸ δὲ 5 ταμιεῖον ἦν. κατακοιμίζουσα δὲ ἀεὶ τὴν Λευκίππην ἡ μήτηρ, ἔκλειεν ἔνδοθεν τὴν ἐπὶ τοῦ στενωποῦ θύραν· ἔξωθεν δέ τις ἕτερος ἐπέκλειε

---

[1] κατά F.
[2] Hercher suggests ἐρωτικώτερον, "something more amatory," which may perhaps be right. ἐποπτικόν Lumb.
[3] After στενωπὸς the words ὁδὸς ἐπὶ were deleted by Herscher.
[4] ἐπέκειτο Hirschig.

94

19. After a few days had elapsed, I said to Leucippe: " How [1] long, my dearest, are we to stop at kisses? Favourable is such a beginning! Let us add to them something with real love in it. Let us fetter one another with an indissoluble bond; for if but once Aphrodite initiate us into her mysteries, no other god will ever prove stronger than she." By constantly reiterating my request, I had persuaded the maiden to receive me one night in her chamber, with the connivance of Clio, who was her chambermaid. This was how her chamber lay: there was a large wing of the house divided into four rooms, two on the right and two on the left, separated by a narrow passage down the middle; there was a single door at the beginning of the passage, which was usually locked. This was the abode the women used. The two inner rooms opposite one another belonged to the maiden and her mother; as for the two outer rooms nearer the entrance, the one next to Leucippe's was occupied by Clio, and the other was used as the steward's store. Her mother was in the habit, when she put Leucippe to bed, of locking the passage door from the inside, and somebody else would also lock it

---

[1] Anthony Hodges, translating Achilles Tatius in 1638, paraphrases the opening words of Clitophon in a pretty lyric:

> " Dunces in love, how long shall we
> Be poring on our A, B, C?
> For such are kisses, which torment
> Rather than give my soule content:
> Letters from which you scarce will prove
> The wisest scholler can spell love.
> What though the lilly of your hand,
> Or corall lip I may command?
> It is but like him up to th' chin,
> Whose mouth can touch, but take none in."

καὶ τὰς κλεῖς ἔβαλλε διὰ τῆς ὀπῆς· ἡ δὲ λα-
βοῦσα ἐφύλαττε καὶ περὶ τὴν ἕω καλέσασα
τὸν εἰς τοῦτο ἐπιτεταγμένον, διέβαλλε πάλιν τὰς
6 κλεῖς, ὅπως ἀνοίξειε. ταύταις οὖν ἴσας μηχανη-
σάμενος ὁ Σάτυρος γενέσθαι, τὴν ἄνοιξιν πειρᾶ-
ται καὶ ὡς εὗρε δυνατήν, τὴν Κλειὼ [1] ἐπεπείκει,
τῆς κόρης συνειδυίας, μηδὲν ἀντιπρᾶξαι τῇ [2] τέχνῃ.
ταῦτα ἦν τὰ συγκείμενα.

20. Ἦν δέ τις αὐτῶν οἰκέτης πολυπράγμων
καὶ λάλος καὶ λίχνος καὶ πᾶν ὅ τι ἂν εἴποι
τις, ὄνομα Κώνωψ. οὗτός μοι ἐδόκει πόρρωθεν
ἐπιτηρεῖν τὰ πραττόμενα ἡμῖν· μάλιστα δέ, ὅπερ
ἦν, ὑποπτεύσας μή τι νύκτωρ ἡμῖν πραχθῇ,
διενυκτέρευε μέχρι πόρρω τῆς ἑσπέρας, ἀναπετά-
σας τοῦ δωματίου τὰς θύρας, ὥστε ἔργον ἦν
2 αὐτὸν λαθεῖν. ὁ οὖν Σάτυρος βουλόμενος αὐτὸν
εἰς φιλίαν ἀγαγεῖν, προσέπαιζε πολλάκις καὶ
κώνωπα ἐκάλει καὶ ἔσκωπτε τοὔνομα σὺν γέλωτι.
καὶ οὗτος εἰδὼς τοῦ Σατύρου τὴν τέχνην, προσε-
ποιεῖτο μὲν ἀντιπαίζειν καὶ αὐτός, ἐνετίθει δὲ τῇ
3 παιδιᾷ τῆς γνώμης τὸ ἄσπονδον. λέγει δὴ πρὸς
αὐτόν· "Ἐπειδὴ καταμωκᾷ μου καὶ τοὔνομα,
φέρε σοι μῦθον ἀπὸ κώνωπος εἴπω.

21. "Ὁ λέων κατεμέμφετο τὸν Προμηθέα πολλάκις, ὅτι μέγαν μὲν αὐτὸν ἔπλασε καὶ καλὸν
καὶ τὴν μὲν γένυν ὥπλισε τοῖς ὀδοῦσι, τοὺς
δὲ πόδας ἐκράτυνε τοῖς ὄνυξιν, ἐποίησέ τε τῶν
ἄλλων θηρίων δυνατώτερον. 'Ὁ δὲ τοιοῦτος,'

---

[1] The τε after Κλειὼ and καὶ before τῆς κόρης must be
removed—so Jacobs.
[2] MSS. τῇ κόρῃ, which Salmasius saw to be a gloss.

from the outside and pass the keys through the hole; she used to take and keep them, and in the morning, calling the servant whose business this was, she would pass the keys back again for him to open the door. Satyrus obtained a duplicate set of these keys and experimented with unlocking the door; finding that this was practicable, he persuaded Clio, with the maiden's consent, to raise no objections to our plan. Such, then, were the arrangements we had made.

20. There was one of their servants called Conops —a meddlesome, talkative, greedy rascal, deserving any bad name you liked to call him. I noticed that he seemed to be watching from a distance all that we were about; and being particularly suspicious that we were intending (as was indeed the case) to make some attempt by night, he would constantly sit up until very late, leaving open the doors of his room, so that it was a difficult business to escape him. Satyrus, wishing to conciliate him, used often to joke with him, calling him the Conops or Gnat, and good-humouredly punned upon his name; he saw through the device, and while he pretended to make jokes in return, he shewed in his humour his cross-grained and intractable nature. "Since," said he, "you even mock at my name, allow me to relate to you a fable derived from the gnat.

21. "The lion often used to complain to Prometheus that he had made him great and handsome, that he had armed his jaw with teeth and made his feet strong with claws, and made him stronger than all the other beasts: 'And yet,' he would say,

2 ἔφασκε, 'τὸν ἀλεκτρυόνα φοβοῦμαι.' καὶ ὁ
Προμηθεὺς ἐπιστὰς ἔφη· 'Τί με μάτην αἰτιᾷ;
τὰ μὲν γὰρ ἐμὰ πάντα ἔχεις ὅσα πλάττειν
ἠδυνάμην, ἡ δὲ σὴ ψυχὴ πρὸς τοῦτο μόνον
μαλακίζεται.' ἔκλαιεν οὖν ἑαυτὸν ὁ λέων καὶ
τῆς δειλίας κατεμέμφετο καὶ τέλος ἀποθανεῖν
3 ἤθελεν. οὕτω δὲ γνώμης ἔχων ἐλέφαντι περι-
τυγχάνει καὶ προσαγορεύσας εἱστήκει διαλεγόμενος. καὶ ὁρῶν διὰ παντὸς τὰ ὦτα κινοῦντα,
'Τί πάσχεις;' ἔφη, 'καὶ τί δήποτε οὐδὲ μικρὸν
4 ἀτρεμεῖ σου τὸ οὖς;' καὶ ὁ ἐλέφας, κατὰ τύχην
παραπτάντος αὐτῷ κώνωπος, ''Ορᾷς,' ἔφη, 'τουτὶ
τὸ βραχὺ τὸ βομβοῦν; ἢν εἰσδύῃ μου τῇ τῆς ἀκοῆς
ὁδῷ, τέθνηκα.' καὶ ὁ λέων, 'Τί οὖν,' ἔφη,
'ἀποθνήσκειν ἔτι με δεῖ, τοσοῦτον ὄντα καὶ
ἐλέφαντος εὐτυχέστερον, ὅσον κρείττων κώνωπος ἀλεκτρυών;' ὁρᾷς, ὅσον ἰσχύος ὁ κώνωψ
5 ἔχει, ὡς καὶ ἐλέφαντα φοβεῖν." συνεὶς οὖν ὁ
Σάτυρος τὸ ὕπουλον αὐτοῦ τῶν λόγων, ἠρέμα
μειδιῶν, "'Ακουσον κἀμοῦ τινα λόγον," εἶπεν,
"ἀπὸ κώνωπος καὶ λέοντος, ὃν ἀκήκοά τινος τῶν
φιλοσόφων· χαρίζομαι δέ σοι τοῦ μύθου τὸν
ἐλέφαντα.

22. " Λέγει τοίνυν κώνωψ ἀλαζὼν ποτε πρὸς
τὸν λέοντα· 'Εἶτα κἀμοῦ βασιλεύειν νομίζεις
ὡς καὶ τῶν ἄλλων θηρίων; ἀλλ' οὔτε ἐμοῦ

---

[1] Pliny, *Natural History*, x. 21 : "Hereupon it is, that
marching proudly as they [cocks] do, the very lions (which

' powerful as I am, I am terrified of a cock.'[1] ' Why thus blame me in vain?' said Prometheus, his attention thus attracted to the matter: ' you have everything that I could give you at the moment of creation : your spirit is feeble in this one respect.' The lion wept much at his evil case and cursed his cowardice and at last determined to slay himself : but while he was in this frame of mind, he happened to meet the elephant, and after hailing him, stopped gossiping with him. He noticed that his ears kept moving the whole time, and asked him : ' What is the matter with you? Why is it that your ear never keeps still even for a moment?' It so chanced that at that instant a gnat was flying about him, and the elephant replied : ' Do you see this tiny little buzzing creature? If once it were to get into the channel through which I hear, it would be the death of me.' ' Well,' said the lion, ' there is surely no reason for me to die after all, seeing that I am big enough and as much better off than the elephant, as the cock is a nobler creature than the gnat.' You see then how powerful is the gnat, so that even the elephant is afraid of him." Satyrus understood the innuendo that lay beneath this story, and, with a slight smile, " Listen," said he, " to a fable of mine as well, taken from the gnat and the lion, which I once heard from a learned man : and I will make you a present of the elephant of your story.

22. " The rascally braggart gnat said one day to the lion : ' I suppose that you think that you are king over me as over all other beasts? But you have

of all beasts be most courageous) stand in fear and awe of them, and will not abide the sight of them."

κάλλιων, οὔτε ἀλκιμώτερος ἔφυς, οὔτε μείζων
2 ἐπεὶ τίς σοι πρῶτόν ἐστιν ἀλκή; ἀμύσσεις τοῖς
ὄνυξι καὶ δάκνεις τοῖς ὀδοῦσι. ταῦτα γὰρ οὐ
ποιεῖ μαχομένη γυνή; ποῖον δὲ μέγεθος ἢ κάλλος
σε κοσμεῖ; στέρνον πλατύ, ὦμοι παχεῖς καὶ
πολλὴ περὶ τὸν αὐχένα κόμη. τὴν κατόπιν οὖν
αἰσχύνην οὐχ ὁρᾷς; ἐμοὶ δὲ μέγεθος μὲν ὁ
ἀὴρ ὅλος, ὅσον μου καταλαμβάνει τὸ πτερόν,
κάλλος δὲ αἱ τῶν λειμώνων κόμαι· αἱ μὲν γάρ
εἰσιν ὥσπερ ἐσθῆτες, ἃς ὅταν θέλω παῦσαι τὴν
3 πτῆσιν ἐνδύομαι. τὴν δὲ ἀνδρείαν μου μὴ καὶ
γελοῖον ᾖ καταλέγειν· ὄργανον γὰρ ὅλος εἰμὶ
πολέμου· μετὰ μὲν σάλπιγγος παρατάττομαι,
σάλπιγξ δέ μοι καὶ βέλος τὸ στόμα· ὥστε εἰμὶ
καὶ αὐλητὴς καὶ τοξότης. ἐμαυτοῦ δὲ ὀιστὸς
καὶ τόξον γίνομαι· τοξεύει γάρ με[1] διαέριον τὸ
πτερόν, ἐμπεσὼν δὲ ὡς ἀπὸ βέλους ποιῶ τὸ
τραῦμα· ὁ δὲ παταχθεὶς ἐξαίφνης βοᾷ καὶ τὸν
τετρωκότα ζητεῖ. ἐγὼ δὲ παρὼν οὐ πάρειμι·
ὁμοῦ δὲ καὶ φεύγω καὶ μένω, καὶ περιϊππεύω
τὸν ἄνθρωπον τῷ πτερῷ, γελῶ δὲ αὐτὸν βλέπων
4 περὶ τοῖς τραύμασιν ὀρχούμενον. ἀλλὰ τί δεῖ
λόγων; ἀρχώμεθα μάχης.' ἅμα λέγων ἐμπίπτει
τῷ λέοντι, καὶ εἰς τοὺς ὀφθαλμοὺς ἐμπηδῶν καὶ
εἴ τι ἄλλο ἄτριχον τῶν προσώπων, περιϊπτά-

---

[1] The MSS. have μου: με is the ingenious and certain
reading of Cruceius or della Croce, the early Italian translator
of Achilles Tatius.

not better looks than I, or more courage or even
greatness. What, in the first place, is your courage?
You scratch with your claws and bite with your
teeth: and so does any woman when she fights. Then
what about your size or your looks of which you are
so proud? You have a broad chest, muscular
shoulders and plenty of hair about your neck: but
you cannot see what a wretched sight you are from
behind.[1] *My* greatness is that of the whole air
which is traversed by my wings, and my beauty is
the flowers of the meadows, which are as it were
my garments which I put on when I am tired of
flying. I fear it will make you laugh to hear all the
catalogue of my valour: I am wholly an instrument
of war; I am ready for the fray at the sound of the
trumpet, and my mouth being at once trumpet and
weapon I am both bandsman and archer. I am at
once my own arrow and my own bow; my wings
shoot me through the air, and as I pounce I make
a wound like an arrow: the person who is struck
suddenly cries out and looks for him who dealt
the wound. I am there and not there: at the
same moment I retire and advance: I use my
wings as cavalry use their horses to circle round
the man I am attacking; and I laugh at him when
I see him dancing with the pain of my wounds.
But what need of words? Let us begin the battle.'
So speaking, he fell upon the lion, alighting upon
his eyes and any other part of his face that was un-
protected by hair, flying around and at the same time

---

[1] I do not feel quite sure of the reason for this taunt—
whether the lion was supposed to be particularly unsightly
in his hinder parts, or simply that the rest of the body, after
the fine maned front, seems to be a poor and scraggy thing.

ACHILLES TATIUS

μενος ἅμα καὶ τῷ βόμβῳ καταυλῶν. ὁ δὲ λέων
ἠγρίαινέ τε καὶ μετεστρέφετο πάντη καὶ τὸν
ἀέρα περιέχασκεν, ὁ δὲ κώνωψ ταύτῃ πλέον
τὴν ὀργὴν ἐτίθετο παιδιὰν καὶ ἐπ' αὐτοῖς ἐτί-
5 τρωσκε τοῖς χείλεσιν. καὶ ὁ μὲν ἔκλινεν εἰς
τὸ λυποῦν μέρος, ἀνακάμπτων ἔνθα τοῦ τραύματος ἡ πληγή, ὁ δὲ ὥσπερ παλαιστὴς τὸ σῶμα
σκευάζων εἰς τὴν συμπλοκὴν ἀπέρρει τῶν τοῦ
λέοντος ὀδόντων, αὐτὴν μέσην διαπτὰς κλειο-
6 μένην τὴν γένυν. οἱ δὲ ὀδόντες κενοὶ τῆς θήρας
περὶ ἑαυτοὺς ἐκροτάλιζον. ἤδη τοίνυν ὁ λέων
ἐκεκμήκει σκιαμαχῶν πρὸς τὸν ἀέρα τοῖς ὀδοῦσι
καὶ εἱστήκει παρειμένος ὀργῇ· ὁ δὲ κώνωψ
περιϊπτάμενος αὐτοῦ τὴν κόμην, ἐπηύλει μέλος
7 ἐπινίκιον. μακρότερον δὲ ποιούμενος τῆς πτή-
σεως τὸν κύκλον ὑπὸ περιττῆς ἀπειροκαλίας
ἀράχνης λανθάνει νήμασιν ἐμπλακείς, καὶ τὴν
ἀράχνην οὐκ ἔλαθεν ἐμπεσών. ὡς δὲ οὐκέτι
εἶχε φυγεῖν, ἀδημονῶν εἶπεν, ' Ὦ τῆς ἀνοίας·
προυκαλούμην γὰρ ἐγὼ λέοντα, ὀλίγος δέ με
ἤγρευσεν ἀράχνης χιτών. ' " ταῦτα εἰπών, " Ὥρα
τοίνυν," ἔφη, " καὶ σὲ ¹ τὰς ἀράχνας φοβεῖσθαι·"
καὶ ἅμα ἐγέλασε.
   23. Καὶ ὀλίγας διαλιπὼν ἡμέρας, εἰδὼς αὐτὸν
γαστρὸς ἡττώμενον, φάρμακον πριάμενος ὕπνου
βαθέος, ἐφ' ἑστίασιν αὐτὸν ἐκάλεσεν. ὁ δὲ ὑπώπτευε μέν τινα μηχανὴν καὶ ὤκνει τὸ πρῶτον·
ὡς δὲ ἡ βελτίστη γαστὴρ κατηνάγκασε, πείθεται.
2 ἐπεὶ δὲ ἧκε πρὸς τὸν Σάτυρον, εἶτα δειπνήσας
ἔμελλεν ἀπιέναι, ἐγχεῖ τοῦ φαρμάκου κατὰ τῆς

σοὶ Cobet.

piping with his drone. The lion began to be furious, jumping round in every direction and making empty bites at the air: then the gnat all the more made sport of his anger, and wounded him actually on the lips. The lion turned towards the direction in which he was hurt, bending over to where he felt the blow of the wound, but the gnat, like a wrestler, prepared his body against the hold and slipped out of the snap of the lion's teeth, and flew clean through the middle of his jaw as it closed, so that his teeth clashed idly against one another. By this time the lion was tired out with fighting vainly against the air with his teeth, and stood quite worn out with his own passion, while the gnat hovered round his mane, chanting a song of victory: but as he took a wider sweep of flight in his unmannerly exultation, he became entangled unawares in the meshes of a spider's web, though the spider was not at all unaware of his arrival. Now unable to escape, he began to cry in despair: 'Fool that I was: I challenged the lion, while a paltry spider's web has caught me!'" Thus did Satyrus speak: and, "Now," said he, with a smile, "you had better beware of spiders."

23. After letting a few days pass, he (knowing that Conops was always the slave of his belly) bought a drug of the nature of a strong sleeping-draught, and asked him to dinner. At first he suspected some trick and hesitated: then, his beloved belly being too strong for him, he accepted. He came to Satyrus, and after dinner was just on the point of going away, when Satyrus poured some of the drug

τελευταίας κύλικος ὁ Σάτυρος αὐτῷ· καὶ ὁ μὲν
ἔπιε, καὶ μικρὸν διαλιπών, ὅσον εἰς τὸ δωμάτιον
αὐτοῦ φθάσαι, καταπεσὼν ἔκειτο, τὸν ὕπνον
3 καθεύδων τοῦ φαρμάκου. ὁ δὲ Σάτυρος εἰστρέχει πρός με καὶ λέγει· "Κεῖταί σοι καθεύδων
ὁ Κύκλωψ·[1] σὺ δὲ ὅπως Ὀδυσσεὺς ἀγαθὸς γένῃ."
ἅμα ἔλεγε καὶ ἥκομεν ἐπὶ τὰς θύρας τῆς ἐρωμένης·
καὶ ὁ μὲν ὑπελείπετο, ἐγὼ δὲ εἰσῄειν, ὑποδεχο-
μένης με τῆς Κλειοῦς ἀψοφητί, τρέμων τρόμον
4 διπλοῦν, χαρᾶς ἅμα καὶ φόβου. ὁ μὲν γὰρ τοῦ
κινδύνου φόβος ἐθορύβει τὰς τῆς ψυχῆς ἐλπίδας,
ἡ δὲ ἐλπὶς τοῦ τυχεῖν ἐπεκάλυπτεν ἡδονῇ τὸν
φόβον· οὕτω καὶ τὸ ἐλπίζον ἐφοβεῖτό μου καὶ
ἔχαιρε τὸ λυπούμενον. ἄρτι δέ μου προσελ-
θόντος εἴσω τοῦ θαλάμου τῆς παιδός, γίνεταί τι
τοιοῦτο περὶ τὴν τῆς κόρης μητέρα· ἔτυχε γὰρ
5 ὄνειρος αὐτὴν ταράξας. ἐδόκει τινὰ λῃστὴν
μάχαιραν ἔχοντα γυμνὴν ἄγειν ἁρπασάμενον
αὐτῆς τὴν θυγατέρα καὶ καταθέμενον ὑπτίαν,
μέσην ἀνατέμνειν[2] τῇ μαχαίρᾳ τὴν γαστέρα
κάτωθεν ἀρξάμενον ἀπὸ τῆς αἰδοῦς. ταραχθεῖσα
οὖν ὑπὸ δείματος, ὡς εἶχεν, ἀναπηδᾷ καὶ ἐπὶ τὸν
τῆς θυγατρὸς θάλαμον τρέχει, ἐγγὺς γὰρ ἦν,
6 ἄρτι μου κατακλιθέντος. ἐγὼ μὲν δὴ τὸν ψόφον
ἀκούσας ἀνοιγομένων τῶν θυρῶν, εὐθὺς ἀνεπή-
δησα· ἡ δὲ ἐπὶ τὴν κλίνην παρῆν. συνεὶς οὖν
τὸ κακὸν ἐξάλλομαι καὶ διὰ τῶν θυρῶν ἵεμαι
δρόμῳ, καὶ ὁ Σάτυρος ὑποδέχεται τρέμοντα καὶ

[1] Göttling's brilliant and certain emendation for Κώνωψ:
an ignorant copyist would inevitably alter it into the familiar
name.

[2] Cobet restored the present infinitive for the MSS. aorist
ἀνατεμεῖν which however may be right.

into his parting glass: he drank it, had just time to
get to his own room, and then fell down and lay
sleeping a drugged sleep. Then Satyrus hurried to
me and said: "Your Cyclops is asleep; see that you
prove yourself a brave Ulysses.[1]" He was still
speaking when we came to my beloved's door. He
left me, and I entered, Clio letting me in on tiptoe,
trembling with the double emotion of joy and fear:
the fear of the danger we were running troubled
the hopes of my heart, while the hope of success
dulled with pleasure the fear I had conceived; hope
was afraid and apprehension rejoiced. But hardly
had I entered the maiden's chamber, when a strange
event befell her mother: she was troubled by a
dream in which she saw a robber with a naked sword
snatch her daughter from her, throw her down on
her back, and then rip her up the middle of the
belly with the blade, beginning from the groin.
Frightened and disturbed, just as she was, she
jumped up and rushed to her daughter's chamber,
which was quite close, when I had but just lain down:
I, hearing the noise of the doors opening, leaped
quickly up; but she was already at the bed-side.
Then I understood the mischief, sprang away, and
ran through the door-way, where Satyrus was
waiting for me, all trembling and disordered as I

---

[1] A reference to the famous story in the ninth book of the
Odyssey.

τεταραγμένον. εἶτα ἐφεύγομεν διὰ τοῦ σκότους καὶ ἐπὶ τὸ δωμάτιον ἑαυτῶν ἤλθομεν.

24. Ἡ δὲ πρῶτον μὲν ὑπὸ ἰλίγγου κατέπεσεν, εἶτα ἀνενεγκοῦσα τὴν Κλειὼ κατὰ κόρρης, ὡς εἶχε, ῥαπίζει καὶ ἐπιλαβομένη τῶν τριχῶν, ἅμα πρὸς τὴν θυγατέρα ἀνῴμωξεν, "᾽Απώλεσάς μου,"

2 λέγουσα, "Λευκίππη, τὰς ἐλπίδας. οἴμοι, Σώστρατε· σὺ μὲν ἐν Βυζαντίῳ πολεμεῖς ὑπὲρ ἀλλοτρίων γάμων, ἐν Τύρῳ δὲ καταπεπολέμησαι καὶ τῆς θυγατρός σού τις τοὺς γάμους σεσύληκεν. οἴμοι δειλαία, τοιούτους σου γάμους ὄψεσθαι οὐ

3 προσεδόκων. ὤφελον ἔμεινας ἐν Βυζαντίῳ· ὤφελον ἔπαθες πολέμου νόμῳ τὴν ὕβριν· ὤφελόν σε κἂν Θρᾷξ νικήσας ὕβρισεν· οὐκ εἶχεν ἡ συμφορὰ διὰ τὴν ἀνάγκην ὄνειδος· νῦν δέ, κακό-

4 δαιμον, ἀδοξεῖς ἐν οἷς δυστυχεῖς· ἐπλάνα δέ με καὶ τὰ τῶν ἐνυπνίων φαντάσματα, τὸν δὲ ἀληθέστερον ὄνειρον οὐκ ἐθεασάμην· νῦν ἀθλιώτερον ἀνετμήθης τὴν γαστέρα· αὕτη δυστυχεστέρα τῆς μαχαίρας τομή, οὐδὲ εἶδον τὸν ὑβρίσαντά σε, οὐδὲ οἶδά μου τῆς συμφορᾶς τὴν τύχην. οἴμοι τῶν κακῶν· μὴ καὶ δοῦλος ἦν;"

25. Ἐθάρρησεν οὖν ἡ παρθένος, ὡς ἂν ἐμοῦ διαπεφευγότος, καὶ λέγει· "Μὴ λοιδόρει μου, μῆτερ, τὴν παρθενίαν· οὐδὲν ἔργον μοι πέπρακται τοιούτων ῥημάτων ἄξιον,[1] οὐδὲ οἶδα τοῦτον ὅστις

2 ἦν, εἴτε δαίμων, εἴτε ἥρως, εἴτε λῃστής. ἐκείμην δὲ πεφοβημένη, μηδὲ ἀνακραγεῖν διὰ τὸν φόβον δυναμένη· φόβος γὰρ γλώττης ἐστὶ δεσμός. ἓν οἶδα μόνον, οὐδείς μου τὴν παρθενίαν κατῄσχυνε."

3 καταπεσοῦσα οὖν ἡ Πάνθεια πάλιν ἔστενεν·

[1] Inserted by Cobet.

was : then we fled through the darkness and came to our own rooms.

24. Panthea first of all fell down in a swoon : when she recovered, she straightway boxed Clio's ears and caught her by the hair, at the same time crying out to her daughter : "Leucippe, you have destroyed all my hopes. Ah, my poor Sostratus, you are fighting at Byzantium to protect other people's marriages, while at Tyre you have already been defeated and another has ravished your daughter's marriage. Woe is me, Leucippe : I never thought to see your wedding in this wise : would that you had remained at Byzantium ; would that you had suffered violence after the custom of war ; yes, would even that a conquering Thracian had been your ravisher : a misfortune brought about by force does not carry shame with it. But now, wretched girl, you have lost your fame at the same time as your happiness. Even the visions of the night have beguiled me—this is truer than any dream : you have suffered a worse fate than being, as I saw you, ripped up ; this is a crueller wound than the cutting of the sword—and I could not see your ravisher, nor do I know how the whole wretched business came about : alas, alas, was he perhaps a slave ?"

25. This, showing that I had escaped, gave the maiden fresh courage. "Do not, mother," said she, "thus disparage my virginity ; nothing has happened to justify what you have said, and I know not who was here—god, demigod, or burglar. I was lying stricken with fright, and I was too much afraid, even to cry out : fear is a shackle on the tongue. Only one thing I know, that nobody has offended my virginity." Then Panthea again fell down and wept :

ἡμεῖς δὲ ἐσκοποῦμεν, καθ' ἑαυτοὺς γενόμενοι, τί
ποιητέον εἴη, καὶ ἐδόκει κράτιστον εἶναι φεύγειν,
πρὶν ἢ ἕως γένηται καὶ τὸ πᾶν ἡ Κλειὼ βασα-
νιζομένη κατείπῃ.

26. Δόξαν οὖν οὕτως εἰχόμεθα ἔργου, σκηψά-
μενοι πρὸς τὸν θυρωρὸν ἀπιέναι πρὸς ἐρωμένην,
καὶ ἐπὶ τὴν οἰκίαν ἐρχόμεθα τὴν Κλεινίου. ἦσαν
δὲ λοιπὸν μέσαι νύκτες, ὥστε μόλις ὁ θυρωρὸς
ἀνέῳξεν ἡμῖν. καὶ ὁ Κλεινίας, ἐν ὑπερῴῳ γὰρ
τὸν θάλαμον εἶχε, διαλεγομένων ἡμῶν ἀκούσας,
2 κατατρέχει τεταραγμένος. καὶ ἐν τοσούτῳ τὴν
Κλειὼ κατόπιν ὁρῶμεν σπουδῇ θέουσαν· ἦν γὰρ
δρασμὸν βεβουλευμένη. ἅμα τε οὖν ὁ Κλεινίας
ἤκουσεν ἡμῶν ἃ πεπόνθαμεν καὶ τῆς Κλειοῦς
ἡμεῖς, ὅπως φύγοι, καὶ πάλιν ἡμῶν ἡ Κλειὼ τί
3 ποιεῖν μέλλομεν. παρελθόντες οὖν εἴσω τῶν
θυρῶν, τῷ Κλεινίᾳ διηγούμεθα τὰ γεγονότα καὶ
ὅτι φεύγειν διεγνώκαμεν. λέγει ἡ Κλειώ, "Κἀγὼ
σὺν ὑμῖν· ἢν γὰρ περιμείνω τὴν ἕω, θάνατός μοι
πρόκειται, τῶν βασάνων γλυκύτερος."

27. Ὁ οὖν Κλεινίας τῆς χειρός μου λαβόμενος
ἄγει τῆς Κλειοῦς μακρὰν καὶ λέγει· "Δοκῶ μοι
καλλίστην γνώμην εὑρηκέναι, ταύτην μὲν ὑπεξαγ-
αγεῖν, ἡμᾶς δὲ ὀλίγας ἡμέρας ἐπισχεῖν, κἂν οὕτω
2 δοκῇ, συσκευασαμένους ἀπελθεῖν. οὐδὲ γὰρ νῦν
οἶδε τῆς κόρης ἡ μήτηρ τίνα κατέλαβεν, ὡς ὑμεῖς
φατέ, ὅ τε καταμηνύσων οὐκ ἔσται, τῆς Κλειοῦς
ἐκ μέσου γενομένης· τάχα δὲ καὶ τὴν κόρην

but Satyrus and I, when we were alone in our rooms, were considering what we had best do, and we decided that the best course would be to fly before morning came and Clio revealed the whole story under torture.

26. This resolved, we set about it at once. We told the porter that we were going out to see my mistress,[1] and went to Clinias' house. It was still deep night, and his porter made some difficulty about opening to us; but Clinias, whose bedroom was upstairs, heard us talking to him and came running down in disorder: and just at that moment we saw Clio behind us, running; she too had made up her mind to run away. So all together Clinias heard our story from us, and we Clio's, how she had fled, and Clio our next intentions. We all therefore went indoors, related to Clinias all that had happened, and told him that we had made up our mind to fly. Then said Clio: "I am with you too: if I wait until morning, my only resource is death, which I prefer to torture."

27. Then Clinias took me by the hand and led me away from Clio. "I think," said he, "that I have conceived the best idea: namely, to send her away privily, and ourselves remain a few days; then, if we like, we can ourselves go after making all necessary preparations. At present, so you tell me, the girl's mother does not even know whom she caught; and when Clio has once disappeared there will be nobody able to inform her. And perhaps you will be able to persuade the girl to escape with

[1] Not, of course, Leucippe, but some girl of lower station. Young Greeks and Romans were almost encouraged in light love-affairs to keep them from the graver offences of meddling with women of their own rank.

συμφυγεῖν πείσετε." ἔλεγε δὲ καὶ αὐτὸς ὅτι
3 κοινωνὸς γενήσεται τῆς ἀποδημίας. ταῦτα ἔδοξε·
καὶ τὴν μὲν Κλειὼ τῶν οἰκετῶν αὐτοῦ τινι παραδίδωσι, κελεύσας ἐμβαλέσθαι σκάφει, ἡμεῖς δὲ
αὐτοῦ καταμείναντες ἐφροντίζομεν περὶ τῶν
ἐσομένων, καὶ τέλος ἔδοξεν ἀποπειραθῆναι τῆς
κόρης καὶ εἰ μὲν θελήσει συμφυγεῖν, οὕτω
πράττειν· εἰ δὲ μή, μένειν αὐτοῦ, παραδόντας
ἑαυτοὺς τῇ τύχῃ. κοιμηθέντες οὖν ὀλίγον τῆς
νυκτὸς ὅσον τὸ λοιπόν, περὶ τὴν ἔω πάλιν ἐπὶ τὴν
οἰκίαν ἐπανήλθομεν.

28. Ἡ οὖν Πάνθεια ἀναστᾶσα περὶ τὰς βασάνους τῆς Κλειοῦς ηὐτρεπίζετο καὶ καλεῖν αὐτὴν
ἐκέλευεν. ὡς δὲ ἦν ἀφανής, πάλιν ἐπὶ τὴν
θυγατέρα ἵεται καί "Οὐκ ἐρεῖς," ἔφη, "τὴν
συσκευὴν τοῦ δράματος; ἰδοὺ καὶ ἡ Κλειὼ
2 πέφευγεν." ἡ δὲ ἔτι μᾶλλον ἐθάρρησε καὶ λέγει·
"Τί πλέον εἴπω σοι, τίνα δὲ ἄλλην προσαγάγω
πίστιν τῆς ἀληθείας μείζονα; εἰ παρθενίας ἐστί
3 τις δοκιμασία, δοκίμασον." "Ἔτι καὶ τοῦτο,"
ἔφη ἡ Πάνθεια, "λείπεται, ἵνα καὶ μετὰ μαρτύρων δυστυχῶμεν." ταῦτα ἅμα λέγουσα, ἀνεπήδη-
σεν ἔξω.

29. Ἡ δὲ Λευκίππη καθ' ἑαυτὴν γενομένη καὶ
τῶν τῆς μητρὸς γεμισθεῖσα ῥημάτων παντοδαπή
τις ἦν. ἤχθετο, ἠσχύνετο, ὠργίζετο. ἤχθετο
μὲν πεφωραμένη, ἠσχύνετο δὲ ὀνειδιζομένη, ὠργίζετο δὲ ἀπιστουμένη. αἰδὼς δὲ καὶ λύπη καὶ
2 ὀργὴ τρία τῆς ψυχῆς κύματα· ἡ μὲν γὰρ αἰδὼς

you." At the same time he told us that he was prepared to share our flight abroad. This plan commended itself to us: so he handed Clio over to the charge of one of his servants, telling him to put her aboard a ship, while we waited there and discussed the future. Our final decision was to make an attempt to persuade Leucippe, and if she were willing to accompany us in our flight, to act accordingly: if not, to remain at home and put ourselves in the hands of fortune. We reposed ourselves therefore for the small part of the night that was still left, and returned home again about dawn.

28. When Panthea had risen, she began to set about the preparations for the torturing of Clio, and bade her be summoned. As Clio could not be found, she again hurried to her daughter. "Do you refuse," said she, "to tell how this plot was composed? Now Clio too has fled." On this Leucippe gained still greater courage, saying, "What more can I tell you? What more valid proof can I bring that I am speaking the truth? If there be any test of virginity, apply it to me." "Yes," said Panthea, "that was the one thing lacking—that our disgrace should be publicly known to others too." As she said this, she flounced out of the room.

29. Leucippe, left alone to ponder on her mother's words, was a prey to various differing emotions; grief, shame, and anger. She was grieved at having been found out: she was ashamed because of the reproaches which had been cast upon her: and she was angry because her mother would not believe her. Shame, grief, and anger may be compared to three billows which dash against the soul: shame enters

διὰ τῶν ὀμμάτων εἰσρέουσα τὴν τῶν ὀφθαλμῶν
ἐλευθερίαν καθαιρεῖ· ἡ λύπη δὲ περὶ τὰ στέρνα
διανεμομένη κατατήκει τῆς ψυχῆς τὸ ζωπυροῦν·
ἡ δὲ ὀργὴ περιϋλακτοῦσα τὴν καρδίαν ἐπικλύζει
3 τὸν λογισμὸν τῷ τῆς μανίας ἀφρῷ. λόγος δὲ
τούτων ἁπάντων πατήρ, καὶ ἔοικεν ἐπὶ σκοπῷ
τόξον βάλλειν καὶ ἐπιτυγχάνειν καὶ ἐπὶ τὴν
ψυχὴν πέμπειν τὰ βλήματα καὶ ποικίλα τοξεύματα. τὸ μέν ἐστιν αὐτῷ λοιδορία[1] βέλος καὶ
γίνεται τὸ ἕλκος ὀργή· τὸ δέ ἐστιν ἔλεγχος
ἀτυχημάτων· ἐκ τούτου τοῦ βέλους λύπη γίνε-
ται· τὸ δὲ ὄνειδος ἁμαρτημάτων καὶ καλοῦσιν
4 αἰδὼ τὸ τραῦμα. ἴδιον δὲ τούτων ἁπάντων
τῶν βελῶν βαθέα μὲν τὰ βλήματα, ἄναιμα δὲ
τὰ τοξεύματα. ἐν δὲ τούτων ἁπάντων φάρμακον,
ἀμύνεσθαι βάλλοντα τοῖς αὐτοῖς βλήμασι· λόγος
γὰρ γλώσσης βέλος ἄλλης γλώσσης βέλει
θεραπεύεται· καὶ γὰρ τῆς καρδίας ἔπαυσε τὸ
θυμούμενον καὶ τῆς ψυχῆς ἐμάρανε τὸ λυπού-
5 μενον. ἂν δέ τις ἀνάγκη τοῦ κρείττονος σιγήσῃ
τὴν ἄμυναν, ἀλγεινότερα γίνεται τὰ ἕλκη τῇ σιωπῇ·
αἱ γὰρ ὠδῖνες τῶν ἐκ τοῦ λόγου κυμάτων, οὐκ
ἀποπτύσασαι τὸν ἀφρόν, οἰδοῦσι περὶ ἑαυτὰς
πεφυσημέναι. τοσούτων οὖν ἡ Λευκίππη γεμισθεῖσα ῥημάτων, οὐκ ἔφερε τὴν προσβολήν.[2]

---

[1] Scaliger's suggestion for the MSS. λοιδορίας.
[2] The last sentence of this chapter is rejected by Hercher
as the *scholion* of a copyist. But it does not seem to me
entirely alien to the style of our author.

---

[1] I do not feel very sure of the meaning of this passage : it
is a rhetorical *sententia* not very well fitted into its context.
The obvious interpretation is that shame is caused by things

through the eyes and takes away their freedom [1];
grief diffuses itself about the breast and tends to
extinguish the lively flame of the soul; while anger,
roaring round the heart, overwhelms the reasoning
power with its foam of madness. Of all these speech
is the begetter: it is like a bow shooting and aiming
at its mark and discharging its wounding arrows
of various kinds against the soul. One of its arrows
is upbraiding, the wound it causes, anger. Another
is the conviction of wrong, and the wound caused by it
grief. The third is the reproach for error, and the
wound inflicted by this is called shame. All these
arrows have the same peculiarity; the wounds they
deal are deep, but bloodless, and there is but one
remedy for all of them—to return the same arrows
against the enemy. Speech is the arrow of the
tongue, and the wound it causes can only be cured
by another tongue shooting in return: this quiets
the anger of the heart and deadens the soul's pain.
If the fact that one is dealing with a stronger makes
such a return impossible, the wound grows more
painful by reason of the silence thus enjoined. For
the pains which are the result of these stormy
waves of speech, if they cannot cast off their
foam, swell within and only become the more
severe. Such were the thoughts that surged upon
Leucippe's mind, and she was little able to bear
their onslaught.

seen, and shame may be said to deprive the eyes of their
liberty in that it causes the person ashamed to cast his eyes
down to the ground; but it has been stated only a sentence
above that Leucippe's shame came from the reproaches
levelled at her, and this is the sense of the continuation of
the *sententia*, in which it is stated that the efficient cause of
these distressing emotions is speech.

30. Ἐν τούτῳ δὲ ἔτυχον πέμψας τὸν Σάτυρον πρὸς τὴν κόρην ἀποπειρασόμενον τῆς φυγῆς. ἡ δὲ πρὶν ἀκοῦσαι, πρὸς τὸν Σάτυρον "Δέομαι," ἔφη, "πρὸς θεῶν ξένων καὶ ἐγχωρίων, ἐξαρπάσατέ με τῶν τῆς μητρὸς ὀφθαλμῶν, ὅπη βού-
2 λεσθε· εἰ δέ με ἀπελθόντες καταλίποιτε, βρόχον πλεξαμένη τὴν ψυχήν μου οὕτως ἀφήσω." ἐγὼ δὲ ὡς ταῦτα ἤκουσα, τὸ πολὺ τῆς φροντίδος ἀπερριψάμην. δύο δὲ ἡμέρας διαλιπόντες, ὅτε καὶ ἀποδημῶν ἔτυχεν ὁ πατήρ, παρεσκευαζόμεθα πρὸς τὴν φυγήν.

31. Εἶχε δὲ ὁ Σάτυρος τοῦ φαρμάκου λείψανον, ᾧ τὸν Κώνωπα ἦν κατακοιμίσας· τούτου διακονούμενος ἡμῖν ἐγχεῖ λαθὼν κατὰ τῆς κύλικος τῆς τελευταίας, ἣν τῇ Πανθείᾳ προσέφερεν· ἡ δὲ ἀναστᾶσα ᾤχετο εἰς τὸν θάλαμον αὐτῆς καὶ
2 εὐθὺς ἐκάθευδεν. εἶχε δὲ ἑτέραν ἡ Λευκίππη θαλαμηπόλον, ἣν τῷ αὐτῷ φαρμάκῳ καταβαπτίσας ὁ Σάτυρος (προσεπεποίητο γὰρ καὶ αὐτῆς, ἐξ οὗ τῷ θαλάμῳ προσεληλύθει, ἐρᾶν) ἐπὶ τὴν τρίτην θήραν[1] ἔρχεται τὸν θυρωρόν· κἀκεῖνον
3 ἐβεβλήκει τῷ αὐτῷ πώματι. ὄχημα δὲ εὐτρεπὲς ἡμᾶς πρὸ τῶν πυλῶν ἐξεδέχετο, ὅπερ ὁ Κλεινίας παρεσκεύασε, καὶ ἔφθασεν ἡμᾶς ἐπ᾽ αὐτοῦ περιμένων αὐτός. ἐπεὶ δὲ πάντες ἐκάθευδον, περὶ πρώτας νυκτὸς φυλακὰς προῇμεν ἀψοφητί,
4 Λευκίππην τοῦ Σατύρου χειραγωγοῦντος. καὶ γὰρ ὁ Κώνωψ, ὅσπερ ἡμῖν ἐφήδρευε, κατὰ τύχην ἐκείνην ἀπεδήμει τὴν ἡμέραν, τῇ δεσποίνῃ διακονησόμενος. ἀνοίγει δὴ τὰς θύρας ὁ Σάτυρος

---

[1] θήραν—his third victim—is the ingenious emendation of Boden for θύραν, the third door. Jacobs proposed πεῖραν.

30. It so happened that just at that moment I sent Satyrus to her to see if she were prepared to run away with us. But before she even heard what he had to say, " I implore you," said she to Satyrus, " in the name of our country gods and all there are in the world, take me away, wherever you like, out of my mother's sight. If you go away and leave me behind, I shall end my life by a noose of my own making." When I heard of her words, I felt that the greater part of my anxiety was gone ; we waited a couple of days, while my father was still away,[1] and began to make our preparations for flight.

31. Satyrus still had some of that drug left with which he had put Conops to sleep; and while he was waiting upon us, he poured some of it unobserved into the last cup which he was bringing to Panthea: after rising from the table she went to her chamber and there fell at once asleep. Leucippe had a second chambermaid ; with her, too, ever since she had been placed in that position, Satyrus had pretended to be in love, and he gave her also a dose of the same mixture ; then he proceeded to his third victim, the porter, and successfully drugged him with a similar draught. A carriage was waiting in readiness for us outside the gates, due to the forethought of Clinias, and he himself got into it and waited there for us. When everybody was asleep, at about the first watch of the night, we went out without a sound, Satyrus leading Leucippe by the hand ; fortunately Conops, who was in constant ambush for us, was away on that particular day on some business for his mistress. Satyrus opened the

---

[1] In Palestine : see V. x. § 3.

καὶ προήλθομεν· ὡς δὲ παρῆμεν ἐπὶ τὰς πύλας,
5 ἐπέβημεν τοῦ ὀχήματος. ἦμεν δὲ οἱ πάντες ἕξ,
ἡμεῖς καὶ ὁ Κλεινίας καὶ δύο θεράποντες αὐτοῦ.
ἐπελαύνομεν οὖν τὴν ἐπὶ Σιδῶνα καὶ περὶ μοίρας
τῆς νυκτὸς δύο παρῆμεν ἐπὶ τὴν πόλιν καὶ εὐθὺς
ἐπὶ Βηρυτὸν τὸν δρόμον ἐποιούμεθα, νομίζοντες
6 εὑρήσειν ἐκεῖ ναῦν ἐφορμοῦσαν. καὶ οὐκ ἠτυχή-
σαμεν· ὡς γὰρ ἐπὶ τοῦ Βηρυτίων λιμένος ἤλθομεν, ἀναγόμενον σκάφος εὕρομεν, ἄρτι τὰ πρυ-
μνήσια μέλλον ἀπολύειν. μηδὲν οὖν ἐρωτήσαντες
ποῖ πλεῖ, μετεσκευαζόμεθα ἐπὶ τὴν θάλασσαν
ἐκ τῆς γῆς, καὶ ἦν ὁ καιρὸς μικρὸν ἄνω τῆς ἕω.
ἔπλει δὲ τὸ πλοῖον εἰς Ἀλεξάνδρειαν, τὴν μεγάλην
τοῦ Νείλου πόλιν.

32. Ἔχαιρον τὸ πρῶτον ὁρῶν τὴν θάλασσαν,
οὔπω πελαγίζοντος τοῦ σκάφους ἀλλ' ἐπὶ τοῖς
λιμέσιν ἐποχουμένου. ὡς δὲ ἔδοξεν οὔριον εἶναι
πρὸς ἀναγωγὴν τὸ πνεῦμα, θόρυβος ἦν πολὺς
κατὰ τὸ σκάφος, τῶν ναυτῶν διαθεόντων, τοῦ
κυβερνήτου κελεύοντος, ἑλκομένων τῶν κάλων·
2 ἡ κεραία περιήγετο, τὸ ἱστίον καθίετο, ἡ ναῦς
ἀπεσαλεύετο, τὰς ἀγκύρας ἀνέσπων, ὁ λιμὴν
κατελείπετο· τὴν γῆν ἑωρῶμεν ἀπὸ τῆς νηὸς
κατὰ μικρὸν ἀναχωροῦσαν, ὡς αὐτὴν πλέουσαν·
παιανισμὸς ἦν καὶ πολλή τις εὐχή, θεοὺς σωτῆ-
ρας καλοῦντες,[1] εὐφημοῦντες αἴσιον τὸν πλοῦν
γενέσθαι· τὸ πνεῦμα ἤρετο σφοδρότερον, τὸ ἱστίον
ἐκυρτοῦτο καὶ εἷλκε τὴν ναῦν.

---

[1] Guyet altered these participles into the genitive, but a
nominative pendens does not seem an impossibility in Achilles
Tatius.

doors; we followed; and when we had arrived at
the gates, we entered the carriage: we were six in
all—ourselves, Clinias, and two servants of his. We
took the road to Sidon; arriving there when
another watch of the night was about spent, we
hurried on to Berytus, expecting that we should
find some ship at anchor there. Nor were we
disappointed: for as we arrived at the harbour of
Berytus, we found a ship just sailing, on the
very point of casting loose; so we asked no
questions as to her destination, but embarked all
our belongings aboard; it was then a little before
dawn. It appeared that she was making the voyage
to Alexandria, the great city at the mouth of the
Nile.

32. I was at once full of joy, even at my first
sight of the ocean, before the boat got out to sea
but was still riding in the harbour. When the
breeze seemed favourable for putting off, a busy
commotion arose throughout the ship—the crew
running hither and thither, the helmsman giving his
orders, men hauling on the ropes. The yard-arm
was pulled round, the sail set, the ship leaped
forward, the anchors were pulled in-deck, the
harbour was left; we saw the coast little by little
receding from the ship, as though it were itself in
movement; there were songs of joy and much
prayer directed to the gods saviours, invoking good
omens for a prosperous voyage; meanwhile the
wind freshened, the sail bellied, and the ship sped
along.

33. Ἔτυχε δέ τις ἡμῖν νεανίσκος παρασκηνῶν, ὃς ἐπεὶ καιρὸς ἦν ἀρίστου, φιλοφρονούμενος ἡμᾶς συναριστᾶν ἠξίου. καὶ ἡμῖν δὲ ὁ Σάτυρος παρέφερεν· ὥστε εἰς μέσον καταθέμενοι ἃ εἴχομεν, 2 τὸ ἄριστον ἐκοινοῦμεν, ἤδη δὲ καὶ λόγον. λέγω δὴ πρῶτος· "Πόθεν, ὦ νεανίσκε, καὶ τίνα σε δεῖ καλεῖν;" "'Εγὼ Μενέλαος," εἶπεν· "τὸ δὲ γένος 3 Αἰγύπτιος. τὰ δὲ ὑμέτερα τίνα;" "'Εγὼ Κλειτοφῶν, οὗτος Κλεινίας, Φοίνικες ἄμφω." "Τίς οὖν ἡ πρόφασις ὑμῖν τῆς ἀποδημίας;" "Ἢν σὺ πρῶτος ἡμῖν φράσῃς, καὶ τὰ παρ' ἡμῶν ἀκούσῃ."

34. Λέγει οὖν ὁ Μενέλαος· "Τὸ μὲν κεφάλαιον τῆς ἐμῆς ἀποδημίας ἔρως βάσκανος καὶ θήρα δυστυχής. ἤρων μειρακίου καλοῦ· τὸ δὲ μειράκιον φιλόθηρον ἦν. ἐπεῖχον τὰ πολλά, κρατεῖν οὐκ ἠδυνάμην. ὡς δὲ οὐκ ἔπειθον, εἱπόμην ἐπὶ 2 τὰς ἄγρας κἀγώ. ἐθηρῶμεν οὖν ἱππεύοντες ἄμφω καὶ τὰ πρῶτα ηὐτυχοῦμεν, τὰ λεπτὰ 3 διώκοντες τῶν θηρίων. ἐξαίφνης δὲ σῦς τῆς ὕλης προπηδᾷ καὶ τὸ μειράκιον ἐδίωκε· καὶ ὁ σῦς ἐπιστρέφει τὴν γένυν καὶ ἀντιπρόσωπος ἐχώρει δρόμῳ, καὶ τὸ μειράκιον οὐκ ἐξετρέπετο, βοῶντος ἐμοῦ καὶ κεκραγότος, ''Ελκε τὸν ἵππον, μετένεγκε τὰς ἡνίας, πονηρὸν τὸ θηρίον.' ἀνάξας[1] δὲ ὁ σῦς 4 σπουδῇ ἔτρεχεν ὡς ἐπ' αὐτό· καὶ οἱ μὲν συνέπιπτον ἀλλήλοις, ἐμὲ δὲ τρόμος, ὡς εἶδον,

---

[1] The MSS. have ἀλλάξας or ἀλαλάξας: ᾄξας or ἀνάξας were suggested by Jacobs, and one of them is almost certainly right.

---

[1] παρασκηνῶν means literally " bivouacking near us." It was doubtless the custom (as in modern ships in Eastern

33. There happened to be camping near us [1] on board a young man, who, when breakfast-time [2] arrived, very courteously asked us to take the meal with him. Satyrus was just bringing our victuals; so that we put all that we had into the common stock, and made a joint meal and also shared the conversation. I was the first to speak : " Where do you come from, young sir, and what are you called?" "Menelaus is my name," he replied, "an Egyptian by nationality. What are yours?" " I am Clitophon, this is Clinias, Phoenicians both." "What then is the reason that you are thus leaving your country?" "Tell us your story first, and then we will relate ours to you."

34. Menelaus then began : "The summary of my absence from my native land is an ill-starred love and a hunt with evil event. I loved a fair youth, who was a passionate huntsman. I tried to check him, but my attempts were unsuccessful ; as he would not obey me, I used to go with him on his expeditions. One day we were both out hunting on horseback ; at first we were successful, chasing small beasts only. Suddenly a boar sprang from the wood ; the youth gave chase. Then the boar turned and faced him, charging directly at him. But he would not give ground, though I shouted and yelled, ' Pull in your horse and turn the reins; the beast is dangerous.' The boar made a spring and charged right at him. They closed with one another, but as I saw it I was

waters) for the passengers to bring their bedding and other household effects and make themselves as comfortable as they could on the deck.

[2] ἄριστον is *déjeuner*, and may be regarded indifferently as breakfast or luncheon.

λαμβάνει καὶ φοβούμενος μὴ φθάσῃ τὸ θηρίον
καὶ πατάξῃ τὸν ἵππον, ἐναγκυλισάμενος τὸ
ἀκόντιον, πρὶν ἀκριβῶς καταστοχάσασθαι τοῦ
σκοποῦ, πέμπω τὸ βέλος· τὸ δὲ μειράκιον παρα-
5 θέον ἁρπάζει τὴν βολήν. τίνα οἴει με τότε
ψυχὴν ἔχειν; εἰ καὶ ψυχὴν εἶχον ὅλως, ὡς ἂν ἄλλος
τις ἀποθάνοι ζῶν. τὸ δὲ οἰκτρότερον, τὰς χεῖρας
ὤρεγέ μοι μικρὸν ἔτι ἐμπνέων καὶ περιέβαλλε καὶ
ἀποθνήσκων οὐκ ἐμίσει με τὸν πονηρὸν ὁ ὑπ'
ἐμοῦ πεφονευμένος, ἀλλὰ τὴν ψυχὴν ἀφῆκε τῇ
6 φονευσάσῃ περιπλεκόμενος δεξιᾷ. ἄγουσιν οὖν
με ἐπὶ τὸ δικαστήριον οἱ τοῦ μειρακίου γονεῖς οὐκ
ἄκοντα· καὶ γὰρ παρελθὼν ἀπελογούμην οὐδέν,
θανάτου δὲ ἐτιμώμην ἐμαυτῷ. ἐλεήσαντες οὖν οἱ
δικασταὶ προσετίμησάν μοι τριετῆ φυγήν· ἧς νῦν
τέλος ἐχούσης, αὖθις ἐπὶ τὴν ἐμαυτοῦ καταίρω."
7 ἐπεδάκρυσεν ὁ Κλεινίας αὐτοῦ λέγοντος Πάτρο-
κλον πρόφασιν, ἀναμνησθεὶς Χαρικλέους. καὶ
ὁ Μενέλαος, "Τὰμὰ δακρύεις," ἔφη, "ἢ καὶ σέ τι
τοιοῦτον ἐξήγαγε;" στενάξας οὖν ὁ Κλεινίας
καταλέγει τὸν Χαρικλέα καὶ τὸν ἵππον, κἀγὼ
τἀμαυτοῦ.

35. Ὁρῶν οὖν τὸν Μενέλαον ἔγωγε κατηφῆ
πάνυ τῶν ἑαυτοῦ μεμνημένον, τὸν δὲ Κλεινίαν
ὑποδακρύοντα μνήμῃ Χαρικλέους, βουλόμενος
αὐτοὺς τῆς λύπης ἀπαγαγεῖν, ἐμβάλλω λόγον
ἐρωτικῆς ἐχόμενον ψυχαγωγίας· καὶ γὰρ οὐδὲ ἡ
Λευκίππη παρῆν, ἀλλ' ἐν μυχῷ ἐκάθευδε τῆς

---

[1] In Greek law-suits the defendant was required to state
the penalty he thought would be the just reward for his
offence : the reader will recall the manner in which Socrates
did so at his trial, recorded in Plato's *Apologia*.

overcome with fright, and, fearing that the brute
would get his blow in first and wound the horse,
I poised my javelin without taking sufficiently
careful aim, and let fly. The youth crossed the line
and received it full. What do you think that my
feelings were then? If I had any feelings at all,
they were like those of a living death. More pitiful
still, while he yet faintly breathed he stretched out his
hands to me and embraced me; in his death-throes
he that was slaughtered by me did not loathe my
accursed self, but he gave up the ghost embracing
my murderous hand. His parents dragged me, not at
all unwilling, before the tribunal of justice. I made
no defence there, and proposed the penalty of death.[1]
So the jury took pity upon me, and sentenced
me to three years' banishment; this period has now
come to an end, and I am returning to my own
country." As he spoke, Clinias wept as the Trojan
women wept over Patroclus[2]; he remembered
Charicles. "You weep at my woes," said Menelaus;
"Has some similar adventure exiled you too?"
Then Clinias groaned bitterly and related to him the
story of Charicles and the horse, and I told my tale
too.

35. Seeing that Menelaus was greatly dejected
at the memory of his sorrows, and that Clinias too
was secretly weeping when he recalled Charicles,
I was anxious to banish their grief, and embarked
upon a discussion which would divert the mind by a
love-interest. Leucippe was not present, but was

[2] Homer, *Iliad*, xix. 302. The captive Trojan women
were forced to act as mourners for the dead Patroclus; and
they shed real enough tears, but they were thinking of their
own woes rather than of the dead hero. The scene passed
into a proverb, which is also used by Plutarch.

2 νηός. λέγω δὴ πρὸς αὐτοὺς ὑπομειδιῶν· "Ὡς παρὰ πολὺ κρατεῖ μου Κλεινίας· ἐβούλετο γὰρ λέγειν κατὰ γυναικῶν, ὥσπερ εἰώθει. ῥᾷον δὲ ἂν
3 εἴποι νῦν ἤτοι, ὡς κοινωνὸν ἔρωτος εὑρών. οὐκ οἶδα γὰρ πῶς ἐπιχωριάζει νῦν ὁ εἰς τοὺς ἄρρενας ἔρως." "Οὐ γὰρ πολὺ ἄμεινον," ὁ Μενέλαος ἔφη, "τοῦτο ἐκείνου; καὶ γὰρ ἁπλούστεροι παῖδες γυναικῶν καὶ τὸ κάλλος αὐτοῖς δριμύτερον εἰς
4 ἡδονήν." "Πῶς δριμύτερον," ἔφην, "ὅ τι παρακύψαν μόνον οἴχεται καὶ οὐκ ἀπολαῦσαι δίδωσ τῷ φιλοῦντι, ἀλλ' ἔοικε τῷ τοῦ Ταντάλου
5 πώματι; πολλάκις γὰρ ἐν ᾧ πίνεται πέφευγε, καὶ ἀπῆλθεν ὁ ἐραστὴς οὐχ εὑρὼν πιεῖν· τὸ δὲ ἔτι πινόμενον ἁρπάζεται πρὶν[1] ὁ πίνων κορεσθῇ. καὶ οὐκ ἔστιν ἀπὸ παιδὸς ἀπελθεῖν ἐραστὴν ἄλυπον ἔχοντα τὴν ἡδονήν· καταλείπει γὰρ ἔτι διψῶντα."

36. Καὶ ὁ Μενέλαος, "Ἀγνοεῖς, ὦ Κλειτοφῶν," ἔφη, "τὸ κεφάλαιον τῆς ἡδονῆς. ποθεινὸν γὰρ ἀεὶ τὸ ἀκόρεστον· τὸ μὲν γὰρ εἰς χρῆσιν χρονιώτερον τῷ κόρῳ μαραίνει τὸ τερπνόν· τὸ δὲ ἁρπαζόμενον καινόν ἐστιν ἀεὶ καὶ μᾶλλον ἀνθεῖ· οὐ γὰρ γεγηρακυῖαν ἔχει τὴν ἡδονήν, καὶ[2] ὅσον ἐλαττοῦται τῷ χρόνῳ, τοσοῦτον εἰς μέγεθος

[1] Cobet wished to insert ἄν after πρίν.
[2] Hercher deleted τοῖς ἄλλοις after καί. But τὸ κάλλος (so Lumb) for τοῖς ἄλλοις looks good.

---

[1] Clitophon shewed a very proper spirit in waiting for Leucippe's absence before propounding this *dubbio amoroso;*

asleep in the ship's hold.[1]   I remarked to them with
a smile, " How much more fortunate than I is
Clinias: he was doubtless about to declaim against
women, as is his wont, and now he can speak with
the greater freedom, because he has found another
that shares his ideas in love.   I know not how it is
that this affection for youths is now so fashionable."
" Why," said Menelaus, " is not the one sort much
preferable to the other ?   Youths have a much simpler
nature than women, and their beauty is a keener
stimulant to delight."   " How keener," said I,
" considering that it has no sooner blossomed[2] than
it is gone, giving the adorer no opportunity of
enjoying it ?   It is like the draught of Tantalus ; often
in the very act of drinking it disappears, and the
lover must retire thirsty, and that which is actually
being drunk is whisked away before the drinker has
had his fill.   Never can the lover leave the object of
his affection with unalloyed delight ; it always leaves
him thirsty still."

36. " You know not, Clitophon," said Menelaus,
" the sum of all pleasure : the unsatisfied is the most
desirable of all.   The longer a thing lasts, the more
likely is it to cloy by satiety ; that which is constantly being ravished away from us is ever new
and always at its prime—delight cannot grow old
and the shorter its time the greater is its intensity

Anthony Hodges in his translation (1638) omits the whole
passage from here to the end of the book, and della Croce omits
some and softens down some of the rest.   The discussion is
characteristic, and certainly less gross than the similar example
at the end of [pseudo-]Lucian's *Amores*.

[2] παρακύψαν means literally " peeped out."

2 ἐκτείνεται πόθῳ. καὶ τὸ ῥόδον διὰ τοῦτο τῶν
ἄλλων εὐμορφότερόν ἐστι φυτῶν, ὅτι τὸ κάλλος
αὐτοῦ φεύγει ταχύ. δύο γὰρ ἐγὼ νομίζω κατ᾽
ἀνθρώπους κάλλη πλανᾶσθαι, τὸ μὲν οὐράνιον,
τὸ δὲ πάνδημον, [ὥσπερ τοῦ κάλλους οἱ χορηγοὶ
3 θεαί].[1] ἀλλὰ τὸ μὲν οὐράνιον ἄχθεται θνητῷ
σκήνει[2] δεδεμένον καὶ ζητεῖ πρὸς οὐρανὸν ταχὺ
φεύγειν· τὸ δὲ πάνδημον ἔρριπται κάτω καὶ
ἐγχρονίζει περὶ τοῖς σώμασιν. εἰ δὲ καὶ ποιητὴν
δεῖ λαβεῖν μάρτυρα τῆς οὐρανίας τοῦ κάλλους
ἀνόδου, ἄκουσον Ὁμήρου λέγοντος,

> Τὸν καὶ ἀνηρείψαντο θεοὶ Διὶ οἰνοχοεύειν
> κάλλεος εἵνεκα οἷο, ἵν᾽ ἀθανάτοισι μετείη.

4 οὐδεμία δὲ ἀνέβη ποτὲ εἰς οὐρανὸν διὰ κάλλος
γυνή (καὶ γὰρ γυναιξὶ κεκοινώνηκεν ὁ Ζεύς) ἀλλ᾽
Ἀλκμήνην μὲν ἔχει πένθος καὶ φυγή· Δανάην δὲ
λάρναξ καὶ θάλασσα· Σεμέλη δὲ πυρὸς γέγονε
τροφή. ἂν δὲ μειρακίου Φρυγὸς ἐρασθῇ, τὸν
οὐρανὸν αὐτῷ δίδωσιν, ἵνα καὶ συνοικῇ καὶ
οἰνοχόον ἔχῃ τοῦ νέκταρος· ἡ δὲ πρότερον

---

[1] The bracketed words were deleted by Hercher: they are
probably the insertion of a scholiast. Whether the words
of the bracketed passage be genuine or not, the reference
is to the two kinds of love treated of in Plato's *Symposium.*
[2] So Jacobs for the MSS. κάλλει. Lumb proposes ἀλύσει.

---

[1] This argument—and its contrary used by Clitophon in
his speech above—is a commonplace of discussions of this
kind. Paul Adam paradoxically alleged the opposite:
"*L'éphèbe offre une beauté plus durable que la vierge ; et cet
espoir de durée suffit seul à justifier sa suprématie.*"
[2] See note on this passage in the Greek text.

increased in desire.[1]   This is why the rose is of all
flowers the most beautiful, because its beauty is so
fleeting.   I hold that there are two different kinds of
beauty conversant among men, the one heavenly,
the other vulgar [presided over by their respective
goddesses [2]]; the heavenly sort chafes at being
fettered by its mortal habitation and is ever seeking
to hurry back again to its heavenly home, while the
vulgar kind is diffused on our earth below and stays
long in association with human bodies.   If one may
quote a poet as a witness of the flight of beauty to
heaven, listen to Homer, who tells how

> The gods to be Jove's cup-bearer in heaven him [3]
>   did take,
> To dwell immortal there with them, all for his
>   beauty's sake.

But no woman ever went up to heaven by reason of
her beauty—yes, Zeus had dealings with women too—
but the fate of Alcmene [4] was sorrow and exile, of
Danae [5] an ark and the sea, while Semele [6] became
food for fire.   But if his affections fall upon this
Phrygian youth, he takes him to heaven to be with
him and to pour his nectar for him ; and she [7] whose

---

[3] Ganymede. *Iliad*, xx. 234.

[4] The wife of Amphitryon, in whose semblance Zeus visited
her and begat Heracles.

[5] The daughter of Acrisius, visited by Zeus in the form of
a shower of gold.   Her father in anger put her and her baby
(Perseus) into a chest or ark and sent them adrift at sea ;
they finally arrived at the island of Seriphus.

[6] The daughter of Cadmus, who foolishly prayed that Zeus
might visit her as he visited Hera.   He came therefore with
fire and lightning, by which she was destroyed ; but her
offspring was saved, the god Dionysus.

[7] Hebe.

διάκονος τῆς τιμῆς ἐξέωσται· ἦν γάρ, οἶμαι,
γυνή."

37. Ὑπολαβὼν οὖν ἐγώ, "Καὶ μὴν οὐράνιον,"
ἔφην, "ἔοικε μᾶλλον εἶναι τὸ τῶν γυναικῶν
κάλλος, ὅσον μὴ ταχὺ φθείρεται· ἐγγὺς γὰρ τοῦ
θείου τὸ ἄφθαρτον. τὸ δὲ κινούμενον ἐν φθορᾷ
θνητὴν φύσιν μιμούμενον, οὐκ οὐράνιόν ἐστιν
2 ἀλλὰ πάνδημον. ἠράσθη μειρακίου Φρυγός,
ἀνήγαγεν εἰς οὐρανὸν τὸν Φρύγα· τὸ δὲ κάλλος
τῶν γυναικῶν αὐτὸν τὸν Δία κατήγαγεν ἐξ
οὐρανοῦ. διὰ γυναῖκά ποτε Ζεὺς ἐμυκήσατο, διὰ
γυναῖκά ποτε Σάτυρον ὠρχήσατο, καὶ χρυσὸν
3 πεποίηκεν ἑαυτὸν ἄλλῃ γυναικί. οἰνοχοείτω μὲν
Γανυμήδης, μετὰ δὲ τῶν θεῶν Ἥρα [1] πινέτω, ἵνα
ἔχῃ μειράκιον διάκονον γυνή. ἐλεῶ δὲ αὐτοῦ καὶ
τὴν ἁρπαγήν· ὄρνις ἐπ' αὐτὸν κατέβη ὠμηστής, ὁ
δὲ ἀνάρπαστος γενόμενος ὑβρίζεται, καὶ ἔοικεν
ἐσταυρωμένῳ· [2] καὶ τὸ θέαμά ἐστιν αἴσχιστον,

[1] Göttling's emendation Ἥβη is most attractive, considering
the mention of her at the end of the last chapter: and yet
Ἥρα may still be right, Hera and Ganymede being considered
as the two rivals for the affections of Zeus: as Ganymede
poured out the wine for the heavenly feast, Hera, the queen of
the gods, might properly be said to have him as her butler.

[2] A brilliant emendation by Jacobs for the MSS. τυραν-
νουμένῳ. Morel suggests τυπανουμένῳ, Lumb κεραυνουμένῳ.

---

[1] Europa. cf. Book I. chap. i.
[2] Antiope. See Ovid, Metamorphoses, vi. 110. The whole
passage (a continuation of that quoted upon Book I. chap. i.
fin.) is here instructive :

She portray'd also there
Asterie struggling with an Erne which did away her bear.
And over Leda she had made a Swan his wings to splay.
She added also how by Jove in shape of Satyr gay

was formerly this duty, was deprived of the honour—
she, I fancy, was a woman."

37. Here I interrupted him. "Woman's beauty,"
said I, "seems the more heavenly of the two,
because it does not rapidly fade; the incorruptible
is not far from the divine, while that which is ever
changing and corruptible (in which it resembles our
poor mortality) is not heavenly but vulgar. Zeus was
fired with a Phrygian stripling; true, and he took his
Phrygian up to heaven; but women's beauty actually
brought Zeus down from heaven. For a woman Zeus
once lowed as a bull[1]; for a woman[2] he danced the
satyr's dance; for another woman he changed himself
into gold. Let Ganymede pour out the wine; but
let Hera drink with the gods, so that a woman may
have a youth to serve her. I am even sorry for him
in the manner of his assumption—a savage bird
swooped down upon him, and when he had been
seized by it he was placed in an ignominious position,
looking like one crucified.[3] Can one imagine a
viler sight than a youth hanging from a beast's

The fair Antiope with a pair of children was besped:
And how he took Amphitryo's shape when in Alcmena's bed
He gat the worthy Hercules: and how he also came
To Danae like a Shower of Gold, to Aegine like a Flame,
A Shepherd to Mnemosyne, and like a Serpent sly
To Proserpine.

[3] This is very different from Tennyson's beautiful portrait
in *The Palace of Art*:

> Or else flush'd Ganymede, his rosy thigh
>   Half-buried in the Eagle's down,
> Sole as a flying star shot through the sky
>   Over the pillar'd town.

But pictures also exist in which Ganymede is represented as
in the extremity of anguish and terror, such as one ascribed
to Rembrandt in the Dresden Gallery.

4 μειράκιον ἐξ ὀνύχων κρεμάμενον. Σεμέλην δὲ εἰς
οὐρανὸν ἀνήγαγεν οὐκ ὄρνις ὠμηστής, ἀλλὰ πῦρ.
καὶ μὴ θαυμάσῃς, εἰ διὰ πυρός τις ἀναβαίνει εἰς
οὐρανόν· οὕτως ἀνέβη Ἡρακλῆς. εἰ δὲ Δανάης
τὴν λάρνακα γελᾷς, πῶς τὸν Περσέα σιωπᾷς;
Ἀλκμήνῃ δὲ τοῦτο μόνον δῶρον ἀρκεῖ, ὅτι δι᾽
5 αὐτὴν ἔκλεψεν ὁ Ζεὺς τρεῖς ὅλους ἡλίους. εἰ δὲ
δεῖ μεθέντα τὰς μυθολογίας αὐτὴν εἰπεῖν τὴν ἐν
τοῖς ἔργοις ἡδονήν, ἐγὼ μὲν πρωτόπειρος ὢν εἰς
γυναῖκας, ὅσον ὁμιλῆσαι ταῖς εἰς Ἀφροδίτην
πωλουμέναις· ἄλλος γὰρ ἂν ἴσως εἰπεῖν τι καὶ
πλέον ἔχοι μεμνημένος· εἰρήσεται δέ μοι, κἂν
6 μετρίως ἔχω πείρας. γυναικὶ [1] μὲν οὖν ὑγρὸν μὲν
τὸ σῶμα ἐν ταῖς συμπλοκαῖς, μαλθακὰ δὲ τὰ
χείλη πρὸς τὰ φιλήματα. καὶ διὰ τοῦτο μὲν ἔχει
τὸ σῶμα ἐν τοῖς ἀγκαλίσμασιν, ἐν δὲ ταῖς
σαρξὶν [2] ὅλως ἐνηρμοσμένον, καὶ ὁ συγγιγνόμενος
7 περιβάλλεται ἡδονῇ. [3] ἐγγίζει δὲ τοῖς χείλεσιν
ὥσπερ σφραγῖδας τὰ φιλήματα, φιλεῖ δὲ τέχνῃ
καὶ σκευάζει τὸ φίλημα γλυκύτερον. οὐ γὰρ
μόνον ἐθέλει φιλεῖν τοῖς χείλεσιν, ἀλλὰ καὶ
τοῖς ὀδοῦσι συμβάλλεται καὶ περὶ τὸ τοῦ φιλοῦν-
τος στόμα βόσκεται καὶ δάκνει τὰ φιλήματα·
ἔχει δέ τινα καὶ μαστὸς ἐπαφώμενος ἰδίαν
8 ἡδονήν. ἐν δὲ τῇ τῆς Ἀφροδίτης ἀκμῇ
οἰστρεῖ μὲν ὑφ᾽ ἡδονῆς, περικέχηνε δὲ φιλοῦσα
καὶ μαίνεται· αἱ δὲ γλῶτται τοῦτον τὸν χρόνον
φοιτῶσιν ἀλλήλαις εἰς ὁμιλίαν καὶ ὡς δύνανται

---

[1] γυναικὶ Hercher: γυναιξί.   [2] συνερξέσιν Naber.
[3] ὁσυγγιγνόμενος a, β: F has πως ἐγκειμένον: πᾶσα ἐγκει-
μένη Jacobs: πως ἐγκειμένῳ Hercher. The reading περιβάλλεται ἡδονῇ is Vilborg's for περιβάλλει τὴν ἡδονήν.

talons? But Semele was caught up to heaven—
not by a savage bird, but by fire. It is no matter
for surprise that any should ascend to heaven
through fire: that is how Hercules ascended. You
laugh at Danae's ark, but you say nothing of Perseus.[1]
As for Alcmene, this compliment alone is enough
for her, that for her sake Zeus stole away three
whole courses of the sun.[2] But it is time to leave
mythology and to talk of the delights of reality,
though here I am but a novice; I have only had the
society of women whose favourite haunt is Love;
perhaps somebody else who has been more deeply
initiated might have more to say; but I will make
an attempt, though my experience has been so small.
In a woman then, during lovers' embraces her body
is supple and her lips are soft for kisses. Therefore
both in her embraces and in her tender flesh she
holds the man's body completely fitted in; and he
who is within is surrounded with pleasure. Her
kisses also she presses closely like seals lip to lip,
and she makes love with artistic skill and purposely
renders each kiss all the sweeter. For she not only
likes to kiss with her lips but meets you with her
teeth too and forages round the kisser's mouth; and
her kisses bite you. Her breasts too when you feel
them have a sort of pleasure all their own. Again,
in the orgasm of Love she is maddened with pleasure,
opens her mouth wide as she kisses, and goes crazy.
The lovers' tongues too, while this goes on, haunt
each other's company, and they too struggle to kiss

---

[1] Danae's hero son—a worthy scion of Zeus.
[2] " Tam libens cum ea concubuit, ut unum diem usurparet,
duas noctes congeminaret, ita ut Alcumena tam longam
noctem admiraretur."—Hyginus, *Fabulae*, 29.

βιάζονται κἀκεῖναι φιλεῖν· σὺ δὲ μείζονα ποιεῖς
9 τὴν ἡδονήν, ἀνοίγων τὰ φιλήματα. πρὸς δὲ τὸ
τέρμα αὐτὸ τῆς 'Αφροδίτης ἡ γυνὴ γινομένη
πέφυκεν ἀσθμαίνειν ὑπὸ καυματώδους ἡδονῆς, τὸ
δὲ ἄσθμα σὺν πνεύματι ἐρωτικῷ μέχρι τῶν τοῦ
στόματος χειλέων ἀναθορὸν συντυγχάνει πλανω-
μένῳ τῷ φιλήματι καὶ ζητοῦντι καταβῆναι κάτω·
10 ἀναστρέφον τε σὺν τῷ ἄσθματι τὸ φίλημα καὶ
μιχθὲν ἕπεται καὶ βάλλει τὴν καρδίαν· ἡ δὲ
ταραχθεῖσα τῷ φιλήματι πάλλεται. εἰ δὲ μὴ
τοῖς σπλάγχνοις ἦν δεδεμένη, ἠκολούθησεν ἂν καὶ
ἀνείλκυσεν αὐτὴν ἄνω τοῖς φιλήμασι. παίδων δὲ
φιλήματα μὲν ἀπαίδευτα, περιπλοκαὶ δὲ ἀμαθεῖς,
'Αφροδίτη δὲ ἀργή, ἡδονῆς δὲ οὐδέν."

38. Καὶ ὁ Μενέλαος, " 'Αλλὰ σύ μοι δοκεῖς,"
ἔφη, " μὴ πρωτόπειρος ἀλλὰ γέρων εἰς 'Αφροδίτην τυγχάνειν· τοσαύτας ἡμῶν κατέχεας γυναικῶν περιεργίας. ἐν μέρει δὲ καὶ τὰ τῶν παίδων
2 ἀντάκουσον. γυναικὶ μὲν γὰρ πάντα ἐπίπλαστα
καὶ τὰ ῥήματα καὶ τὰ σχήματα· κἂν εἶναι δόξῃ
καλή, τῶν ἀλειμμάτων ἡ πολυπράγμων μηχανή.
καί ἐστιν αὐτῆς τὸ κάλλος ἢ μύρων, ἢ τριχῶν
βαφῆς, ἢ καὶ φυκωμάτων·[1] ἂν δὲ τῶν πολλῶν
τούτων γυμνώσῃς δόλων, ἔοικε κολοιῷ γεγυμνω-
3 μένῳ τῶν τοῦ μύθου πτερῶν. τὸ δὲ κάλλος τὸ
παιδικὸν οὐκ ἀρδεύεται μύρων ὀσφραῖς, οὐδὲ
δολεραῖς καὶ ἀλλοτρίαις ὀσμαῖς, πάσης δὲ γυναι-

so far as they can. *You* also make the pleasure
greater if you kiss with open mouth. At the end
itself of Love the woman pants—*that's* natural to her
—because of the burning heat of her pleasure. Her
gasps, rushing up with her amorous spirit to her
mouth and lips, meet the kiss that wanders around
and desires to go down. The kiss too turns back in
company with her gasping, and follows mingled with
it and strikes the heart which, profoundly moved by
the kiss, beats fast. Indeed, if the heart were not
bound fast in the flesh, it would follow the kisses and
draw itself upwards with them. On the other hand
the kisses of boys are untutored, their embraces
unskilled, their Love is lazy, and in them is no
pleasure at all."

38. Then Menelaus: "But, my dear sir," said he,
"you seem to me to be, in matters of love, no raw tiro
but a veteran. What a lot of feminine superfluities
you have swamped us with! Hear now in your turn
a counter-argument of facts about boys too. In a
woman, then, all that she says and all her actions too
are figments for the occasion. Does she look
beautiful? You have there nothing but the fussy
trickery of oily paint and perfume; her " beauty " is
that of unguents or hair-dye or †make ups†. If
you strip any woman of all these numerous deceptions,
she looks like a jackdaw stripped of its feathers as in
the story. But the beauty of boys—*that* does not
reek of wet unguents or deceptive scents that are
foreign to it; and the sweat of boys smells sweeter

---

¹ The MSS. φιλημάτων cannot be right: kisses are not a
kind of cosmetic or artificial means of producing beauty.
Jacobs proposed ἐντριμμάτων, which is too far from the text,
and I have, with all diffidence, written φυκωμάτων. Knox
would prefer φαρμάκων. There are other suggestions.

κῶν μυραλοιφίας ἥδιον ὄδωδεν ὁ τῶν παίδων
4 ἱδρώς. ἔξεστι δὲ αὐτῷ καὶ πρὸ τῆς ἐν Ἀφροδίτῃ
συμπλοκῆς καὶ ἐν παλαίστρᾳ συμπεσεῖν καὶ
φανερῶς περιχυθῆναι καὶ οὐκ ἔχουσιν αἰσχύνην
αἱ περιπλοκαί· καὶ οὐ μαλθάσσει τὰς ἐν Ἀφροδίτῃ περιπλοκὰς ὑγρότητι σαρκῶν, ἀλλ᾽ ἀντι-
τυπεῖ πρὸς ἄλληλα τὰ σώματα καὶ περὶ τῆς
5 ἡδονῆς ἀθλεῖ. τὰ δὲ φιλήματα σοφίαν μὲν
οὐκ ἔχει γυναικείαν, οὐδὲ μαγγανεύει τοῖς χείλεσι
σινάμωρον [1] ἀπάτην, ὡς δὲ οἶδε φιλεῖ, καὶ οὐκ
ἔστι τέχνης ἀλλὰ τῆς φύσεως τὰ φιλήματα.
αὕτη δὲ παιδὸς φιλήματος εἰκών· εἰ νέκταρ
ἐπήγνυτο καὶ χεῖλος ἐγίνετο, τοιαῦτα ἂν ἔσχες τὰ
φιλήματα. φιλῶν δὲ οὐκ ἂν ἔχοις κόρον, ἀλλ᾽
ὅσον ἐμφορῇ, διψῇς ἔτι φιλεῖν, καὶ οὐκ ἂν
ἀποσπάσειας τὸ στόμα, μέχρις ἂν ὑφ᾽ ἡδονῆς
ἐκφύγῃς τὰ φιλήτατα."

---

[1] An ingenious correction of Jacobs for the MSS. εἶναι
μωράν.

than all the greasy ointments used by women. More-over you can meet your boy, before any embrace-ments of love, in the wrestling school, and spread yourself round him in embraces which involve no shyness, and he doesn't make an over-soft affair of Love's entanglements through suppleness of the flesh; but instead the two bodies resist each other and have a contest where pleasure is the prize. As for boys' kisses—*they* lack the cleverness of women's and your boy does not perform with his lips a mis-chievous tomfool conjuring trick, but simply kisses as he knows how, and his kisses are not art's but nature's. The image of a boy's kiss is this:—suppose that nectar had congealed and formed a lip; *that's* the kind of kisses you would have had. You would never have too much of love; but, no matter how much you take in the kisses, you still thirst for love; and you would not want to withdraw your mouth until you were to shrink from further kisses through the mere pleasure of them.[1]

---

[1] Besides the similar discussion of this *dubbio amoroso* at the end of the *Amores* of pseudo-Lucian, referred to on p. 123, mention may also be made of a medieval example, the "Ganymede and Helen" (*Zeitschrift für Deutsches Alterthum*, xviii. p. 124), and, in Oriental literature, *Arabian Nights*, 419 *sqq.* The curious may find a full in-vestigation of our author's sources for this dialogue by Friedrich Wilhelm, in vol. lvii. of the *Rheinisches Museum*.

1. Τρίτην δὲ ἡμέραν πλεόντων ἡμῶν, ἐξ αἰθρίας πολλῆς αἰφνίδιον ἀχλὺς περιχεῖται καὶ τῆς ἡμέρας ἀπωλώλει τὸ φῶς· ἐγείρεται δὲ κάτωθεν ἄνεμος ἐκ τῆς θαλάσσης κατὰ πρόσωπον τῆς νηός, καὶ ὁ κυβερνήτης περιάγειν ἐκέλευσε τὴν κεραίαν.

2 καὶ σπουδῇ περιῆγον οἱ ναῦται, πῇ μὲν τὴν ὀθόνην ἐπὶ θάτερα συνάγοντες ἄνω τοῦ κέρως βίᾳ (τὸ γὰρ πνεῦμα σφοδρότερον ἐμπεσὸν ἀνθέλκειν οὐκ ἐπέτρεπε), πῇ δὲ πρὸς θάτερον μέρος, φυλάττοντες τοῦ πρόσθεν μέτρου καθ' ὃ συνέβαινεν οὔριον εἶναι τῇ περιαγωγῇ τὸ πνεῦμα

3 κλίνεται δὲ κοῖλον τοιχίσαν τὸ σκάφος καὶ ἐπὶ θάτερα μετεωρίζεται καὶ πάντη πρηνὲς ἦν, καὶ ἐδόκει τοῖς πολλοῖς ἡμῶν ἀεὶ περιτραπήσεσθαι καθάπαξ ἐμπίπτοντος τοῦ πνεύματος. μετεσκευαζόμεθα οὖν ἅπαντες εἰς τὰ μετέωρα τῆς νηός, ὅπως τὸ μὲν βαπτιζόμενον τῆς νηὸς ἀνακουφίσαιμεν, τὸ δὲ τῇ προσθήκῃ βιασάμενοι

4 κατὰ μικρὸν καθέλοιμεν εἰς τὸ ἀντίρροπον. πλέον δὲ ἠνύομεν οὐδέν· ἀνέφερε γὰρ ἡμᾶς μᾶλλον κορυφούμενον τὸ ἔδαφος τῆς νηὸς ἢ πρὸς ἡμῶν

5 κατεβιβάζετο. καὶ χρόνον μέν τινα διαταλαντουμένην οὕτω τὴν ναῦν τοῖς κύμασιν ἐπαλαίομεν εἰς τὸ ἀντίρροπον καθέλκειν·[1] αἰφνίδιον δὲ μετα-

---

[1] So Headlam for καθελεῖν, which β and F omit.

BOOK III

1. Oɴ the third day of our voyage, the perfect
calm we had hitherto experienced was suddenly
overcast by dark clouds and the daylight disappeared,
a wind blew upwards from the sea full in the ship's
face, and the helmsman bade the sailyard be slewed
round. The sailors hastened to effect this, bunching
up half the sail upon the yard by main force,
for the increasing violence of the gusts obstructed
their efforts; for the rest, they kept enough of the
full spread to make the wind help them to tack.
As a result of this, the ship lay on her side, one
bulwark raised upward into the air and the deck a
steep slope, so that most of us thought that she
must heel over when the gale next struck us.
We transferred ourselves therefore to that part of
the boat which was highest out of water, in
order to lighten that part which was down in
the sea, and so if possible, by our own added
weight depressing the former, to bring the whole
again to a level; but all was of no avail: the high
part of the deck, far from being weighed down by
our presence, merely lifted us higher still away from
the water. For some time we thus ineffectually
struggled to bring to an equilibrium the vessel thus
balanced on the waves: but the wind suddenly

βάλλεται τὸ πνεῦμα ἐπὶ θάτερα τῆς νηὸς καὶ
μικροῦ βαπτίζεται τὸ σκάφος, τοῦ μὲν τέως εἰς
κῦμα κλιθέντος, ἀναθορόντος ὀξείᾳ ῥοπῇ, θατέρου
δέ, ᾗ ᾐωρεῖτο, καταρραγέντος εἰς τὴν θάλασσαν.
6 κωκυτὸς οὖν αἴρεται μέγας ἐκ τῆς νηός, καὶ
μετοικία πάλιν καὶ δρόμος μετὰ βοῆς ἐπὶ τὰς
ἀρχαίας ἕδρας. καὶ τρίτον καὶ τέταρτον καὶ
πολλάκις τὸ αὐτὸ πάσχοντες κοινὴν ταύτην
εἴχομεν τῷ σκάφει τὴν πλάνην. πρὶν μὲν γὰρ
μετασκευάσασθαι τὸ πρῶτον, δίαυλος ἡμᾶς
διαλαμβάνει δεύτερος.

2. Σκευοφοροῦντες οὖν κατὰ τὴν ναῦν διὰ
πάσης ἡμέρας, δόλιχόν τινα τοῦτον δρόμον
μυρίον ἐπονοῦμεν, ἀεὶ τὸν θάνατον προσδοκῶντες.
2 καὶ ἦν, ὡς εἰκός, οὐ μακράν· περὶ γὰρ μεσημβρίαν δείλην ὁ μὲν ἥλιος τέλεον ἁρπάζεται,
ἑωρῶμεν δὲ ἑαυτοὺς ὡς ἐν σελήνῃ. πῦρ μὲν ἀπ᾽
αὐτῆς ἵπταται, μυκᾶται δὲ βροντὴν οὐρανὸς καὶ
τὸν ἀέρα γεμίζει βόμβος, ἀντεβόμβει δὲ κάτωθεν
τῶν κυμάτων ἡ στάσις, μεταξὺ δὲ οὐρανοῦ καὶ
3 θαλάσσης ἀνέμων ποικίλων ἐσύριζε ψόφος. καὶ
ὁ μὲν ἀὴρ εἶχε σάλπιγγος ἦχον· οἱ δὲ κάλοι περὶ
τὴν ὀθόνην πίπτουσιν, ἀντιπαταγοῦντες δὲ ἐτετρί-
γεσαν, ἐφόβει δὲ καὶ τὰ ξύλα τῆς νηὸς ῥηγνύ-
μενα, μὴ κατὰ μικρὸν ἀνοιχθείη τὸ σκάφος τῶν
γόμφων ἀποσπωμένων· γέρρα δὲ περὶ πᾶσαν
4 τὴν ναῦν ἐκεκάλυπτο. καὶ γὰρ ὄμβρος ἐπέκλυζε
πολύς, ἡμεῖς δὲ τὰ γέρρα ὑποδύντες ὥσπερ εἰς
ἄντρον ἐμένομεν, παραδόντες ἑαυτοὺς τῇ τύχῃ,

shifted to the other side so that the ship was almost sent under water, and instantly that part of the boat which had been down in the waves was now violently thrown up, and the part formerly raised on high was crushed down into the waters. Then arose a great wailing from the ship, and all changed their station, running, with shouts and cries, to the position in which they had been before they moved; and the same thing happening a third and a fourth, nay, many times, we thus imitated the motion of the ship; and even before we had finished one transmigration, the necessity for a second and contrary one was upon us.

2. The whole day long then we carried our baggage up and down the ship, running, as it were, a long-distance race a thousand times, with the expectation of death ever before our eyes. Nor did it seem far off, for about mid-day or a little after the sun totally disappeared, and we could see one another no better than by moonlight. Lightning flashed from the sky, the heaven bellowed with thunder so that the whole air rang with the din; this was answered from below by the turmoil of the waves, and between sky and sea whistled the noise of contending winds. In this manner the air seemed to be turned into one vast trumpet; the ropes beat against the sail, creaking as they crossed one another, and there was every reason to fear for the broken planks of the ship that the rivets would no longer keep together and that the whole would fall asunder. The wicker bulwarks were actually under water the whole ship round. For much rain fell too, washing over the decks, so we crept under the wattlings as if into a cave, and there

5 ῥίψαντες τὰς ἐλπίδας. τρικυμίαι δὲ πολλαὶ καὶ
πάντοθεν, αἱ μὲν κατὰ πρόσωπον, αἱ δὲ κατ᾽
οὐρὰν τῆς νηὸς ἀλλήλαις ἀντέπιπτον. ἡ δὲ ναῦς
ἀεὶ πρὸς μὲν τὸ κυρτούμενον τῆς θαλάσσης
ἠγείρετο, πρὸς δὲ τὸ παράδρομον ἤδη καὶ χθα-
μαλὸν τοῦ κύματος κατεδύετο. ἐῴκει δὲ τῶν
6 κυμάτων τὰ μὲν ὄρεσι, τὰ δὲ χάσμασιν. ἦν δὲ
καὶ τὰ ἐγκάρσια τῶν κυμάτων ἑκατέρωθεν
φοβερώτερα· ἀναβαίνουσα μὲν γὰρ ἐπὶ τὴν
ναῦν ἡ θάλασσα διὰ τῶν γέρρων ἐκυλίετο καὶ
7 ἐκάλυπτε πᾶν τὸ σκάφος. τὸ γὰρ κῦμα αἰρόμε-
νον ὑψοῦ, ψαῦον αὐτῶν τῶν νεφῶν, πόρρωθεν
μὲν πρὸς ἀντιπρόσωπον ἐφαίνετο τῷ σκάφει
μέγεθος οἷον[1]. . . . προσιὸν δὲ βλέπων, κατα-
8 ποθήσεσθαι τὴν ναῦν προσεδόκησας. ἦν οὖν
ἀνέμων μάχη καὶ κυμάτων· ἡμεῖς δὲ οὐκ ἠδυνά-
μεθα κατὰ χώραν μένειν ὑπὸ τοῦ τῆς νηὸς
σεισμοῦ. συμμιγὴς δὲ πάντων ἐγίνετο βοή·
ἐρρόχθει τὸ κῦμα, ἐπάφλαζε τὸ πνεῦμα, ὀλολυγ-
μὸς γυναικῶν, ἀλαλαγμὸς ἀνδρῶν, κελευσμὸς
ναυτῶν, πάντα θρήνων καὶ κωκυτῶν ἀνάμεστα.
9 καὶ ὁ κυβερνήτης ἐκέλευε ῥίπτειν τὸν φόρτον·
διάκρισις δὲ οὐκ ἦν ἀργύρου καὶ χρυσοῦ πρὸς
ἄλλο τι τῶν εὐτελῶν, ἀλλὰ πάνθ᾽ ὁμοίως ἠκοντί-
ζομεν ἔξω τῆς νηός· πολλοὶ δὲ καὶ τῶν ἐμπόρων,
αὐτοὶ τῶν οἰκείων λαμβάνοντες ἐν οἷς εἶχον
τὰς ἐλπίδας, ἐώθουν ἐπειγόμενοι. καὶ ἦν ἤδη
ἡ ναῦς τῶν ἐπίπλων γυμνή· ὁ δὲ χειμὼν οὐκ
ἐσπένδετο.

[1] The word to which the size of the billow is compared
seems to be lost. Jacobs suggests that it may have been
ὄρος: a word which could easily be omitted by haplography
owing to its similarity with the first syllable of προσιόν.

we waited, trusting to luck but giving up all hope.
Great waves came from every quarter; some from the
bows, some dashed against one another at the ship's
stern. The vessel rose first as the wave heaved
beneath it, and then sank deep as it retired and
sank low down; the billows were now like mount-
ains, now like valleys. More terrifying still were
those which struck us athwart from either side.
For the water rose up, rolled over the bulwarks,
and deluged the whole vessel; even from a distance
the wave could be seen lifting its head on high so
as almost to touch the clouds, and threatening the
ship, as large as [a mountain]; and when one saw it
as it approached nearer, one would think that it
would swallow it up altogether. It was a fight
between wind and water: we could never keep still
in one spot owing to the shocks imparted to
the vessel. A confused noise of all kinds arose
—roaring of waves, whistling of wind, shrieking
of women, shouting of men, the calling of
the sailors' orders; all was full of wailing and
lamentation. Then the helmsman ordered the
jettison of the cargo. No difference was made
between gold and silver and the cheapest stuff, but
we hurled all alike from the ship's sides; many of
the merchants themselves seized their goods, on
which all their hopes were centred, and hastened
to pitch them overboard. Now the ship was
stripped of all its contents; but the storm was still
unabated.

3. Τέλος ὁ κυβερνήτης ἀπειπὼν ῥίπτει μὲν τὰ πηδάλια ἐκ τῶν χειρῶν, ἀφίησι δὲ τὸ σκάφος τῇ θαλάσσῃ καὶ εὐτρεπίζει ἤδη τὴν ἐφολκίδα καὶ τοῖς ναύταις ἐμβαίνειν κελεύσας, τῆς ἀποβάθρας 2 ἦρχεν· οἱ δὲ εὐθὺς κατὰ πόδας ἐξήλλοντο. ἔνθα δὴ καὶ τὰ δεινὰ ἦν καὶ ἦν μάχη χειροποίητος. οἱ μὲν γὰρ ἐπιβάντες ἤδη τὸν κάλων ἔκοπτον ὃς συνέδει τὴν ἐφολκίδα τῷ σκάφει· τῶν δὲ πλωτήρων ἕκαστος ἔσπευδε μεταπηδᾶν ἔνθα καὶ τὸν κυβερνήτην ἑωράκεσαν ἐφέλκοντα τὸν κάλων· οἱ δὲ ἐκ τῆς ἐφολκίδος μεταβαίνειν οὐκ ἐπέτρεπον. 3 εἶχον δὲ καὶ πελέκεις καὶ μαχαίρας, καὶ πατάξειν ἠπείλουν, εἴ τις ἐπιβήσεται· πολλοὶ δὲ ἐκ τῆς νηὸς ὁπλισάμενοι τὸ δυνατόν, ὁ μὲν κώπης παλαιᾶς τρύφος ἀράμενος, ὁ δὲ τῶν τῆς νηὸς σελμάτων, ἠμύνετο. θάλασσα γὰρ εἶχε νόμον 4 τὴν βίαν καὶ ἦν ναυμαχίας καινὸς τρόπος. οἱ μὲν γὰρ ἐκ τῆς ἐφολκίδος δέει τοῦ καταδῦναι τῷ τῶν ἐπεμβαινόντων ὄχλῳ πελέκεσι καὶ μαχαίραις τοὺς ἐξαλλομένους ἔπαιον· οἱ δὲ σκυτάλαις καὶ κώπαις ἅμα τῷ πηδήματι τὰς πληγὰς κατε- 5 φέροντο·[1] οἱ δὲ καὶ ἄκρου ψαύοντες τοῦ σκάφους ἐξωλίσθανον· ἔνιοι δὲ καὶ ἐπιβαίνοντες τοῖς ἐπὶ τῆς ἐφολκίδος ἤδη διεπάλαιον· φιλίας γὰρ ἢ αἰδοῦς οὐκ ἔτι θεσμὸς ἦν, ἀλλὰ τὸ οἰκεῖον ἕκαστος σκοπῶν ἀσφαλές, τὸ πρὸς τοὺς ἑτέρους εὔγνωμον οὐκ ἐλογίζετο. οὕτως οἱ μεγάλοι κίνδυνοι καὶ τοὺς τῆς φιλίας λύουσι νόμους.

[1] Cobet reads κατέφερον: to him is also due the change of ἐξωλίσθανον from ἐξωλίσθαινον.

3. At length the helmsman threw up his task. He dropped the steering oars from his hands and left the ship to the mercy of the sea ; he then had the jolly-boat got ready, and bidding the sailors follow him, was the first to descend the ladder and enter her. They jumped in close after him, and then was confusion worse confounded and a hand-to-hand fight ensued. They who were already in the boat began to cut the rope which held her to to the ship, while all the passengers made preparations to jump where they saw the helmsman holding on to the rope ; the boat's crew objected to this, and, being armed with axes and swords, threatened to attack any who leaped in ; many, on the other hand, of those still on the ship armed themselves as best they might, one picking up a piece of an old oar, another taking a fragment of one of the ship's benches, and so began to defend themselves. At sea might is right, and there now followed a novel kind of sea-fight ; those already in the jolly-boat, fearing she would be swamped by the number of those desiring to enter her, struck at them as they jumped with their axes and swords, while the passengers returned the blows as they jumped with planks and oars. Some of them merely touched the edge of the boat and slipped into the sea ; some effected their entry and were now struggling with the crew already there. Every law of friendship and pity [1] disappeared, and each man, regarding only his own safety, utterly disregarded all feelings of kindliness towards his neighbours. Great dangers do away with all bonds, even the most dear.

---

[1] αἰδώς, Latin *pietas*. The dutiful affection felt by children to their parents, or between relations generally ; or the respect due from a younger to an older man.

4. Ἔνθα δή τις ἀπὸ τῆς νηὸς νεανίσκος
εὔρωστος λαμβάνεται τοῦ κάλω καὶ ἐφέλκεται
τὴν ἐφολκίδα, καὶ ἦν ἐγγὺς ἤδη τοῦ σκάφους·
ηὐτρεπίζετο δὲ ἕκαστος, ὡς, εἰ πελάσειε, πηδήσων
2 ἐς αὐτήν. καὶ δύο μὲν ἢ τρεῖς ηὐτύχησαν οὐκ
ἀναιμωτί, πολλοὶ δὲ ἀποπηδᾶν πειρώμενοι ἐξεκυ-
λίσθησαν τῆς νηὸς κατὰ τῆς θαλάσσης. ταχὺ
γὰρ τὴν ἐφολκίδα ἀπολύσαντες οἱ ναῦται, πελέκει
κόψαντες τὸν κάλων, τὸν πλοῦν εἶχον ἔνθα
αὐτοὺς ἦγε τὸ πνεῦμα· οἱ δὲ ἐπὶ τῆς νηὸς ἐπει-
3 ρῶντο [1] καταδῦναι τὴν ἐφολκίδα. τὸ δὲ σκάφος
ἐκυβίστα περὶ τοῖς κύμασιν ὀρχούμενον, λανθάνει
δὲ προσενεχθὲν ὑφάλῳ πέτρᾳ καὶ ῥήγνυται πᾶν.
ἀπωσθείσης δὲ τῆς νηὸς ὁ ἱστὸς ἐπὶ θάτερα
πεσὼν τὸ μέν τι κατέκλασε, τὸ δέ τι κατέδυσεν
4 αὐτῆς. ὁπόσοι μὲν οὖν παραχρῆμα τῆς ἅλμης
πιόντες κατεσχέθησαν, οὗτοι μετριωτέραν ὡς ἐν
κακοῖς ἔσχον τὴν συμφοράν, οὐκ ἐνδιατρίψαντες
τῷ τοῦ θανάτου φόβῳ. ὁ γὰρ ἐν θαλάσσῃ
5 θάνατος βραδὺς προαναιρεῖ πρὸ τοῦ παθεῖν· ὁ
γὰρ ὀφθαλμὸς πελάγους γεμισθεὶς ἀόριστον
ἐκτείνει τὸν φόβον, ὡς καὶ διὰ τούτων θάνατον
δυστυχεῖν πλείονα· ὅσον γὰρ τῆς θαλάσσης τὸ
μέγεθος, τοσοῦτος καὶ ὁ τοῦ θανάτου φόβος.
6 ἔνιοι δὲ κολυμβᾶν πειρώμενοι, προσραγέντες ὑπὸ
τοῦ κύματος τῇ πέτρᾳ διεφθείροντο· πολλοὶ δὲ
καὶ ξύλοις ἀπερρωγόσι συμπεσόντες ἐπείροντο
δίκην ἰχθύων· οἱ δὲ καὶ ἡμιθνῆτες ἐνήχοντο.

5. Ἐπεὶ οὖν τὸ πλοῖον διελύθη, δαίμων τις
ἀγαθὸς περιέσωσεν ἡμῖν τῆς πρῴρας μέρος, ἔνθα
περικαθίσαντες ἐγώ τε καὶ ἡ Λευκίππη κατὰ

[1] ἐπηρῶντο V and E, as Orelli had suggested.

4. At that point one of the passengers, a sturdy young man, seized the cable and drew up the jolly-boat until it was quite close to the ship's side, and everybody made ready to jump into it directly it should be close enough. Two or three were successful, though they effected their object not unscathed, and many made the attempt to leap only to fall from the ship into the sea ; for the crew cut the rope with an axe, cast the boat off, and set sail wherever the wind was driving them, while the passengers did their best to sink it. Our vessel, after much plunging and tossing upon the waves, drove unexpectedly on to a rock hidden under water, and was utterly broken in pieces ; as she slipped off the rock the mast fell on one side, breaking up part of her and carrying the rest beneath the water. Those who instantly perished, their lungs full of salt water, experienced the most tolerable fate in our general evil plight, because they were not kept in suspense by the fear of death. For a slow death at sea lets a man suffer all its pangs before the actual moment of dissolution. The eye, satiated with the waste expanse of the waters, prolongs the agony of fear, so that perishing in these circumstances is far more wretched than in any other : the terror of such a death is great in proportion to the size of the ocean. Some tried to swim, and were killed by being dashed by the waves on to the rock : many others fell upon broken pieces of wood and were spitted upon them like fishes ; others were swimming about already half dead.

5. The ship thus broken up, some favouring deity kept whole for us that part of the prow on which Leucippe and I were seated astride, and we floated as

ῥοῦν ἐφερόμεθα τῆς θαλάσσης· ὁ δὲ Μενέλαος
καὶ ὁ Σάτυρος σὺν ἄλλοις τῶν πλωτήρων ἐπιτυ-
χόντες τοῦ ἱστοῦ καὶ ἐπιπεσόντες ἐνήχοντο.
2 πλησίον δὲ καὶ τὸν Κλεινίαν ἐωρῶμεν περινηχό-
μενον τῇ κεραίᾳ καὶ ταύτην ἠκούσαμεν αὐτοῦ
τὴν βοήν, "῎Εχου τοῦ ξύλου, Κλειτοφῶν·" ἅμα
δὲ λέγοντα κῦμα ἐπεκάλυπτε κατόπιν· καὶ ἡμεῖς
3 ἐκωκύσαμεν. κατὰ ταὐτὸ καὶ ἡμῖν ἐπεφέρετο
τὸ¹ κῦμα· ἀλλὰ τύχῃ τινὶ πλησίον γενόμενον
ἡμῶν κάτωθεν παρατρέχει, ὥστε μόνον ὑψού-
μενον μετέωρον τὸ ξύλον κατὰ τὸν αὐχένα τοῦ
4 κύματος καὶ τὸν Κλεινίαν ἰδεῖν αὖθις. ἀνοιμώξας
οὖν, " Ἐλέησον," ἔφην, "δέσποτα Πόσειδον,
καὶ σπεῖσαι πρὸς τὰ τῆς ναυαγίας σου λείψανα.
πολλοὺς ἤδη τῷ φόβῳ θανάτους ὑπεμείναμεν· εἰ
δὲ ἡμᾶς ἀποκτεῖναι θέλεις, μὴ διαστήσῃς ἡμῶν
τὴν τελευτήν· ἓν ἡμᾶς κῦμα καλυψάτω. εἰ δὲ
καὶ θηρίων ἡμᾶς βορὰν πέπρωται γενέσθαι, εἷς
ἡμᾶς ἰχθὺς ἀναλωσάτω, μία γαστὴρ χωρησάτω,
5 ἵνα καὶ ἐν ἰχθύσι κοινῇ ταφῶμεν." μετὰ μικρὸν
δὲ τῆς εὐχῆς τὸ πολὺ τοῦ πνεύματος περιεπέ-
παυτο, τὸ δὲ ἄγριον ἐστόρεστο τοῦ κύματος· μεστὴ
δὲ ἦν ἡ θάλασσα νεκρῶν σωμάτων. τοὺς μὲν οὖν
ἀμφὶ τὸν Μενέλαον θᾶττον προσάγει τῇ γῇ τὸ
κῦμα· καὶ ἦν ταῦτα τῆς Αἰγύπτου τὰ παράλια·
κατεῖχον δὲ τότε λῃσταὶ πᾶσαν τὴν ἐκεῖ χώραν·
6 ἡμεῖς δὲ περὶ δείλην ἑσπέραν τύχῃ τινὶ τῷ
Πηλουσίῳ προσίσχομεν καὶ ἄσμενοι γῆς λαβό-
μενοι τοὺς θεοὺς ἀνευφημοῦμεν· εἶτα ὠλοφυρό-

¹ An insertion due to Jacobs. The word is particularly
likely to have dropped out owing to its being identical with
the last syllable of the preceding word.

the sea carried us. Menelaus and Satyrus, together with some others of the passengers, happened upon the mast, and swam, using it as a support. Close by we saw Clinias swimming with his hands on the yard-arm, and we heard him cry ; " Keep hold of your piece of wood, Clitophon." As he spoke, a wave overwhelmed him from behind. We cried out at the sight, and at the same time the wave bore down upon us too; but by good fortune when it came near it only heaved us up and passed by beneath us, and we once again saw the spar lifted up on high on the crest of the billow, with Clinias upon it. " Have pity," I wailed and cried, " Lord Poseidon, and make a truce with us, the remnants of your shipwreck. We have already undergone many deaths through fear; if you mean to kill us, do not make our deaths separate; let one wave overwhelm us. If our fate is to become food for sea-beasts, let one fish destroy us and one maw swallow us, that even in the fish we may have a common tomb." It was but a short time after I had uttered this prayer that the wind dropped and the savagery of the waves subsided ; the sea was full of the corpses of the dead; and the tide rapidly brought Menelaus and his servants to land. (This land was the coast of Egypt, then wholly infested by robbers.) We, towards evening, chanced to come ashore at Pelusium ; in joy at our safe arrival we first gave thanks to the

μεθα τὸν Κλεινίαν καὶ τὸν Σάτυρον, νομίζοντες
αὐτοὺς ἀπολωλέναι.

6. Ἔστι δὲ ἐν τῷ Πηλουσίῳ Διὸς ἱερὸν ἄγαλμα
Κασίου· τὸ δὲ ἄγαλμα νεανίσκος, Ἀπόλλωνι
μᾶλλον ἐοικώς· οὕτω γὰρ ἡλικίας εἶχε· προβέβληται δὲ τὴν χεῖρα καὶ ἔχει ῥοιὰν ἐπ᾽ αὐτῇ·
2 τῆς δὲ ῥοιᾶς ὁ λόγος μυστικός. προσευξάμενοι
δὴ τῷ θεῷ καὶ περὶ τοῦ Κλεινίου καὶ τοῦ Σατύρου σύμβολον ἐξαιτήσαντες (καὶ γὰρ ἔλεγον
μαντικὸν εἶναι τὸν θεὸν) περιήειμεν τὸν νεών.
3 κατὰ δὲ τὸν ὀπισθόδομον ὁρῶμεν εἰκόνα διπλῆν,
καὶ ὁ γραφεὺς ἐνεγέγραπτο·[1] Εὐάνθης μὲν ὁ
γραφεύς, ἡ δὲ εἰκὼν Ἀνδρομέδα, καὶ Προμηθεύς,
δεσμῶται μὲν ἄμφω (διὰ τοῦτο γὰρ αὐτούς,
οἶμαι, εἰς ἓν συνήγαγεν ὁ ζωγράφος) ἀδελφαὶ
4 δὲ καὶ τὴν ἄλλην τύχην αἱ γραφαί. πέτραι μὲν
ἀμφοῖν τὸ δεσμωτήριον, θῆρες δὲ κατ᾽ ἀμφοῖν
οἱ δήμιοι, τῷ μὲν ἐξ ἀέρος, τῇ δὲ ἐκ θαλάσσης·
ἐπίκουροι δὲ αὐτοῖς Ἀργεῖοι δύο συγγενεῖς, τῷ
μὲν Ἡρακλῆς, τῇ δὲ Περσεύς· ὁ μὲν τοξεύων
τὸν ὄρνιν τοῦ Διός, ὁ δὲ ἐπὶ τὸ κῆτος τοῦ Ποσειδῶ-
νος ἀθλῶν. ἀλλ᾽ ὁ μὲν ἵδρυται τοξαζόμενος ἐν γῇ,
ὁ δὲ ἐξ ἀέρος κρέμαται τῷ πτερῷ.

7. Ὀρώρυκται μὲν οὖν εἰς τὸ μέτρον τῆς κόρης
ἡ πέτρα· θέλει δὲ τὸ ὄρυγμα λέγειν ὅτι μὴ
τις αὐτὸ πεποίηκε χείρ, ἀλλ᾽ ἔστιν αὐτόχθον·[2]

[1] So Salmasius: ἐγγέγραπτο Vilborg: ἐνέγραπτο.
[2] Most MSS. give αὐτόχθων· one αὐτόχθον which Hercher
adopted, and rightly expelled the ἡ γραφή which followed it.

---

[1] A mountain out in the desert towards the Red Sea.
[2] It is a pity that our author did not explain what this
mystery was. Some have supposed that the large number of

gods and then bewailed Clinias and Satyrus, thinking that they had both perished.

6. At Pelusium is the holy statue of Zeus of Mount Casius [1] ; in it the god is represented so young that he seems more like Apollo. He has one hand stretched out and holds a pomegranate in it, and this pomegranate has a mystical signification.[2] After adoring the deity and asking for an oracle about Clinias and Satyrus (we were told that the god was willing to give prophetic answers) we went round the temple, and near the postern door we saw a double picture, signed by the artist; it had been painted by Evanthes, and represented first Andromeda, then Prometheus, both of them in chains—and this was the reason, I suppose, why the artist had associated the two subjects. In other respects too the two works were akin. In both, the chains were attached to a rock, and in both, beasts were the torturers [3]—his from the air, and hers from the sea ; their deliverers were Argives of the same [4] family, his Hercules and hers Perseus; the one shooting Zeus's eagle and the other contending with the sea-beast of Posidon. The former was represented aiming with his arrow on land, the latter suspended in the air on his wings.

7. In the picture of Andromeda, there was a hollow in the rock of about the size of the maiden, but it was of a sort that would indicate that it was

seeds in a pomegranate typify the fertility and productivity of nature.

[3] Lit. "executioners."

[4] Perseus was the great-grandfather of Hercules. The former's son, Electryon, was the father of the latter's mother, Alcmena.

ἐτράχυνε γὰρ τοῦ λίθου τὸν κόλπον ὁ γραφεύς,
2 ὡς ἔτεκεν αὐτὸν ἡ γῆ. ἡ δὲ ἐνίδρυται τῇ σκέπῃ·
καὶ ἔοικε τὸ θέαμα, εἰ μὲν εἰς τὸ κάλλος ἀπίδοις,
ἀγάλματι καινῷ, εἰ δὲ εἰς τὰ δεσμὰ καὶ τὸ
κῆτος, αὐτοσχεδίῳ τάφῳ. ἐπὶ δὲ τῶν προσώ-
3 πων αὐτῆς κάλλος κεκέρασται καὶ δέος· ἐν μὲν
γὰρ ταῖς παρειαῖς τὸ δέος κάθηται, ἐκ δὲ τῶν
ὀφθαλμῶν ἀνθεῖ τὸ κάλλος. ἀλλ' οὔτε τῶν
παρειῶν τὸ ὠχρὸν τέλεον ἀφοίνικτον ἦν, ἠρέμα
δὲ τῷ ἐρεύθει βέβαπται· οὔτε τὸ τῶν ὀφθαλμῶν
ἄνθος ἐστὶν ἀμέριμνον, ἀλλ' ἔοικε τοῖς ἄρτι
μαραινομένοις ἴοις· οὕτως αὐτὴν ἐκόσμησεν ὁ
4 ζωγράφος εὐμόρφῳ φόβῳ. τὰς δὲ χεῖρας εἰς τὴν
πέτραν ἐξεπέτασεν, ἄγχει δὲ ἄνω δεσμὸς ἑκατέ-
οαν συνάπτων τῇ πέτρᾳ· οἱ καρποὶ[1] δὲ ὥσπερ
ἀμπέλου βότρυες κρέμανται. καὶ αἱ μὲν ὠλέναι
τῆς κόρης ἄκρατον ἔχουσαι τὸ λευκὸν εἰς τὸ
πελιδνὸν μετέβαλον καὶ ἐοίκασιν ἀποθνήσκειν οἱ
5 δάκτυλοι. δέδεται μὲν οὖν οὕτω τὸν θάνατον
ἐκδεχομένη· ἔστηκε δὲ νυμφικῶς ἐστολισμένη,
ὥσπερ Ἀϊδωνεῖ[2] νύμφη κεκοσμημένη. ποδήρης ὁ
χιτών, λευκὸς ὁ χιτών· τὸ ὕφασμα λεπτόν,
ἀραχνίων ἐοικὸς πλοκῇ, οὐ κατὰ τὴν τῶν προ-
βατείων τριχῶν, ἀλλὰ κατὰ τὴν τῶν ἐρίων τῶν
πτηνῶν, οἷον ἀπὸ δένδρων ἕλκουσαι νήματα
6 γυναῖκες ὑφαίνουσιν Ἰνδαί. τὸ δὲ κῆτος ἀντιπρόσωπον τῆς κόρης κάτωθεν ἀναβαῖνον ἀνοίγει
τὴν θάλασσαν· καὶ τὸ μὲν πολὺ τοῦ σώματος
περιβέβληται τῷ κύματι, μόνῃ δὲ τῇ κεφαλῇ
τὴν θάλασσαν ἀποδύεται. ὑπὸ δὲ τὴν ἅλμην

---

[1] A play on the double meaning of καρπός, " wrist " and
" fruit." [2] So β as Jacobs had suggested for Ἀδώνιδι (WF).

not artificially made, but natural, for the painter had
made its surface rough, just as nature had fashioned
it.   She rested within its embrace, and while, if one
gazed upon her beauty, one would compare her to a
newly carven statue, anybody seeing the chains and
the approaching beast would think the rock a hastily
contrived tomb.   Upon her face was a mixture of
beauty and fear ; fear sat upon her cheeks, and
beauty shone from her eyes.   Even so, the pallor
of her cheeks was not utterly without colour,
but there was a gentle flush upon them ; nor was
the flower of beauty in her eyes without care, but
was rather to be compared to violets that have just
begun to fade.   The painter had depicted her with
the terror that did but enhance her charms.   Her
hands were stretched out against the wall of rock,
a bond holding both of them fast to it above her
head, so that her fingers hung like bunches of fruit
from a vine ; the arms of spotless white verging
towards the livid, and the fingers white with the
pallor of death.   Thus was she bound, waiting for her
fate, adorned for a bridal as one who was to be the
bride of the King of Death.   She wore a tunic reaching to her feet, and white, of the thinnest woof like a
spider's web ; not like that woven of the hair of sheep
but of the produce of that winged insect which
Indian women spin into thread from trees and weave
into silk.[1]   The beast is just coming up and opening
the surface of the water, facing the maiden ; most of
its body was still enveloped in the waves, its head
alone being above the surface, but beneath the foam

---

[1] Such seems to be the meaning of this obscure sentence.
The silk-worm, from the fact that it afterwards changes into
a moth, is represented as itself winged.

τοῦ κύματος ἡ τῶν νώτων ἐγέγραπτο φαινομένη
σκιά, τὰ τῶν φολίδων ἐπάρματα, τὰ τῶν αὐχένων
κυρτώματα, ἡ λοφιὰ τῶν ἀκανθῶν, οἱ τῆς οὐρᾶς
7 ἐλιγμοί. γένυς πολλὴ καὶ μακρά· ἀνέῳκτο δὲ
πᾶσα μέχρι τῆς τῶν ὤμων συμβολῆς, καὶ εὐθὺς
ἡ γαστήρ. μεταξὺ δὲ τοῦ κήτους καὶ τῆς κόρης
ὁ Περσεὺς ἐγέγραπτο καταβαίνων ἐξ ἀέρος·
καταβαίνει δὲ ἐπὶ τὸ θηρίον γυμνὸς τὸ πᾶν·
χλαμὺς ἀμφὶ τοῖς ὤμοις μόνον καὶ πέδιλον περὶ
τὼ πόδε πλησίον τοῦ πτεροῦ· πῖλος δὲ αὐτοῦ
τὴν κεφαλὴν καλύπτει· ὁ πῖλος δὲ ὑπηνίττετο
τὴν Ἄϊδος κυνέην. τῇ λαιᾷ τὴν τῆς Γοργοῦς
κεφαλὴν κρατεῖ καὶ προβέβληται δίκην ἀσπίδος·
8 ἡ δὲ ἐστὶ φοβερὰ καὶ ἐν τοῖς χρώμασι· τοὺς
ὀφθαλμοὺς ἐξεπέτασεν, ἔφριξε τὰς τρίχας τῶν
κροτάφων, ἤγειρε τοὺς δράκοντας· οὕτως ἀπειλεῖ
κἂν τῇ γραφῇ. ὅπλον μὲν τοῦτο τῇ λαιᾷ τῷ
Περσεῖ· ὥπλισται δὲ καὶ τὴν δεξιὰν διφυεῖ
9 σιδήρῳ εἰς δρέπανον καὶ ξίφος ἐσχισμένῳ. ἄρχεται μὲν γὰρ ἡ κώπη κάτωθεν ἀμφοῖν ἐκ μιᾶς,
καὶ ἐστιν ἐφ᾽ ἡμίσει τοῦ σιδήρου ξίφος, ἐντεῦθεν
δὲ ἀπορραγέν, τὸ μὲν ὀξύνεται, τὸ δὲ ἐπικάμ-
πτεται. καὶ τὸ μὲν ἀπωξυσμένον μένει ξίφος, ὡς
ἤρξατο, τὸ δὲ καμπτόμενον δρέπανον γίνεται, ἵνα
μιᾷ πληγῇ τὸ μὲν ἐρείδῃ τὴν σφαγήν, τὸ δὲ κρατῇ
τὴν τομήν. τὸ μὲν τῆς Ἀνδρομέδας δρᾶμα τοῦτο.

8. Ἑξῆς δὲ τὸ τοῦ Προμηθέως ἐγεγόνει. δέδεται
μὲν ὁ Προμηθεὺς σιδήρῳ καὶ πέτρᾳ, ὥπλισται δὲ
Ἡρακλῆς τόξῳ καὶ δόρατι. ὄρνις ἐς τὴν τοῦ

---

[1] The monster seems to be drawn from an exaggerated and
more terrific crocodile. Compare the description in Bk. IV.
ch. xix.

the outline of its back was represented as apparent,
as well as its knotted scales, its arched neck, its
pointed prickles, and its twisting tail. Its mouth
was wide and deep, and gaped open to where its neck
joined its shoulders, and straightway there is the belly.[1]
Painted between the beast and the maiden was
Perseus descending from the air; he was advancing to
attack the monster, quite naked except for his mantle
thrown about his shoulders, his winged sandals upon
his feet, and a cap on his head, which signified Pluto's
helmet.[2] In his left hand he bore the Gorgon's
head and held it before him like a shield; it was
frightful, even in the artist's representation, with
its staring, protruding eyes, its bristling hair about
the temples, its waving snakes; even as painted it
seemed to threaten evil. That was the armament of
Perseus's left hand, in his right he held an iron
weapon of double shape, something between a sickle
and a sword; it began below as one, but half
way up it split; half was pointed, and that half
remained a sword, as it began; the other half was
curved, thus becoming like a sickle, so that in a
single blow one might with one portion kill by
piercing and with the other by cutting.[3] So much
for the episode of Andromeda.

8. Next to it was that of Prometheus. Rock and
iron form his bonds, and Hercules is armed with
bow and spear. The bird was feasting upon his

[2] The "cap of darkness," which made the wearer invisible.
It was a gift from the Cyclopes to Pluto at the same time
that they forged Zeus his thunderbolts.

[3] The description of the weapon is not easy to understand,
but it was presumably not unlike a mediaeval halberd.
Perseus is traditionally represented with a *falcatus ensis*, a
ferrum curvo hamo instructum; cp. Ovid, *Met.* iv. 720, 727.

Προμηθέως γαστέρα τρυφᾷ· ἕστηκε γὰρ αὐτὴν
2 ἀνοίγων, ἤδη μὲν οὖν¹ ἀνεῳγμένην· ἀλλὰ τὸ ῥάμ-
φος ἐς τὸ ὄρυγμα καθεῖται,² καὶ ἔοικεν ἐπορύττειν
τὸ τραῦμα καὶ ζητεῖν τὸ ἧπαρ· τὸ δὲ ἐκφαίνεται
τοσοῦτον, ὅσον ἀνέῳξεν ὁ γραφεὺς τὸ διόρυγμα
τοῦ τραύματος· ἐρείδει δὲ τῷ μηρῷ τῷ τοῦ Προμη-
3 θέως τὰς τῶν ὀνύχων ἀκμάς. ὁ δὲ ἀλγῶν πάντῃ
συνέσταλται καὶ τὴν πλευρὰν συνέσπασται καὶ
τὸν μηρὸν ἐγείρει καθ' αὑτοῦ· εἰς γὰρ τὸ ἧπαρ
συνάγει τὸν ὄρνιν· ὁ δὲ ἕτερος αὐτῷ τοῖν ποδοῖν
τὸν σπασμὸν ὄρθιον ἀντιτείνει κάτω καὶ εἰς
4 τοὺς δακτύλους ἀποξύνεται. τὸ δὲ ἄλλο σχῆμα
δείκνυσι τὸν πόνον· κεκύρτωται τὰς ὀφρῦς, συνέσταλται τὸ χεῖλος, φαίνει τοὺς ὀδόντας· ἠλέησας
5 ἂν ὡς ἀλγοῦσαν τὴν γραφήν. ἀναφέρει δὲ
λυπούμενον Ἡρακλῆς· ἕστηκε γὰρ τοξεύων τοῦ
Προμηθέως τὸν δήμιον· ἐνήρμοσται τῷ τόξῳ
βέλος· τῇ λαιᾷ προβέβληται τὸ κέρας ὠθῶν·
ἐπὶ μαζὸν ἕλκει τὴν δεξιάν, ἕλκων τὸ νεῦρον·
6 κεκύρτωται κατόπιν τὸν ἀγκῶνα. πάντα οὖν
ὁμοῦ πτύσσεται, τὸ τόξον, τὸ νεῦρον, τὸ βέλος,
ἡ δεξιά. συνάγεται μὲν ὑπὸ τοῦ νεύρου τὸ
τόξον, διπλοῦται δὲ ὑπὸ τῆς χειρὸς τὸ νεῦρον,
7 κλίνεται δὲ ἐπὶ μαζὸν ἡ χείρ. ὁ δὲ Προμηθεὺς
μεστός ἐστιν ἐλπίδος ἅμα καὶ φόβου· πῆ μὲν
γὰρ εἰς τὸ ἕλκος, πῆ δὲ εἰς τὸν Ἡρακλέα
βλέπει, καὶ θέλει μὲν αὐτὸν ὅλοις τοῖς ὀφθαλμοῖς ἰδεῖν, ἕλκει δὲ τὸ ἥμισυ τοῦ βλέμματος ὁ
πόνος.

¹ οὖν is not in the MSS., but, as Headlam suggests, must
be supplied.
² Hercher's emendation for MSS. κεῖται.

belly, and standing just ripping it open, or rather
had already ripped it open, its beak dipped
into the wound, and it seemed to be digging about
in it, looking for the sufferer's liver, which could
just be seen, by the depth to which the painter had
depicted the wound as being open, and it was
pressing the sharp points of its claws into Prometheus'
thigh. He, in agony, is all drawn up, twisting himself on to his side, and lifts up his thigh; but to his
own harm, for this does but bring the bird nearer to
his liver. The other leg is stretched out straight
right down to his feet, and the tension of it can be
seen actually into the toes. His torture is shewn by
the rest of the representation of him; his eyebrows
are arched, his lips drawn up, his teeth shewn; you
cannot help feeling pity even for what you know is
only a picture. Then Hercules is coming to bring
help to him in his distress; he stands just about to
shoot at his torturer; the arrow is fitted to the bow;
with his left hand he is drawing it to its full extent,
while he holds his right hand back against his breast,
and as he draws the string his arm, viewed from
behind, appears somewhat foreshortened. All seem
in motion at once—the bow, the string, the arrow,
the hand which holds it; the bow is bent by means
of the string, the string is made to run double by
means of the hand, the hand is at rest upon the
hero's breast. The countenance of Prometheus has
a mixed look of hope and fear; he looks partly at his
wound, partly at Hercules; he would like to fix all
his gaze upon the hero, but his agony robs him of
half of the sight of him.[1]

[1] Because the other half is distracted by the wound, from
which he cannot wholly turn his eyes away.

9. Ἐνδιατρίψαντες οὖν ἡμερῶν δύο καὶ ἀναλα-
βόντες ἑαυτοὺς ἐκ τῶν κακῶν, ναῦν Αἰγυπτίαν
μισθωσάμενοι (εἴχομεν δὲ ὀλίγον χρυσίον, ὅπερ
ἐτύχομεν ἐζωσμένοι) διὰ τοῦ Νείλου πλοῦν ἐπ'
Ἀλεξάνδρειαν ἐποιούμεθα, μάλιστα μὲν ἐκεῖ
διεγνωκότες ποιήσασθαι τὴν διατριβὴν καὶ
νομίζοντες ταύτῃ τάχα τοὺς φίλους εὑρήσειν
2 προσενεχθέντας. ἐπεὶ δὲ ἐγενόμεθα κατά τινα
πόλιν, ἐξαίφνης βοῆς ἀκούομεν πολλῆς. καὶ ὁ
ναύτης εἰπών, "Ὁ βουκόλος," μεταστρέφει τὴν
ναῦν, ὡς ἐπαναπλεύσων εἰς τοὐπίσω· καὶ ἅμα
πλήρης ἦν ἡ γῆ φοβερῶν καὶ ἀγρίων ἀνθρώπων·
μεγάλοι μὲν πάντες, μέλανες δὲ τὴν χροιάν, οὐ
κατὰ τὴν τῶν Ἰνδῶν τὴν ἄκρατον, ἀλλ' οἷος ἂν
γένοιτο νόθος Αἰθίοψ, ψιλοὶ τὰς κεφαλάς, λεπτοὶ
τοὺς πόδας, τὸ σῶμα παχεῖς· ἐβαρβάριζον δὲ
3 πάντες. καὶ ὁ κυβερνήτης εἰπών, "Ἀπολώ-
λαμεν," ἔστησε τὴν ναῦν, ὁ γὰρ ποταμὸς ταύτῃ
στενώτατος, καὶ ἐπεμβάντες τῶν λῃστῶν
τέσσαρες, πάντα μὲν τὰ ἐν τῇ νηὶ λαμβάνουσι,
καὶ τὸ χρυσίον ἡμῶν ἀποφέρουσιν, ἡμᾶς δὲ
δήσαντες καὶ κατακλείσαντες εἴς τι δωμάτιον,
ἀπηλλάττοντο, φύλακας ἡμῖν καταλιπόντες, ὡς
εἰς τὴν ἐπιοῦσαν ἄξοντες ἡμᾶς ὡς τὸν βασιλέα·
τούτῳ γὰρ ἐκάλουν τῷ ὀνόματι τὸν λῃστὴν τὸν
μείζονα· καὶ ἦν ὁδὸς ἡμερῶν δύο, ὡς παρὰ τῶν
σὺν ἡμῖν ἑαλωκότων ἠκούσαμεν.

10. Ἐπεὶ οὖν νὺξ ἐγένετο καὶ ἐκείμεθα, ὡς
ἦμεν, δεδεμένοι καὶ ἐκάθευδον οἱ φρουροί, τότε,
ὡς ἐξὸν ἤδη, κλαίειν ἦρχον τὴν Λευκίππην· καὶ
δὴ λογισάμενος ὅσων αὐτῇ γέγονα κακῶν αἴτιος,
κωκύσας ἐν τῇ ψυχῇ βύθιον, τῷ δὲ νῷ κλέψας

9. Having waited therefore two days and some-what refreshed ourselves after our troubles, we hired an Egyptian boat (we had just a little money which we happened to have kept in our belts), and started by the Nile towards Alexandria; there we purposed to make some stay and thought it was just possible that we might find that some of our shipwrecked friends had arrived there. We had arrived at a certain town, when suddenly we heard a great shouting. "The herdsmen," cried the skipper, and tried to put the boat about and sail back; but already the place was full of terrifying savage men, all tall, dark-coloured (yet not absolutely black like an Indian, but more like a bastard Ethiopian), with shaven heads, small feet, and gross bodies: all spoke an outlandish jargon. "We are done for," cried the helmsman, and brought the boat to a standstill, for the river is there very narrow; and four of the robbers boarded her, took all that there was in her, and snatched our money from us; then tying us up they shut us into a little hut and went away, setting a guard over us, with the intention of taking us before their king the following day: "king" is the name they gave to the robber-chief, and it would be a journey of two days, as we learned from those who had been made prisoners along with us.

10. When the night had come on, and we lay, bound as we were, and our guards were asleep, I began, as indeed I might, to mourn Leucippe's fate, and, counting up how great were her woes of which I was the cause, to bewail them deep in my soul,

τοῦ κωκυτοῦ τὸν ψόφον, "῏Ω θεοὶ καὶ δαίμονες,"
ἔφην, " εἴπερ ἐστέ που καὶ ἀκούετε, τί τηλικοῦτον ἠδικήκαμεν, ὡς ἐν ὀλίγαις ἡμέραις το-
2 σούτῳ πλήθει βαπτισθῆναι κακῶν; νῦν δὲ καὶ
παραδεδώκατε ἡμᾶς λῃσταῖς Αἰγυπτίοις, ἵνα μηδὲ
ἐλέου τύχωμεν. λῃστὴν γὰρ ῞Ελληνα καὶ φωνὴ
κατέκλασε καὶ δέησις ἐμάλαξεν· ὁ γὰρ λόγος
πολλάκις τὸν ἔλεον προξενεῖ· τῷ γὰρ πονοῦντι
τῆς ψυχῆς ἡ γλῶττα πρὸς ἱκετηρίαν διακο-
νουμένη τῆς τῶν ἀκουόντων ψυχῆς ἡμεροῖ τὸ
3 θυμούμενον. νῦν δὲ ποία μὲν φωνῇ δεηθῶμεν;
τίνας δὲ ὅρκους προτείνωμεν; κἂν Σειρήνων τις
γένηται πιθανώτερος, ὁ ἀνδροφόνος οὐκ ἀκούει.
μόνοις ἱκετεύειν με δεῖ τοῖς νεύμασι καὶ τὴν
δέησιν δηλοῦν ταῖς χειρονομίαις. ὢ τῶν ἀτυχη-
4 μάτων· ἤδη τὸν θρῆνον ἐξορχήσομαι. τὰ μὲν
οὖν ἐμά, κἂν ὑπερβολὴν ἔχῃ συμφορᾶς, ἧττον
ἀλγῶ, τὰ σὰ δέ, Λευκίππη, ποίῳ στόματι
θρηνήσω; ποίοις ὄμμασι δακρύσω; ὢ πιστὴ μὲν
πρὸς ἀνάγκην ἔρωτος, χρηστὴ δὲ πρὸς ἐραστὴν
5 δυστυχοῦντα. ὡς καλά σου τῶν γάμων τὰ
κοσμήματα· θάλαμος μὲν τὸ δεσμωτήριον, εὐνὴ
δὲ ἡ γῆ, ὅρμοι δὲ καὶ ψέλια κάλοι καὶ βρόχος,
καί σοι νυμφαγωγὸς λῃστὴς παρακαθεύδει· ἀντὶ
6 δὲ ὑμεναίων τίς σοι τὸν θρῆνον ᾄδει. μάτην σοι,
ὦ θάλασσα, τὴν χάριν ὡμολογήσαμεν· μέμφομαί
σου τῇ φιλανθρωπίᾳ· χρηστοτέρα γέγονας πρὸς
οὓς ἀπέκτεινας, ἡμᾶς δὲ σώσασα μᾶλλον ἀπέκτεινας. ἐφθόνησας ἡμῖν ἀλῃστεύτοις ἀποθανεῖν."

while hiding inwardly the sound of my grief. " O all ye gods and guardian angels," said I, " if really ye exist and can hear me, what great wrong have we done to be plunged in such a sea of troubles in so short a space of time ? Now have you also delivered us over into the hands of Egyptian robbers, so that we have not even a chance of pity. A Greek buccaneer might be moved by the human voice, prayer might soften him : for speech is often the go-between of compassion ; the tongue, ministering to him that is in anguish of soul by helping him to express supplication, subdues the fury of the listener's mind. But, as things are, in what language are we to make our prayers ? What oaths can we pour out ? I might be more persuasive than the Sirens, but the murderer would not listen to me ; I can only make my supplications by signs and explain my prayers for mercy by the gestures of my hands. Alack for my mishaps ; already, in dumb show, I shall begin my funeral dirge. For my own woes, intolerable as they are, I care less ; but yours, Leucippe—how can my lips deplore them, my eyes weep for them ? Faithful you were when love's stress came upon you, gentle and good to your unhappy lover : and here are fine trappings for your wedding ! A prison is your bridal chamber, the earth your marriage bed, ropes and cords your necklaces and bracelets, a robber sleeps without as your bridesman, a dirge is your marriage-hymn. Ah, all in vain, O sea, did we give you thanks : now I blame your mercy ; you were kinder to those whom you destroyed, and you have destroyed us yet more grievously by keeping us alive ; you grudged us death save by a robber's hand."

11. Ταῦτα μὲν οὖν ἐθρήνουν ἡσυχῇ, κλαίειν δὲ οὐκ ἠδυνάμην· τοῦτο γὰρ ἴδιον τῶν ὀφθαλμῶν ἐν τοῖς μεγάλοις κακοῖς. ἐν μὲν γὰρ ταῖς μετρίαις συμφοραῖς ἀφθόνως τὰ δάκρυα καταρρεῖ καί ἐστι τοῖς πάσχουσιν εἰς τοὺς κολάζοντας ἱκετηρία, καὶ τοὺς ἀλγοῦντας, ὥσπερ ἀπ᾽ οἰδοῦντος τραύματος, ἐξεκένωσεν· ἐν δὲ τοῖς ὑπερβάλλουσι δεινοῖς φεύγει καὶ τὰ δάκρυα καὶ 2 προδίδωσι καὶ τοὺς ὀφθαλμούς. ἐντυχοῦσα γὰρ αὐτοῖς ἀναβαίνουσιν ἡ λύπη, ἴστησί τε τὴν ἀκμὴν καὶ μετοχετεύει καταφέρουσα σὺν αὐτῇ κάτω· τὰ δὲ ἐκτρεπόμενα τῆς ἐπὶ τοὺς ὀφθαλμοὺς ὁδοῦ εἰς τὴν ψυχὴν καταρρεῖ καὶ χαλεπώτερον αὐτῆς ποιεῖ τὸ τραῦμα. λέγω οὖν πρὸς τὴν Λευκίππην πάντα σιγῶσαν· " Τί σιγᾷς, φιλτάτη, καὶ οὐδέν μοι λαλεῖς; " "῞Οτι μοι," ἔφη, "πρὸ τῆς ψυχῆς, Κλειτοφῶν, τέθνηκεν ἡ φωνή."

12. Ταῦτα ἡμᾶς διαλεγομένους ἔλαθεν ἕως γενομένη· καί τις ἵππον ἐπελαύνων ἔρχεται, κόμην ἔχων πολλὴν καὶ ἀγρίαν· ἐκόμα δὲ καὶ ὁ ἵππος. γυμνὸς ἦν, ἄστρωτος[1] καὶ οὐκ ἔχων[2] φάλαρα· τοιοῦτοι γὰρ τοῖς λῃσταῖς εἰσιν οἱ ἵπποι. ἀπὸ δὲ τοῦ λῃστάρχου παρῆν καί, " Εἴ τις," ἔφη, "παρθένος ἐστὶν ἐν τοῖς εἰλημμένοις, ταύτην ἀπάγειν πρὸς τὸν θεόν, ἱερεῖον ἐσομένην καὶ 2 καθάρσιον τοῦ στρατοῦ." οἱ δὲ ἐπὶ τὴν Λευκίππην εὐθὺς τρέπονται· ἡ δὲ εἴχετό μου καὶ ἐξεκρέματο βοῶσα. τῶν δὲ λῃστῶν οἱ μὲν ἀπέσπων, οἱ δὲ ἔτυπτον· ἀπέσπων μὲν τὴν

---

[1] ἄστρωτος was deleted by Jacobs. F has ἵππος.
[2] εἶχε F.

11. Thus did I silently lament, but I could not weep—a peculiarity of the eyes in excessive sorrows. For when disasters are but moderate, tears flow freely, and serve for the sufferer as intercessions addressed to him that inflicts the suffering; they relieve an aching heart like the draining of a swollen wound. But when misfortunes are overwhelming, even tears fail and are traitors to the eyes; grief meets them as they well up, depresses their rise, conducts them away into other channels, and takes them back again below with itself, and then, diverted from the path of the eyes they flow back upon the soul and aggravate its wound. So I whispered to Leucippe, who lay speechless; " Why do you keep silence, my darling, and say no word to me? " " Because, Clitophon," said she, " my voice is dead, even before the departure of my soul."

12. Thus conversing, we did not notice the approach of dawn, when a man arrived on horseback, with long and wild hair; his horse too had a full mane and tail, and was bare, without coverings or trappings, after the manner of robbers' horses. He came from the robber chief, and " If there chance to be a virgin among the captives," said he, " I am to take [1] her away for the god, to be a propitiatory and cleansing sacrifice for the host." They at once rushed upon Leucippe, who clung to me and hung upon me screaming; the guards, some dragging her away and

---

[1] This sentence is, in the Greek, a mixture of the Oratio Recta and Obliqua. I have, for convenience, put all the English into the former mode of speech.

Λευκίππην, ἔτυπτον δὲ ἐμέ. ἀράμενοι οὖν αὐτὴν
μετέωρον ἀπάγουσιν· ἡμᾶς δὲ κατὰ σχολὴν ἦγον
δεδεμένους.

13. Καὶ ἐπεὶ δύο σταδίους τῆς κώμης προήλθομεν, ἀλαλαγμὸς ἀκούεται πολὺς καὶ σάλπιγγος
ἦχος καὶ ἐπιφαίνεται φάλαγξ στρατιωτική,
πάντες ὁπλῖται. οἱ δὲ λῃσταὶ κατιδόντες, ἡμᾶς
μέσους διαλαβόντες ἔμενον ἐπιόντας, ὡς αὐτοὺς
2 ἀμυνούμενοι. καὶ μετ᾽ οὐ πολὺ παρῆσαν πεντήκοντα τὸν ἀριθμόν,[1] οἱ μὲν ποδήρεις ἔχοντες τὰς
ἀσπίδας, οἱ δὲ πέλτας· οἱ δὲ λῃσταὶ πολλῷ
πλείους ὄντες, βώλους ἀπὸ τῆς γῆς λαμβάνοντες
3 τοὺς στρατιώτας ἔβαλλον. παντὸς δὲ βώλου
χαλεπώτερος βῶλος Αἰγύπτιος, βαρύς τε καὶ
τραχὺς καὶ ἀνώμαλος· τὸ δὲ ἀνώμαλόν ἐστιν αἱ[2]
αἰχμαὶ τῶν λίθων· ὥστε βληθεὶς διπλοῦν ποιεῖ
ἐν ταὐτῷ τὸ τραῦμα, καὶ οἴδημα, ὡς ἀπὸ λίθου,
4 καὶ τομάς, ὡς ἀπὸ βέλους. ἀλλὰ ταῖς γε ἀσπίσιν
ἐκδεχόμενοι τοὺς λίθους ὀλίγον τῶν βαλλόντων
ἐφρόντιζον. ἐπεὶ οὖν ἔκαμον οἱ λῃσταὶ βάλ-
λοντες, ἀνοίγουσι μὲν οἱ στρατιῶται τὴν φάλαγγα, ἐκθέουσι δὲ ἀπὸ τῶν ὅπλων ἄνδρες κούφως
ἐσταλμένοι, φέρων αἰχμὴν ἕκαστος καὶ ξίφος,
καὶ ἀκοντίζουσιν ἅμα, καὶ ἦν οὐδεὶς ὃς οὐκ
5 ἐπέτυχεν. εἶτα οἱ ὁπλῖται προσέρρεον· καὶ ἦν ἡ

---

[1] Here follows πάντες ὁπλῖται, removed by Hercher as an
echo of the same words three lines above.

[2] Inserted by Hercher: it might easily have dropped out
because followed by the same syllable at the beginning of
the next word.

some raining blows upon me,[1] took her up and carried her off on their shoulders ;[2] us they conveyed, bound, with no such speed.

13. We had progressed about a quarter of a mile from the village, when there came to our ears loud shouting and the sound of trumpets, and a regiment of soldiers appeared, all heavily armed. When the robbers saw them, they placed us in the middle of their band and waited for their advance, with the intention of resisting them. Soon they came on, about fifty in number, some with long shields and some with small targets ; the robbers, who were far their superior in numbers, picked up clods from the ground and began hurling them at the soldiers. The Egyptian clod is more effective for this purpose than any other, being heavy, jagged, and unlike others, in that the jagged points of it are stones, so that when it is thrown and strikes, it can inflict a double sort of wound—a swelling, as from the blow of a stone, and an actual cut, like that of an arrow. The soldiers, however, received the stony clods on their shields and seemed to make light of the casting of their adversaries ; and when the robbers began to tire by reason of their efforts in throwing, they opened their massed ranks, and from behind the shields out ran men lightly armed, each carrying a javelin and a sword, and as they hurled their javelins there was none that failed in his aim. Then the heavy-armed soldiers came in a flood ; the battle was

---

[1] A good example of the over-elaboration of antithesis, which is intolerable in English. Literally translated, the sentence is ; " Of the guards, some dragged and some beat : while they dragged Leucippe, they beat me."

[2] Or perhaps " on horseback."

μάχη στερρά, πληγαὶ δὲ παρ' ἀμφοτέρων καὶ
τραύματα καὶ σφαγαί. καὶ τὸ μὲν ἔμπειρον
παρὰ τοῖς στρατιώταις ἀνεπλήρου τοῦ πλήθους
τὸ ἐνδεές. ἡμεῖς δὲ ὅσοι τῶν αἰχμαλώτων ἦμεν,
ἐπιτηρήσαντες τὸ πονοῦν τῶν λῃστῶν μέρος, ἅμα
συνελθόντες διακόπτομέν τε αὐτῶν τὴν φάλαγγα
6 καὶ ἐπὶ τοὺς ἐναντίους ἐκτρέχομεν. οἱ δὲ στρατιῶται τὸ μὲν πρῶτον ἐπεχείρουν ἀναιρεῖν οὐκ εἰδότες,
ὡς δὲ εἶδον γυμνοὺς καὶ δεσμὰ ἔχοντας, ὑπονοή-
σαντες τὴν ἀλήθειαν, δέχονται τῶν ὅπλων εἴσω,
καὶ ἐπ' οὐρὰν παραπέμψαντες εἴων ἡσυχάζειν.
7 ἐν τούτῳ δὲ καὶ ἱππεῖς πλείους προσέρρεον· καὶ
ἐπεὶ πλησίον ἐγένοντο, κατὰ κέρας ἑκάτερον
ἐκτείναντες τὴν φάλαγγα περιΐππευον αὐτοὺς ἐν
κύκλῳ, καὶ ἐν τούτῳ συναγαγόντες αὐτοὺς εἰς
ὀλίγον κατεφόνευον. καὶ οἱ μὲν ἔκειντο τεθνη-
κότες, οἱ δὲ καὶ ἡμιθνῆτες ἐμάχοντο· τοὺς δὲ
λοιποὺς ἐζώγρησαν.

14. Ἦν δὲ περὶ δείλην ὁ καιρός· καὶ ὁ στρατηγὸς διαλαβὼν ἡμῶν ἕκαστον, ἐπυνθάνετο τίνες
εἴημεν καὶ πῶς ληφθείημεν· διηγεῖτο δὲ ἄλλος
ἄλλο τι, κἀγὼ τἀμὰ εἶπον. ἐπεὶ οὖν ἅπαντα
ἔμαθεν, ἐκέλευσεν ἀκολουθεῖν, αὐτὸς δὲ ὅπλα
δώσειν ὑπέσχετο. διεγνώκει γὰρ ἀναμείνας
στρατιὰν ἐπελθεῖν τῷ μεγάλῳ λῃστηρίῳ· ἐλέ-
2 γοντο δὲ ἀμφὶ τοὺς μυρίους εἶναι. ἐγὼ δὲ ἵππον
ᾔτουν, σφόδρα γὰρ ᾔδειν ἱππεύειν γεγυμνασ-
μένος. ὡς δέ τις παρῆν, περιάγων τὸν ἵππον
ἐπεδεικνύμην ἐν ῥυθμῷ τὰ τῶν πολεμούντων
σχήματα, ὥστε καὶ τὸν στρατηγὸν σφόδρα
ἐπαινέσαι. ποιεῖται δή με ἐκείνην τὴν ἡμέραν
ὁμοτράπεζον καὶ παρὰ τὸ δεῖπνον ἐπυνθάνετο

severe, with plenty of blows, wounds, and slaughter on both sides : the experience of the soldiers compensated for their inferiority in numbers. We prisoners, seeing that one flank of the robbers was weakening, made a concerted rush, broke through their line, and ran to join the enemy ; they at first did not realise the position, and were ready to slay us, but when they saw that we were unarmed and bound, they suspected the truth, received us within the protection of their lines, and sent us to the rear and allowed us to remain there quietly. Meanwhile a large body of horse charged up ; on their approach they spread out their wings and completely surrounded the robbers, and thus herding them together into a narrow space began to butcher them. Some were lying killed, some, half-dead, went on fighting ; the rest they took alive.

14. It was now late afternoon, and the general took each of us separately aside, enquiring of us who we were and how we had been captured ; each related his own story, and I mine. So when he had heard all, he bade us follow him, and said that he would give us arms. His intention was to wait for the rest of his forces and then attack the great robbers' stronghold ; there were said to be about ten thousand of them there. I asked for a horse, being well versed in the art of riding, and when one came, I rode him about and went through the various evolutions of cavalry fighting, so that the general was greatly pleased with me ; on that same day he made me a companion of his own table, and at dinner he asked me about my story, and, when he

3 τἀμὰ καὶ ἀκούων ἠλέει. συμπαθὴς δέ πως
εἰς ἔλεον ἄνθρωπος ἀκροατὴς ἀλλοτρίων κακῶν,
καὶ ὁ ἔλεος πολλάκις φιλίαν προξενεῖ· ἡ γὰρ
ψυχὴ μαλαχθεῖσα πρὸς τὴν ὧν ἤκουσε λύπην,
συνδιατεθεῖσα κατὰ μικρὸν τῇ τοῦ πάθους
ἀκροάσει τὸν οἶκτον εἰς φιλίαν καὶ τὴν λύπην
4 εἰς τὸν ἔλεον συλλέγει. οὕτως οὖν διέθηκα τὸν
στρατηγὸν ἐκ τῆς ἀκροάσεως ὡς καὶ αὐτὸν
δάκρυα προαγαγεῖν· πλέον δὲ ποιεῖν εἴχομεν
οὐδέν, τῆς Λευκίππης ὑπὸ τῶν λῃστῶν ἐχομένης.
ἔδωκε δέ μοι καὶ θεράποντα τὸν ἐπιμελησόμενον
Αἰγύπτιον.

15. Τῇ δὲ ὑστεραίᾳ πρὸς τὴν διάβασιν παρεσκευάζετο καὶ ἐπεχείρει τὴν διώρυχα χῶσαι, ἥτις
ἦν ἐμποδών. καὶ γὰρ ἑωρῶμεν τοὺς λῃστὰς μετὰ
πλείστης δυνάμεως ἐπὶ θάτερα τῆς διώρυχος
ἑστῶτας ἐν τοῖς ὅπλοις· βωμὸς δέ τις αὐτοῖς
αὐτοσχέδιος ἦν πηλοῦ πεποιημένος καὶ σορὸς
2 τοῦ βωμοῦ πλησίον. ἄγουσι δή τινες δύο τὴν
κόρην, ὀπίσω τὼ χεῖρε δεδεμένην· καὶ αὐτοὺς
μὲν οἵτινες ἦσαν οὐκ εἶδον, ἦσαν γὰρ ὡπλισμένοι,
3 τὴν δὲ κόρην Λευκίππην οὖσαν ἐγνώρισα. εἶτα
κατὰ τῆς κεφαλῆς σπονδὴν χέαντες,[1] περιάγουσι
τὸν βωμὸν κύκλῳ καὶ ἐπηύλει τις αὐτῇ, καὶ ὁ
ἱερεύς, ὡς εἰκός, ᾖδεν ᾠδὴν Αἰγυπτίαν· τὸ γὰρ
σχῆμα τοῦ στόματος, καὶ τῶν προσώπων τὸ
4 διειλκυσμένον ὑπέφαινεν ᾠδήν. εἶτα ἀπὸ συνθήματος πάντες ἀναχωροῦσι τοῦ βωμοῦ μακράν·
τῶν δὲ νεανίσκων ὁ ἕτερος ἀνακλίνας αὐτὴν

---

[1] MSS. περιχέαντες. The περι doubtless came from the
next word, and its removal was suggested by Hercher who
proposed also καταχέαντες. Lumb suggested πέριξ χέαντες.

heard it, was moved with pity. When a man hears
of another's misfortunes, he is inclined towards
pity, and pity is often the introduction to friendship ;
the heart is softened by grief for what it hears, and
gradually feeling the same emotions at the mournful
story converts its commiseration into friendship and
the grief into pity. So much did I move the general
by my recital that I forced him to weep. More we
could not do, Leucippe being in the robbers' power.
He also gave me an Egyptian servant to attend to
me.

15. On the next day he made preparations to
fill up and so cross over a wide trench which lay in
our way : for on the other side of it we could see the
robbers standing in great numbers and fully armed ;
they had an improvised altar made of mud and a
coffin near it. Then two of them led up the girl,
her hands tied behind her back. I could not see
who they were,[1] as they were in full armour, but I
recognized her as Leucippe. First they poured
libations over her head and led her round the altar
while, to the accompaniment of a pipe, a priest
chanted what seemed to be an Egyptian hymn ; this
at least was indicated by the movements of his lips
and the contortions of his features.[2] Then, at a
concerted sign, all retired to some distance from the
altar ; one of the two young attendants laid her down

[1] The reason for this will be made clear in chapters xxi
and xxii.
[2] I do not think that this necessarily means that the
Egyptian language was of so "crack-jaw" a kind that the
face of anybody singing it would be distorted beyond recognition ; but rather that the narrator was standing too far off
to hear the words, and could only guess as to their nature by
observing the facial movements of the singer.

ὑπτίαν, ἔδησεν ἐκ παττάλων ἐπὶ τῆς γῆς ἐρηρεισ-
μένων, οἷον ποιοῦσιν οἱ κοροπλάθοι τὸν Μαρσύαν
ἐκ τοῦ φυτοῦ δεδεμένον· εἶτα λαβὼν ξίφος
βάπτει κατὰ τῆς καρδίας καὶ διελκύσας τὸ ξίφος
5 εἰς τὴν κάτω γαστέρα, ῥήγνυσι· τὰ σπλάγχνα
δὲ εὐθὺς ἐξεπήδησεν, ἃ ταῖς χερσὶν ἐξελκύσαντες
ἐπιτιθέασι τῷ βωμῷ, καὶ ἐπεὶ ὠπτήθη, κατατε-
μόντες ἅπαντες εἰς μοίρας ἔφαγον. ταῦτα δὲ
ὁρῶντες οἱ μὲν στρατιῶται καὶ ὁ στρατηγὸς καθ᾽
ἓν τῶν πραττομένων ἀνεβόων καὶ τὰς ὄψεις
ἀπέστρεφον τῆς θέας, ἐγὼ δὲ ἐκ παραλόγου
6 καθήμενος ἐθεώρουν. τὸ δὲ ἦν ἔκπληξις· μέτρον
γὰρ οὐκ ἔχον τὸ κακὸν ἐνεβρόντησέ με. καὶ
τάχα ὁ τῆς Νιόβης μῦθος οὐκ ἦν ψευδής, ἀλλὰ
κἀκείνη τοιοῦτόν τι παθοῦσα ἐπὶ τῇ τῶν παίδων
ἀπωλείᾳ δόξαν παρέσχεν ἐκ τῆς ἀκινησίας ὡσεὶ
λίθος γενομένη. ἐπεὶ δὲ τέλος εἶχεν, ὥς γε
ᾤμην, τὸ ἔργον, τὸ σῶμα ἐνθέντες τῇ σορῷ κατα-
λείπουσι, πῶμα ἐπ᾽ αὐτῆς ἐπιθέντες, τὸν δὲ
βωμὸν καταστρέψαντες, φεύγουσιν ἀμεταστρεπτί.
οὕτω γὰρ αὐτοῖς ποιεῖν ἔτυχε μεμαντευμένος ὁ
ἱερεύς.

16. Ἑσπέρας δὲ γενομένης, ἡ διῶρυξ ἐκέχω-
στο πᾶσα· οἱ δὲ στρατιῶται διαβάντες αὐλίζονται
μικρὸν ἄνω τῆς διώρυχος καὶ περὶ δεῖπνον ἦσαν·
ὁ δὲ στρατηγὸς ἐπεχείρει με παρηγορεῖν ἀνιαρῶς
2 ἔχοντα. περὶ δὲ πρώτην νυκτὸς φυλακὴν πάντας ἐπιτηρήσας καθεύδοντας, πρόειμι,[1] τὸ ξίφος
3 ἔχων, ἐπικατασφάξων ἐμαυτὸν τῇ σορῷ. ἐπεὶ
δὲ πλησίον ἐγενόμην, ἀνατείνω τὸ ξίφος, " Λευκίππη," λέγων, " ἀθλία καὶ πάντων ἀνθρώπων

[1] So Hercher for πρόσειμι of the MSS.

on her back, and strapped her so by means of pegs
fixed in the ground, just as the statuaries represent
Marsyas fixed to the tree ; then he took a sword and
plunging it in about the region of the heart, drew
it down to the lower part of the belly, opening up
her body ; the bowels gushed out, and these they
drew forth in their hands and placed upon the altar ;
and when they were roasted, the whole body of them
cut them up into small pieces, divided them into
shares and ate them. The soldiers and the general
who were looking on cried out as each stage of the
deed was done and averted their eyes from the
sight. I sat gazing in my consternation, rooted to
the spot by the horror of the spectacle ; the im-
measurable calamity struck me, as by lightning,
motionless. Perhaps the story of Niobe was no
fiction ; she too, suffering some such woe as I, may,
at the destruction of her children, have become
so fixed and motionless, that she seemed to be made
of stone. When the business came, as I thought, to
an end, the two attendants placed her body in the
coffin, put the lid upon it, overturned the altar, and
hurried away without looking round ; such were the
instructions given to them by the priest in the
liturgy which he chanted.

16. Evening come, the whole trench was filled up,
the soldiers crossed it, pitched their camp a little
beyond it, and set about preparing their supper,
while the general tried to console me in my misery.
Nevertheless about the first watch of the night,
waiting until all were asleep, I took my sword and
went forth, intending to kill myself over the coffin.
When I had arrived at the spot, I held out the
sword, and, " Leucippe," said I, " wretched Leucippe,

δυστυχεστάτη, οὐ τὸν θάνατον ὀδύρομαί σου
μόνον, οὐδὲ ὅτι τέθνηκας ἐπὶ ξένης, οὐδὲ ὅτι σοι
γέγονεν ἐκ βίας σφαγή, ἀλλ᾽ ὅτι ταῦτα τῶν
σῶν ἀτυχημάτων παίγνια, ἀλλ᾽ ὅτι καθάρσιον
γέγονας ἀκαθάρτων σωμάτων καί σε ζῶσαν
ἀνέτεμον, οἴμοι, καὶ βλέπουσαν ὅλην τὴν ἀνατομήν, ἀλλ᾽ ὅτι σοῦ τῆς γαστρὸς τὰ μυστήρια
ἐμέρισαν καὶ τὴν ταφὴν κακοδαίμονι βωμῷ καὶ
4 σορῷ. καὶ τὸ μὲν σῶμα ταύτῃ κατατέθειται,
τὰ δὲ σπλάγχνα ποῦ; εἰ μὲν ἐδεδαπανήκει τὸ
πῦρ, ἥττων ἡ συμφορά· νῦν δὲ ἡ τῶν σπλάγχνων
σου ταφὴ λῃστῶν γέγονε τροφή. ὢ πονηρᾶς
ἐπὶ βωμοῦ δᾳδουχίας· ὢ τροφῶν καινὰ μυστήρια.
5 καὶ ἐπὶ τοιούτοις θύμασιν ἔβλεπον ἄνωθεν οἱ
θεοὶ καὶ οὐκ ἐσβέσθη τὸ πῦρ, ἀλλὰ μιαινόμενον
ἠνείχετο καὶ ἀνέφερε τοῖς θεοῖς τὴν κνίσσαν.
λάβε οὖν, Λευκίππη, τὰς πρεπούσας σοι χοὰς
παρ᾽ ἐμοῦ."

17. Ταῦτα εἰπὼν ἀνατείνω ἄνω τὸ ξίφος, ὡς
καθήσων ἐμαυτῷ κατὰ τῆς σφαγῆς· καὶ ὁρῶ
δύο τινὰς ἐξ ἐναντίας (σεληναία δὲ ἦν) σπουδῇ
θέοντας. ἐπέσχον οὖν λῃστὰς εἶναι δοκῶν,
ἂν ὑπ᾽ αὐτῶν ἀποθάνοιμι. ἐν τούτῳ δὲ ἐγγὺς
ἐγένοντο καὶ ἀναβοῶσιν ἄμφω· Μενέλαος δὲ ἦν
2 καὶ ὁ Σάτυρος. ἐγὼ δὲ ἄνδρας ἰδὼν ἐκ παραλόγου ζῶντας καὶ φίλους, οὔτε περιεπτυξάμην, οὔτε
ἐξεπλάγην ὑφ᾽ ἡδονῆς· τοσοῦτον ἡ λύπη με
3 τῆς συμφορᾶς ἐξεκώφωσε.[1] λαμβάνονται δὴ

---

[1] So Salmasius for ἐξεκούφισε. Hemsterhuis reads ἐξεκώ-
φησε.

---

[1] The appalling ill taste of this rhetorical outburst
prevents the English translation from being anything but

most ill-fated of mankind, it is not thy death alone
that I mourn, nor thy death in a strange land, nor
the violence of thy murder, but I grieve at the
mockeries added to thy woes—that thou didst
become a purifying sacrifice for the bodies of the
most impure of men; that, still alive, thou wast
ripped up and couldst see the torture with thine
own eyes; that division was made of the secret and
inner parts of thy belly, to receive its burial upon this
ill-starred altar and in this ill-starred coffin. Here
lies the shell of thy carcase, but its entrails where?
If the fire had consumed them, thy fate would have
been more tolerable; but now has the burial of them
been at the same time the robbers' sustenance.[1]
Accursed requiem at an accursed altar! Horrible
and new-fangled banquet! At a sacrifice such as
this the gods looked down—and yet the fire was
not quenched, but was allowed to pollute itself and
carry up to heaven the savour of such an offering!
Receive then, Leucippe, from me the only fitting
expiatory offering."

17. With these words I raised my sword on high,
intending to plunge it into my throat, when I saw
two figures—the moon was shining—running towards
me from in front. I therefore stayed my hand,
thinking them to be two of the robbers, in order
to meet my death at their hands. They approached
and shouted aloud; they were Menelaus and Satyrus!
When I saw that they were friends, and all unexpectedly still alive, I neither embraced them, nor
had I the astonishment of joy; my grief for my
misfortunes had made me dumb. They seized my

ludicrous. Compare chap. v. §4 of this book, where the
hero prays for burial, together with his beloved, in the belly
of the same whale.

μου τῆς δεξιᾶς καὶ ἐπεχείρουν ἀφαιρεῖσθαι τὸ
ξίφος· ἐγὼ δέ, "Πρὸς θεῶν," ἔφην, "μή μοι
φθονήσητε θανάτου καλοῦ, μᾶλλον δὲ φαρμάκου
τῶν κακῶν· οὐδὲ γὰρ ζῆν ἔτι δύναμαι, κἂν νῦν
με βιάσησθε, Λευκίππης οὕτως ἀνῃρημένης.
4 τοῦτο μὲν γὰρ ἀφαιρήσεσθέ μου τὸ ξίφος, τὸ δὲ
τῆς ἐμῆς λύπης ξίφος ἔνδον καταπέπηγε καὶ
τέμνει κατ' ὀλίγον. ἀθανάτῳ σφαγῇ ἀποθνήσκειν με βούλεσθε;" λέγει οὖν ὁ Μενέλαος,
"Ἀλλ' εἰ διὰ τοῦτο θέλεις ἀποθανεῖν, ὥρα σοι
τὸ ξίφος ἐπισχεῖν· Λευκίππη δέ σοι νῦν ἀναβιώ-
5 σεται." βλέψας οὖν πρὸς αὐτόν, "Ἔτι μου
καταγελᾷς," ἔφην, "ἐπὶ τηλικούτῳ κακῷ; εὖ
γε, Μενέλαε, Ξενίου μέμνησαι Διός." ὁ δὲ
κρούσας τὴν σορόν, "Ἐπεὶ τοίνυν ἀπιστεῖ
Κλειτοφῶν," ἔφη, "σύ μοι, Λευκίππη, μαρτύρη-
6 σον, εἰ ζῇς." ἅμα δὲ εἶπε, καὶ δίς που καὶ τρὶς
ἐπάταξε τὴν σορόν, καὶ κάτωθεν ἀκούω φωνῆς
πάνυ λεπτῆς. τρόμος οὖν εὐθὺς ἴσχει με καὶ
πρὸς τὸν Μενέλαον ἀπέβλεπον, μάγον εἶναι
7 δοκῶν. ὁ δὲ ἤνοιγεν ἅμα τὴν σορὸν καὶ ἡ
Λευκίππη κάτωθεν ἀνέβαινε, φοβερὸν θέαμα, ὦ
θεοί, καὶ φρικωδέστατον. ἀνέῳκτο μὲν ἡ γαστὴρ
αὐτῆς πᾶσα καὶ ἦν ἐντέρων κενή· ἐπιπεσοῦσα
δέ μοι περιπλέκεται καὶ συνέφυμεν καὶ ἄμφω
κατεπέσομεν.

18. Μόλις οὖν ἀναζωπυρήσας λέγω πρὸς τὸν
Μενέλαον, "Οὐκ ἐρεῖς μοι, τί ταῦτα; οὐχὶ
Λευκίππην ὁρῶ; ταύτην οὐ κρατῶ καὶ ἀκούω

hand and tried to wrest away the sword from me;
but "By all the gods," said I, "do not grudge
me a death that is honourable, nay, is a cure for
my woes; I cannot endure to live, even though you
now constrain me, after Leucippe has thus been
murdered. You can take away this sword of mine
from me, but the sword of my grief has already
stuck fast within me, and is little by little wounding
me to death. Do you prefer that I should die by a
death that never dies?" "If this is your reason for
killing yourself," said Menelaus, "you may indeed
withold your sword; your Leucippe will now at once
live once more." "Do you still mock me," said I,
looking steadily at him, "in this my great woe?
Bravo, Menelaus—you had regard to Zeus, the
god that protects the guest.[1]" But he knocked
upon the lid of the coffin, and said, "Since Clitophon
is still an unbeliever, do you, Leucippe, bear me
witness if you are yet alive." As he spoke, he
struck the coffin two or three times in different places,
and I heard a faint voice come from beneath; a
shuddering instantly took hold of me, and I looked
hard at Menelaus, thinking him a wizard; then he
opened the coffin, and out came Leucippe—a shocking
and horrible sight, God wot. Her belly seemed
ripped open and deprived of all its entrails, but
she fell upon my neck and embraced me; we clung
together and both fell to the ground.

18. When I had with difficulty come again to
myself, I said to Menelaus, "Tell me, what is this?
Is not this Leucippe whom I see, and hold, and hear

---

[1] Menelaus being an Egyptian, a Tyrian such as Clitophon
would be able in Egypt to invoke Ζεὺς Ξένιος in his dealings
with him.

λαλούσης; ἃ οὖν χθὲς ἐθεασάμην, τίνα ἦν; ἢ γὰρ
2 ἐκεῖνά ἐστιν ἢ ταῦτα ἐνύπνια. ἀλλ' ἰδοὺ καὶ
φίλημα ἀληθινὸν καὶ ζῶν, ὡς κἀκεῖνο τὸ τῆς
Λευκίππης γλυκύ." "'Ἀλλὰ νῦν," ὁ Μενέλαος
ἔφη, " καὶ τὰ σπλάγχνα ἀπολήψεται καὶ τὰ
στέρνα συμφύσεται καὶ ἄτρωτον ὄψει. ἀλλ'
ἐπικάλυψαί σου τὸ πρόσωπον· καλῶ γὰρ τὴν
3 Ἑκάτην ἐπὶ τὸ ἔργον." ἐγὼ δὲ πιστεύσας
ἐνεκαλυψάμην. ὁ δὲ ἄρχεται τερατεύεσθαι καὶ
λόγον τινὰ καταλέγειν· καὶ[1] ἅμα λέγων περιαιρεῖ
τὰ μαγγανεύματα τὰ ἐπὶ τῇ γαστρὶ τῆς Λευ-
4 κίππης καὶ ἀποκατέστησεν εἰς τὸ ἀρχαῖον. λέγει
δέ μοι, "'Ἀποκάλυψαι." κἀγὼ μόλις μὲν καὶ
φοβούμενος (ἀληθῶς γὰρ ᾤμην τὴν Ἑκάτην
παρεῖναι) ὅμως δ' οὖν ἀπέστησα τῶν ὀφθαλμῶν
τὰς χεῖρας καὶ ὁλόκληρον τὴν Λευκίππην ὁρῶ
5 ἔτι μᾶλλον οὖν ἐκπλαγεὶς ἐδεόμην τοῦ Μενελάου,
λέγων· "Ὦ φίλτατε Μενέλαε, εἰ διάκονός τις εἰ
θεῶν, δέομαί σου, ποῦ[2] γῆς εἰμὶ καὶ τίνα[3] ποτὲ
ταῦτα ὁρῶ;" καὶ ἡ Λευκίππη, "Παῦσαι," ἔφη,
"Μενέλαε, δεδιττόμενος αὐτόν· λέγε δὲ πῶς τοὺς
λῃστὰς ἠπάτησας."

19. Ὁ οὖν Μενέλαος λέγει· "Οἶδας, ὡς
Αἰγύπτιός εἰμι τὸ γένος· φθάνω γάρ σοι ταῦτα
εἰπὼν ἐπὶ τῆς νηός. ἦν οὖν μοι τὰ πλεῖστα τῶν
κτημάτων περὶ ταύτην τὴν κώμην καὶ οἱ ἄρχοντες
2 αὐτῆς γνώριμοι. ἐπεὶ οὖν τῇ ναυαγίᾳ περι-
επέσομεν, εἶτά με προσέρριψε τὸ κῦμα τοῖς τῆς
Αἰγύπτου παραλίοις, λαμβάνομαι μετὰ τοῦ

---

[1] καί, supplied by Hercher, seems to be necessary to join
this clause to the last.   [2] So Jacobs, for MSS. ποῖ.
[3] The correction of Cobet for MSS. τί.

her speaking? What was it then that I saw
yesterday? Either that was a dream, or else this is.
But certainly this is a real, living kiss, as was of old
Leucippe's sweet embrace." "Yes," said Menelaus,
" and now she will get her entrails back again, the
wound in her breast shall close, and you shall see
her whole and sound. But cover your face, I am
going to invoke the assistance of Hecate in the task."
I believed him and veiled myself, while he began to
conjure and to utter some incantation; and as he
spoke he removed the deceptive contrivances which
had been fitted to Leucippe's belly, and restored it
to its original condition. Then he said to me, " Un-
cover yourself"; with some hesitation and full of
fright (for I really thought that Hecate was there),
I at length removed my hands from my eyes and saw
Leucippe whole and restored. Still more greatly
astonished, I implored Menelaus, saying; " Menelaus,
my best of friends, if you are really a minister of the
gods, where am I and what is this I see?" Hereupon
Leucippe broke in. "Stop teasing and frightening
him, Menelaus," said she, "and tell him how you
cheated the robbers."

19. So Menelaus began his story. "You know,"
said he, "that I am an Egyptian by birth; I told
you so before, on the ship; most of my property is
near this village, and the chief people here are
acquaintances of mine. Well, when we had suffered
shipwreck, the tide brought me to the shores of
Egypt, and I, with Satyrus, was captured by the

Σατύρου πρὸς τῶν ταύτῃ[1] παραφυλαττόντων
λῃστῶν. ὡς δὲ ἄγομαι πρὸς τὸν λήσταρχον,
ταχύ με τῶν λῃστῶν τινες γνωρίσαντες λύουσί
μου τὰ δεσμά, θαρρεῖν τε ἐκέλευον καὶ συμπονεῖν
3 αὐτοῖς, ὡς ἂν οἰκεῖον. ἐξαιτοῦμαι δὴ καὶ τὸν
Σάτυρον ὡς ἐμόν. οἱ δέ, ' Ἀλλ' ὅπως,' ἔφασαν,
' ἐπιδείξεις ἡμῖν σεαυτὸν τολμηρὸν πρῶτον.'
κἂν τούτῳ χρησμὸν ἴσχουσι κόρην καταθῦσαι καὶ
καθῆραι τὸ λῃστήριον καὶ τοῦ μὲν ἥπατος
ἀπογεύσασθαι τυθείσης, τὸ δὲ λοιπὸν σῶμα σορ-
ῷ παραδόντας ἀναχωρῆσαι, ὡς ἂν τὸ τῶν
ἐναντίων στρατόπεδον ὑπερβάλοι τῆς θυσίας τὸν
τόπον. λέγε δὴ τὰ ἐπίλοιπα, Σάτυρε, σὸς γὰρ
ἐντεῦθεν ὁ λόγος."

20. Καὶ ὁ Σάτυρος λέγει· "Ἅμα δὲ βιαζόμενος
ἐπὶ τὸ στρατόπεδον ἔκλαιον, ὦ δέσποτα, καὶ
ὠδυρόμην, τὰ περὶ τῆς Λευκίππης πυθόμενος,
καὶ ἐδεόμην Μενελάου παντὶ τρόπῳ σῶσαι τὴν
2 κόρην. δαίμων δέ τις ἀγαθὸς ἡμῖν συνήργησεν.
ἐτύχομεν τῇ προτεραίᾳ τῆς θυσίας ἡμέρᾳ καθεζό-
μενοι πρὸς τῇ θαλάσσῃ λυπούμενοι καὶ περὶ
τούτων σκοποῦντες, τῶν δὲ λῃστῶν τινες ναῦν
ἰδόντες ἀγνοίᾳ πλανηθεῖσαν, ὥρμησαν ἐπ' αὐτήν.
3 οἱ δὲ ἐπὶ τῆς νηὸς συνέντες οἳ τυγχάνουσιν,
ἐπεχείρουν ἐλαύνειν εἰς τοὐπίσω· ὡς δὲ φθάνου-
σιν οἱ λῃσταὶ καταλαβόντες, πρὸς ἄμυναν
4 τρέπονται. καὶ γάρ τις ἐν αὐτοῖς ἦν τῶν τὰ

---

[1] Jacobs' correction for MSS. ταύτην.

robbers who were on guard in this part of it.
When I was brought before the robber-chief, some
of them at once recognized me, struck off my chains,
and bade me be of good cheer and join their company,
as a friend ought to do. I begged to have Satyrus
too, as being my servant. 'Yes,' said they, 'if you
will first prove yourself a courageous companion.'
At this time it happened that they had received an
oracle that that they should sacrifice a maiden and
so purify the robber-camp, devouring her liver after
her sacrifice; they were then to put the rest of her
body in a coffin and retire from the spot, and all this
was to be done so that the opposing army would
have to march over the spot where the sacrifice had
taken place.[1] Do you now relate the rest, Satyrus;
from this point the story is yours."

20. "When I was brought by force to the robbers'
camp," said Satyrus, continuing the story, "I wept,
master, and lamented when I heard about Leucippe,
and implored Menelaus to save the maiden, and
some kindly deity assisted us. On the day before
the sacrifice we happened to be sitting on the sea-
shore and thinking how we could effect this end,
when some of the robbers seeing a ship wandering
and ignorant of her course, attacked her; those on
board, realising the character of their assailants, tried
to put her about, but the robbers being too quick for
them, they made preparations to resist. Now there

---

[1] So that the magic should take them, presumably, as they
crossed the place. If, on the other hand, we wish to understand the sentence in the sense that the horror of the
cannibal sacrifice was to affright and overawe the enemy, the
rendering would be more easily reached if we were to read
τῆς θυσίας τὸ ἄτοπον, which would then be the subject of
ὑπερβάλοι, and τὸ τῶν ἐναντίων στρατόπεδον its object.

Ὁμήρου τῷ στόματι δεικνύντων ἐν τοῖς θεάτροις·
τὴν Ὁμηρικὴν οὖν[1] σκευὴν ὁπλισάμενος καὶ
αὐτὸς καὶ τοὺς ἀμφ' αὐτὸν οὕτως σκευάσας, ἐπε-
5 χείρουν μάχεσθαι. πρὸς μὲν οὖν τοὺς πρώτους
ἐπελθόντας καὶ μάλα ἐρρωμένως ἀντετάξαντο·
πλειόνων δὲ ἐπιπλευσάντων σκαφῶν λῃστρικῶν
καταδύουσι τὴν ναῦν καὶ τοὺς ἄνδρας ἐκπεσόντας
6 ἀνῄρουν. λανθάνει δὴ κίστη ἐκτραπεῖσά τις, καὶ
τῷ ναυαγίῳ καθ' ἡμᾶς τῷ ῥοῒ κομισθεῖσα, ἣν ὁ
Μενέλαος ἀναιρεῖται, καὶ ἀναχωρήσας ποι παρόντος ἅμα κἀμοῦ (προσεδόκα γάρ τι σπουδαῖον
ἔνδον εἶναι) ἀνοίγει τὴν κίστην καὶ ὁρῶμεν
χλαμύδα καὶ ξίφος, τὴν μὲν κώπην ἔχον παλαι-
στῶν τεσσάρων, τὸν δὲ σίδηρον ἐπὶ τῇ κώπῃ
βραχύτατον, δακτύλων ὅσον οὐ πλείω τριῶν.
7 ὡς δὲ ἀνελόμενος τὸ ξίφος ὁ Μενέλαος ἔλαθε
μεταστρέψας κατὰ τὸ τοῦ σιδήρου μέρος, τὸ
μικρὸν ἐκεῖνο ξίφος ὥσπερ ἀπὸ χηραμοῦ τῆς
κώπης κατατρέχει τοσοῦτον, ὅσον εἶχεν ἡ κώπη
τὸ μέγεθος· ὡς δὲ ἀνέστρεψεν εἰς τοὔμπαλιν,
αὖθις ὁ σίδηρος εἴσω κατεδύετο. τούτῳ δὲ ἄρα,
ὡς εἰκός, ὁ κακοδαίμων ἐκεῖνος ἐν τοῖς θεάτροις
ἐχρῆτο πρὸς τὰς κιβδήλους σφαγάς.

21. " Λέγω οὖν πρὸς τὸν Μενέλαον, ' Θεὸς ἡμῖν,
ἂν θέλῃς χρηστὸς γενέσθαι, συναγωνιεῖται. δυνη-
σόμεθα γὰρ καὶ τὴν κόρην σῶσαι καὶ τοὺς λῃστὰς
2 λαθεῖν. ἄκουσον δὲ ποίῳ τρόπῳ. δέρμα προ-
βάτου λαβόντες ὡς ὅτι ῥαδινώτατον συρράψωμεν
εἰς σχῆμα βαλαντίου, μέτρον ὅσον γαστρὸς ἀν-
θρωπίνης, εἶτα ἐμπλήσαντες θηρείων σπλάγχνων

---

[1] A connecting particle of some sort seems to be necessary
to the sense, and Cobet's οὖν is as good as any other.

was among the passengers one of those actors who recite Homer in the public theatres: he armed himself with his Homeric gear and did the same for his companions, and did his best to repel the invaders. Against the first comers of the attacking party they made a good fight, but several of the pirate boats coming up, the enemy sank the ship and murdered the passengers as they jumped off. They did not notice that a certain chest fell from the boat and this, after the ship had gone to pieces, was washed ashore near us by the tide. Menelaus found it, and retiring with it—I was with him—expected that there might be something of value in it, and opened it. We saw there a cloak and a dagger; the latter had a handle a foot [1] long with a very short blade fitted to it not more than three inches in length. Menelaus took out the dagger and casually turned it over, blade downwards, when the blade suddenly shot out from the handle so that handle and blade were now of equal size; and when turned back again, the blade sank back to its original length. This had doubtless been used in the theatre by that unlucky actor for sham murders.

21. "'We shall have the help of Heaven,' said I to Menelaus, 'if you will shew yourself a good fellow: we shall be able to trick the robbers and save the girl. Listen to my plan. We must take a sheep's skin, as thin a one as we can get, and sew it into the form of a pouch, about the size of a man's belly; then we must fill it with some animal's

---

[1] Literally, "four palm-breadths," which may be taken roughly as three inches each, though perhaps in reality a little more. The δάκτυλος "finger," here rather "thumb," may in the same way be taken as an inch.

καὶ αἵματος, τὴν πλαστὴν ταύτην γαστέρα
ῥάψωμεν, ὡς [1] μὴ ῥᾳδίως τὰ σπλάγχνα
διεκπίπτοι, καὶ ἐνσκευάσαντες τὴν κόρην τοῦτον
τὸν τρόπον καὶ στολὴν ἔξωθεν περιβαλόντες
μίτραις τε καὶ ζώμασιν ἐνδεδυμένην, τὴν σκευὴν
3 ταύτην ἐπικρύψωμεν. πάντως δὲ καὶ ὁ χρησμὸς
ἡμῖν εἰς τὸ λαθεῖν χρήσιμος· ὁλοκλήρως [2] γὰρ
αὐτὴν ἐσταλμένην δι' αὐτῆς [3] ἀνατμηθῆναι μέσην
τῆς ἐσθῆτος λέγει ὁ χρησμός. ὁρᾷς τοῦτο τὸ
4 ξίφος ὡς ἔχει μηχανῆς· ἂν γὰρ ἐρείσῃ τις ἐπί
τινος σώματος, φεύγει πρὸς τὴν κώπην, ὥσπερ εἰς
κουλεόν· καὶ οἱ μὲν ὁρῶντες δοκοῦσι βαπτίζεσθαι
τὸν σίδηρον κατὰ τοῦ σώματος, ὁ δὲ εἰς τὸν
χηραμὸν τῆς κώπης ἀνέδραμε, μόνην δὲ καταλείπει τὴν αἰχμήν, ὅσον τὴν πλαστὴν γαστέρα
τεμεῖν. καὶ τὴν κώπην ἐν χρῷ τοῦ σφαζομένου
τυχεῖν· κἂν ἀποσπάσῃ τις τὸν σίδηρον ἐκ τοῦ
τραύματος, κατατρεῖ πάλιν ἐκ τοῦ χηραμοῦ τὸ
ξίφος, ὅσον τῆς κώπης ἀνακουφίζεται τὸ μετέωρον
5 καὶ τὸν αὐτὸν τρόπον τοὺς ὁρῶντας ἀπατᾷ· δοκεῖ
γὰρ τοσοῦτον καταβῆναι ἐν [4] τῇ σφαγῇ, ὅσον
ἄνεισιν ἐκ τῆς μηχανῆς. τούτων οὖν γενομένων,
οὐκ ἂν εἰδεῖεν οἱ λῃσταὶ τὴν τέχνην. τά τε γὰρ
δέρματα ἀποκέκρυπται, τά τε σπλάγχνα τῇ
σφαγῇ προπηδήσεται, ἅπερ ἡμεῖς ἐξελόντες ἐπὶ
6 τῷ βωμῷ θύσομεν. καὶ τὸ ἐντεῦθεν οὐκέτι
προσίασιν οἱ λῃσταὶ τῷ σώματι, ἀλλ' ἡμεῖς εἰς
τὴν σορὸν καταθήσομεν. ἀκήκοας τοῦ λῃστάρχου
μικρῷ πρόσθεν εἰπόντος, δεῖν τι τολμηρὸν ἐπι-

---

[1] Hercher proposed to insert ἄν after ὡς.
[2] A very ingenious restoration by Hercher for the MSS.
meaningless ὁ σίδηρος. Lumb suggests ποδήρει.

entrails and blood, sew up this sham stomach so that
its contents cannot easily leak out, and fit her to it
by putting a dress outside and fastening it with
bands and girdles we can thus hide the whole
contrivance. The oracle is extremely useful to us
for our stratagem, as it has ordered that she is to be
fully adorned and must thus be ripped up through
her clothes. You see the mechanism of this dagger ;
if it is pressed against a body, the blade retreats into
the handle, as into a sheath ; all those who are
looking on think that it is actually plunged into the
flesh, whereas it has really sprung back into the
hollow of the handle, leaving only this point exposed,
which is just enough to slit the sham stomach, and
the handle will be flush with the thing struck :
when it is withdrawn from the wound, the blade
leaps forth from its cavity in proportion as the hilt is
raised and deceives the spectators just as when it
was plunged in : they think that so much of it
penetrated at the stroke as now springs out by its
mechanism. This being so, the robbers cannot per-
ceive the trick, for the sheepskin is hidden away : at
the blow the entrails will gush forth and we will take
them and sacrifice them on the altar. After that
the robbers will not approach the body, and we will
put it into the coffin. You heard the robber-chief
say a little while ago that you must give them some

---

³ So Jacobs for διὰ ταύτης (ταύτην F): the oracle did not
speak of " this dress," but had simply indicated that the cut
was to be made through her clothes.

⁴ καταβῆναι ἐν is Cobet's restoration from the MSS. καταβαίνειν.

δείξασθαι πρὸς αὐτούς· ὥστε ἔστι σοι προσελθεῖν
αὐτῷ καὶ ὑποσχέσθαι ταύτην τὴν ἐπίδειξιν.'
ταῦτα λέγων, ἐδεόμην Δία Ξένιον καλῶν καὶ
κοινῆς ἀναμιμνήσκων τραπέζης [1] καὶ κοινῆς
ναυαγίας.

22. "Ὁ δὲ χρηστὸς οὗτος, 'Μέγα μέν,' ἔφη,
'τὸ ἔργον, ἀλλ᾽ ὑπὲρ φίλου, κἂν ἀποθανεῖν
δεήσῃ, καλὸς ὁ κίνδυνος, γλυκὺς ὁ θάνατος.'
2 'Νομίζω δέ,' ἔφην, 'ζῆν καὶ Κλειτοφῶντα. ἢ
γὰρ κόρη πυθομένῳ μοι καταλιπεῖν αὐτὸν εἶπε
παρὰ τοῖς ἑαλωκόσι τῶν λῃστῶν δεδεμένον· οἱ
δὲ τῶν λῃστῶν πρὸς τὸν λήσταρχον ἐκφυγόν-
τες ἔλεγον πάντας τοὺς ὑπ᾽ αὐτῶν εἰλημμένους
τὴν εἰς τὸ στρατόπεδον μάχην ἐκπεφευγέναι·
ὥστε ἀποκείσεταί σοι παρ᾽ αὐτῷ ἡ χάρις καὶ
ἅμα ἐλεῆσαι κόρην ἀθλίαν ἐκ τοσούτου κακοῦ.'
3 ταῦτα λέγων πείθω, καὶ συνέπραξεν ἡ Τύχη
ἐγὼ μὲν οὖν περὶ τὴν τοῦ μηχανήματος ἤμην
σκευήν. ἄρτι δὲ τοῦ Μενελάου μέλλοντος τοῖς
λῃσταῖς περὶ τῆς θυσίας λέγειν, ὁ λήσταρχος
φθάσας κατὰ δαίμονα, 'Νόμος ἡμῖν,' ἔφη, 'τοὺς
πρωτομύστας τῆς ἱερουργίας ἄρχεσθαι, μάλιστα
4 ὅταν ἄνθρωπον καταθύειν δέῃ. ὥρα τοίνυν εἰς
αὔριόν σοι παρασκευάζεσθαι πρὸς τὴν θυσίαν·
δεήσει δὲ καὶ τὸν σὸν οἰκέτην ἅμα σοὶ μυηθῆναι.'
'Καὶ μάλα,' οὗτος ἔφη, 'προθυμησόμεθα μη-
5 δενὸς ὑμῶν χείρους γενέσθαι. στεῖλαι δὲ ἡμᾶς
αὐτοὺς δεήσει τὴν κόρην ὡς ἁρμοδίως πρὸς τὴν
ἀνατομήν.' 'Ὑμῶν,' ὁ λήσταρχος ἔφη, 'τὸ
6 ἱερεῖον.' στέλλομεν δὴ τὴν κόρην τὸν προειρη-

---

[1] καὶ χρηστῆς, deleted by Hercher, seems to have crept in
from the opening of the next chapter. καὶ χρήσεως Lumb.

proof of your courage, so that you can now go to him
and undertake this service as the proof required.'
After these words I prayed, calling upon Zeus the
god of strangers, remembering before him the common table at which we had eaten and our common
shipwreck.

22. "'It is a great undertaking,' said this good
fellow, 'but for a friend—even if one must perish—
danger is noble and death sweet.' 'I think,' I added,
'that Clitophon also is still alive: the maiden told
me that she had left him in bonds among the robbers'
captives, and those of the band who had escaped to
the robber-chief mentioned that their prisoners had
all slipped out of the battle and reached the enemy's
camp: you will thus be earning his warmest
gratitude and at the same time rescue a poor girl
from so cruel a fate.' He agreed with what I said,
and Fortune favoured us. So I set about making the
preparations for our stratagem, while Menelaus was
just about to broach the subject of the sacrifice to
the robbers, when the robber-chief by the instigation
of Providence anticipated him, saying: 'It is a
custom among us that those who are being initiated
into our band should perform the sacred rites;
particularly when there is a question of sacrificing
a human being. It is time therefore to get yourself
ready for to-morrow's sacrifice, and your servant will
have to be initiated at the same time as yourself.'
'Certainly,' said Menelaus, 'and we shall try to show
ourselves as good men as any of you. But it must
be our business to arrange the maiden as may be
most convenient for the operation.' 'Yes,' said the
robber-chief, 'the victim is wholly your charge.'
We therefore dressed her up in the manner I have

μένον τρόπον καθ' ἑαυτούς, καὶ θαρρεῖν παρε-
κελευσάμεθα, διεξελθόντες ἕκαστα, καὶ ὡς μένειν
εἴσω τῆς σοροῦ χρή, κἂν θᾶττον αὐτὴν ὁ ὕπνος
ἀφῇ, τὴν ἡμέραν ἔνδον μένειν· ''Ην δέ τι ἡμῖν
ἐμποδὼν γένηται, σῷζε σαυτὴν ἐπὶ τὸ στρατόπεδον.' ταῦτα εἰπόντες ἐξάγομεν αὐτὴν ἐπὶ τὸν
βωμόν· καὶ τὰ λοιπὰ οἶδας."

23. Ὡς οὖν ἤκουσα, παντοδαπὸς ἐγινόμην καὶ
διηπόρουν ὅ τι ποιήσω πρὸς τὸν Μενέλαον
ἀντάξιον. τὸ δ' οὖν κοινότατον, προσπεσὼν
κατησπαζόμην καὶ προσεκύνουν ὡς θεόν, καί
μου κατὰ τῆς ψυχῆς ἀθρόα κατεχεῖτο ἡδονή.
2 ὡς δὲ τὰ κατὰ Λευκίππην εἶχέ μοι καλῶς,
" Ὁ δὲ Κλεινίας," εἶπον, "τί γέγονεν;" ὁ δὲ
Μενέλαος, "Οὐκ οἶδα," ἔφη· "μετὰ γὰρ τὴν
ναυαγίαν εὐθὺς εἶδον μὲν αὐτὸν τῆς κεραίας
3 λαβόμενον, ὅποι δὲ κεχώρηκεν οὐκ οἶδα." ἀνεκώ-
κυσα οὖν ἐν μέσῃ τῇ χαρᾷ· ταχὺ γὰρ ἐφθόνησέ
μοι δαίμων τις τῆς καθαρᾶς ἡδονῆς· τὸν δι'
ἐμὲ[1] φαινόμενον οὐδαμοῦ, τὸν μετὰ Λευκίππην
ἐμὸν δεσπότην, τοῦτον ἐκ πάντων κατέσχεν ἡ
θάλασσα, ἵνα μὴ τὴν ψυχὴν μόνον ἀπολέσῃ,
4 ἀλλὰ καὶ τὴν ταφήν· ''Ω θάλασσα ἄγνωμον,
ἐφθόνησας ἡμῖν ὁλοκλήρου τοῦ τῆς φιλανθρωπίας
σου δράματος." ἄπιμεν οὖν εἰς τὸ στρατόπεδον

---

[1] It is not quite obvious why the (supposed) death of
Clinias was Clitophon's fault, and editors have wished to
alter the reading δι' ἐμέ for this reason. It is, however,
possible to argue that, since Clinias did not originally intend
to leave his home, and only embarked on the voyage to be
Clitophon's companion, Clitophon was in some measure responsible for death encountered on that voyage.

previously described, apart from the others, and told her to be of good courage; we went through all the details with her, telling her to stay inside the coffin, and even if she awoke early from sleep, to wait inside until day appeared. 'If anything goes amiss with us,' we said, 'take flight to the hostile camp.' With these injunctions we led her out to the altar, and the rest you know."

23. On hearing this story I felt almost out of my senses, and was utterly at a loss how I could make any recompense to Menelaus for his great services to me. I adopted the commonest form of gratitude, falling at his feet, embracing him, and worshipping him as a god, while my heart was inundated with a torrent of joy. But now that all was well in the matter of Leucippe, "What has happened," I asked, "to Clinias?" "I do not know," said Menelaus. "Directly after the shipwreck I saw him clinging to the yard-arm, but I do not know whither he was carried." I gave a cry of sorrow even in the midst of my joy; for some god quickly grudged me unalloyed happiness; and now he that was lost through my doing, he who was everything to me after Leucippe, he of all men was in the clutches of the sea, and had lost not only his life,[1] but any hope of burial. "Unkindly ocean," I cried, "thus to deprive us of the full measure of the mercy thou hast shewn us!" We then returned all

---

[1] It is usual to explain this passage by referring to the belief common in the ancient world that the souls of those drowned at sea do not find a rest in the next world, but remain wandering about the waves. But ψυχή can mean *life* as well as *soul*, so that the explanation suggested is not absolutely necessary.

κοινῇ καὶ τῆς σκηνῆς εἴσω παρελθόντες τῆς ἐμῆς,
τὸ λοιπὸν τῆς νυκτὸς διετρίψαμεν, καὶ τὸ πρᾶγμα
οὐκ ἔλαθε τοὺς πολλούς.

24. Ἅμα δὲ τῇ ἕῳ ἄγω τὸν Μενέλαον τῷ
στρατηγῷ καὶ ἅπαντα λέγω· ὁ δὲ συνήδετο καὶ
τὸν Μενέλαον ποιεῖται φίλον, πυνθάνεται δέ,
πόση δύναμίς ἐστι τοῖς ἐναντίοις· ὁ δὲ ἔλεγε
πᾶσαν ἐμπεπλῆσθαι τὴν ἑξῆς κώμην ἀνδρῶν
ἀπονενοημένων καὶ πολὺ συνηθροῖσθαι ληστή-
2 ριον, ὡς εἶναι μυρίους. λέγει οὖν ὁ στρατηγός,
"'Αλλ' ἡμῖν αὗται πέντε χιλιάδες ἱκαναὶ πρὸς
εἴκοσι τῶν ἐκείνων. ἀφίξονται δὲ ὅσον οὐδέπω
πρὸς τούτοις ἕτεροι δισχίλιοι τῶν ἀμφὶ τὸ Δέλτα
καὶ τὴν Ἡλίου πόλιν τεταγμένων ἐπὶ τοὺς
3 βαρβάρους." καὶ ἅμα λέγοντος αὐτοῦ παῖς
εἰστρέχει τις, λέγων ἀπὸ τοῦ Δέλτα πρόδρομον
ἥκειν τοὐκεῖθεν στρατοπέδου καὶ πέντε λέγειν
ἄλλων ἡμερῶν διατρίβειν τοὺς δισχιλίους· τοὺς
γὰρ βαρβάρους τοὺς κατατρέχοντας πεπαῦσθαι,
μελλούσης δὲ ἥκειν τῆς δυνάμεως, τὸν ὄρνιν αὐτοῖς
ἐπιδημῆσαι τὸν ἱερόν, φέροντα τοῦ πατρὸς τὴν
ταφήν· ἀνάγκη δ' ἦν[1] τὴν ἔξοδον ἐπισχεῖν
τοσούτων ἡμερῶν.

25. "Καὶ τίς ὁ ὄρνις οὗτος, ὅστις," ἔφην,
"τοσαύτης τιμῆς ἠξίωται; ποίαν δὲ καὶ κομίζει
ταφήν;" "Φοῖνιξ μὲν ὁ ὄρνις ὄνομα, τὸ δὲ γένος
Αἰθίοψ, μέγεθος κατὰ ταῶν· τῇ χροιᾷ ταῶς ἐν
2 κάλλει δεύτερος. κεκέρασται μὲν τὰ πτερὰ

---

[1] ἀνάγκη δ' ἦν Vilborg: ἀνάγκη δ' ἦσαν the MSS.: ἠναγ-
κάσθησαν Göttling: ἀνάγκην δὲ εἶναι Hercher. There are other
suggestions.

together to the camp, and entering my tent passed the rest of the night there, and our adventures soon became the common property of the army.

24. At early dawn I took Menelaus to the general and told him the whole story ; he was delighted to hear it, and made him one of his companions. To his enquiry as to the size of the enemy's forces, Menelaus replied that the whole of the village before us was full of desperate fighters, and that the robber-camp was so thickly manned that they must amount to ten thousand. " But these five thousand of ours," replied the general, " are a match for twenty of theirs, and besides that, very shortly another two thousand will arrive of the troops stationed in the Delta and about Heliopolis ready to fight against these savages." While he was still speaking, a courier arrived, saying that a messenger had arrived from the camp in the Delta with the news that the two thousand would have to wait for five more days ; the savages had stopped making incursions, but just as the force was ready to start, their Sacred Bird had arrived, bearing with him the sepulchre of his father. They were therefore compelled to delay their march for that space of time.

25. " What bird is that," said I, " which is so greatly honoured ? And what is this sepulchre that he carries ? " " The bird is called the Phoenix ; " was the answer, " he comes from Ethiopia, and is of about a peacock's size, but the peacock is inferior to him in beauty of colour. His wings are a mixture of gold and

χρυσῷ καὶ πορφύρᾳ· αὐχεῖ δὲ τὸν Ἥλιον
δεσπότην καὶ ἡ κεφαλὴ μαρτυρεῖ, ἐστεφάνωσε
γὰρ αὐτὴν κύκλος εὐφυής· ἡλίου δέ ἐστιν ὁ τοῦ
3 κύκλου στέφανος εἰκών. κυάνεός ἐστιν, ῥόδοις
ἐμφερής, εὐειδὴς τὴν θέαν, ἀκτῖσι κομᾷ, καὶ
εἰσιν αὗται πτερῶν ἀνατολαί. μερίζονται δὲ
αὐτοῦ Αἰθίοπες μὲν τὴν ζωήν, Αἰγύπτιοι δὲ τὴν
4 τελευτήν· ἐπειδὰν γὰρ ἀποθάνῃ (σὺν χρόνῳ δὲ
τοῦτο πάσχει μακρῷ), ὁ παῖς αὐτὸν ἐπὶ τὸν
Νεῖλον φέρει, σχεδιάσας αὐτῷ καὶ τὴν ταφήν.
σμύρνης γὰρ βῶλον τῆς εὐωδεστάτης, ὅσον
ἱκανὸν πρὸς ὄρνιθος ταφήν, ὀρύττει τε τῷ
στόματι καὶ κοιλαίνει κατὰ μέσον, καὶ τὸ ὄρυγμα
5 θήκη γίνεται τῷ νεκρῷ. ἐνθεὶς δὲ καὶ ἐναρμόσας
τὸν ὄρνιν τῇ σορῷ, καὶ κλείσας¹ τὸ χάσμα
γηΐνῳ χώματι, ἐπὶ τὸν Νεῖλον οὕτως ἵπταται
τὸ ἔργον φέρων. ἕπεται δὲ αὐτῷ χορὸς ἄλλων
ὀρνίθων ὥσπερ δορυφόρων καὶ ἔοικεν ὁ ὄρνις
ἀποδημοῦντι βασιλεῖ, καὶ τὴν πόλιν οὐ πλανᾶται
6 τὴν Ἡλίου· ὄρνιθος αὕτη μετοικία νεκροῦ. ἕστηκεν οὖν ἐπὶ μετεώρου σκοπῶν καὶ ἐκδέχεται
τοὺς προπόλους τοῦ θεοῦ. ἔρχεται δή τις ἱερεὺς
Αἰγύπτιος, βιβλίον ἐξ ἀδύτων φέρων, καὶ δοκιμά-

---

¹ καὶ κλείσας Hercher: καὶ εἰς the MSS. κλείσας τε Jacobs:
κλείσας Castiglioni: καὶ βύσας Hirschig.

---

¹ " By report," says Pliny (*H.N.* x. 2), " he is as big as an
eagle ; for colour, as yellow and bright as gold (namely, all
about the neck) ; the rest of the body a deep red purple ;
the tail azure blue, intermingled with feathers among, of rose

scarlet [1]; he is proud to acknowledge the Sun as his lord, and his head is witness of his allegiance, which is crowned with a magnificent halo—a circular halo is the symbol of the sun. It is of a deep magenta colour, like that of the rose, of great beauty, with spreading rays where the feathers spring. The Ethiopians enjoy his presence during his life-time, the Egyptians at his death; when he dies—and he is subject to death after a long period of years—his son makes a sepulchre for him and carries him to the Nile. He digs out with his beak a ball of myrrh of the sweetest savour and hollows it out in the middle sufficiently to take the body of a bird; the hollow that he has dug out is employed as a coffin for the corpse. He puts the bird in and fits it into the receptacle, and then, after sealing up the cavity with clay, flies to the Nile, carrying with him the result of his labours. An escort of other birds accompanies him, as a bodyguard attends a migrating king, and he never fails to make straight for Heliopolis, the dead bird's last destination. Then he perches upon a high spot and awaits the coming of the attendants of the god [2]; an Egyptian priest goes out, carrying with him a book from the sacred shrine, and assures himself that he is the genuine bird from his likeness to

---

carnation colour, and the head bravely adorned with a crest and pinnage finely wrought; having a tuft and a plume thereupon, right fair and goodly to be seen." *Cf.* also Herodotus ii. 73, from which most of the details in the rest of this chapter are taken.

[2] The Sun — worshipped in Heliopolis, the Sun's City. Pliny's account is very similar. except that he makes the dying bird construct his own coffin, and be carried by his offspring to a city of the Sun in the direction of Panchaea (Socotra?), an Arabian spice-island in the Red Sea.

7 ζει τὸν ὄρνιν ἐκ τῆς γραφῆς. ὁ δὲ οἶδεν ἀπιστού-
μενος καὶ τὰ ἀπόρρητα φαίνει τοῦ σώματος καὶ
τὸν νεκρὸν ἐπιδείκνυται καί ἐστιν ἐπιτάφιος
σοφιστής. ἱερέων δὲ παῖδες Ἡλίου τὸν ὄρνιν τὸν
νεκρὸν παραλαβόντες θάπτουσι. ζῶν μὲν οὖν
Αἰθίοψ ἐστὶ τῇ τροφῇ, ἀποθανὼν δὲ Αἰγύπτιος
γίνεται τῇ ταφῇ."

the picture which he possesses. The bird knows that he may be doubted, and displays every part, even the most private, of his body. Afterwards he exhibits the corpse and delivers, as it were, a funeral panegyric on his departed father; then the attendant-priests of the Sun take the dead bird and bury him. It is thus true that during life the Phoenix is an Ethiopian by right of nurture, but at his death he becomes an Egyptian by right of burial."

Δ΄

1. Ἔδοξεν οὖν τῷ στρατηγῷ, μαθόντι τήν τε
τῶν ἐναντίων παρασκευὴν καὶ τὴν τῶν συμμάχων
ἀναβολήν, εἰς τὴν κώμην ἀναστρέψαι πάλιν,
ὅθενπερ ἐξωρμήσαμεν, ἔστ᾽ ἂν οἱ σύμμαχοι
παραγένωνται· ἐμοὶ δέ τις οἶκος ἀπετέτακτο
ἅμα τῇ Λευκίππῃ μικρὸν ἀνωτέρω τῆς τοῦ
2 στρατηγοῦ καταγωγῆς. καὶ ὡς εἴσω παρῆλθον,
περιπτυξάμενος αὐτὴν οἷός τε ἤμην ἀνδρίζεσθαι.
ὡς δὲ οὐκ ἐπέτρεπε, "Μέχρι πότε," εἶπον,
3 "χηρεύομεν τῶν τῆς Ἀφροδίτης ὀργίων; οὐχ
ὁρᾷς οἷα ἐκ παραλόγου γίνεται; ναυαγία, καὶ
λῃσταί, καὶ θυσίαι, καὶ σφαγαί· ἀλλ᾽ ἕως ἐν
γαλήνῃ τῆς Τύχης ἐσμέν, ἀποχρησώμεθα τῷ
καιρῷ, πρίν ἢ χαλεπώτερον ἡμᾶς ἐπισχεῖν." ἡ
δέ, "᾽Αλλ᾽ οὐ θέμις," ἔφη, "τοῦτο ἤδη γενέσθαι.
4 ἡ γάρ μοι θεὸς Ἄρτεμις ἐπιστᾶσα πρώην κατὰ
τοὺς ὕπνους, ὅτε ἔκλαιον μέλλουσα σφαγήσεσθαι,
'Μὴ νῦν,' ἔφη, 'κλαῖε· οὐ γὰρ τεθνήξῃ· βοηθὸς
γὰρ ἐγώ σοι παρέσομαι· μενεῖς δὲ παρθένος,
ἔστ᾽ ἄν σε νυμφοστολήσω· ἄξεται δέ σε ἄλλος
5 οὐδεὶς ἢ Κλειτοφῶν.' ἐγὼ δὲ τῇ μὲν ἀναβολῇ
ἠχθόμην, ταῖς δὲ τοῦ μέλλοντος ἐλπίσιν ἡδόμην."[1]
ὡς δὲ ἤκουσα τὸ ὄναρ, ἀναμιμνήσκομαι προσό-

---

[1] In previous editions and translations Leucippe's speech
has been brought to an end with the pronouncement of Artemis, and the following sentence (I was disappointed . . .)

BOOK IV

1. WHEN the general heard of the amount and equipment of his adversaries' forces as well as the delay of his own succours, he decided to turn back to to the village whence we had set out until the reinforcements should appear. Leucippe and I had a house assigned to us a little beyond the general's lodging. After entering it, I took her in my arms and desired to exercise the rights of a husband ; but as she would not allow me to do so, "How long," said I, " are we to be deprived of the rites of Aphrodite ? Do you take no account of all our mishaps and adventures, shipwrecks, robbers, sacrifices, murders ? While we are now in Fortune's calm, let us make good use of our opportunity, before some other more cruel fate impedes us." " No," said she, "this cannot be now at once. Yesterday, when I was weeping at the thought of my coming sacrifice, the goddess Artemis stood before me in a dream and said, 'Weep no more ; thou shalt not die, for I will be thy helper, but thou must remain a virgin, until I deck thee as bride, and none other than Clitophon shall be thy spouse.' I was disappointed to hear that our happiness must thus be postponed, but glad for the hopes of the future." Hearing her dream, I remembered that

---

made the beginning of Clitophon's reflexions ; but on the whole it seems slightly preferable to make Leucippe speak as far as the word "future."

6 μοιον ἰδὼν ἐνύπνιον· ἐδόκουν γὰρ τῇ παρελθούσῃ
νυκτὶ νεὼν Ἀφροδίτης ἰδεῖν καὶ τὸ ἄγαλμα ἔνδον
εἶναι τῆς θεοῦ· ὡς δὲ πλησίον ἐγενόμην προσευξό-
7 μενος, κλεισθῆναι τὰς θύρας. ἀθυμοῦντι δέ μοι
γυναῖκα ἐκφανῆναι κατὰ τὸ ἄγαλμα τὴν μορφὴν
ἔχουσαν, καὶ " Νῦν," εἶπεν, "οὐκ ἔξεστί σοι
παρελθεῖν εἴσω τοῦ νεώ· ἦν δὲ ὀλίγον ἀναμείνῃς
χρόνον, οὐκ ἀνοίξω σοι μόνον, ἀλλὰ καὶ ἱερέα
8 σε ποιήσω τῆς θεοῦ." καταλέγω δὴ τοῦτο τῇ
Λευκίππῃ τὸ ἐνύπνιον καὶ οὐκέτι ἐπεχείρουν
βιάζεσθαι· ἀναλογιζόμενος δὲ τὸν τῆς Λευκίππης
ὄνειρον, οὐ μετρίως ἐταραττόμην.

2. Ἐν τούτῳ δὴ Χαρμίδης, τοῦτο γὰρ ἦν ὄνομα
τῷ στρατηγῷ, ἐπιβάλλει τῇ Λευκίππῃ τὸν ὀφθαλμόν, ἀπὸ τοιαύτης ἀφορμῆς αὐτὴν ἰδών· ἔτυχον
ποτάμιον θηρίον ἄνδρες τεθηρακότες θέας ἄξιον·
ἵππον δὲ αὐτὸν τοῦ Νείλου καλοῦσιν οἱ Αἰγύπ-
2 τιοι. καὶ ἔστι μὲν ἵππος, ὡς ὁ λόγος βούλεται,
τὴν γαστέρα καὶ τοὺς πόδας, πλὴν ὅσον ἐν χηλῇ
σχίζει τὴν ὁπλήν· μέγεθος δὲ κατὰ τὸν βοῦν τὸν
μέγιστον· οὐρὰ βραχεῖα καὶ ψιλὴ τριχῶν, ὅτι
3 καὶ τὸ λοιπὸν τοῦ σώματος οὕτως ἔχει· κεφαλὴ
περιφερής, οὐ σμικρά· ἐγγὺς ἵππου παρειαί·
μυκτὴρ ἐπὶ μέγα κεχηνὼς καὶ πνέων πυρώδη
καπνόν, ὡς ἀπὸ πηγῆς πυρός· γένυς εὐρεῖα, ὅση
καὶ παρειά, μέχρι τῶν κροτάφων ἀνοίγει τὸ
στόμα. ἔχει δὲ καὶ κυνόδοντας καμπύλους, κατὰ
μὲν τὴν ἰδέαν καὶ τὴν θέσιν ὡς συός,[1] τὸ δὲ
μέγεθος εἰς τριπλάσιον.

---

[1] So Eustathius and Jacobs. The MSS. have ἵππος. It
is much more likely that the teeth resembled a boar's tusks
(except in their size) than those of a horse.

I too had had a similar vision; during the night just past I thought I saw before me Aphrodite's temple and the goddess's image within it; but when I came near to make my prayers, the doors were shut. I was distressed at this, but then a woman appeared exactly like the statue, saying; "At present you cannot enter the temple, but if you wait for a short time, I will not only open it to you but make you a priest of the goddess." I related this dream to Leucippe and did not continue my attempts to constrain her, and yet, when I considered and compared Leucippe's own dream, I was not a little disturbed.

2. Meanwhile Charmides (that was the general's name) cast his eyes upon Leucippe, and this is how the business began. It so happened that some men were chasing a river-beast that is well worth seeing—the Nile-horse,[1] as the Egyptians call it. It is like a horse (as the name implies) with regard to its belly and its feet, except that it has cloven hooves; it is about the size of the largest kind of ox; and it has a tail both short and hairless, as is indeed the rest of its body. Its head is round, and of considerable size, with its cheeks like those of a horse; its nostrils wide and breathing out hot vapour,[2] as from a spring of fire; its jaws enormous as its cheeks, and its mouth gaping open right up to its temples; its eye-teeth crooked, in shape and position like those of a wild boar, but about three times as big.

[1] The whole of this chapter is of course a distorted picture of the hippopotamus.
[2] Compare Job xli. 19 *sqq.* with this passage.

3. Καλεῖ δὴ πρὸς τὴν θέαν ἡμᾶς ὁ στρατηγός· καὶ ἡ Λευκίππη συμπαρῆν. ἡμεῖς μὲν οὖν ἐπὶ τὸ θηρίον τοὺς ὀφθαλμοὺς εἴχομεν, ἐπὶ τὴν Λευκίππην δὲ ὁ στρατηγός· καὶ εὐθὺς ἑαλώκει. 2 βουλόμενος οὖν ἡμᾶς παραμένειν ἐπὶ πλεῖστον, ἵν᾽ ἔχοι τοῖς ὀφθαλμοῖς αὐτοῦ χαρίζεσθαι, περιπλοκὰς ἐζήτει λόγων· πρῶτον μὲν τὴν φύσιν τοῦ θηρίου καταλέγων, εἶτα καὶ τὸν τρόπον τῆς ἄγρας, ὡς ἔστι μὲν ἀδηφαγώτατον καὶ ποιεῖται τροφὴν ὅλον λήϊον, ἀπάτῃ δὲ πάσχει 3 τὴν ἄγραν. Ἐπιτηρήσαντες γὰρ αὐτοῦ τὰς διατριβάς, ὄρυγμα ποιησάμενοι, ἐπικαλύπτουσιν ἄνωθεν καλάμῃ καὶ χώματι· ὑπὸ δὲ τὴν τῶν καλάμων μηχανὴν ἱστάναι κάτω ξύλινον οἴκημα τὰς θύρας ἀνεῳγμένον εἰς τὸν ὄροφον τοῦ βόθρου, 4 καὶ τὴν πτῶσιν τοῦ θηρίου λοχᾶν· τὸν μὲν γὰρ ἐπιβάντα φέρεσθαι εὐθὺς καὶ τὸ οἴκημα φωλεοῦ δίκην ὑποδέχεσθαι καὶ τοὺς κυνηγέτας ἐκθορόντας εὐθὺς ἐπικλείειν τοῦ πώματος τὰς θύρας καὶ ἔχειν οὕτω τὴν ἄγραν, ἐπεὶ πρός γε τὸ 5 καρτερὸν οὐδεὶς ἂν αὐτοῦ κρατήσειε βίᾳ. "τά τε γὰρ ἄλλα ἐστὶν ἀλκιμώτατος καὶ τὸ δέρμα, ὡς ὁρᾶτε, φέρει παχὺ[1] καὶ οὐκ ἐθέλει πείθεσθαι σιδήρου τραύματι, ἀλλ᾽ ἐστίν, ὡς εἰπεῖν, ἐλέφας Λιγύπτιος. καὶ γὰρ δεύτερος φαίνεται εἰς ἀλκὴν ἐλέφαντος Ἰνδοῦ."

4. Καὶ ὁ Μενέλαος, "Ἦ γὰρ ἐλέφαντα," ἔφη, "ἤδη τεθέασαί ποτε; " "Καὶ μάλα," ὁ Χαρμίδης εἶπεν, "καὶ ἀκήκοα παρὰ τῶν ἀκριβῶς εἰδότων τῆς γενέσεως αὐτοῦ τὸν τρόπον ὡς παράδοξος."[2] 2 "᾽Αλλ᾽ ἡμεῖς γε οὐκ εἴδομεν εἰς ταύτην," ἔφην ἐγώ,

---

[1] MSS. τραχύ, rough. The correction is due to Hercher.

3. The general called us to watch the spectacle, and Leucippe was with us. We kept our eyes fixed on the animal, the general kept his on Leucippe, and he was straightway Love's prisoner. Desiring to keep us by him as long as possible, in order thus to feast his eyes, he span out his conversation about the beast; first he described its appearance and character, and then the way it is captured. It is the greediest of all animals, sometimes taking a whole field of corn at a meal, and it is caught by strategy. The huntsmen, you see, observe its tracks, and then dig a pit, roofing it in with straw and earth; under this arrangement of thatch they place at the bottom a wooden box with its cover open up to the top of the pit, and wait for the beast to fall in. When it arrives, in it tumbles, and the box receives it like a trap; the huntsmen then rush out and close the lid and thus gain possession of their prey, since he is so strong that no one can master him by mere force. " Not only is he extremely strong, but his hide, as you may see, is of great thickness, and cannot be penetrated by the steel.[1] He is, one might say, the elephant of Egypt, and indeed in strength he is only second to the Indian elephant."

4. " Why," said Menelaus, " have you ever seen an elephant?" " Certainly," replied Charmides, " and I have heard from experts the extraordinary circumstances connected with its birth." " We," said I, " have never seen one up to this time,

---

[1] " I shoot the hippopotamus with bullets made of platinum,
    Because, if I use leaden ones, his hide is sure to
    flatten 'em."   *The Bad Child's Book of Beasts.*

---

[2] τὸν τρόπον ὡς παράδοξος F only, all other MSS. having τὴν φύσιν ὡς παράδοξον.

"τὴν ἡμέραν, ὅτι μὴ γραφῇ." "Λέγοιμ' ἂν
ὑμῖν," εἶπε, "καὶ γὰρ ἄγομεν σχολήν. κυεῖ
μὲν αὐτὸν ἡ μήτηρ χρονιώτατον· δέκα γὰρ
ἐνιαυτοῖς πλάττει τὴν σποράν· μετὰ δὲ τοσαύτην
ἐτῶν περίοδον τίκτει, ὅταν ὁ τόκος γέρων γένηται.
3 διὰ τοῦτο, οἶμαι, καὶ ἀποτελεῖται μέγας τὴν
μορφήν, ἄμαχος τὴν ἀλκήν, πολὺς τὴν βιοτήν,
βραδὺς τὴν τελευτήν· βιοῦν[1] γὰρ αὐτὸν λέγουσιν
4 ὑπὲρ τὴν Ἡσιόδου κορώνην. τοιαύτη δέ ἐστιν
ἐλέφαντος ἡ γένυς, οἵα τοῦ βοὸς ἡ κεφαλή· σὺ
μὲν γὰρ ἂν ἰδὼν εἴποις κέρας ἔχειν αὐτὸ τὸ στόμα
διπλοῦν· ἔστι δὲ τοῦτο ἐλέφαντος καμπύλος
ὀδούς. μεταξὺ δὲ τῶν ὀδόντων ἀνίσταται[2] αὐτῷ
προβοσκίς, κατὰ σάλπιγγα μὲν καὶ τὴν ὄψιν
καὶ τὸ μέγεθος, εὐπειθὴς δὲ τῶν πρὸς τὸν
5 ἐλέφαντα· προνομεύει γὰρ αὐτῷ τὰς βοσκὰς
καὶ πᾶν ὅ τι ἂν ἐμποδὼν εὕρῃ σιτίον· ἐὰν μὲν
γὰρ ᾖ ὄψον ἐλέφαντος, ἔλαβέ τε εὐθὺς καὶ
ἐπιπτυχθεῖσα κάτω πρὸς τὴν γένυν τῷ στόματι
τὴν τροφὴν διακονεῖ· ἂν δέ τι τῶν ἁβροτέρων[3]
ἴδῃ, τούτῳ περιβάλλει, κύκλῳ τὴν ἄγραν περι-
σφίγξας καὶ τὸ πᾶν ἀνεκούφισε καὶ ὤρεξεν ἄνω
6 δῶρον δεσπότῃ. ἐπικάθηται γάρ τις αὐτῷ
ἀνὴρ Αἰθίοψ, καινὸς ἐλέφαντι ἱππεὺς ὤν· καὶ
κολακεύει καὶ φοβεῖται καὶ τῆς φωνῆς αἰσθάνε-

---

[1] So Cobet for the MSS. βίον γὰρ αὐτοῦ or αὐτῷ.
[2] So Hercher for MSS. ἀνθίσταται.
[3] Jacobs' suggestion for ἁδροτέρων of the MSS. (ἀνδροτέρων
W): λαροτέρων Lumb: ἀνθρωπείων Hercher.

except in a picture." "In that case," he said, " I
will describe it to you, as we have plenty of time.
The female has a long period of pregnancy; for she
takes ten years[1] to give form to the seed in her
womb, and after that period she brings forth, her
offspring being thus already old. This is the reason,
I imagine, that he grows in the end to such an
enormous bulk, is unconquerable by reason of his
strength, and is so long-lived and slow to come to
his end; they say that he lives longer than the crow
in Hesiod.[2] The elephant's jaw is like the head of
an ox, because to the observer his mouth appears
to have two horns; these are, however, in reality the
elephant's curved tusks. Between them grows his
trunk, in appearance and size not unlike a trumpet,
and very convenient for all that the beast may
require; it takes up his food for him or anything that
he finds to eat; if it is proper nutriment for an
elephant, he takes it at once, and then bending
inwards towards his jaw, delivers it to his mouth;
but if he sees that it is anything too rich for him, he
seizes it, twists up his find in a circle, raises it on
high, and offers it as a gift to his master. This
master is an Ethiopian who sits on his back, a sort
of elephant horseman; the beast fawns on him and
fears him, and attends to his voice and submits to

[1] Pliny, *H.N.* viii. 10. "The common sort of men think
that they go with young for ten years, but Aristotle that
they go but two years."

[2] Although the extant works of Hesiod, as we have them,
do not include this allusion, we fortunately have a reference
to it in Pliny, and Hesiod's exact words preserved to us in
Plutarch, *de defectu oraculorum* (*Morals*, 415 c):

ἐννέα τοι ζώει γενεὰς λακέρυζα κορώνη
ἀνδρῶν ἡβώντων.

Nine ages of men in their flower doth live
The cawing crow.

ται καὶ μαστίζοντος ἀνέχεται· ἡ δὲ μάστιξ αὐτῷ
7 πέλεκυς σιδηροῦς. εἶδον δέ ποτε καὶ θέαμα
καινόν· ἀνὴρ Ἕλλην ἐνέθηκε τὴν κεφαλὴν κατὰ
μέσην τοῦ θηρίου τὴν κεφαλήν· ὁ δὲ ἐλέφας
ἐκεχήνει καὶ περιήσθμαινε τὸν ἄνθρωπον ἐγκεί-
μενον. ἀμφότερα οὖν ἐθαύμαζον, καὶ τὸν ἄνθρωπον τῆς εὐτολμίας καὶ τὸν ἐλέφαντα τῆς
8 φιλανθρωπίας. ὁ δὲ ἄνθρωπος ἔλεγεν ὅτι καὶ
μισθὸν εἴη δεδωκὼς τῷ θηρίῳ· προσπνεῖν γὰρ
αὐτῷ καὶ μόνον οὐκ ἀρωμάτων Ἰνδικῶν· εἶναι δὲ
καὶ κεφαλῆς νοσούσης φάρμακον. οἶδεν οὖν τὴν
θεραπείαν ὁ ἐλέφας καὶ προῖκα οὐκ ἀνοίγει τὸ
στόμα, ἀλλ' ἐστὶν ἰατρὸς ἀλαζὼν καὶ τὸν μισθὸν
πρῶτον αἰτεῖ. κἂν δῷς, πείθεται καὶ παρέχει τὴν
χάριν καὶ ἁπλοῖ τὴν γένυν καὶ τοσοῦτον ἀνέχεται[1]
κεχηνώς, ὅσον ὁ ἄνθρωπος βούλεται· οἶδε γὰρ ὅτι
πέπρακε τὴν ὀδμήν."

5. "Καὶ πόθεν," ἔφην, "οὕτως ἀμόρφῳ θηρίῳ
τοσαύτη τῆς εὐωδίας ἡδονή;" "Ὅτι," ἔφη Χαρμίδης, "τοιαύτην ποιεῖται καὶ τὴν τροφήν. Ἰνδῶν
γὰρ ἡ γῆ γείτων ἡλίου· πρῶτοι γὰρ ἀνατέλλοντα
τὸν θεὸν ὁρῶσιν Ἰνδοί, καὶ αὐτοῖς θερμότερον
τὸ φῶς ἐπικάθηται, καὶ τηρεῖ τὸ σῶμα τοῦ πυρὸς
2 τὴν βαφήν. γίνεται δὲ παρὰ τοῖς Ἕλλησιν
ἄνθος Αἰθίοπος χροιᾶς· ἔστι δὲ παρ' Ἰνδοῖς
οὐκ ἄνθος ἀλλὰ πέταλον, οἷα παρ' ἡμῖν τὰ πέταλα
τῶν φυτῶν· ὃ ἐκεῖ[2] μὲν κλέπτει[3] τὴν πνοὴν καὶ

---

[1] The MSS. have ἐκδέχεται, which cannot be construed.
The alteration is due to Jacobs.

[2] Jacobs' insertion (it was perhaps present in the MS.
translated by della Croce): without it the sense is not satisfactory. The MSS. have ὁ μὲν or ἡ μὲν or τὸ μὲν.

[3] Thus Cobet for MSS. κλέπτον or κλέπτων.

be beaten by him, the instrument with which he is beaten being an iron axe. I once saw an extraordinary sight; there was a Greek who had put his head right into the middle of the animal's jaws; it kept its mouth open and breathed upon him as he remained in that position. I was surprised at both, the audacity of the man and the amiability of the elephant; but the man told me that he had in fact given the animal a fee for it, because the beast's breath was only less sweet than the scents of India, and a sovereign remedy for the headache. The elephant knows that he possesses this power of healing, and will not open his mouth for nothing; he is one of those rascally doctors that insist on having their fee first. When you give it him, he graciously consents, stretches open his jaws, and keeps them agape as long as the man desires; he knows that he has let out on hire the sweetness of his breath."

5. "From what source," said I, "does this ugly beast get this delightful scent of his?" "From the character of his food," said Charmides. "The country of the Indians is close to the sun: they are the first to see the sun-god rising; his rays are very hot when they strike them, and their body preserves the tint due to exposure to his fire.[1] We Greeks have a certain flower as dark as a negro's skin: in India it is not a flower, but a leaf, such as we find on trees in our country: there, it conceals its

---

[1] Ovid, *Met.* ii. 235 (of Phaethon's fatal drive):—

The Aethiopians at that time (as men for truth uphold)
—The blood by force of that same heat drawn to the outer part
And there adust from that time forth—became so black and swart.

τὴν ὀδμὴν οὐκ ἐπιδείκνυται· ἢ γὰρ ἀλαζονεύεσθαι
πρὸς τοὺς εἰδότας ὀκνεῖ τὴν ἡδονὴν ἢ τοῖς πολίταις
φθονεῖ. ἂν δὲ τῆς γῆς μικρὸν ἐξοικήσῃ καὶ
ὑπερβῇ τοὺς ὅρους, ἀνοίγει τῆς κλοπῆς τὴν
ἡδονὴν καὶ ἄνθος ἀντὶ φύλλου γίνεται καὶ τὴν
3 ὀδμὴν ἐνδύεται. μέλαν τοῦτο ῥόδον Ἰνδῶν· ἔστι
δὲ τοῖς ἐλέφασι σιτίον, ὡς τοῖς βουσὶ παρ' ἡμῖν
ἡ πόα. ἅτε οὖν ἐκ πρώτης γονῆς αὐτῷ τραφείς,
ὄδωδέ τε πᾶς κατὰ τὴν τροφὴν καὶ τὸ πνεῦμα
πέμπει κάτωθεν εὐωδέστατον, ὃ τῆς πνοῆς αὐτῷ
γέγονε πηγή."

6. Ἐπεὶ οὖν ἐκ τῶν λόγων ἀπηλλάγημεν τοῦ
στρατηγοῦ, μικρὸν διαλιπών, ὅτι οὐ δύναταί τις
τρωθεὶς ἀνέχεσθαι θλιβόμενος τῷ πυρί, τὸν
Μενέλαον μεταπέμπεται, καὶ τῆς χειρὸς λαβόμενος λέγει· "Ἀγαθὸν εἰς φιλίαν οἶδά σε ἐξ ὧν
ἔπραξας εἰς Κλειτοφῶντα· κἀμὲ δὲ εὑρήσεις οὐ
2 χείρονα. δέομαι δὲ παρὰ σοῦ χάριτος, σοὶ μὲν
ῥᾳδίας, ἐμοὶ δὲ ἀνασώσεις τὴν ψυχήν, ἂν θέλῃς.
Λευκίππη με ἀπολώλεκε· σῶσον δὲ σύ. ὀφεί-
λεταί σοι παρ' αὐτῆς ζωάγρια, μισθὸς δὲ σοὶ μὲν
χρυσοῖ πεντήκοντα τῆς διακονίας, αὐτῇ δέ, ὅσους
3 ἂν θέλῃ." λέγει οὖν ὁ Μενέλαος· "Τοὺς μὲν
χρυσοῦς ἔχε καὶ φύλαττε τοῖς τὰς χάριτας
πιπράσκουσιν· ἐγὼ δὲ φίλος ὤν, πειράσομαι
γενέσθαι σοι χρήσιμος." ταῦτα εἰπὼν ἔρχεται

---

[1] This remarkable plant is said to be simply the clove.
Its Greek name καρυόφυλλον, which some think derived from

fragrance and gives no evidence of its scent; for it either hesitates to vaunt its qualities before those who know them well, or grudges them to those of its own country. But if it remove but a little from its own haunts and pass the borders of its own land, it throws open the sweetness that it has hidden, turns into a flower instead of a leaf, and becomes invested with scent. This is the black rose of the Indians; it is the food of the elephant, as is grass to our oxen. Nurtured on it from birth, the whole animal acquires the scent of its food and sends forth its breath endowed with the sweetest savour—its breathing is the origin of its fragrance." [1]

6. Not very long after the general had made an end of these stories (for he who has suffered Cupid's attack cannot long endure torture in his fire), he sent for Menelaus and took him by the hand, saying: "Your services to Clitophon shew that you have a genius for friendship; and you shall find the same in me. I ask of you a favour which is quite easy for you to perform; and by granting it you can save my life, if you will. Leucippe is the death of me; do you come to the rescue. She is already in your debt for saving her life; your reward for the service you can do me will be fifty pieces of gold, while she can have as much as she likes." "No," said Menelaus, "keep your money for those who make their friendship a matter of barter; I, who am already your friend, will try to be of service to you." With these words, he

an Eastern word قرنفول, *qarunfūl*, altered to appear to have a Greek origin ("nut-leaf"), still persists (through middle Latin) in the French *girofle*.

πρός με καὶ πάντα καταγορεύει· ἐβουλευόμεθα
οὖν τί δεῖ πράττειν. ἔδοξε δὲ αὐτὸν ἀπατῆσαι·
4 τό τε γὰρ ἀντιλέγειν οὐκ ἀκίνδυνον ἦν, μὴ καὶ
βίαν προσαγάγῃ, τό τε φεύγειν ἀδύνατον, πάντῃ
μὲν ληστῶν περικεχυμένων, τοσούτων δὲ στρα-
τιωτῶν ἀμφ' αὐτὸν ὄντων.

7. Μικρὸν οὖν διαλιπὼν ὁ Μενέλαος, ἀπελθὼν
πρὸς τὸν Χαρμίδην, "Κατείργασται τὸ ἔργον," ἔφη·
"καίτοι τὸ πρῶτον ἠρνεῖτο ἰσχυρῶς ἡ γυνή, δεο-
μένου δέ μου καὶ ὑπομιμνήσκοντος τῆς εὐεργεσίας,
2 ἐπένευσεν. ἀξιοῖ δὲ δικαίαν δέησιν, ὀλίγην αὐτῇ
χαρίσασθαι προθεσμίαν ἡμερῶν, 'ἔστ' ἂν εἰς τὴν
Ἀλεξάνδρειαν ἀφίκωμαι. κώμη γὰρ αὕτη, καὶ ἐν
ὄψει τὰ γινόμενα, καὶ πολλοὶ μάρτυρες.'" "Εἰς
μακράν," ὁ Χαρμίδης εἶπε, "δίδωσι τὴν χάριν.
3 ἐν πολέμῳ δὲ τίς ἐπιθυμίαν ἀναβάλλεται;
στρατιώτης δὲ ἐν χερσὶν ἔχων μάχην, οἶδεν εἰ
ζήσεται; τοσαῦται τῶν θανάτων εἰσὶν ὁδοί·
αἴτησαί μοι παρὰ τῆς Τύχης τὴν ἀσφάλειαν, καὶ
μενῶ. ἐπὶ πόλεμον νῦν ἐξελεύσομαι βουκόλων·
ἔνδον μου τῆς ψυχῆς ἄλλος πόλεμος κάθηται.
στρατιώτης με πορθεῖ τόξον ἔχων, βέλος ἔχων·
4 νενίκημαι, πεπλήρωμαι βελῶν· κάλεσον, ἄνθρωπε,
ταχὺ τὸν ἰώμενον· ἐπείγει τὸ τραῦμα. ἅψω πῦρ
ἐπὶ τοὺς πολεμίους· ἄλλας δᾷδας ὁ ἔρως ἀνῆψε
κατ' ἐμοῦ· τοῦτο πρῶτον, Μενέλαε, σβέσον τὸ
5 πῦρ. καλὸν τὸ οἰώνισμα πρὸ πολέμου συμβολῆς

came to me and related the whole story, and we took counsel what to do. Our conclusion was that it was best to cozen him; for open opposition was not without danger, in case he should employ force, while flight was impossible, as we were surrounded on every side both by the robbers and by his own very large retinue of soldiers.

7. Menelaus therefore waited a short time, and then returned to Charmides. " Your business is done," he said. " At first she refused most vehemently, but when I implored her, reminding her that she was under obligations to me, she consented. She makes, however, a reasonable request, and that is a short delay of a few days; 'Until,' she says, 'I arrive at Alexandria; this is only a village, where everything is in the public view, and there are too many here who see everything that goes on.'" " It is a long time to wait," said Charmides, " for her favours. When one is at war, how can one postpone one's desires? And when a soldier is just going into battle, how can he know whether he will survive? There are so many different roads to death; if you can get my safety guaranteed to me by Fate, I will wait. I am just going out to fight against buccaneers; but within my soul there is a different kind of conflict. A warrior,[1] armed with bow and arrows, is ravaging me: I am beaten, I am covered with wounds; call, my friend, call quickly the physician that can heal me; the wound is dangerous. I shall carry fire into the country of my enemies; but Love has lit up another kind of torch against me; do you, Menelaus, quench this fire first. Love's congress would be a fair omen

---

[1] Cupid.

ἐρωτικὴ συμπλοκή. Ἀφροδίτη με πρὸς Ἄρεα
ἀποστειλάτω." καὶ ὁ Μενέλαος, "Ἀλλ᾽ ὁρᾷς,"
ἔφη, "ὡς οὐκ ἔστι ῥᾴδιον λαθεῖν αὐτὴν ἐνθάδε
6 τὸν ἄνδρα ὄντα καὶ ταῦτα ἐρῶντα." καὶ ὁ
Χαρμίδης, "Ἀλλὰ τοῦτό γε ῥᾴδιον," ἔφη, "τὸν
Κλειτοφῶντα ἀποφορτίσασθαι."

Ὁρῶν οὖν ὁ Μενέλαος τοῦ Χαρμίδου τὴν
σπουδὴν καὶ φοβηθεὶς περὶ ἐμοῦ, ταχύ τι σκή-
7 πτεται [1] πιθανὸν καὶ λέγει· "Βούλει τὴν ἀλήθειαν
ἀκοῦσαι τῆς ἀναβολῆς; ἢ γὰρ αὕτη [2] χθὲς ἀφῆκε
τὰ ἔμμηνα καὶ ἀνδρὶ συνελθεῖν οὐ θέμις." "Οὐκοῦν
ἀναμενοῦμεν," ὁ Χαρμίδης εἶπεν, "ἐνταῦθα τρεῖς
8 ἡμέρας ἢ τέτταρας, αὗται γὰρ ἱκαναί. ὃ δὲ
ἔξεστιν, αἰτοῦ παρ᾽ αὐτῆς· εἰς ὀφθαλμούς ἡκέτω
τοὺς ἐμοὺς καὶ λόγων μεταδότω· ἀκοῦσαι θέλω
φωνῆς, χειρὸς θιγεῖν, ψαῦσαι σώματος· αὗται
γὰρ ἐρώντων παραμυθίαι. ἔξεστι δὲ αὐτὴν καὶ
φιλῆσαι· τοῦτο γὰρ οὐ κεκώλυκεν ἡ γαστήρ."

8. Ὡς οὖν ταῦτα ὁ Μενέλαος ἐλθὼν ἀπαγ-
γέλλει μοι, πρὸς τοῦτο ἀνεβόησα, ὡς θᾶττον
ἂν ἀποθάνοιμι ἢ περιίδω Λευκίππης φίλημα
ἀλλοτριούμενον. "Οὐ τί γάρ," ἔφην, "ἐστὶ
2 γλυκύτερον; τὸ μὲν γὰρ ἔργον τῆς Ἀφροδίτης
καὶ ὅρον ἔχει καὶ κόρον, καὶ οὐδέν ἐστιν, ἐὰν
ἐξέλῃς αὐτοῦ τὰ φιλήματα· φίλημα δὲ καὶ
ἀόριστόν ἐστι καὶ ἀκόρεστον καὶ καινὸν ἀεί.
τρία γὰρ τὰ κάλλιστα ἀπὸ τοῦ στόματος ἄνεισιν,
3 ἀναπνοὴ καὶ φωνὴ καὶ φίλημα· τοῖς μὲν γὰρ

---

[1] So Cobet for MSS. σκέπτεται.
[2] ἢ γὰρ αὕτη Vilborg: αὕτη γὰρ Cobet: ἢ γὰρ γυνὴ Fritzsche:
ἢ γὰρ αὐτὴ MSS. (αὐτῇ WG): ἡ γὰρ αὐτόχθες anonymously in
Schaefer.

before we join in battle; let it be Aphrodite that
sends me out on my way to Ares." "But you
must see," said Menelaus, "that it is not easy for
her here to trick the one who is her man, especially
as he is greatly in love with her." "Tush," said
Charmides, "it is easy enough to send off Clitophon
somewhere else."

Menelaus saw that Charmides was in earnest,
and began to fear for my safety; he therefore
hastily concocted a plausible excuse saying: "Do
you wish to know the real reason of the delay?
Only yesterday she began the monthly of women,
so that she cannot be approached by a man."
"Very well then," said Charmides, "we must
wait here three or four days, which will be quite
enough. But ask her to do what is possible; let
her at any rate come into my sight and converse
with me; I wish to hear her voice, to hold her hand,
to touch her—the consolation of lovers. Yes, and
I may kiss her too; in her condition there is no
objection to this."

8. When Menelaus came and told me this, I
cried out that I would much rather die than see
Leucippe's kiss bestowed upon another. "What,"
I said, "can be sweeter than her kiss? Love's full
enjoyment comes to an end and one is soon sated
with it—it is nothing, if you take away the kisses
from it; the kiss does not come to an end, never
brings satiety, and is always fresh. Three very
charming things come from the mouth; the breath,
the voice, and the kiss; we kiss those whom we

χείλεσιν ἀλλήλους φιλοῦμεν, ἀπὸ δὲ τῆς ψυχῆς
ἡ τῆς ἡδονῆς ἐστι πηγή. πίστευσόν μοι λέγοντι,
Μενέλαε (ἐν γὰρ τοῖς κακοῖς ἐξορχήσομαι τὰ
μυστήρια), ταῦτα μόνα παρὰ Λευκίππης ἔχω
κἀγώ· ἔτι μένει παρθένος· μέχρι μόνων τῶν
4 φιλημάτων ἐστί μου γυνή. εἰ δέ τις ἁρπάσει
μου καὶ ταῦτα, οὐ φέρω τὴν φθοράν, οὐ μοιχεύε-
ταί μου τὰ φιλήματα." "Οὐκοῦν," ἔφη ὁ Μενέλαος, "βουλῆς ἡμῖν ἀρίστης δεῖ καὶ ταχίστης.
5 ἐρῶν γάρ τις, εἰς ὅσον μὲν ἔχει τὴν ἐλπίδα τοῦ
τυχεῖν, φέρει, εἰς αὐτὸ τὸ τυχεῖν ἀποτεινόμενος·
ἐὰν δὲ ἀπογνῷ, τὸ ἐπιθυμοῦν μεταβαλὼν ἀντι-
λυπῆσαι μέχρι τοῦ δυνατοῦ τολμᾷ τὸ κωλῦον.
6 ἔστω δὲ καὶ ἰσχύς, ὥστε τι δρᾶσαι μετὰ τοῦ μὴ
παθεῖν· τοῦτο δὲ τῆς ψυχῆς τὸ μὴ φοβούμενον
ἀγριαίνει μᾶλλον τὸ θυμούμενον. καὶ γὰρ ὁ
καιρὸς ἐπείγει τῶν πραγμάτων τὸ ἄπορον."

9. Σκοπούντων οὖν ἡμῶν εἰστρέχει τις τεθορυβημένος, καὶ λέγει τὴν Λευκίππην ἄφνω βαδί-
ζουσαν καταπεσεῖν καὶ τὼ ὀφθαλμὼ διαστρέφειν.
ἀναπηδήσαντες οὖν ἐθέομεν ἐπ' αὐτὴν καὶ ὁρῶμεν
2 ἐπὶ τῆς γῆς κειμένην. προσελθὼν οὖν ἐπυθόμην
ὅ τι πάθοι. ἡ δὲ ὡς εἶδέ με, ἀναπηδήσασα παίει
με κατὰ τῶν προσώπων, ὕφαιμον βλέπουσα. ὡς
δὲ καὶ ὁ Μενέλαος οἷός τε ἦν ἀντιλαμβάνεσθαι,
παίει κἀκεῖνον τῷ σκέλει. συνέντες οὖν, ὅτι
μανία εἴη τις [1] τὸ κακόν, βίᾳ συλλαβόντες

---

[1] After τις the MSS. have ἐπί, which Hirschig proposed to
omit and Jacobs proposed to change into ἐστί.

love with the lips, but the spring of the pleasure comes from the soul. Believe me, Menelaus, when I tell you (for in my troubles I will reveal to you the most sacred secrets), that this is all that even I have received from Leucippe; she is still a virgin; only as far as kisses go she is my spouse; and if another is to ravish these from me, I will not tolerate the rape; there can be no adultery with my kisses." "It is clear, then," said Menelaus, "that we need good and speedy counsel. For when a man is in love, he can bear it so long as he cherishes a hope of success, striving eagerly to that very success; once drive him to despair, and he will transform his desire into a passion to inflict pain in return upon that which stands in his way. And suppose he has power also, so as to inflict, without suffering, an injury, then the fact that his spirit is without fear inflames his fury further; and the opportunity urges him to deal drastically with his difficult situation." [1]

9. We were still looking for a plan when a man rushed in, greatly disturbed, and told us that Leucippe, while walking abroad, had suddenly fallen down, her eyes rolling; so we jumped up and ran to her, and found her lying on the ground. I went up to her and asked her what was the matter, but no sooner had she seen me than, her eyes all bloodshot, she struck me in the face; and when Menelaus tried to constrain her, she kicked him. This made us understand that she was afflicted with some kind of madness, so that we forcibly seized her and tried to

---

[1] I do not feel at all sure of the exact meaning of Menelaus' last sentence. It might also mean: "Yes, and the occasion [the short time we have in which to act] increases our difficulties in dealing with the situation."

ἐπειρώμεθα κρατεῖν· ἡ δὲ προσεπάλαιεν ἡμῖν,
οὐδὲν φροντίζουσα κρύπτειν ὅσα γυνὴ μὴ ὁρᾶσθαι
3 θέλει. θόρυβος οὖν πολὺς περὶ τὴν σκηνὴν
αἴρεται, ὥστε καὶ αὐτὸν εἰσδραμεῖν τὸν στρατηγὸν
καὶ τὰ γινόμενα ὁρᾶν. ὁ δὲ τὰ πρῶτα σκῆψιν
ὑπώπτευε τὴν ἀσθένειαν καὶ τέχνην ἐπ' αὐτὸν καὶ
τὸν Μενέλαον ὑπεβλέπετο· ὡς δὲ κατὰ μικρὸν
ἑώρα τὴν ἀλήθειαν, ἔπαθέ τι καὶ αὐτὸς καὶ
ἠλέησε. κομίσαντες οὖν βρόχους ἔδησαν τὴν
4 ἀθλίαν. ὡς δὲ εἶδον αὐτῆς περὶ τὰς χεῖρας τὰ
δεσμά, ἐδεόμην Μενελάου, τῶν πολλῶν ἀπηλλαγ-
μένων ἤδη, " Λύσατε," λέγων, "ἱκετεύω, λύσατε·
οὐ φέρουσι δεσμὸν χεῖρες ἁπαλαί· ἐάσατέ με σὺν
αὐτῇ· μόνος ἐγὼ περιπτυξάμενος αὐτῇ δεσμὸς
5 ἔσομαι· μαινέσθω κατ' ἐμοῦ. τί γάρ με καὶ ζῆν
ἔτι δεῖ; οὐ γνωρίζει με Λευκίππη παρόντα.
κεῖται δέ μοι δεδεμένη, καὶ ὁ ἀναιδὴς ἐγὼ λῦσαι
δυνάμενος οὐκ ἐθέλω. ἐπὶ τούτῳ ἡμᾶς σέσωκεν
ἡ Τύχη ἐκ τῶν λῃστῶν, ἵνα γένῃ μανίας παιδιά;
6 ὦ δυστυχεῖς ἡμεῖς, ὅταν εὐτυχήσωμεν. τοὺς
οἴκοι φόβους ἐκπεφεύγαμεν, ἵνα ναυαγίαν¹ δυσ-
τυχήσωμεν· ἐκ τῆς θαλάσσης περιγεγόναμεν . . . .
ἐκ τῶν λῃστῶν ἀνασεσώσμεθα· μανίᾳ γὰρ ἐτηρού-
7 μεθα. ἐγὼ μέν, ἂν σωφρονήσῃς, φιλτάτη,
φοβοῦμαι πάλιν τὸν δαίμονα, μή τί σοι κακὸν
ἐργάσηται. τίς οὖν ἡμῶν κακοδαιμονέστερος, οἳ
φοβούμεθα καὶ τὰ εὐτυχήματα; ἀλλ' εἰ μόνον
μοι σωφρονήσειας καὶ σεαυτὴν ἀπολάβοις,
παιζέτω πάλιν ἡ Τύχη."

---

¹ So Jacobs for ναυάγια (ναυαγία W).

hold her; she struggled against us, however, and cared nothing about what a woman doesn't want to be seen. As a result, a great hubbub arose in the tent, so that the general himself hurried in and saw what was happening. At first he suspected that this illness of hers was but a pretence against his advances, and looked suspiciously at Menelaus; when he saw the truth, as he soon did, he too grieved and felt pity for her. Ropes were therefore brought, and the poor girl tied up. But when I saw the bonds about her wrists, I could not but implore Menelaus (the others had gone away), saying, " Loose them, I beseech you, loose them ; these tender hands cannot bear fetters. Leave me with her ; I alone will, with my embrace, be the rope to bind her; let her madness rage against me. For what profits it me to live longer ? I am here, and Leucippe knows me not; there my love lies bound, and I, heartless wretch, could loose her and will not. Has Fate only saved us from the hands of the robbers for you to become the sport of madness, ill-starred that we were, when we seemed to be most fortunate? We escaped the terrors that awaited us at home, only to suffer shipwreck; we were saved from the sea, ... [1]; we were rescued from the robbers, only to find madness waiting for us. Yes, dearest, even if you recover, I still fear the visitation of God has some ill to work upon you. Who can be more wretched than we are, who are in fear even of what seems our good fortune? But do you but once get well and come again to your senses, and let Fortune again play what pranks she will ! "

---

[1] The rhetorical structure of the sentence seems to shew that something is here lost, such as " only to fall into the hands of robbers."

10. Ταῦτά με λέγοντα παρηγόρουν οἱ ἀμφὶ τὸν Μενέλαον, φάσκοντες μὴ ἔμμονα εἶναι τὰ τοιαῦτα νοσήματα, πολλάκις δὲ καὶ ἡλικίας ζεούσης ὑπάρχειν· τὸ γὰρ αἷμα πάντη νεάζον, καὶ ὑπὸ πολλῆς ἀκμῆς ἀναζέον, ὑπερβλύζει πολλάκις τὰς φλέβας, καὶ τὴν κεφαλὴν ἔνδον περικλύζον βαπτίζει τοῦ
2 λογισμοῦ τὴν ἀναπνοήν· δεῖ οὖν ἰατροὺς μεταπέμπειν καὶ θεραπείαν προσφέρειν. πρόσεισιν οὖν τῷ στρατηγῷ ὁ Μενέλαος καὶ δεῖται τὸν τοῦ στρατοπέδου ἰατρὸν μετακαλέσασθαι. κἀκεῖνος ἄσμενος ἐπείσθη· χαίρουσι γὰρ οἱ ἐρῶντες εἰς τὰ
3 ἐρωτικὰ προστάγματα.[1] καὶ ὁ ἰατρὸς παρῆν καὶ λέγει· "Νῦν μὲν ὕπνον αὐτῇ παρασκευάσομεν, ὅπως τὸ ἄγριον τῆς ἀκμῆς ἡμερώσωμεν· ὕπνος γὰρ πάντων νοσημάτων φάρμακον· ἔπειτα δὲ
4 καὶ τὴν λοιπὴν θεραπείαν προσοίσομεν." δίδωσιν οὖν ἡμῖν φάρμακόν τι μικρόν, ὅσον ὀρόβου μέγεθος, καὶ κελεύει λύσαντας εἰς ἔλαιον ἐπαλεῖψαι τὴν κεφαλὴν μέσην· σκευάσειν δὲ ἔφη καὶ
5 ἕτερον εἰς γαστρὸς αὐτῇ κάθαρσιν. ἡμεῖς μὲν οὖν ἃ ἐκέλευσεν ἐποιοῦμεν· ἡ δὲ ἐπαλειφθεῖσα μετὰ μικρὸν ἐκάθευδε τὸ ἐπίλοιπον τῆς νυκτὸς μέχρι τῆς ἕω. ἐγὼ δὲ δι' ὅλης τῆς νυκτὸς ἀγρυπνῶν, ἔκλαιον παρακαθήμενος καὶ βλέπων ἔλεγον τὰ δεσμά, "Οἴμοι, φιλτάτη, δέδεσαι καὶ καθεύδουσα,
3 οὐδὲ τὸν ὕπνον ἐλεύθερον ἔχεις. τίνα ἄρα σου τὰ φαντάσματα; ἆρα κἂν κατὰ τοὺς ὕπνους σωφρονεῖς, ἢ μαίνεταί σου καὶ τὰ ὀνείρατα;" ἐπεὶ δὲ

---

[1] προστάγματα W: πράγματα the other MSS.: ταράγματα Lumb. προστάγματα had been conjectured also by Hercher and Headlam.

10. At these words of mine Menelaus' companions tried to comfort me; such troubles, they said, were not lasting, but often occurred at the hot season of youth, when the blood, being young and new, and boiling at its approach to full age, overflows the veins and floods the brain, drowning the fount of reason. It was proper, therefore, to send for doctors and attempt to find a cure. Accordingly, Menelaus approached the general and asked that the army doctor might be called in; the general assented with pleasure, for those in love are glad enough to obey the behests which love lays upon them. When the physician had come: "First," said he, "we must make her sleep, in order to overcome the violent crisis of the disease from which she is suffering— sleep is the remedy for all illness—and after that we will prescribe a further course of treatment." With this intention he gave us a small medicament about the size of a nut, bidding us dissolve it in oil and rub the crown of her head with it; later, he said, he would prepare another to purge her. We followed out his instructions, and after being rubbed with the drug she quickly fell asleep and remained so for the rest of the night until morning. I kept watch the whole night long, and as I sat I could not but weep and say, as I beheld her bonds, "Alas, my darling, you are a prisoner even while you slumber; even your sleep is not free. I wonder of what you are dreaming; are you, in your sleep, in your right senses, or are your dreams too those of a mad-woman?" But even when she woke, she again

ἀνέστη, πάλιν ἄσημα ἐβόα· καὶ ὁ ἰατρὸς παρῆν
καὶ τὴν ἄλλην θεραπείαν ἐθεράπευεν.

11. Ἐν τούτῳ δὴ ἔρχεταί τις παρὰ τοῦ τῆς
Αἰγύπτου σατράπου, κομίζων ἐπιστολὴν τῷ
στρατηγῷ· ἐπέσπευδε δὲ αὐτόν, ὡς εἰκός, ἐπὶ τὸν
πόλεμον τὰ γράμματα, ἐκέλευσε γὰρ εὐθὺς πάντας
ἐν τοῖς ὅπλοις γενέσθαι ὡς ἐπὶ τοὺς βουκόλους.
2 αὐτίκα δὴ μάλα ἐξορμήσαντες, εὐθὺς ἕκαστος,
ὡς εἶχε τάχους, ἐπὶ τὰ ὅπλα ἐχώρουν καὶ παρῆσαν ἅμα τοῖς λοχαγοῖς. τότε μὲν οὖν αὐτοῖς
δοὺς τὸ σύνθημα καὶ κελεύσας αὐτοῖς στρατο-
πεδεύεσθαι, καθ' αὑτὸν ἦν· τῇ δὲ ὑστεραίᾳ ἅμα
τῇ ἡμέρᾳ τὸ στράτευμα ἐξῆγεν ἐπὶ τοὺς πολεμίους.
3 εἶχε δὲ αὐτοῖς οὕτω τῆς κώμης ἡ θέσις. ὁ Νεῖλος
ῥεῖ μὲν ἄνωθεν ἐκ Θηβῶν τῶν Αἰγυπτίων εἰς ὢν [1]
ἄχρι Μέμφεως καὶ ἔστι μικρὸν κάτω κώμη [2]
(Κερκάσωρος ὄνομα τῇ κώμῃ) πρὸς τῷ τέλει τοῦ
4 μεγάλου ῥεύματος. ἐντεῦθεν δὲ περιρρήγνυται τῇ
γῇ καὶ ἐξ ἑνὸς ποταμοῦ γίνονται τρεῖς, δύο μὲν
ἑκατέρωθεν λελυμένοι, ὁ δὲ εἷς ὥσπερ ἦν ῥέων
πρὶν λυθῆναι, καὶ τὴν γῆν εἰς τὰ σχίσματα Δέλτα
5 ποιῶν.[3] ἀλλ' οὐδὲ τούτων ἕκαστος τῶν ποταμῶν
ἀνέχεται μέχρι θαλάσσης ῥέων, ἀλλὰ περισχί-
ζεται ἄλλος ἄλλῃ κατὰ πόλεις, καί εἰσιν αἱ
σχίσεις μείζονες τῶν παρ' Ἕλλησι ποταμῶν· τὸ

---

[1] After Αἰγυπτίων the MSS. have καί ἐστιν εἰς τοῦτο (or
τοσοῦτον) ῥέων. Various suggestions have been made. See
Vilborg's critical apparatus and indeed for all chapters 11–13.
Hercher's ingenious simplification of εἰς ὤν, following a hint
given by Jacobs, should probably be accepted. In the next
line the name of the village is restored by Wesseling from κέρας
Σύρος (which means nothing) of the MSS.

[2] This κώμη is not in the MSS. and was supplied by

cried out some meaningless words; the doctor was
at hand, and gave her the other medicine.

11. While this was going on, a messenger came
from the Satrap of Egypt, bidding the army set
forth, and it appears as if the letter must have
ordered the general to make haste to give battle, for
he at once ordered all his men to arm themselves to
engage with the buccaneers. They therefore hurried
with all speed to their arms and were soon in
readiness with their company-commanders. He
then gave them the watchword, bade them encamp,
and stayed where he was; on the next morning
at day-break he led them out against the enemy.
Now the situation of the village held by the robbers
was as follows. The Nile flows down in a single
stream from Thebes of Egypt as far as Memphis; a
little below is a village (Cercasorus is its name), at
the end of the undivided body of the river. From
that point it breaks up round the land, and three
rivers are formed out of one; two streams discharge
themselves on either side, while the middle one
flows on in the same course as the unbroken river,
and forms the Delta in between the two outer
branches. None of these three channels reaches
the sea in an unbroken state; each, on reaching
various cities, splits up further in different directions.
The resulting branches are all of them larger than
the rivers of Greece, and the water, although so

Wesseling. It might easily have dropped out by haplography,
owing to the following κώμη.

³ It does not seem necessary to expunge this clause, as
some editors wish to do, but to remove it from after εἰς to the
end of the sentence. I translate εἰς τὰ σχίσματα as if it were
εἴσω τῶν σχισμάτων, which may indeed have been the original
reading. See Vilborg's critical note, and his commentary, p. 86.

δὲ ὕδωρ πανταχοῦ μεμερισμένον οὐκ ἐξασθενεῖ, ἀλλὰ καὶ πλεῖται καὶ πίνεται καὶ γεωργεῖται.

12. Νεῖλος ὁ πολὺς πάντα αὐτοῖς γίνεται, καὶ ποταμὸς καὶ γῆ καὶ θάλασσα καὶ λίμνη· καί ἐστι τὸ θέαμα καινόν, ναῦς ὁμοῦ καὶ δίκελλα, κώπη καὶ ἄροτρον, πηδάλιον καὶ πτύον,[1] ναυτῶν ὁμοῦ καὶ γεωργῶν καταγωγή, ἰχθύων ὁμοῦ καὶ βοῶν. ὃ πέπλευκας, φυτεύεις· καὶ ὃ φυτεύεις, τοῦτο

2 πέλαγος γεωργούμενον. ἔχει γὰρ ὁ ποταμὸς ἐπιδημίας· κάθηται δὲ αὐτὸν Αἰγύπτιος ἀναμένων καὶ ἀριθμῶν αὐτῷ τὰς ἡμέρας. καὶ ὁ Νεῖλος οὐ ψεύδεται, ἀλλ' ἔστι ποταμὸς μετὰ προθεσμίας τὸν χρόνον τηρῶν καὶ τὸ ὕδωρ μετρῶν, ποταμὸς

3 ἀλῶναι μὴ θέλων ὑπερήμερος. ἔστι δὲ ἰδεῖν ποταμοῦ καὶ γῆς φιλονεικίαν. ἐρίζετον ἀλλήλοις ἑκάτερον, τὸ μὲν ὕδωρ, τοσαύτην γῆν πελαγίσαι· ἡ δὲ γῆ, τοσαύτην χωρῆσαι γλυκεῖαν θάλασσαν. καὶ νικῶσι μὲν τὴν ἴσην νίκην οἱ δύο, οὐδαμοῦ δὲ

4 φαίνεται τὸ νικώμενον· τὸ γὰρ ὕδωρ τῇ γῇ συνεκτείνεται.

Περὶ δὲ τὰς τῶν βουκόλων ταύτας νομὰς ἀεὶ πολὺ ἐγκάθηται· ὅταν γὰρ τὴν πᾶσαν γῆν πελαγίσῃ, καὶ λίμνας ἐνταῦθα ποιεῖ· αἱ δὲ λίμναι, κἂν ὁ Νεῖλος ἀπέλθῃ, μένουσιν οὐδὲν ἧττον, τὸ ὕδωρ ἔχουσαι, τὸν δὲ πηλὸν τοῦ ὕδατος·

5 ἐπὶ ταύτας αὐτοὶ καὶ βαδίζουσι καὶ πλέουσιν, οὐδὲ ναῦς ἑτέρα δύναται πλεῖν, ἀλλ' ὅσον ἄνθρω-

---

[1] MSS. τρόπαιον, which has been explained as Δήμητρος τρόπαιον, and translated "sheaf." Salmasius proposed κρώπιον (reaping-hook): δρέπανον Naber. Apparently Knox has reached the truth with πτύον: the τρο- comes from the preceding ἄροτρον. He compares Theophylact, *Hist.* p. 95.

much subdivided, does not lose its utility, but is used for boats, for drinking, and for agricultural irrigation.

12. This great Nile is the centre of their existence —their river, their land, their sea, their lake; it is a strange sight to see close together the boat and the hoe, the oar and the plough, the rudder and the winnowing-fan—the meeting-place of sailors and husbandmen, of fishes and oxen.[1] Where you have sailed, there you sow; where you sow, there is a sea subject to tillage. For the river has its due seasons, and the Egyptian sits and waits for it, counting the days. Nor does the Nile ever deceive; it is a river that keeps its appointments both in the times of its increase and the amount of water that it brings, a river that never allows itself to be convicted of being unpunctual. You may see a conflict between river and land : each struggles with the other, the water to make a sea of so wide an expanse of soil, and the soil to absorb so much fresh water. In the end it is a drawn battle, and neither of the two parties can be said to suffer defeat, for water and land are coextensive and identical.

About the haunts of the robbers previously mentioned there is always plenty of water standing ; when it floods the land, it forms lakes, and these remain undiminished when the Nile goes down, full of water, and also of the water's mud. The natives can either walk or row over them, but only in boats just large enough to contain a single passenger (any

---

[1] Compare the epigram of Philippus of Thessalonica, *Anth. Pal.* ix. 299, where two oxen, used to ploughing, complain that they are compelled to pull a drag-net.

πον ἐπιβῆναι· ἀλλὰ πᾶν τὸ ξένον τοῦ τόπου ὁ
πηλὸς ἐμπίπτων κρατεῖ. τοῖς δὲ μικρὰ μὲν καὶ
κοῦφα πλοῖα καὶ ὀλίγον ὕδωρ αὐτοῖς ἀρκεῖ. εἰ δὲ
τέλεον ἄνυδρον εἴη, ἀράμενοι τοῖς νώτοις οἱ πλω-
τῆρες τὸ πλοῖον φέρουσιν, ἄχρις ἂν ἐπιτύχωσιν
6 ὕδατος. ἐν ταύταις δὴ ταῖς λίμναις μέσαι νῆσοί
τινές εἰσι σποράδην πεποιημέναι· αἱ μὲν οἰκοδομη-
μάτων ἔρημοι, παπύροις πεφυτευμέναι· τῶν δὲ παπύρων διεστᾶσιν αἱ φάλαγγες πεπυκνωμέναι τοσοῦτον ὅσον παρ' ἑκάστην ἄνδρα στῆναι μόνον·
τὸ μεταξὺ δὲ τοῦτο τῆς πυκνώσεως αὐτῶν ἄνωθεν
7 ἀναπληροῦσιν αἱ τῶν παπύρων κόμαι. ὑπο-
τρέχοντες οὖν ἐκεῖ καὶ βουλεύονται καὶ λοχῶσι
καὶ λανθάνουσι, τείχεσι ταῖς παπύροις χρώμενοι.
εἰσὶ δὲ τῶν νήσων τινὲς καλύβας ἔχουσαι, καὶ
αὐτοσχεδὸν [1] μεμίμηνται πόλιν ταῖς λίμναις
8 τετειχισμένην. βουκόλων αὗται καταγωγαί· τῶν
πλησίον οὖν μία, μεγέθει καὶ καλύβαις πλείοσι
διαφέρουσα (ἐκάλουν δὲ αὐτήν, οἶμαι, Νίκωχιν),
ἐνταῦθα πάντες συνελθόντες ὡς εἰς τόπον ὀχυρώ-
τατον, ἐθάρρουν καὶ πλήθει καὶ τόπῳ. εἷς γὰρ
αὐτὴν διεῖργε στενωπὸς τὸ μὴ πᾶσαν νῆσον γενέσθαι. ἦν δὲ σταδίου μὲν τὸ μέγεθος, τὸ δὲ πλάτος
ὀργυιῶν δώδεκα· λίμναι δὲ τῇδε κἀκεῖσε τὴν
πόλιν περιέρρεον.

13. Ἐπεὶ τοίνυν ἑώρων τὸν στρατηγὸν προσ-
πελάζοντα, τεχνάζονταί τι τοιοῦτον. συναγαγόντες πάντας τοὺς γέροντας καὶ ἐπιθέντες αὐτοῖς

___

[1] αὐτοσχέδιος is an adjective of three terminations. Unless
there is evidence that in these late writers it was used as one
of two terminations, we ought either to alter the MSS.
αὐτοσχέδιον to αὐτοσχεδίαν or to the adverb αὐτοσχεδόν. I
have preferred the latter alternative.

kind strange to the locality the mud there chokes
and stops); theirs are small and light vessels,[1] drawing very little water; if there is no water at all, the
boatmen pick up their craft and carry it on their
backs until they come to water again. In the middle
of these lakes lie some islands dotted here and
there. Some of them have no houses upon them,
but are planted with papyrus, and the stems of it
grow so close that there is only just room for a man
to stand between them ; over the head of this thick
jungle the leaves of the plant make a close covering.
Robbers therefore can slip in there, make their plans,
devise ambushes or lie hid, using the papyrus-plants
as their fortifications. Others of the islands have
cabins upon them, and present the appearance, the
huts being closely packed together, of a town
protected by water. These are the resorts of the
buccaneers ; one of them, larger than the others and
with a greater number of cabins upon it, was called,
I think, Nicochis ; there, as their strongest fastness,
they all collected, and took courage both from their
numbers and the strength of the position. It was
made a peninsula by a narrow causeway, a furlong in
length and twelve fathoms broad, on either side of
which the waters of the lake entirely surrounded the
town.

13. When they saw the general approaching they
devised the following stratagem. They collected all
their old men and provided them with branches of

---

[1] These must have been like our old-fashioned coracles.
Pliny (*H.N.* xiii. 11) tells us of what they were made:
"The very body and pole of the papyrus itself serveth very
well to twist and weave therewith little boats"; *cf.* Lucan,
iv. 136.

ἱκετηρίας ῥάβδους φοινικίνας, ὄπισθεν ἐπιτάτ-
τουσι τῶν νέων τοὺς ἀκμαιοτάτους, ἀσπίσι καὶ
2 λόγχαις ὡπλισμένους. ἔμελλον δὲ οἱ μὲν
γέροντες ἀνίσχοντες τὰς ἱκετηρίας πετάλων
κόμαις καλύψειν τοὺς ὄπισθεν· οἱ δὲ ἑπόμενοι
τὰς λόγχας ἐπισυρεῖν ὑπτίας, ὡς ἂν ἥκιστα
ὀφθεῖεν. κἂν μὲν ὁ στρατηγὸς πεισθῇ ταῖς τῶν
γερόντων λιταῖς, μηδέν τι νεωτερίζειν τοὺς
λογχοφόρους εἰς μάχην· εἰ δὲ μή, καλεῖν αὐτὸν
ἐπὶ τὴν πόλιν, ὡς σφᾶς[1] αὐτοὺς διδόντων εἰς
3 θάνατον. ὅταν δὲ ἐν μέσῳ γένωνται τῷ στενωπῷ,
τοὺς μὲν γέροντας ἀπὸ συνθήματος διαδιδράσκειν
καὶ ῥίπτειν τὰς ἱκετηρίας, τοὺς δὲ ὡπλισμένους
παραδραμόντας[2] ὅ τι καὶ δύναιντο ποιεῖν.

4 Παρῆσαν οὖν ἐσκευασμένοι τοῦτον τὸν τρόπον
καὶ ἐδέοντο τοῦ στρατηγοῦ αἰδεσθῆναι μὲν αὐτῶν
τὸ γῆρας, αἰδεσθῆναι δὲ τὰς ἱκετηρίας, ἐλεῆσαί
τε τὴν πόλιν, διδόναι[3] δὲ αὐτῷ ἰδίᾳ μὲν ἀργυρίου
τάλαντα ἑκατόν, πρὸς δὲ τὸν σατράπην ἄγειν
ἄνδρας ἑκατόν, θέλοντας αὐτοὺς ὑπὲρ τῆς πόλεως
διδόναι, ὡς ἂν ἔχοι καὶ πρὸς ἐκεῖνον λάφυρον
5 φέρειν. καὶ ὁ λόγος αὐτοῖς οὐκ ἐψεύδετο, ἀλλ'
ἔδωκαν ἄν, εἰ λαβεῖν ἠθέλησεν. ὡς δὲ οὐ προσίετο
τοὺς λόγους, " Οὐκοῦν," ἔφασαν οἱ γέροντες, " εἰ
ταῦτά σοι δέδοκται, οἴσομεν τὴν εἱμαρμένην.
6 ἐν κακοῖς σὺ πάρασχε τὴν χάριν· μὴ ἔξω φονεύ-
σῃς πυλῶν, μηδὲ τῆς πόλεως μακράν, ἀλλ' ἐπὶ
τὴν πατρῴαν γῆν, ἐπὶ τὴν τῆς γενέσεως ἑστίαν

---

[1] Cobet's correction for MSS. σφῶν.
[2] παραδραμόντας Vilborg: περιδραμόντας MSS.: ἐπιδραμόντας
Castiglioni: προδραμόντας Hercher.
[3] So Cobet for ἐδίδοσαν: Vilborg suggests ἔτι δώσειν.

palm, to make them look like suppliants, while behind
them they drew up the flower of their youth, armed
with shield and spear; the veterans were to hold the
branches aloft, so as to hide those in the rear behind
the foliage, while the latter were to keep their spears
horizontal and trail them along the ground, so that
they might not be apparent. If the general were
overcome by the old men's prayers, the armed
warriors were not to make any attempt to join
battle; but if he were not, they were to invite him
to enter their city, as if they were there to give
themselves up to their fate; and when they arrived
at the middle of the causeway, the old men, at a
signal previously arranged, were to run away,
throwing down the branches, while the men in arms
were to charge past and fight their hardest.

They were there then in their places, drawn up
according to this plan, and implored the general to
shew respect to their grey hairs and to the suppli-
catory palm-branches, and to have pity upon the town;
they were ready, they said, to give him for his
private purse a hundred talents of silver, and to
send to the Satrap a hundred men willing to offer
themselves as hostages for the city, so that he might
be able to carry his superior some spoils of war. This
offer of theirs was quite genuine, and if the general
had chosen to accept their terms, they would have
paid the money and given the hostages; but as he
would not agree, " Very well," said the old men, " if
that is your decision we must accept what is fated
for us. Only grant us one favour in our distress;
do not kill us without our gates, or far from our
town, but take us to the spot where our fathers
lived, to the hearths where we were born, and let

ἄγε, τάφον ἡμῖν ποίησον τὴν πόλιν. ἰδού σοι
πρὸς τὸν θάνατον ἡγούμεθα." ταῦτα ἀκούσας
ὁ στρατηγός, τὴν μὲν παρασκευὴν τῆς μάχης
ἀφίησι, κελεύει δὲ ἔρχεσθαι καθ᾽ ἡσυχίαν τῷ
στρατῷ.

14. Ἦσαν δὲ τῶν πραττομένων σκοποὶ πόρρωθεν, οὓς οἱ βουκόλοι προκαθίσαντες ἐκέλευον,
εἰ διαβαίνοντας ἴδοιεν τοὺς πολεμίους, τὸ χῶμα
τοῦ ποταμοῦ κόψαντας ἐπαφεῖναι τὸ ὕδωρ πᾶν
τοῖς ἐναντίοις. ἔχει γὰρ οὕτω τὰ τοῦ Νείλου
2 ῥεύματα. καθ᾽ ἑκάστην διώρυχα χῶμα ἔχουσιν
Αἰγύπτιοι, ὡς ἂν μὴ πρὸ καιροῦ τῆς χρείας
ὑπερέχων ὁ Νεῖλος τὴν γῆν ἐπικλύσῃ. ὅταν δὲ
δεηθῶσιν ἀρδεῦσαι τὸ πεδίον, ἀνέῳξαν ὀλίγον τοῦ
χώματος, εἰς ὅσον ἰλύεται.[1] ἦν οὖν τῆς κώμης
ὄπισθεν διῶρυξ τοῦ ποταμοῦ μεγάλη καὶ πλατεῖα·
3 ταύτῃ οἱ τεταγμένοι τὸ ἔργον, ὡς εἶδον εἰσιόντας
τοὺς πολεμίους, διακόπτουσι ταχὺ τὸ χῶμα τοῦ
ποταμοῦ. πάντα οὖν ὁμοῦ γίνεται· οἱ μὲν γέροντες
οἱ κατὰ πρόσωπον ἄφνω διίστανται· οἱ δὲ τὰς
λόγχας ἐγείραντες ἐκτρέχουσι· τὸ δὲ ὕδωρ ἤδη
παρῆν. καὶ ᾠκοῦντο μὲν αἱ λίμναι πάντοθεν
οἰδοῦσαι, ὁ δὲ ἰσθμὸς ἐπεκλύζετο, πάντα δὲ ἦν
4 ὥσπερ θάλασσα. ἐμπεσόντες οὖν οἱ βουκόλοι,
τοὺς μὲν κατὰ πρόσωπον καὶ τὸν στρατηγὸν
αὐτὸν διαπείρουσι ταῖς λόγχαις, ἀπαρασκεύους
τε ὄντας καὶ πρὸς τὸ ἀδόκητον τεταραγμένους.
5 τῶν δὲ ἄλλων ἀδιήγητος θάνατος ἦν· οἱ μὲν γὰρ
εὐθὺς ἐκ πρώτης προσβολῆς μηδὲ κινήσαντες τὰς

---

[1] So Knox (or εἰς ὅσα ἰ.) for εἰς ὃ σαλεύεται. This clause is
not found in all the MSS.: εἰς ὅσον δεύεται Jacobs: εἰς ὅσα
δεύεται Lumb.

our town be also our tomb. Look, we will lead
the way for you to our death." The general,
hearing this request, released his troops from their
battle formation, and bade them follow after him
at leisure.

14. There were some scouts who were watching the
course of events from a distance; they had been
posted by the buccaneers, who had ordered them,
when they saw the enemy crossing, to break down
the dykes and let all the water in upon them as they
advanced. For this is the arrangement adopted with
the waters of the Nile: at the mouth of every canal
the Egyptians keep a dyke, so that the river should
not overflow its banks and inundate the land before
the time of need; when they wish to irrigate the soil,
they open the dyke a little way, until it is turned
into a swamp. There was in this way behind the
town a long and wide canal from the river; and
those appointed for the task, when they saw the
entry of the hostile forces, quickly cut through
the dyke. All happened in a moment; the old men
in front suddenly disappeared, the others raised
their spears and rushed forward, and the water
flowed in at once; the lagoons rose, the water
swelling on every side, the isthmus was flooded
and the whole country became like a sea. The
buccaneers fell on their enemies and transfixed with
their spears those in front, including the general;
for they were unarmed and quite disordered at the
unexpected attack. As for the rest, the ways in
which they met their death were too many to describe.
Some at the first rush never even drew their weapons,
but perished at once; others had no time in which

αἰχμὰς ἀπώλλυντο· οἱ δὲ οὐ λαβόντες σχολὴν
ἀμύνασθαι, ἅμα γὰρ ἐμάνθανον καὶ ἔπασχον.
ἐνίους δὲ ἔφθανε τὸ παθεῖν πρὸ τοῦ μαθεῖν. οἱ
δὲ ὑπ᾽ ἐκπλήξεως παραλόγου τὸν θάνατον εἱστή-
κεσαν περιμένοντες· οἱ δὲ καὶ κινηθέντες μόνον
κατωλίσθανον, ὑποσκελίζοντος αὐτοὺς τοῦ ποτα-
μοῦ· οἱ δὲ καὶ φεύγειν ὁρμήσαντες εἰς τὸ βαθὺ
6 τῆς λίμνης ἐγκυλισθέντες ὑπεσύρησαν. τῶν μὲν
γὰρ ἐπὶ τῆς γῆς ἑστώτων, τὸ ὕδωρ ἦν ἄχρις
ὀμφαλοῦ, ὥστε καὶ ἀνέκρουεν αὐτῶν τὰς ἀσπίδας
καὶ ἐγύμνου πρὸς τὰ τραύματα τὰς γαστέρας. τὸ
δὲ κατὰ τὴν λίμνην ὕδωρ πάντῃ[1] ὑπὲρ κεφαλὴν
7 ἀνδρὸς ἦν. διακρῖναι δὲ οὐκ ἦν, τί λίμνη καὶ τί
πεδίον· ἀλλὰ καὶ ὁ διὰ τῆς γῆς τρέχων δέει τοῦ
μὴ διαμαρτεῖν βραδύτερος ἦν πρὸς τὴν φυγήν,
ὥστε ταχέως ἡλίσκετο· καὶ ὁ κατὰ τῆς λίμνης
8 πλανηθείς, δόξας γῆν εἶναι, κατεδύετο. καὶ ἦν
καινὰ ἀτυχήματα, καὶ ναυάγια τοσαῦτα, καὶ
ναῦς οὐδαμοῦ. ἀμφότερα δὲ καινὰ καὶ παράλογα, ἐν ὕδατι πεζομαχία, καὶ ἐν τῇ γῇ ναυαγία.
9 οἱ μὲν δὴ τοῖς πεπραγμένοις ἐπαρθέντες μέγα
ἐφρόνουν, ἀνδρείᾳ νομίζοντες κεκρατηκέναι καὶ
οὐκ ἀπάτης κλοπῇ. ἀνὴρ γὰρ Αἰγύπτιος καὶ τὸ
δειλόν, ὅπου φοβεῖται, δεδούλωται, καὶ τὸ μά-
χιμον, ἐν οἷς θαρρεῖ, παρώξυνται· ἀμφότερα δὲ οὐ
κατὰ μέτρον, ἀλλὰ τὸ μὲν ἀσθενέστερον δυστυχεῖ,
τὸ δὲ προπετέστερον κρατεῖ.

15. Δέκα δὲ τῇ Λευκίππῃ διεληλύθεσαν
ἡμέραι τῆς μανίας, ἡ δὲ νόσος οὐκ ἐκουφίζετο.

---

[1] I accept Hercher's suggestion. Lumb proposes στάντος.
παντός (παντῶς G) over the head of every man, is very
feeble.

to make their defence; they were cut down in
the same moment that they realised they were
being attacked; others even before they realised it.
Others, struck into immobility by the unexpected
event, stood and waited for death. Some slipped
directly they attempted to move, the water under-
mining their footsteps; others, as they attempted to
flee, rolled into the deep part of the lake, and were
dragged under. As for those who were standing on
the firm ground, the water came up as far as their
navels, and thereby turned up their shields, thus
exposing their bodies to the blows of the enemy.
The water in the lagoon was everywhere above the
height of a man's head; indeed, it was impossible to
tell which was lake and which was land; those who
attempted to run away upon land had to go slowly for
fear of making a mistake, and so were quickly
captured; while those who mistook their way into
the lake, thinking it to be land, were drowned. It
was a paradoxical kind of mishap, innumerable
wrecks, but no ship. Both indeed were new and
strange, a land-fight in the water and a shipwreck on
land. The conquerors were greatly elated by the
result, and in high conceit with themselves, imagining
that they had gained their victory by their bravery,
and not by an underhand stratagem; for the
Egyptian is subject to the most slavish cowardice
when he is afraid and the most fool-hardy rashness
when encouraged by his position; in neither case
has he any moderation—he either bows to fortune
with over-great pusillanimity, or displays in success
more than idiotic temerity.

15. Ten days had now passed since the madness
came upon Leucippe, and there was no improvement

ἅπαξ οὖν ποτὲ καθεύδουσα, ταύτην ἀφίησιν
ὀνειροπολουμένη[1] τὴν φωνήν, " Διὰ σὲ μαίνομαι,
Γοργία." ἐπεὶ οὖν ἕως ἐγένετο, λέγω τῷ Μενε-
λάῳ τὸ λεχθὲν καὶ ἐσκόπουν εἴ τις εἴη που κατὰ
2 τὴν κώμην Γοργίας. προελθοῦσι δὲ ἡμῖν νεανίσκος
προσέρχεταί τις καὶ προσαγορεύσας με, "Σωτὴρ
ἥκω σός," ἔφη, "καὶ τῆς σῆς γυναικός." ἐκπλαγεὶς οὖν καὶ θεόπεμπτον εἶναι νομίσας τὸν
ἄνθρωπον, "Μὴ Γοργίας," εἶπον, "τυγχάνεις ;"
"Οὐ μὲν οὖν," εἶπεν, "ἀλλὰ Χαιρέας· Γοργίας
3 γάρ σε ἀπολώλεκεν." ἔτι μᾶλλον ἔφριξα καὶ
λέγω· "Τίνα ταύτην ἀπώλειαν, καὶ τίς ἐστιν
ὁ Γοργίας; δαίμων γάρ μοί τις αὐτὸν ἐμήνυσε
νύκτωρ· σὺ δὲ διηγητὴς γενοῦ τῶν θείων μηνυ-
μάτων." "Γοργίας ἦν μέν," ἔφη, "Αἰγύπτιος
στρατιώτης· νῦν δὲ οὐκ ἔστιν ἀλλ' ἔργον γέγονε
4 τῶν βουκόλων. ἤρα δὲ τῆς σῆς γυναικός· ὢν δὲ
φύσει φαρμακεύς, σκευάζει τι φάρμακον ἔρωτος
καὶ πείθει τὸν διακονούμενον ὑμῖν Αἰγύπτιον
λαβεῖν τὸ φάρμακον καὶ ἐγκαταμίξαι τῷ τῆς
Λευκίππης ποτῷ. λανθάνει δὲ ἀκράτῳ χρη-
σάμενος τῷ φαρμάκῳ, καὶ τὸ φίλτρον εἰς μανίαν
5 αἴρεται. ταῦτα γάρ μοι χθὲς ὁ τοῦ Γοργίου
θεράπων διηγήσατο, ὃς ἔτυχεν αὐτῷ συστρα-
τευσάμενος ἐπὶ τοὺς βουκόλους· ἔσωσε δὲ αὐτόν,
ὡς εἰκός, ὑπὲρ ὑμῶν ἡ Τύχη. αἰτεῖ δὲ χρυσοῦς
τέτταρας ὑπὲρ τῆς ἰάσεως· ἔχει γάρ, φησίν,
ἑτέρου φαρμάκου σκευήν, δι' οὗ λύσει τὸ πρό-

---

[1] Lobeck's emendation for προπολουμένην, which can hardly
be construed. There have been other suggestions: Cobet
simply changed the participle into the nominative case,
while others preferred a suggestion in some MSS., πυρπολου-
μένην (πυρπολουμένη G) " these fevered words."

in her malady. On one occasion, however, while asleep, she uttered these words in her dream: " It is through you that I have lost my senses, Gorgias." When morning came, I told Menelaus what she had said, and enquired if there were any Gorgias in the place. As we walked out, a young man came up to us and, addressing me, " I come," he said, " to be the salvation of you and your beloved.[1]" I was struck dumb at this and thought that he must be divinely sent to me. " You do not happen to be Gorgias, I suppose ? " said I. " No," said he, " but Chaereas. It is Gorgias that has been your undoing." I could not but shiver at this, and said, " What is this undoing, and who is Gorgias ? Some god communicated to me his name in the night; it is for you to be the interpreter of the heavenly message." " Gorgias *was*," he said, " an Egyptian soldier : now he is no more, but has become the victim of the buccaneers. He fell in love with your chosen, and being naturally an expert in drugs, he prepared a love-philtre and bribed your Egyptian servant to take it and mix it in Leucippe's drink : but the servant by a mistake administered the philtre un-diluted, and it had the effect of producing madness. All this was told me yesterday by Gorgias' servant, who was fighting by his side against the robbers ; it seems that good fortune has kept him safe for you ; he asks four pieces of gold to cure her, for he says that he possesses another preparation of drugs

---

[1] γυνή, both here and in several other passages, is used in the sense of a *prospective* wife, like the German *Braut*. This cannot be exactly rendered in English by any of the ordinary equivalents of γυνή, so that it must be expressed by alternatives or circumlocutions.

6 τερον." "Ἀλλὰ σοὶ μέν," ἔφην, "ἀγαθὰ γένοιτο
τῆς διακονίας· τὸν δὲ ἄνθρωπον, ὃν λέγεις, ἄγε
πρὸς ἡμᾶς." καὶ ὁ μὲν ἀπῆλθεν· ἐγὼ δὲ πρὸς
τὸν Αἰγύπτιον εἰσελθών, τύπτων τε αὐτὸν πὺξ
κατὰ τῶν προσώπων καὶ δευτέραν καὶ τρίτην,
θορυβῶν δὲ ἅμα λέγω· "Εἰπόν, τί δέδωκας
Λευκίππῃ; καὶ πόθεν μαίνεται;" ὁ δὲ φοβηθεὶς
καταλέγει πάντα ὅσα ἡμῖν ὁ Χαιρέας διηγήσατο.
τὸν μὲν οὖν εἴχομεν ἐν φυλακῇ καθείρξαντες.

16. Κἂν τούτῳ παρῆν ὁ Χαιρέας, ἄγων τὸν
ἄνθρωπον. λέγω οὖν πρὸς ἀμφοτέρους· "Τοὺς
μὲν τέτταρας χρυσοῦς ἤδη λάβετε μισθὸν ἀγαθῆς
μηνύσεως· ἀκούσατε δὲ ὡς ἔχω περὶ τοῦ φαρμάκου.
ὁρᾶτε ὡς καὶ τῶν παρόντων τῇ γυναικὶ κακῶν
2 αἴτιον γέγονε φάρμακον. οὐκ ἀκίνδυνον δὲ ἐπι-
φαρμάσσειν τὰ σπλάγχνα ἤδη πεφαρμαγμένα.
φέρε εἴπατε, ὅ τι καὶ ἔχει τὸ φάρμακον τοῦτο καὶ
παρόντων ἡμῶν σκευάσατε· χρυσοῖ δὲ ὑμῖν ἄλλοι
3 τέτταρες μισθός, ἂν οὕτω ποιῆτε." καὶ ὁ ἄνθρωπος, "Δίκαια," ἔφη, "φοβῇ· τὰ δὲ ἐμβαλλό-
μενα κοινὰ καὶ πάντα ἐδώδιμα· αὐτὸς δὲ τούτων
ἀπογεύσομαι τοσοῦτον, ὅσον κἀκείνη λάβοι." καὶ
ἅμα κελεύει τινὰ πριάμενον κομίζειν, ἕκαστον
εἰπών· ὥς τε ταχὺ μὲν ἐκομίσθη, παρόντων δὲ
ἡμῶν συνέτριψε πάντα ὁμοῦ καὶ δίχα διελών,
"Τὸ μὲν αὐτός," ἔφη, "πίομαι πρῶτος, τὸ δὲ
4 δώσω τῇ γυναικί. κοιμηθήσεται δὲ πάντως δι'
ὅλης τῆς νυκτὸς λαβοῦσα· περὶ δὲ τὴν ἕω καὶ

which is an antidote to the former." "May God
bless you," said I, "for this service you are
rendering to us! Please bring hither the man of
whom you speak." He departed on this errand,
while I went in to find my Egyptian, and I beat him
about the face with my fist more than once or twice,
shouting and saying to him, "Tell me, what did you
give to Leucippe? What is it that has made her
mad?" He was greatly frightened, and related to
us the whole story just as Chaereas had told it
to us; so we shut him up in prison and kept him
there.

16. Meanwhile Chaereas came back, bringing his
man with him, and I addressed myself to both of
them: "Here are your four pieces of gold as a
reward for your good tidings; but listen to what I
have to say about the remedy. You see how a
drugged potion has been the cause of the girl's
present evil state; it cannot surely be without
danger to add yet further drugs to organs already
drugged. Tell us then of what ingredients it is
composed, and make it up here in our presence; if
you will do this, there will be a reward of four more
gold pieces for you." "Your fears are quite
justified," said he; "but the ingredients are quite
common and all harmless to take; I will myself
drink a portion equal to hers." So saying, he sent
someone out to buy them and bring them back,
naming each; and when they had arrived, which
was in no long time, he pounded them all up before
our eyes and divided the compound into two parts.
"I will myself drink the one first," he said, "and
the other I will give to the maiden. After she has
taken it she will sleep the whole night through, and

τὸν ὕπνον καὶ τὴν νόσον ἀποθήσεται." λαμβάνει
δὴ τοῦ φαρμάκου πρῶτος αὐτός, τὸ δὲ λοιπὸν
5 κελεύει περὶ τὴν ἑσπέραν δοῦναι πιεῖν. "Ἐγὼ
δὲ ἄπειμι," ἔφη, "κοιμηθησόμενος· τὸ γὰρ φάρμακον οὕτω βούλεται." ταῦτα εἰπὼν ἀπῆλθε,
τοὺς τέτταρας χρυσοῦς παρ᾽ ἐμοῦ λαβών. "Τοὺς
δὲ λοιπούς," ἔφην, "δώσω, εἰ ῥαΐσειεν ἐκ τῆς
νόσου."

17. Ἐπεὶ οὖν καιρὸς ἦν αὐτῇ πιεῖν τὸ φάρμακον, ἐγχέας προσηυχόμην αὐτῷ· "Ὦ γῆς
τέκνον, φάρμακον, ὦ δῶρον Ἀσκληπιοῦ, ἀλή-
θευσόν¹ σου τὰ ἐπαγγέλματα, εὐτυχέστερον ἐμοῦ
γενοῦ καὶ σῶζέ μοι τὴν φιλτάτην. νίκησον τὸ
φάρμακον ἐκεῖνο τὸ βάρβαρον καὶ ἄγριον."
2 ταῦτα δοὺς τῷ φαρμάκῳ τὰ συνθήματα καὶ
καταφιλήσας τὸ ἔκπωμα, δίδωμι τῇ Λευκίππῃ
πιεῖν. ἡ δέ, ὡς ὁ ἄνθρωπος εἶπε, μετὰ μικρὸν
ἔκειτο καθεύδουσα· κἀγὼ παρακαθήμενος, ἔλεγον
πρὸς αὐτὴν ὡς ἀκούουσαν· "Ἆρά μοι σωφρονή-
σεις² ἀληθῶς; ἆρά μέ ποτε γνωριεῖς²; ἆρά σου
3 τὴν φωνὴν ἐκείνην ἀπολήψομαι; μάντευσαί τι
καὶ νῦν καθεύδουσα· καὶ γὰρ χθὲς τοῦ Γοργίου
κατεμαντεύσω δικαίως. εὐτυχεῖς ἄρα μᾶλλον
κοιμωμένη· γρηγοροῦσα μὲν γὰρ μανίαν δυσ-
4 τυχεῖς, τὰ δὲ ἐνύπνιά σου σωφρονεῖ." ταῦτά μου
διαλεγομένου ὡς πρὸς ἀκούουσαν Λευκίππην,
μόλις ἡ πολύευκτος ἕως ἀναφαίνεται, καὶ ἡ
Λευκίππη φθέγγεται, καὶ ἦν ἡ φωνή· "Κλειτοφῶν." ἀναπηδήσας οὖν πρόσειμί τε αὐτῇ καὶ

---

¹ So Cobet for the MSS. ἀληθεύσειαν. Not only would the
change of person be awkward, but the verb should be singular.
Lumb proposes ἀληθεύσαι ἄν.

when morning comes she will arise at once from her sleep and from the disease." So he first took his portion of the drug, and bade the rest be given her to drink in the evening. "But I," he added, "must go away and rest, as the drug requires." With these words he departed, taking the four gold pieces I had given him. "I will give you the other four," I said, "on her recovery."

17. So when the time came to give her the medicine, I poured it out and prayed over it thus: "Drug, child of earth, gift of Aesculapius, bring true thy promises; be more fortunate than I and save me my dearest. Overcome that other cruel and savage philtre." When I had thus conjured the medicine I kissed the cup, and gave it to Leucippe to drink; and she, as the man had predicted, soon lay fast asleep. I sat by her, and addressed her as though she could hear my words; "Will you really regain your senses once more? Will you know me again? Shall I hear again that dear voice of yours? Give me some token of hope, now, in your sleep, just as yesterday you rightly divined the name of Gorgias. Happier are you while at rest; when awake, you suffer the misfortune of madness, while your dreams have sound sense." Thus did I harangue Leucippe, as though she could hear me, and at last appeared the dawn for which I had prayed so long; Leucippe spoke, and the word she uttered was "Clitophon." I jumped up, went to her, and asked her how she

---

² Both optatives (σωφρονήσειας, γνωρίσειας) in the MSS.: corrected by Cobet. γνωρίσεις Vilborg.

πυνθάνομαι πῶς ἔχει. ἡ δὲ ἐῴκει μὲν μηδὲν ὧν
ἔπραξεν ἐγνωκέναι, τὰ δεσμὰ δὲ ἰδοῦσα ἐθαύμαζε
5 καὶ ἐπυνθάνετο τίς ὁ δήσας εἴη. ἐγὼ δὲ ἰδὼν
σωφρονοῦσαν, ὑπὸ πολλῆς χαρᾶς ἔλυον μὲν μετὰ
θορύβου τὰ δεσμά, μετὰ ταῦτα δὲ ἤδη τὸ πᾶν
αὐτῇ διηγοῦμαι. ἡ δὲ ᾐσχύνετο ἀκροωμένη καὶ
6 ἠρυθρία καὶ ἐνόμιζε τότε αὐτὰ ποιεῖν. τὴν μὲν
οὖν ἀνελάμβανον παραμυθούμενος, τοῦ δὲ φαρμάκου τὸν μισθὸν ἀποδίδωμι μάλα ἄσμενος.
ἦν δὲ τὸ πᾶν ἡμῖν ἐφόδιον σῶον· ὃ γὰρ ὁ Σάτυρος
ἔτυχεν ἔχων ἐζωσμένος, ὅτε ἐναυαγήσαμεν, οὐκ
ἀφῄρητο ὑπὸ τῶν λῃστῶν, οὔτε αὐτὸς οὔτε ὁ
Μενέλαος οὐδὲν ὧν εἶχεν.

18. Ἐν τούτῳ δὲ καὶ τοὺς λῃστὰς ἐπελθοῦσα
δύναμις μείζων ἀπὸ τῆς μητροπόλεως παρεστή-
σατο καὶ πᾶσαν αὐτῶν εἰς ἔδαφος κατέστρεψε
τὴν πόλιν. ἐλευθερωθέντος δὲ τοῦ ποταμοῦ τῆς
τῶν βουκόλων ὕβρεως, παρεσκευαζόμεθα τὸν ἐπὶ
τὴν Ἀλεξάνδρειαν πλοῦν. συνέπλει δὲ ἡμῖν καὶ ὁ
Χαιρέας, φίλος ἤδη γενόμενος ἐκ τῆς τοῦ φαρ-
2 μάκου μηνύσεως. ἦν δὲ τὸ μὲν γένος ἐκ τῆς
νήσου τῆς Φάρου, τὴν δὲ τέχνην ἁλιεύς, ἐστρα-
τεύετο δὲ μισθῷ κατὰ τῶν βουκόλων τὴν ἐν ταῖς
ναυσὶ στρατείαν· ὥστε μετὰ τὸν πόλεμον τῆς
3 στρατείας ἀπήλλακτο. ἦν οὖν ἐξ ἀπλοίας
μακρᾶς πλεόντων πάντα μεστά, καὶ πολλή τις
ὄψεως ἡδονή, ναυτῶν ᾠδή, πλωτήρων κρότος,
χορεία νεῶν, καὶ ἦν ἅπας ὁ ποταμὸς ἑορτή· ἐῴκει

was; she seemed to know nothing of what had
happened, but was astonished to see her bonds, and
asked who had fettered her. Seeing her in her senses
again, I was overjoyed to confusion and undid the
bonds, and then related to her the whole course of
events; she was quite ashamed when she heard it;
she blushed, and could hardly be persuaded that she
was not still beside herself. I therefore did my
best to comfort and calm her, and paid the fee for
the drug with the utmost good will. All the money
which we had provided for our journey was safe;
that which Satyrus had happened to tie up in his
girdle when we were shipwrecked had not been taken
from him by the robbers, and neither he nor Menelaus
had lost any of their possessions.

18. While all this was going on there came from
the capital against the robbers a larger force, which
settled their business and razed their town to the
ground. The river freed from the buccaneers' violence,
we proposed to sail to Alexandria, and Chaereas was to
accompany us; for he had become on friendly terms
with us on account of the information he had been
able to give us about the philtre. He was of the
Island of Pharos by birth and a fisherman by trade;
he had served in the fleet sent against the buccaneers,
and had taken his discharge after the conclusion of
the war. Long had boats been absent from the
Nile,[1] but the river was now thronged with passengers,
and the whole presented a delightful spectacle—
the singing of the boatmen, the rhythm of the oars,
and the procession of the boats; it was like a great
fair, and the whole of our voyage seemed to be on

---

[1] Owing to its having been long infested by the pirates,
who had now been destroyed.

δὲ ὁ πλοῦς κωμάζοντι ποταμῷ. ἔπινον δὲ καὶ
τοῦ Νείλου τότε πρῶτον ἄνευ τῆς πρὸς οἶνον
ὁμιλίας, κρῖναι θέλων τοῦ πώματος τὴν ἡδονήν·
4 οἶνος γὰρ φύσεως ὕδατος κλοπή. ἀρυσάμενος
οὖν ὑάλου τῆς διαφανοῦς κύλικα, τὸ ὕδωρ ἑώρων
ὑπὸ λευκότητος πρὸς τὸ ἔκπωμα ἁμιλλώμενον
καὶ τὸ ἔκπωμα νικώμενον. γλυκὺ δὲ πινόμενον
ἦν καὶ ψυχρὸν ἐν μέτρῳ τῆς ἡδονῆς· οἶδα γὰρ
ἐνίους τῶν παρ᾽ Ἕλλησι ποταμῶν καὶ τιτρώσ-
κοντας· τούτῳ συνέκρινον αὐτοὺς τῷ ποταμῷ.
5 διὰ τοῦτο αὐτὸν ἄκρατον ὁ Αἰγύπτιος πίνων οὐ
φοβεῖται, Διονύσου μὴ δεόμενος. ἐθαύμασα δὲ
αὐτῶν[1] καὶ τὸν τρόπον τοῦ ποτοῦ· οὔτε γὰρ
ἀρύσαντες πίνειν ἐθέλουσιν, οὔτε ἐκπωμάτων
ἀνέχονται, ἔκπωμα αὐτουργὸν ἔχοντες· ἔκπωμα
6 γὰρ αὐτοῖς ἐστιν ἡ χείρ. εἰ γάρ τις αὐτῶν
διψήσειε πλέων, προκύψας ἐκ τῆς νηὸς τὸ μὲν
πρόσωπον εἰς τὸν ποταμὸν προβέβληκε, τὴν δὲ
χεῖρα εἰς τὸ ὕδωρ καθῆκε καὶ κοίλην βαπτίσας
καὶ πλησάμενος ὕδατος, ἀκοντίζει κατὰ τοῦ
στόματος τὸ πῶμα καὶ τυγχάνει τοῦ σκοποῦ· τὸ
δὲ κεχηνὸς περιμένει τὴν βολὴν καὶ δέχεται καὶ
κλείεται, καὶ οὐκ ἐᾷ τὸ ὕδωρ αὖθις ἔξω πεσεῖν.

19. Εἶδον δὲ καὶ ἄλλο θηρίον τοῦ Νείλου,
ὑπὲρ τὸν ἵππον τὸν ποτάμιον εἰς ἀλκὴν ἐπαινού-
μενον· κροκόδειλος δὲ ὄνομα ἦν αὐτῷ. παρήλ-
λακτο δὲ καὶ τὴν μορφὴν εἰς ἰχθὺν ὁμοῦ καὶ
θηρίον.[2] μέγας μὲν γὰρ ἐκ κεφαλῆς εἰς οὐράν,
2 τὸ δὲ εὖρος τοῦ μεγέθους οὐ κατὰ λόγον. δορὰ

---

[1] Hirschig's correction, which seems right, from αὐτοῦ, the
subject of the next sentence being in the plural.
[2] θηρίον is followed in the MSS. by μέγα, which Jacobs
saw was a mere dittography from the following word.

a river keeping festival. That was the first occasion
on which I drank the water of the Nile without
mixing it with wine, as I wished to test its excellence
as a drink; wine spoils its character. I filled a
transparent glass with it, and saw that in the matter
of limpidity [1] it vied with, nay, it defeated the vessel
that contained it; to the taste it was sweet and cool
enough to be delightful, whereas some of the Greek
rivers with which I compared it are so cold as to be
painful. For this reason the Egyptian does not feel
the need of the juice of Bacchus, and fears not to
drink the water without mixture. I was also
surprised at the manner in which they drink it: they
do not draw it in the usual way, nor use vessels to
drink it from, having a vessel provided by nature—
their hand. If one of them, while on ship-board,
is thirsty, he leans his face forward over the side
above the river, and then, making a hollow of his
hand, plunging it beneath the surface, and filling it
with water, he jerks it up into his mouth and does
not miss the mark; his open mouth awaits, receives
and keeps it when it is thrown, and then shuts, not
allowing it to fall out again.

19. I also saw another beast, a denizen of the Nile,
which is even more celebrated for its strength than
the hippopotamus: it is called the crocodile. Its form
partakes both of that of a beast and that of a fish;
it is of great length from head to tail, though it is
not proportionately broad. Its hide is wrinkled and

---

[1] Excellent water as it is, this is not at the present day
one of its characteristics, though the slight opacity is quite
harmless, and can to some extent be made to settle.

μὲν φολίσι ῥυσή· πετραία[1] δὲ τῶν νώτων ἡ χροιὰ
καὶ μέλαινα· ἡ γαστὴρ δὲ λευκή· πόδες τέτταρες,
εἰς τὸ πλάγιον ἠρέμα κυρτούμενοι, καθάπερ
χερσαίας χελώνης· οὐρὰ μακρὰ καὶ παχεῖα καὶ
3 ἐοικυῖα στερεῷ σώματι. οὐ γὰρ ὡς τοῖς ἄλλοις
περίκειται θηρίοις, ἀλλ᾽ ἔστι τῆς ῥάχεως ἐν
ὀστοῦν τελευτὴ καὶ μέρος αὐτοῦ τῶν ὅλων.
ἐντέτμηται δὲ ἄνωθεν εἰς ἀκάνθας ἀναιδεῖς, οἷαι
4 τῶν πριόνων εἰσὶν αἱ αἰχμαί. αὕτη δὲ αὐτῷ καὶ
μάστιξ ἐπὶ τῆς ἄγρας γίνεται, τύπτει γὰρ αὐτῇ
πρὸς οὓς ἂν διαπαλαίῃ καὶ πολλὰ ποιεῖ τραύματα
πληγῇ μιᾷ. κεφαλὴ δὲ αὐτῷ τοῖς νώτοις συν-
υφαίνεται καὶ εἰς μίαν στάθμην ἰθύνεται, ἔκλεψε
γὰρ αὐτοῦ τὴν δειρὴν ἡ φύσις. ἔστι δὲ τοῦ
ἵππου[2] βλοσυρώτερος τὰ ὄμματα, καὶ ἐπὶ πλέον
5 ἐπὶ τὰς γένυς ἐκτείνεται καὶ ἀνοίγεται πᾶς. τὸν
μὲν γὰρ ἄλλον χρόνον, παρ᾽ ὅσον οὐ κέχηνε τὸ
θηρίον, ἔστι κεφαλή, ὅταν δὲ χάνῃ πρὸς τὰς
ἄγρας, ὅλον στόμα γίνεται. ἀνοίγει δὲ τὴν γένυν
τὴν ἄνω, τὴν δὲ κάτω στερεὰν ἔχει· καὶ ἀπόστασίς
ἐστι πολλή, καὶ μέχρι τῶν ὤμων τὸ χάσμα, καὶ
6 εὐθὺς ἡ γαστήρ. ὀδόντες δὲ πολλοί, καὶ ἐπὶ
πλεῖστον τεταγμένοι· φασὶ δὲ ὅτι τὸν ἀριθμὸν
τυγχάνουσιν, ὅσας ὁ θεὸς εἰς ὅλον ἔτος ἀναλάμ-
πει τὰς ἡμέρας· τοσοῦτον ἔργον αἴρει τῶν
γενύων πεδίον. ἂν δὲ ἐκπεράσῃ πρὸς τὴν γῆν,
ὅσον ἔχει δυνάμεως ἀπιστήσεις, ἰδὼν τὴν τοῦ
σώματος ὁλκήν.

[1] Note Hercher's ingenious conjecture, τεφραία, ash-coloured.
It is attractive, as the rest of the epithets in the sentence are
of colours. πετραίαις Schneider.

[2] So Hirschig for λοιποῦ, which made no sense: he also
suggested ὄμματα and πᾶς for the MSS. σώματα and πᾶσα. For
λοιποῦ Lumb proposes λύκου.

scaly, the skin of its back black and hard as stones,
whereas that of its belly is white; it has four feet,
with curved, bandy legs, like those of a tortoise; its
tail is long and thick, like the solid part of its body;
unlike that of other animals, it is the bony continuation of the spine, of which it is indeed an integral part.
On the upper side it is divided into cruel spines, like
the teeth of a saw; the animal uses it like a scourge
against its prey, striking with it anything against
which it is struggling, and inflicting several wounds
with a single blow. Its head grows directly on to its
shoulders, forming with them a single straight line;
for a neck is not one of the gifts with which it has
been favoured by nature. Its eyes are more grim and
staring than those of a horse; it is generally in the
condition of having its mouth wide open. For the
rest of the time, when not agape, that part of the
beast is a head; but when it yawns after its prey, it
is all mouth. It lifts its upper jaw, keeping the
lower one rigid. So wide apart do they go that
the opening reaches all the way to the shoulders and
the entrance to its belly is visible.[1] Its teeth are
numerous, placed one behind the other; they are
said to be identical in number with the days God
gives light to for a year—a mighty crop to spring up
in the field of its jaws! When it comes up from the
river on to the land, you would be surprised at the
creature's enormous strength if you observed the way
it drags its body.

[1] Compare the description of the beast about to attack
Andromeda in III. vii.

Ε′

1. Τριῶν δὲ πλεύσαντες ἡμερῶν εἰς ᾽Αλεξάν-
δρειαν ἤλθομεν. ἀνιόντι δέ μοι κατὰ τὰς ῾Ηλίου
καλουμένας πύλας, συνηντᾶτο εὐθὺς τῆς πόλεως
ἀστράπτον τὸ κάλλος, καί μου τοὺς ὀφθαλμοὺς
2 ἐγέμισεν ἡδονῆς.   στάθμη μὲν κιόνων ὄρθιος
ἑκατέρωθεν ἐκ τῶν ῾Ηλίου πυλῶν εἰς τὰς Σελήνης
πύλας· οὗτοι γὰρ τῆς πόλεως οἱ πυλωροί.   ἐν
3 μέσῳ δὴ τῶν κιόνων τῆς πόλεως τὸ πεδίον· ὁδὸς
δὲ διὰ τοῦ πεδίου πολλὴ καὶ ἔνδημος ἀποδημία.
ὀλίγους δὲ τῆς πόλεως σταδίους προελθών, ἦλθον
εἰς τὸν ἐπώνυμον ᾽Αλεξάνδρου τόπον.   εἶδον δὲ
ἐντεῦθεν ἄλλην πόλιν καὶ σχιζόμενον ταύτῃ
4 τὸ κάλλος· ὅσος γὰρ κιόνων ὄρχατος εἰς τὴν
εὐθυνωρίαν, τοσοῦτος ἕτερος εἰς τὰ ἐγκάρσια.
ἐγὼ δὲ μερίζων τοὺς ὀφθαλμοὺς εἰς πάσας τὰς
ἀγυιάς, θεατὴς ἀκόρεστος ἤμην καὶ τὸ κάλλος
5 ὅλως οὐκ ἐξήρκουν ἰδεῖν.   τὰ μὲν ἔβλεπον, τὰ
δὲ ἔμελλον, τὰ δὲ ἠπειγόμην ἰδεῖν, τὰ δὲ οὐκ
ἤθελον παρελθεῖν· ἐκράτει τὴν θέαν τὰ ὁρώμενα, εἷλκε τὰ προσδοκώμενα.   περιάγων οὖν
ἐμαυτὸν εἰς πάσας τὰς ἀγυιὰς καὶ πρὸς τὴν
ὄψιν δυσερωτιῶν, εἶπον καμών· "᾽Οφθαλμοί,
6 νενικήμεθα."   εἶδον δὲ δύο καινὰ καὶ παράλογα,
μεγέθους πρὸς κάλλος ἅμιλλαν καὶ δήμου πρὸς
πόλιν φιλονεικίαν καὶ ἀμφότερα νικῶντα· ἡ μὲν

BOOK V

1. AFTER a voyage lasting for three days, we arrived at Alexandria. I entered it by the Sun Gate, as it is called, and was instantly struck by the splendid beauty of the city, which filled my eyes with delight. From the Sun Gate to the Moon Gate—these are the guardian divinities of the entrances—led a straight double row of columns, about the middle of which lies the open part of the town, and in it so many streets that walking in them you would fancy yourself abroad while still at home. Going a few hundred yards further, I came to the quarter called after Alexander, where I saw a second town; the splendour of this was cut into squares, for there was a row of columns intersected by another as long at right angles. I tried to cast my eyes down every street, but my gaze was still unsatisfied, and I could not grasp all the beauty of the spot at once; some parts I saw, some I was on the point of seeing, some I earnestly desired to see, some I could not pass by; that which I actually saw kept my gaze fixed, while that which I expected to see would drag it on to the next. I explored therefore every street, and at last, my vision unsatisfied, exclaimed in weariness, "Ah, my eyes, we are beaten." Two things struck me as especially strange and extraordinary—it was impossible to decide which was the greatest, the size of the place or its beauty, the city itself or its inhabitants; for

γὰρ ἠπείρου μείζων ἦν, ὁ δὲ πλείων ἔθνους.
καὶ εἰ μὲν εἰς τὴν πόλιν ἀπεῖδον, ἠπίστουν εἰ
πληρώσει τις δῆμος αὐτὴν ἀνδρῶν, εἰ δὲ εἰς
τὸν δῆμον ἐθεασάμην, ἐθαύμαζον, εἰ χωρήσει
τις αὐτὸν πόλις. τοιαύτη τις ἦν ἰσότητος
τρυτάνη.

2. Ἦν δέ πως κατὰ δαίμονα ἱερομηνία τοῦ
μεγάλου θεοῦ, ὃν Δία μὲν Ἕλληνες, Σέραπιν
δὲ καλοῦσιν Αἰγύπτιοι· ἦν δὲ καὶ πυρὸς δαδου-
2 χία. καὶ τοῦτο μέγιστον ἐθεασάμην· ἑσπέρα
μὲν γὰρ ἦν καὶ ὁ ἥλιος κατεδύετο καὶ νὺξ ἦν
οὐδαμοῦ, ἀλλ' ἄλλος ἀνέτελλεν ἥλιος κατα-
κερματίζων· τότε γὰρ εἶδον πόλιν ἐρίζουσαν
περὶ κάλλους οὐρανῷ. ἐθεασάμην δὲ καὶ τὸν
Μειλίχιον Δία, καὶ τὸν Διὸς Οὐρανίου [1] νεών.
3 προσευξάμενοι δὴ τῷ μεγάλῳ θεῷ καὶ ἱκετεύ-
σαντες στῆναι ἡμῖν ποτὲ τὰ δεινά, εἰς τὴν
καταγωγὴν ἤλθομεν, ἣν ἔτυχεν ὁ Μενέλαος ἡμῖν
μεμισθωμένος. οὐκ ἐῴκει δὲ ἄρα ὁ θεὸς ἐπινεύειν
ταῖς ἡμετέραις εὐχαῖς, ἀλλ' ἔμενεν ἡμᾶς καὶ ἄλλο
τῆς Τύχης γυμνάσιον.

3. Ὁ γὰρ Χαιρέας πρὸ πολλοῦ τῆς Λευκίππης ἐλάνθανεν ἐρῶν καὶ διὰ τοῦτο μεμηνύ-
κει τὸ φάρμακον, ἅμα μὲν ἀφορμὴν οἰκειότητος
ἑαυτῷ θηρώμενος, ἅμα δὲ καὶ ἑαυτῷ σῴζων
2 τὴν κόρην. εἰδὼς οὖν ἀμήχανον τὸ τυχεῖν,
συντίθησιν ἐπιβουλήν, λῃστήριον [2] ὁμοτέχνων
συγκροτήσας, ἅτε θαλάσσιος ὢν ἄνθρωπος, καὶ
συνθέμενος αὐτοῖς ἃ δεῖ ποιεῖν, ἐπὶ ξενίαν ἡμᾶς

[1] So C. B. Hase for the MSS. οὐράνιον.
[2] Scaliger's emendation for the MSS. λῃστῶν, which
cannot be construed. Or λῃστῶν may be kept, and ἀγέλην
(Jacobs) or χεῖρα (Hercher) inserted after ὁμοτέχνων.

the former was larger than a continent, the latter
outnumbered a whole nation. Looking at the city,
I doubted whether any race of men could ever fill it;
looking at the inhabitants, I wondered whether any
city could ever be found large enough to hold them
all. The balance seemed exactly even.

2. It so fortuned that it was at that time the
sacred festival of the great god whom the Greeks
call Zeus, the Egyptians Serapis, and there was a
procession of torches. It was the greatest spectacle I
ever beheld, for it was late evening and the sun had
gone down; but there was no sign of night—it was
as though another sun had arisen, but distributed
into small parts in every direction; I thought that
on that occasion the city vied with the sky for
beauty. I also visited the Gracious Zeus and his
temple in his aspect as god of Heaven; and then
praying to the great god and humbly imploring him
that our troubles might be at last an end, we came
back to the lodgings which Menelaus had hired for
us. But the god, it seems, was not prepared to
assent to our prayers, but still another of the trials
and exercises of Fate was in store for us.

3. This was the cause of it. Chaereas had for some
time been secretly in love with Leucippe; that was
the reason that he had informed us about the drug
which had been administered to her; he was seeking
an opportunity of beginning a close acquaintance
with her, and desired to save her to his own
advantage. Knowing that it was impossible other-
wise to succeed in his desires, he contrived a plot.
Being himself a sea-faring man, he got together a
pirate-band of fellows of his own sort; and, after
instructing them how they were to act, asked us to

εἰς τὴν Φάρον καλεῖ, σκηψάμενος γενεθλίων
3 ἄγειν ἡμέραν. ὡς οὖν προήλθομεν τῶν θυρῶν,
οἰωνὸς ἡμῖν γίνεται πονηρός· χελιδόνα κίρκος
διώκων τὴν Λευκίππην πατάσσει τῷ πτερῷ εἰς
τὴν κεφαλήν. ταραχθεὶς οὖν ἐπὶ τούτῳ, καὶ
ἀνανεύσας εἰς οὐρανόν, "Ὦ Ζεῦ, τί τοῦτο,"
ἔφην, "φαίνεις ἡμῖν τέρας; ἀλλ' εἰ τῷ ὄντι
σὸς ὄρνις οὗτος, ἄλλον ἡμῖν σαφέστερον δεῖξον
4 οἰωνόν." μεταστραφεὶς οὖν (ἔτυχον γὰρ παρε-
στὼς ἐργαστηρίῳ ζωγράφου) γραφὴν ὁρῶ κειμένην, ἥτις ὑπηνίττετο προσόμοιον· Φιλομήλας[1]
γὰρ εἶχε φθορὰν καὶ τὴν βίαν Τηρέως καὶ τῆς
γλώττης τὴν τομήν. ἦν δὲ ὁλόκληρον τῇ γραφῇ
τὸ διήγημα τοῦ δράματος, ὁ πέπλος, ὁ Τηρεύς, ἡ
5 τράπεζα. τὸν πέπλον ἡπλωμένον εἱστήκει
κρατοῦσα θεράπαινα· Φιλομήλα παρειστήκει
καὶ ἐπετίθει τῷ πέπλῳ τὸν δάκτυλον καὶ ἐδείκνυε τῶν ὑφασμάτων τὰς γραφάς· ἡ Πρόκνη
πρὸς τὴν δεῖξιν ἐνενεύκει καὶ δριμὺ ἔβλεπε καὶ
ὠργίζετο τῇ γραφῇ. Θρᾲξ ὁ Τηρεὺς ἐνύφαντο
6 Φιλομήλᾳ παλαίων πάλην Ἀφροδισίαν. ἐσπά-
ρακτο τὰς κόμας ἡ γυνή, τὸ ζῶσμα ἐλέλυτο,
τὸν χιτῶνα κατέρρηκτο, ἡμίγυμνος τὸ στέρνον
ἦν, τὴν δεξιὰν ἐπ' ὀφθαλμοὺς ἤρειδε τοῦ Τηρέως,

---

[1] The MSS. have Πρόκνης. But it was Philomela, not
Procne, that was ravished by Tereus, and Πρόκνης must be a
copyist's mistake. The credit of the correction is claimed by
Hercher: but it is due, before him, to the Italian translator
Coccio, followed by Rowland Smith.

dinner at Pharos,[1] professing that it was his birth-
day. We were but just leaving our door when an
evil omen happened to us; a hawk chasing a swallow
struck Leucippe's head with his wing. At this I was
somewhat disturbed, and, looking up to heaven,
" What is this portent," said I, " O Zeus, that thou
displayest to us? If in very deed this bird[2] comes
from thee, show us some other clearer augury."
Turning round (I happened to be standing by a
painter's studio) I saw a picture hanging there, the
subject of which had a similar hidden significance,
representing the rape of Philomela, the violence
employed by Tereus, and the cutting out of her
tongue. The whole story was fully represented in
the picture, including the tapestry, Tereus himself,
and the fatal table.[3] A serving-maid was standing
and holding up the tapestry unfolded; Philomela
stood near with her finger on it, pointing out the
subjects of the embroideries; Procne was bowing
her head to show that she understood what was being
pointed out to her; there was a savage look in her
eyes and she had become furious at what she saw
depicted there. The subject embroidered on it was
the Thracian Tereus struggling with Philomela in a
lustful strife; her hair was dishevelled, her girdle
undone, her tunic torn, and her bosom half naked;
with her right hand she aimed for Tereus' eyes, while

[1] An island in the bay of Alexandria, famous for the light-
house upon it.

[2] ὄρνις, like οἰωνός, can mean both a " bird" and an
" omen."

[3] As explained in ch. v. the πέπλος is the substitute for
speech employed by the dumb Philomela, the table the scene
of the cannibal feast. The whole story is one of the most
famous of ancient mythology, and is often told—best, perhaps,
in the sixth book of Ovid's *Metamorphoses*.

τῇ λαιᾷ τὰ διερρωγότα τοῦ χιτῶνος ἐπὶ τοὺς
μαστοὺς εἷλκεν.[1] ἐν ἀγκάλαις εἶχε τὴν Φιλομήλαν ὁ Τηρεύς, ἕλκων πρὸς ἑαυτὸν ὡς ἐνῆν τὸ
σῶμα καὶ σφίγγων ἐν χρῷ τὴν συμπλοκήν·
7 ὧδε μὲν τὴν τοῦ πέπλου γραφὴν ὕφηνεν ὁ
ζωγράφος. τὸ δὲ λοιπὸν τῆς εἰκόνος, αἱ γυναῖκες
ἐν κανῷ τὰ λείψανα τοῦ δείπνου τῷ Τηρεῖ
δεικνύουσι, κεφαλὴν παιδίου καὶ χεῖρας· γελῶσι
8 δὲ ἅμα καὶ φοβοῦνται. ἀναπηδῶν ἐκ τῆς κλίνης
ὁ Τηρεὺς ἐγέγραπτο, καὶ ἕλκων τὸ ξίφος ἐπὶ
τὰς γυναῖκας τὸ σκέλος ἤρειδεν ἐπὶ τὴν τρά-
πεζαν· ἡ δὲ οὔτε ἕστηκεν, οὔτε πέπτωκεν, ἀλλ᾽
ἐδείκνυε ῥοπὴν[2] μέλλοντος πτώματος.

4. Λέγει οὖν ὁ Μενέλαος· "'Εμοὶ δοκεῖ τὴν
εἰς Φάρον ὁδὸν ἐπισχεῖν. ὁρᾷς γὰρ οὐκ ἀγαθὰ
δύο σύμβολα, τό τε τοῦ ὄρνιθος καθ᾽ ἡμῶν πτερὸν
καὶ τῆς εἰκόνος τὴν ἀπειλήν. Λέγουσι δὲ οἱ τῶν
συμβόλων ἐξηγηταὶ σκοπεῖν τοὺς μύθους τῶν
εἰκόνων, ἂν ἐξιοῦσιν ἡμῖν ἐπὶ πρᾶξιν συντύχωσι,
καὶ ἐξομοιοῦν τὸ ἀποβησόμενον τῷ τῆς ἱστορίας
2 λόγῳ. ὁρᾷς οὖν ὅσων γέμει κακῶν ἡ γραφή·
ἔρωτος παρανόμου, μοιχείας ἀναισχύντου, γυναι-
κείων ἀτυχημάτων. ὅθεν ἐπισχεῖν κελεύω τὴν
ἔξοδον." ἐδόκει μοι λέγειν εἰκότα, καὶ παραιτοῦμαι
τὸν Χαιρέαν ἐκείνην τὴν ἡμέραν. ὁ μὲν οὖν
σφόδρα ἀνιώμενος ἀπηλλάττετο, φήσας αὔριον ἐφ᾽
ἡμᾶς ἀφίξεσθαι.

5. Ἡ δὲ Λευκίππη λέγει πρός με (φιλόμυθον
γάρ πως τὸ τῶν γυναικῶν γένος)· "Τί βούλεται τῆς

---

[1] εἷλκεν (Scaliger) and ἐν (Jacobs) for MSS. ἔκλειεν.

[2] The MSS. γραφήν is intolerably flat : I have substituted
for it Jacobs' ῥοπήν.

with her left she tried to draw her torn garments over her breasts. He held her in his arms, drawing her form towards him within them, and tightening his embrace round her, body to body; such was the picture of the tapestry which the painter had made. As for the rest of the painting, the women were shewing Tereus the remains of the feast in a basket, the child's head and hands; their expression was a mixture of laughter and fear. Tereus was depicted leaping up from his seat and drawing his sword against the women; his leg was pressing against the table, which neither stood nor fell, but displayed the unstable balance of an impending fall.

4. " In my opinion," said Menelaus, "we should not continue our journey to Pharos; for you may observe that we have had two bad signs, the touching of us by the bird's wing and the threat which this picture implies. Those who profess to interpret signs bid us pay attention to the stories of pictures, if such happen to meet our eye as we set forth to our business, and to conclude that what is likely to happen to us will be of the same character as the event of the painted story. You see then how full of miseries is this drawing—unlawful love, shameless adultery, women's woes; I therefore recommend you to desist from this expedition of yours." His words seemed to me not without reason, and I prayed Chaereas to have us excused for that day; he left us in considerable displeasure, saying that he would return to us on the morrow.

5. Said Leucippe to me—all womankind is fond of stories—" What is the meaning of the subject of this

243

εἰκόνος ὁ μῦθος ; καὶ τίνες αἱ ὄρνιθες [1] αὗται ; καὶ
τίνες αἱ γυναῖκες, καὶ τίς ὁ ἀναιδὴς ἐκεῖνος ἀνήρ ;"
κἀγὼ καταλέγειν ἄρχομαι· "'Αηδών, καὶ χελιδών,
καὶ ἔποψ, πάντες ἄνθρωποι, καὶ πάντες ὄρνιθες.
2 ἔποψ ὁ ἀνήρ· αἱ δύο γυναῖκες, Φιλομήλα χελιδών,
καὶ Πρόκνη ἀηδών. πόλις αὐταῖς 'Αθῆναι. Τηρεὺς
ὁ ἀνήρ· Πρόκνη Τηρέως γυνή. βαρβάροις δέ, ὡς
ἔοικεν, οὐχ ἱκανὴ πρὸς 'Αφροδίτην μία γυνή, μάλιστα ὅταν αὐτῷ καιρὸς διδῷ πρὸς ὕβριν τρυφᾶν.
3 καιρὸς οὖν γίνεται τῷ Θρᾳκὶ τούτῳ χρήσασθαι
τῇ φύσει Πρόκνης ἡ φιλοστοργία· πέμπει γὰρ
ἐπὶ τὴν ἀδελφὴν τὸν ἄνδρα τὸν Τηρέα. ὁ δὲ
ἀπῄει μὲν ἔτι Πρόκνης ἀνήρ, ἀναστρέφει δὲ
Φιλομήλας ἐραστής, καὶ κατὰ τὴν ὁδὸν ἄλλην
4 αὑτῷ ποιεῖται τὴν Φιλομήλαν Πρόκνην. τὴν
γλῶτταν τῆς Φιλομήλας φοβεῖται, καὶ ἕδνα τῶν
γάμων αὐτῇ δίδωσι μηκέτι λαλεῖν, καὶ κείρει τῆς
φωνῆς τὸ ἄνθος. ἀλλὰ πλέον ἤνυσεν [2] οὐδέν·
ἡ γὰρ Φιλομήλας τέχνη σιωπῶσαν ηὗρηκε φωνήν.
5 ὑφαίνει γὰρ πέπλον ἄγγελον καὶ τὸ δρᾶμα πλέκει
ταῖς κρόκαις, καὶ μιμεῖται τὴν γλῶτταν ἡ χείρ,
καὶ Πρόκνης τοῖς ὀφθαλμοῖς τὰ τῶν ὤτων μηνύει
καὶ πρὸς αὐτὴν ἃ πέπονθε τῇ κερκίδι λαλεῖ.

---

[1] By an inadvertence of the author's or an imperfection of
the text no mention of birds was made in the description of
the picture immediately preceding: the metamorphosis should
have been the last scene after the over-set table. Achilles
Tatius follows the less usual tradition in making Procne the
nightingale and Philomela the swallow ; conditions are more
usually reversed, and such is the tradition in modern poetry,
where "Philomel" has become a synonym for the nightingale.
But the tale in the text is not without support ; a discussion
may be found in Muncker's note on Hyginus, *Fab.* 45.

[2] Villoison's correction for MSS ὤνησεν.

picture? What are these birds? Who are those
women and that vile man?" I began to relate to
her the whole history: "They are the nightingale,"
said I, "the swallow, and the hoopoe—all human
creatures, and all birds as well; the man became
the hoopoe, Philomela the swallow, and Procne the
nightingale. Both these women had their home in
Athens, and the man, Tereus, was Procne's husband.
One wife at a time, it seems, is not enough for
a barbarian's love, especially if opportunity occur
for him to give rein to his wantonness; and this
Thracian's opportunity came through the natural
affection of Procne, who sent her husband to bring
her sister to her. He started on his journey still
the husband of Procne, but he came back[1] the lover
of Philomela, and by the way he made her a second
Procne; then, fearing Philomela's tongue, his bridegroom's present[2] to her was that she should be
dumb, and he shore away the glory of her speech. But
this profited him nothing; Philomela's art provided
her with a silent voice. She weaves a tell-tale
tapestry, working her story into the threads; her hand
takes the place of her tongue and sets out for Procne's
eyes what Procne should have learned by her ears
—she tells her sister of her sufferings by means of

[1] Accounts differ as to the means Tereus employed to take
Philomela from her father Pandion. The more usual one,
apparently followed here, is that his was a genuine mission
from Procne, who wished to see her sister; another relates
that he told Pandion that Procne was dead, and that he
wished to have Philomela, his deceased wife's sister, in a
second marriage.

[2] The ἕδνα is the opposite of the dowry—the present given
by the groom to the bride. It may well have corresponded
to the Germanic *Morgengabe*, his reward to her for her
virginity.

6 ἡ Πρόκνη τὴν βίαν ἀκούει παρὰ τοῦ πέπλου καὶ
ἀμύνασθαι καθ᾽ ὑπερβολὴν ζητεῖ τὸν ἄνδρα.
ὀργαὶ δὲ δύο, καὶ δύο γυναῖκες εἰς ἓν πνέουσαι καὶ
ὕβρει κεράσασαι τὴν ζηλοτυπίαν δεῖπνον ἐπινο-
7 οῦσι τῶν γάμων ἀτυχέστερον. τὸ δὲ δεῖπνον ἦν
ὁ παῖς Τηρέως, οὗ μήτηρ μὲν ἦν πρὸ τῆς ὀργῆς
ἡ Πρόκνη· τότε δὲ τῶν ὠδίνων ἐπελέλησττο.
οὕτως αἱ τῆς ζηλοτυπίας ὠδῖνες νικῶσι καὶ τὴν
γαστέρα· μόνον γὰρ ἐρῶσαι [1] αἱ γυναῖκες ἀνιᾶσαι
τὸν τὴν εὐνὴν λελυπηκότα, κἂν πάσχωσιν ἐν
οἷς ποιοῦσιν οὐχ ἧττον κακόν, τὴν τοῦ πάσχειν
8 λογίζονται συμφορὰν τῇ τοῦ ποιεῖν ἡδονῇ. ἐδείπνη-
σεν ὁ Τηρεὺς δεῖπνον Ἐρινύων, αἱ δὲ ἐν κανῷ τὰ
λείψανα τοῦ παιδίου παρέφερον, γελῶσαι φόβῳ.
ὁ Τηρεὺς ὁρᾷ τὰ λείψανα τοῦ παιδίου καὶ πενθεῖ
τὴν τροφήν, καὶ ἐγνώρισεν ὧν τοῦ δείπνου πατήρ·
γνωρίσας μαίνεται καὶ σπᾶται τὸ ξίφος καὶ ἐπὶ
τὰς γυναῖκας τρέχει, ἃς δέχεται ὁ ἀήρ. καὶ ὁ
Τηρεὺς αὐταῖς συναναβαίνει, καὶ ὄρνις γίνεται·
9 καὶ τηροῦσιν ἔτι τοῦ πάθους τὴν εἰκόνα· φεύγει
μὲν ἀηδών, διώκει δὲ ὁ Τηρεύς. οὕτως ἐφύλαξε
τὸ μῖσος καὶ μέχρι τῶν πτερῶν."

6. Τότε μὲν οὖν οὕτως ἐξεφύγομεν τὴν ἐπιβου-
λήν· ἐκερδήσαμεν δὲ οὐδὲν ἢ μίαν ἡμέραν. Τῇ
γὰρ ὑστεραίᾳ παρῆν ἕωθεν ὁ Χαιρέας· καὶ ἡμεῖς

---

[1] Jacobs, for MSS. ὁρῶσαι. After this word the necessary
article αἱ was supplied by Hirschig : it had disappeared by
haplography.

her shuttle. When Procne read of the deed of
violence by means of the tapestry, she sought how
she might take an overwhelming vengeance upon
her husband. With two women, double was their
wrath; they conspired together for one object,
spurred on by jealousy [1] and sense of violence done,
and contrived a banquet even more hideous than the
unhallowed nuptials; Tereus' own child [2] was to be
his dish, whose mother had been Procne before her
fury; but now she had forgotten the pangs by which
she gave him birth. So far greater were the agonies
of jealousy than those of the womb; women care
for nothing but to avenge themselves on him who
has wronged their bed, even if they suffer in their
revenge a woe equal to that which they inflict, and
they balance the pain of what they suffer by the sweetness of the vengeance which they exact. So Tereus
dined on this devils' dish, while they carried to him
in a basket the remains of his son with a mixture of
fear and mocking laughter; he sees those remains,
mourns for what he has eaten—he knew that he was
the father of the very food he had swallowed;
knowing it, he draws his sword and rushes upon the
women, but the air receives them from his vengeance;
he mounts with them, and like them becomes a bird.
They still preserve the image of the passions they feel
—the swallow flies, Tereus pursues; his hate is as great
as ever, even when they are all clothed with wings."

6. For the moment then we had by this incident
escaped the plot laid against us; but we only gained
one day. On the morrow came Chaereas at dawn:

[1] Strictly speaking it is the ζηλοτυπία which spurs on
Procne, the ὕβρις which was the cause of Philomela's revenge. But by a perfectly natural extension both are made
to apply to each of the women.   [2] Itys.

αἰδεσθέντες ἀντιλέγειν οὐκ εἴχομεν. ἐπιβάντες
οὖν σκάφους, ἤλθομεν εἰς τὴν Φάρον· ὁ δὲ
Μενέλαος ἔμεινεν αὐτοῦ, φήσας οὐχ ὑγιῶς ἔχειν.
2 πρῶτον μὲν οὖν ἡμᾶς ὁ Χαιρέας ἐπὶ τὸν πύργον
ἄγει καὶ δείκνυσι τὴν κατασκευὴν κάτωθεν
3 θαυμασίαν τινὰ καὶ παράλογον. ὄρος ἦν ἐν μέσῃ
τῇ θαλάσσῃ κείμενον, ψαῦον αὐτῶν τῶν νεφῶν.
ὑπέρρει δὲ ὕδωρ κάτωθεν αὐτοῦ τοῦ ποιήματος·
τὸ δὲ ἐπὶ θαλάσσης εἱστήκει κρεμάμενον· ἐς δὲ
τὴν τοῦ ὄρους ἀκρόπολιν ὁ τῶν νεῶν κυβερνήτης
ἀνέτελλεν ἄλλος ἥλιος.[1] μετὰ δὲ ταῦτα ἡγεῖτο
ἡμῖν ἐπὶ τὴν οἰκίαν· ἦν δὲ ἐπ' ἐσχάτων τῇ νήσῳ
κειμένη ἐπ' αὐτῇ τῇ θαλάσσῃ.

7. Ἑσπέρας οὖν γενομένης, ὑπεξέρχεται μὲν ὁ
Χαιρέας, πρόφασιν ποιησάμενος τὴν γαστέρα.
Μετὰ μικρὸν δὲ βοή τις ἐξαίφνης περὶ τὰς θύρας
ἦν, καὶ εὐθὺς εἰστρέχουσιν ἄνθρωποι μεγάλοι καὶ
πολλοί, μαχαίρας ἐσπασμένοι, καὶ ἐπὶ τὴν κόρην
2 πάντες ὥρμησαν. ἐγὼ δὲ ὡς εἶδον φερομένην μοι[2]
τὴν φιλτάτην, οὐκ ἐνεγκὼν ἵεμαι διὰ τῶν ξιφῶν·
καί με παίει τις κατὰ τοῦ μηροῦ μαχαίρα καὶ
ὤκλασα· ἐγὼ μὲν δὴ καταπεσὼν ἐρρεόμην αἵματι·
οἱ δὲ ἐνθέμενοι τῷ σκάφει τὴν κόρην ἔφευγον.
3 θορύβου δὲ καὶ βοῆς οἷα ἐπὶ λῃσταῖς γενομένης, ὁ
στρατηγὸς τῆς νήσου παρῆν· ἦν δέ μοι γνώριμος
ἐκ τοῦ στρατοπέδου γενόμενος. δεικνύω δὴ τὸ
τραῦμα καὶ δέομαι διῶξαι τοὺς λῃστάς. ὥρμει
δὲ πολλὰ πλοῖα ἐν τῇ πόλει· τούτων ἑνὶ ἐπιβὰς

---

[1] Hirschig's insertion: or you may, with Hercher, substitute ἥλιος for ἄλλος. Jacobs proposed δαλός.

[2] I think Hercher must be right in substituting μοι—the dativus incommodi—for the ill-placed and weak possessive μου. The alteration is very slight.

for very shame we could make no further excuses and got aboard a boat to go to Pharos; Menelaus stayed behind, saying that he was not well. Chaereas first took us to the light-house and shewed us the most remarkable and extraordinary structure upon which it rested; it was like a mountain, almost reaching the clouds, in the middle of the sea. Below the building flowed the waters; it seemed to be as it were suspended above their surface, while at the top of this mountain rose a second sun to be a guide for ships. After this he took us to his house, which was on the shore at the extremity of the island.

7. As soon as evening was come, Chaereas went out, alleging as a pretence the demands of nature. Not long after there was a sudden tumult at the door, and in rushed a large number of tall men, their swords drawn, all directing themselves upon the maiden. Seeing my dearest being taken from me, I could not bear it, and rushed into the fray; one of them wounded me with his sword in the thigh, and I sank to the ground. While I was thus falling, streaming with blood, they put her aboard a boat and made off. Such was the noise and tumult caused by the pirates that the commander of the island came up, who happened to be an acquaintance of mine because he had been in our former camp. I shewed him my wound and implored him to pursue the pirates. There were plenty of ships anchored there about the town; the commander entered one of them and

ὁ στρατηγός, ἐδίωκεν ἅμα τῇ παρούσῃ φρουρᾷ,
κἀγὼ δὲ συνανέβην φοράδην κομισθείς.

4 Ὡς δὲ εἶδον οἱ λῃσταὶ προσιοῦσαν ἤδη τὴν ναῦν
εἰς ναυμαχίαν, ἱστᾶσιν ἐπὶ τοῦ καταστρώματος
ὀπίσω τὼ χεῖρε δεδεμένην τὴν κόρην· καί τις αὐτῶν
μεγάλῃ τῇ φωνῇ, "Ἰδοὺ τὸ ἆθλον ὑμῶν," εἰπών,
ἀποτέμνει αὐτῆς τὴν κεφαλὴν καὶ τὸ λοιπὸν σῶμα
5 ὠθεῖ κατὰ τῆς θαλάσσης. ἐγὼ δὲ ὡς εἶδον,
ἀνέκραγον οἰμώξας καὶ ὥρμησα ἐμαυτὸν ἐπαφεῖναι·
ὡς δὲ οἱ παρόντες κατέσχον, ἐδεόμην ἐπισχεῖν τε
τὴν ναῦν, καί τινα ἁλέσθαι κατὰ τῆς θαλάσσης,
εἴ πως κἂν πρὸς ταφὴν λάβοιμι τῆς κόρης τὸ
6 σῶμα. καὶ ὁ στρατηγὸς πείθεται καὶ ἵστησι τὴν
ναῦν· καὶ δύο τῶν ναυτῶν ἀκοντίζουσιν ἑαυτοὺς
ἔξω τῆς νηὸς καὶ ἁρπάσαντες τὸ σῶμα ἀναφέρου-
σιν. ἐν τούτῳ δὲ οἱ λῃσταὶ μᾶλλον ἐρρωμενέ-
στερον ἤλαυνον· ὡς δὲ ἦμεν πάλιν πλησίον,
ὁρῶσιν οἱ λῃσταὶ ναῦν ἑτέραν, καὶ γνωρίσαντες,
ἐκάλουν πρὸς βοήθειαν· πορφυρεῖς δὲ ἦσαν
7 πειρατικοί. ἰδὼν δὲ ὁ στρατηγὸς δύο ναῦς ἤδη
γενομένας, ἐφοβήθη, καὶ πρύμναν ἐκρούετο· καὶ
γὰρ οἱ πειραταὶ τοῦ φυγεῖν ἀποτραπόμενοι προὔ-
8 καλοῦντο εἰς μάχην. ἐπεὶ δὲ ἀνεστρέψαμεν εἰς
γῆν, ἀποβὰς τοῦ σκάφους καὶ τῷ σώματι περι-
χυθείς, ἔκλαιον· "Νῦν μοι Λευκίππη τέθνηκας
ἀληθῶς θάνατον διπλοῦν, γῇ καὶ θαλάσσῃ
διαιρούμενον. τὸ μὲν γὰρ λείψανον ἔχω σου
9 τοῦ σώματος· ἀπολώλεκα δὲ σέ. οὐκ ἴση τῆς
θαλάσσης πρὸς τὴν γῆν ἡ νομή. μικρόν μοί
σου μέρος καταλέλειπται ἐν ὄψει τοῦ μείζονος·
αὕτη δὲ ἐν ὀλίγῳ τὸ πᾶν σου κρατεῖ. ἀλλ'

went in chase, his bodyguard with him, while I followed them, carried aboard in a litter.

Directly the pirates saw our ship putting out to give them battle, they brought the maiden up on deck with her hands tied behind her; and one of them cried out with a tremendous voice, "Here is the prize for which you are contending," cut off her head, and threw the body down into the sea. When I saw this, I cried out and wept, and would have cast myself in too; restrained from doing so by my companions, I begged them to stop the ship, and that somebody might be sent down into the water to see if I could rescue the maiden's body with a view to its burial. The commander agreed, and stopped the ship; two of the sailors jumped overboard, got hold of the trunk and, brought it back to us. Meanwhile the pirates rowed with still greater vigour; we were again nearing them when they sighted another ship, and, on recognising it, called to it for help; its crew were purple-fishers, also pirates. When the commander saw that there were now two ships against him, he became disquieted and ordered the rowers to reverse; the pirates indeed had already desisted from their flight and were challenging us to give battle. We reached the land; I disembarked, and there, embracing the body, I gave vent to my tears: "Now," I cried, "now, Leucippe, are you really dead; and a double death, with its share both in land and sea. The poor remains of your body I possess, but you I have lost; the division between land and sea is no fair one; though there seems to be left to me the greater part of you, it is really the less, while that which seems to possess but a small

ἐπεί μοι τῶν ἐν τῷ προσώπῳ φιλημάτων
ἐφθόνησεν ἡ Τύχη, φέρε σου καταφιλήσω τὴν
σφαγήν."

8. Ταῦτα καταθρηνήσας καὶ θάψας τὸ σῶμα,
πάλιν εἰς τὴν Ἀλεξάνδρειαν ἔρχομαι, καὶ θερα-
πευθεὶς ἄκων τὸ τραῦμα, τοῦ Μενελάου με
2 παρηγοροῦντος, διεκαρτέρησα ζῶν. καὶ ἤδη
μοι γεγόνεσαν μῆνες ἕξ, καὶ τὸ πολὺ τοῦ πένθους
ἤρχετο μαραίνεσθαι· χρόνος γὰρ λύπης φάρμακον καὶ πεπαίνει τῆς ψυχῆς τὰ ἕλκη. μεστὸς
γὰρ ἥλιος ἡδονῆς· καὶ τὸ λυπῆσαν πρὸς ὀλίγον,
κἂν ᾖ καθ' ὑπερβολήν, ἀναζεῖ μέν, ἐφ' ὅσον ἡ
ψυχὴ καίεται, τῇ δὲ τῆς ἡμέρας ψυχαγωγίᾳ
νικώμενον καταψύχεται. καί μού τις κατόπιν
βαδίζοντος ἐν ἀγορᾷ τῆς χειρὸς ἄφνω λαβόμενος
ἐπιστρέφει, καὶ οὐδὲν εἰπὼν προσπτυξάμενός
3 με πολλὰ κατεφίλει. ἐγὼ δὲ τὸ μὲν πρῶτον
οὐκ ᾔδειν ὅστις ἦν, ἀλλ' εἱστήκειν ἐκπεπληγ-
μένος καὶ δεχόμενος τὰς προσβολὰς τῶν ἀσπασ-
μάτων, ὡς φιλημάτων σκοπός· ἐπεὶ δὲ μικρὸν
διέσχε, καὶ τὸ πρόσωπον εἶδον, Κλεινίας δὲ
ἦν, ἀνακραγὼν ὑπὸ χαρᾶς, ἀντιπεριβάλλω τε
αὐτὸν καὶ τὰς αὐτὰς ἀπεδίδουν περιπλοκάς,
καὶ μετὰ ταῦτα εἰς τὴν καταγωγὴν ἀνήλθομεν
τὴν ἐμήν. καὶ ὁ μὲν τὰ αὑτοῦ μοι διηγεῖτο,
ὅπως ἐκ τῆς ναυαγίας περιεγένετο· ἐγὼ δὲ τὰ
περὶ τῆς Λευκίππης ἅπαντα.

9. "Εὐθὺς μὲν γάρ," ἔφη, "ῥαγείσης τῆς
νηὸς ἐπὶ τὸ κέρας ᾖξα, καὶ ἄκρου λαβόμενος
μόλις, ἀνδρῶν ἤδη πεπληρωμένου, περιβαλὼν
τὰς χεῖρας ἐπεχείρουν ἔχεσθαι παρακρεμάμενος.

part of you has really all.[1] Come, since Fate has grudged me kisses on your face, I will kiss instead your wounded neck."

8. After this dirge, and after burying the body, I returned again to Alexandria; there my wound was tended, though against my will, Menelaus exhorting and comforting me, and I endured to live. Six months had now passed, and the intensity of my anguish began a little to fade : for time is the medicine of grief, healing the wounds of the soul—the light of the sun brings with it joy, and grief, however overwhelming it be, boils only while the soul is aflame, and cools when it is finally overcome by the influence of lapse of time. I was walking in the market-place when somebody behind me suddenly took hold of my hand and swung me round, and, without a word, seized me in his arms and kissed me warmly. At first I did not know who it was, but stood like one struck dumb, receiving his embraces—a mere target for kisses ; but in a moment or so, when I saw his face, and it was Clinias, I shouted aloud for joy, and embraced him in return and gave him back the same endearments. After this we both went back to my lodgings, where he related to me his story, how he had escaped from the shipwreck, while I told him all that had come to pass in the matter of Leucippe.

9. "Immediately," said he, "after the break-up of the ship, I climbed on to the yard ; I obtained a hold of it with some difficulty, as it was already crowded, but I put my hands round it and tried to hang from it and keep it within my clutch. We had

---

[1] The head being the noblest part of the anatomy. No translation can make this laboured rhetoric anything but ridiculous.

ὀλίγον δὲ ἡμῶν ἐμπελαγισάντων, κῦμα μέγιστον ἆραν τὸ ξύλον προσρήγνυσιν ὄρθιον ὑφάλῳ
πέτρᾳ κατὰ θάτερον, ᾧ ἐγὼ ἔτυχον κρεμάμενος.
2 τὸ δὲ προσαραχθὲν βίᾳ πάλιν εἰς τοὐπίσω
δίκην μηχανῆς ἀπεκρούετο καί με ὥσπερ ἀπὸ
σφενδόνης ἐξερρίπισε. τοὐντεῦθεν δὲ ἐνηχόμην
τὸ ἐπίλοιπον τῆς ἡμέρας, οὐκέτι ἔχων ἐλπίδα
3 σωτηρίας. ἤδη δὲ καμὼν καὶ ἀφεὶς ἐμαυτὸν
τῇ τύχῃ, ναῦν ὁρῶ κατὰ πρόσωπον φερομένην,
καὶ τὰς χεῖρας ἀνασχών, ὃν ἠδυνάμην τρόπον,
ἱκετηρίαν ἐδεόμην τοῖς νεύμασιν. οἱ δέ, εἴτε
ἐλεήσαντες, εἴτε καὶ τὸ πνεῦμα αὐτοὺς κατήγαγεν, ἔρχονται κατ᾽ ἐμέ, καί τις τῶν ναυτῶν
πέμπει μοι κάλων ἅμα τῆς νηὸς παραθεούσης.
κἀγὼ μὲν ἐλαβόμην, οἱ δὲ ἐφείλκυσάν με ἐξ
αὐτῶν τῶν τοῦ θανάτου πυλῶν. ἔπλει δὲ τὸ
πλοῖον εἰς Σιδῶνα· καί μέ τινες γνωρίσαντες
ἐθεράπευσαν.

10. "Δύο δὲ πλεύσαντες ἡμέρας ἐπὶ τὴν πόλιν
ἥκομεν, καὶ δέομαι τῶν ἐν τῷ πλοίῳ Σιδωνίων,
Ξενοδάμας δὲ ὁ ἔμπορος ἦν καὶ Θεόφιλος ὁ
τούτου πενθερός, μηδενὶ Τυρίων, εἰ περιτύχοιεν,
κατειπεῖν ὡς ἐκ ναυαγίας περιγενοίμην, ὡς ἂν
2 μὴ μάθοιεν συναποδεδημηκότα. ἤλπιζον γὰρ
λήσειν, εἰ τὰ ἀπὸ τούτων ἐν ἡσυχίᾳ γένοιτο, πέντε
μόνον ἡμερῶν μοι μεταξὺ γενομένων, αἷς οὐκ
ἔτυχον ὀφθείς. τοῖς δὲ κατὰ τὴν οἰκίαν τὴν
ἐμήν, ὡς οἶδας, προηγορεύκειν λέγειν[1] τοῖς

---

[1] The insertion of λέγειν is due to Jacobs. It may have
been omitted by an over-clever scribe who thought it was
only a gloss on προηγορεύκειν.

not long drifted upon it, when a mighty billow lifted the spar on high and dashed it, almost in a perpendicular position, upon a rock beneath the surface of the water, the impact being at the opposite end of it to that upon which I was hanging. After it actually struck, it sprang back again violently like a catapult, and shot me from it as though I had been flung from a sling. After that I swam for the rest of the day, though I no longer cherished any hope of being saved. I was already worn out and had given myself up to fate, when I saw a ship bearing towards me from straight in front; and so, lifting up my hands as well as I could, I entreated and prayed for their pity by gestures. They, either taking compassion upon me or because the wind so impelled them, came quite close by me, and one of the sailors flung me a rope without the vessel pausing in her course; I caught hold of it and so they dragged me up from the very gates of death. The vessel was bound for Sidon, and some of those who were on board knew who I was and looked after me.

10. "After a voyage of two days we arrived at that city, and I asked the Sidonians on board (Xenodamas the merchant, and Theophilus his father-in-law) not to mention to any Tyrian that they might meet how I had escaped from the shipwreck, so that it might not be known that I had fled from the country with you. I hoped, that if they kept quiet on these matters, my absence might escape notice; there were only five days while I had been away and not been seen about, and, as you know,[1] I had instructed those of my household to tell anybody that came making

---

[1] This detail is not, as a matter of fact, mentioned in the account of the flight of Clinias and Clitophon from Tyre.

πυνθανομένοις, εἰς κώμην ἀποδεδημηκέναι μέχρι
3 δέκα ὅλων ἡμερῶν. καὶ τοῦτόν γε τὸν λόγον
εὗρον περὶ ἐμοῦ κατεσχηκότα. οὔπω δὲ ὁ
σὸς πατὴρ ἐκ τῆς Παλαιστίνης ἔτυχεν ἥκων,
ἀλλὰ δύο ἄλλων ὕστερον ἡμερῶν, καὶ καταλαμβάνει πεμφθέντα παρὰ τοῦ τῆς Λευκίππης πατρὸς γράμματα, ἅπερ ἔτυχε μετὰ μίαν
ἡμέραν τῆς ἡμετέρας ἀποδημίας κεκομισμένα,
δι' ὧν ὁ Σώστρατος ἐγγυᾷ σοὶ τὴν θυγατέρα.
4 ἐν ποικίλαις ἦν οὖν συμφοραῖς ἀναγνοὺς τὰ
γράμματα καὶ τὴν ὑμετέραν ἀκούσας φυγήν,
τὸ μέν, ὡς τὸ τῆς ἐπιστολῆς ἀπολέσας ἆθλον,
τὸ δέ, ὅτι παρὰ μικρὸν οὕτως ἡ Τύχη τὰ
πράγματα ἔθηκε· καὶ γὰρ οὐδὲν ἂν τούτων
5 ἐγεγόνει, εἰ θᾶττον ἐκομίσθη τὰ γράμματα. καὶ
τῶν μὲν πεπραγμένων οὐδὲν πρὸς τὸν ἀδελφὸν
ἡγήσατό πω δεῖν γράφειν, ἀλλὰ καὶ τῆς μητρὸς
6 τῆς κόρης ἐδεήθη τὸ παρὸν ἐπισχεῖν· 'Τάχα
γὰρ ἂν αὐτοὺς ἐξευρήσομεν· καὶ οὐ δεῖ[1] τὸ
συμβὰν ἀτύχημα μανθάνειν Σώστρατον. ἀσ-
μένως δὲ ὅπου ποτ' ἂν ὦσιν, ὅταν[2] μάθωσι τὴν
ἐγγύην, ἀφίξονται, εἴγε αὐτοῖς ἐξέσται φανερῶς
7 ἔχειν ὑπὲρ οὗ πεφεύγασιν.' ἐπολυπραγμόνει
δὲ παντὶ σθένει, ποῖ κεχωρήκατε· καὶ ὡς ὀλίγον
πρὸ τούτων τῶν ἡμερῶν ἔρχεται Διόφαντος ὁ
Τύριος ἐξ Αἰγύπτου πεπλευκώς, καὶ λέγει πρὸς
αὐτὸν ὅτι σε ἐνθάδε ἐθεάσατο· κἀγὼ μαθών,
ὡς εἶχον, εὐθὺς ἐπιβὰς νηός, ὀγδόην ταύτην

---

[1] The MSS. have δεῖν. Jacobs' alteration should be
accepted. G has δεῖ.

[2] Jacobs substituted ὅπου for ὅποι and ὅταν for a meaningless ὄντες, omitting the following καί before ἀφίξονται. There
are other suggestions.

inquiries that I had gone away to my country seat
for ten full days; and I found that, as a fact, this
report about me held the field.   Your father did not
return from his absence in Palestine [1] until two days
later; and he then found a letter had arrived from
Leucippe's father [2]—it had come the very day after
our flight—betrothing his daughter to you.   He was
doubly distressed when he read the letter and heard
of your flight; first, because of the loss of the prize [3]
which the letter brought, and second, because
Fortune had arranged that you should suffer by so
narrow a margin; none of all these misfortunes
would have happened if the letter had come a little
sooner.   He decided that he had better not write to
his brother an account of what had happened, and
he also asked the girl's mother [4] to keep silence for
the present; 'We shall probably soon find them,'
he said, 'and there is no necessity for Sostratus to
know the misfortune that has befallen us. Wherever
they are, they will be only too glad to come back
when they hear of the betrothal, as they may thus
openly attain the very object of their flight.'   He
did his very utmost to find out where you had
gone; and just a few days ago there came one,
Diophantus of Tyre, who had lately come by sea
from Egypt, and told him that he had seen you
there.   When I learned how things were, I instantly took ship hither, and this is now the eighth

---

[1] It is mentioned in II. xxx. that Hippias had gone away
for a few days, but his destination is not there given.

[2] Sostratus.

[3] Not very clear; was Leucippe herself the prize? And if
so, could Hippias be said to have lost her? Or is the reference to her dowry, which would thus come from the family
of Sostratus to that of Hippias?   [4] Panthea.

ἡμέραν πᾶσάν σε περιῆλθον ζητῶν τὴν πόλιν.
πρὸς ταῦτα οὖν σοι βουλευτέον ἐστίν, ὡς τάχα
καὶ τοῦ πατρὸς ἥξοντος ἐνταῦθα τοῦ σοῦ."

11. Ταῦτα ἀκούσας ἀνώμωξα ἐπὶ τῇ τῆς Τύχης
παιδιᾷ, "Ὦ δαῖμον," λέγων, "νῦν μὲν Σώστρατός
μοι Λευκίππην ἐκδίδωσι καί μοι γάμος ἐκ μέσου
πολέμου πέμπεται, μετρήσας ἀκριβῶς τὰς ἡμέ-
2 ρας, ἵνα μὴ φθάσῃ τὴν φυγήν. ὢ τῶν ἐξώρων
εὐτυχημάτων· ὢ μακάριος ἐγὼ παρὰ μίαν
ἡμέραν· μετὰ θάνατον γάμοι, μετὰ θρῆνον
ὑμέναιοι. τίνα μοι δίδωσι νύμφην ἡ Τύχη,
3 ἣν οὐδὲ ὁλόκληρόν μοι δέδωκε νεκράν;" "Οὐ
θρήνων νῦν καιρός," ὁ Κλεινίας εἶπεν· "ἀλλὰ
σκεψώμεθα πότερον εἰς τὴν πατρίδα σοι[1] νῦν
ἀνακομιστέον, ἢ τὸν πατέρα ἐνταῦθα ἀναμενε-
τέον." "Οὐδέτερον," εἶπον· "ποίῳ γὰρ ἂν[2]
ἴδοιμι προσώπῳ τὸν πατέρα, μάλιστα μὲν οὕτως
αἰσχρῶς φυγών, εἶτα καὶ τὴν παρακαταθήκην
αὐτῷ[3] τἀδελφοῦ διαφθείρας; φεύγειν οὖν ἐντεῦ-
4 θεν ὑπολείπεται πρὶν ἥκειν αὐτόν." ἐν τούτῳ
δὴ ὁ Μενέλαος εἰσέρχεται, καὶ ὁ Σάτυρος μετ'
αὐτοῦ, καὶ τόν τε Κλεινίαν περιπτύσσονται καὶ
μανθάνουσι παρ' ἡμῶν τὰ πεπραγμένα. καὶ
ὁ Σάτυρος, "Ἀλλ' ἔστι σοι," ἔφη, "καὶ τὰ
παρόντα θέσθαι καλῶς καὶ ἐλεῆσαι ψυχὴν ἐπὶ
σοὶ φλεγομένην. ἀκουσάτω δὴ καὶ ὁ Κλεινίας,
5 ἡ γὰρ Ἀφροδίτη μέγα τούτῳ παρέσχεν ἀγαθόν.
ὃ δὲ οὐκ ἐθέλει λαβεῖν. γυναῖκα γὰρ ἐξέμηνεν

[1] Cobet's change from σοῦ. A dative is necessary for use
with the verbal substantive, and it was probably changed
into σοῦ by coming at the right place for a possessive.

[2] ἂν inserted by Cobet.

[3] αὐτῷ (restored by Cobet) had doubtless been changed
into αὐτοῦ by the proximity of the genitive in the next word.

day that I have been scouring the city in search
of you. You have to make up your mind as to
your future plans, as your father will probably be
here."

11. Hearing this story, I cried aloud at the prank
that Fortune had played me : "Cruel goddess," I
said, "this is the time that Sostratus chooses to give
me Leucippe—an espousal coming from the field of
war [1]—so exactly measuring his time that his message
should not arrive before our flight. Alas for my
untimely good luck ! How happy could I have
been with one day's difference ! After death comes
a wedding, after the dirge the marriage-hymn. What
sort of a bride is this that Fate gives me ? Why,
she has not even given her to me in the shape of a
whole corpse." "This is not the time," said Clinias,
"for lamentations ; but let us consider whether it
would be best for you to return at once to your own
country or to wait for your father here." "Neither,"
said I : "with what sort of countenance could I meet
my father, after first fleeing from him in an underhand
manner, and then being the destruction of the
charge entrusted to him by his brother ? There is
nothing that I can do except to make my escape
before he arrives." While I was thus speaking, in
came Menelaus and Satyrus with him ; after embracing Clinias they heard the whole story from us.
"You have the chance," said Satyrus, "of putting
your fortunes in a fine position and at the same time
of shewing pity to a soul that is all afire for your
sake. Let Clinias hear the state of affairs as well ;
Aphrodite offers this fellow a real prize, and he will
not stretch out his hand to take it. She has made to

---

[1] The πόλεμος Θρᾳκικός of I. iii. § 6.

ἐπ' αὐτὸν πάνυ καλήν, ὥστε ἂν ἰδὼν αὐτὴν
εἴποις ἄγαλμα, Ἐφεσίαν τὸ γένος, ὄνομα Μελίτ-
6 ην· πλοῦτος πολὺς καὶ ἡλικία νέα. τέθνηκε
δὲ αὐτῆς προσφάτως ὁ ἀνὴρ κατὰ θάλασσαν·
βούλεται δὲ τοῦτον ἔχειν δεσπότην· οὐ γὰρ
ἄνδρα ἐρῶ· καὶ δίδωσιν ἑαυτὴν καὶ πᾶσαν ἑαυτῆς
τὴν οὐσίαν. δι' αὐτὸν γὰρ τέτταρας [1] μῆνας νῦν
ἐνθάδε διέτριψεν, ἀκολουθῆσαι δεομένη. ὁ δὲ
οὐκ οἶδα τί παθὼν ὑπερηφανεῖ, νομίζων αὐτῷ
Λευκίππην ἀναβιώσεσθαι."

12. Καὶ ὁ Κλεινίας, "Οὐκ ἀπὸ τρόπου δοκεῖ
μοι," φησίν, "ὁ Σάτυρος λέγειν. κάλλος γὰρ
καὶ πλοῦτος καὶ ἔρως εἰ συνῆλθον ἐπὶ σέ, οὐχ
ἕδρας οὐδὲ ἀναβολῆς· τὸ μὲν γὰρ κάλλος ἡδονήν,
ὁ δὲ πλοῦτος τρυφήν, ὁ δὲ ἔρως αἰδὼ προξενεῖ.[2]
2 μισεῖ δὲ ὁ θεὸς τοὺς ἀλαζόνας. φέρε πείσθητι
τῷ Σατύρῳ καὶ χάρισαι[3] τῷ θεῷ." κἀγὼ
στενάξας, "Ἄγε με," εἶπον, "ὅποι θέλεις, εἰ καὶ
Κλεινίᾳ τοῦτο δοκεῖ· μόνον ὅπως τὸ γύναιόν μοι
μὴ παρέχῃ πράγματα, ἐπείγουσα πρὸς τὸ ἔργον,
3 ἔστ' ἂν εἰς τὴν Ἔφεσον ἀφικώμεθα. φθάνω γὰρ
ἐπομοσάμενος ἐνταῦθα μὴ συνελθεῖν, ἔνθα Λευκίππην ἀπολώλεκα." ταῦτα ἀκούσας ὁ Σάτυρος,

[1] The MSS. have δύο: but we know from ch. xxii. below
that Melite had waited *four* months at Alexandria hoping
for the love of Clitophon, so that we must write τέτταρας
with Jacobs, supposing that a copyist misread δ' as δύο.

[2] προξενεῖ G (the other MSS. omit), as Hercher also proposed. Cobet reads δίδωσι.

[3] So Mitscherlich for MSS. ἴδρυσαι. ἱέρωσαι Jacobs.

[1] If we may judge from the Ephesian Matron of Petronius
(chs. cxi.–cxii.) the ladies of Ephesus were celebrated for the
strength of their affections as well as for the sprightliness of
their wit.

dote on him a woman so beautiful that you might
take her for a lovely statue; she is an Ephesian [1] by
race, her name is Melite; [2] she is very rich, and
young. Her husband has lately been lost at sea,
and now she is willing to take this fellow to be—I
will not say her husband, but—her lord and master;
she offers him herself and all that she possesses. On
his account she has now spent four months here
asking him to be her companion on her journey
home, but he, for some reason which I cannot
fathom, is too proud to consent; I suppose that he
thinks that his Leucippe will come to life again."

12. "Satyrus," said Clinias, "seems to me to talk
reason. When beauty, wealth, and love beckon you
all at once, it is no time for sitting down and
procrastination: her beauty will bring you pleasure,
her wealth luxurious living, and her love the respect [3]
of men. God hates the proud, so come, allow yourself
to be persuaded by Satyrus and obey God's will."
"Take me where you will," I said, with a groan,
"if Clinias too approved; but on the one condition
that this tiresome woman shall not trouble and press
me to become her husband in deed until we arrive
at Ephesus; I have some time ago taken an oath
that I will have nothing to do with any woman here
where I lost Leucippe." Immediately that Satyrus

---

[2] Throughout, MSS. α have Μελίττη, β have Μελίτη with Π[3].
It may either be that Clitophon was to marry her, but to
have more domination over herself and her riches than an
ordinary husband; or, more probably, that he was not to be
her husband, but in the more advantageous position of *amant
en titre.*

[3] αἰδώς is here difficult to translate: it may mean self
respect, or respect shewn to others, or respect shewn by
others. I have preferred the third possibility.

προστρέχει πρὸς τὴν Μελίτην εὐαγγέλια φέρων.
καὶ μικρὸν αὖθις διαλιπὼν ἐπανέρχεται, λέγων
ἀκούσασαν τὴν γυναῖκα ὑφ' ἡδονῆς παρὰ μικρὸν
τὴν ψυχὴν ἀφεῖναι· δεῖσθαι δὲ ἥκειν ὡς αὐτὴν
δειπνήσοντα τὴν ἡμέραν γάμων προοίμιον.
ἐπείσθην καὶ ᾠχόμην.

13. Ἡ δὲ ὡς εἶδέ με, ἀναθοροῦσα περιβάλλει
καὶ πᾶν μου τὸ πρόσωπον ἐμπίμπλησι φιλημάτων. ἦν δὲ τῷ ὄντι καλὴ καὶ γάλακτι μὲν ἂν
εἶπες αὐτῆς τὸ πρόσωπον κεχρῖσθαι, ῥόδον δὲ
2 ἐμπεφυτεῦσθαι ταῖς παρειαῖς. ἐμάρμαιρεν αὐτῆς
τὸ βλέμμα μαρμαρυγὴν Ἀφροδίσιον· κόμη πολλὴ
καὶ βαθεῖα καὶ κατάχρυσος τῇ χροιᾷ, ὥστε
3 ἔδοξα οὐκ ἀηδῶς ἰδεῖν τὴν γυναῖκα. τὸ μὲν οὖν
δεῖπνον ἦν πολυτελές· ἡ δὲ ἐφαπτομένη τῶν
παρακειμένων, ὡς δοκεῖν ἐσθίειν, οὐκ ἠδύνατο
τυχεῖν ὁλοκλήρου τροφῆς, πάντα δὲ ἔβλεπεν ἐμέ.
οὐδὲν γὰρ ἡδὺ τοῖς ἐρῶσι πλὴν τὸ ἐρώμενον· τὴν
γὰρ ψυχὴν πᾶσαν ὁ ἔρως καταλαβών, οὐδὲ αὐτῇ
4 χώραν δίδωσι τῇ τροφῇ. ἡ δὲ τῆς θέας ἡδονὴ
διὰ τῶν ὀμμάτων εἰσρέουσα τοῖς στέρνοις ἐγ-
κάθηται· ἕλκουσα δὲ τοῦ ἐρωμένου τὸ εἴδωλον
ἀεί, ἐναπομάττεται τῷ τῆς ψυχῆς κατόπτρῳ, καὶ
ἀναπλάττει τὴν μορφήν· ἡ δὲ τοῦ κάλλους ἀπορ-
ροὴ δι' ἀφανῶν ἀκτίνων ἐπὶ τὴν ἐρωτικὴν ἑλκο-
μένη καρδίαν ἐναποσφραγίζει κάτω τὴν σκιάν.
5 λέγω δὴ πρὸς αὐτὴν συνείς· "Ἀλλὰ σύ γε οὐδενὸς μετέχεις τῶν σαυτῆς,[1] ἀλλ' ἔοικας τοῖς ἐν
γραφαῖς ἐσθίουσιν." ἡ δέ, "Ποῖον γὰρ ὄψον,"

---

[1] σαυτῆς a: σῶν αὐτῆς β.

heard this, he hurried to Melite to take her the good news and very soon returned to report that when she had heard his message she very nearly expired from delight; also, that I must go that very day to dine with her as the prelude to our coming union. I agreed to this and repaired to her.

13. When she saw me, she jumped up, embraced me and covered my face with kisses. She was indeed beautiful; you might describe her face as of the colour and texture of milk,[1] the rose also growing in her cheeks; her look shone with a splendour proper to the goddess of love, and her hair was long and thick and golden, so that I had to admit that it was not without pleasure that I beheld her. The dinner she provided was sumptuous; she took a portion of the meats set before her, so as to appear to eat, but could swallow nothing of the food; she did nothing but gaze upon me. To lovers there is no delight save in the object of love, which occupies the whole of their soul, and leaves no place in it for the pleasures of the table. The pleasure which comes from vision enters by the eyes and makes its home in the breast; bearing with it ever the image of the beloved, it impresses it upon the mirror of the soul and leaves there its image; the emanation given off by beauty travels by invisible rays to the lovesick heart and imprints upon it its photograph. Realizing the position, I said to her, "How is this? Do you take nothing of the dainties you have yourself provided? You consume no more than those who are painted as eating." "What costly dish," said

---

[1] A literal translation would be: "that her face had been anointed with milk." I have had to have recourse to something of a paraphrase.

ἔφη, "μοι πολυτελὲς ἢ ποῖος οἶνος τιμιώτερος
τῆς σῆς ὄψεως;" καὶ ἅμα λέγουσα κατεφίλησέ
με, προσιέμενον οὐκ ἀηδῶς τὰ φιλήματα· εἶτα
διασχοῦσα, εἶπεν· "Αὕτη μοι τροφή."

14. Τότε μὲν οὖν ἐν τούτοις ἦμεν· ἑσπέρας δὲ
γενομένης, ἡ μὲν ἐπεχείρει με κρατεῖν ἐκεῖ κοιμη-
σόμενον· ἐγὼ δὲ παρῃτούμην, εἰπὼν ἃ καὶ πρὸς
τὸν Σάτυρον ἔτυχον προαγορεύσας. μόλις οὖν
2 ἀφίησιν ἀνιωμένη· τῇ δὲ ὑστεραίᾳ συνέκειτο ἡμῖν
εἰς τὸ τῆς Ἴσιδος ἱερὸν ἀπαντῆσαι, διαλεξομένοις
τε ἀλλήλοις καὶ πιστωσομένοις ἐπὶ μάρτυρι τῇ
θεῷ. συμπαρῆσαν δὲ ἡμῖν ὅ τε Μενέλαος καὶ ὁ
Κλεινίας· καὶ ὠμνύομεν, ἐγὼ μὲν ἀγαπῆσαι[1]
ἀδόλως, ἡ δὲ ἄνδρα ποιήσασθαι, καὶ πάντων
3 ἀποφῆναι δεσπότην. "Ἄρξει δέ," εἶπον ἐγώ,
"τῶν συνθηκῶν ἡ εἰς Ἔφεσον ἡμῶν ἄφιξις·
ἐνταῦθα γάρ, ὡς ἔφην, Λευκίππῃ παραχωρήσεις."
δεῖπνον οὖν ἡμῖν ηὐτρεπίζετο πολυτελές· καὶ
ὄνομα μὲν ἦν τῷ δείπνῳ γάμοι, τὸ δὲ ἔργον
4 συνέκειτο ταμιεύεσθαι. καί τι μέμνημαι καὶ
γελοῖον παρὰ τὴν ἑστίασιν τῆς Μελίτης· ὡς
γὰρ ἐπευφήμουν τοῖς γάμοις οἱ παρόντες, νεύσασα
πρός με ἡσυχῇ, "Καινόν," εἶπεν, "ἐγὼ μόνη
πέπονθα καὶ οἷον ἐπὶ τοῖς ἀφανέσι ποιοῦσι

---

[1] Some editors change ποιήσασθαι and ἀποφῆναι into futures:
I have preferred to make ἀγαπῆσειν into an aorist, as being
more idiomatic and requiring less alteration.

she, "what wine could be more agreeable to me than
the sight of you?" As she spoke, she kissed me,
and it was not without pleasure that I received her
kisses; then, as she tore herself from me—"That is
my sustenance," she said.

14. For the time we continued in this manner;
and when evening came she did her best to make
me pass the night there. I, however, begged to be
excused, using the same words to her that I had
previously spoken to Satyrus. She let me go, though
hardly and in distress; and it was agreed upon
between us that the next day we should meet
at the temple of Isis in order to discuss our future
and take the goddess as witness to our troth.
Menelaus and Clinias came there with us, and we
took oaths, I to love her honourably, and she to
make me her husband and declare me master
of all that she possessed. "Our actual arrival at
Ephesus," I said, "must be time enough for you for
the completion of our nuptials; here, as I said, you
must be content to give place to Leucippe." A rich
banquet was then prepared for us: it was called a
wedding breakfast, though we had agreed to defer the
consummation of the marriage. I remember a good
joke made by Melite during the feast; the guests
were calling down blessings upon our espousals,
when she quietly nodded towards me, saying: "I
seem to be unique in having an unheard of experience, and one that generally happens only in the
case of the dead whose bodies cannot be found;
I have often seen a tenantless catafalque,[1] but

---

[1] κενοτάφιον can be represented in English, and we have
adopted the same word, cenotaph, for an empty memorial or
tomb. But we have no proper expression for κενογάμιον, a
mariage blanc.

νεκροῖς. κενοτάφιον μὲν γὰρ εἶδον, κενογάμιον δὲ
οὔ." ταῦτα μὲν οὖν ἔπαιζε σπουδῇ.

15. Τῇ δὲ ἐπιούσῃ στελλόμεθα πρὸς ἀποδη-
μίαν· κατὰ τύχην δὲ καὶ τὸ πνεῦμα ἐκάλει ἡμᾶς.
καὶ ὁ Μενέλαος μέχρι τοῦ λιμένος ἐλθὼν καὶ
ἀσπασάμενος, εὐτυχεστέρας εἰπὼν νῦν ἡμᾶς
τυχεῖν θαλάσσης, ἀπετράπετο αὖθις, νεανίσκος
πάνυ χρηστὸς καὶ θεῶν ἄξιος, καὶ ἅμα δακρύων
ἐμπεπλησμένος· καὶ ἡμῖν δὲ πᾶσι κατεφέρετο
2 δάκρυα. τῷ δὲ Κλεινίᾳ ἐδόκει μή με καταλιπεῖν,
ἀλλὰ μέχρις Ἐφέσου συμπλεύσαντα καί τινα
ἐνδιατρίψαντα τῇ πόλει χρόνον, ἐπανελθεῖν, εἰ
3 τἀμὰ ἐν καλῷ κείμενα καταμάθοι. γίνεται δὴ
κατ' οὐρὰν ἡμῶν ὁ ἄνεμος· ἑσπέρα τε ἦν, καὶ
δειπνήσαντες ἐκείμεθα κοιμησόμενοι. ἰδίᾳ δὲ
ἐμοί τε καὶ τῇ Μελίτῃ καλύβη τις ἦν ἐπὶ τοῦ
4 σκάφους περιπεφραγμένη. περιβαλοῦσα οὖν με
κατεφίλει καὶ ἀπῄτει τὸν γάμον, "Νῦν μέν,"
λέγουσα, "Λευκίππης τοὺς ὅρους ἐξήλθομεν καὶ
τῶν συνθηκῶν τοὺς ὅρους ἀπειλήφαμεν· ἐντεῦθεν
ἡ προθεσμία. τί με δεῖ νῦν εἰς Ἔφεσον περι-
μένειν; ἄδηλοι τῆς θαλάσσης αἱ τύχαι· ἄπιστοι
5 τῶν ἀνέμων αἱ μεταβολαί. πίστευσόν μοι, Κλειτοφῶν, καίομαι· ὤφελον ἠδυνάμην δεῖξαί τὸ πῦρ·
ὤφελον εἶχε τὴν αὐτὴν φύσιν τῷ κοινῷ τὸ[1] τοῦ
ἔρωτος πῦρ, ἵνα σοι περιχυθεῖσα κατέφλεξα.
νῦν δὲ πρὸς τοῖς ἄλλοις τοῦτο μόνον τὸ πῦρ
ἰδίαν ὕλην ἔχει καὶ ἐν ταῖς περὶ τοὺς ἐραστὰς
συμπλοκαῖς ἀνακαιόμενον λάβρον τῶν συμπλε-

---

[1] τό is not in the MSS., having doubtless disappeared
before τοῦ. It was supplied by Jacobs.

never a tenantless marriage-bed"—a jest that was
half in earnest.

15. On the next day we made our preparations for
departure, being by good chance invited by a
favourable wind. Menelaus came with us to the
harbour and bade us god-speed, telling us that on
this occasion we should find a sea that was more
friendly to us; he then left us, a young man who
was the truest of friends and of a nature better
than mortal; his eyes filled with tears and we were
all constrained to weep in return. Clinias decided
not to leave me, but to sail with me as far as Ephesus,
and, after remaining some time in that city, to return
if he found my future prospects in fair case. The
wind was fair behind us; it was now evening and
we had dined and were retiring to rest; Melite and
I had a cabin to ourselves which had been built [1]
on the upper deck; and there she flung her arms
about me, kissed me, and asked me for the full rites of
marriage: "Now," said she, "we have traversed
Leucippe's boundaries and reached those of your
promises; now begins the time when they are to
be fulfilled. Why must I wait for our arrival at
Ephesus? No one can be sure of what will happen
at sea, and no trust can be placed in the changeful
winds. Believe me, Clitophon, I am all afire—would
that I could shew it to you—would that the fire of
love had a like nature with that of the common
element, in order that I might set you aflame by
my embrace; but, as it is, this fire of mine, unlike
other kinds, has its fuel in itself, and in lovers'
embraces it seems to burn up furiously but to spare

---

[1] Literally, "fenced round"; doubtless a temporary
structure.

6 κομένων φείδεται. ὦ πυρὸς μυστικοῦ, πυρὸς ἐν
ἀπορρήτῳ δᾳδουχουμένου, πυρὸς τοὺς ὅρους αὐτοῖ
φυγεῖν μὴ θέλοντος. μυηθῶμεν οὖν, ὦ φίλτατε,
τὰ τῆς Ἀφροδίτης μυστήρια."

16. Κἀγὼ εἶπον· " Μή με βιάσῃ λῦσαι θεσμὸν
ὁσίας νεκρῶν. οὔπω τῆς ἀθλίας ἐκείνης τοὺς
ὅρους παρήλθομεν, ἕως ἂν γῆς ἐπιβῶμεν ἑτέρας.
οὐκ ἤκουσας ὡς ἐν θαλάσσῃ τέθνηκεν; ἔτι πλέω
Λευκίππης τὸν τάφον. τάχα που περὶ τὴν ναῦν
2 αὐτῆς εἰλεῖται τὸ εἴδωλον. λέγουσι δὲ τὰς ἐν
ὕδατι ψυχὰς ἀνῃρημένας μηδὲ εἰς ᾅδου καταβαίνειν ὅλως, ἀλλ' αὐτοῦ περὶ τὸ ὕδωρ ἔχειν τὴν
πλάνην, καὶ ἐπιστήσεται τάχα ἡμῖν συμπλεκο-
μένοις. ἐπιτήδειον δέ σοι δοκεῖ τὸ χωρίον εἶναι
πρὸς γάμον; γάμος ἐπὶ κύματος, γάμος ὑπὸ
θαλάσσης φερόμενος; θάλαμον ἡμῖν θέλεις γενέ-
3 σθαι μὴ μένοντα;" "Σὺ μέν," ἔφη, "σοφίζῃ,
φίλτατε· πᾶς δὲ τόπος τοῖς ἐρῶσι θάλαμος·
οὐδὲν γὰρ ἄβατον τῷ θεῷ. ἐν θαλάσσῃ δὲ μὴ
καὶ οἰκειότερόν ἐστιν Ἔρωτι καὶ Ἀφροδισίοις
μυστηρίοις; θυγάτηρ Ἀφροδίτη θαλάσσης.
4 χαρισώμεθα τῇ γαμηλίῳ θεῷ, τιμήσωμεν αὐτῆς
γάμῳ τὴν μητέρα. ἐμοὶ μὲν γὰρ δοκεῖ τὰ
παρόντα γάμων εἶναι σύμβολα. ζυγὸς μὲν
οὗτος ὑπὲρ κεφαλῆς κρεμάμενος, δεσμοὶ δὲ περὶ

---

[1] She was said to be 'Ἀφρογένεια, foam-born, and to have
risen from the sea by the shore of the island of Cytheɪa.

[2] The symbolism is very elaborate. The yard crossing the
mast at right angles reminds Melite of a yoke, and so of
Hera ζυγία; in the same way the cables stand for the bonds

the object of those embraces. O strange and mystic fire, fire that glows in secret and will not transgress the limits of the victim on whom it preys! Let us then, my dearest, become initiates in the sacred rites of Aphrodite."

16. "No," said I, "force me not to do violence to the duty owed to the dead; we have not traversed the limits consecrated to that poor girl until we land in another country. Did you not hear that she perished at sea? I am now sailing over Leucippe's grave, and perhaps her shade is even now hovering round the ship. They say that the souls of those who have met their end in the deep never go down to Hades, but wander in the same spot about the face of the waters; she may perhaps be present at our embraces. Then does this seem to you a spot suitable for the completion of our marriage? A marriage on the ocean wave, a marriage tossed by the deep? Could you bear that ours should be an unstable and rocking marriage-bed?" "You quibble, my dearest," she cried; "lovers find every spot a possible marriage-bed, and Love is a god who finds nowhere inaccessible to him. Indeed where could a place be found more appropriate than on the sea for love and the mysteries of Aphrodite? Aphrodite is the sea's daughter.[1] Let us propitiate that goddess who presides over marriages and honour her mother by this marriage of ours. Yes, all that I see about seems to me to be emblematic of marriage: here is the yoke[2] of marriage that hangs above our heads,

---

of marriage, which (like the yoke) are quite familiar to us in the figurative language of to-day. The succeeding comparisons are even more far-fetched.

τὴν κεραίαν τεταμένοι· καλά γε, ὦ δέσποτα, τὰ
μαντεύματα· ὑπὸ ζυγὸν ὁ θάλαμος, καὶ κάλω
5 δεδεμένοι. ἀλλὰ καὶ πηδάλιον τοῦ θαλάμου
πλησίον· ἰδοὺ τοὺς γάμους ἡμῶν ἡ Τύχη κυ-
βερνᾷ· νυμφοστολήσουσι δὲ ἡμᾶς Ποσειδῶν καὶ
Νηρεΐδων χορός· ἐνταῦθα γὰρ καὶ αὐτὸς Ἀμφι-
τρίτην γαμεῖ. λιγυρὸν δὲ συρίζει περὶ τοὺς
κάλως καὶ τὸ πνεῦμα· ἐμοὶ μὲν ὑμέναιον ᾄδειν [1]
6 δοκεῖ τὰ τῶν ἀνέμων αὐλήματα. ὁρᾷς δὲ καὶ τὴν
ὀθόνην κεκυρτωμένην, ὥσπερ ἐγκύμονα γαστέρα·
δεξιόν μοι καὶ τοῦτο τῶν οἰωνισμάτων· ἔσῃ μοι
7 ταχὺ καὶ πατήρ." ἰδὼν οὖν αὐτὴν σφόδρα
ἐγκειμένην, " Φιλοσοφήσωμεν," εἶπον, " ὦ γύναι,
μέχρις λαβώμεθα γῆς. ὄμνυμι γάρ σοι τὴν
θάλασσαν αὐτὴν καὶ τὴν τοῦ πλοῦ τύχην, ὡς
ἐσπούδακα καὶ αὐτός. ἀλλ' εἰσὶ καὶ θαλάσσης
8 νόμοι. πολλάκις ἤκουσα παρὰ τῶν ναυτικωτέρων,
καθαρὰ δεῖν Ἀφροδισίων εἶναι τὰ σκάφη, τάχα
μὲν ὡς ἱερά, τάχα δὲ ἵνα μή τις ἐν τηλικούτῳ
κινδύνῳ τρυφᾷ. μὴ ἐνυβρίσωμεν, ὦ φιλτάτη, τῇ
θαλάσσῃ· μὴ συμμίξωμεν γάμον ὁμοῦ καὶ φόβον.
τηρήσωμεν ἑαυτοῖς καθαρὰν τὴν ἡδονήν." ταῦτα
λέγων καὶ μειλισσόμενος τοῖς φιλήμασιν ἔπειθον,
καὶ τὸ λοιπὸν οὕτως ἐκαθεύδομεν.

17. Πέντε δὲ τῶν ἑξῆς ἡμερῶν διανύσαντες
τὸν πλοῦν ἥκομεν εἰς τὴν Ἔφεσον. οἰκία μεγάλη

[1] A most ingenious correction of MSS. ἄγειν, made by
Hemsterhuis.

there are the ties of marriage which depend from the
yard—fine omens, my lord and master—our couch is
beneath the yoke, and the ties are securely fastened.
Here too is the rudder close to our couch, and
Fortune is the helmsman that directs our espousals;
our groomsman and bridesmaids are Poseidon and
his train of Nereids; for it was here that he wedded
Amphitrite. The wind too whistles tunefully in the
rigging: I think that the breath of the gale is singing
our bridal song. Then you also see the sail bellying
out, like a woman's fertile womb: this seems to me
the most propitious of omens; I shall soon see
you a father." Seeing that she was in a coming-on
humour, " Let us abstain," I said, " like philosophers,
dear lady, until we touch land. I swear to you by
this very sea and by the good luck of our voyage, that I
too am as anxious as you for fruition; but the sea too
has its statutes, and I have often heard from sea-
faring men that ships should always be pure from
the rites of love, perhaps because they themselves
are sacred,[1] or perhaps that there should be no
dalliance in the dangerous state in which ship-board
always is. Therefore, my dearest, do not let us
inflict this insult on the sea—we do not want our
marriage to have in it a large admixture of fear—
let us keep our pleasure pure and undefiled." Using
these words I did my best to appease her with my
kisses, and finally succeeded; we then went to sleep
in the cabin, just as we were, for the rest of the
time on board.

17. It took us five days sail after this to reach
Ephesus. Her house there was large and one of the

---

[1] I do not know why ships are sacred *per se*, unless it be
for the *tutela navis*—the figure-head gods.

καὶ πρώτη τῶν ἐκεῖ· θεραπεία πολλὴ καὶ ἡ ἄλλη
2 παρασκευὴ πολυτελής. κελεύει δὴ δεῖπνον ὡς
ὅτι ἐκπρεπέστατον ἑτοιμάζειν· "Ἡμεῖς δὲ τέως,"
ἔφη, "χωρήσωμεν εἰς τοὺς ἀγρούς." ἀπεῖχον δὲ
τῆς πόλεως σταδίους τέτταρας. ἐπικαθίσαντες
3 οὖν ὀχήματι, ἐξήλθομεν· καὶ ἐπεὶ τάχιστα
παρεγενόμεθα, διεβαδίζομεν τοὺς ὀρχάτους τῶν
φυτῶν, καὶ ἐξαίφνης προσπίπτει τοῖς γόνασιν
ἡμῶν γυνή, χοίνιξι[1] παχείαις δεδεμένη, δίκελλαν
κρατοῦσα, τὴν κεφαλὴν κεκαρμένη, ἐρρυπωμένη
τὸ σῶμα, χιτῶνα ἀνεζωσμένη ἄθλιον πάνυ, καὶ
"Ἐλέησόν με," ἔφη, "δέσποινα, γυνὴ γυναῖκα,
ἐλευθέραν μέν, ὡς ἔφυν, δούλην δὲ νῦν, ὡς δοκεῖ τῇ
4 Τύχῃ," καὶ ἅμα ἐσιώπησε. λέγει οὖν ἡ Μελίτη·
"Ἀνάστηθι, ὦ γύναι· λέγε, τίς εἶ, καὶ πόθεν, καὶ
τίς σοι τοῦτον περιέθηκε τὸν σίδηρον· κέκραγε
γάρ σου καὶ ἐν κακοῖς ἡ μορφὴ τὴν εὐγένειαν."
"Ὁ σός," εἶπεν, "οἰκέτης, ὅτι αὐτῷ μὴ πρὸς
5 εὐνὴν ἐδούλευον. ὄνομα Λάκαινα, Θετταλὴ τὸ
γένος· καί σοι προσφέρω μου ταύτην τὴν τύχην
ἱκετηρίαν. ἀπόλυσόν με τῆς καθεστώσης συμφο-
ρᾶς· πάρασχε[2] δέ μοι τὴν ἀσφάλειαν, ἔστ' ἂν
ἀποτίσω τὰς δισχιλίας· τοσούτου γάρ με ὁ
6 Σωσθένης ἀπὸ τῶν λῃστῶν ἐωνήσατο. ποριοῦμεν
δέ, εὖ ἴσθι, τὴν ταχίστην· εἰ δὲ μή, σοὶ δουλεύ-
σομεν. ὁρᾷς δὲ καὶ πληγαῖς ὡς κατέξηνέ με

---

[1] The MSS. have σχοίνοισι, which can be feminine: but
the epithet παχείαις is much more appropriate to the thick,
stock-like χοίνικες than to the thin σχοῖνοι, which should
mean ropes made of reeds or withies. χοίνιξι is found in the
margin of cod. Anglicanus 16 D. XVIII.
[2] So Salmasius for MSS. παρασχεῖν. The infinitive cannot
be construed.

most important in the city, her servants numerous
and her furniture costly. She first ordered a most
elaborate dinner to be prepared; "Meanwhile," said
she, "we will visit my country seat." This was
about half a mile from the city, and we entered a
carriage and set out for it. On our arrival we were
walking through the rows of plants in the garden
when suddenly there threw herself at our feet a
woman wearing heavy fetters and holding a hoe, her
head shorn, her person dirty, clad in a short and
wretched garment. "Have pity on me," she cried,
"my lady, let a woman pity a woman, and one
that was once[1] free, and was born so, though now,
by the decree of Fortune, a slave." After these words
she remained silent; so "Rise, woman," said
Melite, "say who you are and whence you come,
and to whom you owe these fetters. Even in your
misery your appearance proclaims aloud that you are
of gentle birth." "It is your steward," she replied,
"because I would not be a slave to his lusts. My
name is Lacaena, I come from Thessaly. I lay
before you this my fate with all supplication. Save
me from this threatening disaster, grant me security
until I can pay you the two thousand pieces of gold;
that was the sum for which Sosthenes bought me
from the hands of the pirates, and be sure that I can
raise it with very small delay; if not, I will be your
slave. Yes, and you can see how he has torn my

---

[1] The editors have pointed out that the words ἐλευθέραν
μέν, ὡς ἔφυν, δούλην δὲ νῦν form an iambic line; they may
possibly be a quotation from some tragedy.

273

πολλαῖς." καὶ ἅμα διανοίξασα τὸν χιτῶνα,
δείκνυσι τὰ νῶτα διαγεγραμμένα ἔτι οἰκτρότερον.
7 ὡς οὖν ταῦτ᾽ ἠκούσαμεν, ἐγὼ μὲν συνεχύθην· καὶ
γάρ τι ἐδόκει Λευκίππης ἔχειν· ἡ δὲ Μελίτη
ἔφη· " Θάρρει, γύναι· τούτων γάρ σε λύσομεν,
εἴς τε τὴν οἰκείαν προῖκα ἀποπέμψομεν. τὸν
Σωσθένην καλεσάτω τις ἡμῖν."
8 Ἡ μὲν οὖν εὐθὺς τῶν δεσμῶν ἠλευθεροῦτο· ὁ
δὲ παρῆν τεταραγμένος. λέγει οὖν ἡ Μελίτη·
"Ὦ κακὴ κεφαλή, τίνα[1] ποτὲ κἂν τῶν ἀχρειο-
τάτων οἰκετῶν τεθέασαι παρ᾽ ἡμῖν οὕτως ᾐκισ-
μένον; τίς αὕτη; λέγε μηδὲν ψευσάμενος."
9 " Οὐκ οἶδα," εἶπεν, " ὦ δέσποινα, πλὴν ἔμπορός
τις, ὄνομα Καλλισθένης, ταύτην μοι πέπρακε,
φάσκων ἐωνῆσθαι μὲν αὐτὴν ἀπὸ λῃστῶν, εἶναι
δὲ ἐλευθέραν. ὄνομα δὲ αὐτὴν ὁ ἔμπορος ἐκάλει
10 Λάκαιναν." ἡ δὲ τὸν μὲν τῆς διοικήσεως, ἧς
εἶχεν, ἀπέπαυσεν, αὐτὴν δὲ παραδίδωσι θερα-
παίναις, κελεύσασα λοῦσαι καὶ ἐσθῆτα ἀμφιέσαι
καθαρὰν καὶ εἰς ἄστυ ἀγαγεῖν. διοικήσασα δέ
τινα τῶν κατὰ τοὺς ἀγρούς, ὧν ἕνεκεν παρῆν,
ἐπιβᾶσα τοῦ ὀχήματος ἅμα ἐμοί, ἐπανῄειμεν εἰς
τὴν πόλιν, καὶ περὶ τὸ δεῖπνον ἦμεν.

18. Ἑστιωμένῳ δέ μοι μεταξὺ σημαίνει νεύσας
ὁ Σάτυρος προανίστασθαι, καὶ ἦν τὸ πρόσωπον
ἐσπουδακώς. σκηψάμενος οὖν ἐπί τινι τῶν
κατὰ τὴν γαστέρα ἐπείγειν, διανίσταμαι. καὶ
ἐπεὶ προῆλθον, λέγει μὲν οὐδέν, ἐπιστολὴν δὲ
2 ὀρέγει. λαβὼν δέ, πρὶν ἀναγνῶναι,[2] κατεπλάγην

[1] Gaselee's emendation for MSS. τοιαῦτα. Jacobs proposed
τίνα σὺ πώποτε.
[2] ἀναγνῶναι is followed in the MSS. by an unnecessary με.
It was removed by Cobet.

flesh with many stripes," and, as she spoke, she opened her tunic and shewed us her back most piteously marked and scarred. When we heard her story, while I was greatly moved, finding some look of Leucippe about her, Melite said, "Be of good cheer, woman: I will both deliver you from your present apprehension and will send you back to your own country without ransom. Let someone call Sosthenes hither to us."

The woman was at once freed from her fetters, and Sosthenes appeared before us greatly disordered. "Wretch," said Melite to him, "have you ever seen even the most worthless of my slaves disfigured like this at my hands? Who is this woman? No lies, now: tell me the whole story." "I know nothing, Madam," said he, "save that a dealer named Callisthenes sold her to me, saying that he had bought her from some pirates, and that she was of free birth. The dealer said that her name was Lacaena." Melite deposed him from his steward-ship, and handed over the woman to her serving-maids, bidding them wash her, clothe her in clean garments, and bring her to town. Then, having settled the business connected with her country place, the object of her journey thither, she entered the carriage with me and returned to the city, where we set about our dinner.

18. I was about at the middle of the banquet when Satyrus indicated to me by signs to come aside, with a grave expression on his face. I therefore made some excuse about belly-trouble, and left the table. When I had come to him, he said nothing, but handed me a letter. Even as I took it from him, before I began to read it, I was thunder-struck; for

εὐθύς· ἐγνώρισα γὰρ Λευκίππης τὰ γράμματα.
ἐγέγραπτο δὲ τάδε·

Λευκίππη Κλειτοφῶντι τῷ δεσπότῃ μου.

3 Τοῦτο γάρ σε δεῖ καλεῖν, ἐπεὶ καὶ τῆς δεσ-
ποίνης ἀνὴρ εἶ τῆς ἐμῆς. ὅσα μὲν διὰ σὲ
πέπονθα, οἶδας· ἀνάγκη δὲ νῦν ὑπομνῆσαί σε.
4 διὰ σὲ τὴν μητέρα κατέλιπον καὶ πλάνην
εἱλόμην· διὰ σὲ πέπονθα ναυαγίαν καὶ λῃστῶν
ἠνεσχόμην· διὰ σὲ ἱερεῖον γέγονα καὶ καθαρμὸς
καὶ τέθνηκα ἤδη δεύτερον· διὰ σὲ πέπραμαι
καὶ ἐδέθην σιδήρῳ καὶ δίκελλαν ἐβάστασα, καὶ
ἔσκαψα γῆν καὶ ἐμαστιγώθην, ἵνα σὺ ὃ γέγονας
ἄλλῃ γυναικί, κἀγὼ τῷ ἑτέρῳ ἀνδρὶ [1] γένωμαι ;
5 μὴ γένοιτο. ἀλλ᾽ ἐγὼ μὲν ἐπὶ τοσαύταις ἀνάγ-
καις διεκαρτέρησα· σὺ δὲ ἄπρατος, ἀμαστίγωτος
γαμεῖς. εἴ τις οὖν τῶν πεπονημένων διὰ σὲ
κεῖται χάρις, δεήθητί σου τῆς γυναικὸς ἀπο-
πέμψαι, ὡς ἐπηγγείλατο· τὰς δὲ δισχιλίας, ἃς
ὁ Σωσθένης ὑπὲρ ἐμοῦ κατεβάλετο, πίστευσον
ἡμῖν, καὶ ἐγγύησαι πρὸς τὴν Μελίτην ὅτι
6 πέμψομεν. ἐγγὺς γὰρ τὸ Βυζάντιον· ἐὰν δὲ καὶ
ἀποτίσῃς, νόμιζε μισθόν μοι δεδωκέναι τῶν ὑπὲρ
σοῦ πόνων. ἔρρωσο, καὶ ὄναιο τῶν καινῶν
γάμων. ἐγὼ δὲ ἔτι σοι ταῦτα γράφω παρθένος.

19. Τούτοις ἐντυχὼν πάντα ἐγινόμην ὁμοῦ· ἀνε-
φλεγόμην, ὠχρίων, ἐθαύμαζον, ἠπίστουν, ἔχαιρον,
2 ἠχθόμην. λέγω οὖν πρὸς τὸν Σάτυρον· " Πότερον
ἐξ ᾄδου ἥκεις φέρων τὴν ἐπιστολήν; ἢ τί ταῦτα

---

[1] The MSS. have τῶν ἑτέρων ἀνδρῶν. The correction is due
to Cobet.

I recognized Leucippe's writing! This was the tenor of it.

Leucippe, to my lord Clitophon.

Lord I must call you, as you are my lady's husband. You know what I have suffered for your sake, but perforce I must remind you of it. For you I left my mother and took up the life of a wanderer; for you I suffered shipwreck and fell into the hands of pirates; for you I became a victim for sacrifice and an expiatory offering and twice entered the valley of the shadow of death; for you I was sold and fettered, I carried a hoe, I tilled the ground, I underwent the scourge—and was this all that I might become to another man what you have become to another woman? Never. I, through all these trials, have persevered to the end; you were never sold, never scourged, but you are marrying. If you have any gratitude for all that I have suffered for your sake, ask your wife to send me home as she promised; lend me the two thousand pieces of gold which Sosthenes paid for me, and go bail to Melite that I will send them to her. Byzantium is not far off, and even if you have to pay the money yourself, consider it a return for the miseries endured for your sake. Fare you well, and be happy in your new espousals: I who write this to you am still a virgin.

19. At this message I was moved with many emotions at once; I was flushed and pale, I was astonished and incredulous, I was full of joy and sorrow. "Do you come bringing this letter from Hades?" I said to Satyrus, "or what does this mean?

θέλει; Λευκίππη πάλιν ἀνεβίω;” “Μάλιστα,”
ἔφη· “καί ἐστιν ἣν εἶδες ἐν τοῖς ἀγροῖς. καὶ
τότε μὲν οὖν οὐδ’ ἂν ἄλλος αὐτὴν ἰδὼν γνωρίσειεν,
ἔφηβον οὕτω γενομένην· τοῦτο γὰρ ἡ τῶν τριχῶν
3 αὐτῆς κουρὰ μόνον ἐνήλλαξεν.” “Εἶτα ἕστηκας,”
ἔφην, “ἐπὶ τηλικούτοις ἀγαθοῖς καὶ μέχρι τῶν
ὤτων μόνον εὐφραίνεις, ἀλλ’ οὐ δεικνύεις καὶ τοῖς
ὄμμασι τἀγαθά;” “Μὴ σύ γε,” εἶπεν ὁ Σάτυρος·
“ἀλλ’ ἑνὸς κάτασχε, μὴ πάντας ἀπολέσῃς, ἕως
ἂν[1] περὶ τούτων ἀσφαλέστερον βουλευσώμεθα.
4 γυναῖκα ὁρᾷς πρώτην Ἐφεσίων μαινομένην ἐπὶ
σοί, ἡμᾶς δὲ ἐρήμους ἐν μέσαις ἄρκυσιν.” “Ἀλλ’
οὐ δύναμαι,” ἔφην· “ἐπέρχεται γὰρ διὰ πασῶν
5 τῶν τοῦ σώματος ὁδῶν ἡ χαρά. ἀλλ’ ἰδού μοι
διὰ τῶν γραμμάτων ἐγκαλεῖ.” καὶ ἅμα αὖθις
ἐντυγχάνων τοῖς γράμμασιν, ὡς ἐκείνην δι’ αὐτῶν
βλέπων καὶ ἀναγινώσκων καθ’ ἓν ἔλεγον· “Δίκαια
ἐγκαλεῖς, φιλτάτη. πάντα δι’ ἐμὲ ἔπαθες·
6 πολλῶν σοι γέγονα κακῶν αἴτιος.” ὡς δὲ εἰς τὰς
μάστιγας καὶ εἰς τὰς βασάνους ἐγενόμην ἃς ὁ
Σωσθένης αὐτῇ παρετρίψατο, ἔκλαιον ὥσπερ
αὐτὰς τὰς βασάνους βλέπων αὐτῆς· ὁ γὰρ
λογισμὸς πέμπων τῆς ψυχῆς τὰ ὄμματα πρὸς
τὴν ἀπαγγελίαν τῶν γραμμάτων, ἐδείκνυε τὰ
ὁρώμενα ὡς δρώμενα. πάνυ δὲ ἠρυθρίων ἐφ’ οἷς
μοι τὸν γάμον ὠνείδιζεν, ὥσπερ ἐπ’ αὐτοφώρῳ
μοιχὸς κατειλημμένος. οὕτως ᾐσχυνόμην καὶ
τὰ γράμματα.

[1] Inserted by Cobet.

Has Leucippe come to life again?" "She has," he replied, "and it was she whom you saw at the country place. No one would recognise her in that case, looking, as she did, like a boy—the cutting-off of her hair had alone so changed her." "Do you stop there," I cried, "at such good news, bringing these good tidings to my ears only, without also delighting my eyes by the sight of her?" "Stay," said Satyrus, "take no rash action, lest you ruin us all, until we have been able to decide upon some safe course in this matter. You see here a woman, one of the greatest among the Ephesians, doting upon you, and us without help in the midst of the toils." "I cannot," I replied; "joy is coursing through all the veins of my body. Look, she reproaches me in the letter she has written." As I spoke I went through it again, imagining that I could see her in it, and as I read it sentence by sentence, I exclaimed: "Your reproaches are just, my darling. All your sufferings have been for[1] me; I am the cause of all your woes." And when I came to the account of the scourges and the torments which Sosthenes had inflicted upon her, I wept as though I could myself see the tortures; consideration so fixed the eyes of my soul upon the message conveyed by the writing that the scene seemed positively enacted before me. I blushed deeply at the reproaches she heaped upon me in the matter of my marriage, just as if I had been caught in the very act of adultery; so ashamed did her letter make me.

[1] δι' ἐμέ, like διὰ σέ in the letter, has the double meaning of "for my sake" and "by my fault." It is not easy to express both together in English.

20. "Οἴμοι, πῶς ἀπολογήσομαι, Σάτυρε;" ἔφην·
"ἑαλώκαμεν. Λευκίππη κατέγνωκεν ἡμῶν· τάχα
δὲ καὶ μεμισήμεθα. ἀλλὰ πῶς ἐσώθη, φράσον
σύ; καὶ τίνος σῶμα ἐθάψαμεν;" "Αὐτή σοι κατὰ
καιρὸν φράσει· τὸ δὲ νῦν," ὁ Σάτυρος ἔφη,
"ἀντιγράψαι σε δεῖ, καὶ ἱλάσασθαι τὴν κόρην.
2 κἀγὼ γὰρ αὐτῇ διωμοσάμην, ὡς ἄκων αὐτὴν¹
ἔγημας." "Εἶπας γάρ," ἔφην, "ὅτι καὶ ἔγημα;
ἀπολώλεκάς με." "Τῆς εὐηθείας· ὅλη γὰρ ἡ
πόλις οὐκ οἶδε τὸν γάμον;" "'Αλλ' οὐκ ἔγημα,
μὰ τὸν Ἡρακλέα, Σάτυρε, καὶ τὴν παροῦσαν
3 τύχην." "Παίζεις, ὦ 'γαθέ· συγκαθεύδεις."
"Οἶδα μὲν ἄπιστα λέγων, ἀλλ' οὔπω πέπρακται·
καθαρὸς εἰς ταύτην τὴν ἡμέραν Μελίτης Κλειτο-
4 φῶν. ἀλλὰ τί γράψω, λέγε· σφόδρα γάρ με
ἐξέπληξε τὸ συμβάν, ὥστε ἀπόρως ἔχω." "Οὐκ
εἰμί σου σοφώτερος," Σάτυρος εἶπεν· "ἀλλὰ καὶ
αὐτός σοι ὁ Ἔρως ὑπαγορεύσει. μόνον διὰ
ταχέων." ἄρχομαι δὴ γράφειν.

Κλειτοφῶν Λευκίππῃ χαίρειν.²

5 Χαῖρέ μοι, ὦ δέσποινα Λευκίππη. δυστυχῶ
μὲν ἐν οἷς εὐτυχῶ, ὅτι σὲ παρὼν παροῦσαν ὡς
ἀποδημοῦσαν ὁρῶ διὰ γραμμάτων. εἰ μὲν οὖν
τὴν ἀλήθειαν περιμένεις, μηδὲν προκαταγινώ-
σκουσά μου, μαθήσῃ τὴν σήν με παρθενίαν

¹ Hercher, following Orelli and Jacobs, wished to omit
or alter αὐτήν (= Melite) as an awkward and ambiguous
change of object. But I think that αὐτή is here equivalent

20. " Alas, Satyrus," said I, "how shall I make
my excuses to her? I am caught. Leucippe has
condemned me, and perhaps I have become the
object of her hatred. But tell me, how was she
saved, and whose body was it that we buried?" " She
will recount the whole story to you," said Satyrus,
"in due time; for the present it is your business to
answer her and attempt to placate her. I swore to
her that it was against your will that you had married
your lady." "What?" said I, " Did you tell her
that I was married? You have ruined me." "What
nonsense! Does not the whole town know of your
marriage?" " I swear by Hercules, Satyrus, and by
this my present good fortune, that it has been no
marriage." " You are jesting, my friend; you pass
the night with her." " I know that I am telling you
what seems incredible, but nothing has yet happened:
to this day Clitophon is chaste as far as Melite is
concerned. But tell me what to write; I am so
stupefied by what has happened that I am all at a loss."
" I am certainly no better scholar than you," said
Satyrus: " surely it is Love himself that will dictate.
Only be quick about it." So I began to write:—

Clitophon to Leucippe, greeting.

*Hail, my lady Leucippe! I am happy at the same
moment that I am unhappy, because I find you present in
your letter and yet still absent from me. If you will wait
for the truth, not condemning me in advance, you will find*

---

to the Latin *ipsa* or *ipsima*, the mistress: *cf.* the Pytha-
gorean phrase αὐτὸς ἔφα, the master said it, and many similar
examples in Attic comedy. ταύτην Castiglioni.

² Κλειτοφῶν Λ. χαίρειν added by Jacobs.

μεμιμημένον, εἴ τις ἐστὶ καὶ ἐν ἀνδράσι παρθενια·
εἰ δέ με χωρὶς ἀπολογίας ἤδη μεμίσηκας, ὄμνυμί
σοι τοὺς σώσαντάς σε θεούς, ὡς ἐν βραχεῖ σοι τὸ
ἔργον ἀπολογήσομαι. ἔρρωσό μοι φιλτάτη, καὶ
ἵλεως γένοιο.

21. Δίδωμι δὴ τῷ Σατύρῳ τὴν ἐπιστολήν, καὶ
δέομαι τὰ εἰκότα εἰπεῖν πρὸς αὐτὴν περὶ ἐμοῦ.
ἐγὼ δὲ αὖθις ἐπὶ τὸ συμπόσιον ἀπῄειν, ἡδονῆς
ἅμα καὶ λύπης γεγεμισμένος. ᾔδειν γὰρ τὴν
Μελίτην οὐκ ἀνήσουσάν με τῆς νυκτὸς τὸ μὴ οὐ
γενέσθαι [1] τοὺς γάμους ἡμῖν· ἐμοὶ δὲ ἀδύνατον ἦν
Λευκίππην ἀπολαβόντι γυναῖκα ἑτέραν κἂν ἰδεῖν.
2 τὸ μὲν οὖν πρόσωπον ἐβιαζόμην μηδὲν ἀλλοῖον
παρέχειν ἢ πρὶν ἦν· οὐ πάντῃ δὲ κρατεῖν ἠδυνάμην.
ὡς δὲ ἐνικώμην, σκήπτομαι φρίκην μοι ὑποδρα-
μεῖν. ἡ δὲ συνῆκε μὲν ὅτι κατὰ τῆς ὑποσχέσεως
προοιμιάζομαι· ἐλέγχειν δὲ οὐκ ἠδύνατο τὸ προ-
3 οίμιον. ἐγὼ μὲν δὴ ἄδειπνος ἀνίσταμαι κοιμη-
σόμενος· ἡ δὲ κατὰ πόδας, ὡς εἶχεν, ἐφ᾽ ἡμιτελεῖ
τῷ δείπνῳ συνανίσταται. ὡς δὲ εἰς τὸν θάλαμον
παρήλθομεν, ἐγὼ μὲν ἔτι μᾶλλον ἐπέτεινον τῆς
νόσου τὴν ὑπόκρισιν· ἡ δὲ ἐλιπάρει, καὶ ἔλεγε·
"Τί ταῦτα ποιεῖς; μέχρι τίνος με ἀπολλύεις;
ἰδοὺ καὶ τὴν θάλασσαν διεπλεύσαμεν· ἰδοὺ καὶ
4 Ἔφεσος, ἡ προθεσμία τῶν γάμων. ποίαν ἔτι
περιμένομεν ἡμέραν; μέχρι τίνος ὡς ἐν ἱερῷ
συγκαθεύδομεν; ποταμὸν παρατιθεὶς πολὺν κω-

---

[1] οὐ γένεσθαι : so Cobet for MSS. συγγένεσθαι.

*that I have imitated your virginity, if there be any virginity
in men; but if you have already begun to hate me, though
I have had no chance of making my defence before you, I
swear to you by the gods that have saved you that I will
shortly make before you a full explanation of the whole
matter. Farewell, my dearest, and think kindly of me.*

21. I handed the letter to Satyrus, and asked him
to put my case before her in a favourable light; I
then returned to the banquet, full both of delight and
distress, as I knew that in the approaching night
Melite would not permit that our marriage should
fail to be consummated, and it was quite impossible
for me, with Leucippe once again restored to me, even
to look at another woman. However, I tried to
preserve my expression unaltered from what it was
before; but I could not entirely control my emotions,
and, as I felt them becoming too strong for me, I
pretended that I felt a shivering creeping through
me. She suspected this was a prevaricating prelude
to evade my promise; but she was unable at present
to prove that I was in fact thus prevaricating. I
then arose from the table without my dinner, saying
that I must retire to bed; she also instantly leapt to
her feet and followed me, leaving the meal half-eaten.
When we arrived at my bed-chamber, I made a
still further pretence of indisposition; but she
importuned me the more, saying: "Why do you
do this? How long are you going thus to break my
heart? We have finished our sea-journey; here is
Ephesus, the place promised for the completion of
our marriage. For what day are we waiting now?
How long are we to spend our nights as if we were
in church? You set before my eyes a fair river and

283

λύεις πίνειν. τοσοῦτον χρόνον ὕδωρ ἔχουσα διψῶ,
ἐν αὐτῇ καθεύδουσα τῇ πηγῇ. τοιαύτην ἔχω
5 τὴν εὐνήν, οἵαν ὁ Τάνταλος τὴν τροφήν." ταῦτα
ἔλεγε καὶ ἔκλαιεν, ἐπιθεῖσά μου τοῖς στέρνοις
τὴν κεφαλὴν οὕτως ἐλεεινῶς, ὥστε συμπαθεῖν
μέ τι τὴν ψυχήν. οὐκ εἶχον δὲ ὅστις γένωμαι·
6 καὶ γὰρ ἐδόκει μοι δίκαια ἐγκαλεῖν. λέγω
οὖν πρὸς αὐτήν· "Ὄμνυμί σοι, φιλτάτη, τοὺς
πατρῴους θεούς, ἦ μὴν σφόδρα καὶ αὐτὸς ἐπεί-
γομαί σου τὴν σπουδὴν ἀμείψασθαι. ἀλλ' οὐκ
οἶδα," ἔφην, "τί πέπονθα. νόσος γάρ μοι
7 ἐξαίφνης ἐνέπεσεν· οἶδας δὲ ὅτι ὑγιείας χωρὶς
οὐδέν ἐστιν 'Αφροδίτη." καὶ ἅμα λέγων ἀπέ-
ψων αὐτῆς τὰ δάκρυα, καὶ ὅρκοις ἑτέροις
ἐπιστούμην, ὡς οὐκ εἰς μακρὰν ὧν θέλει τεύξεται.
τότε μὲν οὖν καὶ μάλα μόλις ἠνέσχετο.

22. Τῇ δὲ ὑστεραίᾳ καλέσασα τὰς θεραπαινίδας, αἷς τὴν ἐπιμέλειαν τῆς Λευκίππης ἐνεχείρισεν,
ἐπηρώτα μὲν τὸ πρῶτον, εἰ δεξιῶς αὐτῇ κέχρηνται·
φασκουσῶν δὲ μηδὲν τῶν δεόντων παραλιπεῖν αὐτῇ,
ἄγειν ἐκέλευσε τὴν ἄνθρωπον πρὸς αὐτήν. ὡς
2 δὲ ἦλθε· "Τὰ μὲν ἐμὰ ὅπως ἔσχεν," ἔφη, "πρὸς
σὲ φιλανθρωπίας, περισσὸν εἰδυίᾳ σοι λέγειν.
δικαία τυγχάνειν·[1] ἀλλ' ἐν οἷς ἂν δύνῃ, τὴν
ἴσην ἀπότισαί μοι χάριν. ἀκούω τὰς Θετταλὰς
ὑμᾶς ὧν ἂν ἐρασθῆτε μαγεύειν οὕτως, ὥστε

---

[1] So Jacobs for δίκαια τυγχάνειν found in a only.

then forbid me to drink. All this time I have water to hand, and yet I thirst, though I sleep at the water's very fount; my bed is like the banquet of Tantalus." Thus she spoke and wept, laying her head on my bosom so very pitiably that I really felt my heart to some extent moved with sympathy for her. I was in great confusion, particularly as I could not but admit that her reproaches were just. I therefore said to her: "I swear to you, my dearest, by the gods of my fathers, that I too am equally anxious with you to return your passion. But I do not know," said I, "what is the matter with me. Some sudden illness has come upon me, and you know that love without sound health is worse than nothing." While I spoke, I kept wiping away her tears, and I vowed with new oaths that it should not be long before she should obtain that which she desired. Then, and only with difficulty, did she consent to refrain.

22. On the morrow she sent for the serving-maids to whom she had entrusted the care of Leucippe, and asked them first of all whether they had attended her with all skill and care; when they answered that she had lacked nothing of all that was necessary, she ordered that she should be brought before her. On her arrival, "I need not recount to you," she said, "because you already know, the kindness that I have felt towards you; you deserve it; now, as far as you are able, reward me with an equal favour. I understand that you Thessalian[1] women, when you fall in love, are able to conjure in such a

---

[1] It was a common-place of classical literature (*e.g.* in the *Golden Ass* of Apuleius) that the women of Thessaly were skilful witches, particularly in love affairs.

μὴ πρὸς ἑτέραν ἔτι τὸν ἄνθρωπον ἀποκλίνειν
γυναῖκα, πρός τε τὴν μαγεύουσαν οὕτως ἔχειν, ὡς
3 πάντα νομίζειν ἐκείνην αὐτῷ. ἐμοὶ τοῦτο, φιλτάτη, φλεγομένῃ πάρασχε φάρμακον. τὸν νεανίσκον εἶδες, τὸν ἅμα ἐμοὶ χθὲς βαδίζοντα ; " "Τὸν
ἄνδρα," ἔφη, "λέγεις τὸν σόν ; " ὑπολαβοῦσα
πάνυ κακοήθως ἡ Λευκίππη, "τοῦτο γὰρ
ἀκήκοα παρὰ τῶν κατὰ τὴν οἰκίαν." "Ποῖον
ἄνδρα ; " Μελίτη εἶπεν· "οὐδὲν κοινόν ἐστιν
4 ἢ ¹ τοῖς λίθοις. ἀλλά με παρευδοκιμεῖ τις νεκρά·
οὔτε γὰρ ἐσθίων οὔτε κοιμώμενος ἐπιλαθέσθαι
δύναται τοῦ Λευκίππης ὀνόματος· τοῦτο γὰρ
αὐτήν καλεῖ. ἐγὼ δέ, φίλη, μηνῶν τεττάρων
ἐν Ἀλεξανδρείᾳ δι' αὐτὸν διέτριψα, δεομένη,
λιπαροῦσα, ὑπισχνουμένη· τί γὰρ οὐ λέγουσα;
5 τί δὲ οὐ ποιοῦσα τῶν ἀρέσαι δυναμένων; ὁ δὲ
σιδηροῦς τις, ἢ ξύλινος, ἤ τι τῶν ἀναισθήτων
ἦν ἄρα πρὸς τὰς δεήσεις τὰς ἐμάς. μόλις δὲ
τῷ χρόνῳ πείθεται· ἐπείσθη δὲ μέχρι τῶν
ὀμμάτων. ὄμνυμι γάρ σοι τὴν Ἀφροδίτην
αὐτήν, ὡς ἤδη πέμπτην ἡμέραν αὐτῷ συγκαθεύδουσα, οὕτως ἀνέστην ὡς ἀπ' εὐνούχου. ἔοικα
δὲ εἰκόνος ἐρᾶν· μέχρι γὰρ τῶν ὀμμάτων ἔχω
6 τὸν ἐρώμενον. δέομαι δέ σου γυναικὸς γυνὴ
τὴν αὐτὴν δέησιν, ἣν καὶ σύ μου χθὲς ἐδεήθης·
δός μοί τι ἐπὶ τοῦτον τὸν ὑπερήφανον· σώσεις
7 γάρ μου τὴν ψυχὴν διαρρεύσασαν ἤδη." ὡς
οὖν ἤκουσεν ἡ Λευκίππη, ἠσθῆναι μὲν ἐδόκει

¹ The phrase is very much abbreviated if it has to mean
"I have no more to do with him than with a stone." Hercher
reads ἐμοὶ καὶ for ἢ, Jacobs ἡμῖν ἢ. Helmbold deletes ἢ.

way that your lover never inclines to any other woman, and is so firmly attached to the woman who has bewitched him that he considers her his all-in-all. Now, dear woman, I am afire; prepare me this magic draught. Did you see that young man who was walking with me yesterday?" "Do you mean your husband?" said Leucippe, interrupting her maliciously; "at least, I heard that he was such from the people of your household." "Husband indeed!" cried Melite; "as good a husband as a stone would be! Some dead woman seems to be my successful rival: both at board and in bed he does not seem to be able to forget the name of Leucippe— that is what he calls her. I, my dear, have been spending four months at Alexandria for his sake, beseeching, importuning, promising—what did I leave unsaid or undone that I thought could please him? But to all my prayers he was just as if he was made of iron, or wood, or some other senseless thing. At last, and with great difficulty, I won him over; but then only as far as seeing goes—I swear to you by the goddess of love herself that it is now five days that I have slept by his side, and every time I have left his bed as though it had been that of an eunuch. I seem to have fallen in love with a statue—I have a lover who is nothing more than an eye-pleaser. Now I make to you the same prayer that you made to me yesterday, that a woman should pity a woman: give me something that will be effectual on this proud fellow. Thus you can save my breaking[1] heart." Leucippe, on hearing this, was naturally delighted that nothing further had passed

[1] The Greek idiom is a little different: "flowing away," "melting."

τῷ μηδὲν πρὸς τὴν ἄνθρωπόν μοι πεπρᾶχθαι·
φήσασα δὲ ἀνερευνήσειν, εἰ συγχωρήσειεν αὐτῇ,
βοτάνας γενομένη κατὰ τοὺς ἀγρούς, ἀπιοῦσα
ᾤχετο· ἀρνουμένη γὰρ οὐκ ᾤετο πίστιν ἕξειν·
8 ὅθεν οἶμαι καὶ ἐπηγγείλατο. ἡ μὲν δὴ Μελίτη
ῥᾴων ἐγεγόνει καὶ μόνον ἐλπίσασα. τὰ γὰρ ἡδέα
τῶν πραγμάτων, κἂν μήπω παρῇ, τέρπει ταῖς
ἐλπίσιν.

23. Ἐγὼ δὲ τούτων ἐπιστάμενος οὐδέν, ἠθύ-
μουν μέν, σκοπῶν πῶς ἂν διακρουσαίμην καὶ
τὴν ἐπιοῦσαν νύκτα τὴν γυναῖκα, καὶ πῶς ἂν
2 συντυχεῖν Λευκίππῃ δυναίμην. ἐδόκει δέ μοι . . .
κἀκείνη τὴν ἴσην σπουδὴν ποιεῖσθαι τοῦ ἀπελθεῖν
δι᾿ αὐτὴν εἰς τοὺς ἀγρούς, καὶ περὶ τὴν ἑσπέραν
αὖθις ἥκειν. ἔμελλε τῇ Λευκίππῃ [1] παρέξειν
3 ὄχημα καὶ . . . ἡμεῖς δὲ ἐπὶ τὸν πότον ἦμεν· [2]
ἄρτι δὲ κατακλιθέντων ἡμῶν θόρυβος πολὺς κατὰ
τὸν ἀνδρῶνα ἀκούεται καὶ συνδρομή, καὶ εἰστρέχει
τις τῶν θεραπόντων, ἀσθμαίνων ἅμα καὶ λέγων·
4 "Θέρσανδρος ζῇ καὶ πάρεστιν." ἦν δὲ ὁ Θέρσανδρος οὗτος ὁ τῆς Μελίτης ἀνήρ, ὃν ἐνόμιζε
τεθνηκέναι κατὰ θάλασσαν. τῶν γὰρ συνόντων
αὐτῷ τινὲς οἰκετῶν, ὡς περιετράπη τὸ σκάφος,
σωθέντες καὶ νομίσαντες ἀπολωλέναι, τοῦτο
ἀπαγγείλαντες ἔτυχον. ἅμα οὖν ὁ οἰκέτης εἶπε,
καὶ ὁ Θέρσανδρος κατὰ πόδας εἰστρέχει· πάντα
γὰρ τὰ περὶ ἐμοῦ πυθόμενος κατὰ τὴν ὁδόν,

---

[1] τῇ Μελίτῃ cdd. a: ἡ Μελίτη Vilborg.
[2] So Hercher for MSS. ἦμεν. The two lacunae in § 2 were
indicated by Jacobs.

---

[1] The text is here corrupt, and one or two words must
certainly be lost. The translation represents the sense of

between myself and Melite. She said that, if leave were given her, she would look for the necessary herbs in the fields, and set off thither; for she thought that she would not be believed if she said that she had no knowledge of magic, and this was the reason, I suppose, that she promised to do her best. Melite, through the action of hope alone, became somewhat more calm: the thought of future joys, even though they are not yet apparent, exercises a soothing effect by means of hope.

23. I knew nothing of all this, and was in great distress; I was wondering how to put off Melite for the coming night, and how I could manage to meet Leucippe face to face; ... she seemed to me to be aiming at the same object, in going with some help from Melite, into the country and returning towards evening.[1] Melite was going to provide a carriage for Leucippe. ... We were now coming to the time for taking wine, and had but just sat down to it, when a great shouting and sound of running about arose in the men's quarters, and a servant came running in, panting, and crying out: "Thersander is alive and here!" Now this Thersander was Melite's husband, believed by her to have perished at sea: some of the servants, who happened to be with him when his boat was overturned, had afterwards been saved, and, thinking that he had perished, had spread the report of his death. The servant was still speaking when Thersander rushed in close on his heels: he had heard all about me on his way back, and was hurrying

the passage, though even so it is inconsistent with ch. xxvi. § 12, where Melite says that Leucippe (instead of returning to Ephesus in the evening) was to spend the night in the country gathering the magic herbs by moonlight.

5 ἔσπευδε φθάσας καταλαβεῖν με. ἡ μὲν δὴ
Μελίτη ἀνέθορεν ὑπ' ἐκπλήξεως τοῦ παραλόγου
καὶ περιβάλλειν ἐπεχείρει τὸν ἄνδρα. ὁ δὲ τὴν
μὲν ὡς εἶχεν ὠθεῖ μάλα ἐρρωμένως· ἐμὲ δὲ ἰδὼν
καὶ εἰπών, "Ὁ μοιχὸς οὗτος," ἐμπηδᾷ, καὶ
ῥαπίζει με κατὰ κόρρης πληγὴν θυμοῦ γέμουσαν.
ἑλκύσας δὲ τῶν τριχῶν, ῥάσσει πρὸς τοὔδαφος,
6 καὶ προσπίπτων κατακόπτει με πληγαῖς. ἐγὼ
δὲ ὥσπερ ἐν μυστηρίῳ μηδὲν ᾔδειν,[1] μήτε ὅστις
ἄνθρωπος ἦν, μήτε οὗ χάριν ἔτυπτεν, ὑποπτεύσας
δέ τι κακὸν εἶναι, ἐδεδοίκειν ἀμύνασθαι, καίτοι
7 δυνάμενος. ἐπεὶ δὲ ἔκαμεν, ὁ μὲν τύπτων, ἐγὼ δὲ
φιλοσοφῶν, λέγω πρὸς αὐτὸν ἀναστάς· "Τίς ποτε
εἶ, ὦ ἄνθρωπε; καὶ τί με οὕτως ἠκίσω;" ὁ δὲ ἔτι
μᾶλλον ὀργισθεὶς ὅτι καὶ φωνὴν ἀφῆκα, ῥαπίζει
πάλιν, καὶ καλεῖ δεσμὰ καὶ πέδας. δεσμεύουσιν
οὖν με καὶ ἄγουσιν εἴς τι δωμάτιον.

24. Ἐν ᾧ δὲ ταῦτα ἐπράττετο, λανθάνει με[2]
διαρρυεῖσα ἡ τῆς Λευκίππης ἐπιστολή· ἔτυχον
γὰρ αὐτὴν εἴσω τοῦ χιτωνίσκου προσδεδεμένην
ἐκ τῶν τῆς ὀθόνης θυσάνων ἔχων. καὶ ἡ Μελίτη
ἀναιρεῖται λαθοῦσα· ἐδεδίει γὰρ μή τινα τῶν
2 πρός με αὐτῆς γραμμάτων ἦν. ὡς δὲ ἀνέγνω καθ'
ἑαυτὴν γενομένη, καὶ τὸ τῆς Λευκίππης εὗρεν
ὄνομα, βάλλεται μὲν εὐθέως τὴν καρδίαν,
γνωρίσασα τοὔνομα· οὐ μὴν αὐτὴν ἐνόμιζεν εἶναι
τῷ πολλάκις αὐτὴν ἀκοῦσαι τετελευτηκέναι.
3 ὡς δὲ προϊοῦσα, καὶ τοῖς λοιποῖς τῶν γεγραμμένων
ἐνέτυχε, πᾶσαν μαθοῦσα τὴν ἀλήθειαν, ἐμεμέ-
ριστο πολλοῖς ἅμα τὴν ψυχήν, αἰδοῖ καὶ ὀργῇ

[1] A verb is necessary, and Hercher's ᾔδειν seems probable.
[2] Cobet's correction for MSS. μου.

so as to be sure to catch me. Melite jumped up, thunderstruck at the strangeness of the situation, and made as if to embrace her husband; but he thrust her violently from him, and, seeing me, "There is the gallant," he cried; he leaped at me and struck me on the forehead a blow full of fury. He then seized me by the hair, bore me to the floor, and, falling upon me, rained blows on me. I knew as little as though I were at the celebration of some secret mystery who the man was or why he was beating me; though, suspecting that there was something wrong, I was afraid to defend myself, though I could have done so. When he grew tired of pounding me (and I of my reasoning), I rose and said: "Who are you, sir, and why have you assaulted me in this way?" He was still more angry at my speech and struck me again, and then called for chains and fetters; his servants bound me and threw me into a closet.

24. While all this was happening, I did not observe that I had dropped Leucippe's letter: I had happened to have fastened it under my coat to the border of my shirt. Melite privately picked it up, fearing that it was one of her letters to me. When she was alone she read it, and directly she found the name of Leucippe, she was cut to the heart on recognizing the name; she never guessed that the woman could be she, as she had heard so often that she had perished. When she went on and finished the rest of what was written, and so learned the whole truth, her heart was the scene of conflicting emotions—shame, and anger, and love, and jealousy.

καὶ ἔρωτι καὶ ζηλοτυπίᾳ. ἠσχύνετο τὸν ἄνδρα,
ὠργίζετο τοῖς γράμμασιν, ὁ ἔρως ἐμάραινε τὴν
ὀργήν, ἐξῆπτε τὸν ἔρωτα ἡ ζηλοτυπία, καὶ τέλος
ἐκράτησεν ὁ ἔρως.

25. Ἦν δὲ πρὸς ἑσπέραν, καὶ ἔτυχεν Θέρσανδρος ἐκ τῆς πρώτης ὀργῆς πρὸς ἑταῖρόν τινα τῶν
ἐγχωρίων ἐκθορών. ἡ δὲ διαλεχθεῖσα τῷ τὴν
φυλακὴν τὴν ἐμὴν πεπιστευμένῳ, εἰσέρχεται πρός
με λαθοῦσα τοὺς ἄλλους, θεράποντας δύο τοῦ
δωματίου προκαθίσασα, καὶ καταλαμβάνει χαμαὶ
2 καταβεβλημένον. παραστᾶσα οὖν πάντα ἤθελεν
εἰπεῖν ὁμοῦ· τὸ σχῆμα τοῦ προσώπου τοσαῦτα
εἶχεν, ὅσα εἰπεῖν ἤθελεν. "Ὦ δυστυχὴς ἐγὼ καὶ
ἐπὶ τῷ ἐμαυτῆς κακῷ τεθεαμένη σε, τὸ μὲν
πρῶτον ἀτέλεστα ἐρασθεῖσα καὶ μετὰ πάσης
ἀνοίας, ἢ καὶ μισουμένη τὸν μισοῦντα φιλῶ, καὶ
ὀδυνωμένη τὸν ὀδυνῶντα ἐλεῶ, καὶ οὐδὲ ὕβρις
3 τὸν ἔρωτα παύει. ὦ ζεῦγος κατ' ἐμοῦ γοήτων,
ἀνδρὸς καὶ γυναικός. ὁ μὲν τοσοῦτόν μου χρόνον
κατεγέλα· ἡ δὲ ἀπῆλθε κομιοῦσά μοι φίλτρον.
ἐγὼ δὲ ἡ κακοδαίμων, ἠγνόουν αἰτοῦσα παρὰ τῶν
4 ἐχθίστων κατ' ἐμαυτῆς φάρμακον." καὶ ἅμα τὴν
ἐπιστολὴν τῆς Λευκίππης μοι προσέρριψεν.
ἰδὼν οὖν καὶ γνωρίσας ἔφριξα, καὶ ἔβλεπον εἰς
γῆν ὡς ἐληλεγμένος. ἡ δὲ ἐτραγῴδει πάλιν·
"Οἴμοι δειλαία τῶν κακῶν· καὶ γὰρ τὸν ἄνδρα
ἀπώλεσα διὰ σέ· οὔτε γὰρ ἂν ἔχοιμί σε τοῦ

She felt shame as regarded her husband, and anger at the letter: love made her anger inclined to cool, while jealousy fired her love, though love was in the end victorious.

25. It was now towards evening; Thersander, in his first fit of rage, had rushed out to the house of one of his friends who lived close by. Melite addressed herself to the man to whom had been entrusted the charge of watching over me, and came secretly to me, setting a couple of her servants at the door to watch. She found me lying on the ground, and, as she stood over me, she seemed to design to give utterance to all her thoughts at once: in the expression of her face gleamed all the different emotions to which she would have liked to give vent in speech. "How wretched am I," she said, "who saw you first to my own undoing, who loved with a love that had no fulfilment and was mere folly, who was hated and love him that hated me, who was wounded and pity him that wounded me; and even the insults I have suffered do not extinguish my love. A fine pair you are of magicians, male and female, working your arts against me: one of you was laughing at me the whole time, while the other went off to bring me a love-philtre—I, poor I, did not know that I was begging for a magical drug, to be used against myself, from my deadliest enemies." As she spoke, she threw down Leucippe's letter in front of me; when I saw it and recognised what it was, I shuddered, and kept my eyes fixed on the ground like a man caught in the commission of some crime. Then she went on again in the same emotional style: "Wretched, wretched woman that I am! I have lost my husband for you, and now, after this, I may

λοιποῦ χρόνου, κἂν μέχρι τῶν ὀμμάτων τῶν
5 κενῶν, ἐπεὶ μὴ δεδύνησαι τούτων πλέον. οἶδα ὅτι
ὁ ἀνήρ με μισεῖ καὶ μοιχείαν κατέγνωκεν ἐπὶ σοί,
μοιχείαν ἄκαρπον, μοιχείαν ἀναφρόδιτον, ἧς
μόνον τὴν λοιδορίαν κεκέρδακα. αἱ μὲν γὰρ
ἄλλαι γυναῖκες μισθὸν τῆς αἰσχύνης ἔχουσι τὴν
τῆς ἐπιθυμίας ἡδονήν· ἐγὼ δὲ ἡ δυστυχὴς τὴν
μὲν αἰσχύνην ἐκαρπωσάμην, τὸ δὲ τῆς ἡδονῆς
6 οὐδαμοῦ. ἄπιστε καὶ βάρβαρε, ἐτόλμησας
οὕτως ἐρῶσαν γυναῖκα κατατῆξαι, καὶ ταῦτα
Ἔρωτος καὶ σὺ δοῦλος ὤν; οὐκ ἐφοβήθης αὐτοῦ
τὰ μηνίματα; οὐκ ᾐδέσθης αὐτοῦ τὸ πῦρ; οὐκ
ἐτίμησας αὐτοῦ τὰ μυστήρια; οὐ κατέκλασέ σε
7 ταῦτα τὰ ὄμματα δακρύοντα; ὦ καὶ λῃστῶν
ἀγριώτερε· δάκρυα γὰρ καὶ λῃστὴς αἰσχύνεται.
οὐδέν σε ἠρέθισεν εἰς ἀφροδίτην κἂν μίαν, οὐ
δέησις, οὐ χρόνος, οὐχ ἡ τῶν σωμάτων συμπλοκή·
ἀλλά, τὸ πάντων ὑβριστικώτατον, προσαπτό-
μενος, καταφιλῶν, οὕτως ἀνέστης ὡς ἄλλη γυνή.
8 τίς αὕτη τῶν γάμων ἡ σκιά; οὐ μὲν δὴ γεγηρακυῖα
συνεκάθευδες, οὐδὲ ἀποστρεφομένη σου τὰς
περιπλοκάς, ἀλλὰ καὶ νέα καὶ φιλούσῃ, εἴποι δὲ
ἂν ἄλλος ὅτι καὶ καλῇ. εὐνοῦχε καὶ ἀνδρόγυνε
καὶ κάλλους[1] βάσκανε, ἐπαρῶμαί σοι δικαιοτάτην
ἀράν· οὕτως σε ἀμύναιτο ὁ Ἔρως εἰς τὰ σά."
ταῦτα ἔλεγε, καὶ ἅμα ἔκλαιεν.

---

[1] After κάλλους the MSS. have καλοῦ: but this must be a
copyist's repetition, and was rightly suspected by Jacobs.

not even possess you to the extent of seeing you,
which is as much pleasure as you have yet vouch-
safed me ; I know that my husband has come to
hate me, and has believed me guilty of adultery on
your account—a fruitless, pleasureless adultery, from
which my only gain has been abuse. Other women
at least obtain as a reward of their shame the
pleasurable satisfaction of their desires ; I have
reaped the shame well enough, poor I, but have
nowhere found the pleasure. Faithless, savage
wretch ! How could you bear to see a woman thus
pining away for love, when you too were Love's slave ?
Did you not fear his wrath ? Had you no apprehension of his fire ? No respect for his mysteries ?
Could not these weeping eyes of mine melt you ?
More brutal than a pirate ! A pirate is at least
moved by tears. Could nothing rouse you even to
one trance of love, not my prayers, not the time you
spent in my company, not our mutual embrace,
breast to breast ? No, and what is of all the most
cruel insult to me, you have clung to me and kissed
me, and then risen from my side as passionless as
another woman. What is this wretched shadow of a
marriage ? It was not as if your mate had been an old
woman or one who rejected your embraces ; I am
young and inclined to love, and anybody else would
say that I was fair. Miserable eunuch—woman-
man—beauty's wet-blanket[1]; I call down upon you
the justest curse of all: may Love requite you in your
passions the same treatment that you have meted
out to mine." Thus she spoke, and at the same
moment burst into tears.

[1] βάσκανε : impotence is supposed to be in a special degree
due to magic. The *frigidi ad venerem* are regularly called in
mediaeval Latin *maleficiati*.

26. Ὡς δὲ ἐσιώπων ἐγὼ κάτω νενευκώς, μικρὸν
διαλιποῦσα, λέγει μεταβαλοῦσα· "Ἃ μὲν εἶπον,
ὦ φίλτατε, θυμὸς ἔλεγε καὶ λύπη· ἃ δὲ νῦν
μέλλω λέγειν, ἔρως λέγει. κἂν ὀργίζωμαι, καίο-
2 μαι· κἂν ὑβρίζωμαι, φιλῶ· σπεῖσαι κἂν νῦν,
ἐλέησον· οὐκέτι δέομαι πολλῶν ἡμερῶν καὶ
γάμου μακροῦ, ὃν ἡ δυστυχὴς ὠνειροπόλουν
ἐπὶ σοί· ἀρκεῖ μοι κἂν μία συμπλοκή. μικροῦ
δέομαι φαρμάκου πρὸς τηλικαύτην νόσον· σβέσον μοι ὀλίγον τοῦ πυρός. εἰ δέ τί σοι προπετῶς
ἐθρασυνάμην, σύγγνωθι, φίλτατε· ἔρως ἀτυχῶν
3 καὶ μαίνεται. ἀσχημονοῦσα οἶδα, ἀλλ' οὐκ αἰσχύ-
νομαι τὰ τοῦ Ἔρωτος ἐξαγορεύουσα μυστήρια.
πρὸς ἄνδρα λαλῶ μεμυημένον. οἶδας τί πάσχω·
τοῖς δὲ ἄλλοις ἀνθρώποις ἀθέατα τὰ βέλη τοῦ
θεοῦ, καὶ οὐκ ἄν τις ἐπιδεῖξαι δύναιτο τὰ
τοξεύματα, μόνοι δὲ οἴδασιν οἱ ἐρῶντες τὰ τῶν
4 ὁμοίων τραύματα. ἔτι μόνον ἔχω ταύτην τὴν
ἡμέραν· τὴν ὑπόσχεσιν ἀπαιτῶ. ἀναμνήσθητι[1]
τῆς Ἴσιδος, αἰδέσθητι τοὺς ὅρκους τοὺς ἐκεῖ.
εἰ μὲν γὰρ καὶ συνοικεῖν ἤθελες, ὥσπερ ὤμοσας,
οὐκ ἂν ἐφρόντισα Θερσάνδρων μυρίων· ἐπεὶ
δὲ Λευκίππην εὑρόντι σοι γάμος ἀδύνατος ἄλλης
γυναικός, ἑκοῦσά σοι κἀγὼ τοῦτο παραχωρῶ.
οἶδα νικωμένη· οὐκ αἰτῶ πλέον ἢ δύναμαι τυχεῖν.
κατ' ἐμοῦ γὰρ πάντα καινά· ἀναβιοῦσι καὶ
5 νεκροί. ὦ θάλασσα, πλέουσαν μέν με διέ-

---

[1] Jacobs' correction (or ἀλλὰ μνήσθητι) for ἅμα μνήσθητι.

26. I still kept silent, my head bowed to the ground, and after a little while she went on in changed mood : "What I have just said, my dearest, has been the utterance of anger and grief; what I am now going to say comes from the prompting of love. Though I be angry, yet I burn ; though I be insulted and despised, still I love. Come to terms now and pity me ; no longer do I ask for length of days and a long life's wedded love, which I was unhappy enough to dream of, in your company. Now one embrace will be enough for me. I ask but for a little medicine for my long disease; quench but for a moment, the fire with which I burn. If I raged against you without restraint, forgive me, my dear ; an unhappy love becomes actually mad. I know that I am lost to all sense of shame—but I feel no shame in speaking openly of Love's mysteries : I speak to one who is already an adept in them. You know what I suffer ; other men have never seen that god's darts, and none can clearly discern the shots of his bow, save that lovers alone recognize the wounds suffered by their kind. I still have this day, and this day only, and I claim the fulfilment of your promise. Remember Isis, respect the oaths you swore before her altar ; if you had been willing to be my lover, as there you swore, I would have recked nought of ten thousand Thersanders. If, now you have found Leucippe, marriage with another woman is no longer possible for you, I willingly grant you even this. I know I am beaten ; I ask for nothing more than I am able to obtain. All sorts of miracles happen to my hurt : even the dead come to life. Cruel sea, to let me sail safely over thee,

σωσας, σώσασα δὲ μᾶλλον ἀπολώλεκας, δύο
ἀποστείλασα κατ᾽ ἐμοῦ νεκρούς· ἦρκει γὰρ
Λευκίππη μόνη ζήσασα, ἵνα μηκέτι λυπῆται
Κλειτοφῶν· νῦν δὲ καὶ ὁ ἄγριος Θέρσανδρος

6 ἡμῖν πάρεστι. τετύπτησαι βλεπούσης μου, καὶ
βοηθεῖν ἡ δυστυχὴς οὐκ ἠδυνάμην. ἐπὶ τοῦτο
τὸ πρόσωπον πληγαὶ κατηνέχθησαν, ὦ θεοί·

7 δοκῶ, τυφλὸς Θέρσανδρος ἦν. ἀλλὰ δέομαι,
Κλειτοφῶν δέσποτα, δεσπότης γὰρ εἶ ψυχῆς
τῆς ἐμῆς, ἀπόδος σεαυτὸν τήμερον πρῶτα καὶ
ὕστατα. ἐμοὶ δὲ ἡμέραι τὸ βραχὺ τοῦτο πολλαί.
οὕτω μηκέτι Λευκίππην ἀπολέσειας,[1] οὕτω μη-

8 κέτι μηδὲ ψευδῶς ἀποθάνοι. μὴ ἀτιμάσῃς τὸν
ἔρωτα τὸν ἐμόν, δι᾽ ὃν τὰ μέγιστα εὐτυχεῖς.
οὗτός σοι Λευκίππην ἀποδέδωκεν· εἰ γάρ σου
μὴ ἠράσθην ἐγώ, εἰ γάρ σε μὴ ἐνταῦθα ἤγαγον,

9 ἦν ἂν ἔτι σοι Λευκίππη νεκρά. εἰσίν, ὦ
Κλειτοφῶν, καὶ Τύχης δωρεαί. ἤδη τις θησαυρῷ
περιτυχών, τὸν τόπον τῆς εὑρέσεως ἐτίμησε,
βωμὸν ἤγειρε, θυσίαν προσήνεγκεν, ἐστεφάνωσε
τὴν γῆν· σὺ δὲ παρ᾽ ἐμοὶ θησαυρὸν ἔρωτος

10 εὑρὼν ἀτιμάζεις τὰ εὐεργετήματα; νόμιζέ σοι
τὸν Ἔρωτα δι᾽ ἐμοῦ λέγειν· ''Ἐμοὶ χάρισαι
τοῦτο, Κλειτοφῶν, τῷ σῷ μυσταγωγῷ. μὴ ἀμύη-
τού τὴν Μελίτην ἀπέλθῃς καταλιπών· καὶ τὸ
ταύτης ἐμόν ἐστι πῦρ.' ἄκουσον δὲ ὡς καὶ τἆλλα

---

[1] The optative is necessary for the construction. Cobet
restored it for the MSS. ἀπολέσῃς. Valley proposed ἀπολέσαις.

and then, after bringing me safe home, to work
my deeper destruction by twice giving up thy dead.
It was enough for Leucippe to be alive for Clitophon
to desist from his grief; and now here is that
savage, Thersander, with us. You have been
beaten, Clitophon, before my eyes, and I was
unhappy enough not to be able to help you. Did
blows rain upon that face, ye gods? Surely
Thersander must have been blind. Now I beseech
you, my lord Clitophon—you are the lord of my
heart—surrender yourself to me now for the first
and last time: the few short moments will be to
me like many days. If you agree to this, may
you never lose your Leucippe, may she never even
falsely [1] seem to die again. Do not despise my
love: through it all your great happiness has come. It
has given you back Leucippe; for if I had never
fallen in love with you, if I had not brought you
hither, Leucippe would still have been dead as
far as you are concerned. Yes, Clitophon, there
are such things as the gifts of Fortune! When
a man finds a treasure, he always honours the place
of its discovery; he puts up an altar, he brings an
offering for sacrifice, he puts a garland upon the
ground; you have found with me the treasure of
love, and do you do nothing to requite the good it
has brought you? Imagine that Love is speaking
thus to you through me: 'Grant this favour to
me, Clitophon, who will lead thee into my mysteries: do not depart and leave Melite without
initiation; her fire too is from me.' Then listen

---

[1] As when she was first apparently ripped up by the
buccaneers and afterwards apparently decapitated by the
pirates.

11 μοι μέλει περὶ σοῦ. λυθήσῃ μὲν γὰρ ἄρτι τῶν
δεσμῶν, κἂν Θερσάνδρῳ μὴ δοκῇ· καταγωγῆς δὲ
τεύξῃ τοσούτων ἡμερῶν, ὅσων ἂν θέλῃς, πρὸς ἐμὸν
σύντροφον. ἕωθεν δὲ καὶ τὴν Λευκίππην παρέσε-
12 σθαι προσδόκα· διανυκτερεύσειν γὰρ ἔλεγεν εἰς
τὸν ἀγρὸν βοτανῶν ἕνεκεν [1] χάριν, ὡς ἐν ὄψει
τῆς σελήνης αὐτὰς ἀναλάβοι. οὕτως γάρ μου
κατεγέλα· ᾔτησα γὰρ φάρμακον παρ' αὐτῆς ὡς
Θετταλῆς κατὰ σοῦ. τί γὰρ ἠδυνάμην ἔτι
ποιεῖν ἀποτυγχάνουσα, ἢ βοτάνας ζητεῖν καὶ
φάρμακα; αὕτη γὰρ τῶν ἐν ἔρωτι δυστυχούντων
13 ἡ καταφυγή. ὁ Θέρσανδρος δέ, ὡς καὶ περὶ
τούτου θαρρήσῃς, ἐξεπήδησε πρὸς ἑταῖρον αὐτοῦ,
ἐξιστάμενος ἐμοὶ τῆς οἰκίας ὑπ' ὀργῆς· δοκεῖ δὲ
ἔμοιγε θεός τις αὐτὸν ἐντεῦθεν ἐξεληλακέναι, ἵνα
σου τὰ τελευταῖα ταῦτα δυνηθῶ τυχεῖν. ἀλλά
μοι σαυτὸν ἀπόδος."

27. Ταῦτα φιλοσοφήσασα (διδάσκει γὰρ ὁ
Ἔρως καὶ λόγους) ἔλυε τὰ δεσμὰ καὶ τὰς χεῖρας
κατεφίλει, καὶ τοῖς ὀφθαλμοῖς καὶ τῇ καρδίᾳ
προσέφερε καὶ εἶπεν, " Ὁρᾷς, πῶς πηδᾷ, καὶ
πάλλει πυκνὸν παλμὸν ἀγωνίας γέμοντα καὶ
ἐλπίδος, γένοιτο δὲ καὶ ἡδονῆς· καὶ ἔοικεν
2 ἱκετεύειν σε τῷ πηδήματι." ὡς οὖν με ἔλυσε,

---

[1] Cobet wished to omit ἕνεκεν as a gloss on χάριν, but
such double prepositions as χάριν ἕνεκα are found in late
Greek.

how I have taken care for all that concerns you.
Soon shall you be loosed from these bonds, however
little Thersander likes it, and you shall find a place
of refuge for as long as you desire with a foster-
brother of mine. There in the morning wait for
Leucippe to come to you; she said that she was
going to spend the night in the country looking
for herbs, in order to cull them by moonlight.[1]
That was how she tricked me: for I asked her,
thinking her a woman from Thessaly, for a philtre
to be used upon you. What else could I do after
all my failures but have recourse to herbs and
magical drugs? That is the only resort for hopeless
lovers. As for Thersander (I tell you this to
assure you on this point too) he flung away from
me out of the house in a rage, and has hurried to
visit one of his friends; I cannot but think that
some god has sent him away from here in order that
I may be successful in gaining from you this last
boon. Then do you give yourself to me!"

27. After these subtle arguments—Love is a
fine master of rhetoric—she loosed my bonds and
kissed my hands, and placed them, first on her
eyes and then upon her heart,[2] saying: "You see
how it leaps and its flutterings betoken anguish
and hope—soon may they betoken pleasure—and
seems by that very leaping to cry your mercy." As

---

[1] The moon was almost a necessity for conjuring of this
kind (Theocritus ii. 10), and herbs plucked by its light far
more efficacious (Horace, *Sat.* I. viii. 21). In modern magic
herbs gathered at night on St. John's Eve are very powerful.
See also note (1) on p. 289.

[2] Lieb Liebchen, leg's Händchen aufs Herze mein;
Ach, hörst du, wie's pocht im Kämmerlein?
HEINE.

ACHILLES TATIUS

καὶ περιέβαλε κλαίουσα, ἔπαθόν τι ἀνθρώπινον,
καὶ ἀληθῶς ἐφοβήθην τὸν Ἔρωτα, μή μοι
γένηται μήνιμα ἐκ τοῦ θεοῦ, καὶ ἄλλως ὅτι
Λευκίππην ἀπειλήφειν, καὶ ὅτι μετὰ ταῦτα τῆς
Μελίτης ἀπαλλάττεσθαι ἔμελλον, καὶ ὅτι οὐδὲ
γάμος ἔτι τὸ πραττόμενον ἦν, ἀλλὰ φάρμακον
3 ὥσπερ ψυχῆς νοσούσης. περιβαλούσης οὖν
ἠνειχόμην καὶ περιπλεκομένης πρὸς τὰς περιπλοκὰς οὐκ ἀντέλεγον, καὶ ἐγένετο ὅσα ὁ Ἔρως
ἤθελεν, οὔτε στρωμνῆς ἡμῶν δεηθέντων, οὔτε
ἄλλου τινὸς τῶν εἰς παρασκευὴν ἀφροδισίων.
4 αὐτουργὸς γὰρ ὁ Ἔρως καὶ αὐτοσχέδιος σοφιστής, καὶ πάντα τόπον αὐτῷ τιθέμενος μυστήριον. τὸ δὲ ἀπερίεργον εἰς Ἀφροδίτην ἥδιον
μᾶλλον τοῦ πολυπράγμονος· αὐτοφυῆ γὰρ ἔχει
τὴν ἡδονήν.

she loosed my fetters and threw her arms about
me, now all in tears, I felt the claims of humanity
too strong for me, and I was really afraid that
the god of love would visit his wrath upon me ;
and besides I felt that I had regained Leucippe,
and was in the near future about to be rid of
Melite, and that anything that might take place
could not possibly be regarded as a marriage, but
only as medicine to an aching heart. I made no
attempt therefore to escape from her encircling
arms, and when she embraced me closer I did
not resist her embraces, and soon all happened as
Love would have it ; nor did we feel at all the
lack of a due couch or of any of the other ac-
cessories of pleasure. Love needs no teaching other
than his own, and is an admirable improviser ; he
can make any place a proper spot for the celebration
of his mysteries. And as regards such enjoyment,
that which has not been too carefully prepared is
better far than the meticulously elaborated ; it has
in itself its own genuine and natural pleasure.

1. Ἐπεὶ οὖν τὴν Μελίτην ἰασάμην, λέγω πρὸς αὐτήν· "Ἀλλ' ὅπως μοι τῆς φυγῆς παράσχῃς τὴν ἀσφάλειαν, καὶ τἆλλα ὡς ὑπέσχου περὶ Λευκίππης." "Μὴ φροντίσῃς," εἶπε, "τοῦ γε κατ' ἐκείνην μέρους, ἀλλ' ἤδη νόμιζε Λευκίππην ἔχειν. σὺ δὲ ἔνδυθι τὴν ἐσθῆτα τὴν ἐμήν, καὶ 2 κλέπτε τὸ πρόσωπον τῷ πέπλῳ. ἡγήσεται δέ σοι τῆς ἐπὶ τὰς θύρας ὁδοῦ Μελανθώ· περιμένει δέ σε καὶ νεανίσκος ἐπ' αὐταῖς ταῖς θύραις,[1] ᾧ προστεταγμένον ἐστὶν ἐξ ἐμοῦ κομίσαι σε εἰς τὴν οἰκίαν, οὗ καὶ Κλεινίαν καὶ Σάτυρον εὑρή- 3 σεις, καὶ Λευκίππη σοι παρέσται." ταῦτα ἅμα λέγουσα, ἐσκεύασέ με ὡς ἑαυτήν, καὶ καταφιλοῦσα, "Ὡς εὐμορφότερος," ἔφη, "παρὰ πολὺ γέγονας τῇ στολῇ· τοιοῦτον Ἀχιλλέα ποτ' ἐθεασάμην ἐν γραφῇ. ἀλλά μοι, φίλτατε, σώζοιο, καὶ τὴν ἐσθῆτα ταύτην φύλαττε μνήμην· ἐμοὶ δὲ τὴν σὴν κατάλιπε, ὡς ἂν ἔχοιμι ἐνδυο- 4 μένη σοι περικεχύσθαι." δίδωσι δέ μοι καὶ

---

[1] Corrected by Cobet from the accusative.

BOOK VI

1. When therefore I had done my best to give Melite her cure, I said to her: "Now you must take care to ensure my safe escape, and to perform the rest of the promise which you made me about Leucippe." "Do not be anxious on her account," she answered; "you can consider that Leucippe is already yours. But do you put on my clothes, and cover your face with this garment. Melantho will shew you the way to the door, and then, just outside, there is waiting for you a young man who has instructions from me to convey you to the house where you will find Clinias and Satyrus, and Leucippe will soon be there with you." With these words, she dressed me up to resemble herself; and then, kissing me, "How much more beautiful still," said she, "you look in these clothes; you are like the Achilles that I once saw in a picture.[1] I wish you good luck, my dearest; keep these garments to remind you of me, and leave me yours; when I put them on I shall still have the illusion of being in your embrace." She then gave me a hundred pieces of gold, and

---

[1] He was concealed by his mother Thetis in female attire at the court of King Lycomedes in Scyros so that he might not have to go to the Trojan war, which would be fatal to him, but was discovered by choosing a helmet and spear from among an array of gifts set out for the maidens of the court.

χρυσοῦς ἑκατόν, καὶ καλεῖ τὴν Μελανθώ· θεράπαινα δὲ ἦν αὕτη τῶν πιστῶν, καὶ ἐφήδρευε
ταῖς θύραις. ὡς δὲ εἰσῆλθε, λέγει περὶ ἐμοῦ τὰ
συγκείμενα, καὶ κελεύει πάλιν ἀναστρέφειν πρὸς
αὐτήν, ἐπειδὰν ἔξω γένωμαι τῶν θυρῶν.

2. Ἐγὼ μὲν δὴ τοῦτον τὸν τρόπον ὑπεκδύο-
μαι· καὶ ὁ φύλαξ τοῦ οἰκήματος ἀνεχώρησε,
νομίσας τὴν δέσποιναν εἶναι, νευσάσης αὐτῷ
τῆς Μελανθοῦς· καὶ διὰ τῶν ἐρήμων τῆς οἰκίας
ἐπί τινα θύραν οὐκ ἐν ὁδῷ κειμένην ἔρχομαι·
καί με ὁ πρὸς τῆς Μελίτης ταύτῃ προστεταγ-
2 μένος ἀπολαμβάνει. ἀπελεύθερος δὲ αὐτὸς τῶν
συμπεπλευκότων ἦν ἡμῖν καὶ ἄλλως ἐμοὶ κεχα-
ρισμένος. ὡς δὲ ἀνέστρεψεν ἡ Μελανθώ, καταλαμβάνει τὸν φρουρὸν ἄρτι ἐπικλείσαντα τὸ
3 οἴκημα, καὶ ἀνοίγειν ἐκέλευσεν αὖθις. ὡς δὲ
ἤνοιξε, καὶ παρελθοῦσα ἐμήνυσε τῇ Μελίτῃ
τὴν ἔξοδον τὴν ἐμήν, καλεῖ τὸν φύλακα.
κἀκεῖνος, ὡς τὸ εἰκός, θέαμα ἰδὼν παραδοξό-
τατον, τῆς κατὰ τὴν ἔλαφον ἀντὶ παρθένου
4 παροιμίας, ἐξεπλάγη καὶ ἔστη σιωπῇ. λέγει
οὖν πρὸς αὐτόν· "Οὐκ ἀπιστοῦσά σοι μὴ οὐκ
ἐθελήσῃς ἀφεῖναι Κλειτοφῶντα, ταύτης ἐδεήθην
τῆς κλοπῆς, ἀλλ' ἵνα σοι πρὸς Θέρσανδρον ἡ
τῆς αἰτίας ἀπόλυσις ᾖ, ὡς οὐ συνεγνωκότι.
5 χρυσοὶ δέ σοι οὗτοι δῶρον δέκα, δῶρον μέν,
ἂν ἐνταῦθα μείνῃς, παρὰ Κλειτοφῶντος· ἐὰν
δὲ νομίσῃς φυγεῖν βέλτιον, ἐφόδιον." καὶ ὁ

called Melantho, who was her serving-maid and among those whom she could entirely trust; she had been sitting at the door. On her entry, she told her the arrangements that had been made about me, and bade her come back again to her directly that I was outside the house.

2. I thus slipped out. The warder of the cell made way for me, thinking that I was his mistress, at a sign from Melantho, and I passed through the empty passages of the house to a door which was somewhat out of the way; and there the young man received me who had been appointed by Melite for this service. He was a freedman, one of those who had been with us on the voyage,[1] and I had made friends with him previously. Melantho then went back and found the warder just locking the doors of the cell; she told him to open them again, and after he had complied with her request, she went in, told Melite of my safe evasion, and called in the keeper. He, as might only be expected, when he saw this extraordinary substitution, like that of the deer for the maiden in the fable,[2] stood struck dumb. "It was no distrust in you," said Melite to him, "lest you should be unwilling to let Clitophon out, that made me employ this stratagem, but so that in Thersander's eyes you might be free of all blame, as one not privy to the plot. Here is a present for you of ten pieces of gold—a present from Clitophon if you choose to stay here, or journey-money if you think it would be better to take flight." "Certainly,

---

[1] The voyage from Alexandria to Ephesus.

[2] When Iphigenia was about to be sacrificed to Diana at Aulis, as happened with Isaac and the ram. Hercher wished to omit the comparison as the note of a scribe, but it seems to me not unlike the style of our author.

Πασίων (τοῦτο γὰρ ἦν ὄνομα τῷ φύλακι),
" Πάνυ," ἔφη, " δέσποινα, τὸ σοὶ δοκοῦν κἀμοὶ
6 δοκεῖ καλῶς ἔχειν." [1] ἔδοξεν οὖν τῇ Μελίτῃ
τὸ νῦν ἀναχωρεῖν· ὅταν δὲ ἐν καλῷ θῆται [2] τὰ
πρὸς τὸν ἄνδρα καὶ γένηται τὰ τῆς ὀργῆς
ἐν γαλήνῃ, τότε μετιέναι. καὶ ὁ μὲν οὕτως
ἔπραξεν.

3. Ἐμοὶ δὲ ἡ συνήθης Τύχη πάλιν ἐπιτίθεται
καὶ συντίθεται κατ' ἐμοῦ δρᾶμα καινόν· ἐπάγει
γάρ μοι τὸν Θέρσανδρον εὐθὺς παρελθόντα.
μεταπεισθεὶς γὰρ ὑπὸ τοῦ φίλου πρὸς ὃν ᾤχετο,
μὴ ἀπόκοιτος γενέσθαι, δειπνήσας πάλιν ἀνέ-
2 στρεφεν ἐπὶ τὴν οἰκίαν. ἦν δὲ τῆς Ἀρτέμιδος
ἱερομηνία, καὶ μεθυόντων πάντα μεστά· ὥστε
καὶ δι' ὅλης τῆς [3] νυκτὸς τὴν ἀγορὰν ἅπασαν
κατεῖχε πλῆθος ἀνθρώπων. κἀγὼ μὲν ἐδόκουν
τοῦτο μόνον εἶναι δεινόν· ἐλελήθει δὲ καὶ ἄλλο
τεχθέν μοι χαλεπώτερον.

3 Ὁ γὰρ Σωσθένης ὁ τὴν Λευκίππην ἐωνημένος,
ὃν ἡ Μελίτη τῆς τῶν ἀγρῶν ἐκέλευσεν ἀπο-
στῆναι διοικήσεως, μαθὼν παρεῖναι τὸν δεσπότην,
τούς τε ἀγροὺς οὐκέτι ἀφῆκε, τήν τε Μελίτην
4 ἤθελεν ἀμύνασθαι. καὶ πρῶτον μὲν φθάσας
καταμηνύει μου πρὸς τὸν Θέρσανδρον· ὁ γὰρ
διαβαλὼν αὐτὸς ἦν· ἔπειτα καὶ περὶ Λευκίππης
λέγει πάνυ τι πιθανῶς πλασάμενος. ἐπεὶ γὰρ
αὐτὸς αὐτῆς ἀπεγνώκει τυχεῖν, μαστροπεύει πρὸς
τὸν δεσπότην, ὡς ἂν αὐτὸν τῆς Μελίτης ἀπαγ-
άγοι· " Κόρην ἐωνησάμην, ὦ δέσποτα, καλήν,

[1] An iambic trimeter. A possible quotation from a play?
[2] Cobet's correction for MSS. θῇ.
[3] A necessary insertion by Cobet.

Mistress," said Pasion (that was the warder's name), " I shall agree to whatever you think best." Melite advised him to go away for a time, and afterwards, when the relations between her and her husband were restored to tranquillity, and the latter's rage was calmed, to return. This was the course he actually followed.

3. As for me, Fortune, as usual, was hostile to me, and contrived a new plot against me; this was no less than to bring Thersander to meet me face to face. He had been persuaded by the friend to whom he had repaired not to sleep away from home, and, after dining, he was returning to his own house. It was the monthly festival of Artemis, and the whole place was full of drunken roysterers; the whole night long the entire market-place was occupied by crowds of people. I thought that this was my only danger; I never dreamed of another worse one that had been contrived for me.

For Sosthenes, the man who had purchased Leucippe, who had been dismissed by Melite from his post as steward of the country estate, when he heard that his master had arrived, did not resign from his post but sought about how he might take vengeance on Melite. In the first place he began by telling Thersander all about me—his was the slander that led to my capture—and then he came with a plausible story that he had made up about Leucippe. Unable himself to gain possession of her for his own purposes, he adopted the character of pimp to his master, in order to widen the breach between him and Melite. " I have bought a girl, Master," he said, " who is beautiful, aye a perfect

5 ἀλλὰ χρῆμά τι κάλλους ἄπιστον· οὕτως αὐτὴν
πιστεύσειας ἀκούων, ὡς ἰδών. ταύτην ἐφύλατ-
τόν σοι· καὶ γὰρ ἠκηκόειν ζῶντά σε· καὶ ἐπί-
στευον, ὅπερ ἤθελον. ἀλλ᾽ οὐκ ἐξέφαινον, ἵνα
τὴν δέσποιναν ἐπ᾽ αὐτοφώρῳ καταλάβοις καὶ
μή σου καταγελῴη[1] μοιχὸς ἄτιμος καὶ ξένος.
6 ἀφῄρηται δὲ ταύτην χθὲς ἡ δέσποινα καὶ
ἔμελλεν ἀποπέμψειν· ἡ τύχη δὲ ἐτήρησέ σοι,
ὥστε τοσοῦτον κάλλος λαβεῖν. ἔστι δὲ νῦν ἐν
τοῖς ἀγροῖς, οὐκ οἶδ᾽ ὅπως πρὸς αὐτῆς ἀπεσταλ-
μένη. πρὶν οὖν αὖθις ἐπανελθεῖν, εἰ θέλεις,
κατακλείσας αὐτὴν φυλάξω σοι, ὡς ὑπὸ σοὶ
γένοιτο."

4. Ἐπῄνεσεν ὁ Θέρσανδρος καὶ ἐκέλευσε τοῦτο
ποιεῖν. ἔρχεται δὴ σπουδῇ μάλα ὁ Σωσθένης
εἰς τοὺς ἀγρούς, καὶ τὴν καλύβην ἑωρακὼς
ἔνθα ἡ Λευκίππη διανυκτερεύειν ἔμελλε, δύο
τῶν ἐργατῶν παραλαβών, τοὺς μὲν κελεύει τὰς
θεραπαινίδας, αἵπερ ἦσαν ἅμα τῇ Λευκίππῃ
παροῦσαι, περιελθεῖν[2] δόλῳ, καὶ καλεσαμένους
ὅτι πορρωτάτω διατρίβειν ἔχοντας ἐφ᾽ ὁμιλίᾳ·
2 δύο δὲ ἄλλους διάγων, ὡς εἶδε τὴν Λευκίππην
μόνην, εἰσπηδήσας καὶ τὸ στόμα ἐπισχὼν συν-
αρπάζει καὶ κατὰ θάτερα τῆς τῶν θεραπαινίδων
ἐκτροπῆς χωρεῖ, φέρων εἴς τι δωμάτιον ἀπόρρητον, καὶ καταθέμενος λέγει πρὸς αὐτήν· '''Ηκω
σοι φέρων σωρὸν ἀγαθῶν, ἀλλ᾽ ὅπως εὐτυχή-
3 σασα μὴ ἐπιλήσῃ μου. μὴ γὰρ φοβηθῇς ταύτην

---

[1] The optative is necessary and was restored by Jacobs
from the MSS. καταγελᾷ.

[2] I accept Hercher's περιελθεῖν for MSS. περιελεῖν. περι-
έρχομαι is regularly used with the meaning *overreach*, *entrap*,
which is not found among the meanings of περιαιρέω.

miracle of beauty : believe it from hearsay, as though
you actually saw her. I had been keeping her for
you ; I had heard that you were alive, and I believed
it, because I desired it to be so. However, I did not
make public my belief, in order that you might be
able to catch my lady in the very act, and that a
worthless paramour, a foreigner too, might not have
the laugh of you. Yesterday my mistress took the
girl from me, and purposed to send her away, but
fortune has kept her for you, so that you will be able
to get possession of this fair prize. She is now at the
country estate, whither she has been sent for some
object or other ; if you like, I can shut her up
before she comes back, so that she may be at your
disposal."

4. Thersander praised him for his suggestion, and
bade him act accordingly. Sosthenes therefore
repaired with all haste to the country estate, and
after inspecting the hut where Leucippe was to pass
the night, took two of the labourers, and ordered
them to employ the arts of deception upon the
serving-maids who were with Leucippe by calling
them away and keeping them at a distance on the
pretence of having something to communicate to
them ; then, taking two others, when he saw that
Leucippe was alone, he burst in upon her, and, after
gagging her, seized her and went off in the opposite
direction to that in which the maids had gone. He
took her to a cottage in a secret spot, and deposit-
ing her there, spoke as follows : " I have come
bringing you a mass of good fortune ; see that
you do not forget me when you are happy. Do not
be frightened at the way you have thus been carried

τὴν ἁρπαγήν, μηδὲ ἐπὶ κακῷ τῷ σῷ γεγονέναι δόξῃς· αὕτη γὰρ τὸν δεσπότην τὸν ἐμὸν ἐραστήν σοι προξενεῖ." ἡ μὲν δὴ τῷ παραλόγῳ τῆς συμφορᾶς ἐκπλαγεῖσα ἐσιώπησεν· ὁ δὲ ἐπὶ τὸν Θέρσανδρον ἔρχεται καὶ λέγει τὰ πεπραγμένα· ἔτυχε δὲ ὁ Θέρσανδρος ἐπανιὼν εἰς τὴν 4 οἰκίαν. τοῦ δὲ Σωσθένους αὐτῷ μηνύσαντος τὰ περὶ τῆς Λευκίππης καὶ κατατραγῳδοῦντος αὐτῆς τὸ κάλλος, μεστὸς γενόμενος ἐκ τῶν εἰρημένων ὡσεὶ κάλλους φαντάσματος, φύσει καλοῦ, παννυχίδος οὔσης, καὶ ὄντων μεταξὺ τεττάρων σταδίων ἐπὶ τοὺς ἀγρούς, ἡγεῖσθαι κελεύσας, ἐπ' αὐτὴν χωρεῖν ἔμελλεν.

5. Ἐν τούτῳ δὲ ἐγὼ τὴν ἐσθῆτα τῆς Μελίτης εἶχον ἠμφιεσμένος, καὶ ἀπερισκέπτως ἐμπίπτω κατὰ πρόσωπον αὐτοῖς· καί με ὁ Σωσθένης πρῶτος γνωρίσας, "'Αλλ' ἰδού," φησίν, "οὗτος ὁ μοιχὸς βακχεύων ἡμῖν ἔπεισι καὶ τῆς σῆς 2 γυναικὸς ἔχων λάφυρα." ὁ μὲν οὖν νεανίσκος ἔτυχε προηγούμενος, καὶ προϊδὼν ἀποφεύγει, μὴ λαβὼν καιρὸν ὑπὸ δέους κἀμοὶ προμηνῦσαι. ἐμὲ δὲ ἰδόντες συλλαμβάνουσι· καὶ ὁ Θέρσανδρος βοᾷ, καὶ πλῆθος τῶν παννυχιζόντων συνέρρεεν. 3 ἔτι μᾶλλον οὖν ὁ Θέρσανδρος ἐδεινοπάθει, ῥητὰ μὲν καὶ ἄρρητα βοῶν, τὸν μοιχόν, τὸν λωποδύτην· ἀπάγει[1] δέ με εἰς τὸ δεσμωτήριον καὶ 4 παραδίδωσιν ἔγκλημα μοιχείας ἐπιφέρων. ἐμὲ δὲ ἐλύπει τούτων μὲν οὐδέν, οὔτε ἡ τῶν δεσμῶν ὕβρις, οὔτε ἡ τῶν λόγων αἰκία·[2] καὶ γὰρ ἐθάρ-

---

[1] The simple verb ἄγει, found in the MSS., seems hardly to bear the requisite meaning "leads me off," so that I have adopted Cobet's ἀπάγει.

[2] Salmasius' certain correction for MSS. αἰτία

off, or think that it portends any harm to you ; it is
the means by which my master is to become your
lover." Thunderstruck at the incredible nature of
her misfortune, she kept silence, while Sosthenes
went off to Thersander, who was just returning
home, and related what he had done, at the same
time praising Leucippe's beauty to the skies in high-
flown language, with the result that the latter was
excited by his words as though by some fair vision,
instinct with beauty ; and as the festival was going
to last through the night, and it was only half a mile
to the country place, he bade the steward lead on
and set out to visit her.

5. I was meanwhile going on, clad in Melite's
garments, and suddenly without any warning fell in
with them face to face. Sosthenes was the first to
recognize me ; and, " Hulloa," he cried, " here is the
gallant coming roystering to meet us, and actually with
your wife's spoils upon him." Now the young man who
was acting as my guide was a little in front, and when
he saw what was going to happen, he ran away, his
fear preventing him from taking time to warn me.
Thersander's companions, when they spied me, laid
hands upon me, and he himself raised so great a
commotion that a crowd of the revellers collected.
Thersander then took to more and more violent
language, shouting all kinds of abusive terms at me,
and calling me now adulterer, now thief ; he then
haled me off to the prison and handed me over to
the constables, laying an information of adultery
against me. I cared nothing for all this, the insult
offered to me by the fetters and the abusive words :
I felt confident that at the hearing I should be able

ρουν τῷ λόγῳ περιέσεσθαι μὴ μοιχὸς εἶναι,
γῆμαι δὲ ἐμφανῶς. δέος δέ με περὶ τῆς Λευκίππης εἶχεν, οὔπω σαφῶς αὐτὴν ἀπολαβόντα.
5 ψυχαὶ δὲ πεφύκασι μάντεις τῶν κακῶν, ἐπεὶ
τῶν γε ἀγαθῶν ἥκιστα ἐκ μαντείας εὐστοχοῦ-
μεν.[1] οὐδὲν οὖν ὑγιὲς ἐνενόουν περὶ τῆς Λευκίππης, ἀλλ᾽ ἦν ὕποπτά μοι πάντα καὶ μεστὰ
δείματος. ἐγὼ μὲν οὖν οὕτως εἶχον τὴν ψυχὴν
κακῶς.

6. Ὁ δὲ Θέρσανδρος ἐμβαλών με εἰς τὸ δεσμωτήριον, ὡς εἶχεν ὁρμῆς ἐπὶ τὴν Λευκίππην ἵεται.
ὡς δὲ παρῆσαν ἐπὶ τὸ δωμάτιον, καταλαμβάνουσιν
αὐτὴν χαμαὶ κειμένην, ἐν νῷ καθεστηκυῖαν ὧν
ἔτυχεν ὁ Σωσθένης εἰπών, ἐμφαίνουσαν τοῖς προσ-
2 ώποις λύπην ὁμοῦ καὶ δέος. ὁ γὰρ νοῦς οὔ μοι
δοκεῖ λελέχθαι καλῶς ἀόρατος εἶναι τὸ παράπαν·
φαίνεται γὰρ ἀκριβῶς ὡς ἐν κατόπτρῳ τῷ προσώπῳ. ἡσθείς τε γὰρ ἐξέλαμψε τοῖς ὀφθαλμοῖς
εἰκόνα χαρᾶς, καὶ ἀνιαθεὶς συνέστειλε τὸ πρόσωπον
3 εἰς τὴν ὄψιν τῆς συμφορᾶς. ὡς οὖν ἤκουσεν ἡ
Λευκίππη ἀνοιγομένων τῶν θυρῶν, ἦν δὲ ἔνδον
λύχνος, ἀνανεύσασα μικρόν, αὖθις τοὺς ὀφθαλμοὺς
κατέβαλεν. ἰδὼν δὲ ὁ Θέρσανδρος τὸ κάλλος
ἐκ παραδρομῆς, ὡς ἁρπαζομένης ἀστραπῆς, μάλιστα γὰρ ἐν τοῖς ὀφθαλμοῖς κάθηται τὸ κάλλος,
ἀφῆκε τὴν ψυχὴν ἐπ᾽ αὐτὴν καὶ εἱστήκει τῇ θέᾳ
δεδεμένος, ἐπιτηρῶν πότε αὖθις ἀναβλέψει πρὸς
4 αὐτόν. ὡς δὲ ἔνευσεν εἰς τὴν γῆν, λέγει· "Τί κάτω
βλέπεις, γύναι; τί δέ σου τὸ κάλλος τῶν ὀφθαλμῶν εἰς γῆν καταρρεῖ; ἐπὶ τοὺς ὀφθαλμοὺς
μᾶλλον ῥεέτω τοὺς ἐμούς."

[1] Hirschig's correction for MSS. εὐτυχοῦμεν.

to clear myself of the charge of adultery, and to prove that my marriage had been open and public; but I was still afflicted with fear in the matter of Leucippe, because I had not yet definitely recovered her. The mind is ever inclined to be a prophet of ill, because we are seldom successful in the presages of good fortune that we make; I had therefore no consoling thought about Leucippe, but was full of suspicions and fears. Such was my uncomfortable state of mind.

6. Thersander, after thrusting me into the gaol, started with all rapidity on his journey to Leucippe. Arriving at the cottage where she was, they found her lying on the ground and turning over in her mind what Sosthenes had said to her; the expression of her face shewed the presence together in her both of grief and fear. For I do not think that it is rightly said that the mind is entirely invisible: it can be accurately discerned in the face as in a mirror. When it is in a state of delight, it causes the appearance of joy to shine from the eyes; when in sorrow, it contracts the face in a manner that tells of the disaster that has occurred. So when Leucippe heard the doors open, and there was a lamp within, she looked up for a moment, and then let her eyes drop again. Thersander, after obtaining this cursory sight of her beauty, sudden as a flash of lightning, for the chiefest seat of beauty is in the eyes, found his whole heart set on her and stood spell-bound by the sight, waiting for her to look up again at him. But as she still kept her eyes fixed on the ground, "Why look down, maiden?" said he. "Why waste the loveliness of your eyes upon the earth? Rather let it sink deep into mine."

7. Ἡ δὲ ὡς ἤκουσεν, ἐνεπλήσθη [1] δακρύων, καὶ
εἶχεν αὐτῆς ἴδιον κάλλος καὶ τὰ δάκρυα. δάκρυον
γὰρ ὀφθαλμὸν ἀνίστησι καὶ ποιεῖ προπετέστερον·
κἂν μὲν ἄμορφος ᾖ καὶ ἄγροικος, προστίθησιν
εἰς δυσμορφίαν· ἐὰν δὲ ἡδὺς καὶ τοῦ μέλανος
ἔχων τὴν βαφὴν ἠρέμα τῷ λευκῷ στεφανούμενος,
ὅταν τοῖς δάκρυσιν ὑγρανθῇ, ἔοικε πηγῆς ἐγκύμονι
2 μαζῷ.[2] χεομένης δὲ τῆς τῶν δακρύων ἅλμης
περὶ τὸν κύκλον, τὸ μὲν [3] πιαίνεται, τὸ δὲ μέλαν
πορφύρεται, καί ἐστιν ὅμοιον, τὸ μὲν ἴῳ, τὸ δὲ
ναρκίσσῳ· τὰ δὲ δάκρυα τῶν ὀφθαλμῶν ἔνδον
3 εἰλούμενα γελᾷ. τοιαῦτα Λευκίππης ἦν τὰ
δάκρυα, αὐτὴν τὴν λύπην εἰς κάλλος νενικηκότα·
εἰ δὲ ἠδύνατο παγῆναι πεσόντα, καινὸν ἂν εἶχεν
ἤλεκτρον ἡ γῆ. ὁ δὲ Θέρσανδρος ἰδών, πρὸς μὲν
τὸ κάλλος ἐκεχήνει, πρὸς δὲ τὴν λύπην ἐξεμεμήνει,
4 καὶ τοὺς ὀφθαλμοὺς δακρύων ἐγκύους εἶχεν. ἔστι
μὲν γὰρ φύσει δάκρυον ἐπαγωγότατον ἐλέου τοῖς
ὁρῶσι· τὸ δὲ τῶν γυναικῶν μᾶλλον, ὅσῳ θαλερώ-
τερον, τοσούτῳ καὶ γοητότερον. ἐὰν δὲ ἡ δακρύ-
ουσα ᾖ καὶ καλή, καὶ ὁ θεατὴς ἐραστής, οὐδὲ
ὀφθαλμὸς ἀτρεμεῖ, ἀλλὰ τὸ δακρύον ἐμιμήσατο.
5 ἐπειδὴ γὰρ εἰς τὰ ὄμματα τῶν καλῶν τὸ κάλλος
κάθηται, ῥέον ἐκεῖθεν ἐπὶ τοὺς ὀφθαλμοὺς τῶν
ὁρώντων ἵσταται καὶ τῶν δακρύων τὴν πηγὴν
συνεφέλκεται. ὁ δὲ ἐραστὴς δεξάμενος ἄμφω, τὸ

[1] So Cobet for the simple ἐπλήσθη of the MSS.
[2] These three words form the end of an hexameter, and
are probably a quotation from a poem.
[3] I do not think that Berger's insertion of λευκόν here is
necessary. The sense is quite obvious without it; the eye is
considered, as a whole, white, with the exception of its dark
centre.

7. On hearing these words, she burst into tears;
and her tears too had a peculiar beauty of their
own. Tears set off the eye and make its character
more prominent: if it be ugly or coarse, they make
it less pleasing still; if it be handsome, the pupil
jet-black and surrounded by the white into which it
insensibly shades, it becomes like a rich fountain-
spring when it is bedewed with tears. The brine of
the tear-drops coming down into the white of the
eye makes it rich and shining, while the black takes
on from the same cause a deep purple hue; it comes
to resemble a violet, while the rest of the eye is like
a narcissus, and the tears which are rolling within
the eye almost seem to smile. Such were Leucippe's
tears, which overcame her very grief and made it
into beauty; if they could have solidified after they
had fallen, the world would have possessed a new
variety of amber.[1] When Thersander saw her thus,
he was struck dumb with her beauty and maddened
by the sight of her grief, and his own eyes filled
with tears. Indeed tears are by their very nature
exceedingly provocative of a beholder's pity; those
of a woman in particular have the more magic in their
effects in proportion as they are the more abundant;
be the woman fair, and he that sees her lover, his eye
too cannot remain unmoved, but copies her weeping.
Since, in the case of the beauteous, their beauty is in
great part in their eyes, it therefore proceeding thence
to the eyes of the beholder makes its home there and
draws forth the fount of tears. Both—the beauty

---

[1] Ordinary amber was fabled to be derived from the
tears of the Heliades weeping for their dead brother
Phaethon.

μὲν κάλλος εἰς τὴν ψυχὴν ἥρπασε, τὸ δὲ δάκρυον
εἰς τοὺς ὀφθαλμοὺς ἐτήρησεν, ὁραθῆναι δὲ εὔχεται,
καὶ ἀποψήσασθαι δυνάμενος, οὐκ ἐθέλει, ἀλλὰ
τὸ δάκρυον, ὡς δύναται, κατέχει, καὶ φοβεῖται
6 μὴ πρὸ καιροῦ φύγῃ. ὁ δὲ καὶ τῶν ὀφθαλμῶν
τὴν κίνησιν ἐπέχει, μὴ πρὶν τὸ ἐρώμενον ἰδεῖν
ταχὺ θελήσῃ πεσεῖν· μαρτυρίαν γὰρ ταύτην
7 νενόμικεν ὅτι καὶ φιλεῖ. τοιοῦτό τι τῷ Θερσάνδρῳ
συνεβεβήκει· ἐδάκρυε γὰρ [1] παθὼν μέν τι, κατὰ
τὸ εἰκός, ἀνθρώπινον, καλλωπιζόμενος δὲ πρὸς
τὴν Λευκίππην, ὡς διὰ τοῦτο δεδακρυμένος, ὅτι
8 κἀκείνη δακρύει. λέγει οὖν πρὸς τὸν Σωσθένην
προσκύψας· "Νῦν μὲν αὐτὴν θεράπευσον· ὁρᾷς
γὰρ ὡς ἔχει λύπης· ὥστε ὑπεκστήσομαι καὶ μάλα
ἄκων, ὡς μὴ ὀχληρὸς εἴην. ὅταν δὲ ἡμερώτερον
9 διατεθῇ, τότε αὐτῇ διαλεχθήσομαι. σὺ δέ, ὦ
γύναι, θάρρει· ταχὺ γάρ σου ταῦτα τὰ δάκρυα
ἰάσομαι." εἶτα πρὸς τὸν Σωσθένην πάλιν,
ἐξιών· "Ὅπως εἴπῃς τὰ εἰκότα περὶ ἐμοῦ· ἕωθεν
δὲ ἧκε πρός με κατορθώσας," ἔφη. ἐπὶ τούτοις
ἀπηλλάττετο.

8. Ἐν ᾧ δὲ ταῦτα ἐπράττετο, ἔτυχεν ἐπὶ τὴν
Λευκίππην, μετὰ τὴν πρός με ὁμιλίαν, εὐθὺς εἰς
τοὺς ἀγροὺς τὴν Μελίτην νεανίσκον ἀποστείλα-
σαν, ἐπείγειν αὐτὴν εἰς τὴν ἐπάνοδον, μηδὲν ἔτι
2 δεομένην φαρμάκων. ὡς οὖν ἧκεν οὗτος εἰς τοὺς
ἀγρούς, καταλαμβάνει τὰς θεραπαινίδας ζητούσας

---

[1] I have ventured to leave out the words πρὸς ἐπίδειξιν here
found in the MSS. They are extremely unsuitable to this
part of the sentence, giving a meaning indeed exactly contrary to that which is required. They were probably a gloss
on καλλωπιζόμενος which has found its way into a wrong part
of the text.

and the tears—are received into the lover's being: the beauty he takes to his heart, but his tears he keeps in his eyes, and hopes that it will be apparent that he is in such a state; even if he could wipe them away, he will not do so, but keeps them hanging there as best he may, and fears lest they should disappear before they have had their effect. He will even refrain from moving his eyes, so that the tears may not too quickly fall before the beloved sees them: he thinks that they form a true witness that he loves. This was the case with Thersander: he wept partly because he felt some human compassion, as was only natural, and partly to make a shew to Leucippe that he was weeping too because she wept. He therefore whispered to Sosthenes: "Do you look after her for the present—you see in how sorrowful a plight she is—and I will retire, though much against my will, so as not to trouble her: when she has come to a calmer state, I will then put my arguments before her. And you, maiden, be of good cheer; I will soon cure you of these tears." Then, as he was going out, he spoke again to Sosthenes: "See that you give her a good account of me, and come to me in the morning when you have put all right." With these words he left the cottage.

8. While all this was happening, it chanced that Melite, after her visit to me, had sent a young man to the country seat after Leucippe, to bid her hasten to return, as there was no longer any need for the philtre. On his arrival there, he found the serving-

τὴν Λευκίππην, καὶ πάνυ τεταραγμένας· ὡς δὲ
οὐκ ἦν οὐδαμοῦ, δρόμῳ φθάσας ἀπήγγειλε τὸ
3 συμβάν. ἡ δὲ ὡς ἤκουσε τὰ περὶ ἐμοῦ, ὡς εἴην
εἰς τὸ δεσμωτήριον ἐμβληθείς, εἶτα περὶ τῆς
Λευκίππης, ὡς ἀφανὴς ἐγένετο, νέφος αὐτῇ[1]
4 κατεχύθη λύπης. καὶ τὸ μὲν ἀληθὲς οὐκ εἶχεν
εὑρεῖν, ὑπενόει δὲ τὸν Σωσθένην. βουλομένη δὲ
φανερὰν αὐτῆς τὴν ζήτησιν ποιήσασθαι διὰ τοῦ
Θερσάνδρου, τέχνην λόγων ἐπενόησεν, ἥτις με-
μιγμένην εἶχε τῷ σοφίσματι τὴν ἀλήθειαν.

9. Ἐπεὶ γὰρ ὁ Θέρσανδρος εἰσελθὼν εἰς τὴν
οἰκίαν ἐβόα πάλιν, "Τὸν μοιχὸν ἐξέκλεψας σύ,
τῶν δεσμῶν ἐξέλυσας, καὶ τῆς οἰκίας ἐξαπέστειλας·
σὸν τὸ ἔργον· τί οὖν οὐκ ἠκολούθεις αὐτῷ; τί δὲ
ἐνταῦθα μένεις; ἀλλ' οὐκ ἄπει πρὸς τὸν ἐρώμενον,
ἵνα αὐτὸν ἴδῃς στερροτέροις δεσμοῖς δεδεμένον;" ἡ
Μελίτη, "Ποῖον μοιχόν;" ἔφη. "τί πάσχεις;
εἰ γὰρ θέλεις, τὴν μανίαν ἀφείς, ἀκοῦσαι τὸ πᾶν,
2 μαθήσῃ ῥᾳδίως τὴν ἀλήθειαν. ἐν οὖν σου δέομαι,
γενοῦ μοι δικαστὴς ἴσος, καὶ καθήρας μέν σου τὰ
ὦτα τῆς διαβολῆς, ἐκβαλὼν δὲ τῆς καρδίας τὴν
ὀργήν, τὸν δὲ λογισμὸν ἐπιστήσας κριτὴν ἀκέραιον,
ἄκουσον. ὁ νεανίσκος οὗτος οὔτε μοιχὸς ἦν ἐμὸς
οὔτε ἀνήρ· ἀλλὰ τὸ μὲν γένος ἀπὸ Φοινίκης, Τυρίων
οὐδενὸς δεύτερος. ἔπλευσε δὲ καὶ αὐτὸς οὐκ
εὐτυχῶς, ἀλλὰ πᾶς ὁ φόρτος αὐτοῦ γέγονε τῆς
3 θαλάσσης. ἀκούσασα τὴν τύχην ἠλέησα, καὶ
ἀνεμνήσθην σου, καὶ παρέσχον ἑστίαν, 'Τάχα,'

---

[1] Cobet wished to alter αὐτῇ into αὐτῆς, and it is quite
true that the genitive is the common post-Homeric construction. But Achilles Tatius may well have reverted
to the earlier use to avoid the possible confusion occasioned
by αὐτῆς seeming to agree with λύπης.

maids looking for Leucippe, and greatly disordered;
as she could not be found anywhere, he hurried back
and related all he knew to his mistress. Having
first heard my case, how I had been clapped into
gaol, and now about the disappearance of Leucippe,
a cloud of grief descended upon her. She had no
means of finding out the truth, but suspected
Sosthenes; and desiring to shed light on her enquiry
by means of Thersander, she devised an artful plan
to be put into effect by means of questions, mingling
a little truth with the story she had made up.

9. When Thersander then came into the house,
and began shouting again: " You have spirited away
your gallant; you have loosed him from his fetters;
you have got him out of the house! This is all your
work; why do you not follow him? Why do you
stay here? Why do you not get off to your beloved
and see him now fettered in stronger bonds?"
" Gallant indeed!" said Melite. " What is the
matter with you? If you can but drop this fury
of yours, and hear the whole story, you will have
no difficulty in realising the truth. I only ask
one thing of you—be an impartial judge, clear
your ears of all the slander you have heard; expel
anger from your heart and put reason into its place,
the only unbiased arbiter. This young man has
been neither my gallant nor my husband; he is a
Phoenician by birth, and of a stock second to none
among the people of Tyre. He too had an unfortunate voyage, and the whole cargo that he had
shipped became the prey of the sea. I heard of his
mishap and took pity on him; I thought of you, and
offered him my hospitality. ' Perhaps,' I said,

λέγουσα, 'καὶ Θέρσανδρος οὕτω πλανᾶται· τάχα,'
λέγουσα, 'τις κἀκεῖνον ἐλεήσει γυνή. εἰ δὲ τῷ
ὄντι τέθνηκε κατὰ τὴν θάλασσαν, ὡς ἡ φήμη
λέγει, φέρε πάντα τιμῶμεν[1] τὰ ναυάγια.' πόσους
4 καὶ ἄλλους ἔθρεψα νεναυαγηκότας; πόσους
ἔθαψα τῆς θαλάσσης νεκρούς, εἰ ξύλον ἐκ
ναυαγίας τῇ γῇ προσπεσὸν ἐλάμβανον, 'Τάχα,'
λέγουσα, 'ἐπὶ ταύτης τῆς νηὸς Θέρσανδρος
5 ἔπλει·' εἷς δὴ καὶ οὗτος ἦν τῶν ἐκ τῆς θαλάσσης
σωζομένων ἔσχατος. ἐχαριζόμην σοὶ τιμῶσα
τοῦτον. ἔπλευσεν ὥσπερ σύ· ἐτίμων, φίλτατε,
τῆς σῆς[2] συμφορᾶς τὴν εἰκόνα. πῶς οὖν ἐνταῦθα
6 συνεπηγόμην; ὁ λόγος ἀληθής. ἔτυχε μὲν πενθῶν
γυναῖκα· ἡ δὲ ἄρα ἐλάνθανεν οὐκ ἀποθανοῦσα·
τοῦτό τις αὐτῷ καταγορεύει καὶ ὡς ἐνταῦθα εἴη,
παρά τινι τῶν ἡμετέρων ἐπιτρόπων· Σωσθένην δὲ
ἔλεγε. καὶ οὕτως εἶχε· τὴν γὰρ ἄνθρωπον ἥκον-
7 τες εὕρομεν. διὰ τοῦτο ἠκολούθησέ μοι. ἔχεις
τὸν Σωσθένην, πάρεστιν ἡ γυνὴ κατὰ τοὺς ἀγρούς.
ἐξέτασον τῶν λεχθέντων ἕκαστον. εἴ τι ἐψευ-
σάμην, μεμοίχευμαι."

10. Ταῦτα δὲ ἔλεγε, προσποιησαμένη τὸν ἀφα-
νισμὸν τῆς Λευκίππης μὴ ἐγνωκέναι· ταμιευ-
σαμένη αὖθις, εἰ ζητήσει ὁ Θέρσανδρος εὑρεῖν τὴν
ἀλήθειαν, τὰς θεραπαινίδας ἀγαγεῖν, αἷς συν-
απελθοῦσα ἔτυχεν, ἂν μὴ[2] παραγένηται περὶ τὴν
ἕω, λεγούσας, ὅπερ ἦν, οὐδαμοῦ φαίνεσθαι τὴν

---

[1] After τιμῶμεν MSS. here have αὐτοῦ or αὐτά, which Jacobs
changed into αὐτῆς, omitting τά. But it seems more likely,
with Hercher, that αὐτοῦ is the mere insertion of a scribe.
ναύτου Lumb: ⟨ἀντ'⟩ αὐτοῦ Jackson: ⟨ὡς⟩ αὐτοῦ Wifstrand.
[2] Jacobs' necessary insertions.

'Thersander is now a wanderer like him; perhaps some woman will take pity on him too. And if he has really perished at sea, as the report tells, let us do our best then for all the victims of shipwreck.' How many others in such a plight did I not befriend? How many of the sea's dead did I not bury, if but a plank of a wreck were washed ashore? and 'Perhaps,' I would say, 'Thersander used to sail on the very ship of which this was a part?' This man, then, was the last of my refugees saved from the waters; I thought that I was doing what I could for you by looking after him. He had gone on a voyage like you; I was honouring, my dear, the parallel to your fate. How then did I happen to be here in his company? I will tell you the whole true story. He happened to be mourning for the loss of his wife; but though he had lost her, she was not dead. Somebody informed him of this, and also that she was here, in the possession of one of our bailiffs; and told him the bailiff's name, Sosthenes. This was actually the case; we found the woman here when we arrived. This was the reason that he came with me. You have Sosthenes at your disposal, and she is here at our country place; make inquiries as to the truth of every particular that I have told you. If my story is false in any respect, I admit myself convicted of unfaithfulness."

10. This was the story she told, pretending that she knew nothing of Leucippe's abduction; but on the other hand she held in reserve her power, if Thersander should attempt to discover the truth, of bringing forward the serving-maids in whose company Leucippe had departed, to say, if she did not reappear in the morning, that she could not be

2 κόρην· οὕτω γὰρ αὐτὴν ἐγκεῖσθαι πρὸς τὴν
ζήτησιν φανερῶς, ὡς καὶ τὸν Θέρσανδρον ἐπαναγ-
κάσαι. ταῦτα οὖν ὑποκριναμένη πιθανῶς, κἀκεῖνα
προσετίθει· "Πίστευσον, ἄνερ· οὐδέν μου, φίλτατε, παρὰ τὸν τῆς συμβιώσεως κατέγνωκας
3 χρόνον· μηδὲ νῦν τοιοῦτον ὑπολάβοις. ἡ δὲ
φήμη διαπεφοίτηκεν ἐκ τῆς εἰς τὸν νεανίσκον
τιμῆς, οὐκ εἰδότων τῶν πολλῶν τὴν αἰτίαν τῆς
4 κοινωνίας. καὶ γὰρ σὺ φήμῃ τέθνηκας. Φήμη
δὲ καὶ Διαβολὴ δύο συγγενῆ κακά· θυγάτηρ ἡ
Φήμη τῆς Διαβολῆς. καί ἐστι μὲν ἡ Διαβολὴ
μαχαίρας ὀξυτέρα, πυρὸς σφοδροτέρα, Σειρήνων
πιθανωτέρα· ἡ δὲ Φήμη ὕδατος ὑγροτέρα, πνεύ-
5 ματος δρομικωτέρα, πτερῶν ταχυτέρα. ὅταν οὖν
ἡ Διαβολὴ τοξεύσῃ τὸν λόγον, ὁ μὲν δίκην βέλους
ἐξίπταται καὶ τιτρώσκει μὴ παρόντα καθ' οὗ
πέμπεται· ὁ δὲ ἀκούων ταχὺ πείθεται, καὶ ὀργῆς
αὐτῷ πῦρ ἐξάπτεται καὶ ἐπὶ τὸν βληθέντα
μαίνεται. τεχθεῖσα δὲ ἡ Φήμη τῷ τοξεύματι,
ῥεῖ μὲν εὐθὺς πολλὴ καὶ ἐπικλύζει τὰ ὦτα τῶν
ἐντυχόντων, διαπνεῖ δὲ ἐπὶ πλεῖστον καταιγίζουσα
τῷ τοῦ λόγου πνεύματι, καὶ ἐξίπταται κουφι-
6 ζομένη τῷ τῆς γλώττης πτερῷ. ταῦτά με τὰ δύο
πολεμεῖ· ταῦτά σου τὴν ψυχὴν κατέλαβε[1] καὶ
ἀπέκλεισέ μου τοῖς λόγοις τῶν ὤτων σου τὰς
θύρας."

[1] Hercher's correction for MSS. κατέβαλε.

---

[1] The text seems here to be corrupt. It is not certain
whether Melite is trying to make Thersander also help in
the search for Leucippe, or disclose his own intentions, or

found anywhere. She could thus openly continue her search for the girl, and at the same time compel Thersander to reveal his own plans.[1] In addition to the plausible story that she had already contrived, she went on as follows : " Trust me, my husband ; in all the period of our married life, you have never, my dear, had anything with which to reproach me, and do not now suspect me of anything of the kind. This rumour got abroad because of the care which I took of the young man ; the community did not know the real reason of our association , and by rumour, you, too, were dead. Rumour and Slander are two kindred Furies : Rumour is Slander's daughter. Slander is sharper than any sword, stronger than fire, more persuasive than a Siren ; Rumour is more slippery than water, runs faster than the wind, flies quicker than any winged bird. When Slander shoots forth a lying report, it flies like an arrow and wounds him at whom it is aimed even though he is not present where the word is spoken ; the hearer quickly believes it, the fire of his anger is kindled, and he is soon furious and mad against the object of the shot. Rumour, brought into being by the act of shooting, at once flows onward gaining in volume, and overwhelms the ears of all whom she meets ; she travels far, like a wind, carried storm-wise on the gale of words ; she flies,[2] borne aloft by the wings of the human tongue. These two plagues are my enemies : they have captured your mind, and by their arguments they have shut against me the doors of your ears."

[1] come round to her own point of view. A word or two has probably dropped out.

[2] The metaphors seem a little mixed, but they are only repeating the three similes applied to Rumour in § 4 above.

11. Ἅμα λέγουσα, χειρός τε ἔθιγε καὶ καταφιλεῖν ἤθελεν. ἐγεγόνει δὲ ἡμερώτερος, καὶ αὐτὸν ἔσαινε τῶν λεγομένων τὸ πιθανόν, καὶ τὸ τῆς Λευκίππης σύμφωνον τῷ λόγῳ τοῦ Σωσθένους μέρος τῆς ὑπονοίας μετέφερεν. οὐ μέντοι τέλεον ἐπίστευσε· ζηλοτυπία γὰρ ἅπαξ ἐμπεσοῦσα ψυχῇ 2 δυσέκνιπτόν ἐστιν. ἐθορυβήθη οὖν ὅτι τὴν κόρην ἤκουσεν εἶναί μου γυναῖκα, ὥστε ἐμίσει με μᾶλλον. τότε μὲν οὖν εἰπὼν ἐξετάσειν περὶ τῶν εἰρημένων, κοιμησόμενος ᾤχετο καθ' αὐτόν. ἡ δὲ Μελίτη κακῶς εἶχε τὴν ψυχήν, ὡς ἐκπεσοῦσα πρός με τῆς ὑποσχέσεως.

3 Ὁ δὲ Σωσθένης προπέμψας[1] μέχρι τινὸς τὸν Θέρσανδρον, καὶ καθυποσχόμενος περὶ τῆς Λευκίππης, αὖθις ἀναστρέφει πρὸς αὐτὴν καὶ σχηματίσας τὸ πρόσωπον εἰς ἡδονήν, "Κατωρθώσαμεν," εἶπεν, "ὦ Λάκαινα. Θέρσανδρος ἐρᾷ σου, καὶ μαίνεται· ὥστε τάχα καὶ γυναῖκα ποιή- 4 σεταί σε. τὸ δὲ κατόρθωμα τοῦτο ἐμόν. ἐγὼ γάρ σου πρὸς αὐτὸν περὶ τοῦ κάλλους πολλὰ ἐτερατευσάμην, καὶ τὴν ψυχὴν αὐτοῦ φαντασίας ἐγέμισα. τί κλαίεις; ἀνάστηθι, καὶ θῦε ἐπὶ τοῖς εὐτυχήμασιν Ἀφροδίτῃ. μνημόνευε δὲ κἀμοῦ."

12. Καὶ ἡ Λευκίππη, "Τοιαῦτά σοι," ἔφη, "γένοιτο εὐτυχήματα, οἷα ἐμοὶ κομίζων πάρει." ὁ δὲ Σωσθένης τὴν εἰρωνείαν οὐ συνείς, ἀλλὰ νομίζων αὐτὴν τῷ ὄντι λέγειν, φιλοφρονούμενος προσετίθει· "Βούλομαι δέ σοι καὶ τὸν Θέρσανδρον, ὅστις ἐστίν, εἰπεῖν, ὡς ἂν μᾶλλον ἡσθείης.

[1] So Jacobs for MSS. παραπέμψας. The sense requires "accompanied" rather than "sent for."

11. While she was still speaking, she took his hand and made as though to kiss him. He was already somewhat calmed by her words; and was both coaxed by the plausibility of what she said and had part of his suspicions removed by the harmony of her story with that of Sosthenes. However, he did not yet completely trust her: for when jealousy has once entered the heart, it is hard indeed to remove its stain. Then he was greatly vexed at hearing that the maiden was my wife, and this made him but hate me the more. For the time, he said that he would make further inquiries about the story that she had told him, and retired alone to bed; Melite, the while, was greatly distressed in that she had failed to perform her promise to me.

Sosthenes, after accompanying Thersander on part of his journey home and encouraging him to hope for Leucippe's favours, turned back again and went to her. He composed his face to wear an expression of delight, and, "We have succeeded, Lacaena," he said. "Thersander is in love with you, madly in love, so that he is likely to make you his wife. All this success was my doing; for it was I who dilated at great length to him of your beauty, and have filled his heart with a violent fancy for you. Why do you weep? Up, and sacrifice to Aphrodite for your good fortune; and then mind you remember me too."

12. "I pray," said Leucippe, "that you may have just such good fortune as you come and bring me now." Sosthenes did not in the least understand her sarcasm, and went on in high good humour: "I want to tell you all about Thersander, to give you the better conceit of your good luck. He is the

327

2 Μελίτης μὲν ἀνὴρ ἦν εἶδες ἐν τοῖς ἀγροῖς· γένει
δὲ πρῶτος ἁπάντων τῶν Ἰώνων· πλοῦτος μείζων
τοῦ γένους, ὑπὲρ τὸν πλοῦτον ἡ χρηστότης.
τὴν δὲ ἡλικίαν οἷός ἐστιν εἶδες, ὅτι νέος καὶ
3 καλός, ὃ μάλιστα τέρπει γυναῖκα." πρὸς τοῦτο
οὐχ ὑπήνεγκεν ἡ Λευκίππη ληροῦντα τὸν Σωσθένην, ἀλλ', " Ὦ κακὸν σὺ θηρίον, μέχρι τίνος
μοι ¹ μιαίνεις τὰ ὦτα; τί ἐμοὶ καὶ Θερσάνδρῳ
4 κοινόν; καλὸς ἔστω Μελίτῃ, καὶ πλούσιος τῇ
πόλει, χρηστός τε καὶ μεγαλόψυχος τοῖς δεο-
μένοις· ἐμοὶ δὲ οὐδὲν μέλει τούτων, εἴτε ἐστὶ καὶ
Κόδρου εὐγενέστερος, εἴτε Κροίσου πλουσιώτερος.
5 τί μοι καταλέγεις σωρὸν ἀλλοτρίων ἐγκωμίων;
τότε ἐπαινέσω Θέρσανδρον ὡς ἄνδρα ἀγαθόν,
ὅταν εἰς τὰς ἀλλοτρίας μὴ ἐνυβρίζῃ γυναῖκας."
13. Καὶ ὁ Σωσθένης σπουδάσας εἶπε· "Παίζεις;" "Ποῖ ² παίζω;" ἔφη· "ἔα με, ἄνθρωπε,
μετὰ τῆς ἐμαυτῆς συντρίβεσθαι τύχης καὶ τοῦ
κατέχοντός με δαίμονος. οἶδα γὰρ οὖσα ἐν
πειρατηρίῳ." "Δοκεῖς μοι," ἔφη, "μαίνεσθαι
2 μανίαν ἀνήκεστον. πειρατήριον ταῦτα εἶναί σοι
δοκεῖ, πλοῦτος καὶ γάμος καὶ τρυφή, ἄνδρα
τοιοῦτον λαβούσῃ παρὰ τῆς Τύχης, ὃν οὕτω
φιλοῦσιν οἱ θεοί, ὡς αὐτὸν καὶ ἐκ μέσων τῶν τοῦ
θανάτου πυλῶν ἀναγαγεῖν·" εἶτα κατέλεγε τὴν
ναυαγίαν, ἐκθειάζων ὡς ἐσώθη, καὶ τερατευόμενος

¹ Inserted by Jacobs.
² Cobet wished to alter ποῖ (ποῦ G) to πῶς. ποῖα Jacobs.
Castiglioni deletes.

---

¹ The allusion is here less to his patriotic self-sacrifice for
his country's salvation than to the fact that he was the last
of a long line of kings.

husband of Melite, the lady whom you saw at the
country place; he is the very highest of all the Ionians
in birth, his riches are above his birth, and his
amiability above his riches. His looks you could
see for yourself; how he is young and well-favoured,
things that women particularly appreciate." At this
point Leucippe could no longer bear the vapourings
of Sosthenes, but burst out: " You vile beast, how
much longer are you going on polluting my ears?
What do I care about Thersander? Let him be
well-favoured for his Melite, and rich for his city,
and amiable and generous for those who need it;
I care for none of all these, whether he be nobler
than Codrus,[1] or richer than Croesus. Why go on
piling up another's praises to me? I shall esteem
Thersander as a good man, when he stops forcing
his attentions on other men's wives."

13. Sosthenes' tone then changed to earnest. " I
suppose you are joking?" said he. "What could
be my object[2] in joking?" she cried. "Leave me
alone, fellow, with my ill-fortune and the fate that
constrains me; I know now that I have fallen among
pirates." "You seem to me," he replied, "to
be mad; and incurably mad. Is this what you
call falling among pirates—wealth, marriage, luxury,
when you get from Fortune a husband such as
Thersander, whom the gods love so dearly that
they saved him from the very gates of death?"
And he went on to relate to her the story of his
shipwreck, making his escape a matter of divine

---

[2] As stated in the note on the Greek text, I have here kept
the MSS. reading ποῖ. πῶς is the regular word—"Joking
indeed!" or, "How could I be joking?"; but ποῖ, meaning
literally "Whither do I joke?", can be translated so as to
make good sense.

ACHILLES TATIUS

3 ὑπὲρ τὸν δελφῖνα τὸν Ἀρίονος. ὡς δὲ οὐδὲν ἡ
Λευκίππη οὐκέτι μυθολογοῦντα πρὸς αὐτὸν εἶπε,
"Σκέψαι," ἔφη, " κατὰ σέ,[1] τί ἄμεινον, καὶ ὅπως
μηδὲν τούτων πρὸς Θέρσανδρον ἐρεῖς, μὴ παρο-
ξύνῃς χρηστὸν ἄνδρα. ὀργισθεὶς γὰρ ἀφόρητός
4 ἐστι. χρηστότης γὰρ τυγχάνουσα μὲν χάριτος,
ἐπὶ[2] μᾶλλον αὔξεται· προπηλακισθεῖσα δὲ εἰς
ὀργὴν ἐρεθίζεται. τὸ γὰρ περιττὸν εἰς φιλαν-
θρωπίαν ἴσον ἔχει τὸν θυμὸν εἰς τιμωρίαν." τὰ
μὲν δὴ κατὰ Λευκίππην εἶχεν οὕτως.

14. Κλεινίας δὲ καὶ ὁ Σάτυρος πυθόμενοί
με ἐν τῷ δεσμωτηρίῳ[3] καθεῖρχθαι (διηγγέλκει
γὰρ αὐτοῖς ἡ Μελίτη) τῆς νυκτὸς εὐθὺς ἐπὶ
τὸ οἴκημα σπουδῇ παρῆσαν. καὶ ἤθελον μὲν
αὐτοῦ καταμεῖναι σὺν ἐμοί, ὁ δὲ ἐπὶ τῶν δεσμῶν
οὐκ ἐπέτρεπεν, ἀλλ' ἐκέλευεν ἀπαλλάττεσθαι
2 αὐτοὺς τὴν ταχίστην. ὁ μὲν δὴ τούτους
ἀπήλασεν ἄκοντας, ἐγὼ δὲ ἐντειλάμενος αὐτοῖς
περὶ τῆς Λευκίππης, εἰ παραγένοιτο, περὶ τὴν
ἕω σπουδῇ πρός με ἥκειν, καὶ τὰς τῆς Μελίτης
διηγησάμενος ὑποσχέσεις, τὴν ψυχὴν εἶχον ἐπὶ
τρυτάνης ἐλπίδος καὶ φόβου, καὶ ἐφοβεῖτό μου τὸ
ἐλπίζον καὶ ἤλπιζε τὸ φοβούμενον.

15. Ἡμέρας δὲ γενομένης, ὁ μὲν Σωσθένης
ἐπὶ τὸν Θέρσανδρον ἔσπευδεν, οἱ δὲ ἀμφὶ τὸν
Σάτυρον ἐπ' ἐμέ. ὡς δὲ εἶδεν ὁ Θέρσανδρος
τὸν Σωσθένην, ἐπυνθάνετο πῶς ἔχει τὰ κατὰ
2 τὴν κόρην εἰς πειθὼ πρὸς αὐτόν. ὁ δὲ τὸν μὲν
ὄντα λόγον οὐ λέγει, σοφίζεται δέ τι μάλα

---

[1] So Cobet for σοῦ.   κατὰ σοῦ would presumably mean " to
your disadvantage."
[2] ἐπὶ is Jacobs' clever change for MSS. ἔτι.

providence, and embroidering it with more miracles
than Arion and his dolphin. Leucippe made no
answer to him as he was recounting his marvels; so
he went on: "You had better regard your own
interests, and not indulge in any of this kind of talk
to Thersander, in case you should anger a naturally
amiable man; for once roused to fury, there is no
stopping him. Amiability grows and multiplies if
it meets with gratitude, while if it meets with
contempt it is irritated into anger; the more a man
is naturally inclined to friendliness, the more forward is he to avenge a slight." So much then for
Leucippe's plight.

14. Clinias and Satyrus learning, by the information
of Melite, that I was shut up in gaol, at once came
hurriedly by night to the prison, and were anxious
to stay there with me; but the gaoler refused and
bade them begone about their business as quick as
might be. They were thus driven away by him,
though greatly against their will, after I had conjured
them to come to me without delay in the morning
to tell me if Leucippe had reappeared; I also
related to them all Melite's promises, and then I
had to stay with my heart on the balance between
hope and fear, my hopes afraid and my terrors with
a vestige of hope.

15. As soon as it was day Satyrus and his friends
returned to me, while Sosthenes hurried to
Thersander. Directly that Thersander saw him, he
began to question him as to what progress was
being made in the attempt to win Leucippe for him;
to which question he did not reply the truth, but
contrived an ingenious and plausible story. "She

---

³ Π³ recto begins here] ωτη[.

ACHILLES TATIUS

πιθανῶς· " Ἀρνεῖται μὲν γάρ," [1] εἶπεν· " οὐ
μὴν ἡγοῦμαι τὴν ἄρνησιν αὐτῆς οὕτως ἔχειν
ἁπλῶς, ἀλλ' ὑπονοεῖν μοι δοκεῖ σε χρησάμενον
3 ἅπαξ ἀφήσειν καὶ ὀκνεῖ τὴν ὕβριν." " Ἀλλὰ
τούτου γε ἕνεκεν," [2] εἶπεν ὁ Θέρσανδρος, " θαρ-
ρείτω· τὸ γὰρ ἐμὸν οὕτως ἔχει πρὸς αὐτήν,
ὡς ἀθάνατον εἶναι. ἓν δὲ μόνον φοβοῦμαι, καὶ
ἐπείγομαι μαθεῖν περὶ τῆς κόρης, εἰ τῷ ὄντι
γυνὴ τυγχάνει τοῦ νεανίσκου γενομένη, ὡς ἡ
4 Μελίτη μοι διηγήσατο." ταῦτα διαλεγόμενοι
παρῆσαν ἐπὶ τὸ τῆς Λευκίππης δωμάτιον. ἐπεὶ
δὲ πλησίον ἐγένοντο τῶν θυρῶν, ἀκούουσιν αὐτῆς
ποτνιωμένης. ἔστησαν οὖν ἀψοφητὶ κατόπιν τῶν
θυρῶν.

16. " Οἴμοι, Κλειτοφῶν " (τοῦτο γὰρ ἔλεγε
πολλάκις), " οὐκ οἶδας ποῦ γέγονα καὶ ποῦ
καθείργμαι· οὐδὲ γὰρ ἐγώ, τίς σὲ κατέχει τύχη·
2 ἀλλὰ τὴν αὐτὴν ἄγνοιαν δυστυχοῦμεν. ἆρα μή
σε κατέλαβε Θέρσανδρος ἐπὶ τῆς οἰκίας; ἆρα
μὴ καὶ σύ τι πέπονθας ὑβριστικόν; πολλάκις
ἠθέλησα πυθέσθαι παρὰ τοῦ Σωσθένους, ἀλλ'
οὐκ εἶχον ὅπως πύθωμαι. εἰ μὲν ὡς περὶ ἀνδρὸς
ἐμαυτῆς, ἐφοβούμην, μή τί σοι κινήσω κακόν,
παροξύνασα Θέρσανδρον ἐπὶ σέ· εἰ δὲ ὡς περὶ
3 ξένου τινός, ὑπόνοια καὶ [3] τοῦτο ἦν· τί γὰρ
μέλει γυναικὶ περὶ τῶν οὐχ ἑαυτῆς; ποσάκις
ἐμαυτὴν ἐβιασάμην, ἀλλ' οὐκ ἔπειθον τὴν γλῶσ-

[1] I am almost tempted to change the position of the
inverted commas to μέν," γὰρ εἶπεν: cf. such a phrase as Ov.
Tr. 4. 2. 51. " Io " que Miles " io " magna voce " triumphe "
canet.
[2] Π[3] recto ends here] ἐγ.
[3] It would be possible to read κἂν for καί, but I do not

33²

still refuses," he said, " but I do not think that her
refusal is genuine and final; I fancy she suspects
that after once enjoying her favours you will cast her
off, and she shrinks from the insult that is thus offered
to her." " As far as that goes," said Thersander,
" she need have no apprehensions; my feelings towards her are of such a nature that they can never
die. There is only one thing about her of which I am
really afraid, and I am exceedingly anxious to know
the truth about it—whether she is really that young
man's wife, as Melite told me." As they thus
talked, they arrived at the cottage where Leucippe
was, and as they approached the door, they heard
her deliriously murmuring to herself; they therefore took up their position behind the door without
making any noise.

16. " Alas, Clitophon," she was saying over and
over again, " you do not know what has become of
me and where I am imprisoned; and I know not
either what has befallen you: the same ignorance is
the unhappy lot of both of us. Did Thersander
come upon you at the house? Have you too
suffered insult and violence? Many is the time that
I have desired to ask Sosthenes about you, but knew
not how to inquire. If I asked of you as of my
own husband, I was afraid that I might bring some
new trouble upon you by embittering Thersander's
rage against you: if as of a stranger, that too would
have been a matter of suspicion: for what should
a woman care about others than those of her own
family? How often did I try to force myself to ask,

---

think the change is absolutely necessary. The ἦν without ἄν
both corresponds to ἐφοβούμην and expresses the certainty that
suspicion would have been aroused by such a course of action.

σαν εἰπεῖν· ἀλλὰ ταῦτα μόνον ἔλεγον, ''Ἄνερ
Κλειτοφῶν, Λευκίππης μόνης ἄνερ, πιστὲ καὶ
βέβαιε, ὃν οὐδὲ συγκαθεύδουσα πέπεικεν ἄλλη
4 γυνή, κἂν ἡ ἄστοργος ἐγὼ πεπίστευκα· μετὰ
τοσοῦτον ἰδοῦσά σε χρόνον ἐν τοῖς ἀγροῖς οὐ
κατεφίλησα.' νῦν οὖν ἂν Θέρσανδρος ἔλθῃ
πυνθανόμενος, τί πρὸς αὐτὸν εἴπω; ἆρα ἀπο-
καλύψασα τοῦ δράματος τὴν ὑπόκρισιν διηγή-
σομαι τὴν ἀλήθειαν; μή με νομίσῃς ἀνδράποδον
5 εἶναι, Θέρσανδρε. στρατηγοῦ θυγάτηρ εἰμὶ
Βυζαντίων, πρώτου τῶν Τυρίων γυνή· οὐκ εἰμὶ
Θετταλή· οὐ καλοῦμαι Λάκαινα. ὕβρις αὕτη
6 ἐστὶ πειρατική· λελῄστευμαι καὶ τοὔνομα. ἀνήρ
μοι Κλειτοφῶν, πατρὶς Βυζάντιον, Σώστρατος
πατήρ, μήτηρ [1] Πάνθεια. ἀλλ' οὐδὲ πιστεύσειας
ἐμοὶ λεγούσῃ. φοβοῦμαι δὲ καὶ ἐὰν πιστεύσῃς
περὶ Κλειτοφῶντος, μὴ τὸ ἄκαιρόν μου τῆς
ἐλευθερίας τὸν φίλτατον ἀπολέσῃ. φέρε πάλιν
ἐνδύσωμαί μου τὸ δρᾶμα· φέρε πάλιν περίθωμαι
τὴν Λάκαιναν.''

17. Ταῦτα ἀκούσας ὁ Θέρσανδρος μικρὸν
ἀναχωρήσας λέγει πρὸς τὸν Σωσθένην· '' Ἤκουσας ἀπίστων ῥημάτων, γεμόντων ἔρωτος; ὅσα
εἶπεν· ὅσα [2] ὠδύρατο· ὅτι [3] ἑαυτὴν κατεμέμψατο.
ὁ μοιχός μου κρατεῖ πανταχοῦ. δοκῶ, ὁ λῃστὴς
2 καὶ φαρμακεύς ἐστι. Μελίτη φιλεῖ, Λευκίππη
φιλεῖ. ὤφελον, ὦ Ζεῦ, γενέσθαι Κλειτοφῶν.''
'' Ἀλλ' οὐ μαλακιστέον,'' ὁ Σωσθένης ἔφη,

---

[1] Π³ verso begins here μ[.   [2] οια Π³.
[3] The MSS. have τί, which Jacobs altered into οἷα. But
surely it is only that the initial o of ὅτι disappeared after
the final o of the preceding word?

but could not persuade my tongue to speak! I could only keep on saying this: 'My husband Clitophon, husband of Leucippe alone, faithful and steadfast! Another woman could not persuade you to be her own, no, not though she slept by your side, though I, heartless I, believed that you were hers! When I saw you in the garden after so long an interval of time, I would not even kiss you.' And now if Thersander comes again to ask me about myself, what shall I answer him? Shall I strip off the whole make-up and pretence of the long story and declare the truth? Think not, Thersander, that I am some servile chattel! I am the daughter of the commander-in-chief of the Byzantines, the wife of the first in rank among the people of Tyre; no Thessalian I, and my name is not Lacaena: this is but another instance of pirates' violence; my very name too has been stolen from me. My husband is Clitophon, my fatherland Byzantium: Sostratus is my father, Panthea my mother. But you will hardly believe my words—and if you did, I should be afraid for Clitophon's sake; my untimely frankness might be the ruin of him who is dearest to me. Come, let me play my part once more: let me once again assume the character of Lacaena!"

17. When he had heard this Thersander drew away a little, and said to Sosthenes; "Did you hear her love-sick words, almost incredible as they were? What things she uttered! How she wailed! How she reproached herself! That lecher has the better of me everywhere; I think the cut-purse must be a wizard too. Melite loves him, Leucippe loves him; would God that I might become Clitophon!" "No," said Sosthenes, "you must not

" δέσποτα, πρὸς τὸ ἔργον, ἀλλ' ἐπὶ τὴν κόρην
3 ἰτέον αὐτήν. καὶ γὰρ ἂν νῦν ἐρᾷ τοῦ καταράτου
τούτου μοιχοῦ, μέχρι μὲν αὐτὸν οἶδε μόνον, καὶ
οὐ κεκοινώνηκεν ἑτέρῳ, βόσκει [1] τὴν ψυχὴν ἐπ'
αὐτόν· ἂν δὲ ἅπαξ εἰς ταὐτὸν ἔλθῃς (πολλῷ
γὰρ [2] διαφέρεις ἐκείνου εἰς εὐμορφίαν) ἐπιλήσεται [3]
4 τέλεον αὐτοῦ. παλαιὸν γὰρ ἔρωτα μαραίνει
νέος ἔρως, γυνὴ δὲ καὶ μάλιστα τὸ παρὸν φιλεῖ,
τοῦ δὲ ἀπόντος ἕως καινὸν οὐχ εὗρε, μνημονεύει·
προσλαβοῦσα δὲ ἕτερον, τὸν πρότερον τῆς ψυχῆς
5 ἀπήλειψε." ταῦτα ἀκούσας ὁ Θέρσανδρος ἠγέρθη.
λόγος γὰρ ἐλπίδος εἰς τὸ τυχεῖν ἔρωτος ἐς
πειθὼ ῥᾴδιος· τὸ γὰρ ἐπιθυμοῦν, σύμμαχον ὃ
θέλει λαβόν, ἐγείρει τὴν ἐλπίδα.

18. Διαλιπὼν οὖν ὀλίγον ἐφ' οἷς πρὸς ἑαυτὴν
ἐλάλησεν ἡ Λευκίππη, ὡς μὴ δοκοίη τι κατακ-
οῦσαι [4] τῶν ὑπ' αὐτῆς εἰρημένων, εἰσέρχεται
σχηματίσας ἑαυτὸν εἰς τὸ εὐαγωγότερον [5] πρὸς
θέαν, ὡς ᾤετο. ἐπεὶ δὲ εἶδε τὴν Λευκίππην,
ἀνεφλέγη τὴν ψυχήν, καὶ ἔδοξεν αὐτῷ τότε
2 καλλίων γεγονέναι. θρέψας γὰρ ὅλης τῆς
νυκτὸς τὸ πῦρ, ὅσον χρόνον ἀπελείφθη τῆς
κόρης, ἀνεζωπύρησεν ἐξαίφνης ὕλην λαβὼν εἰς
τὴν φλόγα τὴν θέαν, καὶ μικροῦ μὲν προσπεσὼν
περιεχύθη τῇ κόρῃ. καρτερήσας δ' οὖν καὶ
παρακαθίσας διελέγετο, ἄλλοτε ἄλλα ῥήματα

[1] βόσκει Gaselee: πάσχει MSS:]χει Π[3].
[2] Some connecting particle seems to be required for the
sentence in the bracket, and none is present in the MSS.
Jacobs suggested δέ, Cobet γάρ.
[3] Π[3]verso ends here]σε[.
[4] So Cobet: the MSS. have the participle κατακούσας.
[5] εὐάγωγος generally means " ductile " rather than " en-

weaken in your task, my master: you must once more approach the girl yourself. Even if now she is in love with this damned spark, it is only that as long as she has known him alone, and has no experience of others, she sends her heart out to pasture on him; once you step into his place—you are a far more handsome figure than he is—she will utterly forget him. A new love makes an old passion wither away; a woman is best pleased with things present before her, and only remembers the absent as long as she has failed to find something new: when she takes a new lover, she wipes off the impression of the old from her heart." When Thersander heard this exhortation, he roused himself; for words containing the prediction of success in love are efficacious in their power of persuasion: desire takes its own object as its ally, and so awakes the sentiment of hope.

18. He therefore waited for a little while after Leucippe had finished her soliloquy, so that he might not seem to have been listening to it, and then, composing himself to an expression which he thought would make him more acceptable in her sight, went into the hut. At the sight of Leucippe, his heart burned up into fresh love: she seemed to him at that moment to have become more beautiful than ever. All night long—the whole time that he had been absent from her—he had been nursing the fire of his passion; and now, the sight of her adding fresh fuel to its flames, it suddenly burst out, and he was all but falling upon her and embracing her. But he mastered himself and sat down by her side, beginning to converse with her and stringing to-

gaging," and Jacobs may possibly have been right in desiring to change it to ἐπαγωγότερον.

3 συναπτων οὐκ ἔχοντα νοῦν. τοιοῦτοι γὰρ οἱ
ἐρῶντες, ὅταν πρὸς τὰς ἐρωμένας ζητήσωσι
λαλεῖν· οὐ γὰρ ἐπιστήσαντες τὸν λογισμὸν τοῖς
λόγοις, ἀλλὰ τὴν ψυχὴν εἰς τὸ ἐρώμενον ἔχοντες,
τῇ γλώττῃ μόνον χωρὶς ἡνιόχου τοῦ λογισμοῦ
4 λαλοῦσιν. ἅμα οὖν συνδιαλεγόμενος, καὶ ἐπιθεὶς
τὴν χεῖρα τῷ τραχήλῳ, περιέβαλεν, ὡς μέλλων
φιλήσειν. ἡ δὲ προϊδοῦσα τῆς χειρὸς τὴν ὁδόν,
5 νεύει κάτω, καὶ εἰς τὸν κόλπον κατεδύετο. ὁ
δὲ οὐδὲν ἧττον περιβαλών, ἀνέλκειν τὸ πρόσωπον
ἐβιάζετο· ἡ δὲ ἀντικατεδύετο καὶ ἔκρυπτε τὰ
φιλήματα. ὡς δὲ χρόνος ἐγίνετο τῇ τῆς χειρὸς
πάλῃ, φιλονεικία λαμβάνει τὸν Θέρσανδρον
ἐρωτική, καὶ τὴν μὲν λαιὰν ὑποβάλλει τῷ
προσώπῳ κάτω, τῇ δὲ δεξιᾷ τῆς κόμης λαβόμενος, τῇ μὲν εἷλκεν εἰς τοὐπίσω, τῇ δὲ εἰς
6 τὸν ἀνθερεῶνα ὑπερείδων ἀνώθει. ὡς δέ ποτε
ἐπαύσατο τῆς βίας, ἢ τυχών, ἢ μὴ τυχών, ἢ
καμών, λέγει πρὸς αὐτὸν ἡ Λευκίππη· "Οὔτε
ὡς ἐλεύθερος ποιεῖς, οὔτε ὡς εὐγενής· καὶ σὺ
ἐμιμήσω Σωσθένην. ἄξιος ὁ δοῦλος τοῦ δεσπότου.
ἀλλ' ἀπέχου τοῦ λοιποῦ, μηδὲ ἐλπίσῃς τυχεῖν,
πλὴν εἰ μὴ γένῃ Κλειτοφῶν."

19. Ταῦτα ἀκούσας ὁ Θέρσανδρος οὐκ εἶχεν
ὅς τις γένηται· καὶ γὰρ ἦρα, καὶ ὠργίζετο.
θυμὸς δὲ καὶ ἔρως δύο λαμπάδες· ἔχει γὰρ

gether remarks with no particular meaning. This is characteristic of lovers, when they try to talk with the women they love ; they put no sense into what they say, but, their whole heart fixed on the object of its love, they let their tongue prattle on without the guidance of reason. As he conversed with her and put his hand on her shoulder, he began[1] to embrace her, making as though he would kiss her; but she, seeing the course which his hand was about to make, bent her head down and let it drop on her bosom ; at which he did but encircle her neck the more, trying to compel her to lift up her face, while she in return still bent down and tried to avoid his kisses. Some time passing in this wrestling against the force of his hand, Thersander was overcome by love's anger and strife : he put his left hand beneath her face, while with the right he took hold of her hair ; and pulling her head backward with the one and pushing upward beneath her chin with the other, he made her lift up her head. When he presently desisted from the force he was employing, either because he had been successful in his object, or because he had been unsuccessful in it, or because he was tired, Leucippe exclaimed to him, " You are not acting as a free man or as one that is noble ; you behave like Sosthenes; the man is worthy of his master. Stop now, and know that you can never attain your wishes, unless you become Clitophon."

19. At these words Thersander was utterly distracted ; he loved, he was wroth. Anger and love are two flames : yes, anger possesses a second fire, as

---

[1] It might be objected that this would rather render the imperfect περιέβαλλεν than the aorist in the text. But the Greek means that he placed his arm round her neck, trying to bring her face into the right position for a kiss.

καὶ ὁ θυμὸς ἄλλο πῦρ, καί ἐστι τὴν μὲν φύσιν
2 ἐναντιώτατον, τὴν δὲ βίαν ὅμοιον. ὁ μὲν γὰρ
παροξύνει μισεῖν, ὁ δὲ ἀναγκάζει φιλεῖν· καὶ
ἀλλήλων πάροικος ἡ τοῦ πυρός ἐστι πηγή.
ὁ μὲν γὰρ εἰς τὸ ἧπαρ κάθηται, ὁ δὲ τῇ καρδίᾳ
3 περιμαίνεται. ὅταν οὖν ἄμφω τὸν ἄνθρωπον
καταλάβωσι,[1] γίνεται μὲν αὐτοῖς ἡ ψυχὴ τρυτάνη, τὸ δὲ πῦρ ἑκατέρου ταλαντεύεται. μάχονται δὲ ἄμφω περὶ τῆς ῥοπῆς· καὶ τὰ πολλὰ
μὲν ὁ ἔρως εἴωθε νικᾶν, ὅταν εἰς τὴν ἐπιθυμίαν
εὐτυχῇ· ἢν δὲ αὐτὸν ἀτιμάσῃ τὸ ἐρώμενον, αὐτὸς
4 τὸν θυμὸν εἰς συμμαχίαν καλεῖ. κἀκεῖνος ὡς
γείτων πείθεται, καὶ ἀνάπτουσιν ἄμφω τὸ πῦρ.
ἂν δὲ ἅπαξ ὁ θυμὸς τὸν ἔρωτα παρ' αὐτῷ λάβῃ
καὶ τῆς οἰκείας ἕδρας ἐκπεσόντα κατάσχῃ, φύσει[2]
ὢν ἄσπονδος, οὐχ ὡς φίλῳ πρὸς τὴν ἐπιθυμίαν
συμμαχεῖ, ἀλλ' ὡς δ⟨οῦ⟩λον τῆς ἐπιθυμίας πεδήσας
κρατεῖ· οὐκ ἐπιτρέπει δὲ αὐτῷ σπείσασθαι πρὸς
5 τὸ ἐρώμενον, κἂν θέλῃ. ὁ δὲ τῷ θυμῷ βεβαπτισ-
μένος καταδύεται, καὶ εἰς τὴν ἰδίαν ἀρχὴν
ἐκπηδῆσαι θέλων, οὐκέτι ἐστὶν ἐλεύθερος, ἀλλὰ
μισεῖν ἀναγκάζεται τὸ φιλούμενον. ὅταν δὲ ὁ
θυμὸς καχλάζων γεμισθῇ, καὶ τῆς ἐξουσίας
ἐμφορηθεὶς ἀποβλύσῃ, κάμνει μὲν ἐκ τοῦ κόρου,
καμὼν δὲ παρίεται, καὶ ὁ ἔρως ἀμύνεται καὶ

[1] This word, like μάχονται below, is found in the singular
in the MSS. The plurals were restored by Cobet.
[2] The MSS. read φύσει τε. Hirschig deletes τε, but Jacobs
reads γε.

opposite as possible to the other in its nature, but of
equal strength. The one stirs up to hatred, the other
forces on to love; and near to each other are the
sources of both; the one has its seat in the bile,[1]
the other flutters madly round the heart. When
both these passions together attack a man, his soul
becomes a balance between them, with fire in either
of its scales; they fight as to which shall weigh
down the balance, and generally love wins, if it
attain the object of its desire; but if the beloved
scorn it, it calls in anger to be its ally; like a true
neighbour it responds to the call, and both combine
together in making the flames burn more fiercely.
But[2] if once anger, associating with love, has
driven it from its proper place and keeps it without,
it is an implacable foe, and will not fight together
with it as a friend with a view of accomplishing its
desire, but rather keeps it bound as its desire's serf;
it will not allow it, even though it be anxious to do so,
to come to terms with the beloved. Then love is overwhelmed by anger and sinks in its flood; and when
it wishes to revert to its former power, it is no longer
free, but is forced to hate the object of its affections.
Anger, however, first froths up to its full and has
complete fruition of its power; then it grows weary
and begins to weaken from satiety, and when the
weakening has once begun its power relaxes: then

---

[1] Literally, the liver. But the mention of that organ
seems medical, and almost ridiculous to our ears in such a
connexion.

[2] The whole of the rest of this chapter is a τόπος or patch,
half physiological and half psychological, of a character
extremely tiresome to modern readers. It is difficult to
translate into any English that does not appear to us ludicrous, and I have departed more than usual from a closely
literal rendering of the Greek.

ὁπλίζει τὴν ἐπιθυμίαν καὶ τὸν θυμὸν ἤδη καθεύ-
6 δοντα νικᾷ. ὁρῶν δὲ τὰς ὕβρεις, ἃς κατὰ τῶν
φιλτάτων ἐπαρῴνησεν, ἀλγεῖ, καὶ πρὸς τὸ ἐρώμενον ἀπολογεῖται, καὶ εἰς ὁμιλίαν παρακα-
λεῖ, καὶ τὸν θυμὸν ἐπαγγέλλεται καταμαλάττειν
7 ἡδονῇ. τυχὸν μὲν οὖν ὧν ἠθέλησεν, ἵλεως
γίνεται· ἀτιμούμενος δὲ πάλιν εἰς τὸν θυμὸν καταδύεται. ὁ δὲ καθεύδων ἐξεγείρεται καὶ τὰ ἀρχαῖα
ποιεῖ· ἀτιμίᾳ γὰρ ἔρωτος σύμμαχός ἐστι θυμός.
20. Ὁ Θέρσανδρος οὖν, τὸ μὲν πρῶτον ἐλπί-
ζων εἰς τὸν ἔρωτα εὐτυχήσειν, ὅλος Λευκίππης
δοῦλος ἦν· ἀτυχήσας δὲ ὧν ἤλπισεν, ἀφῆκε
τῷ θυμῷ τὰς ἡνίας.[1] ῥαπίζει δὴ κατὰ κόρρης
αὐτήν, "Ὦ κακόδαιμον ἀνδράποδον," λέγων,
"καὶ ἀληθῶς ἐρωτιῶν· πάντων γάρ σου κατή-
2 κουσα. οὐκ ἀγαπᾷς ὅτι σοι λαλῶ; καὶ μεγάλην
εὐτυχίαν δοκεῖς, τὸν σὸν καταφιλῆσαι δεσπότην,
ἀλλὰ ἀκκίζῃ καὶ σχηματίζῃ πρὸς ἀπόνοιαν; ἐγὼ
μέν σε καὶ πεπορνεῦσθαι δοκῶ· καὶ γὰρ μοιχὸν
3 φιλεῖς. ἀλλ' ἐπειδὴ μὴ θέλεις ἐραστοῦ μου
πεῖραν λαβεῖν, πειράσῃ δεσπότου." καὶ ἡ
Λευκίππη, "Κἂν τυραννεῖν ἐθέλῃς, κἀγὼ τυραν-
νεῖσθαι, πλὴν οὐ βιάσῃ." καὶ πρὸς τὸν Σωσθένην ἰδοῦσα, "Μαρτύρησον," εἶπεν αὐτῷ, "πῶς
πρὸς τὰς αἰκίας ἔχω· σὺ γάρ με καὶ μᾶλλον
4 ἠδίκησας." καὶ ὁ Σωσθένης αἰσχυνθεὶς ὡς
ἐληλεγμένος, "Ταύτην," εἶπεν, "ὦ δέσποτα,
ξανθῆναι μάστιξι δεῖ, καὶ μυρίαις βασάνοις

[1] Wyttenbach's correction for MSS. ἡδονάς.

love takes the offensive, puts desire into arms, and wins the mastery over anger which has already begun to doze. It sees the wrongs which it has done to those very dear to it in its moment of frenzy; it feels remorse, it expresses its sorrow to the beloved and issues a call to intimacy, promising to soften anger by the power of pleasure. If it gains the object of its desires, it becomes agreeable and gentle; but if it is once more rejected, it again takes refuge in anger, which is aroused from its slumbers and acts as it did before. Anger is the ally of love suffering under scorn.

20. Thersander then, when he first hoped to be successful in his passion, was wholly Leucippe's slave: but when he was disappointed of his hopes, he gave free rein to his anger. ". Wretched slave," he cried, striking her on the face, " miserable, love-sick girl; I heard all your ravings. Are you not delighted that I even speak to you? Do you not think it a great piece of good fortune to be able to kiss your master? No, instead of that, you give yourself airs and pretend that you are desperate. A harlot you must be, for it is an adulterer that you love. Since, then, you will not take me as a lover, you shall experience me as a master." " Very good," said Leucippe, " if you choose to play the tyrant, and I have to suffer your oppression; but you will never ravish me by violence. I call you to witness," she said, turning to Sosthenes, " how I bear outrage; your treatment of me has been still worse." Sosthenes, full of shame at being thus convicted of his wrong-doing, cried: " A good taste of the lash is what this trollop wants, and an experience of all

περιπεσεῖν, ὡς ἂν μάθῃ δεσπότου μὴ καταφρονεῖν."

21. "Πείσθητι τῷ Σωσθένει," φησὶν ἡ Λευκίππη· "συμβουλεύει γὰρ καλῶς. τὰς βασάνους παράστησον, φερέτω τροχόν· ἰδοὺ χεῖρες, τεινέτω. φερέτω καὶ μάστιγας· ἰδοὺ νῶτον, τυπτέτω. κομιζέτω πῦρ· ἰδοὺ σῶμα, καιέτω.
2 φερέτω καὶ σίδηρον· ἰδοὺ δέρη, σφαζέτω. ἀγῶνα θεάσασθε καινόν· πρὸς πάσας τὰς βασάνους ἀγωνίζεται μία γυνή, καὶ πάντα νικᾷ. εἶτα Κλειτοφῶντα μοιχὸν καλεῖς, αὐτὸς μοιχὸς ὤν; οὐδὲ τὴν Ἄρτεμιν, εἰπέ μοι, τὴν σὴν φοβῇ, ἀλλὰ βιάζῃ παρθένον ἐν πόλει παρθένου;
3 Δέσποινα, ποῦ σοῦ τὰ τόξα;" "Παρθένος;" εἶπεν ὁ Θέρσανδρος· "ὦ τόλμης καὶ γέλωτος· παρθένος τοσούτοις συννυκτερεύσασα πειραταῖς. εὐνοῦχοί σοι γεγόνασιν οἱ λῃσταί; φιλοσόφων ἦν τὸ πειρατήριον; οὐδεὶς ἐν αὐτοῖς εἶχεν ὀφθαλμούς;"

22. Καὶ ἡ Λευκίππη εἶπεν· "Εἰμὶ[1] παρθένος, καὶ μετὰ Σωσθένην· ἐπεὶ πυθοῦ Σωσθένους. οὗτος γὰρ ὄντως γέγονέ μοι[2] λῃστής· ἐκεῖνοι γὰρ ἦσαν ὑμῶν μετριώτεροι, καὶ οὐδεὶς αὐτῶν
2 ἦν οὕτως ὑβριστής. εἰ δὲ ὑμεῖς τοιαῦτα ποιεῖτε, ἀληθινὸν τοῦτο πειρατήριον. εἶτα οὐκ αἰσχύνεσθε ποιοῦντες ἃ μὴ τετολμήκασιν οἱ λῃσταί; λανθάνεις δὲ ἐγκώμιόν μοι διδοὺς πλεῖον διὰ

---

[1] MSS. εἰ, corrected by Jacobs. An alternative is to keep εἰ and put a comma after Σωσθένην, omitting the following ἐπεί: "Ask Sosthenes if I am still a virgin, even after passing through his hands." ἡ Lumb: ναὶ Wakefield.
[2] Corrected from μου by C. B. Hase.

kinds of tortures, until she learns not to look down
on her lord and master."

21. " You had better listen to Sosthenes," said
Leucippe; " he gives you admirable advice. Set
out your tortures, bring up the wheel. Here are my
arms,[1] stretch them out. Bring your scourges too:
here is my back, smite upon it. Bring your fire;
here is my body, burn it. Bring also the sword;
here is my neck, pierce it. Feast your eyes with
a new sight; one woman contends against all manner
of tortures, and overcomes all her trials. Then do
you dare to call Clitophon an adulterer when you
are an adulterer yourself? Tell me, pray, have you
no fear of your own patroness Artemis, that you
would ravish a virgin in the virgin's[2] city? Queen,
where are thy avenging arrows?" "Virgin indeed!"
cried Thersander. " The ridiculous impudence of the
baggage! You a virgin, who passed night after night
among a gang of pirates! I suppose your pirates
were eunuchs? Or was the pirates' lair a Sunday-
school? Or perhaps none of them had eyes?"

22. " Virgin I am," said Leucippe, " even after passing through Sosthenes' hands; if you do not believe
me, ask him. He was the real brigand to me: the
others had more command over their passions than both
of you, and none of them shewed the brutal lust that
you shew. If you behave like this, here is the
true pirates' lair. Do you feel no shame in acting
as the pirates never dared to act? You do not
seem to realize that by this very shamelessness

---

[1] The victim was "spread-eagled" on the wheel, the hands
and feet drawn as far apart as possible.
[2] Diana of the Ephesians, who was in reality rather, I
believe, a goddess of fertility than of chastity.

ταύτης σου τῆς ἀναισχυντίας· καὶ τις ἐρεῖ,
κἂν νῦν μαινόμενος φονεύσῃς· ʻΛευκίππη παρθένος μετὰ βουκόλους, παρθένος καὶ μετὰ Χαι-
3 ρέαν, παρθένος καὶ μετὰ Σωσθένην.' ἀλλὰ
μέτρια ταῦτα· τὸ δὲ μεῖζον ἐγκώμιον, ʻΚαὶ μετὰ
Θέρσανδρον παρθένος, τὸν καὶ λῃστῶν ἀσελγέ-
στερον· ἂν ὑβρίσαι μὴ δυνηθῇ, καὶ φονεύει.'
4 ὁπλίζου τοίνυν ἤδη, λάμβανε κατ' ἐμοῦ τὰς
μάστιγας, τὸν τροχόν, τὸ πῦρ, τὸν σίδηρον·
συστρατευέσθω δέ σοι καὶ ὁ σύμβουλος Σωσθένης. ἐγὼ δὲ καὶ γυμνή, καὶ μόνη, καὶ γυνή,[1] ἓν
ὅπλον ἔχω τὴν ἐλευθερίαν, ἣ μήτε πληγαῖς
κατακόπτεται, μήτε σιδήρῳ κατατέμνεται, μήτε
πυρὶ κατακαίεται. οὐκ ἀφήσω ποτὲ ταύτην ἐγώ·
κἂν καταφλέγῃς, οὐχ οὕτως θερμὸν εὑρήσεις τὸ
πῦρ."

---

[1] καί here follows in the MSS., and Jacobs was probably
right in omitting it.

ot yours, you are piling up the greater eulogies for
me; if you kill me now in your mad passion, people
will say; 'Here is Leucippe, who remained a virgin
after falling among buccaneers, who remained a virgin
after her abduction by Chaereas, who remained a
virgin after passing through the hands of Sosthenes!'
This would be but little; I shall have a still greater
meed of praise; 'She remained a virgin even after
her encounter with Thersander, who is more
lecherous than any robber; if he cannot gratify
his lust, he kills its object!' Take up then all your
instruments of torture, and at once; bring out against
me the scourges, the wheel, the fire, the sword,
and let Sosthenes, your counsellor, take the field
with you. I am defenceless, and alone, and a
woman; but one shield I have, and that is my free
soul, which cannot be subdued by the cutting of the
lash, or the piercing of the sword, or the burning of
the fire. That is a possession I will never surrender;
no, not I: and burn as you will, you will find that
there is no fire hot enough to consume it!"

Z

1. Ταῦτ᾽ ἀκούσας ὁ Θέρσανδρος παντοδαπὸς
ἦν· ἤχθετο, ὠργίζετο, ἐβουλεύετο. ὠργίζετο μέν,
ὡς ὑβρισμένος· ἤχθετο δέ, ὡς ἀποτυχών· ἐβουλεύετο δέ, ὡς ἐρῶν. τὴν οὖν ψυχὴν διασπώ-
μενος, οὐδὲν εἰπὼν πρὸς τὴν Λευκίππην, ἐξεπή-
2 δησεν. ὀργῇ μὲν δῆθεν ἐκδραμών, δοὺς δὲ τῇ ψυχῇ
σχολὴν εἰς τὴν διάκρισιν τῆς τρικυμίας, βουλευό-
μενος ἅμα τῷ Σωσθένει, πρόσεισι τῷ τῶν δεσμῶν ἄρχοντι, δεόμενος διαφθαρῆναί με φαρμάκῳ.
3 ὡς δὲ οὐκ ἔπειθεν (ἐδεδίει γὰρ τὴν πόλιν· καὶ
γὰρ ἄλλον ἄρχοντα πρὸ αὐτοῦ ληφθέντα τοιαύτην ἐργασάμενον φαρμακείαν ἀποθανεῖν) δευτέραν αὐτῷ προσφέρει δέησιν, ἐμβαλεῖν τινα
εἰς τὸ οἴκημα ἔνθα ἔτυχον δεδεμένος, ὡς δὴ
καὶ αὐτὸν ἕνα τῶν δεσμωτῶν, προσποιησάμενος
4 βούλεσθαι τἀμὰ δι᾽ ἐκείνου μαθεῖν. ἐπείσθη,
καὶ ἐδέξατο τὸν ἄνθρωπον. ἔμελλε δὲ ἐκεῖνος
ὑπὸ τοῦ Θερσάνδρου δεδιδαγμένος τεχνικῶς πάνυ
περὶ τῆς Λευκίππης λόγον ἐμβαλεῖν, ὡς εἴη
πεφονευμένη, τῆς Μελίτης συσκευασαμένης τὸν

---

[1] This is not quite a literal translation. τρικυμία is the
third wave, supposed to be bigger than the others, like our

348

BOOK VII

1. AT these words Thersander was utterly distracted : he felt grief, anger, and the need of taking
further counsel ; the first, for his insulting repulse ;
the second, for his ill-success in his desires ; and the
third, because he was still in love. His soul therefore torn every way, he made no reply to Leucippe,
but rushed from the hut. Although he flung away
in a passion, he then allowed his mind the leisure to
try to escape from the grievous quandary [1] in which
he found himself : and, after consulting Sosthenes, he
went to the chief gaoler and asked that I might be
put out of the way by means of poison. He could
not persuade him, because the gaoler was afraid of
the people's vengeance, a predecessor of his having
been found guilty of a similar poisoning and put to
death : so he made a second request, that he would
put a second inmate, in the guise of another
prisoner, into the cell where I was lying shackled,
with a view to learning my whole story by means of
confidences made to him. The gaoler agreed, and
the man was sent : he had had full instructions from
Thersander, and he was to relate to me a story most
artfully composed about Leucippe, to the effect that
she had been killed by the contrivance of Melite.

seventh and the Romans' tenth ; but the word here refers to
the three emotions described as distracting Thersander at
the beginning of the chapter.

5 φόνον. τὸ δὲ τέχνασμα ἦν τῷ Θερσάνδρῳ[1]
εὑρεθέν, ὡς ἂν ἀπογνοὺς ἐγὼ μηκέτι ζῶσαν τὴν
ἐρωμένην, κἂν τὴν δίκην φύγοιμι, μὴ πρὸς
6 ζήτησιν αὐτῆς ἔτι τραποίμην. προσέκειτο δὲ ἡ
Μελίτη τῷ φόνῳ, ἵνα μή, τετελευτηκέναι τὴν
Λευκίππην δοκῶν, τὴν Μελίτην γήμας ὡς ἂν
ἐρῶσαν, αὐτοῦ μένοιμι, κἀκ τούτου παρέχοιμί
τινα φόβον αὐτῷ τοῦ μὴ μετ' ἀδείας Λευκίππην
ἔχειν, ἀλλὰ μισήσας, ὡς τὸ εἰκός, τὴν Μελίτην,
ὡς ἂν ἀποκτείνασάν μου τὴν ἐρωμένην, ἀπαλ-
λαγείην ἐκ τῆς πόλεως τὸ παράπαν.
2. Ὡς οὖν ὁ ἄνθρωπος ἐγένετό μου πλησίον, καὶ
τοῦ δράματος ἤρχετο· ἀνοιμώξας γὰρ πάνυ
κακούργως, "Τίνα βίον," ἔφη, "βιωσόμεθα ἔτι;
καὶ τίνα φυλαξόμεθα πρὸς ἀκίνδυνον ζωήν; οὐ
γὰρ αὐτάρκης ἡμῖν ὁ δίκαιος τρόπος. ἐμπίπ-
τουσαι δὲ αἱ τύχαι βαπτίζουσιν ἡμᾶς. ἔδει γάρ
με μαντεύσασθαι, τίς ἦν ὁ συμβαδίζων μοι, καὶ τί
2 πεπραχὼς εἴη." καθ' ἑαυτὸν δὲ ταῦτα ἔλεγε καὶ
τὰ τοιαῦτα, ζητῶν ἀρχὴν τῆς ἐπ' ἐμὲ τοῦ λόγου
3 τέχνης, ὡς ἂν πυθοίμην τί εἴη παθών. ἀλλ' ἐγὼ
μὲν ἐφρόντιζον ὧν[2] ᾤμωζεν ὀλίγον, ἄλλος δέ τις
τῶν συνδεδεμένων (περίεργον γὰρ ἄνθρωπος
ἀτυχῶν εἰς ἀλλοτρίων ἀκρόασιν κακῶν· ἐπεὶ
φάρμακον αὐτῷ τοῦτο τῆς ὧν ἔπαθε λύπης ἡ πρὸς
ἄλλον εἰς τὸ παθεῖν κοινωνία) "Τί δέ σοι συμ-
4 βέβηκεν," εἶπεν, "ἀπὸ τῆς Τύχης; εἰκὸς γάρ σε
μηδὲν ἀδικήσαντα πονηρῷ περιπεσεῖν δαίμονι.
τεκμαίρομαι δὲ ἐκ τῶν ἐμαυτοῦ." καὶ ἅμα τὰ

---

[1] τό preceded εὑρεθέν in the MSS., but it was rightly
omitted by Cobet. Castiglioni suggests ⟨τοῦ⟩το.
[2] Some MSS. here follow with κατὰ νοῦν εἶχον ὁ δέ, but it
is better omitted.

The plot was composed by Thersander with this object: that if I were acquitted at my trial, I should believe that my loved one existed no more, and should therefore make no efforts to look for her; and Melite was associated with her murder, so that I might not marry Melite with the idea that she was still in love with me, thinking that Leucippe was dead, and so remain in the town and give constant anxiety to Thersander and prevent him from enjoying Leucippe at his ease, but should rather, as was natural, detest Melite as the cause of my darling's murder, and leave Ephesus once and for all.

2. So the fellow became my cell-mate and began to play the part that had been taught him. Heaving a simulated groan, "What kind of life," he said, "am I to live in future? How can I direct my course so as to be out of danger? An honest life has by itself done me no good at all : evil fortune has overwhelmed me, and the waters of fate are closing over my head. I suppose I ought to have guessed the kind of man my fellow-traveller was, and the sort of things he had been doing." This he murmured to himself and other phrases like it, trying to get a conversation begun with me, so that I should ask him what his trouble was. However, I paid little attention to what he said between his groans; but one of our fellow-prisoners (for in misfortune man is a creature always inquisitive to hear about another's woes; community of suffering is something of a medicine for one's own troubles), said to him : "What was the prank that Fortune played you ? I dare say you met with a piece of bad luck, and did nothing wrong, if I may judge from my own misfortunes." So saying, he related his own story, the

οἰκεῖα κατέλεγεν, ἐφ' οἷς ἦν δεδεμένος· ἐγὼ δὲ
οὐδενὶ τούτων προσεῖχον.

3. Ὡς δὲ ἐπαύσατο, τὴν ἀντίδοσιν ᾔτει τοῦ
λόγου τῶν ἀτυχημάτων, " Λέγοις ἄν," εἰπών,
" καὶ σὺ τὰ σαυτοῦ." ὁ δέ, " Βαδίζων ἔτυχον,"
εἶπε, " τὴν ἐξ ἄστεος χθές· ἐπορευόμην [1] δὲ τὴν
2 ἐπὶ τῆς Σμύρνης ὁδόν. προελθόντι δέ μοι σταδίους τέτταρας, νεανίσκος ἐκ τῶν ἀγρῶν προσελθὼν καὶ προσειπὼν καὶ πρὸς μικρὸν συμβαδίσας,
'Ποῖ,' ἔφη, 'ἔχεις τὴν ὁδόν;' 'Ἐπὶ Σμύρνης,'
εἶπον. 'Κἀγώ,' ἔφη, 'τὴν αὐτήν, ἀγαθῇ τύχῃ.'
τοὐντεῦθεν ἐπορευόμεθα κοινῇ, καὶ διελεγόμεθα
3 οἷα εἰκὸς ἐν ὁδῷ. ὡς δὲ εἴς τι πανδοκεῖον ἤλθομεν,
ἠριστῶμεν ἅμα· κατὰ ταὐτὸ δὲ παρακαθίζουσιν
ἡμῖν τινὲς τέτταρες, καὶ προσεποιοῦντο μὲν
ἀριστᾶν κἀκεῖνοι, ἐνεώρων δὲ ἡμῖν πυκνὰ καὶ
4 ἀλλήλοις ἐπένευον. ἐγὼ μὲν οὖν ὑπώπτευον τοὺς
ἀνθρώπους διανοεῖσθαι εἰς ἡμᾶς, οὐ μὴν ἠδυνάμην
συνιέναι τί αὐτοῖς ἐθέλει τὰ νεύματα· ὁ δὲ ὠχρὸς
ἐγίνετο κατὰ μικρὸν καὶ ὀκνηρότερον ἤσθιεν, ἤδη
5 δὲ καὶ τρόμος εἶχεν αὐτόν. ὡς δὲ ταῦτα εἶδον,
ἀναπηδήσαντες συλλαμβάνουσιν ἡμᾶς καὶ ἱμᾶσιν
εὐθὺς δεσμεύουσι· παίει δὲ κατὰ κόρρης τις
ἐκεῖνον· καὶ παταχθείς, ὥσπερ βασάνους παθὼν
μυρίας, καταλέγει μηδενὸς ἐρωτῶντος αὐτόν· 'Ἐγὼ
τὴν κόρην ἀπέκτεινα, καὶ ἔλαβον χρυσοῦς ἑκατὸν
παρὰ Μελίτης τῆς Θερσάνδρου γυναικός· αὕτη
6 γάρ με ἐπὶ τὸν φόνον ἐμισθώσατο. ἀλλ' ἰδοὺ
τοὺς χρυσοῦς ὑμῖν τοὺς ἑκατὸν φέρω· ὥστε τί
με ἀπόλλυτε [2] καὶ ἑαυτοῖς φθονεῖτε κέρδους;'"

Ἐγὼ δὲ ὡς ἤκουσα Θερσάνδρου καὶ Μελίτης

---

[1] So Cobet: ἐποιούμην.   [2] ⟨οὐκ⟩ ἀπολύετε Merkelbach.

reason why he was in prison. However, I paid no attention to any of his talk.

3. This concluded, he asked the other for the story of his troubles: " Now do you," said he, " relate what happened to you." " I happened yesterday," replied the other, " to be leaving the town on foot; I was proceeding on the road to Smyrna. When I had gone about half a mile, a young man from the country came up: he hailed me and accompanied me a little way. ' Where are you going?' said he. ' To Smyrna,' said I. ' So am I,' he said, ' by good luck.' So from there we went on together, and there passed between us the usual conversation of people journeying together, and when we arrived at an inn, we took our mid-day meal in one another's company. Then four fellows came and sat down with us: they too pretended to eat, but they kept casting glances at us and nodding and winking at each other. I suspected that they entertained some bad purpose against us, but I could not understand what their signs and nods meant: my companion, however, began to turn pale and ate more and more slowly, and was finally overcome with a fit of trembling. When they saw this, the men jumped up, and, over-powering us, quickly tied us up with leather thongs: one of them struck my companion on the head, and he, as if he had experienced a thousand tortures, began to blurt out, though no one had questioned him: ' Yes, I killed the girl, and took the bribe of a hundred pieces of gold from Melite, Thersander's wife, which was the hire she gave me for the crime. Here is the money: why be the death of me and deprive yourselves of this chance of gain?' "

I had not been attending previously, but when I

τοὔνομα, τὸν ἄλλον οὐ προσέχων χρόνον, τῷ δὲ
λόγῳ τὴν ψυχὴν ὥσπερ ὑπὸ μύωπος παταχθείς,
ἐγείρω καὶ πρὸς αὐτὸν μεταστραφεὶς λέγω· " Τίς
ἡ Μελίτη"; ὁ δέ, " Μελίτη ἐστίν," ἔφη, " τῶν
7 ἐνταῦθα πρώτη γυναικῶν. αὕτη νεανίσκου τινὸς
ἠράσθη· Τύριον, οἶμαι, φασὶν αὐτόν· κἀκεῖνος
ἔτυχεν ἐρωμένην ἔχων, ἣν εὗρεν ἐν τῇ τῆς
Μελίτης οἰκίᾳ πεπραμένην. ἡ δὲ ὑπὸ ζηλοτυπίας
πεφλεγμένη τὴν γυναῖκα ταύτην ἀπατήσασα
συλλαμβάνει καὶ παραδίδωσι ᾧ νῦν ἔφην [1] κακῇ
8 τύχῃ μοι συνωδευκότι, φονεῦσαι κελεύσασα. ὁ
μὲν οὖν τὸ ἀνόσιον ἔργον τοῦτο δρᾷ· ἐγὼ δὲ ὁ
ἄθλιος, οὔτε ἰδὼν αὐτόν, οὔτε ἔργου τινὸς κοινω-
νήσας ἢ λόγου, συναπηγόμην αὐτῷ δεδεμένος, ὡς
τοῦ ἔργου κοινωνός. τὸ δὲ χαλεπώτερον, μικρὸν
τοῦ πανδοκείου προελθόντες, τοὺς ἑκατὸν χρυσοῦς
λαβόντες παρ' αὐτοῦ, τὸν μὲν ἀφῆκαν φυγεῖν,
ἐμὲ δὲ ἄγουσι πρὸς τὸν στρατηγόν."

4. Ὡς δὲ ἤκουσά μου τὸν μῦθον τῶν κακῶν,
οὔτε ἀνῴμωξα οὔτε ἔκλαυσα· οὔτε γὰρ φωνὴν
εἶχον οὔτε δάκρυα· ἀλλὰ τρόμος μὲν εὐθὺς
περιεχύθη μου τῷ σώματι καὶ ἡ καρδία μου
ἐλέλυτο, ὀλίγον δέ τί μοι τῆς ψυχῆς ὑπελέλειπτο.
2 μικρὸν δὲ νήψας ἐκ τῆς μέθης τοῦ λόγου, " Τίνα
τρόπον τὴν κόρην," ἔφην, " ἀπέκτεινεν ὁ μισθωτός,
καὶ τί πεποίηκε τὸ σῶμα;" ὁ δὲ ὡς ἅπαξ ἐνέβαλέ

---

[1] ᾧ νῦν ἔφην MSS. (ἔφη cod. M): ὡς νῦν ἐφάνη Jacobs: τῷ νῦν
δὴ Cobet: τῷ νῦν ἐπὶ Lumb.

heard the names of Thersander and Melite, I
started up, seeming to be stung to the heart by
what he said as though by the sting of a gadfly:
and I turned to him and said, " Who is Melite ? "
" Melite," said he, " is a lady of the highest rank
among those of this place. She was in love with
a certain young man—a Tyrian, they say—and
this Tyrian happened to be in love with a girl whom
he afterwards found as a bought slave in Melite's
house. She, fired by jealousy, got hold of this
girl by fraud and handed her over to the man who
I just said travelled with me (to my bad luck),
bidding him put her out of the way. He did indeed
commit the crime : but the unhappy I, who had
never even seen him or taken any part with him in
word or deed, was now being dragged away with
him as if I were an accomplice. Worse still, when
we had gone a little way from the inn, those who
had arrested us accepted his hundred pieces of gold
and let him go, while they dragged me hither before
the magistrate."

4. When I heard this trumped-up story of woe, I
did not cry aloud nor weep; for I had neither voice
nor tears in me. At once a great trembling took
hold of all my body; my heart seemed turned to
water, and I felt that there was but little of my
spirit left in me. When I was slightly recovered
from the paralysis[1] occasioned by his story, I
questioned him: " How did the hired murderer
kill the girl, and what did he do with her body ?"
He, the sting once fairly planted and the work done

[1] The literal meaning of the Greek is " when I was something sobered from the intoxication caused by his story " :
but we use the metaphor of intoxication rather about joy
than about grief.

μοι τὸν μύωπα, καὶ ἔργον εἰργάσατο οὕτω κατ'
ἐμοῦ δι' ὃ παρῆν, ἐσιώπα καὶ ἔλεγεν οὐδέν.
3 πάλιν δέ μου πυθομένου, " Δοκεῖς," ἔφη, " κἀμὲ
κεκοινωνηκέναι τῷ φόνῳ; ταῦτα ἤκουσα μόνα τοῦ
πεφονευκότος, ὡς κτείνας εἴη τὴν κόρην· ποῦ δὲ
καὶ τίνα τρόπον, οὐκ εἶπεν." ἐπῆλθε[1] δέ μοι
τότε δάκρυα καὶ τοῖς ὀφθαλμοῖς τὴν λύπην
4 ἀπεδίδουν. ὥσπερ γὰρ ἐν ταῖς τοῦ σώματος
πληγαῖς οὐκ εὐθὺς ἡ σμῶδιξ ἐπανίσταται, ἀλλὰ
παραχρῆμα μὲν οὐκ ἔχει τὸ ἄνθος ἡ πληγή, μετὰ
μικρὸν δὲ ἀνέθορε· καὶ ὀδόντι συός τις παταχθεὶς
εὐθὺς μὲν ζητεῖ τὸ τραῦμα, καὶ οὐκ οἶδεν εὑρεῖν,
τὸ δὲ ἔτι δέδυκε καὶ κέκρυπται κατειργασμένον
σχολῇ τῆς πληγῆς τὴν τομήν· μετὰ ταῦτα δὲ
ἐξαίφνης λευκή τις ἀνέτειλε γραμμή, πρόδρομος
τοῦ αἵματος,[2] σχολὴν δὲ ὀλίγην λαβὸν ἔρχεται
5 καὶ ἀθρόον ἐπιρρεῖ· οὕτω καὶ ψυχὴ παταχθεῖσα
τῷ τῆς λύπης βέλει, τοξεύσαντος λόγου, τέτρωται
μὲν ἤδη καὶ ἔχει τὴν τομήν, ἀλλὰ τὸ τάχος τοῦ
βλήματος οὐκ ἀνέῳξεν οὔπω τὸ τραῦμα, τὰ δὲ
δάκρυα ἐδίωξε τῶν ὀφθαλμῶν μακράν. δάκρυον
γὰρ αἷμα τραύματος ψυχῆς· ὅταν ὁ τῆς λύπης
ὀδοὺς κατὰ μικρὸν τὴν καρδίαν ἐκφάγῃ, κατέρ-
ρηκται μὲν τῆς ψυχῆς τὸ τραῦμα, ἀνέῳκται δὲ
τοῖς ὀφθαλμοῖς ἡ τῶν δακρύων θύρα, τὰ δὲ μετὰ
6 μικρὸν τῆς ἀνοίξεως ἐξεπήδησεν. οὕτω κἀμὲ[3]
τὰ μὲν πρῶτα τῆς ἀκροάσεως τῇ ψυχῇ προσπε-
σόντα, καθάπερ[4] τοξεύματα, κατεσίγασε καὶ

---

[1] The simple verb ἦλθε, as found in the MSS., can hardly
stand. ἐπῆλθε is Cobet's suggestion.
[2] Hirschig's certain correction for the τραύματος of the
MSS.

for which he was sent to the prison, kept silence
and answered me not a word. When I asked again,
"Do you think," said he, "that I was an accessory in
the murder? All I heard from the miscreant was,
that he had killed the girl: he did not tell me
where or how." Then came a flood of tears,
making a vent for my grief through my eyes. It is
like bodily blows—the weal does not come up at
once; the bruise does not show directly after the
stroke, but comes out suddenly after a little while.
If a man gets a slash from a boar's tusk he looks at
once to find the wound but cannot find it, because
it is deep-set, and, far down in the flesh, has slowly
completed the incision made by the blow; but then
suddenly a white streak appears, the precursor of
the blood, which after a short interval wells to the
surface and flows in abundance. Just in the same
way, when the soul is smitten by the dart of grief,
the spoken word directing the arrow, it receives the
cutting wound: but the rapidity of the blow prevents
the wound at first from opening, and keeps the tears
far from the eyes. Tears may be considered the
blood that flows from the wound of the soul: and
after the biting tooth of grief has been for some
time gnawing at the heart, only then does the soul's
wound begin to gape, and the portal of tears open
in the eyes, and they gush out directly it is opened.
So in my case; the news, attacking my soul like an
arrow, had struck it to silence and shut off the fount

---

³ This word is governed by κατεσίγασε, and must thus be
in the accusative, as Hercher suggested, instead of the
dative κἀμοί of the MSS.

⁴ τοξεύματα has the definite article τά in the MSS. It was
rightly expunged by Jacobs.

τῶν δακρύων ἀπέφραξε τὴν πηγήν, μετὰ ταῦτα
δὲ ἔρρει, σχολασάσης τῆς ψυχῆς τῶν κακῶν.

5. Ἔλεγον οὖν· "Τίς με δαίμων ἐξηπάτησεν
ὀλίγῃ χαρᾷ; τίς μοι Λευκίππην ἔδειξεν εἰς καινὴν
ὑπόθεσιν συμφορῶν; ἀλλ᾽ οὐδὲ ἐκόρεσά μου τοὺς
ὀφθαλμούς, οἷς μόνοις ηὐτύχησα, οὐδὲ ἐνεπλήσθην
κἂν βλέπων. ἀληθής μοι γέγονεν ὀνείρων ἡδονή.
2 οἴμοι, Λευκίππη, ποσάκις μοι τέθνηκας. μὴ γὰρ
θρηνῶν ἀνεπαυσάμην; ἀεί σε πενθῶ, τῶν θανάτων
διωκόντων ἀλλήλους; ἀλλ᾽ ἐκείνους μὲν πάντας
ἡ Τύχη ἔπαιξε κατ᾽ ἐμοῦ· οὗτος δὲ οὔκ ἐστι τῆς
3 Τύχης ἔτι παιδιά. πῶς ἄρα μοι, Λευκίππη,
τέθνηκας; ἐν μὲν γὰρ τοῖς ψευδέσι θανάτοις
ἐκείνοις παρηγορίαν εἶχον ὀλίγην· τὸ μὲν πρῶτον,
ὅλον σου τὸ σῶμα, τὸ δὲ δεύτερον, κἂν τὴν
κεφαλὴν δοκῶν μὴ ἔχειν εἰς τὴν ταφήν· νῦν δὲ
τέθνηκας θάνατον διπλοῦν, ψυχῆς καὶ σώματος.
δύο ἐξέφυγες λῃστήρια, τὸ δὲ τῆς Μελίτης
4 πεφόνευκέ σε πειρατήριον. ὁ δὲ ἀνόσιος καὶ
ἀσεβὴς ἐγὼ τὴν ἀνδροφόνον σου κατεφίλησα
πολλάκις καὶ συνεπλάκην μεμιασμένας συμπλο-
κάς, καὶ τὴν Ἀφροδίτης χάριν αὐτῇ παρέσχον πρὸ
σοῦ."

6. Μεταξὺ δέ μου θρηνοῦντος Κλεινίας εἰσέρχεται, καὶ καταλέγω τὸ πᾶν αὐτῷ, καὶ ὅτι
μοι δέδοκται πάντως ἀποθανεῖν. ὁ δὲ παρεμυθεῖτο·
2 "Τίς γὰρ οἶδεν, εἰ ζῇ πάλιν; μὴ γὰρ οὐ πολλάκις

of tears; but afterwards, when it had lain quiet for a time under its woe, they began to flow.

5. I began therefore thus to commune with myself: "What god is it that has thus cheated me by a few moments of joy, and let me have just a glance at Leucippe only to form a new starting-point for miseries? I did not even satisfy my eyes—they were as far as my happiness extended—and take my fill even of gazing at her: all my happiness has been no more than that of a dream. Alas, Leucippe, how often have I seen you die! Have I ever been able to cease from bewailing you? Am I always to be mourning you, one death coming hot upon the heels of another? Yet on all the former occasions Fate was but playing a bad joke on me: this time she is jesting no longer. And now how wholly have I lost you! Each time then, when you falsely seemed to die, I had at least a little consolation; the first time, your whole corpse at least I thought I had, and the second time, all but your head, for me to bury: but now you have died a double death, life and body too. Two brigands' bands did you escape, and now the contrivance of Melite, a very pirate-venture of her own, has been your destruction. Accursed and wicked I, that kissed your murderess time and again, that joined with her in a crime-stained embrace, and that imparted to her, before you, the joys of Aphrodite!"

6. As I was thus making moan, in came Clinias, and I related the whole story to him, telling him at the same time that I was resolved on self-destruction. He did his best to comfort me: "Who can know," he said, "but that she will come to life again? Has she not died more than once and more than

τέθνηκε; μὴ γὰρ οὐ πολλάκις ἀνεβίω; τί δὲ προπετῶς ἀποθνήσκεις; ὃ καὶ κατὰ σχολὴν ἔξεστιν,
ὅταν μάθῃς σαφῶς τὸν θάνατον αὐτῆς." "Ληρεῖς·
3 τούτου γὰρ ἀσφαλέστερον πῶς ἂν μάθοις; δοκῶ
δέ εὑρηκέναι τοῦ θανάτου καλλίστην ὁδόν, δι' ἧς
οὐδὲ ἡ θεοῖς ἐχθρὰ Μελίτη παντάπασιν ἀθῴως
ἀπαλλάξεται. ἄκουσον δὲ τὸν τρόπον. παρε-
σκευασάμην, ὡς οἶδας, πρὸς τὴν ἀπολογίαν τῆς
μοιχείας, εἰ κληρωθείη τὸ δικαστήριον. νῦν δέ
μοι δέδοκται πᾶν τοὐναντίον, καὶ τὴν μοιχείαν
ὁμολογεῖν, καὶ ὡς ἀλλήλων ἐρῶντες ἐγώ τε καὶ
4 Μελίτη κοινῇ τὴν Λευκίππην ἀνῃρήκαμεν. οὕτω
γὰρ κἀκείνη δίκην δώσει, κἀγὼ τὸν ἐπάρατον
βίον καταλίποιμ' ἄν.[1]" "Εὐφήμησον," ὁ Κλεινίας
ἔφη· "καὶ τολμήσεις οὕτως ἐπὶ τοῖς αἰσχίστοις
ἀποθανεῖν, νομιζόμενος φονεύς, καὶ ταῦτα Λευκίππης;" "Οὐδέν," εἶπον, "αἰσχρόν, ὃ λυπεῖ
5 τὸν ἐχθρόν." καὶ ἡμεῖς ἐν τούτοις ἦμεν, τὸν δὲ
ἄνθρωπον ἐκεῖνον, τὸν μηνυτὴν τοῦ ψευδοῦς φόνου,
μετὰ μικρὸν ἀπολύει ὁ ἐπὶ[2] τῶν δεσμῶν, φάσκων
τὸν ἄρχοντα κελεῦσαι κομίζειν αὐτὸν δώσοντα
6 λόγον ὧν αἰτίαν ἔσχεν. ἐμὲ δὲ παρηγόρει Κλεινίας
καὶ ὁ Σάτυρος, εἴ πως δύναιντο πεῖσαι, μηδὲν ὧν
διενοήθην εἰς τὴν δίκην εἰπεῖν· ἀλλ' ἐπέραινον
οὐδέν. ἐκείνην μὲν οὖν τὴν ἡμέραν καταγωγήν
τινα μισθωσάμενοι κατῳκίσαντο, ὡς ἂν μηκέτι
παρὰ τῷ τῆς Μελίτης εἶεν συντρόφῳ.

[1] ἄν added by Jacobs, perhaps needlessly.
[2] ὁ ἐπί, though necessary to the sense, is not found in the
MSS. Its insertion is due to a friend of Schaefer's.

once been restored to life? Why so rashly resolve to die? There is plenty of time to do so at leisure, when you know for certain that she is dead." "Your talk is folly," said I: "how could one possibly learn anything with greater certainty than this? But I think I have found the best way to put an end to myself, and by it that accursed Melite too will not escape altogether without vengeance. Listen to my plan. I had resolved, as you know, if my case came into court, to put up a defence against the charge of adultery. But I have now determined to act in a precisely contrary manner—to confess the truth of the charge, and to add that Melite and I, deeply in love with one another, made the plot for the murder of Leucippe. Thus she too will be condemned, and I shall have a chance of getting rid of my life which I now but execrate." "Speak not so,[1]" said Clinias. "What? Could you bear to be condemned to death on the vilest of all charges, reputed a murderer and that the murderer of Leucippe?" "Nothing," I answered, "is vile that hurts the enemy." Shortly after we were engaged upon these discussions the chief gaoler removed the fellow who had been sent to tell the story of the sham murder, on the pretext that the magistrate had ordered him to be fetched to answer to the charges made against him. Clinias and Satyrus did their very best to dissuade me from my purpose, exhorting me to make no such statement as I had intended at my trial: but their efforts were of no avail. They therefore on the same day hired a lodging and took up their abode there, so as no longer to be living with Melite's foster-brother.

[1] Either "speak words of better omen," or "be silent."

ACHILLES TATIUS

7. Τῇ δὲ ὑστεραίᾳ ἀπηγόμην ἐπὶ τὸ δικαστήριον. παρασκευὴ δὲ πολλὴ ἦν τοῦ Θερσάνδρου κατ' ἐμοῦ, καὶ πλῆθος ῥητόρων οὐχ ἧττον δέκα· καὶ τῆς Μελίτης σπουδῇ πρὸς τὴν ἀπολογίαν παρε-
2 σκεύαστο. ἐπεὶ δὲ ἐπαύσαντο λέγοντες, αἰτήσας κἀγὼ λόγον, " Ἀλλ' οὗτοι μέν," ἔφην, " ληροῦσι πάντες, καὶ οἱ Θερσάνδρῳ καὶ οἱ Μελίτῃ συνει-πόντες· ἐγὼ δὲ πᾶσαν ὑμῖν ἐρῶ τὴν ἀλήθειαν.
3 ἦν ἐρωμένη μοι πάλαι Βυζαντία μὲν γένος, Λευκίππη δὲ τοὔνομα. ταύτην τεθνάναι δοκῶν, ἥρπαστο γὰρ ὑπὸ λῃστῶν ἐν Αἰγύπτῳ, Μελίτῃ περιτυγχάνω, κἀκεῖθεν ἀλλήλοις συνόντες, ἥκομεν ἐνταῦθα κοινῇ καὶ τὴν Λευκίππην εὑρίσκομεν Σωσθένει δουλεύουσαν, διοικητῇ τινὶ τῶν Θερ-
4 σάνδρου χωρίων. ὅπως δὲ τὴν ἐλευθέραν ὁ Σω-σθένης εἶχε δούλην, ἢ τίς ἡ κοινωνία τοῖς λῃσταῖς πρὸς αὐτόν, ὑμῖν καταλείπω σκοπεῖν. ἐπεὶ τοίνυν ἔμαθεν ἡ Μελίτη τὴν προτέραν εὑρόντα με γυναῖκα, φοβηθεῖσα μὴ πρὸς αὐτὴν ἀποκλίναιμι τὸν νοῦν, συμβουλεύεται τὴν ἄνθρωπον ἀνελεῖν.
5 κἀμοὶ συνεδόκει, (τί γὰρ οὐ δεῖ τἀληθῆ λέγειν;) ἐπεὶ τῶν αὐτῆς με κύριον ἀποφανεῖν [1] ὑπισχνεῖτο. μισθοῦμαι ἕνα δή τινα πρὸς τὸν φόνον· ἑκατὸν δὲ ὁ μισθὸς ἦν τοῦ φόνου χρυσοῖ. καὶ ὁ μὲν δὴ τὸ ἔργον δράσας οἴχεται, κἀκ τότε γέγονεν ἀφανής·
6 ἐμὲ δὲ ὁ ἔρως εὐθὺς ἠμύνατο. ὡς γὰρ ἔμαθον ἀνῃρημένην, μετενόουν καὶ ἔκλαιον καὶ ἤρων καὶ νῦν ἐρῶ. διὰ τοῦτο ἐμαυτοῦ κατεῖπον, ἵνα με

---

[1] Cobet's correction for MSS. ἀποφαίνειν.

7. On the following day I was taken to the court. Thersander had made a great show in his appearance against me, and had an array of no less than ten counsel, and every preparation for her defence had been made with great care by Melite. When they had all finished their speeches, I asked to be allowed to speak too. " Every word," said I, " that has been spoken by these lawyers, both those appearing for Thersander and for Melite, is pure nonsense. I will declare to you the whole true story. Long ago I was in love with a maiden; she was a Byzantine by birth, and her name was Leucippe. I believed that she was dead—she had been carried off by brigands in Egypt—and then fell in with Melite. A familiarity grew up between us, and from that country we came together hither, where we found Leucippe in the position of a slave belonging to Sosthenes, who was one of the bailiffs of Thersander's country estates. How Sosthenes had obtained this free girl as a slave, and what were his relations with the brigands, I leave you to investigate. Now when Melite learned that I had found my former mistress, she was afraid that I should again become attached to her, and began to plot to put her out of the way. I fell in with her schemes— there is nothing that stops me from revealing the truth—because she promised to make me lord and master of all her substance. I therefore hired a fellow to commit the murder; the price of it was a hundred pieces of gold. After his crime, he escaped, and from that time nothing more has been heard of him; as for me, love soon took its revenge: I felt remorse, I bewailed my crime ; I was in love with her and I still am. This is the reason that I have accused

πέμψητε πρὸς τὴν ἐρωμένην. οὐ γὰρ φέρω νῦν
ζῆν, καὶ μιαιφόνος γενόμενος, καὶ φιλῶν ἣν
ἀπέκτεινα."

8. Ταῦτα εἰπόντος ἐμοῦ, πάντας ἔκπληξις κατ-
έσχε ἐπὶ τῷ παραλόγῳ τοῦ πράγματος, μάλιστα
δὲ τὴν Μελίτην. καὶ οἱ μὲν τοῦ Θερσάνδρου
ῥήτορες μεθ᾽ ἡδονῆς ἀνεβόησαν ἐπινίκιον· οἱ δὲ
τῆς Μελίτης ἀνεπύθοντο τί ταῦτα εἴη τὰ λεχθέντα.
2 ἡ δὲ τὰ μὲν ἐτεθορύβητο, τὰ δὲ ἠρνεῖτο, τὰ δὲ
διηγεῖτο σπουδῇ μάλα καὶ σαφῶς, τὴν μὲν
Λευκίππην εἰδέναι λέγουσα, καὶ ὅσα εἶπον, ἀλλὰ
τόν γε φόνον οὔ· ὥστε κἀκείνους, διὰ τὸ τὰ πλείω
μοι συνᾴδειν, ὑπόνοιαν ἔχειν κατὰ τῆς Μελίττης,
καὶ ἀπορεῖν ὅτῳ χρήσαιντο λόγῳ πρὸς τὴν
ἀπολογίαν.

9 Ἐν τούτῳ δὲ ὁ Κλεινίας, θορύβου πολλοῦ
κατὰ τὸ δικαστήριον ὄντος, ἀνελθών, " Κἀμοί
τινα λόγον," εἶπε, "συγχωρήσατε· περὶ γὰρ
2 ψυχῆς ἀνδρὸς ὁ ἀγών." ὡς δὲ ἔλαβε, δακρύων
γεμισθείς, "Ἄνδρες," εἶπεν, "Ἐφέσιοι, μὴ προπετῶς καταγνῶτε θάνατον ἀνδρὸς ἐπιθυμοῦντος
ἀποθανεῖν, ὅπερ φύσει τῶν ἀτυχούντων ἐστὶ
φάρμακον· κατέψευσται γὰρ ἑαυτοῦ τὴν τῶν
ἀδικούντων αἰτίαν, ἵνα πάθῃ τὴν τῶν δυστυχούν-
3 των τιμωρίαν. ἃ δὲ ἠτύχησε διὰ βραχέων ἐρῶ.
ἐρωμένην εἶχεν, ὡς εἶπεν· τοῦτο γὰρ οὐκ ἐψεύ-
σατο· καὶ ὅτι λῃσταὶ ταύτην ἥρπασαν, καὶ τὰ
περὶ Σωσθένους, καὶ πάνθ᾽ ὅσα πρὸ τοῦ φόνου
4 διηγήσατο, πέπρακται τὸν τρόπον τοῦτον. αὕτη

myself, that you may send me after her whom I love. I can bear life no longer—I who am a murderer and still in love with the maiden whom I slew."

8. At this speech of mine all in court were struck dumb with astonishment at the extraordinary turn affairs had taken, Melite most of all. Thersander's advocates were already joyfully upraising a paean of triumph, while Melite's questioned her as to the statements that had been made. At some she professed to be overcome with surprise and distress; some she denied, others she confessed openly and clearly; she said that she knew Leucippe, and admitted the truth of what I said, except as regards the murder; to such an extent that her counsel, on account of most of her statements corroborating mine, began to suspect that she might indeed be guilty, and were at a great loss what arguments to use in her defence.

9. While the whole court was becoming a place of uproar, Clinias came forward. "Give me too leave to speak," he said, "the case involves a man's life." Leave given, he began, his eyes full of tears: "Men of Ephesus, do not be too hasty to pass the death sentence upon a man who desires to die, the last remedy of the miserable; he has lied, accusing himself of the crimes committed by the guilty, in order that he may suffer the fate of the unfortunate. I will briefly relate to you the whole course of his troubles. He was in love with a maiden, as he told you; here his speech was true enough; and that brigands carried her off, and the part about Sosthenes, and the whole story that he told up till the murder, all has actually happened as he related.

γέγονεν ἐξαίφνης ἀφανής, οὐκ οἶδ' ὅπως, οὔτε εἰ
τις ἀπέκτεινεν αὐτήν, οὔτε εἰ ζῇ κλαπεῖσα· πλὴν
ἓν τοῦτο οἶδα μόνον, τὸν Σωσθένην αὐτῆς ἐρῶντα
καὶ αἰκισάμενον βασάνοις πολλαῖς, ἐφ' οἷς οὐκ
ἐτύγχανε, καὶ φίλους ἔχοντα λῃστάς. οὗτος οὖν
ἀνῃρῆσθαι δοκῶν τὴν γυναῖκα, ζῆν οὐκέτι θέλει,
5 καὶ διὰ τοῦτο ἑαυτοῦ φόνον κατεψεύσατο. ὅτι
μὲν γὰρ ἐπιθυμεῖ θανάτου, καὶ αὐτὸς ὡμολόγησε,
καὶ ὅτι διὰ λύπην τὴν ἐπὶ γυναικί. σκοπεῖτε
δὲ εἴ τις ἀποκτείνας τινὰ ἀληθῶς ἐπαποθανεῖν
6 αὐτῷ θέλει καὶ ζῆν δι' ὀδύνην οὐ φέρει. τίς
οὕτω φιλόστοργος φονεύς, ἢ ποῖον μῖσός ἐστιν
οὕτω φιλούμενον; μή, πρὸς θεῶν, μὴ πιστεύσητε,
μηδὲ ἀποκτείνητε ἄνθρωπον ἐλέου μᾶλλον ἢ
τιμωρίας δεόμενον.

"Εἰ δὲ αὐτὸς ἐπεβούλευσεν, ὡς λέγει, τὸν
φόνον, εἰπάτω τίς ἐστιν ὁ μεμισθωμένος, δειξάτω
7 τὴν ἀνῃρημένην. εἰ δὲ μήτε ὁ ἀποκτείνας ἐστί,
μήτε ἡ ἀνῃρημένη, τίς ἤκουσε ποτε τοιοῦτον
φόνον; 'Ἥρων,' φησί, 'Μελίτης· διὰ τοῦτο
Λευκίππην ἀπέκτεινα.' πῶς οὖν Μελίτης φόνον
κατηγορεῖ ἧς ἤρα, διὰ Λευκίππην δὲ νῦν ἐθέλει
8 ἀποθανεῖν ἣν ἀπέκτεινεν; οὕτω γὰρ ἄν τις καὶ
μισοῖ[1] τὸ φιλούμενον, καὶ φιλοῖ τὸ μισού-
μενον; ἆρ' οὖν οὐ πολὺ μᾶλλον ἂν καὶ ἐλεγχό-
μενος ἠρνήσατο τὸν φόνον, ἵνα καὶ σώσῃ τὴν ἐρω-

---

[1] Cobet suggested μισοίη and χιλοίη for MSS. μισοῖ and
φιλοῖ (V has μισεῖ .... φιλεῖ).

True it is that she has suddenly disappeared ; I know
not how, nor whether somebody has really murdered
her, or whether she has been spirited away and is
still alive; but this alone I do know, that Sosthenes
was in love with her, that he afflicted her with divers
torments, because of what he failed to get, and that
he consorts with brigands as his friends.   Clitophon
is a man who here, thinking that his mistress is no
more, no longer cares to live, and this is why he has
falsely accused himself of murder.   Why, he has
himself confessed that he longs for death, and that
for grief for a maiden lost ; consider, then, if it is really
probable that one individual should kill another, and
then desire to be united in death with his victim,
finding life intolerable from his sorrow for the victim's
death ?   Was there ever so affectionate a murderer, or
hatred so akin to love ?   Believe him not, I implore
you in the name of heaven, believe him not, and do
not put to death a man who deserves pity rather
than punishment.

"Then, if he himself contrived the murder, as he
says he did, let him describe the hireling he employed,
let him produce the dead girl's corpse; if, as in the
present case, there exists neither murderer nor
victim, was such a crime ever heard of before?
Again, ' I loved Melite,' he says, ' and therefore I
killed Leucippe.'   How is it then that he accuses of
murder Melite whom he loved, and is now desirous
of dying for Leucippe whom he killed ?   Is it possible
that anyone could thus hate the object of his love
and love the object of his hatred ?   Nay, is it not
rather far more probable that, if charged with the
murder, he would have denied it, in order both to

μένην, καὶ ὑπὲρ τῆς ἀνῃρημένης [1] μὴ μάτην
ἀποθάνῃ;

9 "Διὰ τί οὖν Μελίτης κατηγόρησεν, εἰ μηδὲν
αὐτῇ τοιοῦτο πέπρακται; ἐγὼ καὶ τοῦτο πρὸς
ὑμᾶς ἐρῶ, καὶ πρὸς τῶν θεῶν μή με νομίσητε δια-
βάλλειν θέλοντα τὴν γυναῖκα ποιήσασθαι τὸν

10 λόγον, ἀλλ᾽ ὡς τὸ πᾶν ἐγένετο. Μελίτη μὲν
ἐπεπόνθει τι [2] πρὸς τοῦτον ἐρωτικὸν καὶ περὶ τοῦ
γάμου διείλεκτο, πρὶν ὁ θαλάττιος οὗτος ἀνεβίω
νεκρός. ὁ δὲ οὐκ εἶχεν οὕτως, ἀλλὰ καὶ πάνυ
ἐρρωμένως τὸν γάμον ἀπεκρούετο, κἂν τούτῳ
τὴν ἐρωμένην εὑρών, ὡς ἔφη, παρὰ τῷ Σωσθένει
ζῶσαν, ἣν ᾤετο νεκράν, πολὺ μᾶλλον πρὸς τὴν

11 Μελίτην εἶχεν ἀλλοτριώτερον. ἡ δὲ πρὶν
μαθεῖν ἐρωμένην οὖσαν αὐτῷ τὴν παρὰ τῷ
Σωσθένει, ταύτην ἠλέησέ τε καὶ ἔλυσε τῶν
δεσμῶν, οἷς ἦν ὑπὸ τοῦ Σωσθένους δεδεμένη,
καὶ εἰς τὴν οἰκίαν τε εἰσεδέξατο καὶ τἆλλα ὡς
πρὸς ἐλευθέραν δυστυχήσασαν ἐφιλοτιμήσατο.
ἐπειδὴ δὲ ἔμαθεν, ἔπεμψεν εἰς τοὺς ἀγροὺς δια-
κονησομένην αὐτῇ· καὶ μετὰ ταῦτά φασιν ἀφανῆ

12 γεγονέναι. καὶ ὅτι ταῦτα οὐ ψεύδομαι, ἡ Μελίτη
συνομολογήσει καὶ θεράπαιναι δύο, μεθ᾽ ὧν
αὐτὴν ἐπὶ τοὺς ἀγροὺς ἐξέπεμψεν. ἓν μὲν δὴ
τοῦτο πρὸς ὑπόνοιαν ἤγαγε τοῦτον, μὴ ἄρα
φονεύσασα εἴη τὴν Λευκίππην διὰ ζηλοτυπίαν
αὕτη· ἕτερον δέ τι αὐτῷ πρὸς τὴν τῆς ὑπονοίας

[1] Jacobs' correction for MSS. ἐρωμένης, which is a mere repetition from ἐρωμένην immediately before.
[2] A necessary insertion by Mitscherlich.

save her whom he loved and not to die for nothing
on account of the victim?

" Why then, you may ask, has he brought this
accusation against Melite, if she committed no crime
of this sort at all? I will explain this to you too,
and I call heaven to witness that you should not
think that I am arguing in order to traduce this
lady's character, but simply relating the story as it
actually happened. Melite had fallen in love with
the defendant, and the matter of marriage had been
mentioned between them before the sea gave up its
dead in the person of Thersander. Clitophon was
not at all inclined to agree, but resisted the proposal
stoutly; and at this moment finding his mistress,
whom he believed dead, a slave in the power of
Sosthenes and alive, he was still less inclined to have
anything to do with Melite. She, before she found
out that Sosthenes' slave was beloved by him, had
taken pity on her and released her from the chains
with which Sosthenes had loaded her; she took her
into her own house, and generally treated her in the
way in which one would treat a free woman who had
fallen into misfortune. When she did learn the truth,[1]
she sent her into the country to perform some service
for her, and it is after this that she is said to have
disappeared; Melite will acknowledge that this
part of my story is true, as well as the two serving-
maids whom she sent with her into the country.
This single fact aroused a suspicion in Clitophon's
mind, with the idea that she might have put an end
to Leucippe from jealousy; and his suspicion was

[1] Clinias is here mistaken. Melite sent Leucippe away
to gather the herbs *before* she knew of her relations with
Clitophon.

βεβαίωσιν ἐν τῷ δεσμωτηρίῳ συμβὰν καὶ καθ'
13 αὑτοῦ καὶ κατὰ τῆς Μελίτης ἐξηγρίανε. τῶν
δεσμωτῶν τις ὀδυρόμενος ἑαυτοῦ τὴν συμφορὰν
ἔλεγεν ὁδεύοντί[1] τινι κεκοινωνηκέναι κατ' ἄγνοιαν
ἀνδρὶ φονεῖ, δεδρακέναι δὲ ἐκεῖνον γυναικὸς φόνον
ἐπὶ μισθῷ· καὶ τοὔνομα ἔλεγε· Μελίτην μὲν
εἶναι τὴν μισθωσαμένην, Λευκίππην δὲ τὴν ἀνηρη-
14 μένην. εἰ δὲ ταῦτα γέγονεν οὕτως, ἐγὼ μὲν
οὐκ οἶδα, μαθεῖν δὲ ὑμῖν[2] ἐξέσται. ἔχετε τὸν
δεδεμένον· εἰσὶν αἱ θεράπαιναι· ἔστιν ὁ Σωσθένης.
ὁ μὲν ἐρεῖ, πόθεν ἔσχε τὴν Λευκίππην δούλην·
αἱ δέ, πῶς γέγονεν ἀφανής· ὁ δὲ περὶ τοῦ
μισθωτοῦ καταγορεύσει. πρὶν δὲ μάθητε τούτων
ἕκαστον, οὔτε ὅσιον οὔτε εὐσεβὲς νεανίσκον ἄθλιον
ἀνελεῖν, πιστεύσαντας μανίας λόγοις· μαίνεται
γὰρ ὑπὸ λύπης."

10. Ταῦτα εἰπόντος τοῦ Κλεινίου, τοῖς μὲν
πολλοῖς ἐδόκει πιθανὸς ὁ λόγος, οἱ δὲ τοῦ
Θερσάνδρου ῥήτορες, καὶ ὅσοι τῶν φίλων συμπαρῆσαν, ἐπεβόων ἀνελεῖν τὸν ἀνδροφόνον, τὸν
2 αὐτοῦ κατειπόντα θεοῦ προνοίᾳ. Μελίτη τὰς

---

[1] ὁδεύοντι Gaselee: ὁδεύων Hercher: ἐν ὁδῷ Salmasius.
[2] So Cobet, for MSS. ὑμᾶς.

---

[1] The relevance of this is not immediately apparent, as it
is only the circumstances of Leucippe's final disappearance
which have brought suspicion on Clitophon, and the manner
of her coming to Ephesus would have no effect on his guilt
or innocence. I think the train of thought can be gathered

confirmed by a second event which occurred in the prison, one which aroused bitterness in his heart against both himself and Melite. One of the prisoners was bewailing his lot, and began to relate how he had fallen in by the way with a man who was—though he did not know it—a murderer; that this fellow had murdered a woman for money: and he mentioned the names; it was Melite who had hired him to commit the crime, and Leucippe who had been done to death. Whether all this really happened, I do not know; you will be able to find out; you have the prisoner of whom I spoke, and the serving-maids and Sosthenes are all in existence. Sosthenes can tell you whence he obtained Leucippe as a slave [1]; the maids, how she disappeared; and the prisoner, who the hireling was. Until you have ascertained everyone of these particulars, it is not right, it is not consonant with your oaths, to condemn to death this wretched young man, accepting as evidence words spoken under the influence of madness; for he certainly has gone mad from grief."

10. When Clinias had finished this speech, the majority of those present were convinced by his argument; but Thersander's counsel, and those of his friends who were present in court with him, shouted for the sentencing of the murderer, who had been brought by God's providence to become his own accuser. Melite offered her serving-maids

from § 4 above: Clinias is trying to throw the suspicion of making away with her upon Sosthenes; he has had one disreputable deal over Leucippe with pirates, and it is now quite probable that he has done the same a second time, and got rid of her again through their agency.

θεραπαινίδας ἐδίδου καὶ Θέρσανδρον ἠξίου διδόναι Σωσθένην· τάχα γὰρ αὐτὸν εἶναι τὸν Λευκίππην ἀνῃρηκότα· καὶ οἱ συναγορεύοντες αὐτῇ
3 ταύτην[1] μάλιστα προεφέροντο πρόκλησιν. ὁ
δὲ Θέρσανδρος φοβηθεὶς λάθρα τινὰ τῶν προστα-
τῶν[2] εἰς τὸν ἀγρὸν ἀποστέλλει πρὸς τὸν Σωσθένην, κελεύσας τὴν ταχίστην ἀφανῆ γενέσθαι,
πρὶν τοὺς ἐπ᾽ αὐτὸν πεμφθέντας ἥκειν· ὃς δὴ
ἐπιβὰς ἵππῳ σπουδῇ μάλα πρὸς αὐτὸν ἔρχεται
καὶ τὸν κίνδυνον λέγει καὶ ὡς, εἰ ληφθείη παρών,
4 εἰς βασάνους ἀπαχθήσεται. ὁ δὲ ἔτυχε μὲν
ἐν τῷ τῆς Λευκίππης δωματίῳ παρών, κατεπᾴδων
αὐτῆς· κληθεὶς δὲ ὑπὸ τοῦ παρόντος σὺν βοῇ
καὶ ταραχῇ πολλῇ προέρχεται, καὶ ἀκούσας τὰ
ὄντα, μεστὸς γενόμενος δέους, καὶ ἤδη νομίζων
τοὺς δημίους ἐπ᾽ αὐτὸν παρεῖναι, ἐπιβὰς ἵππῳ
σπουδῇ μάλα ἐλαύνει ἐπὶ Σμύρνης· ὁ δὲ ἄγγελος
πρὸς τὸν Θέρσανδρον ἀναστρέφει. ἀληθὴς δέ
ἐστιν, ὡς ἔοικεν, ὁ λόγος, ὅτι μνήμην ἐκπλήσσειν
5 πέφυκε φόβος· ὁ γοῦν Σωσθένης περὶ ἑαυτοῦ
φοβηθείς, ἁπαξαπάντων ἐξελάθετο τῶν ἐν ποσὶν
ὑπ᾽ ἐκπλήξεως, ὡς μηδὲ τοῦ τῆς Λευκίππης
δωματίου κλεῖσαι τὰς θύρας. μάλιστα γὰρ τὸ
τῶν δούλων γένος ἐν οἷς ἂν φοβηθῇ σφόδρα
δειλόν ἐστιν.

[1] Rightly corrected by Cobet from MSS. ταῦτα.
[2] This word, which would properly mean "champions," is
not quite satisfactory. Salmasius proposed παραστατῶν,
which is only a little better, though defended in a careful
note by Jacobs: I should have preferred προσπόλων, if it
were not so poetical a word.

to be questioned, and required Thersander to produce
Sosthenes, for perhaps it was he who had murdered
Leucippe ; her advocates indeed laid great stress
on this challenge[1] which they put forward. Thersander was much alarmed at it, and privately sent
one of his supporters to Sosthenes at his country
place, advising him to make himself scarce at once,
before the messengers sent for him could reach him ;
the envoy took horse with all speed, and when he
had reached him, explained the danger that he was
in ; if he stayed where he was, he said, and were
there arrested, he would certainly be put to the
torture. Sosthenes happened to be at Leucippe's
hut, trying his blandishments upon her ; when the
messenger called out his name with much shouting
and noise, he came out, heard the state of affairs,
and was overcome by fear ; and thinking that the
police were already on his heels, he took horse and
rode off at full gallop for Smyrna, while the other
returned to Thersander. True it is, it seems, that
fear paralyses the memory ; at any rate Sosthenes,
in his fright for his own skin, utterly forgot all his
immediate duties in the momentary shock, and did
not remember even to lock the doors of Leucippe's
hut. The whole tribe of slaves is greatly inclined to
cowardice in any circumstances where there is the
slightest room for fear.

[1] One of the most essential institutions of Greek litiga-
tion ; one side would put forward a salient point to be tested,
the refusal by the other side to accept it as a test bringing
the case to an end. πρόκλησις may mean either a challenge or
an offer, or something between the two ; it is very often indeed
(as here) an *offer* to produce one's own slaves to be questioned
under torture as to the veracity of one's own evidence, or a
challenge to the other party to produce *his* slaves to be treated
in the same way, with the hope of shaking his evidence.

ACHILLES TATIUS

11. Ἐν τούτῳ δὲ ὁ Θέρσανδρος πρώτης [1] προκλήσεως ἀπὸ τῆς Μελίτης οὕτω γενομένης παρελθών, "Ἱκανῶς μέν," εἶπεν, "οὗτος, ὅστις ποτέ ἐστι, κατελήρησε μυθολογῶν. ἐγὼ δὲ ὑμῶν τεθαύμακα τῆς ἀναλγησίας, εἰ φονέα ἐπ᾿ αὐτοφώρῳ λαβόντες, μεῖζον γὰρ τῆς φωρᾶς τὸ αὐτὸν ἑαυτοῦ κατειπεῖν, οὐ δὴ κελεύετε τῷ δημίῳ, καθέζεσθε δὲ γόητος ἀκούοντες πιθανῶς μὲν ὑποκρινομένου, πιθανῶς δὲ δακρύοντος· ὃν νομίζω καὶ αὐτὸν κοινωνὸν γενόμενον τοῦ φόνου περὶ ἑαυτοῦ φοβεῖσθαι· ὥστε οὐκ οἶδα τί δεῖ βασάνων ἔτι περὶ πράγματος οὕτω σαφῶς ἐλη-
2 λεγμένου. δοκῶ δὲ καὶ ἄλλον τινὰ ἐργάσασθαι φόνον· ὁ γὰρ Σωσθένης οὗτος, ὃν αἰτοῦσι παρ᾿ ἐμοῦ, τρίτην ταύτην ἡμέραν γέγονεν ἀφανής, καί ἐστιν οὐ πόρρω τινὸς ὑπονοίας, μὴ ἄρα τῆς τούτων ἐπιβουλῆς γέγονεν ἔργον· αὐτὸς γὰρ ἐτύγχανεν ὁ τὴν μοιχείαν μοι κατειπών. ὥστε εἰκότως ἀποκτεῖναί μοι δοκοῦσιν αὐτόν, καὶ τοῦτο εἰδότες, ὡς ἂν οὐκ ἔχοιμι παρασχεῖν τὸν ἄνθρωπον, πρόκλησιν περὶ αὐτοῦ πεποίηνται πάνυ
3 κακούργως. εἴη μὲν οὖν κἀκεῖνον φανῆναι καὶ μὴ τεθνάναι· τί δὲ καί, εἰ παρῆν, ἔδει παρ᾿ αὐτοῦ μαθεῖν; εἴ τινα κόρην ἐωνήσατο; τοιγαροῦν ἐωνημένος ἔστω· καὶ εἰ ταύτην ἔσχε Μελίτη; λέγει καὶ τοῦτο δι᾿ ἐμοῦ. ἀπήλλακται μὲν δὴ Σωσθένης ταῦτα εἰπών· τοὐντεῦθεν

[1] Most MSS. have πρώτης: πρὼ τῆς W πρὸ τῆς M which modern editors before Vilborg relied on. A friend of Gaselee suggested πρὸς τὴν πρόκλησιν " against the challenge ": πρός and πρό are written very nearly alike in MSS., and the change of case would naturally follow the change of the former preposition into the latter.

11. While all this was happening, Thersander
appeared after the first challenge in the lawsuit was
made from Melite's side in this way, and said: " We
have surely had enough," said he, " of the raving
moonshine put forward by this fellow, whoever he
is. I am really astonished at your callousness; you
have caught a murderer in the act—a man's own
accusation of himself is even stronger than a capture
in flagrante, and yet you do not call upon the officer
to lead him away to death, but sit there listening
to this charlatan with his plausible acting and his
plausible tears. I rather suspect that he too,
being an accomplice in the murder, is afraid for his
own skin, and so I see no need for the process of
torturing slaves for further evidence in a case so
clearly proved as this. Nay more, I fancy that
they have committed a second murder; this Sosthenes, whom they call upon me to produce, has
now been missing for more than two full days, and
there is every ground for suspicion that his disappearance is due to their plotting; he it was that
informed me of the adultery. So I think that they
have made away with him, and now, certain that
I cannot produce the fellow, have most craftily put
forward the challenge for him. Now suppose for a
moment that he were not dead, and had appeared
here in court: whatever could be learned from his
presence? If he once bought a certain girl? It is
granted at once that he bought her. If Melite was
at one time in possession of her? That too he
acknowledges, by my lips. When he has given this
evidence, Sosthenes is dismissed from the case;

375

δὲ ὁ λόγος μοι πρὸς Μελίτην καὶ Κλειτοφῶντα.
4 τί μου τὴν δούλην λαβόντες πεποιήκατε; δούλη
γὰρ ἦν ἐμή, Σωσθένους αὐτὴν ἐωνημένου· καὶ εἰ
περιῆν καὶ μὴ πρὸς αὐτῶν ἐπεφόνευτο, πάντως ἂν
ἐδούλευεν ἐμοί."
5 Τοῦτον δὲ τὸν λόγον ὁ Θέρσανδρος πάνυ
κακοήθως παρενέβαλεν, ἵνα κἂν ὕστερον ἡ
Λευκίππη φωραθῇ ζῶσα, πρὸς δουλείαν αὐτὴν
ἀγάγῃ. εἶτα προσετίθει· "Κλειτοφῶν μὲν οὖν
ὡμολόγησεν ἀνῃρηκέναι, καὶ ἔχει τὴν δίκην,
Μελίτη δὲ ἀρνεῖται· πρὸς ταύτην αἱ τῶν θερα-
6 παινίδων εἰσὶ βάσανοι. ἂν γὰρ φανῶσι παρὰ
ταύτης λαβοῦσαι τὴν κόρην, εἶτα οὐκέτι πάλιν
ἀγαγοῦσαι, τί γέγονε; τί δὲ ὅλως ἐξεπέμπετο;
καὶ πρὸς τίνα; ἆρ' οὐκ εὔδηλον τὸ πρᾶγμα, ὡς
συσκευασάμενοι μὲν ἦσάν τινας ὡς κτενοῦντας;
7 αἱ δὲ θεράπαιναι τούτους μέν, ὡς εἰκός, οὐκ
ᾔδεσαν, ἵνα μὴ μετὰ πλειόνων μαρτύρων γενόμενον
τὸ ἔργον κίνδυνον ἔχῃ μείζονα· κατέλιπον δὲ αὐτὴν
ἔνθα ἦν ὁ τῶν λῃστῶν λόχος λανθάνων, ὥστε
ἐνεχώρει μηδὲ ἐκείνας τὸ γενόμενον ἑωρακέναι.
ἐλήρησε δὲ καὶ περὶ δεσμώτου τινός, ὡς εἰπόντος
8 περὶ τοῦ φόνου. καὶ τίς ὁ δεσμώτης οὗτος, ὃς τῷ
στρατηγῷ μὲν οὐδὲν εἶπε, τούτῳ δὲ μόνῳ τὰ ἀπόρρητα διελέγετο τοῦ φόνου, πλὴν εἰ μὴ κοινωνοῦντα
ἐγνώρισεν; οὐ παύσεσθε φληνάφων ἀνεχόμενοι

from this point begins my arraignment of Melite
and Clitophon. What have you done with my slave,
whom you took from me? For my slave she was, as
Sosthenes had bought her, and if she were still alive
and had not been murdered by them, she would still
be my slave."

This last remark was interjected by Thersander
with wicked cunning, so that if later on it were
detected that Leucippe were still alive, he would
be able to keep her in slavery to him. Then he
went on: "Clitophon has acknowledged that he
murdered her, and the verdict is settled on his case:
Melite denies it; well, her serving-maids may be
tortured to refute her denial. Supposing it is established that they received the girl from her, but
never brought her back again, what is the conclusion? Why was she ever sent off into the
country? To whom? Is not the whole affair perfectly clear, that the conspirators had suborned
men to do away with her? About them, naturally
enough, no information was given to the serving-
maids—the greater the number of those privy to
the scheme, the greater danger would it involve;
the maids left her near the spot where the robber-
band was lying in hiding, and it was so quite
possible that they did not even see what happened.
Then this fellow uttered some frantic nonsense
about some prisoner, who is supposed to have spoken
of the murder. Who is this prisoner, who has said
nothing to the magistrate, but has related to
Clitophon alone all the secrets of the murder, which he
certainly would not have done if he had not recognised him as a participator in it? It is surely time
that you ceased to pay any attention to these empty

κενῶν, καὶ τηλικοῦτον ἔργον τιθέμενοι παιδιάν;
οἴεσθε χωρὶς θεοῦ τοῦτον ἑαυτοῦ κατειπεῖν;"

12. Ταῦτα λέγοντος τοῦ Θερσάνδρου καὶ διομνυ-
μένου περὶ τοῦ Σωσθένους οὐκ εἰδέναι τί γέγονεν,
ἔδοξε τῷ προέδρῳ τῶν δικαστῶν—ἦν δὲ τοῦ
βασιλικοῦ γένους, καὶ τὰς μὲν φονικὰς ἐδίκαζε
δίκας, κατὰ δὲ τὸν νόμον συμβούλους ἐκ τῶν
γεραιτέρων εἶχεν, οὓς ἐπιγνώμονας ἐλάμβανε τῆς
γνώσεως—ἔδοξεν οὖν αὐτῷ διασκοπήσαντι σὺν
τοῖς παρέδροις αὐτοῦ, θάνατον μὲν ἐμοῦ κατα-
γνῶναι κατὰ τὸν νόμον, ὃς ἐκέλευσε τὸν αὐτοῦ
κατειπόντα φόνον τεθνάναι· περὶ δὲ Μελίτης
κρίσιν γενέσθαι δευτέραν ἐν ταῖς βασάνοις τῶν
θεραπαινίδων· Θέρσανδρον δὲ ἐπομόσαι περὶ τοῦ
Σωσθένους ἐν γράμμασιν, ἦ μὴν οὐκ εἰδέναι τι
γέγονεν· κἀμὲ δέ, ὡς ἤδη κατάδικον, βασανισθῆναι
2 περὶ τοῦ Μελίτην τῷ φόνῳ συνεγνωκέναι. ἄρτι
δέ μου δεθέντος καὶ τῆς ἐσθῆτος τοῦ σώματος
γεγυμνωμένου, μετεώρου τε ἐκ τῶν βρόχων κρε-
μαμένου καὶ τῶν μὲν μάστιγας κομιζόντων, τῶν
δὲ πῦρ καὶ τροχόν, ἀνοιμώξαντος δὲ τοῦ Κλεινίου
καὶ ἐπικαλοῦντος τοὺς θεούς, ὁ τῆς Ἀρτέμιδος
3 ἱερεὺς δάφνην ἐστεμμένος προσιὼν ὁρᾶται. σημεῖον δὲ τοῦτό ἐστιν ἠκούσης θεωρίας τῇ θεῷ·

---

[1] The only possible answer to Melite's πρόκλησις.
[2] This, with the mention of the satrap of Egypt in Book
III, suggests that the story takes place under the Persian
rule. But we had better conclude that Achilles knew that
the "King-archon" at Athens managed murder-cases, but
misapplies his knowledge. There is a great contrast to
Chariton's Chaereas and Callirrhoe, in which historical
probability is most carefully preserved.

babblings, making this serious business a matter of ridicule; can you think that this fellow would ever have brought this accusation against himself without the direct interposition of Providence?"

12. This was Thersander's speech, and he followed it by his oath [1] that he knew nothing of what had become of Sosthenes. The president of the judges then delivered his sentence: he was of the royal [2] house, and it was his business to sit in capital charges; but he had, as the law provided, assessors chosen from the elders of the town, whom he had selected as experts in jurisprudence. After consultation with the assessors, his sentence was that I was to be put to death, in accordance with the law which provided that a murderer [3] admitting his crime was to be condemned, but that as concerning Melite, there must be a second trial, the result of which would depend upon the evidence given by the serving-maids when put to the question; that Thersander was to make an additional affidavit in writing that he did not know what had become of Sosthenes, and that I, already judged guilty, was to be questioned under torture as to the connivance of Melite in my crime. I was therefore at once fettered, stripped naked of my clothes, and slung up on the cords, the attendants were some of them bringing the scourges, some the fire and wheel; Clinias was crying aloud and calling upon the gods for help, when Artemis' bishop was descried approaching, crowned with bay. This is the indication that a sacred embassy to the goddess has arrived,

[3] A good example of the injustice which may occur in the absence of the excellent rule requiring production of the body for the success of a charge of murder.

τοῦτο δὲ ὅταν γένηται, πάσης εἶναι δεῖν τιμωρίας
ἐκεχειρίαν ἡμερῶν τοσούτων, ὅσων οὐκ ἐπετέλεσαν
τὴν θυσίαν οἱ θεωροί· οὕτω μὲν δὴ τότε τῶν
δεσμῶν ἐλύθην. ἦν δὲ ὁ τὴν θεωρίαν ἄγων Σώ-
4 στρατος, ὁ τῆς Λευκίππης πατήρ. οἱ γὰρ Βυζάντιοι, τῆς Ἀρτέμιδος ἐπιφανείσης ἐν τῷ πολέμῳ τῷ
πρὸς τοὺς Θρᾷκας, νικήσαντες ἐλογίσαντο δεῖν
αὐτῇ θυσίαν ἀποστέλλειν, τῆς συμμαχίας ἐπινί-
κιον· ἦν δὲ καὶ ἰδίᾳ τῷ Σωστράτῳ νύκτωρ ἡ θεὸς
ἐπιστᾶσα. τὸ δὲ ὄναρ ἐσήμαινε τὴν θυγατέρα
εὑρήσειν ἐν Ἐφέσῳ καὶ τοῦ ἀδελφοῦ τὸν υἱόν.

13. Παρὰ δὲ τὸν αὐτὸν χρόνον καὶ ἡ Λευκίππη,
τὰς μὲν τοῦ δωματίου θύρας ἀνεῳγμένας ὁρῶσα,
τὸν δὲ Σωσθένην μὴ παρόντα, περιεσκόπει μὴ πρὸ
θυρῶν εἴη. ὡς δὲ ἦν οὐδαμοῦ, θάρσος αὐτῇ καὶ
ἐλπὶς ἡ συνήθης εἰσέρχεται· μνήμη γὰρ αὐτῇ
τοῦ πολλάκις παρὰ δόξαν σεσῶσθαι, πρὸς τὸ
παρὸν τῶν κινδύνων τὴν ἐλπίδα προυξένει ἀπο-
2 χρῆσθαι[1] τῇ Τύχῃ. καί, ἦν γὰρ τῶν ἀγρῶν
πλησίον τὸ τῆς Ἀρτέμιδος ἱερόν, ἐκτρέχει τε ἐπ'
αὐτό, καὶ ἔχεται τοῦ νεώ. τὸ δὲ παλαιὸν ἄβατος
ἦν γυναιξὶν ἐλευθέραις οὗτος ὁ νεως, ἀνδράσι δὲ
3 ἐπετέτραπτο καὶ παρθένοις. εἰ δέ τις εἴσω παρ-
ῆλθε γυνή, θάνατος ἦν ἡ δίκη, πλὴν εἰ μὴ δούλη
τις ἦν ἐγκαλοῦσα τῷ δεσπότῃ. ταύτῃ[2] δὲ ἐξῆν
ἱκετεύειν τὴν θεόν, οἱ δὲ ἄρχοντες ἐδίκαζον αὐτῇ

---

[1] So Cobet: ἀποχρῆσαι V: ἀποχρῆται W, R, G: ἀποχρῆτε M.
[2] So Salmasius and cod. G for ταύτην.

and when such an event occurs, there is bound to be
a respite from all judicial punishments until the
ambassadors have completed the sacrifice which they
have come to perform : I was therefore temporarily
released from my chains. Now the head of the
sacred embassy was Sostratus, Leucippe's father ; for
Artemis had appeared to the Byzantines during their
war against the Thracians, and after their consequent
victory, they decided that they must send her a
sacrifice as a recognition of her aid during the war.
Nay more, the goddess had appeared to Sostratus
separately by night, and his dream foretold him
that he would find his daughter and his brother's son
at Ephesus.

13. To return to Leucippe ; about the same time
that all this was occurring, she perceived that the
doors of her hut had been left open and that Sosthenes
was not there : then she looked round to see if he
were outside in front of the doors. As he was
nowhere to be found, her accustomed courage and
hope returned to her : she remembered that more
than once she had been brought safely through,
against all expectation, and in the matter of her
present dangers she dared to hope that Fortune
would once again come to her help. Now quite
near to the country house was the temple of
Artemis : so she ran thither, and there clutched
hold with her hands of the shrine within it : the
shrine was anciently forbidden to free matrons,
but open to men and maidens : if any other woman
entered it, death was the penalty of her intrusion,
unless she were a slave with a legal complaint against
her master : such a one was permitted to come as a
suppliant to the goddess, while the magistrates de-

τε καὶ τῷ δεσπότῃ· καὶ εἰ μὲν ὁ δεσπότης οὐδὲν
ἔτυχεν ἀδικῶν, αὖθις τὴν θεράπαιναν ἐλάμβανεν,
ὀμόσας μὴ μνησικακήσειν τῆς καταφυγῆς· εἰ δὲ
ἔδοξεν ἡ θεράπαινα[1] δίκαια λέγειν, ἔμενεν αὐτοῦ
4 δούλη τῇ θεῷ. ἄρτι δὲ τοῦ Σωστράτου τὸν ἱερέα
παραλαβόντος, καὶ ἐπὶ τὰ δικαστήρια παρελ-
θόντος, ὡς ἂν ἐπίσχῃ τὰς δίκας, εἰς τὸ ἱερὸν ἡ
Λευκίππη παρῆν, ὥστε μικροῦ τινος ἀπελείφθη
τοῦ μὴ τῷ πατρὶ συντυχεῖν.

14. Ὡς δὲ ἀπηλλάγην ἐγὼ τῶν βασάνων, διελέ-
λυτο μὲν τὸ δικαστήριον, ὄχλος τε ἦν περὶ ἐμὲ καὶ
θόρυβος, τῶν μὲν ἐλεούντων, τῶν δὲ ἐπιθειαζόντων,[2] τῶν δὲ ἀναπυνθανομένων. ἔνθα καὶ ὁ Σώ-
2 στρατος ἐπιστὰς ὁρᾷ με καὶ γνωρίζει. καὶ γάρ, ὡς
ἔφην ἐν ἀρχῇ τῶν λόγων, ἐν Τύρῳ ποτ᾽ ἐγεγόνει
περὶ τὴν τῶν Ἡρακλείων ἑορτήν, καὶ χρόνου
πολλοῦ διατρίψας ἔτυχεν ἐν Τύρῳ, πρὸ πολλοῦ
τῆς ἡμετέρας φυγῆς· ὥστε ταχύ[3] μου τὴν μορφὴν
συνεβάλετο, καὶ διὰ τὸ ἐνύπνιον φύσει προσδοκῶν
3 εὑρήσειν ἡμᾶς. προσελθὼν οὖν μοι· "Κλειτοφῶν
οὗτος, Λευκίππη δὲ ποῦ;" ἐγὼ μὲν οὖν γνωρίσας
αὐτὸν εἰς γῆν κατένευσα· οἱ δὲ παρόντες αὐτῷ
διηγοῦντο ὅσα εἶπον κατ᾽ ἐμαυτοῦ· καὶ ὃς ἀνοιμώξας, καὶ κοψάμενος τὴν κεφαλήν, ἐμπηδᾷ μου

---

[1] MSS. ἔδοξε τὴν θεράπαιναν; corrected by Jacobs.
[2] So MSS. ἐκθειαζόντων Hercher: ἐπιτωθαζόντων Hirschig.
ἐκθειάζω means "to deify," ἐπιθειάζω "to appeal to the gods
against."
[3] I think that Hercher's ταχύ (for τάχα) must be accepted.
In prose τάχα means "perhaps," ταχύ "quickly."

cided the case between her and the master. If the
master were found to have committed no offence
against her, he used to take the serving-girl back,
after taking an oath that he would bear no malice
against her on account of her flight : but if sentence
were given for the servant, then she stayed there as
the goddess's slave. Sostratus was just taking with
him the bishop and coming to the law-court to stop
the execution of the sentence at the moment when
Leucippe arrived at the temple, and she only missed
meeting her father by a few moments.

14. I was thus reprieved from the question, and
the court had broken up : I was surrounded by a
noisy mob, some expressing their pity, some calling
upon the gods [1] to punish me, others questioning me
about my story, when Sostratus, who had stopped
near me, recognized who I was ; for, as I mentioned
at the beginning of my story, he had [2] once been in
Tyre when the feast of Heracles was being celebrated, and had remained there for some days a considerable time before our flight : so that he at once realised from my appearance who I was, and he
naturally expected to find us in Ephesus on account
of his dream. He therefore came up to me, saying ;
" Here is Clitophon, but where is Leucippe ? " As
soon as I recognized him, I bent down my head,
while the bystanders related to him the accusations
I had brought against myself : at which he cried
aloud, and buffeted his face, and then rushed at me

---

[1] See note on the Greek text. If ἐπιθειαζόντων be the true
reading, it might perhaps also mean "calling upon the gods"
in amazement at their timely intervention.

[2] A mistake. Sostratus had recommended (II. xiv.) that a
sacred embassy should be sent to the Tyrian Hercules, but
Callisthenes actually conducted it.

τοῖς ὀφθαλμοῖς καὶ μικροῦ δεῖν ἐξώρυξεν αὐτούς·
οὐδὲ γὰρ ἐπεχείρουν κωλύειν ἐγώ, παρεῖχον δὲ τὸ
4 πρόσωπον εἰς τὴν ὕβριν. ὁ δὲ Κλεινίας προσελθὼν εἶργε παρηγορῶν αὐτὸν ἅμα καὶ λέγων· "Τί
ποιεῖς, ἄνθρωπε; τί μάτην ἐξηγρίωσαι κατ' ἀν-
δρός, ὃς μᾶλλον σοῦ Λευκίππην φιλεῖ; θάνατον
γοῦν ὑπέστη παθεῖν, ὅτι τεθνάναι ταύτην ἔδοξεν·"
5 ἄλλα τε πολλὰ ἔλεγε παραμυθούμενος αὐτόν. ὁ
δὲ ὠδύρετο καλῶν τὴν Ἄρτεμιν· "'Επὶ τοῦτό με,
δέσποινα, ἤγαγες ἐνταῦθα; τοιαῦτά σου τῶν ἐνυπνίων τὰ μαντεύματα; κἀγὼ μὲν ἐπίστευόν σου
τοῖς ὀνείροις καὶ εὑρήσειν παρὰ σοὶ προσεδόκων
τὴν θυγατέρα. καλὸν δέ μοι δῶρον δέδωκας·
6 εὗρον τὸν ἀνδροφόνον αὐτῆς παρὰ σοί." καὶ ὁ
Κλεινίας ἀκούσας τοῦ τῆς 'Αρτέμιδος ἐνυπνίου
περιχαρὴς ἐγένετο, καὶ λέγει· "Θάρρει, πάτερ, ἡ
Ἄρτεμις οὐ ψεύδεται· ζῇ σοι Λευκίππη· πίστευσόν
μου τοῖς μαντεύμασιν. οὐχ ὁρᾷς καὶ τοῦτον ὡς
ἐκ τῶν βασάνων νῦν κρεμάμενον ἐξήρπασεν; "

15. 'Εν τούτῳ δὲ ἔρχεταί τις τῶν τοῦ νεὼ
προπόλων ἐπὶ τὸν ἱερέα σπουδῇ μάλα θέων, καὶ
λέγει πάντων ἀκουόντων· "Κόρη τις ἐπὶ τὴν
Ἄρτεμιν ξένη κατέφυγεν." ἐγὼ μὲν δὴ τοῦτο
ἀκούσας ἀναπτεροῦμαι, καὶ τὰ ὄμματα ἀνεγείρω,
καὶ ἀναβιοῦν ἠρχόμην· ὁ δὲ Κλεινίας πρὸς τὸν
Σώστρατον, "'Αληθῆ μου, πάτερ," εἶπε, "τὰ μαν-
τεύματα·" καὶ ἅμα πρὸς τὸν ἄγγελον εἶπε· "Μὴ
2 καλή;" "Οὐκ ἄλλην τοιαύτην," ἔφη, "μετὰ τὴν
384

and made as if he would almost tear out my eyes ;
I made no resistance and did not try to prevent him,
but rather freely offered my face to his violence.
At this Clinias came forward and addressed him,
trying to restrain him : "What are you doing, Sir ?"
he said, "Why do you exhibit so wrong a passion
against a man who loves Leucippe even better than
you do ? He has at any rate offered himself up to
be put to death because he thought that the maiden
had perished :" and he exhorted him with these and
many other like words. He, however, went on lam-
enting, calling upon Artemis ; "Was it for this, great
queen, that thou didst bring me hither? Was the
interpretation of the vision thou sentest me to be
after this fashion ? Yes, and I believed thy dream,
and trusted to find my daughter here with thee.
Now it is a fine gift that thou hast made me ; I have
found her murderer here in thy city." When Clinias
heard of the dream in which Artemis had appeared,
he was overcome with joy ; "Be of good cheer, ven-
erable Sir ;" he said, "Artemis is no liar : your
Leucippe is alive ; believe my powers of interpretation. Do you not see how she has delivered Clitophon
too, who was actually strung up for execution, from
the tortures that were awaiting him ? "

15. While he was thus speaking, one of the temple-
keepers came running his fastest to the bishop, and
cried, in the hearing of all, "A maiden, a foreigner,
has taken sanctuary with Artemis." At these words
I was all in a flutter with hope ; I opened my eyes
and began to live once more. Clinias turned to
Sostratus, saying ; "You see, aged Sir, that my divi-
nations are coming true ;" and at once, speaking to
the messenger, "Is she not fair?" "Never saw I

"Ἄρτεμιν εἶδον," πρὸς τοῦτο ἐγὼ πηδῶ καὶ βοῶ,
" Λευκίππην λέγεις." " Καὶ μάλα," ἔφη· " καλεῖ-
σθαι γὰρ τοῦτο ἔλεγεν αὕτη,[1] καὶ πατρίδα Βυζάν-
3 τιον καὶ πατέρα Σώστρατον ἔχειν." ὁ μὲν δὴ Κλεινίας ἀνεκρότησε παιανίσας· ὁ δὲ Σώστρατος ὑπὸ
χαρᾶς κατέπεσεν· ἐγὼ δὲ ἐξάλλομαι μετὰ τῶν
δεσμῶν εἰς ἀέρα καὶ ἐπὶ τὸ ἱερὸν ὡς ἀπὸ μηχανῆς
βληθεὶς ἐπετόμην· οἱ δὲ φυλάσσοντες ἐδίωκον, νομίζοντες ἀποδιδράσκειν, καὶ ἐβόων τοῖς ἐντυγχάνουσι
4 λαβέσθαι. ἀλλ᾽ εἶχον οἱ πόδες μου τότε πτερά·
καὶ μόλις οὖν τινες μαινομένου μου πρὸς τὸν
δρόμον λαμβάνονται· καὶ οἱ φύλακες ἅμα παρῆσαν καὶ ἐπεχείρουν με τύπτειν. ἐγὼ δὲ ἤδη
θαρρῶν ἠμυνόμην· οἱ δὲ εἷλκόν με εἰς τὸ δεσμωτήριον.

16. Καὶ ἐν τούτῳ παρῆν ὁ Κλεινίας καὶ ὁ
Σώστρατος. καὶ ὁ μὲν Κλεινίας ἐβόα· "Ποῖ
ἄγετε τὸν ἄνθρωπον; οὐκ ἔστι φονεὺς ἐφ᾽ ᾗ κατα-
δεδίκασται." καὶ ὁ Σώστρατος ἐν μέρει ταὐτὰ
ἔλεγε, καὶ ὡς εἴη αὐτὸς τῆς ἀνῃρῆσθαι δοκούσης
πατήρ. οἱ δὲ παρόντες, μαθόντες τὸ πᾶν, εὐφή-
μουν τε τὴν Ἄρτεμιν καὶ περιίσταντό με καὶ
2 ἄγειν εἰς τὸ δεσμωτήριον οὐκ ἐπέτρεπον. οἱ δὲ
φύλακες οὐκ εἶναι κύριοι τοῦ μεθεῖναι καταδικα-
σθέντα πρὸς θάνατον ἄνθρωπον ἔλεγον, ἕως ὁ
ἱερεύς, τοῦ Σωστράτου δεηθέντος, ἐνηγγυήσατο

[1] αὕτη codd. β: αὑτὴν codd. α: αὑτὴ Cobet.

---

[1] A combination of two constructions: (a) " Never saw I
fairer, save the goddess," and (b) " The fairest I ever saw

such another, " he replied, "save [1] the goddess alone."
At this I leaped up and shouted: "It must be
Leucippe of whom you speak." "Certainly," said
he; "that was the name by which she said that she
was called, and that her country was Byzantium and
her father Sostratus." Then Clinias clapped his
hands, shouting with triumph, while Sostratus fell
to the ground for joy, and I leaped up on high,
chains and all, and flew off to the temple like
a bullet from the gun: my warders pursued me,
thinking that I was running away, and called all those
whom we met to catch me. But my feet had wings,
and it was with the greatest difficulty that at length
some of them stopped me in my mad course, and
then my guards came up and set about beating me: to
which I, now back in my old good spirits, resisted
stoutly, and they began dragging me off to the prison.

16. Meanwhile, up came Clinias and Sostratus, the
former crying out; "Whither are you dragging this
man? He is not guilty of the murder for which he
was sentenced:" and Sostratus in his turn corroborated his story and said that he was the father of the
girl who had been believed to have been murdered.
The bystanders when they heard the whole story,
blessed the name of Artemis; and making a ring
round me, refused to allow me to be taken off to
prison. The warders said that they did not possess the
power of letting out a man who had been condemned
to death; but presently the bishop, at the request
of Sostratus, went bail that he would be responsible

after the goddess." *cf.* Milton, *P.L.* iv. 324, " Fairest of her
daughters Eve." With the sentiment *cf.* Ovid, *Her.* xviii.
69 [Leander addressing the moon (Artemis)]: A Veneris facie
non est prior ulla tuaque—Save Venus' face and thine there
is none surpasses Hero's.

αὐτὸν ἔχειν καὶ παράξειν[1] εἰς τὸν δῆμον, ὅταν
δέῃ. οὕτω μὲν δὴ τῶν δεσμῶν ἀπολύομαι καὶ
ἐπὶ τὸ ἱερὸν ταχὺ μάλα ἠπειγόμην· καὶ ὁ Σώστρατος κατὰ πόδας, οὐκ οἶδα εἰ τὰ ὅμοια ἐμοὶ
3 χαίρων. οὐκ ἔστι δὲ οὕτως ἄνθρωπος δρομικώ-
τατος, ὃν οὐ τῆς φήμης φθάνει τὸ πτερόν· ἢ καὶ
τότε ἡμᾶς ἐπὶ Λευκίππην προύλαβεν, ἀπαγγέλ-
λουσα πάνται καὶ τὰ τοῦ Σωστράτου καὶ τἀμά.
ἰδοῦσα δὲ ἡμᾶς, ἐξεπήδησε τοῦ νεώ, καὶ τὸν μὲν
πατέρα περιεπτύξατο, τοὺς δὲ ὀφθαλμοὺς εἶχεν
4 ἐπ' ἐμέ. ἐγὼ δὲ εἱστήκειν, αἰδοῖ τῇ πρὸς τὸν
Σώστρατον κατέχων ἐμαυτόν (καὶ ἅπαντα ἔβλεπον
εἰς τὸ ἐκείνης πρόσωπον) ἐπ' αὐτὴν ἐκθορεῖν.
οὕτως ἀλλήλους ἠσπαζόμεθα τοῖς ὄμμασιν.

---

[1] MSS. παρέξειν. The correction is due to Hirschig.

for the prisoner and produce him for public trial when the time came. Released thus then from my bonds, I hurried away with all possible speed to the temple, with Sostratus close at my heels, who probably felt the same kind of joy as my own. But, run a man never so swiftly, yet the winged tongue of speech gets to his destination before him : on this occasion again it anticipated us in our visit to Leucippe, relating the whole story to her, both Sostratus' adventures and mine ; and when she saw us, she rushed forth from the shrine, and while her arms were folded round her father's neck, she kept her eyes fixed on me. There I stood, my shame for the way I had treated Sostratus restraining me—though all the time I was gazing steadfastly at her face— from falling into her arms ; and so we greeted one another only with our eyes.

Η΄

1. Ἄρτι δὲ ἡμῶν μελλόντων καθέζεσθαι καὶ περὶ τούτων διαλέγεσθαι, Θέρσανδρος σπουδῇ μάλα, μάρτυρας ἄγων τινάς, ἔρχεται πρὸς τὸν νεών, καὶ μεγάλῃ τῇ φωνῇ πρὸς τὸν ἱερέα, "Μαρτύρομαι," ἔφη, "τῶνδε ἐναντίον, ὅτι μὴ δεόντως ἐξαιρῇ δεσμῶν καὶ θανάτου κατεγνω-σμένον ἄνθρωπον ἐκ τῶν νόμων ἀποθανεῖν.
2 ἔχεις δὲ καὶ δούλην ἐμήν, γυναῖκα μάχλον καὶ πρὸς ἄνδρας ἐπιμανῆ· ταύτην ὅπως μοι φυλάξῃς." ἐγὼ δὲ πρὸς τὸ "δούλην καὶ γυναῖκα μάχλον" ὑπεραλγήσας τὴν ψυχήν, οὐκ ἤνεγκα τῶν ῥημάτων τὰ τραύματα, ἀλλ' ἔτι λαλοῦντος αὐτοῦ, "Σὺ μὲν οὖν," ἔφην, "καὶ τρίδουλος καὶ ἐπιμανὴς καὶ μάχλος· αὕτη δὲ καὶ ἐλευθέρα καὶ παρθένος καὶ
3 ἀξία τῆς θεοῦ." ὡς δὲ ταῦτ' ἤκουσε, "Καὶ λοιδορεῖς," φήσας, "δεσμῶτα καὶ κατάδικε;" παίει με κατὰ τῶν προσώπων μάλα βιαίως καὶ ἐπάγει δευτέραν· οἱ δὲ τῶν ῥινῶν αἵματος ἔρρεον κρουνοί· ὅλον γὰρ αὐτοῦ τὸν θυμὸν εἶχεν ἡ πληγή.
4 ὡς δὲ καὶ τρίτην ἀπροφυλάκτως ἔπαισε, λανθάνει

BOOK VIII

1. WE were just about to sit down and talk of
all this that had happened, when Thersander came
rushing into the shrine, bringing some of his supporters as witnesses; and, addressing himself to
the bishop, shouted out: "I testify before these
witnesses that you have no right to release from his
bonds and from the death-sentence a man who has
been capitally condemned with all the solemnity of
the law. And you have here a slave-girl of mine,
a harlot who cannot be stopped from madness for
men; see that you keep her safe for me." At the
words "slave and harlot," I was grievously affected,
and could not bear [1] the wounds inflicted by his words;
but while he was still speaking, "Triply [2] slave
yourself," I interrupted, "and lecher, you run after
harlots, while she is a free woman and a virgin, and
well worthy of the goddess whom she serves." On
hearing this, "Do you dare to revile me," he cried,
"gaol-bird and convicted felon?" and as he spoke,
he gave me a violent blow on the face and followed
it up with another, so that out flowed the streams of
blood from my nostrils, as there was all the force of
his fury behind the blow. He aimed a third, but
taking less care in its direction, he accidentally struck

Achilles Tatius intended to depict him so, or whether it is a
fault in the drawing.
   [2] Literally, "a slave through three generations." Reference is probably made here to his being a slave to his lusts.

μου τῷ στόματι περὶ τοὺς ὀδόντας προσπταίσας
τὴν χεῖρα, καὶ τρωθεὶς τοὺς δακτύλους, μόλις τὴν
χεῖρα συνέστειλεν ἀνακραγών. καὶ οἱ ὀδόντες
ἀμύνουσι τὴν τῶν ῥινῶν ὕβριν· τιτρώσκουσι γὰρ
αὐτοὶ τοὺς παίοντας δακτύλους, καὶ ἃ πεποίηκεν
5 ἔπαθεν ἡ χείρ. καὶ ὁ μὲν ἐπὶ τῇ πληγῇ μάλα
ἄκων[1] ἀνακραγὼν συνέστειλε τὴν χεῖρα καὶ
οὕτως ἐπαύσατο. ἐγὼ δὲ ἰδὼν οἷον ἔχει κακόν,
τοῦτο μὲν οὐ προσεποιησάμην· ἐφ' οἷς δὲ ἐτυραν-
νήθην τραγῳδῶν, ἐνέπλησα βοῆς τὸ ἱερόν.

2. " Ποῖ[2] φύγωμεν ἔτι τοὺς βιαίους; ποῖ
καταδράμωμεν; ἐπὶ τίνα θεῶν μετὰ τὴν Ἄρτεμιν;
ἐν αὐτοῖς τυπτόμεθα τοῖς ἱεροῖς· ἐν τοῖς τῆς
αὐλαίας παιόμεθα χωρίοις. ταῦτα ἐν ἐρημίαις
μόναις γίνεται, ὅπου μηδεὶς μάρτυς, μηδὲ ἄνθρωπός
ἐστι· σὺ δὲ αὐτῶν ἐν ὄψει τυραννεῖς τῶν θεῶν.
2 καὶ τοῖς μὲν πονηροῖς αἱ τῶν ἱερῶν ἀσφάλειαι
διδόασι καταφυγήν, ἐγὼ δὲ μηδένα ἀδικήσας,
ἱκέτης δὲ τῆς Ἀρτέμιδος γενόμενος, τύπτομαι
παρ' αὐτῷ τῷ βωμῷ, βλεπούσης, οἴμοι, τῆς θεοῦ.
3 ἐπὶ τὴν Ἄρτεμιν αἱ πληγαί. καὶ οὐ μέχρι πληγῶν
ἡ παροινία, ἀλλὰ καὶ ἐπὶ τῶν προσώπων τις
λαμβάνει τραύματα, ὡς ἐν πολέμῳ καὶ μάχῃ,
καὶ μεμίανται[3] τὸ ἔδαφος ἀνθρωπίνῳ αἵματι.
τοιαῦτα σπένδει τίς θεῷ; οὐ βάρβαροι ταῦτα

---

[1] So Hercher: μαλ' ἀλγῶν Schmidt: μαλ' Cobet: μαλακὸν MSS.
[2] Jacobs' correction for MSS. ποῦ.
[3] μέν followed in the MSS. I think Hercher must be
right to omit it.

his hand on my mouth, right on the teeth, and wounding his knuckles badly, uttered a cry of pain, and drew back his hand, though the wound made it quite hard to do so; thus my teeth avenged the violence offered to my nose, wounding the fingers that had given the blow, and the striking hand was repaid in its own coin. He could not repress a cry at the wound, but drew back his hand and so desisted from his assault: while I saw the accident that had happened to him, but pretended not to do so; but instead I made a tremendous fuss and outcry at the violent and overbearing treatment meted out to me, filling the temple with my cries.

2. "Now whither are we to flee from violence? What is to be our refuge? To which of the gods are we to have recourse, if Artemis cannot protect us? We are assaulted in her very temple; we are beaten before the very sanctuary-veil. Such things as this happen only in deserted places where there are no witnesses at hand or even none of the human race; you shew your brutal violence in the sight of the gods themselves. Even evil-doers have a refuge in the safety of the sanctuary; but I, who have offended against no man, and had taken up the position of Artemis' suppliant, am struck before her very altar, with the goddess, oh shame, looking on. These blows are aimed at Artemis herself: and the mad folly of her desecrator did not stop at mere blows; people are wounded, yes, wounded on the face, wounds such as one receives in wars and battles, and the holy pavement has been defiled with human blood. Is this a libation fit for the goddess? Are not these the offerings poured by

393

καὶ Ταῦροι, καὶ ἡ Ἄρτεμις ἡ Σκυθῶν; ὁ παρ'
ἐκείνοις μόνος νεὼς οὕτως αἱμάσσεται· τὴν Ἰωνίαν
Σκυθίαν πεποίηκας, καὶ ἐν Ἐφέσῳ ῥεῖ τὰ ἐν
Ταύροις αἵματα. λαβὲ καὶ ξίφος κατ' ἐμοῦ.
4 καίτοι τί δέῃ σιδήρου; τὰ τοῦ ξίφους πεποίηκεν
ἡ χείρ. ἀνδροφόνος αὕτη καὶ μιαιφόνος δεξιὰ
τοιαῦτα δέδρακεν οἷα ἐκ φόνου γίνεται."

3. Ταῦτά μου βοῶντος ὁ [1] ὄχλος συνερρύη τῶν
ἐν τῷ ἱερῷ παρόντων· καὶ οὗτοι [2] ἐκάκιζον αὐτὸν
καὶ ὁ ἱερεὺς αὐτός, " Οὐκ αἰσχύνῃ [3] τοιαῦτα ποιῶν
οὕτω φανερῶς καὶ ἐν τῷ ἱερῷ;" ἐγώ τε τεθαρρηκώς,
" Τοιαῦτα," ἔφην, "ὦ ἄνδρες, πέπονθα, ἐλεύθερός
τε ὤν, καὶ πόλεως οὐκ ἀσήμου, ἐπιβουλευθεὶς μὲν
εἰς τὴν ψυχὴν ὑπὸ τούτου, σωθεὶς δὲ ὑπὸ τῆς
2 Ἀρτέμιδος, ἣ τοῦτον ἀπέφηνε συκοφάντην. καὶ
νῦν προελθεῖν με δεῖ καὶ ἀπονίψασθαι τὸ πρόσωπον ἔξω. μὴ γὰρ ἐνταῦθα τοῦτο ποιήσαιμι
ἔγωγε, μὴ καὶ τὸ ἱερὸν ὕδωρ τῷ τῆς ὕβρεως αἵματι
3 μιανθῇ." τότε μὲν δὴ μόλις ἀφελκύσαντες
αὐτὸν ἐξάγουσι τοῦ ἱεροῦ. τοσοῦτον δὲ εἶπεν
ἀπιών· "Ἀλλὰ τὸ μὲν σὸν ἤδη κέκριται, καὶ ὅσον
οὐδέπω πείσῃ δίκην· τὸ δὲ τῆς ψευδοπαρθένου
ταύτης ἑταίρας ἡ σύριγξ τιμωρήσεται."

---

[1] ὁ added by Jacobs.
[2] So Salmasius for οὕτως. Jackson reads οὗτοί τ'.
[3] αἰσχύνῃ Salmasius: αἰσχύνεται.

---

[1] The inhabitants of the Crimea, who sacrificed to their
Artemis any strangers who entered their country.
[2] St. Paul's exact words, Acts xxi. 39, οὐκ ἀσήμου πόλεως

barbarians and the natives of Tauri,[1] and is not this rather the Artemis worshipped by the Scythians? Only among them is the shrine drenched with blood after this fashion. You have converted Ionia into Scythia, Thersander, and here in Ephesus flows blood that should only flow at Tauri. Come, use your sword against me! But what need is there of the steel? Your hand has done the work of the sword. Yes, that murderous and bloody hand of yours has performed the work that is done at a human sacrifice."

3. As I shouted out these complaints, a great crowd came together of all those who were in the temple: and they began to abuse Thersander, as did the bishop himself, who said: "Are you not ashamed of acting thus, openly and in the temple?" At this, I took courage and added: "This is what I have suffered, Sirs, though I am a free man and a citizen of no mean city[2]; this rascal conspired against my life, but Artemis saved me and proved him a trumper-up of false charges. Now I must go and wash my face outside; God forbid that the holy water[3] of the temple should be polluted by the blood of violence." At this, they dragged him away with some difficulty and induced him to leave the temple, but thus much he was able to say as he went; "Your case is already judged and finished, and it will not be long before you pay the penalty that is due; as for this prostitute, this sham virgin, she shall be tested by the ordeal of the pan-pipes.[4]"

πολίτης, of which the present passage sounds a reminiscence.

[3] Not in stoups, as in modern churches, but a fountain for purposes of ablution.

[4] This will be explained in chapter vi.

4. Ὡς δὲ ἀπηλλάγη ποτέ, κἀγὼ ἐξελθὼν ἐκάθηρα τὸ πρόσωπον. τοῦ δὲ δείπνου καιρὸς ἦν, καὶ ὑπεδέξατο ἡμᾶς ὁ ἱερεὺς μάλα φιλοφρόνως. ἐγὼ δὲ εἰς τὸν Σώστρατον ὀρθοῖς τοῖς ὀφθαλμοῖς ἰδεῖν οὐκ ἠδυνάμην, συνειδὼς οἷα αὐτὸν διετεθείκειν. καὶ ὁ Σώστρατος δὲ τὰς τῶν ὀφθαλμῶν ὁρῶν ἀμύξεις τῶν ἐμῶν ἃς ἔτυχον ὑπ' αὐτοῦ παθών, ἀντῃσχύνετό με βλέπειν· καὶ ἡ Λευκίππη δὲ τὰ πολλὰ εἰς γῆν ἔβλεπε· καὶ
2 ἦν ὅλον τὸ συμπόσιον αἰδώς. προϊόντος δὲ τοῦ πότου καὶ τοῦ Διονύσου κατὰ μικρὸν ἐξιλασκομένου τὴν αἰδὼ (ἐλευθερίας γὰρ οὗτος πατήρ)[1] ἄρχει λόγου πρῶτος ὁ ἱερεὺς πρὸς τὸν Σώστρατον· " Τί οὐ λέγεις, ὦ ξένε, τὸν περὶ ὑμᾶς μῦθον ὅστις ἐστί; δοκεῖ γάρ μοι περιπλοκάς τινας ἔχειν οὐκ ἀηδεῖς, οἴνῳ δὲ μάλιστα πρέπουσιν
3 οἱ τοιοῦτοι λόγοι." καὶ ὁ Σώστρατος προφάσεως λαβόμενος ἄσμενος, "Τὸ μὲν κατ' ἐμὲ τοῦ λόγου μέρος ἁπλοῦν," εἶπεν· "ὅτι Σώστρατος ὄνομα, Βυζάντιος τὸ γένος, τούτου θεῖος, πατὴρ ταύτης. τὸ δὲ λοιπόν, ὅπερ ἐστὶ μῦθος, λέγε,
4 τέκνον Κλειτοφῶν, μηδὲν αἰδούμενος. καὶ γὰρ εἴ τί μοι συμβέβηκε λυπηρόν, μάλιστα μὲν οὐ σόν ἐστιν, ἀλλὰ τοῦ δαίμονος· ἔπειτα τῶν ἔργων παρελθόντων ἡ διήγησις τὸν οὐκέτι πάσχοντα ψυχαγωγεῖ μᾶλλον ἢ λυπεῖ."
5. Κἀγὼ πάντα τὰ κατὰ τὴν ἀποδημίαν τὴν ἀπὸ Τύρου διηγοῦμαι, τὸν πλοῦν, τὴν ναυαγίαν, τὴν Αἴγυπτον, τοὺς βουκόλους, τῆς Λευκίππης

---

[1] Possibly a reference to the Latin name of Bacchus, *Liber pater.*

4. At last he went, and I too went out and washed
my face. It was then time for dinner, and the
bishop most hospitably invited us to dine with him.
I was unable to look Sostratus in the face, conscious
of the way I had treated him : while he, observing
the scratches round my eyes of which he had been
the inflicter, was in return ashamed to face me ;
and Leucippe for the most part kept her eyes fixed
on the ground; so that the whole dinner was one long
shamefastness. However, as we began to drink
more deep and Dionysus little by little dissolved our
shyness (rightly is he called the father of freedom [1]),
the bishop was the first to speak, addressing himself
to Sostratus. "Will you not tell us, stranger," said
he, "the story in which you are all involved? Some
of its ins and outs are likely to be not without
interest, and tales of this sort are most suitable for
the time when the wine is going round." Sostratus
was very glad to get hold of an excuse for breaking
the ice. "My part of the story," he said, "is very
simple. Sostratus is my name, and I am a Byzantine
by birth ; the uncle of one of your guests, and the
father of the other. As for all the rest, do you,
my boy Clitophon, relate whatever the story is,
and do not be shy about it. Even if I have gone
through a great deal of trouble, the greater part
of it is not your fault, but that of Fortune ; and
besides, the recital of trials past is more likely to
raise the spirits [2] of a man who is no longer sufferng
under them than to depress him."

5. At this I related the whole story which de-
veloped from our flight from Tyre—our voyage, the
shipwreck, our adventures in Egypt, the buccaneers,

[2] Not quite a literal translation : ψυχαγωγέω means "to
allure," and so "to delight."

τὴν ἀπαγωγήν, τὴν παρὰ τῷ βωμῷ πλαστὴν
γαστέρα, τὴν Μενελάου τέχνην, τὸν ἔρωτα τοῦ
στρατηγοῦ καὶ τὸ Χαιρέου φάρμακον, τὴν τῶν
λῃστῶν ἁρπαγήν, καὶ τὸ τοῦ μηροῦ τραῦμα
2 καὶ ἔδειξα τὴν οὐλήν. ἐπεὶ δὲ κατὰ τὴν
Μελίτην ἐγενόμην, ἐξῆρον τὸ πρᾶγμα [1] ἐμαυτοῦ
πρὸς τὴν σωφροσύνην μεταποιῶν καὶ οὐδὲν ἐψευ-
δόμην· τὸν Μελίτης ἔρωτα, καὶ τὴν σωφροσύνην τὴν ἐμήν, ὅσον ἐλιπάρησε χρόνον, ὅσον ἀπέ-
τυχεν, ὅσα ἐπηγγείλατο, ὅσα ὠδύρατο· τὴν ναῦν
διηγησάμην, τὸν εἰς Ἔφεσον πλοῦν, καὶ ὡς ἄμφω
συνεκαθεύδομεν, καί, μὰ ταύτην τὴν Ἄρτεμιν,
3 ὡς ἀπὸ γυναικὸς ἀνέστη γυνή. ἓν μόνον παρῆκα
τῶν ἐμαυτοῦ δραμάτων, τὴν μετὰ ταῦτα πρὸς
Μελίτην αἰδῶ· ἐπεὶ καὶ τὸ δεῖπνον εἶπον,
καὶ ὡς ἐμαυτοῦ κατεψευσάμην, καὶ μέχρι τῆς
θεωρίας τὸν λόγον συνεπέρανα, καί, "Τὰ μὲν
ἐμὰ ταῦτα," ἔφην· "τὰ δὲ Λευκίππης τῶν ἐμῶν
4 μείζονα. πέπραται, δεδούλευκε, γῆν ἔσκαψε,
σεσύληται τῆς κεφαλῆς τὸ κάλλος· τὴν κουρὰν
ὁρᾷς." καὶ καθ᾽ ἕκαστον ὡς ἐγένετο διεξήειν.
5 κἂν τῷδε κατὰ τὸν Σωσθένην καὶ Θέρσανδρον
γενόμενος, ἐξῆρον καὶ τὰ αὐτῆς ἔτι μᾶλλον ἢ

---

[1] πρᾶγμα is a little feeble, and I should believe Hercher's
δρᾶμα to be right were it not for δραμάτων in § 3 below.

the carrying away of Leucippe, the mock stomach used at the altar (Menelaus' artful device), the general's love and the remedy administered by Chaereas, how Leucippe was carried off by the pirates and the wound I received in the thigh during the fight with them, of which I showed them the scar. When I came to the part of the story in which Melite was concerned, I gave such a turn to the sequence of events that I made them appear greatly to the advantage of my continence, yet without any departure from the truth; I related the story of Melite's love for me, my own chastity with regard to her—the long time during which she besought me to take pity on her, her ill-success in her prayers, her promises, her laments; I told all about the ship, our voyage to Ephesus, how we shared the same couch, and how (I swore by Artemis present before us) she rose from it as one woman would rise from another's bed. Only one thing I omitted in all my adventures, and that was the somewhat delicate matter of my connexion with Melite after the events just mentioned; but I recounted my dinner with her, and how, later, I made the false accusation against myself, and I completed the story as far as the arrival of the sacred embassy. " These are my adventures," said I, " but those of Leucippe have been more thrilling than mine. She has been bought and sold, she has been a slave, she has dug the ground, she has been robbed of the crowning glory of her hair; you can still see where her head was shaved ": and I then related all that had happened to her in detail. When I came to the part where she fell in with Sosthenes and Thersander, I made much more of her adventures than I had of

τἀμά, ἐρωτικῶς[1] αὐτῇ χαριούμενος ἀκούοντος
τοῦ πατρός· ὡς πᾶσαν αἰκίαν ἤνεγκεν εἰς τὸ
σῶμα καὶ ὕβριν, πλὴν μιᾶς· ὑπὲρ δὲ ταύτης τὰς
ἄλλας πάσας ὑπέστη· "Καὶ ἔμεινε, πάτερ,
τοιαύτη μέχρι τῆς παρούσης ἡμέρας, οἵαν αὐτὴν

6 ἐξέπεμψας, ἀπὸ Βυζαντίου. καὶ οὐκ ἐμὸν τοῦτο
ἐγκώμιον, ὅτι φυγὴν ἑλόμενος οὐδὲν ἔδρασα
ὑπὲρ ὧν ἔφυγον, ἀλλ᾽ αὐτῆς, ὅτι καὶ ἐν μέσοις
λῃσταῖς ἔμεινε παρθένος, καὶ τὸν μέγαν ἐνίκησε
λῃστήν, Θέρσανδρον λέγω, τὸν ἀναίσχυντον,

7 τὸν βίαιον. ἐφιλοσοφήσαμεν, πάτερ, τὴν ἀποδη-
μίαν· ἐδίωξε γὰρ ἡμᾶς ἔρως, καὶ ἦν ἐραστοῦ
καὶ ἐρωμένης φυγή· ἀποδημήσαντες γεγόναμεν
ἀλλήλων ἀδελφοί. εἴ τις ἄρα ἐστὶν ἀνδρὸς
παρθενία, ταύτην κἀγὼ μέχρι τοῦ παρόντος
πρὸς Λευκίππην ἔχω· ἡ μὲν γὰρ ἦρα ἐκ πολλοῦ

8 τοῦ τῆς Ἀρτέμιδος ἱεροῦ. δέσποινα Ἀφροδίτη,
μὴ νεμεσήσῃς ἡμῖν ὡς ὑβρισμένη. οὐκ ἠθέλομεν
ἀπάτορα γενέσθαι τὸν γάμον· πάρεστιν οὖν
ὁ πατήρ· ἧκε καὶ σύ· εὐμενὴς ἡμῖν ἤδη γενοῦ."

9 ταῦτα ἀκούοντες, ὁ μὲν ἱερεὺς ἐκεχήνει, θαυμάζων
ἕκαστον τῶν λεγομένων· ὁ δὲ Σώστρατος καὶ
ἐπεδάκρυεν, εἴ ποτε κατὰ Λευκίππην ἐγεγόνει

---

[1] The MSS. have ἑτέρως, for which Cobet suggested εἰδώς.
But I prefer Jacobs' ἐρωτικῶς.

---

[1] He calls Sostratus "father" either simply as a title of
respect to an older man, or because Sostratus had called him
τέκνον (iv. § 3), or because he hoped soon to be Sostratus'
son-in-law.

[2] True enough. See Book IV. ch. i.

[3] A very necessary qualification. Melite is presently (xi. § 3
and xiv. § 4) to get off by a similar mental reservation. The
reference to Leucippe's anxious expectation (if ἦρα can thus

my own, wishing, as a lover should, to give her the
greatest possible credit while her father was listening ;
how she suffered bodily all manner of insult and
violence, save one, and because of this one alone
withstood all the others : "And in that respect,
father," [1] I added, "she is still the same, up to the
present day, as when you sent her away from
Byzantium. Nor is it to be put down at all to my
credit [2] that after accomplishing this flight I abstained
from the very object for which we had fled: but to
hers, that she remained a virgin when surrounded by
a gang of pirates, and overcame that greatest pirate
of all ; I mean Thersander, the shameless, brutal
wretch. During our journey from Tyre we were
abstemious, my father; it was love that drove us from
our native land, and the flight was that of a lover
and his mistress; but when we had once started we
became no more than a brother and sister to each
other. If there be any such thing as virginity
among us men, then that I have preserved with respect
to Leucippe [3] up to the present moment, while, as
for her, she has long been anxiously hoping for this
temple of Artemis. Lady Aphrodite, be not wroth
with us as though we had slighted thee ; we would
not that our marriage should take place without her
father being present ; now he is here, come thou
also, and look kindly upon us." As they heard this
tale, the bishop listened agape with astonishment, full
of surprise at all the details of the story ; while
Sostratus was shedding tears every time the relation
dealt with the adventures of Leucippe. When I had

be translated) that she might come to the temple of Artemis
is explained by IV. i. § 4, where Artemis announces that she
will assist at Leucippe's marriage, and Clitophon's appeal to
Aphrodite by §§ 6 and 7 of the same chapter.

τὸ δρᾶμα. καὶ ἐπεί ποτε ἐπαυσάμην, "Τὰ μὲν
ἡμέτερα," εἶπον, "ἠκούσατε· ἐν δὲ αἰτῶ μαθεῖν
κἀγὼ παρὰ σοῦ, ἱερεῦ, μόνον· τί ποτέ ἐστιν
ὃ τελευταῖον ἀπιὼν ὁ Θέρσανδρος κατὰ Λευκίππης προσέθηκε, σύριγγα εἰπών;" "'Αλλὰ σύ γε,"
ἔφη, "καλῶς ἀνήρου· καὶ γὰρ εἰδότας ἡμᾶς
τὰ περὶ τὴν σύριγγα τοῖς παροῦσιν ὅμως ἁρμό-
σασθαι προσήκει· κἀγὼ τὸν σὸν ἀμείψομαι μῦθον
εἰπών.

6. "'Ορᾷς τουτὶ τὸ ἄλσος τὸ κατόπιν τοῦ νεώ.
ἐνθάδε ἐστὶ σπήλαιον ἀπόρρητον γυναιξί, καθα-
ραῖς δὲ εἰσελθούσαις οὐκ ἀπόρρητον παρθένοις·
ἀνάκειται δὲ σύριγξ ὀλίγον ἔνδον τῶν τοῦ σπη-
2 λαίου θυρῶν. εἰ μὲν οὖν τὸ ὄργανον καὶ παρ'
ὑμῖν ἐπιχωριάζει τοῖς Βυζαντίοις, ἴστε ὃ λέγω·
εἰ δέ τις ὑμῶν ἧττον ὡμίλησε ταύτῃ τῇ μουσικῇ,
φέρε καὶ οἷόν ἐστιν εἴπω, καὶ τὸν ταύτῃ τοῦ
3 Πανὸς πάντα μῦθον. ἡ σύριγξ αὐλοὶ μέν εἰσι πολλοί, κάλαμος¹ δὲ τῶν αὐλῶν ἕκαστος· αὐλοῦσι
δὲ οἱ κάλαμοι πάντες ὥσπερ αὐλὸς εἷς. σύγκεινται
4 δὲ στοιχηδὸν ἄλλος ἐπ' ἄλλον ἠνωμένος· τὸ
πρόσωπον ἰσοστάσιον καὶ τὸ νῶτον. καὶ ὅσοι
εἰσὶ τῶν καλάμων βραχὺ μικρῷ λειπόμενοι, τούτων
μείζων ὁ μετὰ τοῦτον, καὶ ἐπὶ τῷ δευτέρῳ
τοσοῦτον, ὅσον τοῦ δευτέρου μείζων ὁ μετὰ
τοῦτον τρίτος, καὶ κατὰ λόγον οὕτως ὁ λοιπὸς
τῶν καλάμων χορὸς ἕκαστον τοῦ πρόσθεν ἴσον²

¹ I think the singular (Hercher's correction) is gram-
matically necessary. The MSS. have κάλαμοι.
² The Greek is very hard. ἄνισον Salmasius. A friend
suggests ἕκαστος τοῦ πρόσθεν ἴσον (or ἴσῳ) προύχων.

at last made an end: "You have now both of you heard all that happened to us," I added, "but there is one thing about which I in my turn should like to question you, good bishop. What is it that Thersander meant in his last threats against Leucippe, just as he was going away, when he mentioned the pan-pipes?" "That is a fair question," he replied, "and as I know all about the pan-pipes, it is only right that I should adapt myself to your present wishes. I will make it clear to you as a return for the story you have just told.

6. "You see this grove here behind the shrine. Within it is a grotto that may not be entered by any women except clean maids, and a little within its walls there hangs up a pan-pipes. If this instrument is found as a native institution among you of Byzantium, you will be well acquainted with that of which I speak, but if any of you are less familiar with music of this description, allow me to explain it to you and to tell you the whole story of Pan. The pan-pipes is in reality a set of pipes, and while each reed is a pipe, the whole group of reeds is equal to one pipe [1]; they are fastened together in a row, one after the other, to form a single whole, and the instrument appears the same whether regarded from the back or the front. The reeds differ slightly from one another in length; the shortest is fixed at one end of the row, then comes that which is next above it in size, then, third, the one which is as much longer than the second as the second is longer than the first, and so the whole of them in due order, going up in equal gradations

[1] Because the one pipe can make all the notes of the group of single reeds. On this whole passage see Vilborg, Commentary, 127 ff.

5 ἔχων, τὸ δὲ ἔσω μέσον ἐστὶ τῷ περιττῷ. αἴτιον
δὲ τῆς τοιαύτης τάξεως ἡ τῆς ἁρμονίας διανομή.
τὸ[1] μὲν γὰρ ὀξύτατον ἄνω,[2] καὶ ὅσον εἰς τὸ
κάτω πρῶτον βαρύ,[3] κατὰ κέρας ἑκάτερον ὁ
ἄκρος ἔλαχεν αὐλός· τὰ δὲ μεταξὺ τῶν ἄκρων
τοῦ ῥυθμοῦ διαστήματα, πάντες οἱ μεταξὺ
κάλαμοι, ἕκαστος ἐπὶ τὸν πέλας τὸ ὀξὺ κατα-
φέρων ἐς τὸν τῷ τελευταίῳ συνάπτει βάρει.
6 ὅσα δὲ ὁ τῆς Ἀθηνᾶς αὐλὸς ἐντὸς λαλεῖ, τοσαῦτα
καὶ ὁ τοῦ Πανὸς ἐν τοῖς στόμασιν αὐλεῖ. ἀλλ’
ἐκεῖ μὲν οἱ δάκτυλοι κυβερνῶσι τὰ αὐλήματα,
ἐνταῦθα δὲ τοῦ τεχνίτου τὸ στόμα μιμεῖται τοὺς
δακτύλους. κἀκεῖ μὲν κλείσας ὁ αὐλητὴς τὰς
ἄλλας ὀπάς, μίαν ἀνοίγει μόνην, δι’ ἧς τὸ πνεῦμα
καταρρεῖ, ἐνταῦθα δὲ τοὺς μὲν ἄλλους ἐλευθέρους
ἀφῆκε καλάμους, μόνῳ δὲ τὸ χεῖλος ἐπιτίθησιν,
ὃν ἂν ἐθέλῃ μὴ σιωπᾶν, μεταπηδᾷ τε ἄλλοτε ἐπ’
ἄλλον, ὅποι ποτ’ ἂν ἡ τοῦ κρούματος ἁρμονία
7 καλῇ.[4] οὕτως αὐτῷ περὶ τοὺς αὐλοὺς χορεύει
τὸ στόμα. ἦν δὲ ἡ σύριγξ οὔτε αὐλὸς ἀπ’ ἀρχῆς
οὔτε κάλαμος, ἀλλὰ παρθένος εὐειδὴς οἵαν εἰς
θεοὺς ἐγκρίνειν.[5] ὁ Πὰν οὖν ἐδίωκεν αὐτὴν δρόμον
ἐρωτικόν, τὴν δὲ ὕλη τις δέχεται δασεῖα φεύγου-
σαν· ὁ δὲ Πὰν κατὰ πόδας εἰσθορὼν ὤρεγε τὴν

---

[1] τόσον Düring.
[2] ⟨τὸ⟩ἄνω Düring.
[3] βαρύτα τον καὶ Düring.
[4] ἡ . . . καλῇ is Jacobs’ correction for εἴη . . . καλή of
the MSS.
[5] The MSS. read οἵαν εἶχεν κρίνειν. The suggestion in the
text is due to Knox, and besides making excellent sense is
palaeographically most ingenious, owing to the comparatively
common confusion of ΥϹ with Χ. εἴληχεν κρίνειν Jackson:
οἵα λευκὸν κρίνον Lumb: Hercher deletes.

from the first, and the innermost is (exactly) the middle by reason of the entire number being odd.[1] The reason for this arrangement is to be found in the intervals of the scale: that which gives the highest note is at the top, and the note descends with the length of the reed, so that the two extremities are occupied by the pipes which are musically furthest apart; while, as for the intervals between these extremities, each reed is a note below its neighbour until it comes to the deepest of all at the far end. The sounds which Athene's pipe makes within, the pan-pipes makes at the ends of the reeds, but whereas in the former the note is governed by the movement of the fingers over the holes, in the latter case the performer's lips replace the office of the fingers. With the pipe, the performer stops all the holes but one, through which the breath escapes; but with the pan-pipes all the rest of the reeds are left untouched, and the lips are applied to one alone, the one which is to speak, and thence moves from one reed to another as the necessities of the tune indicate, so that the mouth may be said to dance along the pipes. Now originally the pan-pipes was neither pipe nor reed, but a maiden so fair that one would judge her worthy of a place among the gods.[2] Pan was chasing her, a chase inspired by love, and in her flight she entered a thick wood; he, close on her heels,

---

[1] The whole of this passage is difficult to translate; the description of the instrument is clumsy and involved, and the text is far from secure. I do not flatter myself that I have done more than represent as closely as possible the general sense of the Greek. The words " innermost . . . . odd " are Shorey's.

[2] The story is given in full by Ovid, *Metamorphoses* i. 691.

8 χεῖρα ὡς ἐπ' αὐτήν. καὶ ὁ μὲν ᾤετο τεθηρακέναι
καὶ ἕχεσθαι τῶν τριχῶν, καλάμων δὲ κόμην εἶχεν ἡ
χείρ. τὴν μὲν γὰρ εἰς γῆν καταδῦναι λέγουσι,
9 καλάμους δὲ τὴν γῆν ἀντ' αὐτῆς τεκεῖν. τέμνει
δὴ τοὺς καλάμους ὑπ' ὀργῆς ὁ Πάν, ὡς κλέπτοντας
αὐτοῦ τὴν ἐρωμένην. ἐπεὶ δὲ μετὰ ταῦτα οὐκ
εἶχεν εὑρεῖν, εἰς τοὺς καλάμους δοκῶν λελύσθαι
τὴν κόρην, ἔκλαιε τὴν τομήν, νομίζων τετμηκέναι [1]
10 τὴν ἐρωμένην. συμφορήσας οὖν τὰ τετμημένα
τῶν καλάμων ὡς μέλη τοῦ σώματος, καὶ συνθεὶς
εἰς ἓν σῶμα, εἶχε διὰ χειρῶν τὰς τομὰς τῶν
καλάμων καταφιλῶν, ὡς τῆς κόρης τραύματα·
ἔστενε δὲ ἐρωτικὸν ἐπιθεὶς τὸ στόμα, καὶ ἐνέπνει
ἄνωθεν εἰς τοὺς αὐλοὺς ἅμα φιλῶν. τὸ δὲ πνεῦμα
διὰ τῶν ἐν τοῖς καλάμοις στενωπῶν καταρρέον
αὐλήματα ἐποίει, καὶ ἡ σύριγξ εἶχε φωνήν.
11 ταύτην οὖν τὴν σύριγγά φασιν ἀναθεῖναι μὲν
ἐνθάδε τὸν Πᾶνα, περιορίσαι δὲ εἰς σπήλαιον
αὐτήν, θαμίζειν τε αὐτοῦ καὶ [2] τῇ σύριγγι συνήθως
αὐλεῖν. χρόνῳ δὲ ὕστερον χαρίζεται τὸ χωρίον
τῇ Ἀρτέμιδι, συνθήκας ποιησάμενος πρὸς αὐτήν,
12 μηδεμίαν ἐκεῖ καταβαίνειν γυναῖκα. ὅταν οὖν
αἰτίαν ἔχῃ τις οὐκ εἶναι παρθένος, προπέμπει
μὲν αὐτὴν ὁ δῆμος μέχρι τῶν τοῦ σπηλαίου θυρῶν,
δικάζει δὲ ἡ σύριγξ τὴν δίκην. ἡ μὲν γὰρ παῖς
εἰσέρχεται κεκοσμημένη στολῇ τῇ νενομισμένῃ,
ἄλλος δὲ ἐπικλείει τὰς τοῦ σπηλαίου θύρας.
13 κἂν μὲν ᾖ παρθένος, λιγυρόν τι μέλος ἀκούεται
καὶ ἔνθεον, ἤτοι τοῦ τόπου πνεῦμα ἔχοντος μου-

---

[1] Jacobs' most ingenious correction for MSS. τεθνηκέναι.

[2] καί was formerly read (so in MSS.) after σύριγγι. The
transposition is due to Cobet.

was just stretching out his hand to catch her. He thought that his chase had been successful, and that he was grasping her hair: but his hand only clutched a bunch of reeds; she, it is said, had sunk into the ground, which bore a clump of reeds in her place. Pan, in a passion, cut away the reeds, thinking that they were hiding his beloved from him: but when, after a search lasting some time, he was unable to find her, he realised that she had been transformed into the reeds and regretted his action, thinking that he had actually cut down the object of his love. So he collected the fragments of reed as though they had been the maiden's limbs and put them together as though to form a single body: and then, holding the pieces in his hands, kissed them, as though they had been her wounds. As he put his lips to them he groaned from love, and breathed down upon the reeds while he kissed them; and his breath, pouring down through the holes in them, gave musical notes, and the pan-pipes found its voice. So it is said that Pan there hung up the instrument, shutting it up in a cave, and that it was his custom to resort there often and play on the pipes. Some time after he made a gift of the whole spot to Artemis, making a compact with her that it should be entered by no woman no longer a maid. If therefore any girl is accused of being of doubtful virginity, she is sent by public decree to the door of the grotto, and the pan-pipes decides the ordeal for her; she goes in, clad in the proper dress, and the doors are closed behind her. If she is in reality a virgin, a clear and divine note is heard, either because there is some breeze in the place which enters the pipes and makes a musical

σικὸν εἰς τὴν σύριγγα τεταμιευμένον,[1] ἢ τάχα
καὶ ὁ Πὰν αὐτὸς αὐλεῖ. μετὰ δὲ μικρὸν αὐτόμαται
μὲν αἱ θύραι ἀνεῴχθησαν τοῦ σπηλαίου, ἐκφαίνεται δὲ ἡ παρθένος ἐστεφανωμένη τὴν κεφαλὴν
14 πίτυος κόμαις. ἐὰν δὲ ᾖ τὴν παρθενίαν ἐψευσμένη,
σιωπᾷ μὲν ἡ σύριγξ, οἰμωγὴ δέ τις ἀντὶ μουσικῆς
ἐκ τοῦ σπηλαίου πέμπεται, καὶ εὐθὺς ὁ δῆμος
ἀπαλλάττεται καὶ ἀφίησιν ἐν τῷ σπηλαίῳ τὴν
γυναῖκα. τρίτῃ δὲ ἡμέρᾳ παρθένος ἱέρεια τοῦ
τόπου παρελθοῦσα τὴν μὲν σύριγγα εὑρίσκει
15 χαμαί, τὴν δὲ γυναῖκα οὐδαμοῦ. πρὸς ταῦτα
παρασκευάσασθε πῶς ἂν αὐτοὶ σχῆτε τύχης καὶ
σύνετε. εἰ μὲν γάρ ἐστι παρθένος, ὡς ἔγωγε
βουλοίμην, ἄπιτε χαίροντες τῆς σύριγγος τυχόντες
εὐμενοῦς· οὐ γὰρ ἄν ποτε ψεύσαιτο τὴν κρίσιν·
εἰ δὲ μή, αὐτοὶ γὰρ ἴστε οἷα εἰκὸς ἐν τοσαύταις
αὐτὴν ἐπιβουλαῖς γενομένην ἄκουσαν—"

7. Καὶ εὐθὺς ἡ Λευκίππη, πρὶν τὸν ἱερέα
εἰπεῖν τὸν ἑξῆς λόγον· "Ὡς γέ μοι δοκεῖ, μηδὲ
εἴπῃς· ἐγὼ γὰρ ἑτοίμη εἰς τὸ τῆς σύριγγος σπήλαιον
εἰσελθεῖν καὶ χωρὶς προκλήσεως[2] κατακεκλεῖσθαι."
"'Αγαθὰ λέγεις," ὁ ἱερεὺς εἶπε, "καί σοι συνήδομαι
2 ὑπὲρ σωφροσύνης καὶ τύχης." τότε μὲν οὖν
ἑσπέρας γενομένης, ἕκαστος ἡμῶν ἀπῄει κοιμησόμενος ἔνθα ὁ ἱερεὺς παρεσκεύασεν. ὁ Κλεινίας
δὲ οὐκ ἦν ἡμῖν συνδειπνῶν, ὡς ἂν μὴ φορτικοὶ

---

[1] The MSS. have ταμιεῖον. The word in the text was
suggested by Hercher. ταμεῦον Göttling.
[2] So Hirschig, for MSS. κλήσεως (κλείσεως M): κλίσεως
Lumb.

sound, or possibly because it is Pan himself that is
piping : and after a short time the doors of the
grotto open of their own accord, and out comes the
virgin with a wreath of the foliage of the pine upon
her head. But if she has lied about her virginity,
the pan-pipes is silent, and a groan comes forth from
the cave instead of a musical sound ; the people go
away and leave the woman inside. On the third day
after, the virgin priestess of the spot comes and finds
the pan-pipes lying on the ground, but there is no
trace of the woman. It is advisable therefore that
you should take most careful thought as to the
position that you are in, and be prudent. If she is a
virgin, as I hope and think, go on light-heartedly
and find the pan-pipes in your favour, for there is no
instance of their giving a false decision ; but if not,
for you know that in the various trials to which she
has been subject, it is possible that she, all against
her will—"

7. But Leucippe would not let the bishop finish his
sentence. " I am quite determined," she broke in ;
" say nothing more. I am ready to go into the
grotto of the pan-pipes and to be shut up there
even without any legal challenge." " Good news,"
said the bishop, " and I congratulate you on your discretion [1] and your good fortune." It was by this
time the evening, and we each of us retired to bed
according as the bishop had made disposition for us :
Clinias had not dined with us, as we did not wish to

---

[1] σωφροσύνη is exactly equivalent to the French *sagesse* in
this rather technical shade of meaning. We are unable to
represent it with precision in English. I fear that the
bishop's next words sound a little cynical ; we know that he
was well up in Aristophanes, but I am not sure whether our
author intends him to be speaking here with a smile.

δοκοίημεν εἶναι τῷ ξενοδόκῳ, ἀλλ' ἔνθα καὶ τὴν
3 πρόσθεν ἡμέραν καὶ τὴν τότε. τὸν μέντοι Σώστρατον ἑώρων ὑποθορυβηθέντα τῷ τῆς σύριγγος
διηγήματι, μὴ ἄρα τὰ περὶ τῆς παρθενίας δι'
4 αἰδῶ τὴν πρὸς αὐτὸν ψευδώμεθα. διανεύω δὴ τῇ
Λευκίππῃ νεύματι ἀφανεῖ τὸν φόβον τοῦ πατρὸς
ἐξελεῖν, ἐπισταμένη[1] οἴῳ δὴ τρόπῳ μάλιστα οἴεται
πείσειν. κἀκείνη δὲ ἐδόκει μοι ταὐτὸν ὑποπτεύειν,
ὥστε ταχύ μου[2] συνῆκε. διενοεῖτο δὲ καὶ πρὸ
τοῦ παρ' ἐμοῦ νεύματος, πῶς ἂν κοσμιώτατα
5 προσενεχθείη τῷ πιστώματι. μέλλουσα οὖν
πρὸς ὕπνον ἀναχωρεῖν, καὶ ἀσπαζομένη τὸν πατέρα, ἠρέμα πρὸς αὐτόν, " Θάρρει, πάτερ," ἔφη,
" περὶ ἐμοῦ, καὶ πίστευε τοῖς εἰρημένοις. μὰ
τὴν γὰρ Ἄρτεμιν, οὐδέτερος ἡμῶν οὐδὲν ἐψεύ-
σατο."

6 Τῇ δὲ ὑστεραίᾳ περὶ τὴν θεωρίαν ἦσαν ὅ τε
Σώστρατος καὶ ὁ ἱερεύς, καὶ ηὐτρεπισμέναι ἦσαν
αἱ θυσίαι· παρῆν δὲ καὶ ἡ βουλὴ μεθέξουσα τῶν
ἱερείων. εὐφημίαι δὲ ἦσαν εἰς τὴν θεὸν πολλαί,
καὶ ὁ Θέρσανδρος (ἔτυχε γὰρ καὶ αὐτὸς παρών)
προσελθὼν τῷ προέδρῳ, " Πρόγραψον εἰς αὔριον,"
ἔφη, " τὰς περὶ ἡμῶν δίκας, ἐπεὶ καὶ τὸν καταγνω-
σθέντα σοι χθὲς ἤδη τινὲς ἔλυσαν, καὶ ὁ Σωσθένης
ἐστὶν οὐδαμοῦ." προυγέγραπτο μὲν οὖν εἰς τὴν
ὑστεραίαν ἡ δίκη· παρεσκευαζόμεθα δὲ ἡμεῖς μάλα
εὐτρεπῶς[3] ἔχοντες.

---

[1] I think the dative, restored by Hercher, is necessary.
The MSS. give the accusative. πιστωσαμένην Jackson.
[2] Cobet's correction for MSS. μέν; who also corrected ὡς
into πῶς in the next line.
[3] Corrected by Jacobs from MSS. εὐπρεπῶς.

seem to impose on the hospitality of our good host, but
had stayed in the same lodging where he had been
the day before. I should say that I had noticed
that Sostratus shewed some slight signs of uneasiness
during the story about the pan-pipes; he was
evidently afraid that we had somewhat exaggerated
Leucippe's virginity out of respect to his presence;
I therefore gave Leucippe an imperceptible sign
that she should relieve her father's anxiety, as she
would obviously know best how to convince him;
from the readiness with which she understood my
hint, I rather think that she must have had the same
suspicion about him, so that she quickly understood
me and even before my sign she had been thinking
of the most seemly way to make his assurance doubly
sure. When therefore she was on the point of retiring to bed, she kissed her father good-night, and
said to him in a low voice : " Courage, father, as far
as I am concerned ; and believe our story. I swear
to you by Artemis that neither of us concealed the
truth in any detail."

On the following day Sostratus and the bishop
went about the business of the sacred embassy, and
the sacrifices were handsomely performed, the
members of the council being present and assisting at the service. Many were the blessings and
hymns with which the goddess was invoked, when
Thersander, who had also put in an appearance, went
up to the presiding officer, saying : " I request you
to put down my case for to-morrow ; some persons
have taken it upon themselves to release the prisoner
whom you condemned yesterday, and Sosthenes is
nowhere to be found." The case had therefore been
put down for the following day, and we were making
the most elaborate preparations for our part in it.

ACHILLES TATIUS

8. Ἡκούσης δὲ τῆς κυρίας, ὁ Θέρσανδρος εἶπεν ὧδε· "Οὐκ οἶδα τίνος ἄρξωμαι¹ λόγου καὶ πόθεν, οὐδὲ τίνων κατηγορήσω πρῶτον καὶ τίνων δεύτερον. τά τε γὰρ τετολμημένα πολλὰ ὑπὸ πολλῶν, καὶ οὐδὲν οὐδενὸς τῷ μεγέθει δεύτερον· πάντα δὲ ἀλλήλων γυμνά, καὶ μεθ' ὧν οὐδ' ἂν

2 ἄψωμαι κατηγορῶν.² τά τε γὰρ τῆς ψυχῆς κρατούσης, φοβοῦμαι μὴ ἀτελής μοι ὁ λόγος γένηται, τῆς τῶν ἄλλων μνήμης τὴν γλῶτταν ἐφ' ἕκαστον ἑλκούσης. ἡ γὰρ εἰς τὸ μήπω λεχθὲν ἔπειξις τοῦ λόγου τὸ ὁλόκληρον τῶν ἤδη λεχθέντων

3 παραιρεῖται. ὅταν μὲν γὰρ φονεύωσι τοὺς ἀλλοτρίους οἰκέτας οἱ μοιχοί, μοιχεύωσι δὲ τὰς ἀλλοτρίας γυναῖκας οἱ φονεῖς, λύωσι δὲ ἡμῖν τὰς θεωρίας οἱ πορνοβοσκοί, τὰ δὲ σεμνότατα τῶν ἱερῶν μιαίνωσιν αἱ πόρναι, τὰς ἡμέρας δὲ λογιζόμενος³ ἢ ταῖς δούλαις καὶ τοῖς δεσπόταις, τί δράσειέ τις ἔτι, τῆς ἀνομίας ὁμοῦ καὶ μοιχείας, καὶ ἀσεβείας καὶ μιαιφονίας κεκερασμένης;

4 "Κατεγνώκατέ τινος θάνατον, ἐφ' αἷς δή ποτ' οὖν αἰτίαις, οὐδὲν γὰρ διαφέρει, καὶ δεδεμένον εἰς τὸ δεσμωτήριον ἀπεστείλατε, φυλαχθησόμενον τῇ καταδίκῃ· οὗτος δὲ παρέστηκεν ὑμῖν, ἀντὶ τῶν δεσμῶν λευκὴν ἠμφιεσμένος στολήν, καὶ ἐν τῇ τάξει τῶν ἐλευθέρων ἔστηκεν ὁ δεσμώτης. τάχα

¹ So Cobet for MSS. ἄρξομαι.
² Knox suggests καὶ μεστῶν οὐδ' ἂν ἄψωμαι κατηγοριῶν. Vilborg reads ἔστιν ὧν for μεθ' ὧν and ἄψαιμι for ἄψωμαι or ἄψομαι.
³ With some diffidence I have written ᾖ for ἤ, which at least allows a certain sense to be wrung from the Greek. Dr. Rouse suggests that the original may have been δέ τις ὁριζόμενος, "someone fixing trials for masters and slaves." λογιζόμεναι Vilborg. MSS. have λογιζόμενος (-οι R)ῇ (ἤ W).

8. The appointed time having come, Thersander began, as follows. " I know not where to begin my argument, and with which to begin ; against which to bring my accusation first, and which second. Crime has been piled on crime, by different parties, each as heinous as the rest, and these crimes are but loosely connected with one another; and there are some as well on which I shall hardly be able to touch during my indictment. Since the heart rules the head,[1] I am afraid my speech will be too incoherent to comprehend them all ; before I finish one my tongue will go on to another; my anxiety to proceed to some point on which I have not yet dwelt will blunt the general effect of the whole sum of what I have previously said. When adulterers murder other people's servants, when murderers commit adultery with other people's wives, when whoremongers desecrate sacred embassies, when whores pollute our most sacred temples, when a person is found to fix the day of trials between slave-girls and their masters, is there any further excess of crime that can be committed beyond the welter of contempt for the law, adultery, impiety and blood-guiltiness ?

" You condemned a prisoner to death, on what charges it matters not now, and sent him in chains to prison to be kept there until his execution : and now here he stands before you ; instead of his fetters he is wearing a white robe, and the prisoner is standing in the ranks of those who are free. He

---

[1] The Greek is very difficult. Perhaps " My feelings are too much for me, and so I am afraid . . ." It seems barely possible to get from the Greek the sense more obviously required, " I have them all fully set out in my head, but . . ." Dr. Rouse suggests that for τά τε γάρ we should read ἅτε γάρ.

δὲ καὶ τολμήσει φωνὴν ἀφεῖναι καὶ ἐπιρρητορεύ-
σαί τι κατ' ἐμοῦ, μᾶλλον δὲ καθ' ὑμῶν καὶ τῆς
5 ὑμετέρας ψήφου. λέγε δὲ τῶν προέδρων καὶ τῶν
συμβούλων τὸ δόγμα. ἀκούετε καθάπερ ἐψηφί-
σασθε, καὶ τὴν περὶ τούτου μοι γραφήν. ἔδοξεν
ἀποθνήσκειν Κλειτοφῶντα. ποῦ τοίνυν ὁ δήμιος;
ἀπαγέτω τοῦτον λαβών. δὸς ἤδη τὸ κώνειον.
6 ἤδη τέθνηκε τοῖς νόμοις· κατάδικός ἐστιν ὑπερήμερος.

"Τί λέγεις, ὦ σεμνότατε καὶ κοσμιώτατε ἱερεῦ;
ἐν ποίοις ἱεροῖς γέγραπται νόμοις τοὺς ὑπὸ τῆς
βουλῆς καὶ τῶν πρυτάνεων κατεγνωσμένους καὶ
θανάτοις καὶ δεσμοῖς παραδοθέντας ἐξαρπάζειν
τῆς καταδίκης καὶ τῶν δεσμῶν ἀπολύειν, καὶ
κυριώτερον σαυτὸν ποιεῖν τῶν προέδρων καὶ τῶν
7 δικαστηρίων; ἀνάστηθι τοῦ θώκου, πρόεδρε,
παραχώρησον τῆς ἀρχῆς αὐτῷ καὶ τοῦ δικαστη-
ρίου· οὐκέτι οὐδενὸς εἶ κύριος· οὐδὲν ἔξεστί σοι
κατὰ τῶν πονηρῶν ψηφίσασθαι, καὶ σήμερον ὅ τι
δόξει λύεται. τί ἕστηκας, ἱερεῦ, σὺν ἡμῖν ὡς τῶν
8 πολλῶν εἷς; ἀνάβηθι, καὶ κάθισον ἐν τῷ τοῦ
προέδρου θρόνῳ, καὶ σὺ δίκαζε λοιπὸν ἡμῖν,
μᾶλλον δὲ κέλευε τυραννικῶς, μηδὲ ἀναγινωσκέσθω
σοί τις νόμος μηδὲ γνῶσις δικαστηρίου, μήτε
ὅλως ἄνθρωπον σεαυτὸν ἡγοῦ. μετὰ τῆς Ἀρτέμιδος προσκυνοῦ· καὶ γὰρ τὴν ἐκείνης τιμὴν

will have the impudence, perhaps, to lift up his voice and bring some cavilling, sophisticated accusation against me—rather will it be against you and the vote you gave. Read, usher, the decree pronounced by the presiding judges and their assessors. [*The usher reads the sentence.*] You hear how you decided, and the verdict brought at my suit against this fellow. The vote was that Clitophon was to die. Where then is the public executioner? Let him arrest the prisoner and lead him away to death. Quick, give him the hemlock. He is already dead in the eyes of the law; he is a condemned felon whose date of execution is overdue.

" And now, most reverend and worthy bishop, what have you to say? In what part of the divine law is it written that, when men are condemned by the government and its executive officers and given over for death or chains, you should rescue them from their sentence and have their chains struck off them, arrogating to yourself higher powers than those of presiding judges and courts of law? Come down from the bench, my Lord Chief, and leave your position and the court in his favour; you have no longer power over anybody; it is not within your province to pass sentence on rascals; all your decrees are reversed to-day. Nay, good bishop, why stand among us as though you were one of the common herd? Go up, and take your seat on his Lordship's bench, and be our judge for the future—or rather, just express your sweet will and pleasure, like an autocrat; it is not worth while having any law or precedent of the court read to you. Better still, claim a position above mankind altogether; have worship paid to you along with Artemis, for it is her

415

9 ἐξήρπασας. αὐτῇ μόνῃ τοὺς ἐπ' αὐτὴν κατα-
φεύγοντας ἔξεστι σώζειν· καὶ ταῦτα πρὸ δικαστηρίου γνώσεως. δεδεμένον δὲ οὐδένα λέλυκεν ἡ
θεός, οὐδὲ θανάτῳ παραδοθέντα ἠλευθέρωσε τῆς
τιμωρίας. τῶν δυστυχούντων εἰσίν, οὐ τῶν
10 ἀδικούντων οἱ βωμοί. σὺ δὲ καὶ τοὺς δεθέντας
ἐλευθεροῖς, καὶ τοὺς καταδίκους ἀπολύεις. οὕτως
παρηυδοκίμησας καὶ τὴν Ἄρτεμιν. τίς ᾤκησεν
ἀντὶ δεσμωτηρίου τὸ ἱερόν; φονεὺς καὶ μοιχὸς [1]
παρὰ τῇ καθαρᾷ θεῷ· οἴμοι μοιχὸς παρὰ τῇ
παρθένῳ. συνῆν δὲ αὐτῷ καὶ γυνή τις ἀκόλαστος,
11 ἀποδρᾶσα τὸν δεσπότην.[2] καὶ γὰρ ταύτην, ὡς
εἴδομεν, ὑπεδέχου, καὶ μία γέγονεν αὐτοῖς ἑστία
παρὰ σοὶ καὶ συμπόσιον, τάχα δὲ καὶ συνεκάθευδες, ἱερεῦ, οἴκημα τὸ ἱερὸν ποιήσας. ἡ τῆς
Ἀρτέμιδος οἰκία μοιχῶν γέγονε καὶ πόρνης
12 θάλαμος. ταῦτα μόλις ἐν χαμαιτυπείῳ γίνεται.
εἷς μὲν δή μοι λόγος οὗτος κατ' ἀμφοῖν· τὸν
μέντοι ἀξιῶ τῆς αὐθαδείας δοῦναι τιμωρίαν, τὸν δὲ
ἀποδοθῆναι κελεῦσαι τῇ καταδίκῃ.

" Δεύτερος δέ ἐστί μοι πρὸς Μελίτην μοιχείας
ἀγών, πρὸς ἣν οὐδὲν δέομαι λόγων· ἐν γὰρ τῇ τῶν
θεραπαινῶν βασάνῳ τὴν ἐξέτασιν γενέσθαι δέ-
13 δοκται. ταύτας οὖν αἰτῶ, αἳ κἂν βασανιζόμεναι
φήσωσιν οὐκ εἰδέναι τοῦτον τὸν κατάδικον χρόνῳ

---

[1] I think it quite possible that Jacobs was right in
believing that the words οἴμοι φονεύς have here dropped out.

[2] ἀποδιδράσκω must take an accusative, and this was rightly
altered from the MSS. τοῦ δεσπότου by Cobet.

honour that you have usurped. She alone has had
the power, until now, of affording an asylum to those
who fly to her for help (and that only before the
court has pronounced its verdict; the goddess has
never loosed a criminal from his chains or rescued a
condemned felon from his deserved fate; her altars
are for the unfortunate, not for the guilty), but now
you take it upon yourself to strike the shackles from
the prisoner and acquit the condemned, thus setting
yourself up above the goddess. Who has ever lived
in the temple as if it were a prison? Yes, there was a
murderer and an adulterer in the church of that pure
goddess; alack, alack, an adulterer in the virgin-
shrine! And with him was a woman of the lightest
character, a slave who had run away from her
master: her too, as I myself saw, you took in; you
allowed them to share your hearth and your table;
and I should not be surprised to hear, my lord bishop,
that you shared their bed as well when you turned
the temple into a common lodging. Yes, the church
of Artemis is become a bawdy-house—a whore's bed-
chamber; they would have been ashamed of the
goings-on there in the commonest brothel. My case
against these two men therefore stands together; I
ask that the one may be punished for his presumption,
and that you will order the other to be handed over
to suffer the punishment to which he has been
condemned.

" My second charge is against Melite, for adultery;
and I shall not have to speak at great length against
her, as it has been already resolved that the enquiry
shall be conducted by putting her serving-maids to
the question. I therefore claim them for this
purpose; if, under the torture, they deny that they

πολλῷ συνόντα αὐτῇ καὶ ἐν ἀνδρὸς χώρᾳ ἐν[1] τῇ
οἰκίᾳ τῇ ἐμῇ, οὐκ ἐν μοιχοῦ μόνον, καθεστηκότα,
πάσης αἰτίας αὐτὴν ἀφίημι. ἂν τοίνυν τοὐναντίον, τὴν μὲν κατὰ τὸν νόμον ἀφεῖσθαι τῆς
προικὸς φημὶ δεῖν ἐμοί· τὸν δὲ ὑποσχεῖν τὴν
ὀφειλομένην τοῖς μοιχοῖς τιμωρίαν· θάνατος δέ
ἐστιν αὕτη.[2] ὥστε ὁποτέρως ἂν οὗτος ἀποθάνῃ,[3]
ὡς μοιχὸς ἢ ὡς φονεύς, ἀμφοτέροις ἔνοχος ὤν,
δίκην δεδωκὼς οὐ δέδωκεν· ἀποθανὼν γὰρ ὀφείλει
14 θάνατον ἄλλον. ὁ δέ μοι τρίτος τῶν λόγων πρὸς
τὴν δούλην ἐστὶ τὴν ἐμήν, καὶ τὸν σεμνὸν τοῦτον
πατρὸς ὑποκριτήν, ὃν εἰς ὕστερον, ὅταν τούτων
καταψηφίσησθε, ταμιεύσομαι." ὁ μὲν δὴ ταῦτα
εἰπὼν ἐπαύσατο.

9. Παρελθὼν δὲ ὁ ἱερεύς (ἦν δὲ εἰπεῖν οὐκ
ἀδύνατος, μάλιστα δὲ τὴν Ἀριστοφάνους ἐζη-
λωκὼς κωμῳδίαν) ἤρξατο αὐτὸς λέγειν πάνυ
ἀστείως καὶ κωμῳδικῶς εἰς πορνείαν αὐτοῦ καθαπ-
τόμενος, "Παρὰ τὴν θεόν," λέγων, "λοιδορεῖσθαι
μὲν οὕτως ἀκόσμως τοῖς εὖ βεβιωκόσι στόματός
2 ἐστιν οὐ καθαροῦ. οὗτος δὲ οὐκ ἐνταῦθα μόνον,
ἀλλὰ καὶ πανταχοῦ τὴν γλῶτταν μεστὴν ὕβρεως
ἔχει. καί τοί γε νέος ὢν συνεγίνετο πολλοῖς
αἰδοίοις ἀνδράσι καὶ τὴν ὥραν ἅπασαν εἰς τοῦτο

---

[1] If τῇ οἰκίᾳ τῇ ἐμῇ (τὴν οἰκίαν τὴν ἐμὴν cdd. β) is to be kept,
Jacobs' insertion of ἐν is necessary. But I am not sure that
it is not a gloss to explain ἀνδρὸς χώρᾳ.
[2] Corrected by Jacobs from MSS. αὐτῷ.
[3] So Cobet: αὐτὸς ἀποθάνοι cdd. β: ἀποθάνοι cdd. a.

knew that this gaol-bird kept company with her for
a long time, and actually held a husband's place, not
a mere gallant's, in my house, then I will retract all
charges against her. But if the contrary proves to
be the truth, I claim that, as the law directs, she
must lose her dowry, which then becomes my property,
and that her paramour must suffer the punishment
meted out to adulterers; which is death. So that
for whichever crime he suffers, adultery or murder
(as he is clearly guilty of both), he will escape his due
while he pays the penalty of his crime; whichever
death he dies he will avoid the other which he ought
to undergo. The third part of my charge is against
my slave-girl and this hoary impostor who sets out to
be her father; but I will keep that till later on, after
you have given your verdict against these others."
With these words he ended his speech.

9. The bishop then came forward. He was no
poor hand at speaking, and as good at quip and gibe
as the plays of Aristophanes, and he began his speech
with much humour, touching in a jesting vein on
Thersander's own lecherous depravity. "This[1] fil-
thy abuse," he cried, "in the presence of the
goddess, of those who have led respectable lives, is a
sign of unclean lips! This fellow's tongue is full of
wickedness in more ways than one. When he was
a boy he consorted with many men of standing, and
indeed on this he spent all the period of his youthful

[1] In the whole of the first part of the good bishop's speech
there is a series of double meanings, insinuations, and plays
upon words which are not without wit, but, like the discussion at the end of Book II., are not pleasing to Northern
and Christian ears. I shall not point out the allusions in
notes; they are to be found in almost every sentence down
to the end of § 5.

δεδαπάνηκε. σεμνότητα δ' ἔδρακε [1] καὶ σωφροσύνην ὑπεκρίνατο, παιδείας προσποιούμενος ἐρᾶν καὶ
τοῖς εἰς ταύτην αὐτῷ χρωμένοις πάντα ὑποκύπτων
3 καὶ ὑποκατακλινόμενος ἀεί. καταλιπὼν γὰρ τὴν
πατρῴαν οἰκίαν, ὀλίγον ἑαυτῷ μισθωσάμενος
στενωπεῖον, εἶχεν ἐνταῦθα τὸ οἴκημα, ὁμηρίζων
μὲν τὰ πολλά, πάντας δὲ τοὺς χρησίμους πρὸς
ἅπερ ἤθελε προσηταιρίζετο δεχόμενος. καὶ οὕτω
μὲν ἀσκεῖν τὴν ψυχὴν ἐνομίζετο· [ἦν δὲ ἄρα
4 τοῦτο κακουργίας ὑπόκρισις.[2]] ἔπειτα κἂν τοῖς
γυμνασίοις ἑωρῶμεν, πῶς τὸ σῶμα ὑπηλείφετο
καὶ πῶς πλῆκτρον [3] περιέβαινε καὶ τοὺς μὲν
νεανίσκους, οἷς προσεπάλαιε, πρὸς τοὺς ἀνδρειο-
τέρους μάλιστα συμπλεκόμενος· οὕτως αὐτοῦ
5 κέχρηται καὶ τῷ σώματι. ταῦτα μὲν οὖν ὡραῖος
ὤν· ἐπεὶ δὲ εἰς ἄνδρας ἧκε, πάντα ἀπεκάλυψεν, ἃ
τότε ἀπέκρυπτε. καὶ τοῦ μὲν ἄλλου σώματος
ἔξωρος γενόμενος ἠμέλησε, μόνην δὲ τὴν γλῶτταν
εἰς ἀσέλγειαν ἀκονᾷ καὶ τῷ στόματι χρῆται πρὸς
ἀναισχυντίαν, ὑβρίζων πάντας, ἐπὶ τῶν προσώπων φέρων τὴν ἀναίδειαν, ὃς οὐκ ᾐδέσθη τὸν ὑφ'
ὑμῶν ἱερωσύνῃ τετιμημένον οὕτως ἀπαιδεύτως
6 βλασφημεῖν ὑμῶν ἐναντίον. ἀλλ' εἰ μὲν ἀλλῇ
που βεβιωκὼς ἔτυχον, καὶ μὴ παρ' ὑμῖν, ἔδει μοι

---

[1] δ' ἔδρακε Jacobs: ἔδρακε Gaselee: δεδόρκει Hercher and
ὑπεκρίνετο at end of sentence: δέδρακε MSS.
[2] I deeply suspect this sentence to be an inept gloss. It is
intolerably flat after the witty bishop's sallies.
[3] So Salmasius for MSS. πλέκτρον. Berger reads πρωκτόν.

---

[1] See note on the Greek text. Besides the ineptitude of

bloom: he put on a look of high seriousness, and
counterfeited discretion, making himself out to be
passionately devoted to the training in the way he
should go, and always submitting and subjecting
himself to those who made it their business to be his
masters. Yes, and he left his father's house and hired
a little out-of-the-way hovel, where he took up his
abode: and there he did much joint work and was
also always ready to receive and associate with himself
those who were able to give him what he wanted. He
was certain that in this manner he was developing
the powers of his soul: [but all was in a reality a
cloak for his wickedness [1]:] and then we used to see
him in the public places of exercise too; how carefully he would anoint his body for the fray, with
what agility he would bestride the spur, and how in
the wrestle he never shrank from embrace of youths
who were almost men; such was the training to
which he devoted his body. All this was when he
was in the flower of his early years: when he came
to associate with men, he unveiled all that had
previously been hidden. The rest of his body became no longer suitable for the pursuits in which it
had formerly been engaged, but he sharpened his
tongue to wickedness and employed his lips for
the grossest purposes: there was none whom he
would not use it to defile, his shamelessness appearing openly on his countenance, and he has even gone
so far as publicly and brutally to revile one who has
been honoured by you with the priestly office. If I
had happened to live anywhere else, and had not
passed all my days among you. I might have found

the insertion, it spoils the balance between the accounts of
the young Thersander's spiritual and bodily development.

λόγων περὶ ἐμαυτοῦ καὶ τῶν ἐμοὶ βεβιωμένων·
ἐπεὶ δὲ σύνιστέ μοι πόρρω τῶν τούτου βλασφη-
μιῶν τὸν βίον ἔχοντι, φέρε εἴπω πρὸς ὑμᾶς περὶ
7 ὧν ἐγκέκλημαι. ''Ελυσας,' φησί, 'τὸν θανάτου
κατεγνωσμένον·' καὶ ἐπὶ τούτῳ πάνυ δεινῶς
ἐσχετλίασε, τύραννον ἀποκαλῶν με, καὶ ὅσα δὴ
κατετραγῴδησέ μου. ἔστι δὲ οὐχ ὁ σῴζων τοὺς
συκοφαντηθέντας τύραννος, ἀλλ' ὁ τοὺς μηδὲν
ἀδικοῦντας, μήτε βουλῆς, μήτε δήμου κατεγνω-
8 κότος. ἢ κατὰ ποίους νόμους, εἰπέ, τοῦτον τὸν
ξένον νεανίσκον κατέκλεισας πρῶτον εἰς τὸ δεσμωτήριον; τίς προέδρων κατέγνω; ποῖον δικαστήριον ἐκέλευσε δεθῆναι τὸν ἄνθρωπον; ἔστω γὰρ
πάντα ἀδικήσας, ὅσα ἂν εἴπῃς, ἀλλὰ κριθήτω
πρῶτον, ἐλεγχθήτω, λόγου μεταλαβών· ὁ νόμος
αὐτόν, ὁ καὶ σοῦ καὶ πάντων κύριος, δησάτω·
9 οὐδενὸς γὰρ οὐδείς ἐστιν ἄνευ κρίσεως δυνατώ-
τερος. κλεῖσον οὖν τὰ δικαστήρια, κάθελε τὰ
βουλευτήρια, ἔκβαλε τοὺς στρατηγούς· πάντα
γὰρ ὅσα σὺ πρὸς τὸν πρόεδρον εἴρηκας, ἔοικα
δικαιότερον ἐρεῖν κατὰ σοῦ ἀληθῶς. ἐπανάστηθι
Θερσάνδρῳ, πρόεδρε· μέχρι μόνων ὀνομάτων πρό-
10 εδρος εἶ. οὗτος τὰ σὰ ποιεῖ. μᾶλλον δὲ ὅσα
οὐδὲ σύ· σὺ μὲν γὰρ συμβούλους ἔχεις, καὶ οὐδὲν
ἄνευ τούτων ἔξεστί σοι· ἀλλ' οὔτε τι τῆς ἐξουσίας

it necessary to give you an account of myself and of
my life : but since you know how remote has been
my way of life from the slanders which he has uttered against me, let me discourse to you at greater
length upon the actual charges which he brings
against me. ' You have set free,' he says, ' one condemned to death' : and on this ground he has called
me the hardest names, terming me ' autocrat ' and all
the other grandiloquent nonsense which he was able to
trump up against me. But the autocrat is one who
in this case has done his best to save not merely
those who have been falsely charged, but persons
who have done no wrong whatever, and who have
been condemned neither by the government nor by
the voice of the people. Tell me, Thersander, what
was the law by whose authority you originally threw
this young man, a foreigner, into gaol ? Which of
the presiding justices had condemned him ? Which
court had ordered him to be put into chains ? Suppose for a moment that he had been guilty of all the
crimes in your catalogue, yet must he be first be
judged, conclusive evidence brought against him,
and he be allowed an opportunity to defend himself :
let the law, which is above you and everybody else,
be the one to fetter him : before judgement has
been given, no man has such powers over any other.
Come then, shut up the law-courts, do away with
the councillors' benches, turn out the officers : every
word of your address to the Lord Chief I could
with greater justice apply in your disfavour. Come
down, my Lord, in Thersander's favour : you are the
Chief Justice in name alone. He does your office—
nay, more than yours ; for you have your assessors,
without whom you can come to no decision, and you

δράσειας πρὶν ἐλθεῖν ἐπὶ τοῦτον τὸν θρόνον·
οὐδὲ ἐπὶ τῆς σῆς οἰκίας ποτὲ δεσμὸν ἀνθρώπου
κατέγνως. ὁ δὲ γενναῖος οὗτος πάντα ἑαυτῷ
γίνεται, δῆμος, βουλή, πρόεδρος, στρατηγός.
11 οἴκοι κολάζει καὶ δικάζει καὶ δεθῆναι κελεύει, καὶ
ὁ τῆς δίκης καιρὸς ἑσπέρα ἐστί· καλός γε καὶ
ὁ νυκτερινὸς δικαστής. καὶ νῦν πολλάκις βοᾷ,
' Κατάδικον ἔλυσας θανάτῳ παραδοθέντα.' ποίῳ
12 θανάτῳ; ποῖον κατάδικον; εἰπέ μοι τοῦ θανάτου
τὴν αἰτίαν. ' 'Επὶ φόνῳ κατέγνωσται,' φησί.
πεφόνευκεν οὖν; εἰπέ μοι τίς ἐστιν; ἣν ἀπέκτεινε
καὶ ἔλεγες ἀνῃρῆσθαι, ζῶσαν βλέπεις, καὶ οὐκ ἂν
ἔτι τολμήσειας [1] τὸν αὐτὸν αἰτιᾶσθαι [2] φόνου. οὐ
γὰρ δὴ τοῦτο τῆς κόρης ἐστὶν εἴδωλον· οὐκ ἀνέ-
πεμψεν ὁ 'Αϊδωνεὺς κατὰ σοῦ τὴν ἀνῃρημένην.
13 δυσὶ μὲν οὖν φόνοις ἔνοχος εἶ. τὴν μὲν γὰρ
ἀπέκτεινας τῷ λόγῳ, τὸν δὲ τοῖς ἔργοις ἠθέλησας
μᾶλλον δὲ καὶ ταύτην ἔμελλες· τὸ γὰρ δρᾶμά
σου τὸ ἐπὶ τῶν ἀγρῶν ἠκούσαμεν. ἡ δὲ "Αρτεμις
ἡ μεγάλη θεὸς ἀμφοτέρους ἔσωσε· τὴν μὲν ἐκ τῶν
τοῦ Σωσθένους χειρῶν ἐξαρπάσασα, τὸν δὲ τῶν
14 σῶν. καὶ τὸν μὲν Σωσθένην ἐξήρπασας, ἵνα μὴ
κατάφωρος γένῃ. οὐκ αἰσχύνῃ δέ, ὅτι κατηγορῶν
τοὺς ξένους ἄμφω συκοφαντῶν ἐλήλεγξαι; τὰ
μὲν ἐμὰ ἐπὶ τοσοῦτον εἰρήσθω πρὸς τὰς τούτου

---

[1] Corrected by Cobet from MSS. τολμήσεις (-ης).
[2] Jacobs' successful correction for MSS. αἰτεῖσθαι.

never exercise your legal power until you have taken
your seat on the bench; you have never in your own
house condemned a man to chains: while our good
friend here combines all functions in one—people,
government, judge, officer, all combined. Yes,
he gives sentence, he decides his case, he orders
people into chains at his own house, and further, he
chooses the evening for the time of his court of law:
a pretty thing is a juryman that sits at night! And
now he dares to bawl repeatedly, ' You have set free
Clitophon who was condemned to death?' How,
death? Condemned for what? Tell me the charge
on which he was capitally condemned. 'He was condemned for murder,' says he. Very well then, he has
committed murder: but upon whom? Come, you
see his victim, the very one whom you said had been
slain; now you can hardly dare to accuse Clitophon
of murder. This is not the girl's ghost: the god
of death has not sent her back here merely to con-
fute you. Two murders lie at your door: by your
lies and slanders you have done your best to kill the
girl, the youth by your actions. Worse, you were on
the very point of actually making an end of her;
we know all about your doings on your country
estate. But the great goddess Artemis has saved
them both: she has saved her from the hands of
Sosthenes, and him from yours: Sosthenes you have
got out of the way, that you might not be convicted
in flagrante: but do you feel no shame now that it is
definitely proved that in the course of your prosecut-
ing speech you have made false accusations against
both these foreigners? Gentlemen, I think I have
said enough to defend myself against Thersander's
ridiculous abuse: as for the defence of these

425

βλασφημίας, τὸν δὲ ὑπὲρ τῶν ξένων λόγον αὐτοῖς τούτοις παραδίδωμι."

10. Μέλλοντος δὲ ὑπὲρ ἐμοῦ καὶ τῆς Μελίτης ἀνδρὸς οὐκ ἀδόξου μὲν ῥήτορος, ὄντος δὲ τῆς[1] βουλῆς, λέγειν, φθάσας ῥήτωρ ἕτερος, ὄνομα Σώπατρος, Θερσάνδρου συνήγορος, " Ἀλλ' ἐμός," εἶπεν, " ἐντεῦθεν ὁ λόγος κατὰ τούτων τῶν μοιχῶν, ὦ βέλτιστε Νικόστρατε, (τοῦτο γὰρ ἦν ὄνομα τῷμῷ ῥήτορι) " εἶτα σός· ὁ γὰρ Θέρσανδρος ἃ εἶπε, πρὸς τὸν ἱερέα μόνον ἀπετείνατο, ὀλίγον ἀψάμενος ὅσον ἐπιψαῦσαι καὶ τοῦ κατὰ τὸν 2 δεσμώτην μέρους. ὅταν οὖν ἀποδείξω δυσὶ θανάτοις ἔνοχον ὄντα, τότε ἂν εἴη καὶ σοὶ καιρὸς ἀπολύσασθαι τὰς αἰτίας." ταῦτα εἰπὼν καὶ τερατευσάμενος καὶ τρίψας τὸ πρόσωπον, " Τῆς μὲν τοῦ ἱερέως κωμῳδίας," ἔφη, " ἠκούσαμεν, πάντα ἀσελγῶς καὶ ἀναισχύντως ὑποκριναμένου 3 τὰ εἰς τὸν Θέρσανδρον προσκρούσματα, καὶ τοῦ λόγου τὸ προοίμιον, μέμψεις εἰς Θέρσανδρον, ἐφ' οἷς εἰς αὐτὸν εἶπεν.[2] ἀλλὰ Θέρσανδρος μὲν οὐδὲν ὧν εἶπεν εἰς τοῦτον ἐψεύσατο· καὶ γὰρ δεσμώτην ἔλυσε, καὶ πόρνην ὑπεδέξατο, καὶ συνέγνω μοιχῷ· ἃ δὲ αὐτὸς μᾶλλον ἀναιδῶς ἐσυκοφάντησε, διασύρων τὸν Θερσάνδρου βίον, οὐδεμιᾶς ἀπήλλακται 4 συκοφαντίας. ἱερεῖ δὲ ἔπρεπεν, εἴπερ ἄλλο, καὶ

---

[1] βουλῆς can hardly stand without the article, which was inserted by Jacobs.

[2] Knox suggests for these difficult words καὶ τοῦ λόγου τὸ προοίμιον ἐλέγξει αὐτὸν ἐφ' οἷς εἰς Θέρσανδρον εἶπεν—his introduction will convince him of the charges he laid against Thersander. μέμψεις Göttling for πέμψεις. The insertion of εἰς is due to Hercher.

foreigners, I propose to allow them to speak for
themselves."

10. An advocate, who was a speaker of considerable
merit and also a member of the council was just
rising on behalf of Melite and myself, when
another lawyer, called Sopater, who was counsel for
Thersander, jumped up before him. " No," he cried,
" it is now my turn to address the court against this
adulterous couple, good Sir Nicostratus " (that was
my counsel's name) " and then your turn will come ;
what Thersander said was directed against the bishop
alone, and he did nothing more than touch upon that
part of the case which deals with the gaol-bird.
When I have finished shewing that he is twice over
liable to the capital punishment, it will then be your
business to attempt to palliate the charges brought
against him." Thus he spoke with frantic gesticu-
lation and wiping his face : then he went on, " We
have all been hearers of the bishop's farcical ribaldry
while he indulged in the most brutal, shameless,
trumped-up accusations against Thersander, and all
the first part of his speech, which was nothing but
calling Thersander back the same names that
Thersander had called him. Yet every word that
Thersander said was true ; the bishop did actually
release a criminal from his chains, receive and
entertain a harlot, and consort with an adulterer ; and
as for the shameless false charges he brought when
he represented in the worst light Thersander's way
of life, he refrained from no calumny in the course
of them.[1] I should have thought the most necessary

---

[1] I doubt whether the text is here sound. Sopater is more
likely to say : " As for the complaints that the bishop made
that he was being falsely accused by Thersander—the bishop's
own speech simply teemed with false accusations."

τοῦτο, καθαρὰν ἔχειν τὴν γλῶτταν ὕβρεως· χρή-
σομαι γὰρ τοῖς αὐτοῦ πρὸς αὐτόν. ἃ δὲ μετὰ
τὴν κωμῳδίαν ἐτραγῴδησεν ἤδη, οὕτω φανερῶς
καὶ οὐκέτι δι᾽ αἰνιγμάτων, σχετλιάζων εἰ μοιχόν
τινα λαβόντες ἐδήσαμεν, ὑπερτεθαύμακα τί[1]
τοσοῦτον ἴσχυσε πρίασθαι πρὸς τὴν τοσαύτην
5 σπουδήν. ὑπονοεῖν γὰρ τἀληθές ἐστιν· εἶδε
γὰρ τῶν ἀκολάστων τούτων τὰ πρόσωπα, τοῦ τε
μοιχοῦ καὶ τῆς ἑταίρας. ὡραία μὲν γὰρ αὕτη
καὶ νέα, ὡραῖον δὲ καὶ τοῦτο τὸ μειράκιον, καὶ
οὐδέπω τὴν ὄψιν ἀργαλέον, ἀλλ᾽ ἔτι χρήσιμον
6 πρὸς τὰς τοῦ ἱερέως ἡδονάς. ὁποτέρα σε τούτων
ἐωνήσατο; κοινῇ γὰρ πάντες ἐκαθεύδετε, καὶ
ἐμεθύετε κοινῇ, καὶ τῆς νυκτὸς ὑμῶν οὐδεὶς γέγονε
θεατής. φοβοῦμαι μὴ τὸ τῆς Ἀρτέμιδος ἱερὸν
Ἀφροδίτης πεποιήκατε, καὶ περὶ ἱερωσύνης κρινοῦ-
μεν, εἰ δεῖ σε τὴν τιμὴν ταύτην ἔχειν.

7 "Τὸν δὲ Θερσάνδρου βίον ἴσασι πάντες καὶ ἐκ
πρώτης ἡλικίας μετὰ σωφροσύνης κόσμιον· καὶ
ὡς εἰς ἄνδρας ἐλθὼν ἔγημε κατὰ τοὺς νόμους,
σφαλεὶς μὲν εἰς τὴν περὶ τῆς γυναικὸς κρίσιν (οὐ
γὰρ εὗρεν ἣν ἤλπισε), τῷ δὲ ταύτης γένει καὶ τῇ
8 οὐσίᾳ πεπιστευκώς. εἰκὸς γὰρ αὐτὴν καὶ πρὸς
ἄλλους τινὰς ἡμαρτηκέναι τὸν πρόσθεν χρόνον,
λανθάνειν δὲ ἐπ᾽ ἐκείνοις χρηστὸν ἄνδρα· τὸ δὲ

---

[1] καί wrongly preceded τί in the MSS., and was removed
by Jacobs.

428

priestly quality of all was a pair of lips clean of guile,
to use his own expression against himself. As for
the high-flown rhetoric of his speech, after the farcical
part was over, when he began to speak openly and
no longer in riddles, so grievously angered that we
had caught a lecher and thrown him into chains, I
was very greatly astonished, and wondered what the
price could be that was high enough to arouse in
him this excess of zeal. But I fear one may suspect
the truth: he had taken note of the faces of this
scandalous pair, the adulterer and his punk: she is
young and pretty, and he is a pretty stripling too,
with his cheeks still soft, and one still available for
the bishop's pleasures. Which [1] of them was it,
reverend sir, whose charms won you over? You
slept all in the same place, you tippled all together,
and there was no spectator of how you passed your
night. I greatly fear that Artemis' temple has been
made by you into the temple of Aphrodite, and we
shall have to sit in judgement on your priesthood, to
decide if you are worthy of your cloth.

"As for Thersander's way of life, all here know how
that from his first youth it was elegant and discreet;
and how, when he came to years of manhood, he
married in accordance with the direction of the law,
but unfortunately made a mistake in his estimation
of the character of his wife, for he found her not
what he had hoped, but had put too much trust in
her birth and material position. It is like enough
that earlier in her married life she misconducted
herself with several lovers, but was able to conceal
her relations with them from her excellent husband;

---

[1] ὁποτέρα, feminine, is a subtlety that cannot be rendered
into English. "Which fair one of them . . ."

τελευταῖον τοῦ δράματος, πᾶσαν ἀπεκάλυψε τὴν
9 αἰδῶ, πεπλήρωται δὲ ἀναισχυντίας. τοῦ γὰρ
ἀνδρὸς στειλαμένου τινὰ μακρὰν ἀποδημίαν,
καιρὸν τοῦτον νενόμικεν εὔκαιρον μοιχείας, [καὶ
αὔχημα,[1]] καὶ νεανίσκον εὑροῦσα πόρνον (τοῦτο
γὰρ τὸ μεῖζον ἀτύχημα, ὅτι τοιοῦτον ηὗρε τὸν
ἐρώμενον, ὃς πρὸς μὲν γυναῖκας ἄνδρας ἀπομιμεῖ-
ται, γυνὴ δὲ γίνεται πρὸς ἄνδρας) οὕτως μετὰ
ἀδείας οὐκ ἤρκεσεν ἐπὶ τῆς ξένης αὐτῷ συνοῦσα
φανερῶς, ἀλλὰ καὶ ἐνταῦθα ἤγαγε διὰ τοσούτου
πελάγους συγκαθεύδουσα, κἂν τῷ σκάφει φανερῶς
10 ἀσελγαίνουσα· πάντων ὁρώντων. ὦ μοιχείας
γῇ καὶ θαλάσσῃ μεμερισμένης· ὦ μοιχείας ἀπ'
Αἰγύπτου μέχρις Ἰωνίας ἐκτεταμένης. μοιχεύε-
ταί τις, ἀλλὰ πρὸς μίαν ἡμέραν· ἂν δὲ καὶ δεύτερον
γένηται τὸ ἀδίκημα, κλέπτει τὸ ἔργον, καὶ πάντας
ἀποκρύπτεται· αὕτη δὲ οὐχ ὑπὸ σάλπιγγι μόνον,
11 ἀλλὰ καὶ κήρυκι μοιχεύεται. Ἔφεσος ὅλη τὸν
μοιχὸν ἔγνωκεν· ἡ δὲ οὐκ ᾐσχύνετο τοῦτο ἀπὸ
τῆς ξένης ἐνεγκοῦσα τὸ ἀγώγιμον, ὡς φορτίον
καλὸν ἐωνημένη[2] ἦλθε, μοιχὸν ἐμπεπορευμένη.
' Ἀλλ' ᾤμην,' φησί, 'τὸν ἄνδρα τετελευτηκέναι.'
12 οὐκοῦν, εἰ μὲν τέθνηκεν, ἀπήλλαξαι τῆς αἰτίας·
οὐδὲ γὰρ ἔστιν ὁ τὴν μοιχείαν παθών, οὐδὲ
ὑβρίζεται γάμος οὐκ ἔχων ἄνδρα· εἰ δὲ ὁ γάμος
τῷ τὸν γήμαντα ζῆν οὐκ ἀνῄρηται, τὴν γαμηθεῖσαν

---

[1] Mitscherlich deleted these words.
[2] κάλλους ἐωνημένη Vilborg: κάλλος ἐωνημένη codd. β.

but at the end of her career she threw off even the pretence of modesty and filled up the cup of impudence. Her husband had to go abroad for a long stay, and she considered this a suitable opportunity for unfaithfulness. She found a youth who may be described as a sort of male prostitute—perhaps the most wretched part of the business is that the lover she selected is one of those who ape manhood when they are among women, while they count as women among men. Well, it was not enough for her to put aside all fear and live openly with him in a foreign country, but she must needs bring him here over that wide stretch of sea, sleeping with him and exposing her unseemly lust on the boat for all to see. Oh, think of an adulterous intercourse with its shares both on sea and land, drawn out all the way from Egypt to Ionia! Does a woman fall? Then it is but for a single day: or, if the sin be repeated, she hides what she has done and conceals it from the eyes of all: but Melite does not merely proclaim her unfaithfulness in the market place [1]; she has it put abroad by the town-crier! All Ephesus knew of her gallant; she had thought no shame to import him hither from abroad, trafficking in a lover as though he were merchandise, buying him and bringing him hither as a pretty bit of cargo! 'But I thought,' says she, 'that my husband had perished.' Certainly; if he is dead, you are quit of the charge against you. In that case there is nobody to be injured by the adultery, nor can a marriage be outraged when there is no husband. But if the marriage has not come to an end, owing to the fact that the husband is still alive, then an act of robbery is committed upon

---

[1] Literally, "to the sound of the trumpet."

διαφθείραντος ἄλλου λῃστεύεται. ὥσπερ γὰρ
μὴ μένοντος ὁ μοιχὸς οὐκ ἦν, μένοντος δὴ [1] μοιχὸς
ἐστιν."

11. Ἔτι τοῦ Σωπάτρου λέγοντος, ὑποτεμὼν
αὐτοῦ τὸν λόγον ὁ Θέρσανδρος, " Ἀλλ' οὐκ,"
ἔφη, " λόγων δεῖ.[2] δύο γὰρ προκαλοῦμαι προ-
κλήσεις, Μελίτην τε ταύτην, καὶ τὴν δοκοῦσαν
εἶναι τοῦ θεοπρόπου θυγατέρα, [οὐκέτι βασανίσων,
ὡς μικρῷ πρόσθεν ἔλεγον [3]] τῷ δὲ ὄντι δούλην
ἐμήν." καὶ ἀνεγίνωσκε·

2   " Προκαλεῖται Θέρσανδρος Μελίτην καὶ
Λευκίππην· τοῦτο γὰρ ἤκουσα τὴν πόρνην
καλεῖσθαι· Μελίτην μέν, εἰ μὴ κεκοινώνηκεν
εἰς Ἀφροδίτην τῷδε τῷ ξένῳ παρ' ὃν ἀπεδή-
μουν χρόνον, εἰς τὸ τῆς ἱερᾶς Στυγὸς ὕδωρ
εἰσβᾶσαν καὶ ἐπομοσαμένην ἀπηλλάχθαι τῶν
ἐγκλημάτων· τὴν δὲ ἑτέραν, εἰ μὲν τυγχάνει
γυνή, δουλεύειν τῷ δεσπότῃ· δούλαις γὰρ
μόναις γυναιξὶν ἔξεστιν εἰς τὸν τῆς Ἀρτέμιδος
νεὼν παριέναι· εἰ δέ φησιν εἶναι παρθένος, ἐν
τῷ τῆς σύριγγος ἄντρῳ κλεισθῆναι."

3   Ἡμεῖς μὲν οὖν εὐθὺς ἐδεξάμεθα τὴν πρόκλησιν,
καὶ γὰρ ᾔδειμεν αὐτὴν ἐσομένην· ἡ δὲ Μελίτη
θαρρήσασα τῷ παρ' ὃν ἀπεδήμει χρόνον ὁ Θέρσανδρος μηδέν μοι κοινὸν πρὸς αὐτὴν γεγονέναι
πλὴν λόγων, " Ἀλλὰ καὶ ἔγωγε," ἔφη, " ταύτην
δέχομαι τὴν πρόκλησιν, καὶ ἔτι πλέον αὐτὴ [4]

---

[1] Cobet's correction for δέ.   Jacobs deletes.
[2] λόγων ⟨δεῖ⟩ Jacobs: λέγων.
[3] There was never any mention of putting Leucippe to the
question.   Hercher deletes, Vilborg retains.
[4] Salmasius' correction for αὐτήν.

it by the corruption of the wife by a third party.
Exactly as much as if the marriage did not exist
there would be no adulterer, so, as it does exist, an
adulterer there must be."

11. Sopater was still speaking, but his speech was
interrupted by Thersander, who cried: " There is no
need of further talk. I make two challenges: one
to Melite here, and one to that girl who professes
to be the daughter of the sacred ambassador, [with
no further question of the torture which I mentioned
a little time ago], but is really my slave." And he
began to read out:

" *Thersander challenges Melite and Leucippe*—I
think I have heard that is the harlot's name. *Melite,
if she has not had to do with this foreigner during the
time that I was abroad, is to enter the sacred water of
the Styx, take the oath and be cleared, if she can, of
the charges brought against her. As for the other, if
she is found to be a woman of whom man has had carnal
knowledge, she is to remain in slavery to her proper
master, for such women can only enter the shrine of
Artemis if they are slaves; if, however, she persists in
declaring that she is a virgin, she is to be shut into the
grotto of the pan-pipes.*"

We at once accepted this challenge, having been
sure that it would be made: and Melite, who was
encouraged by the fact that *during the time of
Thersander's absence abroad* nothing more serious
than words had passed between her and me, also
complied. " Certainly," she said, " I accept this
challenge; and I will even add something to it on

προστίθημι· τὸ δὲ μέγιστον, οὐδὲ εἶδον τὸ παράπαν οὔτε ξένον, οὔτε πολίτην ἥκειν εἰς ὁμιλίαν,
καὶ¹ ὧν λέγεις, καὶ ὧν . . . σε δεῖ παθεῖν, ἂν
4 συκοφάντης ἁλῷς·” “Ὅ τι ἄν,” ἔφη, “δόξῃ
προστιμῆσαι τοῖς δικασταῖς.” ἐπὶ τούτοις διελύθη
τὸ δικαστήριον, καὶ εἰς τὴν ὑστεραίαν διώριστο
τὰ τῆς προκλήσεως ἡμῖν γενέσθαι.

12. Τὸ δὲ τῆς Στυγὸς ὕδωρ εἶχεν οὕτως.
παρθένος ἦν εὐειδής, ὄνομα Ῥοδῶπις, κυνηγίων
ἐρῶσα καὶ θήρας· πόδες ταχεῖς, εὔστοχοι χεῖρες,
ζώνη καὶ μίτρα, καὶ ἀνεζωσμένος εἰς γόνυ χιτών,
καὶ κατὰ ἄνδρας κουρὰ τριχῶν. ὁρᾷ ταύτην
Ἄρτεμις, καὶ ἐπήνει, καὶ ἐκάλει, καὶ σύνθηρον
ἐποιήσατο, καὶ τὰ πλεῖστα κοινὰ ἦν αὐταῖς
2 θηράματα. ἀλλὰ καὶ ὤμοσεν ἀεὶ παραμενεῖν,
καὶ τὴν πρὸς ἄνδρας ὁμιλίαν φυγεῖν, καὶ τὴν ἐξ
Ἀφροδίτης ὕβριν μὴ παθεῖν. ὤμοσεν ἡ Ῥοδῶπις,
καὶ ἤκουσεν ἡ Ἀφροδίτη, καὶ ὀργίζεται, καὶ ἀμύ-
3 νασθαι θέλει τὴν κόρην τῆς ὑπεροψίας. νεανίσκος ἦν Ἐφέσιος καλὸς ἐν μειρακίοις, ὅσον
Ῥοδῶπις ἐν παρθένοις. Εὐθύνικον αὐτὸν ἐκάλουν·
ἐθήρα δὲ καὶ αὐτὸς ὡς Ῥοδῶπις, καὶ τὴν Ἀφροδίτην
4 ὁμοίως οὐκ ἤθελεν εἰδέναι. ἐπ' ἀμφοτέρους οὖν ἡ
θεὸς ἔρχεται καὶ τὰς θήρας αὐτῶν εἰς ἓν συνάγει·
τέως γὰρ ἦσαν κεχωρισμένοι· ἡ δὲ Ἄρτεμις
τηνικαῦτα οὐ παρῆν. παραστησαμένη δὲ τὸν

¹ The text is here corrupt and imperfect, and various
emendations that have been proposed have not done much
to cure it. The simplest seems Salmasius' ὁμιλίαν, οἴαν λέγεις.
καὶ τί σε δεῖ. . . .

my own account; the most important part of which is that I never allowed anybody, whether citizen or foreigner, to enter into such relations with me during the time of which you speak. And now, what ought your penalty to be if you are proved to be a maker of false charges?" "Whatever fine," said he, "that the jury like to inflict." These terms settled, the court broke up, and it was decided that the business of the challenge should be determined on the following day.

12. This is the story of the water of the Styx. There was a maiden fair to see, called Rhodopis, passionately fond of hunting and the chase. She was swift of foot and a sure shot: she wore a girdle and a cap, her tunic was girt up at the knee, and her hair was cut short like a man's. Artemis once saw her, and was delighted with her pursuits; she summoned her, associated her with her in the chase, and many is the time that they hunted together: she took an oath that she would always remain with the goddess; that she would shun the company of men, and that she would never suffer the violence that Aphrodite inspires. Rhodopis swore: Aphrodite heard her, was wroth, and desired to punish the maid for her disdain. Now there was a young man at Ephesus, as fair among the striplings of that town as Rhodopis was among its maidens; Euthynicus was his name, and he was as passionate for the chase as was Rhodopis, and he too desired to know nothing of the power of Aphrodite. So the goddess was determined to attack them both, and brought to the same place the quarries they were hunting; for until that time they had never met, and on that occasion Artemis happened to be away. Aphrodite therefore

435

υἱὸν τὸν τοξότην ἡ Ἀφροδίτη εἶπε· "Τέκνον,
ζεῦγος τοῦτο ὁρᾷς ἀναφρόδιτον καὶ ἐχθρὸν ἡμῶν
καὶ τῶν ἡμετέρων μυστηρίων; ἡ δὲ παρθένος καὶ
θρασύτερον ὤμοσε κατ᾽ ἐμοῦ. ὁρᾷς δὲ αὐτοὺς
5 ἐπὶ τὴν ἔλαφον συντρέχοντας; ἄρξαι καὶ σὺ
τῆς θήρας ἀπὸ πρώτης τῆς τολμηρᾶς κόρης· καὶ
πάντως γε τὸ σὸν βέλος εὐστοχώτερόν ἐστιν."
ἐντείνουσιν ἀμφότεροι τὰ τόξα, ἡ μὲν ἐπὶ τὴν
ἔλαφον, ὁ δὲ Ἔρως ἐπὶ τὴν παρθένον· καὶ
ἀμφότεροι τυγχάνουσι, καὶ ἡ κυνηγέτις μετὰ τὴν
6 θήραν ἦν τεθηραμένη. καὶ εἶχεν ἡ μὲν ἔλαφος
εἰς τὰ νῶτα τὸ βέλος, ἡ δὲ παρθένος εἰς τὴν
καρδίαν· τὸ δὲ βέλος, Εὐθύνικον φιλεῖν. δεύτερον
7 δὲ καὶ ἐπὶ τοῦτον οἰστὸν ἀφίησι· καὶ εἶδον
ἀλλήλους Εὐθύνικος καὶ ἡ Ῥοδῶπις. καὶ ἔστησαν μὲν τὸ πρῶτον τοὺς ὀφθαλμοὺς ἑκάτεροι,
μηδέτερος ἐκκλῖναι θέλων ἐπὶ θάτερα· κατὰ
μικρὸν δὲ τὰ τραύματα ἀμφοῖν ἐξάπτεται, καὶ
αὐτοὺς ὁ Ἔρως ἐλαύνει κατὰ τουτὶ τὸ ἄντρον, οὗ
νῦν ἐστιν ἡ πηγή, καὶ ἐνταῦθα τὸν ὅρκον ψεύδονται.
8 ἡ Ἄρτεμις ὁρᾷ τὴν Ἀφροδίτην γελῶσαν, καὶ
τὸ πραχθὲν συνίησι, καὶ εἰς ὕδωρ λύει τὴν κόρην,
ἔνθα τὴν παρθενίαν ἔλυσε. καὶ διὰ τοῦτο, ὅταν
τις αἰτίαν ἔχῃ Ἀφροδισίων, εἰς τὴν πηγὴν εἰσβᾶσα
ἀπολούεται· ἡ δέ ἐστιν ὀλίγη, καὶ μέχρι κνήμης
9 μέσης. ἡ δὲ κρίσις· ἐγγράψασα[1] τὸν ὅρκον
γραμματείῳ μηρίνθῳ δεδεμένον περιεθήκατο τῇ
δέρῃ. κἂν μὲν ἀψευδῆ τὸν ὅρκον, μένει κατὰ
χώραν ἡ πηγή· ἂν δὲ ψεύδηται, τὸ ὕδωρ ὀργίζεται
καὶ ἀναβαίνει μέχρι τῆς δέρης καὶ τὸ γραμματεῖον ἐκάλυψε.

---

[1] Jacobs' emendation for MSS. ἐγγράψας.

sent for her son, the Archer; "My child," said she, "seest thou this pair that reck nought of love and hate us and our mysteries? And the virgin has even sworn a rash oath against me. Seest thou too how they are both following the same hind? Do thou begin the sport and that with this too daring maid; and thy dart shall surely miss not its aim." Both bend their bows—she at the hind, and Love at her; both hit, and after the quarry now is the huntress stricken. The hind received the arrow in its flank, the virgin in her heart; and her arrow was that she should love Euthynicus. Then Love shot another bolt, now at the youth; and then Euthynicus and Rhodopis saw one another. At first they kept their eyes fixed, each on the other, and neither could turn them away: little by little both their wounds began to burn, and then Love drove them to this very cave, where the spring now is, and there they belied their oath. Artemis saw Aphrodite laughing and understood what had happened, and she changed the maiden into a water-spring on the very spot where she had changed her virginity for womanhood. On this account, if a woman is called into question over affairs of love, she has to go down into the spring and bathe. Now the water is low, reaching only half way to the knee, and this is the procedure of the ordeal. She writes her oath on a tablet, which she then suspends by a string round her neck. If she has sworn a true oath, the spring remains in its place; but if she has perjured herself, the water boils up, rises to the height of her neck, and covers the written tablet.

Ταῦτα εἰπόντες, καὶ τοῦ καιροῦ προελθόντος εἰς ἑσπέραν, ἀπ⟂ειμεν κοιμησόμενοι, χωρὶς ἕκαστος. 13. Ἐπὶ δὲ τῇ ὑστεραίᾳ ὁ δῆμος μὲν ἅπας παρῆν· ἡγεῖτο δὲ Θέρσανδρος φαιδρῷ τῷ προσώπῳ καὶ εἰς ἡμᾶς ἅμα βλέπων σὺν γέλωτι, ἐστόλιστο[1] δὲ ἡ Λευκίππη ἱερᾷ στολῇ· ποδήρης ὁ[2] χιτών, ὀθόνης ὁ χιτών, ζώνη κατὰ μέσον τὸν χιτῶνα, ταινία περὶ τὴν κεφαλὴν φοινικοβαφής, ἀσάνδαλος ὁ πούς. καὶ ἡ μὲν εἰσῆλθε πάνυ κοσμίως· ἐγὼ δὲ ὡς εἶδον, εἱστήκειν τρέμων, καὶ ταῦτα πρὸς ἐμαυτὸν ἔλεγον· "Ὅτι μὲν παρθένος ἡ Λευκίππη πεπίστευκα, ἀλλὰ τὸν Πᾶνα, ὦ φιλτάτη, φοβοῦμαι. θεός ἐστι φιλοπάρθενος, καὶ δέδοικα μὴ δευτέρα καὶ σὺ σύριγξ γένῃ. ἀλλ' ἐκείνη μὲν ἔφυγε διώκοντα αὐτὸν ἐν πεδίῳ, καὶ ἐδιώκετο ἐν πλάτει· σὲ δὲ καὶ εἴσω θυρῶν ἀπεκλείσαμεν ὡς ἐν πολιορκίᾳ, ἵνα, κἂν διώκῃ, μὴ δύνῃ φυγεῖν. ἀλλ', ὦ δέσποτα Πάν, εὐγνωμονήσειας, καὶ μὴ παραβαίης τὸν νόμον τοῦ τόπου· ἡμεῖς γὰρ αὐτὸν τετηρήκαμεν. ἐξίτω πάλιν ἡμῖν ἡ Λευκίππη παρθένος· ταύτας πρὸς τὴν Ἄρτεμιν συνθήκας ἔχεις· μὴ ψεύσῃ τὴν παρθένον."

14. Ταῦτά μου πρὸς ἐμαυτὸν λαλοῦντος, μέλος ἐξηκούετο μουσικόν, καὶ ἐλέγετο μηδεπώποτε λιγυρώτερον οὕτως ἀκουσθῆναι· καὶ εὐθὺς ἀνεῳγμένας εἴδομεν τὰς θύρας. ὡς δὲ ἐξέθορεν ἡ Λευκίππη, πᾶς μὲν ὁ δῆμος ἐξεβόησεν ὑφ' ἡδονῆς καὶ τὸν Θέρσανδρον ἐλοιδόρουν, ἐγὼ δὲ ὅστις ἐγεγόνειν οὐκ ἂν εἴποιμι λόγῳ. μίαν μὲν δὴ

---

[1] Corrected by Cobet from MSS. ἐστολίσατο.
[2] I think Hercher's insertion of ὁ is necessary if we compare the exactly similar phrase in III. vii. §5.

We talked over these matters, and as it was now
drawing towards evening, we retired, each to his own
bed, to sleep. **13.** On the following day the whole
population of the town was present, and at their
head was Thersander, with a smiling and confident
face, and he kept looking at us and laughing.
Leucippe had been clad in a sacred robe, which was
a long tunic of linen, with a girdle about her waist,
a scarlet fillet on her head, and bare feet. She thus
entered the cave with calm and orderly bearing;
but I stood and trembled as I saw her go, saying
to myself: "That Leucippe is a virgin, I am sure
enough; but it is Pan, my darling, of whom I am
afraid. He is a god too fond of virgins, and my
fear is that you should be the second to be meta-
morphosed into a pan-pipes. The former heroine
was able to escape him because he pursued her on
a plain, and her chase was in broad, open country:
but you we have shut up within gates, like a
besieged city, so that you will have no chance of
flight if he comes after you. My lord Pan, be kindly,
and break not the law and custom of the spot, which
we, for our part, have kept. Let Leucippe come
back to us a virgin; this was thy compact with Artemis, so defraud thou not the virgin goddess.[1]"

14. I was still murmuring thus to myself, when a
strain of music sounded, and it was said that never
had sweeter notes than those been heard from the
grotto: and then we saw the doors open. Out
sprang Leucippe, and all the people shouted for joy
and began to revile Thersander, while I cannot
express the state of delight in which I found myself.

[1] These last few words might also be taken to mean "so
corrupt not the virgin (Leucippe)."

ταύτην νίκην καλλίστην νενικηκότες, ἀπήειμεν·
ἐπὶ δὲ τὴν δευτέραν κρίσιν ἐχωροῦμεν, τὴν Στύγα.
3 καὶ ὁ δῆμος οὕτω μετεσκευάζετο καὶ πρὸς ταύτην
τὴν θέαν· καὶ πάντα συνεπεραίνετο κἀκεῖ. ἡ
Μελίτη τὸ γραμματεῖον περιέκειτο· ἡ πηγὴ
διαυγὴς [1] καὶ ὀλίγη· ἡ δὲ ἐνέβη εἰς αὐτὴν καὶ ἔστη
4 φαιδρῷ τῷ προσώπῳ. τὸ δὲ ὕδωρ οἷον ἦν κατὰ
χώραν ἔμενε, μηδὲ [2] τὸ βραχύτατον ἀναθορὸν τοῦ
συνήθους μέτρου. ἐπεὶ δὲ ὁ χρόνος, ὃν ἐνδιατρίβειν
ἐν τῇ πηγῇ διώριστο, παρελήλυθει, τὴν μὲν ὁ
πρόεδρος δεξιωσάμενος, ἐκ τοῦ ὕδατος ἐξάγει, δύο
παλαίσματα τοῦ Θερσάνδρου νενικημένου. μέλλων
δὲ καὶ τὸ τρίτον ἡττᾶσθαι, ὑπεκδὺς εἰς τὴν οἰκίαν
ἐκδιδράσκει, φοβηθεὶς μὴ καὶ καταλεύσειεν αὐτὸν
5 ὁ δῆμος· τὸν γὰρ Σωσθένην εἷλκον ἄγοντες νεανίσκοι τέτταρες, δύο μὲν τῆς Μελίτης συγγενεῖς,
δύο δὲ οἰκέται· τούτους γὰρ ἐπεπόμφει ζητήσοντας
αὐτὸν ἡ Μελίτη. συνεὶς δὲ ὁ Θέρσανδρος πόρρωθεν, καὶ καταμηνύσειν τὸ πρᾶγμα εἰδώς, ἂν
ἐν βασάνοις γένηται, φθάσας ἀποδιδράσκει, καὶ
6 νυκτὸς ἐπελθούσης, τῆς πόλεως ὑπεξέρχεται. τὸν
δὲ Σωσθένην εἰς τὴν εἱρκτὴν ἐκέλευσαν οἱ ἄρχοντες ἐμβληθῆναι, τοῦ Θερσάνδρου φυγόντος.
τότε μὲν οὖν ἀπηλλαττόμεθα, κατὰ κράτος ἤδη
γενόμενοι καὶ ὑπὸ πάντων εὐφημούμενοι.

15. Τῇ δὲ ὑστεραίᾳ τὸν Σωσθένην ἦγον ἐπὶ
τοὺς ἄρχοντας οἱ ταύτην ἔχοντες τὴν πίστιν. ὁ
δὲ ἐπὶ βασάνους ἑαυτὸν ἀγόμενον ἰδών, πάντα
σαφῶς λέγει, ὅσα τε ἐτόλμησεν ὁ Θέρσανδρος, καὶ

---

[1] Jacobs' most ingenious correction for MSS. δι' αὐτῆς.
[2] So Hercher and ed. G for μήτε of the other MSS.

We therefore retired, having won one magnificent victory; and we then went on to the second ordeal, that of the Styx. The people also came thither from the cave in order to witness the spectacle; and there too the whole process was gone through. Melite put on the tablet round her neck, the water was clear and shallow; she descended into it and stood there with a smiling and cheerful face. The water remained at exactly its previous depth, rising not even an inch above its accustomed level. When the time had passed during which she had to stand in the spring, the presiding judge took her by the hand and led her out of the water; and so Thersander was defeated in two trials of strength. Guessing that he would be beaten in the third too, he slipped away and hurried to his house, fearing that he would be stoned by the populace: for at that moment came four youths, dragging with them Sosthenes—two of them Melite's kinsmen, and two of them her servants—whom she had sent to look for him. But Thersander had observed what was happening from afar, and knowing that if Sosthenes were put to the torture he would reveal the whole plot, determined to flee before this could happen, and so privately left the city when night fell. After Thersander had left the scene, the magistrates ordered Sosthenes to be put in ward; and we then departed, having thus won the mastery over our enemies, and having blessings called down upon our heads by all the people.

15. On the following day those appointed for the purpose brought Sosthenes before the magistrates. Immediately that he realised that he was being brought out to be put to the question, he told the whole story without concealment, both Thersander's

ὅσα αὐτὸς ὑπηρέτησεν· οὐ παρέλιπε δὲ οὐδὲ ὅσα
ἰδίᾳ πρὸ τῶν τῆς Λευκίππης θυρῶν διελέχθησαν
2 πρὸς ἀλλήλους περὶ αὐτῆς. καὶ ὁ μὲν αὖθις εἰς
τὴν εἰρκτὴν ἐβέβλητο, δώσων δίκην· τοῦ δὲ
Θερσάνδρου φυγὴν ἀπόντος κατέγνωσαν. ἡμᾶς
δὲ ὁ ἱερεὺς ὑπεδέχετο πάλιν τὸν εἰθισμένον
3 τρόπον. καὶ μεταξὺ δειπνοῦντες ἐμυθολογοῦμεν
ἅ τε τὴν προτέραν ἐτύχομεν εἰπόντες, καὶ εἴ τι
ἐπιδεέστερον ἦν ὧν ἐπάθομεν. ἡ Λευκίππη δέ,
ἅτε δὴ μᾶλλον τὸν πατέρα μηκέτι αἰδουμένη, ὡς
ἂν σαφῶς παρθένος εὑρεθεῖσα, τὰ συμβάντα μεθ᾽
4 ἡδονῆς διηγεῖτο. ἐπεὶ δὲ κατὰ τὴν Φάρον ἐγεγόνει καὶ τοὺς λῃστάς, λέγω πρὸς αὐτήν· " Οὐκ
ἐρεῖς ἡμῖν τὸν μῦθον τῶν τῆς Φάρου λῃστῶν καὶ
τῆς ἀποτμηθείσης ἐκεῖ τὸ αἴνιγμα κεφαλῆς, ἵνα
σου καὶ ὁ πατὴρ ἀκούσῃ; τοῦτο γὰρ μόνον ἐνδεῖ
πρὸς ἀκρόασιν τοῦ παντὸς δράματος."

16. " Γυναῖκα," ἔφη, "κακοδαίμονα ἐξαπα-
τήσαντες οἱ λῃσταὶ τῶν ἐπὶ μισθῷ πωλουσῶν τὰ
Ἀφροδίτης, ὡς δὴ ναυκλήρῳ τινὶ γυναῖκα συνεσο-
μένην ἐπὶ τοῦ σκάφους, ταύτην εἶχον ἐπὶ τῆς
νηός, ἀγνοοῦσαν τὴν ἀλήθειαν ἐφ᾽ ὃ παρῆν, ὑπο-
2 τείνουσαν δὲ ἡσυχῇ τινὶ τῶν πειρατῶν· λόγῳ δὲ
ἦν ἐραστὴς ὁ λῃστής. ἐπεὶ δὲ ἁρπάσαντές με, ὡς
εἶδες, ἐνέθεσαν τῷ σκάφει καὶ πτερώσαντες αὐτὸ

attempts and his own contributions towards the success of the plot: and he did not even leave out the conversation which they had had with one another before the doors of the hut where Leucippe was confined. He was therefore thrust back into prison to await his sentence, while against Thersander in absence a decree of banishment was passed. As for us, the bishop entertained us once more in his usual hospitable fashion, and during dinner we conversed on the same subjects as on the previous[1] occasion, making particular mention of any details of our adventures which were then omitted. Leucippe especially, being now no longer shy in her father's company, as her virginity was clearly proved, related her story with the greatest pleasure. When she came to the part connected with the island of Pharos and the pirates: "Tell us," said I to her, "of the stratagem which the Pharian pirates devised and explain the riddle of the decapitated woman for your father too to hear; for that is the only point still lacking to the complete understanding of the whole romance."

16. "She was one of those unfortunate women," said she, "who make a traffic of love. The pirates had imposed upon her, on the pretext that she was to become the wife of a skipper who was aboard; and they kept her on the ship, where she did not know the real reason that they desired her presence, but was secretly intimate with one of the pirates, who was supposed to be her lover. Now when they carried me off, as you saw, and put me aboard and

---

[1] Hercher wished to change προτέραν into προτεραίαν, "the day before." But the previous dinner with the bishop was *four* days before.

ταῖς κώπαις ἔφυγον, ὁρῶντες τὴν διώκουσαν ναῦν
φθάνουσαν, περιελόντες τόν τε κόσμον καὶ τὴν
ἐσθῆτα τῆς ταλαιπώρου γυναικὸς ἐμοὶ περιτι-
θέασι, τοὺς δὲ ἐμοὺς χιτωνίσκους ἐκείνῃ· καὶ
στήσαντες αὐτὴν ἐπὶ τῆς πρύμνης ὅθεν διώκοντες
ὄψοισθε,[1] τὴν κεφαλὴν ἀποτέμνουσιν αὐτῆς, καὶ
τὸ μὲν σῶμα ἔρριψαν, ὡς εἶδες, κατὰ τῆς θαλάσσης, τὴν δὲ κεφαλήν, ὡς ἔπεσεν, εἶχον ἐπὶ τῆς
3 νηὸς τότε. μικρὸν γὰρ ὕστερον καὶ ταύτην ἀπο-
σκευάσαντες ἔρριψαν ὁμοίως, ὅτε μηκέτι τοὺς
διώκοντας εἶχον. οὐκ οἶδα δὲ πότερον τούτου
χάριν προπαρασκευάσαντες ἔτυχον τὴν γυναῖκα,
ἢ διεγνωκότες ἀνδραποδίσαντες πωλῆσαι, ὥσπερ
ὕστερον πεπράκασι κἀμέ· τῷ δὲ διώκεσθαι πρὸς
ἀπάτην τῶν διωκόντων ἀντ' ἐμοῦ σφάττουσι,
νομίζοντες πλέον ἐμπολήσειν ἐκ τῆς ἐμῆς πράσεως
4 ἢ τῆς ἐκείνης. διὰ τοῦτο γὰρ καὶ τὸν Χαιρέαν
τὴν ἀξίαν δόντα δίκην ἐπεῖδον· αὐτὸς γὰρ ἦν ὁ
συμβουλεύσας ἀντ' ἐμοῦ τὴν ἄνθρωπον ἀποκτεί-
5 ναντας ῥῖψαι. ὁ δὲ λοιπὸς τῶν λῃστῶν ὄχλος
οὐκ ἔφασάν με αὐτῷ ἀφήσειν μόνῳ· φθάνειν γὰρ
ἤδη λαβόντα σῶμα ἕτερον, ὃ πραθὲν ἂν παρέσχεν
αὐτοῖς ἀφορμὴν κέρδους· δεῖν δὲ ἀντὶ τῆς θανού-
σης ἐμὲ πραθεῖσαν κοινὴν ἅπασιν αὐτοῖς γενέσθαι
6 μᾶλλον ἢ ἐκείνῳ μόνῳ. ὡς δὲ ἀντέλεγε, δικαιολο-
γούμενος δῆθεν καὶ τὰς συνθήκας προφέρων, ὡς
οὐκ εἰς πρᾶσιν ἁρπάσειεν αὐτοῖς, ἀλλ' ἐρωμένην
αὐτῷ, καί τι θρασύτερον εἶπε, τὶς τῶν λῃστῶν,

Hercher restored the optative for MSS. ὄψεσθε.

went off with all the speed that their oars could effect, they saw that the pursuing vessel was gaining upon them; they therefore stripped the poor woman of her ornaments and clothes, which they put upon me, while they clad her in my garments, and then put her on the prow, where you, the pursuers, could see all that took place, and struck off her head. Her body, as you saw, they threw into the sea, while they picked up her head and kept it for the time on the ship: not long after, when they were no longer being pursued, they made away with her head too and threw it overboard. I do not know whether that was the actual reason that they had arranged to have the woman on the ship, or whether they intended to sell her as a slave, just as they afterwards bartered me away: but at any rate, when they were chased, they killed her in my place to cheat their pursuers, thinking that they would gain a greater profit from my sale than from hers. The result was that I saw Chaereas suffer the fate he deserved—it was he who had advised them to kill the female, and throw her overboard instead of me. The rest of the band of pirates said that they were certainly not going to hand me over to him alone; he had already had his share in the body of one slave, which, if sold, would have afforded them a considerable gain to begin with; and in the place of the dead woman I must be sold and so be a common source of profit to them all rather than to him only. He objected to this, arguing with them and alleging the agreement to which he had come with them; he asserted that he had not carried me off for them to sell, but to be his mistress. He went on to speak in a somewhat

καλῶς ποιῶν, ὄπισθεν ἑστὼς ἀποκόπτει τὴν
7 κεφαλὴν αὐτοῦ. ὁ μὲν οὖν δίκην οὐ μεμπτὴν
δοὺς τῆς ἁρπαγῆς, ἔρριπτο καὶ αὐτὸς κατὰ τῆς
θαλάσσης· οἱ δὲ λῃσταί, δύο πλεύσαντες ἡμερῶν,
ἄγουσί με· οὐκ οἶδ᾽ ὅποι γε, καὶ πιπράσκουσιν
ἐμπόρῳ συνήθει, κἀκεῖνος Σωσθένει.

17. Λέγει δὴ καὶ ὁ Σώστρατος· "'Επεὶ τοίνυν
τοὺς ὑμετέρους μύθους, ὦ παιδία, κατελέξατε,
φέρε ἀκούσατε," ἔφη, "καὶ παρ᾽ ἐμοῦ τὰ οἴκοι
πραχθέντα περὶ Καλλιγόνην τὴν σήν, ὦ Κλειτοφῶν, ἀδελφήν, ἵνα μὴ ἀσύμβολος ὦ[1] μυθολογίας
2 παντάπασι." κἀγὼ ἀκούσας τὸ τῆς ἀδελφῆς
ὄνομα, πάνυ τὴν γνώμην ἐπεστράφην, καί, "'Άγε,
πάτερ," εἶπον, "λέγε· μόνον περὶ ζώσης[2] λέγοις."
ἄρχεται δὴ λέγειν, ἃ φθάνω προειρηκὼς ἅπαντα,
τὸν Καλλισθένην, τὸν χρησμόν, τὴν θεωρίαν,
τὸν λέμβον, τὴν ἁρπαγήν.

3   Εἶτα προσέθηκεν, ὅτι "Μαθὼν κατὰ τὸν
πλοῦν ὡς οὐκ ἦν θυγάτηρ ἐμή, διημαρτήθη δὲ
τὸ πᾶν ἔργον αὐτῷ, ἤρα δὲ ὅμως καὶ σφόδρα
τῆς Καλλιγόνης· προσπεσὼν αὐτῆς τοῖς γόνασι,
'Δέσποινα,' εἶπε, 'μή με νομίσῃς λῃστὴν εἶναί
τινα καὶ κακοῦργον. ἀλλὰ γάρ εἰμι τῶν εὖ
γεγονότων, γένει Βυζάντιος δεύτερος οὐδενός·
ἔρως δέ με λῃστείας ὑποκριτὴν πεποίηκε καὶ
ταύτας ἐπὶ σοὶ πλέξαι τὰς τέχνας. δοῦλον οὖν
με σεαυτῆς ἀπὸ ταύτης τῆς ἡμέρας νόμιζε. καί
σοι προῖκα ἐπιδίδωμι, τὸ μὲν πρῶτον ἐμαυτόν,

---

[1] Dindorf's conjecture; cp. Passow's Lexicon for MSS.
ἀσυμβολήσω.
[2] ἄν, which follows in the MSS., was rightly removed by
Cobet.

violent manner, when one of the pirates, I am
thankful to say, crept behind him and struck off
his head. He thus received the most providential
reward for his violent abduction of me, and was
himself thrown into the sea : the pirates sailed on for
two days more, carrying me to some country or other,
I know not where, and sold me to their regular slave-
dealer, and he in turn to Sosthenes."

17. Then said Sostratus : " Now that you, my
children, have finished your stories, listen to mine :
the story of what happened at home with regard to
Calligone—your sister, Clitophon ; I shall thus not
have contributed absolutely nothing to these excellent recitals." Hearing the name of my sister, I was
all attention : " Speak on, father," said I, " only
may your story be of one who is still in the land of
the living ! " He began by recounting all that I
described some time ago [1]—about Callisthenes, and
the oracle, and the sacred embassy, and the boat,
and the abduction.

He then went on : " Callisthenes, during the
course of the voyage, realised that she was not
my daughter, and that his attempt had therefore
completely failed of its object : yet all the same
he fell in love with Calligone, and that violently.
Throwing himself at her feet, ' Lady ' said he, ' think
not that I am a pirate or common malefactor ; well
born am I, a Byzantine, second to none, by descent :
love made me act a pirate's part and weave this plot
against you. So from this day forward count me your
slave. I bring you as a marriage portion, first of all
myself, and, secondly, greater wealth than your

---

[1] Book II., chs. xiii.–xviii.

ἔπειτα ὅσην οὐκ ἂν ὁ πατὴρ ἐπέδωκέ σοι. τηρήσω
4 δέ σε παρθένον μέχρι περ ἂν σοὶ δοκῇ.' καὶ
ταῦτα εἰπὼν καὶ ἔτι τούτων πλείονα εὐαγωγοτέραν
τὴν κόρην αὐτῷ γενέσθαι παρεσκεύασεν. ἦν δὲ
καὶ ὀφθῆναι καλὸς καὶ στωμύλος καὶ πιθανώ-
τατος, καὶ ἐπειδὴ ἧκεν εἰς τὸ Βυζάντιον, συμ-
βόλαιον ποιησάμενος προικὸς μεγίστης καὶ τἆλλα
πολυτελῶς παρασκευάσας, ἐσθῆτά τε καὶ χρυσὸν
καὶ ὅσα εἰς κόσμον γυναικῶν εὐδαιμόνων, περιεῖ-
πεν εὖ καὶ καλῶς, ἄχραντον τηρῶν, ὡς ἐπηγ-
γείλατο· ὥστε καὶ αὐτὴν ᾑρήκει τὴν κόρην ἤδη.
5 ὁ δὲ καὶ τἆλλα πάντα παρεῖχεν ἑαυτὸν κοσμιώ-
τατον καὶ ἐπιεικῆ καὶ σώφρονα, καὶ ἦν τις
ἐξαίφνης περὶ τὸν νεανίσκον θαυμαστὴ μεταβολή.
ἕδρας τε γὰρ ἐξανίστατο τοῖς πρεσβυτέροις καὶ
ἐπεμελεῖτο φθάνειν προσαγορεύων τοὺς ἐντυγχά-
νοντας, καὶ τὸ τέως ἄκριτον πολυτελὲς ἐκ τῆς
πρὶν ἀσωτίας εἰς τὸ εὔβουλον μεταπίπτον, τὸ
μεγαλόφρον ἐφύλαττε πρὸς τοὺς ἐν χρείᾳ τοῦ
λαβεῖν διὰ πενίαν ὄντας· ὥστε θαυμάζειν ἅπαντας τὸ αἰφνίδιον οὕτως ἐκ τοῦ χείρονος εἰς τὸ
6 πάνυ χρηστὸν μετελθόν. ἐμὲ δὲ οὖν ᾑρήκει
πάντων μᾶλλον, καὶ ὑπερηγάπων αὐτόν, καὶ τὴν
πρὶν ἀσωτίαν φύσεως ἐνόμιζον εἶναι θαυμαστὴν
μεγαλουργίαν, ἀλλ' οὐκ ἀκρασίαν.
7   " Κἀμὲ οὖν ὑπεισῄει τὸ τοῦ Θεμιστοκλέους, ὅτι
κἀκεῖνος τὴν πρώτην ἡλικίαν σφόδρα δόξας ἀκό-

---

[1] "In the first part of his youth his behaviour and doings
were very light and unconstant, as one carried away with a
rash head, and without any order of discretion ; by reason
whereof his manners and conditions seemed marvellously to

father would have allotted to you as your dowry : and I will respect your virginity as long as seems good to you!' By means of these words and others like them he was not unsuccessful in inducing the maiden to look upon him favourably, as he was handsome and both ready and persuasive of speech. On his arrival, too, at Byzantium, he made a marriage settlement of a very large sum of money upon her, and also provided her most handsomely with all else that she could require—clothes, gold, and all the ornaments that wealthy women wear : he treated her with the greatest respect, and, as he had promised, made no attempt on her chastity : with the result that he very soon captured her heart. In the other departments of life too he shewed himself polite, virtuous, and discreet; a most wonderful change had taken place in him ! He would rise from his chair when anyone older than himself entered the room, he would be careful to be the first to salute people whom he met, and his former indiscriminate prodigality turned to prudence, but remained a copious liberality to those who, through their poverty, must needs accept favours. All wondered at this sudden transformation from the bad to the really excellent : I was perhaps of all the most attracted by him, both because I was naturally very fond of him and also because I thought that his former irregularities were more the result of an excess of extravagance, but never of vice.

"I called to mind the case of Themistocles[1]; how he in his early youth appeared to indulge in the

change, and oft-times fell into very ill-favoured events, as himself did afterwards confess, by saying that a ragged colt oft-times proves a good horse, specially if he be well-ridden and broken as he should be."—PLUTARCH.

λαστος εἶναι, πάντας ὑπερέβαλεν Ἀθηναίους
ὕστερον σοφίᾳ τε καὶ ἀνδραγαθίᾳ. καὶ δὴ μετενόουν ἀποσκορακίσας αὐτόν, ὅτε μοι περὶ τοῦ
8 τῆς θυγατρὸς διελέχθη γάμου· καὶ γάρ με σφόδρα
ἐθεράπευε καὶ ἐκάλει πατέρα καὶ κατὰ τὴν ἀγορὰν
ἐδορυφόρει. καὶ τῶν εἰς πόλεμον γυμνασίων
οὐκ ἠμέλει, ἀλλὰ καὶ πάνυ ἐρρωμένως ἐν ταῖς
9 ἱππασίαις διέπρεπεν. ἦν μὲν οὖν καὶ παρὰ τὸν
τῆς ἀσωτίας χρόνον τούτοις χαίρων καὶ χρώμενος,
ἀλλ᾽ ὡς ἐν τρυφῇ καὶ παιδιᾷ· τὸ δὲ ἀνδρεῖον ὅμως
αὐτῷ καὶ τὸ ἔμπειρον λεληθότως ἐτρέφετο. τέλεον δὲ ἦν αὐτῷ τὸ ἔργον πρὸς τὸ καρτερῶς καὶ
ποικίλως διαπρέπειν ἐν τοῖς πολεμικοῖς· ἐπεδίδου
10 δὲ καὶ χρήματα ἱκανὰ τῇ πόλει. κἀκεῖνον ἅμα
ἐμοὶ στρατηγὸν προεβάλοντο· ὅθεν ἔτι μᾶλλον
ὑπερησπάζετό με, ὑπήκοόν μοι κατὰ πάντα
παρέχων ἑαυτόν.

18. Ἐπεὶ δὲ ἐνικήσαμεν τὸν πόλεμον ἐπιφανείᾳ
τῶν θεῶν, ὑποστρέψαντες εἰς τὸ Βυζάντιον, εὐφημοῦντες τὸν Ἡρακλέα καὶ τὴν Ἄρτεμιν, ἐχειροτο-
νήθημεν, ἐγὼ μὲν ἐνταῦθα τῇ Ἀρτέμιδι, ὁ δὲ εἰς
Τύρον Ἡρακλεῖ, λαβόμενός μου τῆς δεξιᾶς ὁ
Καλλισθένης, διηγεῖται πρῶτον τὰ πεπραγμένα
2 αὐτῷ περὶ τὴν Καλλιγόνην, ‘Ἀλλ᾽ ἅπερ ἐποιή-
σαμεν, πάτερ,᾽ εἶπε, ‘τὰ μὲν νεότητος φύσει
πέπρακται βίᾳ, τὰ δὲ μετὰ ταῦτα προαιρέσει.
παρθένον γὰρ τὴν κόρην μέχρι τούτου τετήρηκα,

wildest excesses, but later on excelled all the Athenians in wisdom and bravery. And so I began to be sorry that I had contemptuously rejected him when he had broached the subject of an alliance with my daughter—particularly as he always shewed me the greatest attention, calling me 'Father,' and escorting me through the open squares. Nor did he neglect the training that is necessary for military glory, but greatly distinguished himself in the cavalry exercises : indeed, even in the time of his dissipation he had been fond of horses and familiar with their use; but only as a distraction or a luxury, and he had thus, without knowing it, encouraged in himself the spirit of bravery and skill in horsemanship. It finally became his object to gain distinction in war by his endurance and his versatility : he gave large contributions towards the public services ; and then his fellow-citizens appointed him as an associate-general with me, a position which made him still more deferential and cordial towards me, shewing himself willing to accede to my wishes at every turn.

18. " After we had brought the war to a successful conclusion, owing to the divine manifestations [1] in our favour, we returned to Byzantium, as we desired to express our gratitude to Hercules and Artemis. It was voted I should be the delegate hither to Artemis and he to Hercules at Tyre. Before our departure, Callisthenes took me by the hand and told me the whole story about Calligone. ' As for what I did, father,' said he, ' it began as a deed of violence in the heat of youth, but it has gone on as a matter of sober inclination. Up to this very moment I have respected her chastity. and that in-

---

[1] That of Artemis is mentioned in VII. xii. § 4.

καὶ ταῦτα πολέμοις ὁμιλῶν, ἐν οἷς οὐδεὶς ἀνα-
3 βάλλεται τὰς ἡδονάς. νῦν οὖν εἰς τὴν Τύρον
αὐτὴν ἀπαγαγεῖν ἔγνωκα πρὸς τὸν πατέρα, καὶ
νόμῳ παρ᾽ ἐκείνου λαβεῖν τὸν γάμον. ἂν μὲν οὖν
ἐθελήσῃ μοι δοῦναι τὴν κόρην, ἀγαθῇ τύχῃ
δέξομαι· ἂν δὲ σκαιὸς γένηται καὶ δύσκολος, παρ-
4 θένον αὐτὴν ἀπολήψεται. ἐγὼ γὰρ προῖκα ἐπι-
δοὺς οὐκ εὐκαταφρόνητον, ἀγαπητῶς ἂν λάβοιμι
τὸν γάμον.᾽ ἀναγνώσομαι δέ σοι καὶ τὸ συμ-
βόλαιον, ὃ φθάνω πρὸ τοῦ πολέμου γράψας,
δεόμενος συνοικίσαι τῷ Καλλισθένει τὴν κόρην,
τό τε γένος αὐτοῦ καταλέγων καὶ τὸ ἀξίωμα καὶ
τὰς ἐν τοῖς πολέμοις ἀριστείας· τοῦτο γάρ ἐστιν
5 ἡμῖν τὸ συγκείμενον. ἐγὼ δέ, ἢν τὴν ἔφεσιν
ἀγωνισώμεθα, διέγνωκα πρῶτον μὲν εἰς τὸ Βυζάντιον διαπλεῦσαι, μετὰ ταῦτα δὲ εἰς τὴν Τύρον.᾽᾽
καὶ ταῦτα διαμυθολογήσαντες ἐκοιμήθημεν τὸν
αὐτὸν τρόπον.

19. Τῇ δὲ ὑστεραίᾳ παραγενόμενος ὁ Κλεινίας
ἔφη Θέρσανδρον διὰ τῆς νυκτὸς ἀποδεδρακέναι·
τὴν γὰρ ἔφεσιν οὐχ ὡς ἀγωνιούμενον πεποιῆσθαι·
βουλόμενον δὲ μετὰ προφάσεως ἐπισχεθῆναι τὸν
2 ἔλεγχον ὧν ἐτόλμησε. μείναντες οὖν τῶν ἑξῆς
τριῶν ἡμερῶν, ὅσων ἦν ἡ προθεσμία, προσελ-

war-time, when men are generally not accustomed to defer[1] their pleasures. I have therefore now decided to take her back to her father at Tyre, and there to ask him to give her to me in marriage in accordance with the law.[2] If he will give her to me, I will take her and rejoice at my good fortune; if he makes objections and refuses, he shall take her back, still a virgin: I have given her a marriage portion which is not to be despised, and I would gladly conclude the marriage.' I will read you the letter which I wrote before he went to fight, asking Hippias to unite the girl to Callisthenes: in it is recited his good birth and worth, and also his brave deeds in the field[3]: that is the arrangement that Callisthenes and I made. As for myself, if we are successful in the appeal,[4] I have made up my mind to sail first for Byzantium, and after that to proceed to Tyre." When we had finished all this conversation, we retired to our couches as on the previous occasions.

19. On the following day Clinias came and told us that Thersander had fled in the night; he had appealed without any intention of appearing, and only wished, under this pretence, to put off the trial at which his plot would have come to light. We therefore stayed three days more, the legal time for renewing proceedings, and then appeared before the

---

[1] For reasons given in IV. vii. § 3.

[2] Presumably the law mentioned in II. xiii. § 3. But that was a law at Byzantium, not at Tyre, and Callisthenes may merely mean "in due legal form."

[3] In other minor wars, I suppose.

[4] No mention has been made of this appeal. Perhaps it has dropped out in some imperfection of the text, or it may mean little more than the conclusion of the case, which was still technically unfinished.

θόντες τῷ προέδρῳ, καὶ τοὺς νόμους ἀναγνόντες
καθ' οὓς οὐδεὶς ἔτι τῷ Θερσάνδρῳ λόγος πρὸς
ἡμᾶς ἦν, νηὸς ἐπιβάντες καὶ οὐρίῳ χρησάμενοι
πνεύματι, κατήραμεν εἰς τὸ Βυζάντιον, κἀκεῖ τοὺς
πολυεύκτους ἐπιτελέσαντες γάμους, ἀπεδημήσα-
3 μεν εἰς τὴν Τύρον. δύο δὲ ὕστερον ἡμερῶν τοῦ
Καλλισθένους ἐλθόντες, εὕρομεν τὸν πατέρα μέλ-
λοντα θύειν τοὺς γάμους τῆς ἀδελφῆς εἰς τὴν
ὑστεραίαν. παρῆμεν οὖν ὡς καὶ συνθύσοντες
αὐτῷ καὶ εὐξόμενοι τοῖς θεοῖς τούς τε ἐμοὺς καὶ
τοὺς ἐκείνου γάμους σὺν ἀγαθαῖς φυλαχθῆναι
τύχαις. καὶ διεγνώκαμεν ἐν τῇ Τύρῳ παρα-
χειμάσαντες διελθεῖν[1] εἰς τὸ Βυζάντιον.

[1] It is possible that Jacobs was right when he thought
that some such word as ἦρι or θέρει had dropped out before
διελθεῖν.

Chief Justice, where we had the laws read in accordance with which Thersander could no longer have any cause of action against us. We then took ship and, obtaining a favouring wind, arrived at Byzantium, where we celebrated the marriage for which we had so long prayed, and thence set out for Tyre. We reached it two days after the arrival of Callisthenes, and we there found my father just about to offer the proper sacrifices for my sister's wedding, which was to take place on the following day. At this we were present to join in the sacrifices and to pray the gods that both my marriage and his might be guarded and secured by the best of fortune ; and our intention was to pass the winter at Tyre and afterwards to proceed to Byzantium.[1]

[1] Our author seems to have forgotten that the story began by being Clitophon's narration to himself. The narration took place at Sidon, and there should have been a few words to round up the book to explain how it came about that Clitophon found himself at Sidon, and for the author to thank him for his interesting narration.

INDEX

INDEX

INDEX

INDEX

Printed in Great Britain by
Richard Clay (The Chaucer Press), Ltd.,
Bungay, Suffolk

THE LOEB CLASSICAL LIBRARY

VOLUMES ALREADY PUBLISHED

Latin Authors

MINUCIUS FELIX. Cf. TERTULLIAN.

NEPOS CORNELIUS. J. C. Rolfe.

OVID: THE ART OF LOVE and OTHER POEMS. J. H. Mosley. Revised by G. P. Goold.

OVID: FASTI. Sir James G. Frazer

OVID: HEROIDES and AMORES. Grant Showerman. Revised by G. P. Goold

OVID: METAMORPHOSES. F. J. Miller. 2 Vols. Revised by G. P. Goold.

OVID: TRISTIA and EX PONTO. A. L. Wheeler.

PERSIUS. Cf. JUVENAL.

PERVIGILIUM VENERIS. Cf. CATULLUS.

PETRONIUS. M. Heseltine. SENECA: APOCOLOCYNTOSIS. W. H. D. Rouse. Revised by E. H. Warmington.

PHAEDRUS and BABRIUS (Greek). B. E. Perry.

PLAUTUS. Paul Nixon. 5 Vols.

PLINY: LETTERS, PANEGYRICUS. Betty Radice. 2 Vols.

PLINY: NATURAL HISTORY. 10 Vols. Vols. I–V and IX. H. Rackham. VI.–VIII. W. H. S. Jones. X. D. E. Eichholz.

PROPERTIUS. H. E. Butler.

PRUDENTIUS. H. J. Thomson. 2 Vols.

QUINTILIAN. H. E. Butler. 4 Vols.

REMAINS OF OLD LATIN. E. H. Warmington. 4 Vols. Vol. I. (ENNIUS AND CAECILIUS) Vol. II. (LIVIUS, NAEVIUS PACUVIUS, ACCIUS) Vol. III. (LUCILIUS and LAWS OF XII TABLES) Vol. IV. (ARCHAIC INSCRIPTIONS)

RES GESTAE DIVI AUGUSTI. Cf. VELLEIUS PATERCULUS.

SALLUST. J. C. Rolfe.

SCRIPTORES HISTORIAE AUGUSTAE. D. Magie. 3 Vols.

SENECA, THE ELDER: CONTROVERSIAE, SUASORIAE. M. Winterbottom. 2 Vols.

SENECA: APOCOLOCYNTOSIS. Cf. PETRONIUS.

SENECA: EPISTULAE MORALES. R. M. Gummere. 3 Vols.

SENECA: MORAL ESSAYS. J. W. Basore. 3 Vols.

SENECA: TRAGEDIES. F. J. Miller. 2 Vols.

SENECA: NATURALES QUAESTIONES. T. H. Corcoran. 2 Vols.

SIDONIUS: POEMS and LETTERS. W. B. Anderson. 2 Vols.

SILIUS ITALICUS. J. D. Duff. 2 Vols.

STATIUS. J. H. Mozley. 2 Vols.

SUETONIUS. J. C. Rolfe. 2 Vols.

TACITUS: DIALOGUS. Sir Wm. Peterson. AGRICOLA and GERMANIA. Maurice Hutton. Revised by M. Winterbottom, R. M. Ogilvie, E. H. Warmington.

TACITUS: HISTORIES and ANNALS. C. H. Moore and J. Jackson. 4 Vols.

TERENCE. John Sargeaunt. 2 Vols.

TERTULLIAN: APOLOGIA and DE SPECTACULIS. T. R. Glover. MINUCIUS FELIX. G. H. Rendall.

TIBULLUS. Cf. CATULLUS.

VALERIUS FLACCUS. J. H. Mozley.

VARRO: DE LINGUA LATINA. R. G. Kent. 2 Vols.

VELLEIUS PATERCULUS and RES GESTAE DIVI AUGUSTI. F. W. Shipley.

VIRGIL. H. R. Fairclough. 2 Vols.

VITRUVIUS: DE ARCHITECTURA. F. Granger. 2 Vols.

Greek Authors

ACHILLES TATIUS. S. Gaselee.

AELIAN: ON THE NATURE OF ANIMALS. A. F. Scholfield. 3 Vols.

AENEAS TACTICUS. ASCLEPIODOTUS and ONASANDER. The Illinois Greek Club.

AESCHINES. C. D. Adams.

AESCHYLUS. H. Weir Smyth. 2 Vols.

ALCIPHRON, AELIAN, PHILOSTRATUS: LETTERS. A. R. Benner and F. H. Fobes.

ANDOCIDES, ANTIPHON. Cf. MINOR ATTIC ORATORS.

APOLLODORUS. Sir James G. Frazer. 2 Vols.

APOLLONIUS RHODIUS. R. C. Seaton.

APOSTOLIC FATHERS. Kirsopp Lake. 2 Vols.

APPIAN: ROMAN HISTORY. Horace White. 4 Vols.

ARATUS. Cf. CALLIMACHUS.

ARISTIDES: ORATIONS. C. A. Behr. Vol. I.

ARISTOPHANES. Benjamin Bickley Rogers. 3 Vols. Verse trans.

ARISTOTLE: ART OF RHETORIC. J. H. Freese.

ARISTOTLE: ATHENIAN CONSTITUTION, EUDEMIAN ETHICS, VICES AND VIRTUES. H. Rackham.

ARISTOTLE: GENERATION OF ANIMALS. A. L. Peck.

ARISTOTLE: HISTORIA ANIMALIUM. A. L. Peck. Vols. I.–II.

ARISTOTLE: METAPHYSICS. H. Tredennick. 2 Vols.

ARISTOTLE: METEOROLOGICA. H. D. P. Lee.

ARISTOTLE: MINOR WORKS. W. S. Hett. On Colours, On Things Heard, On Physiognomies, On Plants, On Marvellous Things Heard, Mechanical Problems, On Indivisible Lines, On Situations and Names of Winds, On Melissus, Xenophanes, and Gorgias.

ARISTOTLE: NICOMACHEAN ETHICS. H. Rackham.

ARISTOTLE: OECONOMICA and MAGNA MORALIA. G. C. Armstrong (with METAPHYSICS, Vol. II).

ARISTOTLE: ON THE HEAVENS. W. K. C. Guthrie.

ARISTOTLE: ON THE SOUL, PARVA NATURALIA, ON BREATH. W. S. Hett.

ARISTOTLE: CATEGORIES, ON INTERPRETATION, PRIOR ANALYTICS. H. P. Cooke and H. Tredennick.

ARISTOTLE: POSTERIOR ANALYTICS, TOPICS. H. Tredennick and E. S. Forster.

ARISTOTLE: ON SOPHISTICAL REFUTATIONS.
On Coming to be and Passing Away, On the Cosmos. E. S. Forster and D. J. Furley.

ARISTOTLE: PARTS OF ANIMALS. A. L. Peck; MOTION AND PROGRESSION OF ANIMALS. E. S. Forster.

ARISTOTLE: PHYSICS. Rev. P. Wicksteed and F. M. Cornford. 2 Vols.

ARISTOTLE: POETICS and LONGINUS. W. Hamilton Fyfe; DEMETRIUS ON STYLE. W. Rhys Roberts.

ARISTOTLE: POLITICS. H. Rackham.

ARISTOTLE: PROBLEMS. W. S. Hett. 2 Vols.

ARISTOTLE: RHETORICA AD ALEXANDRUM (with PROBLEMS. Vol. II). H. Rackham.

ARRIAN: HISTORY OF ALEXANDER and INDICA. Rev. E. Iliffe Robson. 2 Vols. New version P. Brunt.

ATHENAEUS: DEIPNOSOPHISTAE. C. B. Gulick. 7 Vols.

BABRIUS and PHAEDRUS (Latin). B. E. Perry.

ST. BASIL: LETTERS. R. J. Deferrari. 4 Vols.

CALLIMACHUS: FRAGMENTS. C. A. Trypanis. MUSAEUS: HERO AND LEANDER. T. Gelzer and C. Whitman.

CALLIMACHUS, Hymns and Epigrams, and LYCOPHRON. A. W. Mair; ARATUS. G. R. Mair.

CLEMENT OF ALEXANDRIA. Rev. G. W. Butterworth.

COLLUTHUS. Cf. OPPIAN.

DAPHNIS AND CHLOE. Thornley's Translation revised by J. M. Edmonds: and PARTHENIUS. S. Gaselee.

DEMOSTHENES I.: OLYNTHIACS, PHILIPPICS and MINOR ORATIONS I.–XVII. AND XX. J. H. Vince.

DEMOSTHENES II.: DE CORONA and DE FALSA LEGATIONE. C. A. Vince and J. H. Vince.

DEMOSTHENES III.: MEIDIAS, ANDROTION, ARISTOCRATES, TIMOCRATES and ARISTOGEITON I. and II. J. H. Vince.

DEMOSTHENES IV.–VI: PRIVATE ORATIONS and IN NEAERAM. A. T. Murray.

DEMOSTHENES VII: FUNERAL SPEECH, EROTIC ESSAY, EXORDIA and LETTERS. N. W. and N. J. DeWitt.

DIO CASSIUS: ROMAN HISTORY. E. Cary. 9 Vols.

DIO CHRYSOSTOM. J. W. Cohoon and H. Lamar Crosby. 5 Vols.

DIODORUS SICULUS. 12 Vols. Vols. I.–VI. C. H. Oldfather. Vol. VII. C. L. Sherman. Vol. VIII. C. B. Welles. Vols. IX. and X. R. M. Geer. Vol. XI. F. Walton. Vol. XII. F. Walton. General Index. R. M. Geer.

DIOGENES LAERTIUS. R. D. Hicks. 2 Vols. New Introduction by H. S. Long.

DIONYSIUS OF HALICARNASSUS: ROMAN ANTIQUITIES. Spelman's translation revised by E. Cary. 7 Vols.

DIONYSIUS OF HALICARNASSUS: CRITICAL ESSAYS. S. Usher. 2 Vols. Vol. I.

EPICTETUS. W. A. Oldfather. 2 Vols.

EURIPIDES. A. S. Way. 4 Vols. Verse trans.

EUSEBIUS: ECCLESIASTICAL HISTORY. Kirsopp Lake and J. E. L. Oulton. 2 Vols.

GALEN: ON THE NATURAL FACULTIES. A. J. Brock.

GREEK ANTHOLOGY. W. R. Paton. 5 Vols.

GREEK BUCOLIC POETS (THEOCRITUS, BION, MOSCHUS). J. M. Edmonds.

GREEK ELEGY AND IAMBUS with the ANACREONTEA. J. M. Edmonds. 2 Vols.

GREEK LYRIC. D. A. Campbell. 4 Vols. Vol. I.

GREEK MATHEMATICAL WORKS. Ivor Thomas. 2 Vols.

HERODES. Cf. THEOPHRASTUS: CHARACTERS.

HERODIAN. C. R. Whittaker. 2 Vols.

HERODOTUS. A. D. Godley. 4 Vols.

HESIOD AND THE HOMERIC HYMNS. H. G. Evelyn White.

HIPPOCRATES and the FRAGMENTS OF HERACLEITUS. W. H. S. Jones and E. T. Withington. 4 Vols.

HOMER: ILIAD. A. T. Murray. 2 Vols.

HOMER: ODYSSEY. A. T. Murray. 2 Vols.

ISAEUS. E. W. Forster.

ISOCRATES. George Norlin and LaRue Van Hook. 3 Vols.

[ST. JOHN DAMASCENE]: BARLAAM AND IOASAPH. Rev. G. R. Woodward, Harold Mattingly and D. M. Lang.

JOSEPHUS. 10 Vols. Vols. I.–IV. H. Thackeray. Vol. V. H. Thackeray and R. Marcus. Vols. VI.–VII. R. Marcus. Vol. VIII. R. Marcus and Allen Wikgren. Vols. IX.–X. L. H. Feldman.

JULIAN. Wilmer Cave Wright. 3 Vols.

LIBANIUS. A. F. Norman. 3 Vols. Vols. I.–II.

LUCIAN. 8 Vols. Vols. I.–V. A. M. Harmon. Vol. VI. K. Kilburn. Vols. VII.–VIII. M. D. Macleod.

LYCOPHRON. Cf. CALLIMACHUS.

LYRA GRAECA, J. M. Edmonds. 2 Vols.

LYSIAS. W. R. M. Lamb.

MANETHO. W. G. Waddell.

MARCUS AURELIUS. C. R. Haines.

MENANDER. W. G. Arnott. 3 Vols. Vol. I.

MINOR ATTIC ORATORS (ANTIPHON, ANDOCIDES, LYCURGUS, DEMADES, DINARCHUS, HYPERIDES). K. J. Maidment and J. O. Burtt. 2 Vols.

MUSAEUS: HERO AND LEANDER. Cf. CALLIMACHUS.

NONNOS: DIONYSIACA. W. H. D. Rouse. 3 Vols.

OPPIAN, COLLUTHUS, TRYPHIODORUS. A. W. Mair.

PAPYRI. NON-LITERARY SELECTIONS. A. S. Hunt and C. C. Edgar. 2 Vols. LITERARY SELECTIONS (Poetry). D. L. Page.

PARTHENIUS. Cf. DAPHNIS and CHLOE.

PAUSANIAS: DESCRIPTION OF GREECE. W. H. S. Jones. 4 Vols. and Companion Vol. arranged by R. E. Wycherley.

PHILO. 10 Vols. Vols. I.–V. F. H. Colson and Rev. G. H. Whitaker. Vols. VI.–IX. F. H. Colson. Vol. X. F. H. Colson and the Rev. J. W. Earp.

PHILO: two supplementary Vols. (*Translation only.*) Ralph Marcus.

PHILOSTRATUS: THE LIFE OF APOLLONIUS OF TYANA. F. C. Conybeare. 2 Vols.

PHILOSTRATUS: IMAGINES; CALLISTRATUS: DESCRIPTIONS. A. Fairbanks.

PHILOSTRATUS and EUNAPIUS: LIVES OF THE SOPHISTS. Wilmer Cave Wright.

PINDAR. Sir J. E. Sandys.

PLATO: CHARMIDES, ALCIBIADES, HIPPARCHUS, THE LOVERS, THEAGES, MINOS and EPINOMIS. W. R. M. Lamb.

PLATO: CRATYLUS, PARMENIDES, GREATER HIPPIAS, LESSER HIPPIAS. H. N. Fowler.

PLATO: EUTHYPHRO, APOLOGY, CRITO, PHAEDO, PHAEDRUS, H. N. Fowler.

PLATO: LACHES, PROTAGORAS, MENO, EUTHYDEMUS. W. R. M. Lamb.

PLATO: LAWS. Rev. R. G. Bury. 2 Vols.

PLATO: LYSIS, SYMPOSIUM, GORGIAS. W. R. M. Lamb.

PLATO: Republic. Paul Shorey. 2 Vols.

PLATO: STATESMAN, PHILEBUS. H. N. Fowler; ION. W. R. M. Lamb.

PLATO: THEAETETUS and SOPHIST. H. N. Fowler.

PLATO: TIMAEUS, CRITIAS, CLITOPHO, MENEXENUS, EPISTULAE. Rev. R. G. Bury.

PLOTINUS: A. H. Armstrong. 7 Vols. Vols. I.–V.

PLUTARCH: MORALIA. 16 Vols. Vols I.–V. F. C. Babbitt. Vol. VI. W. C. Helmbold. Vols. VII. and XIV. P. H. De Lacy and B. Einarson. Vol. VIII. P. A. Clement and H. B. Hoffleit. Vol. IX. E. L. Minar, Jr., F. H. Sandbach, W. C. Helmbold. Vol. X. H. N. Fowler. Vol. XI. L. Pearson and F. H. Sandbach. Vol. XII. H. Cherniss and W. C. Helmbold. Vol. XIII 1–2. H. Cherniss. Vol. XV. F. H. Sandbach.

PLUTARCH: THE PARALLEL LIVES. B. Perrin. 11 Vols.

POLYBIUS. W. R. Paton. 6 Vols.

PROCOPIUS. H. B. Dewing. 7 Vols.

PTOLEMY: TETRABIBLOS. F. E. Robbins.

QUINTUS SMYRNAEUS. A. S. Way. Verse trans.

SEXTUS EMPIRICUS. Rev. R. G. Bury. 4 Vols.

SOPHOCLES. F. Storr. 2 Vols. Verse trans.

STRABO: GEOGRAPHY. Horace L. Jones. 8 Vols.

THEOCRITUS. Cf. GREEK BUCOLIC POETS.

THEOPHRASTUS: CHARACTERS. J. M. Edmonds. HERODES, etc. A. D. Knox.

THEOPHRASTUS: ENQUIRY INTO PLANTS. Sir Arthur Hort, Bart. 2 Vols.

THEOPHRASTUS: DE CAUSIS PLANTARUM. G. K. K. Link and B. Einarson. 3 Vols. Vol. I.

THUCYDIDES. C. F. Smith. 4 Vols.

TRYPHIODORUS. Cf. OPPIAN.

XENOPHON: CYROPAEDIA. Walter Miller. 2 Vols.

XENOPHON: HELLENICA. C. L. Brownson. 2 Vols.

XENOPHON: ANABASIS. C. L. Brownson.

XENOPHON: MEMORABILIA AND OECONOMICUS. E. C. Marchant. SYMPOSIUM AND APOLOGY. O. J. Todd.

XENOPHON: SCRIPTA MINORA. E. C. Marchant. CONSTITUTION OF THE ATHENIANS. G. W. Bowersock.